MODERN CLASSICS OF SCIENCE FICTION

MODERN CLASSICS
OF SCIENCE
FICTION

EDITED BY GARDNER DOZOIS

St. Martin's Press
New York

MODERN CLASSICS OF SCIENCE FICTION. Copyright © 1991 by Gardner Dozois. All rights reserved. Printed in the United States of America. No part of this book may be used or reproduced in any manner whatsoever without written permission except in the case of brief quotations embodied in critical articles or reviews. For information, address St. Martin's Press, 175 Fifth Avenue, New York, N.Y. 10010.

Library of Congress Cataloging-in-Publication Data

Modern classics of science fiction / Gardner Dozois, editor.
          p.   cm.
          ISBN 0-312-07238-4
1. Science fiction, American.   I. Dozois, Gardner R.
          PS648.S3M59   1992
      813′.0876208—dc20   91-40412   CIP

First published in Great Britain by Legend, an imprint of Random Century Group.

First U.S. Edition: February 1992
10   9   8   7   6   5   4   3   2   1

Acknowledgements

Acknowledgement is made for permission to print the following material:

"The Country of the Kind," by Damon Knight. Copyright © 1955 by Fantasy House, Inc. First published in *The Magazine of Fantasy and Science Fiction*, 1955. Reprinted by permission of the author.

"Aristotle and the Gun," by L. Sprague de Camp. Copyright © 1956 by Street and Smith Publications, Inc. First published in *Astounding Science Fiction*, February 1956. Copyright renewed 1986 by L. Sprague de Camp. Reprinted by permission of the author.

"The Other Celia," by Theodore Sturgeon. Copyright © 1957 by Galaxy Publishing Corp. First published in *Galaxy*, 1957. Reprinted by permission of the author's agent, Kirby McCauley.

"Casey Agonistes," by Richard McKenna. Copyright © 1958 by Mercury Press, Inc. First published in *The Magazine of Fantasy and Science Fiction*, September 1958. Reprinted by permission of the author's estate.

"Mother Hitton's Littul Kittons," by Cordwainer Smith. Copyright © 1961 by Galaxy Publishing Corp. First published in *Galaxy*, June 1961. Reprinted by permission of the author's estate and the agents for the estate, Scott Meredith Literary Associates, Inc., 845 Third Avenue, New York, NY 10022.

"The Moon Moth," by Jack Vance. Copyright © 1961 by Galaxy Publishing Corp. First published in *Galaxy*, August 1961. Reprinted by permission of the author.

"The Golden Horn," by Edgar Pangborn. Copyright © 1961 by Mercury Press, Inc. First published in *The Magazine of Fantasy and Science Fiction*, 1961. Reprinted by permission of the author's agent.

"The Lady Margaret," by Keith Roberts. Copyright © 1966 by Keith Roberts. First published in *Impulse 2*, 1966 (as "The Lady Ann"); revised version copyright © 1968 from the book *Pavane*. Reprinted by permission of the author and the author's agent.

"This Moment of the Storm," by Roger Zelazny. Copyright © 1966 by Mercury Press, Inc. First published in *The Magazine of Fantasy and Science Fiction*, 1966. Reprinted by permission of the author.

"Narrow Valley," by R. A. Lafferty. Copyright © 1966 by R. A. Lafferty. First published in *The Magazine of Fantasy and Science Fiction*, September 1966. Reprinted by permission of the author, and the author's agent, Virginia Kidd.

"Driftglass," by Samuel R. Delany. Copyright © 1971 by Samuel R. Delany. First published in *Worlds of If*, June 1967. Reprinted by permission of the author and his agents, Henry Morrison, Inc.

"The Worm That Flies," by Brian W. Aldiss. Copyright © 1968 by Brian W. Aldiss. First published in *The Farthest Reaches* (Packet Books). Reprinted by permission of the author.

"The Fifth Head of Cerberus," by Gene Wolfe. Copyright © 1972 by Gene Wolfe. First published in *Orbit 10* (Berkley). Reprinted by permission of the author, and the author's agent, Virginia Kidd.

"Nobody's Home," by Joanna Russ. Copyright © 1972 by Robert Silverberg. First published in *New Dimensions II* (Doubleday). Reprinted by permission of the author.

"Her Smoke Rose Up Forever," by James Tiptree, Jr. Copyright © 1974 by James Tiptree, Jr. First published in *Final Stage* (Penguin). Reprinted by permission of the author's estate and the estate's agent, Virginia Kidd.

"The Barrow," by Ursula K. Le Guin. Copyright © 1976 by Ursula K. Le Guin. First published in *The Magazine of Fantasy and Science Fiction*, October 1976. Reprinted by permission of the author, and the author's agent, Virginia Kidd.

"Particle Theory," by Edward Bryant. Copyright © 1977 by The Condé Nast Publications, Inc. First published in *Analog Science Fiction/Science Fact*, February 1977. Reprinted by permission of the author.

"The Ugly Chickens," by Howard Waldrop. Copyright © 1980 by Terry Carr. First published in *Universe 10* (Doubleday). Reprinted by permission of the author.

"Going Under," by Jack Dann. Copyright © 1981 by Omni Publications International, Ltd. First published in *Omni*, September 1981. Reprinted by permission of the author.

"Salvador," by Lucius Shepard. Copyright © 1984 by Mercury Press, Inc. First published in *The Magazine of Fantasy and Science Fiction*, April 1984. Reprinted by permission of the author.

"Pretty Boy Crossover," by Pat Cadigan. Copyright © 1986 by Davis Publications, Inc. First published in *Isaac Asimov's Science Fiction Magazine*, January 1986. Reprinted by permission of the author.

"The Pure Product," by John Kessel. Copyright © 1986 by Davis Publications, Inc. First published in *Isaac Asimov's Science Fiction Magazine*, March 1986. Reprinted by permission of the author.

"The Winter Market," William Gibson. Copyright © 1986 by William Gibson. First published in *Stardate*, 1986. Reprinted by permission of the author.

"Chance," by Connie Willis. Copyright © 1986 by Davis Publications, Inc. First published in *Isaac Asimov's Science Fiction Magazine*, May 1986. Reprinted by permission of the author.

"The Edge of the World," by Michael Swanwick. Copyright © 1989 by Michael Swanwick. First published in *Full Spectrum II* (Bantam). Reprinted by permission of the author, and the author's agent, Virginia Kidd.

"Doris Bangs," by Bruce Sterling. Copyright © 1989 by Davis Publications, Inc. First published in *Isaac Asimov's Science Fiction Magazine*, September 1989. Reprinted by permission of the author.

Contents

. ——— .

Time that is intolerant
Of the brave and innocent,
And indifferent in a week
To a beautiful physique,
Worships language and
    forgives
Everyone by whom it lives.

W. H. Auden

MODERN CLASSICS OF SCIENCE FICTION

Preface

Let me talk to you for a moment about a few things that this anthology is *not*.

It is not an evolutionary overview of science fiction, for many of the stories that have had the greatest evolutionary impact on the field, and that would have to be included and analyzed in such an overview, were also stories that I personally didn't much like, and they are not here.

It is not really a historical survey of the various periods of science fiction history, either, since such a survey, to function well, would have to include a balanced selection of representative stories from the various aesthetic factions that are always in contention in any period of genre history, and would have to look beyond first-rate authors to the second-rank authors, from whose work you can often get a more accurate idea of the essential nature of the different kinds of work that are being done . . . but those stories are not here, either. (No story here was selected *because* it is a good example of this trend or that, or of one type of writing or another, although a few of them, by happenstance, may actually turn out to *be* good examples of whatever it is – that is not why they are here, though.)

It isn't a Politically Correct book, either, since to *be* Politically Correct, more care would have had to be taken in selecting the proportionately proper number of writers from each of SF's political cliques and pressure groups – are there enough hard-science writers? enough leftists? enough British writers? enough women? – and no such demographic care was exercised. Nor is it made up of comfortably expedient choices that could be expected to score me a lot of personal brownie points – several of my best friends and closest colleagues have no work here, for instance, which will no doubt hurt their feelings, and there are a number of important and influential genre figures I could usefully have flattered by putting them in these pages and who will probably *not* be flattered by finding that they have been omitted. Nor was the book designed with an eye to insuring me a margin of safety with reviewers, since there are a number of icons, from Heinlein to Dick to Ballard, that I will no doubt be pilloried for leaving out. (Indeed, even as I write this, the critics are gleefully rubbing their hands together in anticipation, getting ready to come forward and tell me what I should have used *instead*, or why I shouldn't have used the stories I *did* use.)

No, from the moment Deborah Beale put forth the suggestion that I should edit a retrospective anthology of the best stories of the last thirty years or so, it was clear to me that there was only one criterion that I *could* use, if the book was to have any sort of validity at all – the stories would have to be the ones that had had the most impact on me as a *reader*.

Not always the ones they're supposed to be, often not the famous ones, or the respectable ones, sometimes not even the ones I'd have *liked* them to be . . . but, rather, the ones that had moved me and shaken me, the ones that got under my skin, the ones that seized me and forced me to be impressed with them, often against my better judgment, the ones that I could not forget, even when sometimes they were stories that I would rather not have ever read at all. The stories that *got* to me, that changed the way I thought, or what I believed, or how I felt, or the way that I felt it. The stories that had penetrated through all the insulating shells of abstract aesthetic appreciation and intellectual admiration, and had hit *me*, hit me in the center of my soul.

Instinct – yes, we're talking about stories selected by instinct, by one reader's emotional reaction to them, rather than stories selected to express some critical theory, or to grind a particular political ax, or because they help buttress some polemic or aesthetic argument about the nature of the field. Already, I can see the lips curling in scorn . . . and yet, I do believe that, in the end, that is all we ever really have to work with.

Even today, at a time when I read hundreds of stories a

month for *Isaac Asimov's Science Fiction Magazine* and for my *Year's Best Science Fiction* anthology . . . even today, I can be reading through the submission pile, and be thinking, yes, this is pretty good, nicely handled, and we can use a hard-science story to balance off the softer stuff in the April issue . . . and then I'll pick up another manuscript and start to read, and all at once I'll forget that I'm reading it. I'll forget that I'm supposed to be evaluating it, I'll forget about the April issue, or what I'm going to have for lunch, I'll forget where I am, or that time is passing . . . I'll submerge in the story and forget everything until I come *out* of the story with a start and a shudder a half-hour or an hour later, and sit there with the manuscript on my lap, staring off into distance and feeling gooseflesh shiver up my spine.

And I think that if there ever comes a time when I'm too worn-out or jaded or cynical to feel that way any longer, if there comes a time when there are no stories, however rare, that can swallow me up and make me shiver with dread or awe or wonder at the end, then that will be the time for me to lay down my blue pencil, and get out of the editing business.

So then, right from the start I resolved to only use stories in this anthology that had been important to *me*, however eccentric those choices might seem to *other* people . . . and not to worry about whether those stories were generally considered to have had any historical or critical importance for the field at large.

A few weeks' work, however, was enough to show me that, even sticking to that criterion, I was still going to end up with a book easily three times larger even than the huge volume that Deborah had envisioned. Larger than was feasible, or even possible. Clearly, other winnowing-screens were needed.

First, figuring that the "Golden Age" of the 1940s and the *Galaxy* era of the early 1950s had already been extensively covered by other anthologies, I arbitrarily decided to reach no further back in time than the late 1950s, about the same period when I myself had started reading science fiction in a systematic and regular way (I cheated a bit – arbitrarily – to get one of my favorites, Damon Knight's "The Country of the Kind," in on the front end of the book). Also, the 1970s and the 1980s are the periods that have been the least extensively mined for anthologies to date, and so I decided to lean slightly in their direction to compensate.

Next, although it was a hard choice, I decided that there were some stories that, although they probably deserved to be in the book, were just too heavily anthologized already. Was there really any point in reprinting Daniel Keyes's "Flowers for Algernon" or Arthur C. Clarke's "The Star" or "The Nine Billion Names of God" or Isaac Asimov's "The Ugly Little Boy" or Harlan Ellison's "Pretty Maggie Moneyeyes" or " 'Repent, Harlequin!' Said the Ticktockman" or Robert A. Heinlein's " 'All You Zombies – ' " or Alfred Bester's "Fondly Fahrenheit" once again, when they were already among the most frequently reprinted stories in the genre? Reluctantly, I decided that there was not – especially as they would be taking slots that could go instead to lesser-known work.

Next, there were many stories that deserved to be used here that were just too *long* to be included, even in a book of this size, especially as every novella that I used would of necessity force the elimination of several good shorter stories that *also* deserved to be here. I settled in the end for using the one novella I felt that I could *not* omit, and all the rest that I would have *liked* to use as well – Jack Vance's "The Dragon Masters," Lucius Shepard's "R & R," Nancy Kress's "Trinity," Poul Anderson's "The Sky People" and "The Night Face," Brian W. Aldiss's "Total Environment," Michael Bishop's "The Samurai and the Willows" and "Death and Designation Among the Asadi," Judith Moffett's "Tiny Tango," John Varley's "In the Hall of the Martian Kings" and "The Persistence of Vision," Joe Haldeman's "Hero," Geoff Ryman's "The Unconquered Country," Samuel R. Delany's "The Star Pit," Connie Willis's "Blued Moon" and "The Last of the Winnebagoes," Theodore Sturgeon's "Baby Is Three," Michael Moorcock's "Pale Roses," Avram Davidson's "Sleep Well of Nights," Algis Budrys's "Rogue Moon," Richard McKenna's "Fiddler's Green," Robert Silverberg's "Born with the Dead" and "Sailing to Byzantium," James Tiptree's "The Girl Who Was Plugged In," Damon Knight's "The Earth

Quarter" and "Dio," J. G. Ballard's "The Voices of Time," Kate Wilhelm's "The Infinity Box," Cordwainer Smith's "On the Storm Planet," Michael Swanwick's "Trojan Horse," George R. R. Martin's "A Song for Lya," Walter Jon Williams's "No Spot of Ground," Bruce Sterling's "Green Days in Brunei," Pat Cadigan's "My Brother's Keeper," John Crowley's "Great Work of Time," Thomas M. Disch's "The Asian Shore," and a dozen others – must wait for the multi-dimensional, infinitely extensible version of this anthology.

There is a finite amount of space even for the shorter stories, alas – and if I'd had even 40,000 words worth of extra room to use, you'd find stories here by Fritz Lieber, Kate Wilhelm, Norman Spinrad, Thomas M. Disch, Ian Watson, Auram Davidson, Robert Silverberg, Greg Bear, Brian Stableford, Pat Murphy, Frederik Pohl, M. John Harrison, Mike Resnick, James Patrick Kelly, Kim Stanley Robinson, and others, which we were ultimately unable to squeeze into the book, no matter how hard we tried.

Last of all, having assembled the stories that burned the brightest in my memory, I went back and reread them all again – thumping them, as it were, to see if any of them rang hollow. A few of them *did*, not holding up to a fresh reading, and I excised them. The majority did *not*.

Tastes being as subjective as they are, I can't claim that these are the best science fiction stories of the last four decades – but certainly it is safe to say that they are *among* the best, at the very least. There is not a story in this book that I wouldn't buy today, if it were somehow crossing my desk for the first time, not even the oldest story here, which will be thirty-six years old by the time you read these words.

The best stories, in fact, seem essentially to be timeless. (We're still reading the *Odyssey*, aren't we?) A good story is like a benign virus – even when it orginates in the minds of men and women long years dead, it can reach across the abyss of the grave, across thousands of miles of distance and hundreds of years of time, across every barrier of custom or prejudice or age, and, touching a living mind, infect that mind with the dream at its heart . . . can leave the one that it infects with dreaming shaken and changed forever, forever dizzy and raddled with a vision that came to them from *outside* the fortress self, burning up with the fever of dreams. And then they may touch someone *else* . . .

Long years from now, long after everyone in this anthology or involved with it have gone to dust, the stories here may still touch someone, and cause that person touched to blink, and put the book down for a second, and stare off through the hollow air, and shiver in wonder.

DAMON KNIGHT
The Country of the Kind

A multi-talented professional whose career as writer, editor, critic, and anthologist spans almost fifty years, Damon Knight has long been a major shaping force in the development of modern science fiction. He wrote the first important book of SF criticism, *In Search of Wonder*, and won a Hugo Award for it. He was the founder of the Science Fiction Writers of America, cofounder of the prestigious Milford Writers' Conference, and, with his wife, writer Kate Wilhelm, is still deeply involved in the operation of the Clarion workshop for new young writers, which was modeled after the Milford Conference. He was the editor of *Orbit*, the longest-running original anthology series in the history of American science fiction, and the most prominent American avant-garde market during the New Wave days of the mid to late '60s. Knight has also produced important works of genre history such as *The Futurians* and *Turning Points*, as well as dozens of influential reprint anthologies, such as *A Science Fiction Argosy*, *Worlds to Come*, *Dimension X*, *The Dark Side*, and *Science Fiction of the Thirties*.

Knight has also been highly influential as a writer, and may well be one of the finest short-story writers ever to work in the genre. Like Bradbury, Ellison, Tiptree, and a number of other SF writers, Knight's reputation rests almost entirely on his short fiction, for somehow his novels, though entertaining, have never reached the level of quality of his best short fiction (although – before the disappointing ending – he wrote *half* of one of the best novels of the '80s in *The Man in the Tree*). Like a handful of other writers during the '50s (Theodore Sturgeon, Alfred Bester, Fritz Leiber, C. M. Kornbluth, Brian W. Aldiss, William Tenn, Ray Bradbury, and Algis Budrys, among others), Knight at his best was engaged in the chore of redrawing the boundaries of the science-fiction short story, redefining its possibilities, and greatly expanding its limits. For this alone – ignoring his accomplishments as a critic and as an

editor – the new writers of the '60s and '70s, who would build on
the foundations laid in the '50s (and several of whom – at the
very least, inarguably, Michael Bishop, James Tiptree, Jr, and
Kate Wilhelm – were directly influenced by him), owe him a
great deal.

There are a number of Knight stories I've never been able to
forget, and which would have served for this anthology –
"Stranger Station," "The Dying Man," "What Rough Beast?,"
"Masks," "Rule Golden," "The Earth Quarter," "Mary" – but
in the final analysis, the one that could not be excluded was
"The Country of the Kind," a story which still strikes me as one
of the best SF stories of our times, and which James Blish once
referred to as "one of the most uncomfortable parables in our
language."

Knight's other books include the novels *A For Anything*, *The
Other Foot*, and *Hell's Pavement*, and the collections *Rule Golden
and Other Stories*, *Turning On*, *Far Out*, and *The Best of Damon
Knight*. His most recent books are the novels *CV*, and its sequel,
The Observers. Coming up is a new novel, *A Reasonable World*, and
a new collection, *One Side Laughing*. Knight lives with his family
in Eugene, Oregon.

The attendant at the car lot was daydreaming when I pulled
up – a big, lazy-looking man in black satin chequered down
the front. I was wearing scarlet, myself; it suited my mood. I
got out, almost on his toes.

"Park or storage?" he asked automatically, turning
around. Then he realized who I was, and ducked his head
away.

"Neither," I told him.

There was a hand torch on a shelf in the repair shed right
behind him. I got it and came back. I knelt down to where I
could reach behind the front wheel, and ignited the torch. I
turned it on the axle and suspension. They glowed cherry
red, then white, and fused together. Then I got up and
turned the flame on both tires until the rubberoid stank and
sizzled and melted down to the pavement. The attendant
didn't say anything.

I left him there, lookng at the mess on his nice clean
concrete.

It had been a nice car, too; but I could get another any
time. And I felt like walking. I went down the winding road,

sleepy in the afternoon sunlight, dappled with shade and smelling of cool leaves. You couldn't see the houses; they were all sunken or hidden by shrubbery, or a little of both. That was the fad I'd heard about; it was what I'd come here to see. Not that anything the dulls did would be worth looking at.

I turned off at random and crossed a rolling lawn, went through a second hedge of hawthorn in blossom, and came out next to a big sunken games court.

The tennis net was up, and two couples were going at it, just working up a little sweat – young, about half my age, all four of them. Three dark-haired, one blonde. They were evenly matched, and both couples played well together; they were enjoying themselves.

I watched for a minute. But by then the nearest two were beginning to sense I was there, anyhow. I walked down onto the court just as the blonde was about to serve. She looked at me frozen across the net, poised on tiptoe. The others stood.

"Off," I told them. "Game's over."

I watched the blonde. She was not especially pretty, as they go, but compactly and gracefully put together. She came down slowly, flat-footed without awkwardness, and tucked the racket under her arm; then the surprise was over and she was trotting off the court after the other three.

I followed their voices around the curve of the path, between towering masses of lilacs, inhaling the sweetness, until I came to what looked like a little sunning spot. There was a sundial, and a birdbath, and towels lying around on the grass. One couple, the dark-haired pair, was still in sight farther down the path, heads bobbing along. The other couple had disappeared.

I found the handle in the grass without any trouble. The mechanism responded, and an oblong section of turf rose up. It was the stair I had, not the elevator, but that was all right. I ran down the steps and into the first door I saw, and was in the top-floor lounge, an oval room lit with diffused simulated sunlight from above. The furniture was all comfortably bloated, sprawling and ugly; the carpet was deep, and there was a fresh flower scent in the air.

The blonde was over at the near end with her back to me,

studying the autochef keyboard. She was half out of her playsuit. She pushed it the rest of the way down and stepped out of it, then turned and saw me.

She was surprised again; she hadn't thought I might follow her down.

I got up close before it occurred to her to move; then it was too late. She knew she couldn't get away from me; she closed her eyes and leaned back against the paneling, turning a little pale. Her lips and her golden brows went up in the middle.

I looked her over and told her a few uncomplimentry things about herself. She trembled, but didn't answer. On an impulse, I leaned over and dialed the autochef to hot cheese sauce. I cut the safety out of circuit and put the quantity dial all the way up. I dialed *soup tureen* and then *punch bowl*.

The stuff began to come out in about a minute, steaming hot. I took the tureens and splashed them up and down the wall on either side of her. Then when the first punch bowl came out I used the empty bowls as scoops. I clotted the carpet with the stuff; I made streamers of it all along the walls, and dumped puddles into what furniture I could reach. Where it cooled it would harden, and where it hardened it would cling.

I wanted to splash it across her body, but it would've hurt, and we couldn't have that. The punch bowls of hot sauce were still coming out of the autochef, crowding each other around the vent. I punched *cancel*, and then *sauterne* (*swt., Calif.*).

It came out well chilled in open bottles. I took the first one and had my arm back just about to throw a nice line of the stuff right across her midriff, when a voice said behind me:

"Watch out for cold wine."

My arm twitched and a little stream of the wine splashed across her thighs. She was ready for it; her eyes had opened at the voice, and she barely jumped.

I whirled around, fighting mad. The man was standing there where he had come out of the stair well. He was thinner in the face than most, bronzed, wide-chested, with alert blue eyes. If it hadn't been for him, I knew it would have worked —the blonde would have mistaken the chill splash for a scalding one.

I could hear the scream in my mind, and I wanted it.

I took a step toward him, and my foot slipped. I went down clumsily, wrenching one knee. I got up shaking and tight all over. I wasn't in control of myself. I screamed, "You – you –" I turned and got one of the punch bowls and lifted it in both hands, heedless of how the hot sauce was slopping over onto my wrists, and I had it almost in the air toward him when the sickness took me – that damned buzzing in my head, louder, louder, drowning everything out.

When I came to, they were both gone. I got up off the floor, weak as death, and staggered over to the nearest chair. My clothes were slimmed and sticky. I wanted to die. I wanted to drop into that dark furry hole that was yawning for me and never come up; but I made myself stay awake and get out of the chair.

Going down in the elevator, I almost blacked out again. The blonde and the thin man weren't in any of the second-floor bedrooms. I made sure of that, and then I emptied the closets and bureau drawers onto the floor, dragged the whole mess into one of the bathrooms and stuffed the tub with it, then turned on the water.

I tried the third floor: maintenance and storage. It was empty. I turned the furnace on and set the thermostat up as high as it would go. I disconnected all the safety circuits and alarms. I opened the freezer doors and dialed them to defrost. I propped the stair well door open and went back up in the elevator.

On the second floor I stopped long enough to open the stairway door there – the water was halfway toward it, creeping across the floor – and then searched the top floor. No one was there. I opened book reels and threw them unwinding across the room; I would have done more, but I could hardly stand. I got up to the surface and collapsed on the lawn: that furry pit swallowed me up, dead and drowned.

While I slept, water poured down the open stair well and filled the third level. Thawing food packages floated out into the rooms. Water seeped into wall panels and machine housings; circuits shorted and fuses blew. The air conditioning stopped, but the pile kept heating. The water rose.

Spoiled food, floating supplies, grimy water surged up the
stair well. The second and first levels were bigger and would
take longer to fill, but they'd fill. Rugs, furnishings, clothing,
all the things in the house would be waterlogged and ruined.
Probably the weight of so much water would shift the house,
rupture water pipes and other fluid intakes. It would take a
repair crew more than a day just to clean up the mess. The
house itself was done for, not repairable. The blonde and the
thin man would never live in it again.

Serve them right.

The dulls could build another house; they built like
beavers. There was only one of me in the world.

The earliest memory I have is of some woman, probably
the cresh-mother, staring at me with an expression of shock
and horror. Just that. I've tried to remember what happened
directly before or after, but I can't. Before, there's nothing
but the dark formless shaft of no-memory that runs back to
birth. Afterward, the big calm.

From my fifth year, it must have been, to my fifteenth,
everything I can remember floats in a pleasant dim sea.
Nothing was terribly important. I was languid and soft; I
drifted. Waking merged into sleep.

In my fifteenth year it was the fashion in love-play for the
young people to pair off for months or longer. "Loving
steady," we called it. I remember how the older people
protested that it was unhealthy; but we were all normal
juniors, and nearly as free as adults under the law.

All but me.

The first steady girl I had was named Elen. She had
blonde hair, almost white, worn long; her lashes were dark
and her eyes pale green. Startling eyes: they didn't look as if
they were looking at you. They looked blind.

Several times she gave me strange startled glances,
something between fright and anger. Once it was because I
held her too tightly, and hurt her; other times, it seemed to be
for nothing at all.

In our group, a pairing that broke up sooner than four
weeks was a little suspect – there must be something wrong
with one partner or both, or the pairing would have lasted
longer.

Four weeks and a day after Elen and I made our pairing, she told me she was breaking it.

I'd thought I was ready. But I felt the room spin half around me till the wall came against my palm and stopped.

The room had been in use as a hobby chamber; there was a rack of plasticraft knives under my hand. I took one without thinking, and when I saw it I thought, *I'll frighten her.*

And I saw the startled, half-angry look in her pale eyes as I went toward her; but this is curious: she wasn't looking at the knife. She was looking at my face.

The elders found me later with the blood on me, and put me into a locked room. Then it was my turn to be frightened, because I realized for the first time that it was possible for a human being to do what I had done.

And if I could do it to Elen, I thought, surely they could do it to me.

But they couldn't. They set me free: they had to.

And it was then I understood that I was the king of the world. . . .

The sky was turning clear violet when I woke up, and shadow was spilling out from the hedges. I went down the hill until I saw a ghostly blue of photon tubes glowing in a big oblong, just outside the commerce area. I went that way, by habit.

Other people were lining up at the entrance to show their books and be admitted. I brushed by them, seeing the shocked faces and feeling their bodies flinch away, and went on into the robing chamber.

Straps, aqualungs, masks and flippers were all for the taking. I stripped, dropping the clothes where I stood, and put the underwater equipment on. I strode out to the poolside, monstrous, like a being from another world. I adjusted the lung and the flippers, and slipped into the water.

Underneath, it was all crystal blue, with the forms of swimmers sliding through it like pale angels. Schools of small fish scattered as I went down. My heart was beating with a painful joy.

Down, far down, I saw a girl slowly undulating through the motions of sinuous underwater dance, writhing around

and around a ribbed column of imitation coral. She had a
suction-tipped fish lance in her hand, but she was not using
it; she was only dancing, all by herself, down at the bottom of
the water.

I swam after her. She was young and delicately made, and
when she saw the deliberately clumsy motions I made in
imitation of hers, her eyes glinted with amusement behind
her mask. She bowed to me in mockery, and slowly glided off
with simple, exaggerated movements, like a child's ballet.

I followed. Around her and around I swam, stiff-legged,
first more child-like and awkward than she, then subtly
parodying her motions; then improving on them until I was
dancing an intricate, mocking dance around her.

I saw her eyes widen. She matched her rhythm to mine,
then, and together, apart, together again we coiled the wake
of our dancing. At last, exhausted, we clung together where a
bridge of plastic coral arched over us. Her cool body was in
the bend of my arm; behind two thicknesses of vitrin – a
world away! – her eyes were friendly and kind.

There was a moment when, two strangers yet one flesh, we
felt our souls speak to one another across that abyss of
matter. It was a truncated embrace – we could not kiss, we
could not speak – but her hands lay confidingly on my
shoulders, and her eyes looked into mine.

That moment had to end. She gestured toward the
surface, and left me. I followed her up. I was feeling drowsy
and almost at peace, after my sickness. I thought . . . I don't
know what I thought.

We rose together at the side of the pool. She turned to me,
removing her mask: and her smile stopped, and melted
away. She stared at me with a horrified disgust, wrinkling
her nose.

"*Pyah!*" she said, and turned, awkward in her flippers.
Watching her, I saw her fall into the arms of a white-haired
man, and heard her hysterical voice tumbling over itself.

"But don't you remember?" the man's voice rumbled.
"You should know it by heart." He turned. "Hal, is there a
copy of it in the clubhouse?"

A murmur answered him, and in a few moments a young
man came out holding a slender brown pamphlet.

I knew that pamphlet. I could even have told you what page the white-haired man opened it to; what sentences the girl was reading as I watched.

I waited. I don't know why.

I heard her voice rising: "To think that I let him *touch* me!" And the white-haired man reassured her, the words rumbling, too low to hear. I saw her back straighten. She looked across at me . . . only a few yards in that scented, blue-lit air; a world away . . . and folded up the pamphlet into a hard wad, threw it, and turned on her heel.

The pamphlet landed almost at my feet. I touched it with my toe, and it opened to the page I had been thinking of:

> . . . sedation until his 15th year, when for sexual reasons it became no longer practicable. While the advisors and medical staff hesitated, he killed a girl of the group by violence.

And farther down:

> The solution finally adopted was three-fold.
> 1. *A sanction* – the only sanction possible to our humane, permissive society. Excommunication: not to speak to him, touch him willingly, or acknowledge his existence.
> 2. *A precaution.* Taking advantage of a mild predisposition to epilepsy, a variant of the so-called Kusko analog technique was employed, to prevent by an epileptic seizure any future act of violence.
> 3. *A warning.* A careful alteration of his body chemistry was effected to make his exhaled and exuded wastes emit a strongly pungent and offensive odor. In mercy, he himself was rendered unable to detect this smell.
> Fortunately, the genetic and environmental accidents which combined to produce this atavism have been fully explained and can never again . . .

The words stopped meaning anything, as they always did at that point. I didn't want to read any farther; it was all nonsense, anyway. I was the king of the world.

I got up and went away, out into the night, blind to the dulls who thronged the rooms I passed.

Two squares away was the commerce area. I found a clothing outlet and went in. All the free clothes in the display cases were drab: those were for worthless floaters, not for me. I went past them to the specials, and found a combination I could stand – silver and blue, with a severe black piping down the tunic. A dull would have said it was "nice." I punched for it. The automatic looked me over with its dull glassy eye, and croaked, "Your contribution book, please."

I could have had a contribution book, for the trouble of stepping out into the street and taking it away from the first passer-by; but I·didn't have the patience. I picked up the one-legged table from the refreshment nook, hefted it, and swung it at the cabinet door. The metal shrieked and dented, opposite the catch. I swung once more to the same place, and the door sprang open. I pulled out clothing in handfuls till I got a set that would fit me.

I bathed and changed, and then went prowling in the big multi-outlet down the avenue. All those places are arranged pretty much alike, no matter what the local managers do to them. I went straight to the knives, and picked out three in graduated sizes, down to the size of my fingernail. Then I had to take my chances. I tried the furniture department, where I had had good luck once in a while, but this year all they were using was metal. I had to have seasoned wood.

I knew where there was a big cache of cherry wood, in good-sized blocks, in a forgotten warehouse up north at a place called Kootenay. I could have carried some around with me – enough for years – but what for, when the world belonged to me?

It didn't take me long. Down in the workshop section, of all places, I found some antiques – tables and benches, all with wooden tops. While the dulls collected down at the other end of the room, pretending not to notice, I sawed off a good oblong chunk of the smallest bench, and made a base for it out of another.

As long as I was there, it was a good place to work, and I could eat and sleep upstairs, so I stayed.

I knew what I wanted to do. It was going to be a man, sitting, with his legs crossed and his forearms resting down along his calves. His head was going to be tilted back, and his eyes closed, as if he were turning his face up to the sun.

In three days it was finished. The trunk and limbs had a shape that was not man and not wood, but something in between: something that hadn't existed before I made it.

Beauty. That was the old word.

I had carved one of the figure's hands hanging loosely, and the other one curled shut. There had to be a time to stop and say it was finished. I took the smallest knife, the one I had been using to scrape the wood smooth, and cut away the handle and ground down what was left of the shaft to a thin spike. Then I drilled a hole into the wood of the figurine's hand, in the hollow between thumb and curled finger. I fitted the knife blade in there; in the small hand it was a sword.

I cemented it in place. Then I took the sharp blade and stabbed my thumb, and smeared the blade.

I hunted most of that day, and finally found the right place – a niche in an outcropping of striated brown rock, in a little triangular half-wild patch that had been left where two roads forked. Nothing was permanent, of course, in a community like this one that might change its houses every five years or so, to follow the fashion; but this spot had been left to itself for a long time. It was the best I could do.

I had the paper ready: it was one of a batch I had printed up a year ago. The paper was treated, and I knew it would stay legible a long time. I hid a little photo capsule in the back of the niche, and ran the control wire to a staple in the base of the figurine. I put the figurine down on top of the paper, and anchored it lightly to the rock with two spots of all-cement. I had done it so often that it came naturally; I knew just how much cement would hold the figurine steady against a casual hand, but yield to one that really wanted to pull it down.

Then I stepped back to look: and the power and the pity of it made my breath come short, and tears start to my eyes.

Reflected light gleamed fitfully on the dark-stained blade that hung from his hand. He was sitting alone in that niche that closed him in like a coffin. His eyes were shut, and his head tilted back, as if he were turning his face up to the sun.

But only rock was over his head. There was no sun for him.

Hunched on the cool bare ground under a pepper tree, I was looking down across the road at the shadowed niche where my figurine sat.

I was all finished here. There was nothing more to keep me, and yet I couldn't leave.

People walked past now and then – not often. The community seemed half deserted, as if most of the people had flocked off to a surf party somewhere, or a contribution meeting, or to watch a new house being dug to replace the one I had wrecked. . . . There was a little wind blowing toward me, cool and lonesome in the leaves.

Up the other side of the hollow there was a terrace, and on that terrace, half an hour ago, I had seen a brief flash of color – a boy's head, with a red cap on it, moving past and out of sight.

That was why I had to stay. I was thinking how that boy might come down from his terrace and into my road, and passing the little wild triangle of land, see my figurine. I was thinking he might not pass by indifferently, but stop: and go closer to look: and pick up the wooden man: and read what was written on the paper underneath.

I believed that sometime it had to happen. I wanted it so hard that I ached.

My carvings were all over the world, wherever I had wandered. There was one in Congo City, carved of ebony, dusty-black; one on Cyprus, of bone; one in New Bombay, of shell; one in Chang-teh, of jade.

They were like signs printed in red and green, in a color-blind world. Only the one I was looking for would ever pick one of them up, and read the message I knew by heart.

TO YOU WHO CAN SEE, the first sentence said, I OFFER YOU A WORLD . . .

There was a flash of color up on the terrace. I stiffened. A minute later, here it came again, from a different direction: it was the boy, clambering down the slope, brilliant against the green, with his red sharp-billed cap like a woodpecker's head.

I held my breath.

He came toward me through the fluttering leaves, ticked off by pencils of sunlight as he passed. He was a brown boy, I could see at this distance, with a serious thin face. His ears stuck out, flickering pink with the sun behind them, and his elbow and knee pads made him look knobby.

He reached the fork in the road, and chose the path on my side. I huddled into myself as he came nearer. *Let him see it, let him not see me*, I thought fiercely.

My fingers closed around a stone.

He was nearer, walking jerkily with his hands in his pockets, watching his feet mostly.

When he was almost opposite me, I threw the stone.

It rustled through the leaves below the niche in the rock. The boy's head turned. He stopped, staring. I think he saw the figurine then. I'm sure he saw it.

He took one step.

"Risha!" came floating down from the terrace.

And he looked up. "Here," he piped.

I saw the woman's head, tiny at the top of the terrace. She called something I didn't hear; I was standing up, tight with anger.

Then the wind shifted. It blew from me to the boy. He whirled around, his eyes big, and clapped a hand to his nose.

"Oh, what a stench!" he said.

He turned to shout, "Coming!" and then he was gone, hurrying back up the road, into the unstable blur of green.

My one chance, ruined. He would have seen the image, I knew, if it hadn't been for that damned woman, and the wind shifting. . . . They were all against me, people, wind and all.

And the figurine still sat, blind eyes turned up to the rocky sky.

There was something inside me that told me to take my disappointment and go away from there, and not come back.

I knew I would be sorry. I did it anyway: took the image out of the niche, and the paper with it, and climbed the slope. At the top I heard his clear voice laughing.

There was a thing that might have been an ornamental mound, or the camouflaged top of a buried house. I went around it, tripping over my own feet, and came upon the boy kneeling on the turf. He was playing with a brown and white puppy.

He looked up with the laughter going out of his face. There was no wind, and he could smell me. I knew it was bad. No wind, and the puppy to distract him – everything about it was wrong. But I went to him blindly anyhow, and fell on one knee, and shoved the figurine at his face.

"Look –" I said.

He went over backwards in his hurry: he couldn't even have seen the image, except as a brown blur coming at him. He scrambled up, with the puppy whining and yapping around his heels, and ran for the mound.

I was up after him, clawing up moist earth and grass as I rose. In the other hand I still had the image clutched, and the paper with it.

A door popped open and swallowed him and popped shut again in my face. With the flat of my hand I beat the vines around it until I hit the doorplate by accident and the door opened. I dived in, shouting, "Wait," and was in a spiral passage, lit pearl-gray, winding downward. Down I went headlong, and came out at the wrong door – an underground conservatory, humid and hot under the yellow lights, with dripping rank leaves in long rows. I went down the aisle raging, overturning the tanks, until I came to a vestibule and an elevator.

Down I went again to the third level and a labyrinth of guest rooms, all echoing, all empty. At last I found a ramp leading upward, past the conservatory, and at the end of it voices.

The door was clear vitrin, and I paused on the near side of it looking and listening. There was the boy, and a woman old enough to be his mother, just – sister or cousin, more likely – and an elderly woman in a hard chair, holding the puppy. The room was comfortable and tasteless, like other rooms.

I saw the shock grow on their faces as I burst in: it was always the same, they knew I would like to kill them, but they never expected that I would come uninvited into a house. It was not done.

There was that boy, so close I could touch him, but the shock of all of them was quivering in the air, smothering, like a blanket that would deaden my voice. I felt I had to shout.

"Everything they tell you is lies!" I said. "See here – here, this is the truth!" I had the figurine in front of his eyes, but he didn't see.

"Risha, go below," said the young woman quietly. He

turned to obey, quick as a ferret. I got in front of him again. "Stay," I said, breathing hard. "Look –"

"Remember, Risha, don't speak," said the woman.

I couldn't stand any more. Where the boy went I don't know; I ceased to see him. With the image in one hand and the paper with it, I leaped at the woman. I was almost quick enough; I almost reached her; but the buzzing took me in the middle of a step, louder, louder, like the end of the world.

It was the second time that week. When I came to, I was sick and too faint to move for a long time.

The house was silent. They had gone, of course . . . the house had been defiled, having me in it. They wouldn't live here again, but would build elsewhere.

My eyes blurred. After a while I stood up and looked around at the room. The walls were hung with a gray close-woven cloth that looked as if it would tear, and I thought of ripping it down in strips, breaking furniture, stuffing carpets and bedding into the oubliette. . . . But I didn't have the heart for it. I was too tired. Thirty years. . . . They had given me all the kingdoms of the world, and the glory thereof, thirty years ago. It was more than one man alone could bear, for thirty years.

At last I stooped and picked up the figurine, and the paper that was supposed to go under it – crumpled now, with the forlorn look of a message that someone has thrown away unread.

I sighed bitterly.

I smoothed it out and read the last part.

YOU CAN SHARE THE WORLD WITH ME. THEY CAN'T STOP YOU. STRIKE NOW – PICK UP A SHARP THING AND STAB, OR A HEAVY THING AND CRUSH. THAT'S ALL. THAT WILL MAKE YOU FREE. ANYONE CAN DO IT.

Anyone. Someone. Anyone.

L. SPRAGUE DE CAMP

Aristotle and the Gun

L. Sprague de Camp is a seminal figure, one whose career spans almost the entire development of modern fantasy and SF. Much of the luster of the "Golden Age" of *Astounding* during the late '30s and the '40s is due to the presence in those pages of de Camp, along with his great contemporaries Robert A. Heinlein, Theodore Sturgeon, and A. E. Van Vogt. At the same time, for *Astounding*'s sister fantasy magazine, *Unknown*, he helped to create a whole new modern style of fantasy writing – funny, whimsical, and irreverent – of which he is still the most prominent practitioner. De Camp's stories for *Unknown* are among the best short fantasies ever written, and include such classics as "The Wheels of If," "The Gnarly Man," "Nothing in the Rules," "The Hardwood Pile," and (written in collaboration with Fletcher Pratt) the famous "Harold Shea" stories that would later be collected as *The Compleat Enchanter*. In science fiction, he is the author of *Lest Darkness Fall*, in my opinion one of the three or four best Alternate Worlds novels ever written, as well as the at-the-time highly controversial novel *Rogue Queen*, and a body of expertly crafted short fiction such as "Judgment Day," "Divide and Rule," and "A Gun for Dinosaur."

"Aristotle and the Gun," published in 1956, would prove to be de Camp's last science-fiction short story for more than a decade. After this, he would devote his energies to turning out a long sequence of critically acclaimed historical novels (including *The Bronze God of Rhodes* and *An Elephant for Aristotle*, two of my favorite historical novels) and, like Isaac Asimov (and at about the same time), a number of non-fiction books on scientific and technical topics. He would not return to writing fantasy and SF to any significant degree until the mid-'70s, and, although his presence enriched several other fields, it was sorely missed in ours. Still, if de Camp *had* to stop writing SF for a time, this was a good story to go out with – de Camp at the height of his powers, writing in his usual vivid, erudite, and slyly witty way about some of the subjects – and the historical personages – that interested him the most.

De Camp's other books include *The Glory That Was, The Search for Zei, The Tower of Zanid, The Great Fetish*, and, with Fletcher Pratt, *The Land of Unreason*. His short fiction has been collected in *The Best of L. Sprague de Camp, A Gun for Dinosaur*, and *The Purple Pterodactyls*. His most recent book is *The Honorable Barbarian*. He lives in Texas with his wife, writer Catherine Crook de Camp.

From:

Sherman Weaver, Librarian
The Palace
Paumanok, Sewanhaki
Sachimate of Lenape
Flower Moon 3, 3097

To:

Messire Markos Koukidas
Consulate of the Balkan Commonwealth
Kataapa, Muskhogian Federation

My dear Consul:

You have no doubt heard of our glorious victory at Ptaksit, when our noble Sachim destroyed the armored chivalry of the Mengwe by the brilliant use of pikemen and archery. (I suggested it to him years ago but never mind.) Sagoyewatha and most of his Senecas fell, and the Oneidas broke before our countercharge. The envoys from the Grand Council of the Long House arrive tomorrow for a peace-pauwau. The roads to the South are open again, so I send you my long-promised account of the events that brought me from my own world into this one.

If you could have stayed longer on your last visit, I think I could have made the matter clear, despite the language difficulty and my hardness of hearing. But perhaps, if I give you a simple narrative, in the order in which things happened to me, truth will transpire.

Know, then, that I was born into a world that looks like

this on on the map, but is very different as regards human affairs. I tried to tell you of some of the triumphs of our natural philosophers, of our machines and discoveries. No doubt you thought me a first-class liar, though you were too polite to say so.

Nonetheless, my tale is true, though for reasons that will appear I cannot prove it. I was one of those natural philosophers. I commanded a group of younger philosophers, engaged in a task called a *project*, at a center of learning named Brookhaven, on the south shore of Sewanhaki twenty parasangs east of Paumanok. Paumanok itself was known as Brooklyn, and formed part of an even larger city called New York.

My project had to do with the study of space-time. (Never mind what that means but read on.) At this center we had learned to get vast amounts of power from sea water by what we called a fusion process. By this process we could concentrate so much power in a small space that we could warp the entity called space-time and cause things to travel in time as our other machines traveled in space.

When our calculations showed that we could theoretically hurl an object back in time, we began to build a machine for testing this hypothesis. First we built a small pilot model. In this we sent small objects back in time for short periods.

We began with inanimate objects. Then we found that a rabbit or rat could also be projected without harm. The time-translation would not be permanent; rather, it acted like one of these rubber balls the Hesperians play games with. The object would stay in the desired time for a period determined by the power used to project it and its own mass, and would then return spontaneously to the time and place from which it started.

We had reported our progress regularly, but my chief had other matters on his mind and did not read our reports for many months. When he got a report saying that we were completing a machine to hurl human beings back in time, however, he awoke to what was going on, read our previous reports, and called me in.

"Sherm," he said, "I've been discussing this project with Washington, and I'm afraid they take a dim view of it."

"Why?" said I, astonished.

"Two reasons. For one thing, they think you've gone off the reservation. They're much more interested in the Antarctic Reclamation Project and want to concentrate all our appropriations and brain power on it.

"For another, they're frankly scared of this time machine of yours. Suppose you went back, say, to the time of Alexander the Great and shot Alexander before he got started? That would change all later history, and we'd go out like candles."

"Ridiculous," I said.

"What, what *would* happen?"

"Our equations are not conclusive, but there are several possibilities. As you will see if you read Report No. 9, it depends on whether space-time has a positive or negative curvature. If positive, any disturbance in the past tends to be ironed out in subsequent history, so that things become more and more nearly identical with what they would have been anyway. If negative, then events will diverge more and more from their original pattern with time.

"Now, as I showed in this report, the chances are overwhelmingly in favor of a positive curvature. However, we intend to take every precaution and make our first tests for short periods, with a minimum –"

"That's enough," said my superior, holding up a hand. "It's very interesting, but the decision has already been made."

"What do you mean?"

"I mean Project A-257 is to be closed down and a final report written at once. The machines are to be dismantled, and the group will be put to work on another project."

"What?" I shouted. "But you can't stop us just when we're on the verge –"

"I'm sorry, Sherm, but I can. That's what the AEC decided at yesterday's meeting. It hasn't been officially announced, but they gave me positive orders to kill the project as soon as I got back here."

"Of all the lousy, arbitrary, benighted –"

"I know how you feel, but I have no choice."

I lost my temper and defied him, threatening to go ahead

with the project anyway. It was ridiculous, because he could easily dismiss me for insubordination. However, I knew he valued my ability and counted on his wanting to keep me for that reason. But he was clever enough to have his cake and eat it.

"If that's how you feel," he said, "the section is abolished here and now. Your group will be broken up and assigned to other projects. You'll be kept on at your present rating with the title of consultant. Then when you're willing to talk sense, perhaps we can find you a suitable job."

I stamped out of his office and went home to brood. I ought now to tell you something of myself. I am old enough to be objective, I hope. And, as I have but a few years left, there is no point in pretence.

I have always been a solitary, misanthropic man. I had little interest in or liking of my fellow man, who naturally paid me back in the same coin. I was awkward and ill at ease in company. I had a genius for saying the wrong thing and making a fool of myself.

I never understood people. Even when I watched and planned my own actions with the greatest care, I never could tell how others would react to them. To me men were and are an unpredictable, irrational, and dangerous species of hairless ape. While I could avoid some of my worst gaffes by keeping my own counsel and watching my every word, they did not like that either. They considered me a cold, stiff, unfriendly sort of person when I was only trying to be polite and avoid offending them.

I never married. At the time of which I speak, I was verging on middle age without a single close friend and no more acquaintances than my professional work required.

My only interest, outside my work was a hobby of the history of science. Unlike most of my fellow philosophers, I was historically minded, with a good smattering of a classical education. I belonged to the History of Science Society and wrote papers on the history of science for its periodical *Isis*.

I went back to my little rented house, feeling like Galileo. He was a scientist persecuted for his astronomical theories by the religious authorities of my world several centuries before my time, as Georg Schwartzhorn was a few years ago in this world's Europe.

I felt I had been born too soon. If only the world were scientifically more advanced, my genius would be appreciated and my personal difficulties solved.

Well, I thought, why is the world not scientifically more advanced? I reviewed the early growth of science. Why had not your fellow countrymen, when they made a start towards a scientific age two thousand to twenty-five hundred years ago, kept at it until they made science the self-supporting, self-accelerating thing it at last became – in my world, that is?

I knew the answers that historians of science had worked out. One was the effect of slavery, which made work disgraceful to a free man and therefore made experiment and invention unattractive because they looked like work. Another was the primitive state of the mechanical arts: things like making clear glass and accurate measuring devices. Another was the Hellenes' fondness for spinning cosmic theories without enough facts to go on, the result of which was that most of their theories were wildly wrong.

Well, thought I, could a man go back to this period and, by applying a stimulus at the right time and place, give the necessary push to set the whole trend rolling off in the right direction?

People had written fantastic stories about a man's going back in time and overawing the natives by a display of the discoveries of his own later era. More often than not, such a time-traveling hero came to a bad end. The people of the earlier time killed him as a witch, or he met with an accident, or something happened to keep him from changing history. But, knowing these dangers, I could forestall them by careful planning.

It would do little or no good to take back some major invention, like a printing press or an automobile, and turn it over to the ancients in the hope of grafting it on their culture. I could not teach them to work it in a reasonable time; and, if it broke down or ran out of supplies, there would be no way to get it running again.

What I had to do was to find a key mind and implant in it

an appreciation of sound scientific method. He would have to be somebody who would have been important in any event, or I could not count on his influence's spreading far and wide.

After study of Sarton and other historians of science, I picked Aristotle. You have heard of him, have you not? He existed in your world just as he did in mine. In fact, up to Aristotle's time our worlds were one and the same.

Aristotle was one of the greatest minds of all time. In my world, he was the first encyclopedist; the first man who tried to know everything, write down everything, and explain everything. He did much good original scientific work, too, mostly in biology.

However, Aristotle tried to cover so much ground, and accepted so many fables as facts that he did much harm to science as well as good. For, when a man of such colossal intellect goes wrong, he carries with him whole generations of weaker minds who cite him as an infallible authority. Like his colleagues, Aristotle never appreciated the need for constant verification. Thus, though he was married twice, he said that men have more teeth than women. He never thought to ask either of his wives to open her mouth for a count. He never grasped the need for invention and experiment.

Now, if I could catch Aristotle at the right period of his career, perhaps I could give him a push in the right direction.

When would that be? Normally, one would take him as a young man. But Aristotle's entire youth, from seventeen to thirty-seven, was spent in Athens listening to Plato's lectures. I did not wish to compete with Plato, an overpowering personality who could argue rings round everybody. His viewpoint was mystical and anti-scientific, the very thing I wanted to steer Aristotle away from. Many of Aristotle's intellectual vices can be traced back to Plato's influence.

I did not think it wise to present myself in Athens either during Aristotle's early period, when he was a student under Plato, or later, when he headed his own school. I could not pass myself off as a Hellene, and the Hellenes of that time had a contempt for all non-Hellenes, whom they called "barbarians." Aristotle was one of the worst offenders in this respect. Of course this is a universal human failing, but it was particularly virulent among Athenian intellectuals. In his later Athenian period, too, Aristotle's ideas would probably be too set with age to change.

I concluded that my best chance would be to catch Aristotle while he was tutoring young Alexander the Great at the court of Philip the Second of Macedon. He would have regarded Macedon as a backward country, even though the court spoke Attic Greek. Perhaps he would be bored with bluff Macedonian stag-hunting squires and lonesome for intellectual company. As he would regard the Macedonians as the next thing to *barbaroi*, another barbarian would not appear at such a disadvantage there as at Athens.

Of course, whatever I accomplished with Aristotle, the results would depend on the curvature of space-time. I had not been wholly frank with my superior. While the equations tended to favor the hypothesis of a positive curvature, the probability was not overwhelming as I claimed. Perhaps my efforts would have little effect on history, or perhaps the effect would grow and widen like ripples in a pool. In the latter case the existing world would, as my superior said, be snuffed out.

Well, at that moment I hated the existing world and would not give a snap of my fingers for its destruction. I was going to create a much better one and come back from ancient times to enjoy it.

Our previous experiments showed that I could project myself back to ancient Macedon with an accuracy of about two months temporally and a half-parasang spatially. The machine included controls for positioning the time traveler anywhere on the globe, and safety devices for locating him above the surface of the earth, not in a place already occupied by a solid object. The equations showed that I should stay in Macedon about nine weeks before being snapped back to the present.

Once I had made up my mind, I worked as fast as I could. I telephoned my superior (you remember what a telephone is?) and made my peace. I said:

"I know I was a damned fool, Fred, but this thing was my

baby; my one chance to be a great and famous scientist. I might have got a Nobel prize out of it."

"Sure, I know, Sherm," he said. "When are you coming back to the lab?"

"Well – uh – what about my group?"

"I held up the papers on that, in case you might change your mind. So if you come back, all will go on organization-wise as before."

"You want that final report on A-257, don't you?" I said, trying to keep my voice level.

"Sure."

"Then don't let the mechanics start to dismantle the machines until I've written the report."

"No; I've had the place locked up since yesterday."

"Okay. I want to shut myself in with the apparatus and the data sheets for a while and bat out the report without being bothered."

"That'll be fine," he said.

My first step in getting ready for my journey was to buy a suit of classical traveler's clothing from a theatrical costume company. This comprised a knee-length pull-over tunic or chiton, a short horseman's cloak or chlamys, knitted buskins, sandals, a broad-brimmed black felt hat, and a staff. I stopped shaving, though I did not have time to raise a respectable beard.

My auxiliary equipment included a purse of coinage of the time, mostly golden Macedonian staters. Some of these coins were genuine, bought from a numismatic supply house, but most were copies I cast myself in the laboratory at night. I made sure of being rich enough to live decently for longer than my nine weeks' stay. This was not hard, as the purchasing power of precious metals was more than fifty times greater in the classical world than in mine.

I wore the purse attached to a heavy belt next to my skin. From this belt also hung a missile-weapon called a *gun*, which I have told you about. This was a small gun, called a pistol or revolver. I did not mean to shoot anybody, or expose the gun at all if I could help it. It was there as a last resort.

I also took several small devices of our science to impress

Aristotle: a pocket microscope and a magnifying glass, a small telescope, a compass, my timepiece, a flashlight, a small camera, and some medicines. I intended to show these things to people of ancient times only with the greatest caution. By the time I had slung all these objects in their pouches and cases from my belt, I had a heavy load. Another belt over the tunic supported a small purse for day-to-day buying and an all-purpose knife.

I already had a good reading knowledge of classical Greek, which I tried to polish by practice with the spoken language and listening to it on my talking machine. I knew I should arrive speaking with an accent, for we had no way of knowing exactly what Attic Greek sounded like.

I decided, therefore, to pass myself off as a traveler from India. Nobody would believe I was a Hellene. If I said I came from the north or west, no Hellene would listen to me, as they regarded Europeans as warlike but half-witted savages. If I said I was from some well-known civilized country like Carthage, Egypt, Babylonia, or Persia, I should be in danger of meeting someone who knew those countries and of being exposed as a fraud.

To tell the truth of my origin, save under extraordinary circumstances, would be most imprudent. It would lead to my being considered a lunatic or a liar, as I can guess that your good self has more than once suspected me of being.

An Indian, however, should be acceptable. At this time, the Hellenes knew about that land only a few wild rumors and the account of Ktesias of Knidos, who made a book of the tales he picked up about India at the Persian court. The Hellenes had heard that India harbored philosophers. Therefore, thinking Greeks might be willing to consider Indians as almost as civilized as themselves.

What should I call myself? I took a common Indian name, Chandra, and Hellenized it to Zandras. That, I knew, was what the Hellenes would do anyway, as they had no "tch" sound and insisted on putting Greek inflectional endings on foreign names. I would not try to use my own name, which is not even remotely Greek or Indian-sounding. (Some day I must explain the blunders in my world that led to Hesperians' being called "Indians.")

The newness and cleanliness of my costume bothered me. It did not look worn, and I could hardly break it in around Brookhaven without attracting attention. I decided that if the question came up, I should say: yes, I bought it when I entered Greece, so as not to be conspicuous in my native garb.

During the day, when not scouring New York for equipment, I was locked in the room with the machine. While my colleagues thought I was either writing my report or dismantling the apparatus, I was getting ready for my trip.

Two weeks went by thus. One day a memorandum came down from my superior, saying: "How is that final report coming?"

I knew then I had better put my plan into execution at once. I sent back a memorandum: "Almost ready for the writing machine."

That night I came back to the laboratory. As I had been doing this often, the guards took no notice. I went to the time-machine room, locked the door from the inside, and got out my equipment and costume.

I adjusted the machine to set me down near Pella, the capital of Macedon, in the spring of the year 340 before Christ in our system of reckoning (976 Algonkian). I set the auto-actuator, climbed inside, and closed the door.

The feeling of being projected through time cannot really be described. There is a sharp pain, agonizing but too short to let the victim even cry out. At the same time there is the feeling of terrific acceleration, as if one were being shot from a catapult, but in no particular direction.

Then the seat in the passenger compartment dropped away from under me. There was a crunch, and a lot of sharp things jabbed me. I had fallen into the top of a tree.

I grabbed a couple of branches to save myself. The mechanism that positioned me in Macedon, detecting solid matter at the point where I was going to materialize, had raised me up above the tree-tops and then let go. It was an old oak, just putting out its spring leaves.

In clutching for branches I dropped my staff, which slithered down through the foliage and thumped the ground below. At least it thumped something. There was a startled yell.

Classical costume is impractical for tree-climbing. Branches kept knocking off my hat, or snagging my cloak, or poking me in tender places not protected by trousers. I ended my climb with a slide and a fall of several feet tumbling into the dirt.

As I looked up, the first thing I saw was a burly, black-bearded man in a dirty tunic, standing with a knife in his hand. Near him stood a pair of oxen yoked to a wooden plow. At his feet rested a water jug.

The plowman had evidently finished a furrow and lain down to rest himself and his beasts when the fall of my staff on him and then my arrival in person aroused him.

Around me stretched the broad Emathian Plain, ringed by ranges of stony hills and craggy mountains. As the sky was overcast, and I did not dare consult my compass, I had no sure way of orienting myself, or even telling what time of day it was. I assumed that the biggest mountain in sight was Mount Bermion, which ought to be to the west. To the north I could see a trace of water. This would be Lake Loudias. Beyond the lake rose a range of low hills. A discoloration on the nearest spur of these hills might be a city, though my sight was not keen enough to make out details, and I had to do without my eyeglasses. The gently rolling plain was cut up into fields and pastures with occasional trees and patches of marsh. Dry brown grasses left over from winter nodded in the wind.

My realization of all this took but a flash. Then my attention was brought back to the plowman, who spoke.

I could not understand a word. But then, he would speak Macedonian. Though this can be deemed a Greek dialect, it differed so from Attic Greek as to be unintelligible.

No doubt the man wanted to know what I was doing in his tree. I put on my best smile and said in my slow fumbling Attic: "Rejoice! I am lost, and climbed your tree to find my way."

He spoke again. When I did not respond, he repeated his words more loudly, waving his knife.

We exchanged more words and gestures, but it was

evident that neither had the faintest notion of what the other was trying to say. The plowman began shouting, as ignorant people will when faced by the linguistic barrier.

At last I pointed to the distant headland overlooking the lake, on which there appeared a discoloration that might be the city. Slowly and carefully I said:

"Is that Pella?"

"*Nai, Pella!*" The man's mien became less threatening.

"I am going to Pella. Where can I find the philosopher Aristoteles?" I repeated the name.

He was off again with more gibberish, but I gathered from his expression that he had never heard of any Aristoteles. So, I picked up my hat and stick, felt through my tunic to make sure my gear was all in place, tossed the rustic a final "*Chaire!*" and set off.

By the time I had crossed the muddy field and come out on a cart track, the problem of looking like a seasoned traveler had solved itself. There were green and brown stains on my clothes from the scramble down the tree; the cloak was torn; the branches had scratched my limbs and face; my feet and lower legs were covered with mud. I also became aware that, to one who has lived all his life with his loins decently swathed in trousers and underdrawers, classical costume is excessively drafty.

I glanced back to see the plowman still standing with one hand on his plow, looking at me in puzzled fashion. The poor fellow had never been able to decide what, if anything, to do about me.

When I found a road, it was hardly more than a heavily used cart track, with a pair of deep ruts and the space between them alternating stones, mud, and long grass.

I walked towards the lake and passed a few people on the road. To one used to the teeming traffic of my world, Macedon seemed dead and deserted. I spoke to some of the people, but ran into the same barrier of language as with the plowman.

Finally a two-horse chariot came along, driven by a stout man wearing a headband, a kind of kilt, and high-laced boots. He pulled up at my hail.

"What is it?" he said, in Attic not much better than mine.

"I seek the philosopher, Aristoteles of Stageira. Where can I find him?"

"He lives in Mieza."

"Where is that?"

The man waved. "You are going the wrong way. Follow this road back the way you came. At the ford across the Bottiais, take the right-hand fork, which will bring you to Mieza and Kition. Do you understand?"

"I think so," I said. "How far is it?"

"About two hundred stadia."

My heart sank to my sandals. This meant five parasangs, or a good two-days' walk. I thought of trying to buy a horse or a chariot, but I had never ridden or driven a horse and saw no prospect of learning how soon enough to do any good. I had read about Mieza as Aristotle's home in Macedon but, as none of my maps had shown it, I had assumed it to be a suburb of Pella.

I thanked the man, who trotted off, and set out after him. The details of my journey need not detain you. I was benighted far from shelter through not knowing where the villages were, attacked by watchdogs, eaten alive by mosquitoes, and invaded by vermin when I did find a place to sleep the second night. The road skirted the huge marshes that spread over the Emathian Plain west of Lake Loudias. Several small streams came down from Mount Bermion and lost themselves in this marsh.

At last I neared Mieza, which stands on one of the spurs of Mount Bermion. I was trudging wearily up the long rise to the village when six youths on little Greek horses clattered down the road. I stepped to one side, but instead of cantering past they pulled up and faced me in a semicircle.

"Who are you?" asked one, a smallish youth of about fifteen, in fluent Attic. He was blond and would have been noticeably handsome without his pimples.

"I am Zandras of Pataliputra," I said, giving the ancient name for Patna on the Ganges. "I seek the philosopher Aristoteles."

"Oh, a barbarian!" cried Pimples. "We know what the Aristoteles thinks of these, eh, boys?"

The others joined in, shouting noncompliments and

bragging about all the barbarians they would some day kill or enslave.

I made the mistake of letting them see I was getting angry. I knew it was unwise, but I could not help myself. "If you do not wish to help me, then let me pass," I said.

"Not only a barbarian, but an insolent one!" cried one of the group, making his horse dance uncomfortably close to me.

"Stand aside, children!" I demanded.

"We must teach you a lesson," said Pimples. The others giggled.

"You had better let me alone" I said, gripping my staff in both hands.

A tall handsome adolescent reached over and knocked my hat off. "That for you, cowardly Asiatic!" he yelled.

Without stopping to think, I shouted an English epithet and swung my staff. Either the young man leaned out of the way or his horse shied, for my blow missed him. The momentum carried the staff past my target and the end struck the nose of one of the other horses.

The pony squealed and reared. Having no stirrups, the rider slid off the animal's rump into the dirt. The horse galloped off.

All six youths began screaming. The blond one, who had a particularly piercing voice, mouthed some threat. The next thing I knew, his horse bounded directly at me. Before I could dodge, the animal's shoulder knocked me head over heels and the beast leaped over me as I rolled. Luckily, horses' dislike of stepping on anything squashy saved me from being trampled.

I scrambled up as another horse bore down upon me. By a frantic leap, I got out of its way, but I saw that the other boys were jockeying their mounts to do likewise.

A few paces away rose a big pine. I dodged in among its lower branches as the other horses ran at me. The youths could not force their mounts in among these branches, so they galloped round and round and yelled. Most of their talk I could not understand, but I caught a sentence from Pimples:

"Ptolemaios! Ride back to the house and fetch bows or javelins!"

Hooves receded. While I could not see clearly through the pine-needles, I inferred what was happening. The youths would not try to rush me on foot, first because they liked being on horseback, and if they dismounted they might lose their horses or have trouble remounting; second, because, as long as I kept my back to the tree, they would have a hard time getting at me through the tangle of branches, and I could hit and poke them with my stick as I came. Though not an unusually tall man in my own world, I was much bigger than any of these boys.

This, however, was a minor consideration. I recognized the name "Ptolemaios" as that of one of Alexander's companions, who in my world became King Ptolemy of Egypt and founded a famous dynasty. Young Pimples, then, must be Alexander himself.

I was in a real predicament. If I stayed where I was, Ptolemaios would bring back missiles for target practice with me as the target. I could of course shoot some of the boys with my gun, which would save me for the time being. But, in an absolute monarchy, killing the crown prince's friends, let alone the crown prince himself, is no way to achieve a peaceful old age, regardless of the provocation.

While I was thinking of these matters and listening to my attackers, a stone swished through the branches and bounced off the trunk. The small dark youth who had fallen off his horse had thrown the rock and was urging his friends to do likewise. I caught glimpses of Pimples and the rest dismounting and scurrying around for stones, a commodity with which Greece and Macedon are notoriously well supplied.

More stones came through the needles, caroming from the branches. One the size of my fist struck me lightly in the shin.

The boys came closer so that their aim got better. I wormed my way around the trunk to put it between me and them, but they saw the movement and spread out around the tree. A stone grazed my scalp, dizzying me and drawing blood. I thought of climbing but, as the tree became more slender with height, I should be more exposed the higher I got. I should also be less able to dodge while perched in the branches.

That is how things stood when I heard hoofbeats again. This is the moment of decision, I thought. Ptolemaios is coming back with missile weapons. If I used my gun, I might doom myself in the long run, but it would be ridiculous to stand there and let them riddle me while I had an unused weapon.

I fumbled under my tunic and unsnapped the safety strap that kept the pistol in its holster. I pulled the weapon out and checked its projectiles.

A deep voice broke into the bickering. I caught phrases: ". . . insulting an unoffending traveler . . . how know you he is not a prince in his own country? . . . the king shall hear of this . . . like newly-freed slaves, not like princes and gentlemen . . ."

I pushed towards the outer limits of the screen of pine needles. A heavy-set, brown-bearded man on a horse was haranguing the youths, who had dropped their stones. Pimples said:

"We were only having a little sport."

I stepped out from the branches, walked over to where my battered hat lay, and put it on. Then I said to the newcomer: "Rejoice! I am glad you came before your boys' play got too rough." I grinned, determined to act cheerful if it killed me. Only iron self-control would get me through this difficulty.

The man grunted. "Who are you?"

"Zandras of Pataliputra, a city in India. I seek Aristoteles the philosopher."

"He insulted us –" began one of the youths, but Brownbeard ignored him. He said:

"I am sorry you have had so rude an introduction to our royal house. This mass of youthful insolence" (he indicated Pimples) "is the Alexandros Philippou, heir to the throne of Makedonia." He introduced the others: Hephaistion, who had knocked my hat off and was now holding the others' horses; Nearchos, who had lost his horse; Ptolemaios, who had gone for weapons; and Harpalos and Philotas. He continued:

"When the Ptolemaios dashed into the house, I inquired the reason for his haste, learned of their quarrel with you, and came out forthwith. They have misapplied their master's teachings. They should not behave thus even to a barbarian like yourself, for in so doing they lower themselves to the barbarian's level. I am returning to the house of Aristoteles. You may follow."

The man turned his horse and started walking it back towards Mieza. The six boys busied themselves with catching Nearchos' horse.

I walked after him, though I had to dog-trot now and then to keep up. As it was uphill, I was soon breathing hard. I panted: "Who – my lord – are you?"

The man's beard came round and he raised an eyebrow. "I thought you would know. I am Antipatros, regent of Makedonia."

Before we reached the village proper, Antipatros turned off through a kind of park, with statues and benches. This, I supposed, was the Precinct of the Nymphs, which Aristotle used as a school ground. We went through the park and stopped at a mansion on the other side. Antipatros tossed the reins to a groom and slid off his horse.

"Aristoteles!" roared Antipatros. "A man wishes to see you."

A man of about my own age – the early forties – came out. He was of medium height and slender build, with a thin-lipped, severe-looking face and a pepper-and-salt beard cut short. He was wrapped in a billowing himation or large cloak, with a colorful scroll-patterned border. He wore golden rings on several fingers.

Antipatros made a fumbling introduction: "Old fellow, this is – ah – what's-his-name from – ah – some place in India." He told of rescuing me from Alexander and his fellow delinquents, adding: "If you do not beat some manners into your pack of cubs soon, it will be too late."

Aristotle looked at me sharply and lisped: "It ith always a pleasure to meet men from afar. What brings you here, my friend?"

I gave my name and said: "Being accounted something of a philosopher in my own land, I thought my visit to the West would be incomplete without speaking to the greatest Western philosopoher. And when I asked who he was, everyone told me to seek out Aristoteles Nikomachou."

Aristotle purred. "It is good of them to thay tho. Ahem. Come in and join me in a drop of wine. Can you tell me of the wonders of India?"

"Yes indeed, but you must tell me in turn of your discoveries, which to me are much more wonderful."

"Come, come, then. Perhaps you could stay over a few days. I shall have many, many things to athk you."

That is how I met Aristotle. He and I hit it off, as we said in my world, from the start. We had much in common. Some people would not like Aristotle's lisp, or his fussy, pedantic ways, or his fondness for worrying any topic of conversation to death. But he and I got along fine.

That afternoon, in the house that King Philip had built for Aristotle to use as the royal school, he handed me a cup of wine flavored with turpentine and asked:

"Tell me about the elephant, that great beast we have heard of with a tail at both ends. Does it truly exist?"

"Indeed it does," I said, and went on to tell what I knew of elephants, while Aristotle scribbled notes on a piece of papyrus.

"What do they call the elephant in India?" he asked.

The question caught me by surprise, for it had never occurred to me to learn ancient Hindustani along with all the other things I had to know for this expedition. I sipped the wine to give me time to think. I have never cared for alcoholic liquors, and this stuff tasted awful to to me. But, for the sake of my objective, I had to pretend to like it. No doubt I should have to make up some kind of gibberish – but then a mental broad-jump carried me back to the stories of Kipling I had read as a boy.

"We call it a *hathi*," I said. "Though of course there are many languages in India."

"How about that Indian wild ath of which Ktesias thpeakth, with a horn in the middle of its forehead?"

"You had better call it a nose-horn (*rhinokerōs*) for that is where its horn really is, and it is more like a gigantic pig than an ass . . ."

As dinner-time neared, I made some artful remarks about going out to find accommodations in Mieza, but Aristotle (to my joy) would have none of it. I should stay right there at the school; my polite protestations of unworthiness he waved aside.

"You mutht plan to stop here for months," he said. "I shall never, never have such a chance to collect data on India again. Do not worry about expense; the king pays all. You are – ahem – the first barbarian I have known with a decent intellect, and I get lonethome for good tholid talk. Theophrastos has gone to Athens, and my other friends come to these back-lands but seldom."

"How about the Macedonians?"

"*Aiboi!* Thome like my friend Antipatros are good fellows, but most are as lackwitted as a Persian grandee. And now tell me of Patal – what is your city's name?"

Presently Alexander and his friends came in. They seemed taken aback at seeing me closeted with their master. I put on a brisk smile and said: "Rejoice, my friends!" as if nothing untoward had happened. The boys glowered and whispered among themselves, but did not attempt any more disturbance at that time.

When they gathered for their lecture next morning, Aristotle told them: "I am too busy with the gentleman from India to waste time pounding unwanted wisdom into your miserable little thouls. Go shoot some rabbits or catch some fish for dinner, but in any case begone!"

The boys grinned. Alexander said: "It seems the barbarian has his uses after all. I hope you stay with us forever, good barbarian!"

After they had gone, Antipatros came in to say good-bye to Aristotle. He asked me with gruff good will how I was doing and went out to ride back to Pella.

The weeks passed unnoticed and the flowers of spring came out while I visited Aristotle. Day after day we strolled about the Precinct of the Nymphs, talking, or sat indoors when it rained. Sometimes the boys followed us, listening; at other times we talked alone. They played a couple of practical jokes on me, but, by pretending to be amused when I was really furious, I avoided serious trouble with them.

I learned that Aristotle had a wife and a little daughter in another part of the big house, but he never let me meet the lady. I only caught glimpses of them from a distance.

I carefully shifted the subject of our daily discourse from the marvels of India to the more basic questions of science. We argued over the nature of matter and the shape of the solar system. I gave out that the Indians were well on the road to the modern concepts – modern in my world, that is – of astronomy, physics, and so forth. I told of the discoveries of those eminent Pataliputran philosophers: Kopernikos in astronomy, Neuton in physics, Darben in evolution, and Mendeles in genetics. (I forgot; these names mean nothing to you, though an educated man of my world would recognize them at once through their Greek disguise.)

Always I stressed *method*: the need for experiment and invention and for checking each theory back against the facts. Though an opinionated and argumentative man, Aristotle had a mind like a sponge, eagerly absorbing any new fact, surmise, or opinion, whether he agreed with it or not.

I tried to find a workable compromise between what I knew science could do on one hand and the limits of Aristotle's credulity on the other. Therefore I said nothing about flying machines, guns, buildings a thousand feet high, and other technical wonders of my world. Nevertheless, I caught Aristotle looking at me sharply out of those small black eyes one day.

"Do you doubt me, Aristoteles?" I said.

"N-no, no," he said thoughtfully. "But it does theem to me that, were your Indian inventors as wonderful as you make out, they would have fabricated you wings like those of Daidalos in the legend. Then you could have flown to Makedonia directly, without the trials of crossing Persia by camel."

"That has been tried, but men's muscles do not have enough strength in proportion to their weight."

"Ahem. Did you bring anything from India to show the skills of your people?"

I grinned, for I had been hoping for such a question. "I did fetch a few small devices," said I, reaching into my tunic and bringing out the magnifying glass. I demonstrated its use.

Aristotle shook his head. "Why did you not show me this before? It would have quieted my doubts."

"People have met with misfortune by trying too suddenly to change the ideas of those around them. Like your teacher's teacher, Sokrates."

"That is true, true. What other devices did you bring?"

I had intended to show my devices at intervals, gradually, but Aristotle was so insistent on seeing them all that I gave into him before he got angry. The little telescope was not powerful enough to show the moons of Jupiter or the rings of Saturn, but it showed enough to convince Aristotle of its power. If he could not see these astronomical phenomena himself, he was almost willing to take my word that they could be seen with the larger telescopes we had in India.

One day a light-armed soldier galloped up to us in the midst of our discussions in the Precinct of Nymphs. Ignoring the rest of us, the fellow said to Alexander: "Hail, O Prince! The king, your father, will be here before sunset."

Everybody rushed around cleaning up the place. We were all lined up in front of the big house when King Philip and his entourage arrived on horseback with a jingle and a clatter, in crested helmets and flowing mantles. I knew Philip by his one eye. He was a big powerful man, much scarred, with a thick curly black beard going gray. He dismounted, embraced his son, gave Aristotle a brief greeting, and said to Alexander:

"How would you like to attend a siege?"

Alexander whooped.

"Thrace is subdued," said the king, "but Byzantion and Perinthos have declared against me, thanks to Athenian intrigue. I shall give the Perintheans something to think about besides the bribes of the Great King. It is time you smelled blood, youngster; would you like to come?"

"Yes, yes! Can my friends come too?"

"If they like and their fathers let them."

"O King!" said Aristotle.

"What is it, spindle-shanks?"

"I trust thith is not the end of the prince's education. He has much yet to learn."

"No, no; I will send him back when the town falls. But he

nears the age when he must learn by doing, not merely by listening to your rarefied wisdom. Who is this?" Philip turned his one eye on me.

"Zandras of India, a barbarian philothopher."

Philip grinned in a friendly way and clapped me on the shoulder. "Rejoice! Come to Pella and tell my generals about India. Who knows? A Macedonian foot may tread there yet."

"It would be more to the point to find out about Persia," said one of Philip's officers, a handsome fellow with a reddish-brown beard. "This man must have just come through there. How about it, man? Is the bloody Artaxerxes still solid on his throne?"

"I know little of such matters," I said, my heart beginning to pound at the threat of exposure. "I skirted the northern-most parts of the Great King's dominions and saw little of the big cities. I know nothing of their politics."

"Is that so?" said Redbeard, giving me a queer look. "We must talk of this again."

They all trooped into the big house, where the cook and the serving wenches were scurrying about. During dinner I found myself between Nearchos, Alexander's little Cretan friend, and a man-at-arms who spoke no Attic. So I did not get much conversation, nor could I follow much of the chatter that went on among the group at the head of the tables. I gathered that they were discussing politics. I asked Nearchos who the generals were.

"The big one at the king's right is the Parmenion," he said, "and the one with the red beard is the Attalos."

When the food was taken away and the drinking had begun, Attalos came over to me. The man-at-arms gave him his place. Attalos had drunk a lot of wine already; but, if it made him a little unsteady, it did not divert him.

"How did you come through the Great King's domain?" he asked. "What route did you follow?"

"I told you, to the north," I said.

"Then you must have gone through Orchoê."

"I –" I began, then stopped. Attalos might be laying a trap for me. What if I said yes and Orchoê was really in the south? Or suppose he had been there and knew all about the place? Many Greeks and Macedonians served the Great King as mercenaries.

"I passed through many places whose names I never got straight," I said. "I do not remember if Orchoê was among them."

Attalos gave me a sinister smile through his beard. "Your journey will profit you little, if you cannot remember where you have been. Come, tell me if you heard of unrest among the northern provinces."

I evaded the question, taking a long pull on my wine to cover my hesitation. I did this again and again until Attalos said: "Very well, perhaps you are really as ignorant of Persia as you profess. Then tell me about India."

"What about it?" I hiccupped; the wine was beginning to affect me, too.

"As a soldier, I should like to know of the Indian art of war. What is this about training elephants to fight?"

"Oh, we do much better than that."

"How so?"

"We have found that the flesh-and-blood elephant, despite its size, is an untrustworthy war beast because it often takes fright and stampedes back through its own troops. So, the philosophers of Pataliputra make artificial elephants of steel with rapid-fire catapults on their backs."

I was thinking in a confused way of the armored war vehicles of my own world. I do not know what made me tell Attalos such ridiculous lies. Partly, I suppose, it was to keep him off the subject of Persia.

Partly it was a natural antipathy between us. According to history, Attalos was not a bad man, though at times a reckless and foolish one. But it annoyed me that he thought he could pump me by subtle questions, when he was about as subtle as a ton of bricks. His voice and manner said as plainly as words: I am a shrewd, sharp fellow; watch out for me, everybody. He was the kind of man who, if told to spy on the enemy, would don an obviously false beard, wrap himself in a long black cloak, and go slinking about the enemy's places in broad daylight, leering and winking and attracting as much attention as possible. No doubt, too, he had prejudiced me against him by his alarming curiosity about my past.

But the main cause for my rash behavior was the strong wine I had drunk. In my own world, I drank very little and so was not used to these carousals.

Attalos was all eyes and ears at my tale of mechanical elephants. "You do not say!"

"Yes, and we do even better than that. If the enemy's ground forces resist the charge of our iron elephants, we send flying chariots, drawn by gryphons, to drop darts on the foe from above." It seemed to me that never had my imagination been so brilliant.

Attalos gave an audible gasp. "What else?"

"Well – ah – we also have a powerful navy, you know, which controls the lower Ganges and the adjacent ocean. Our ships move by machinery, without oars or sails."

"Do the other Indians have these marvels too?"

"Some, but none is so advanced as the Pataliputrans. When we are outnumbered on the sea, we have a force of tame Tritons who swim under the enemy's ships and bore holes in their bottoms."

Attalos frowned. "Tell me, barbarian, how it is that, with such mighty instruments of war, the Palalal – the Patapata –the people of your city have not conquered the whole world?"

I gave a shout of drunken laughter and slapped Attalos on the back. "We *have*, old boy, we have! You Macedonians have just not yet found out that you are our subjects!"

Attalos digested this, then scowled blackly. "You temple-thief! I think you have been making a fool of me! Of *me!* By Herakles, I ought –"

He rose and swung a fist back to clout me. I jerked an arm up to guard my face.

There came a roar of "Attalos!" from the head of the table. King Philip had been watching us.

Attalos dropped his fist, muttered something like "Flying chariots and tame Tritons, forsooth!" and stumbled back to his own crowd.

This man, I remembered, did not have a happy future in store. He was destined to marry his niece to Philip, whose first wife Olympias would have the girl and her baby killed after Philip's assassination. Soon afterwards, Attalos would be murdered by Alexander's orders. It was on the tip of my tongue to give him a veiled warning, but I forebore. I had attracted enough hostile attention already.

Later, when the drinking got heavy, Aristotle came over and shooed his boys off to bed. He said to me: "Let uth walk outside to clear our heads, Zandras, and then go to bed, too. These Makedones drink like sponges. I cannot keep up with them."

Outside, he said: "The Attalos thinks you are a Persian thpy."

"A spy? Me? In Hera's name, why?" Silently I cursed my folly in making an enemy without any need. Would I never learn to deal with this damned human species?

Aristotle said: "He thays nobody could pass through a country and remain as ignorant of it as you theem to be. *Ergo,* you know more of the Persian Empire than you pretend, but wish us to think you have nothing to do with it. And why should you do that, unleth you are yourself a Persian? And being a Persian, why should you hide the fact unleth you are on some hostile mission?"

"A Persian might fear anti-Persian prejudice among the Hellenes. Not that I am one," I hastily added.

"He need not. Many Persians live in Hellas without molestation. Take Artabazos and his sons, who live in Pella, refugees from their own king."

Then the obvious alibi came to me, long after it should have. "The fact is I went even farther north than I said. I went around the northern ends of the Caspian and Euxine seas and so did not cross the Great King's domains save through the Bactrian deserts."

"You did? Then why did you not thay tho? If that is true, you have settled one of our hottest geographical disputes: whether the Caspian is a closed thea or a bay of the Northern Ocean."

"I feared nobody would believe me."

"I am not sure what to believe, Zandras. You are a strange man. I do not think you are a Persian, for no Persian was ever a philothopher. It is good for you that you are not."

"Why?"

"Because I *hate* Persia!" he hissed.

"You do?"

"Yeth. I could list the wrongs done by the Great Kings, but it is enough that they seized my beloved father-in-law by treachery and tortured and crucified him. People like Isokrates talk of uniting the Hellenes to conquer Persia, and Philippos may try it if he lives. I hope he does. However," he went on in a different tone, "I hope he does it without dragging the cities of Hellas into it, for the repositories of civilization have no busineth getting into a brawl between tyrants."

"In India," said I sententiously, "we are taught that a man's nationality means nothing and his personal qualities everything. Men of all nations come good, bad, and indifferent."

Aristotle shrugged. "I have known virtuouth Persians too, but that monstrouth, bloated empire. . . . No state can be truly civilized with more than a few thousand citizens."

There was no use telling him that large states, however monstrous and bloated he thought them, would be a permanent feature of the landscape from then on. I was trying to reform, not Aristotle's narrow view of international affairs, but his scientific methodology.

Next morning King Philip and his men and Aristotle's six pupils galloped off toward Pella, followed by a train of baggage mules and the boys' personal slaves. Aristotle said:

"Let us hope no chance sling-thtone dashes out Alexandros' brains before he has a chance to show his mettle. The boy has talent and may go far, though managing him is like trying to plow with a wild bull. Now, let us take up the question of atoms again, my dear Zandras, about which you have been talking thuch utter rubbish. First, you must admit that if a thing exists, parts of it must also exist. Therefore there is no thuch thing as an indivisible particle . . ."

Three days later, while we were still hammering at the question of atoms, we looked up at the clatter of hooves. Here came Attalos and a whole troop of horsemen. Beside Attalos rode a tall swarthy man with a long gray beard. This man's appearance startled me into thinking he must be another time traveler from my own time, for he wore a hat, coat, and pants. The mere sight of these familiar garments filled me with homesickness for my own world, however much I hated it when I lived in it.

Actually, the man's garb was not that of one from my world. The hat was a cylindrical felt cap with ear flaps. The coat was a brown knee-length garment, embroidered with faded red and blue flowers, with trousers to match. The whole outfit looked old and threadbare, with patches showing. He was a big craggy-looking fellow, with a great hooked nose, wide cheekbones, and deep-set eyes under bushy, beetling brows.

They all dismounted, and a couple of grooms went around collecting the bridles to keep the horses from running off. The soldiers leaned on their spears in a circle around us.

Attalos said: "I should like to ask your guest some more philosophical questions, O Aristoteles."

"Ask away."

Attalos turned, not to me, but to the tall graybeard. He said something I did not catch, and then the man in trousers spoke to me in a language I did not know.

"I do not understand," I said.

The graybeard spoke again, in what sounded like a different tongue. He did this several times, using a different-sounding speech each time, but each time I had to confess ignorance.

"Now you see," said Attalos. "He pretends not to know Persian, Median, Armenian, or Aramaic. He could not have traversed the Great King's dominions from east to west without learning at least one of these."

"Who are you, my dear sir?" I asked Graybeard.

The old man gave me a small dignified smile and spoke in Attic with a guttural accent. "I am Artavazda, or Artabazos as the Hellenes say, once governor of Phrygia but now a poor pensioner of King Philippos."

This, then, was the eminent Persian refugee of whom Aristotle had spoken.

"I warrant he does not even speak Indian," said Attalos.

"Certainly," I said, and started off in English: "*Now is the time for all good men to come to the aid of the party. Four score and seven years ago our fathers brought forth –*"

"What would you call that?" Attalos asked Artavazda.

The Persian spread his hands. "I have never heard the like. But then, India is a vast country of many tongues."

"I was not —" I began, but Attalos kept on:

"What race would you say he belonged to?"

"I know not. The Indians I have seen were much darker, but there might be light-skinned Indians for aught I know."

"If you will listen, General, I will explain," I said. "For most of the journey I was not even in the Persian Empire. I crossed through Bactria and went around the north of the Caspian and Euxine seas."

"Oh, so now you tell another story?" said Attalos. "Any educated man knows the Caspian is but a deep bay opening into the Ocean River to the north. Therefore you could not go around it. So, in trying to escape, you do but mire yourself deeper in your own lies."

"Look here," said Aristotle. "You have proved nothing of the sort, O Attalos. Ever thince Herodotos there have been those who think the Caspian a closed thea —"

"Hold your tongue, Professor," said Attalos. "This is a matter of national security. There is something queer about this alleged Indian, and I mean to find out what it is."

"It is not queer that one who comes from unknown distant lands should tell a singular tale of his journey."

"No, there is more to it than that. I have learned that he first appeared in a treetop on the farm of the freeholder Diktys Pisandrou. Diktys remembers looking up into the tree for crows before he cast himself down under it to rest. If the Zandras had been in the tree, Diktys would have seen him, as it was not yet fully in leaf. The next instant there was the crash of a body falling into the branches, and Zandras' staff smote Diktys on the head. Normal mortal men fall not out of the sky into trees."

"Perhaps he flew from India. They have marvelous mechanisms there, he tells me," said Aristotle.

"If he survives our interrogation in Pella, perhaps he can make me a pair of wings," said Attalos. "Or better yet, a pair for my horse, so he shall emulate Pegasos. Meanwhile, seize and bind him, men!"

The soldiers moved. I did not dare submit for fear they

would take my gun and leave me defenceless. I snatched up the hem of my tunic to get at my pistol. It took precious seconds to unsnap the safety strap, but I got the gun out before anybody laid a hand on me.

"Stand back or I will blast you with lightning!" I shouted, raising the gun.

Men of my own world, knowing how deadly such a weapon can be, would have given ground at the sight of it. But the Macedonians, never having seen one, merely stared at the device and came on. Attalos was one of the nearest.

I fired at him, then whirled and shot another soldier who was reaching out to seize me. The discharge of the gun produces a lightning-like flash and a sharp sound like a close clap of thunder. The Macedonians cried out, and Attalos fell with a wound in his thigh.

I turned again, looking for a way out of the circle of soldiers, while confused thoughts of taking one of their horses flashed through my head. A heavy blow in the flank staggered me. One of the soldiers had jabbed me with his spear, but my belt kept the weapon from piercing me. I shot at the man but missed him in my haste.

"Do not kill him!" screamed Aristotle.

Some of the soldiers backed up as if to flee; others poised their spears. They hesitated for the wink of an eye, either for fear of me or because Aristotle's command confused them. Ordinarily they would have ignored the philosopher and listened for their general's orders, but Attalos was down on the grass and looking in amazement at the hole in his leg.

As one soldier dropped his spear and started to run, a blow on the head sent a flash of light through my skull and hurled me to the ground, nearly unconscious. A man behind me had swung his spear like a club and struck me on the pate with the shaft.

Before I could recover, they were all over me, raining kicks and blows. One wrenched the gun from my hand. I must have lost consciousness, for the next thing I remember is lying in the dirt while the soldiers tore off my tunic. Attalos stood over me with a bloody bandage around his leg, leaning on a soldier. He looked pale and frightened but resolute. The second man I had shot lay still.

"So that is where he keeps his infernal devices!" said Attalos, indicating my belt. "Take it off, men."

The soldiers struggled with the clasp of the belt until one impatiently sawed through the straps with his dagger. The gold in my money pouch brought cries of delight.

I struggled to get up, but a pair of soldiers knelt on my arms to keep me down. There was a continuous mumble of talk. Attalos, looking over the belt, said:

"He is too dangerous to live. Even stripped as he is, who knows but what he will soar into the air and escape by magic?"

"Do not kill him!" said Aristotle. "He has much valuable knowledge to impart."

"No knowledge is worth the safety of the kingdom."

"But the kingdom can benefit from his knowledge. Do you not agree?" Aristotle asked the Persian.

"Drag me not into this, pray," said Artavazda. "It is no concern of mine."

"If he is a danger to Makedonia, he should be destroyed at once," said Attalos.

"There is but little chance of his doing harm now," said Aristotle, "and an excellent chance of his doing us good."

"Any chance of his doing harm is too much," said Attalos. "You philosophers can afford to be tolerant of interesting strangers. But, if they carry disaster in their baggage, it is on us poor soldiers that the brunt will fall. Is it not so, Artabazos?"

"I have done what you asked and will say no more," said Artavazda. "I am but a simple-minded Persian nobleman who does not undertand your Greek subtleties."

"I can increase the might of your armies, General!" I cried to Attalos.

"No doubt, and no doubt you can also turn men to stone with an incantation, as the Gorgons did with their glance." He drew his sword and felt the edge with his thumb.

"You will slay him for mere thuperstition!" wailed Aristotle, wringing his hands. "At least, let the king judge the matter."

"Not superstition," said Attalos, "murder." He pointed to the dead soldier.

"I come from another world! Another age!" I yelled, but Attalos was not to be diverted.

"Let us get this over with," he said. "Set him on his knees, men. Take my sword, Glaukos; I am too unsteady to wield it. Now bow your head, my dear barbarian, and –"

In the middle of Attalos' sentence, he and the others and all my surroundings vanished. Again there came that sharp pain and sense of being jerked by a monstrous catapult . . .

I found myself lying in leaf mold with the pearl-gray trunks of poplars all around me. A brisk breeze was making the poplar leaves flutter and show their silvery bottoms. It was too cool for a man who was naked save for sandals and socks.

I had snapped back to the year 1981 of the calendar of my world, which I had set out from. But where was I? I should be near the site of the Brookhaven National Laboratories in a vastly improved super-scientific world. There was, however, no sign of super-science here; nothing but poplar trees.

I got up, groaning, and looked around. I was covered with bruises and bleeding from nose and mouth.

The only way I had of orienting myself was the boom of a distant surf. Shivering, I hobbled towards the sound. After a few hundred paces, I came out of the forest on a beach. This beach could be the shore of Sewanhaki, or Long Island as we called it, but there was no good way of telling. There was no sign of human life; just the beach curving into the distance and disappearing around headlands, with the poplar forest on one side and the ocean on the other.

What, I wondered, had happened? Had science advanced so fast as a result of my intervention that man had already exterminated himself by scientific warfare? Thinkers of my world had concerned themselves with this possibility, but I had never taken it seriously.

It began to rain. In despair I cast myself down on the sand and beat it with my fists. I may have lost consciousness again.

At any rate, the next thing I knew was the now-familiar sound of hooves. When I looked up, the horseman was almost upon me, for the sand had muffled the animal's footsteps until it was quite close.

I blinked with incredulity. For an instant I thought I must be back in the classical era still. The man was a warrior armed and armored in a style much like that of ancient times. At first he seemed to be wearing a helmet of classical Hellenic type. When he came closer I saw that this was not quite true, for the crest was made of feathers instead of horsehair. The nasal and cheek plates hid most of his face, but he seemed dark and beardless. He wore a shirt of scale mail, long leather trousers, and low shoes. He had a bow and a small shield hung from his saddle and a slender lance slung across his back by a strap. I saw that this could not be ancient times because the horse was fitted with a large, well-molded saddle and stirrups.

As I watched the man stupidly, he whisked the lance out of its boot and couched it. He spoke in an unknown language.

I got up, holding my hands over my head in surrender. The man kept repeating his question, louder and louder, and making jabbing motions. All I could say was "I don't understand" in the languages I knew, none of which seemed familiar to him.

Finally he maneuvered his horse around to the other side of me, barked a command, pointed along the beach the way he had come, and prodded me with the butt of the lance. Off I limped, with rain, blood, and tears running down my hide.

You know the rest, more or less. Since I could not give an intelligible account of myself, the Sachim of Lenape, Wayotan the Fat, claimed me as a slave. For fourteen years I labored on his estate at such occupations as feeding hogs and chopping kindling. When Wayotan died and the present Sachim was elected, he decided I was too old for that kind of work, especially as I was half crippled from the beatings of Wayotan and his overseers. Learning that I had some knowledge of letters (for I had picked up spoken and written Algonkian in spite of my wretched lot) he freed me and made me official librarian.

In theory I can travel about as I like, but I have done little of it. I am too old and weak for the rigors of travel in this world, and most other places are, as nearly as I can determine, about as barbarous as this one. Besides, a few Lenapes come to hear me lecture on the nature of man and the universe and the virtues of the scientific method. Perhaps

I can light a small spark here after I failed in the year 340 B.C.

When I went to work in the library, my first thought was to find out what had happened to bring the world to its present pass.

Wayotan's predecessor had collected a considerable library which Wayotan had neglected, so that some of the books had been chewed by rats and others ruined by dampness. Still, there was enough to give me a good sampling of the literature of this world, from ancient to modern times. There were even Herodotos' history and Plato's dialogues, identical with the versions that existed in my own world.

I had to struggle against more language barriers, as the European languages of this world are different from, though related to, those of my own world. The English of today, for instance, is more like the Dutch of my own world, as a result of England's never having been conquered by the Normans.

I also had the difficulty of reading without eyeglasses. Luckily, most of these manuscript books are written in a large, clear hand. A couple of years ago I did get a pair of glasses, imported from China, where the invention of the printing press has stimulated their manufacture. But, as they are a recent invention in this world, they are not so effective as those of mine.

I rushed through all the history books to find out when and how your history diverged from mine. I found that differences appeared quite early. Alexander still marched to the Indus but failed to die at thirty-two on his return. In fact he lived fifteen years longer and fell at last in battle with the Sarmatians in the Caucasus Mountains.

I do not know why that brief contact with me enabled him to avoid the malaria mosquito that slew him in my world. Maybe I aroused in him a keener interest in India than he would otherwise have had, leading him to stay there longer so that all his subsequent schedules were changed. His empire held together for most of a century instead of breaking up right after his death as it did in my world.

The Romans still conquered the whole Mediterranean, but the course of their conquests and the names of the prominent Romans were all different. Two of the chief religions of my world, Christianity and Islam, never appeared at all. Instead we have Mithraism, Odinism, and Soterism, the last an Egypto-Hellenic synthesis founded by that fiery Egyptian prophet whose followers call him by the Greek word for "savior."

Still, classical history followed the same *general* course that it had in my world, even though the actors bore other names. The Roman Empire broke up, as it did in my world, though the details are all different, with a Hunnish emperor ruling in Rome and a Gothic one in Antioch.

It is after the fall of the Roman Empire that profound differences appear. In my world there was a revival of learning that began about nine hundred years ago, followed by a scientific revolution beginning four centuries later. In your history the revival of learning was centuries later, and the scientific revolution has hardly begun. Failure to develop the compass and the full-rigged ship resulted in North America's (I mean Hesperia's) being discovered and settled via the northern route, by way of Iceland, and more slowly than in my world. Failure to invent the gun meant that the natives of Hesperia were not swept aside by the invading Europeans, but held their own against them and gradually learned their arts of iron-working, weaving, cereal-growing, and the like. Now most of the European settlements have been assimilated, though the ruling families of the Abnakis and Mohegans frequently have blue eyes and still call themselves by names like "Sven" and "Eric."

I was eager to get hold of a work by Aristotle, to see what effect I had had on him and to try to relate this effect to the subsequent course of history. From allusions in some of the works in this library I gathered that many of his writings had come down to modern times, though the titles all seemed different from those of his surviving works in my world. The only actual samples of his writings in the library were three essays, *Of Justice, On Education,* and *Of Passions and Anger.* None of these showed my influence.

I had struggled through most of the Sachim's collection when I found the key I was looking for. This was an Iberic translation of *Lives of the Great Philosophers,* by one Diomedes of Mazaka. I never heard of Diomedes in the literary history of my own world, and perhaps he never existed. Anyway, he had a long chapter on Aristotle, in which appears the following section:

Now Aristotle, during his sojourn at Mytilene, had been an assiduous student of natural sciences. He had planned, according to Timotheus, a series of works which should correct the errors of Empedokles, Demokritos, and others of his predecessors. But, after he had removed to Macedonia and busied himself with the education of Alexander, there one day appeared before him a traveler, Sandos of Palibothra, a mighty philosopher of India.

The Indian ridiculed Aristotle's attempts at scientific research, saying that in his land these investigations had gone far beyond anything the Hellenes had attempted, and the Indians were still a long way from arriving at satisfactory explanations of the universe. Moreover, he asserted that no real progress could be made in natural philosophy unless the Hellenes abandoned their disdain for physical labor and undertook exhaustive experiments with mechanical devices of the sort which cunning Egyptian and Asiatic craftsmen make.

King Philip, hearing of the presence of this stranger in his land and fearing lest he be a spy sent by some foreign power to harm or corrupt the young prince, came with soldiers to arrest him. But, when he demanded that Sandos accompany him back to Pella, the latter struck dead with thunderbolts all the king's soldiers that were with him. Then, it is said, mounting into his chariot drawn by winged gryphons, he flew off in the direction of India. But other authorities say that the man who came to arrest Sandos was Antipatros, the regent, and that Sandos cast darkness before the eyes of Antipatros and Aristotle, and when they recovered from their swoon he had vanished.

Aristotle, reproached by the king for harboring so dangerous a visitor and shocked by the sanguinary ending of the Indian's visit, resolved to have no more to do with the sciences. For, as he explains in his celebrated treatise *On the Folly of Natural Science*, there are three reasons why no good Hellene should trouble his mind with such matters.

One is that the number of facts which must be mastered before sound theories become possible is so vast that if all the Hellenes did nothing else for centuries, they would still not gather the amount of data required. The task is therefore futile.

Secondly, experiments and mechanical inventions are necessary to progress in science, and such work, though all very well for slavish Asiatics, who have a natural bent for it, is beneath the dignity of a Hellenic gentleman.

And, lastly, some of the barbarians have already surpassed the Hellenes in this activity, wherefore it ill becomes the Hellenes to compete with their inferiors in skills at which the latter have an inborn advantage. They should rather cultivate personal rectitude, patriotic valor, political rationality and aesthetic sensitivity, leaving to the barbarians such artificial aids to the good and virtuous life as are provided by scientific discoveries.

This was it, all right. The author had gotten some of his facts wrong, but that was to be expected from an ancient historian.

So! My teachings had been too successful. I had so well shattered the naïve self-confidence of the Hellenic philosophers as to discourage them from going on with science at all.

I should have remembered that glittering theories and sweeping generalizations, even when wrong, are the frosting on the cake; they are the carrot that makes the donkey go. The possibility of pronouncing such universals is the stimulus that keeps many scientists grinding away, year after year, at the accumulation of facts, even seemingly dull and trivial facts. If ancient scientists had realized how much laborious fact-finding lay ahead of them before sound theories would become possible, they would have been so appalled as to drop science altogether. And that is just what happened.

The sharpest irony of all was that I had placed myself where I could not undo my handiwork. If I had ended up in a scientically advanced world, and did not like what I found, I might have built another time machine, gone back, and somehow warned myself of the mistake lying in wait for me. But such a project is out of the question in a backward world like this one, where seamless columbium tubing, for instance, is not even thought of. All I proved by my disastrous adventure is that space-time has a negative curvature, and who in this world cares about that?

You recall, when you were last here, asking me the meaning of a motto in my native language on the wall of my cell. I said I would tell you in connection with my whole fantastic story. The motto says: "Leave Well Enough Alone," and I wish I had.

Cordially yours,

Sherman Weaver.

THEODORE STURGEON
The Other Celia

The late Theodore Sturgeon was one of the true giants of the field, a man who produced stylish, innovative, and poetically intense fiction for more than forty years, a writer who was as important to H. L. Gold's *Galaxy*-era revolution in the '50s as he'd been to John W. Campbell's Golden Age revolution at *Astounding* in the '40s. Sturgeon's stories such as "It," "Microcosmic God," "Killdozer," "Bianca's Hands," "Maturity," "The Other Man," and the brilliant "Baby is Three" – which was eventually expanded into Sturgeon's most famous novel, *More Than Human* – helped to expand the boundaries of the SF story, and push it in the direction of artistic maturity. In Sturgeon's hands, the SF story would be made to do things that no one had ever believed it capable of doing before, and several generations of SF writers to come would cite him as a major – in some cases, *the* major – influence on their work.

Most people would probably have chosen "Baby Is Three" for this book, and it is indeed a seminal work . . . but somehow it was the sly little story that follows, a vivid glimpse of the strangeness that underlies the everyday world, that was the Sturgeon story I've never been able to get out of my mind, and which was the one that insisted that I pick it for this anthology. And, indeed, I think that it is Sturgeon at the very top of his form . . . which places it among the best work ever done in the genre.

Theodore Sturgeon's other books include the novels *Some of Your Blood* (in some ways his best, although it is neither SF or fantasy), *Venus Plus X*, and *The Dreaming Jewels*, and the collections *A Touch of Strange*, *Caviar*, *The Worlds of Theodore Sturgeon*, *Not Without Sorcery*, and *The Stars Are the Styx*. His most recent book is the posthumously published *Godbody*.

If you live in a cheap enough rooming house and the doors are made of cheap enough pine, and the locks are old-fashioned single-action jobs and the hinges are loose, and if you have a hundred and ninety lean pounds to operate with, you can grasp the knob, press the door sidewise against its hinges, and slip the latch. Further, you can lock the door the same way when you come out.

Slim Walsh lived in, and was, and had, and did these things partly because he was bored. The company doctors had laid him up – not off, up – for three weeks (after his helper had hit him just over the temple with a fourteen-inch crescent wrench) pending some more X-rays. If he was going to get just sick-leave pay, he wanted to make it stretch. If he was going to get a big fat settlement – all to the good; what he saved by living in this firetrap would make the money look even better. Meanwhile, he felt fine and had nothing to do all day.

"Slim isn't dishonest," his mother used to tell Children's Court some years back. "He's just curious."

She was perfectly right.

Slim was constitutionally incapable of borrowing your bathroom without looking into your medicine chest. Send him into your kitchen for a saucer and when he came out a minute later, he'd have inventoried your refrigerator, your vegetable bin, and (since he was six feet three inches tall) he would know about a moldering jar of maraschino cherries in the back of the top shelf that you'd forgotten about.

Perhaps Slim, who was not impressed by his impressive size and build, felt that a knowledge that you secretly use hair-restorer, or are one of those strange people who keeps a little mound of unmated socks in your second drawer, gave him a kind of superiority. Or maybe security is a better word. Or maybe it was an odd compensation for one of the most advanced cases of gawking, gasping shyness ever recorded.

Whatever it was, Slim liked you better if, while talking to you, he knew how many jackets hung in your closet, how old that unpaid phone bill was, and just where you'd hidden those photographs. On the other hand, Slim didn't insist on knowing bad or even embarrassing things about you. He just wanted to know things about you, period.

His current situation was therefore a near-paradise. Flimsy doors stood in rows, barely sustaining vacuum on aching vacuum of knowledge; and one by one they imploded at the nudge of his curiosity. He touched nothing (or if he did, he replaced it carefully) and removed nothing, and within a week he knew Mrs Koyper's roomers far better than she could, or cared to. Each secret visit to the rooms gave him a starting point; subsequent ones taught him more. He knew not only what these people had, but what they did, where, how much, for how much, and how often. In almost every case, he knew why as well.

Almost every case. Celia Sarton came.

Now, at various times, in various places, Slim had found strange things in other people's rooms. There was an old lady in one shabby place who had an electric train under her bed; used it, too. There was an old spinster in this very building who collected bottles, large and small, of any value or capacity, providing they were round and squat and with long necks. A man on the second floor secretly guarded his desirables with the unloaded .25 automatic in his top bureau drawer, for which he had a half-box of .38 cartridges.

There was a (to be chivalrous) girl in one of the rooms who kept fresh cut flowers before a photograph on her night-table – or, rather, before a frame in which were stacked eight photographs, one of which held the stage each day. Seven days, eight photographs: Slim admired the system. A new love every day and, predictably, a different love on successive Wednesdays. And all of them movie stars.

Dozens of rooms, dozens of imprints, marks, impressions, overlays, atmospheres of people. And they needn't be odd ones. A woman moves into a room, however standardized; the instant she puts down her dusting powder on top of the flush tank, the room is *hers*. Something stuck in the ill-fitting frame of a mirror, something draped over the long-dead gas jet, and the samest of rooms begins to shrink toward its occupant as if it wished, one day, to be a close-knit, form-fitting, individual integument as intimate as a skin.

But not Celia Sarton's room.

Slim Walsh got a glimpse of her as she followed Mrs Koyper up the stairs to the third floor. Mrs Koyper, who hobbled, slowed any follower sufficiently to afford the most disinterested witness a good look, and Slim was anything but disinterested. Yet for days he could not recall her clearly. It was as if Celia Sarton had been – not invisible, for that would have been memorable in itself–but translucent or, chameleonlike, drably re-radiating the drab wall color, carpet color, woodwork color.

She was – how old? Old enough to pay taxes. How tall? Tall enough. Dressed in . . . whatever women cover themselves with in their statistical thousands. Shoes, hose, skirt, jacket, hat.

She carried a bag. When you go to the baggage window at a big terminal, you notice a suitcase here, a steamer-trunk there; and all around, high up, far back, there are rows and ranks and racks of luggage not individually noticed but just *there*. This bag, Celia Sarton's bag, was one of them.

And to Mrs Koyper, she said – she said – she said whatever is necessary when one takes a cheap room; and to find her voice, divide the sound of a crowd by the number of people in it.

So anonymous, so unnoticeable was she that, aside from being aware that she left in the morning and returned in the evening, Slim let two days go by before he entered her room; he simply could not remind himself about her. And when he did, and had inspected it to his satisfaction, he had his hand on the knob, about to leave, before he recalled that the room was, after all, occupied. Until that second, he had thought he was giving one of the vacancies the once-over. (He did this regularly; it gave him a reference-point.)

He grunted and turned back, flicking his gaze over the room. First he had to assure himself that he was in the right room, which, for a man of his instinctive orientations, was extraordinary. Then he had to spend a moment of disbelief in his own eyes, which was all but unthinkable. When that passed, he stood in astonishment, staring at the refutation of everything his – hobby – had taught him about people and the places they live in.

The bureau drawers were empty. The ashtray was clean. No toothbrush, toothpaste, soap. In the closet, two wire hangers and one wooden one covered with dirty quilted silk, and nothing else. Under the grime-gray dresser scarf, nothing. In the shower stall, the medicine chest, nothing and nothing again, except what Mrs Koyper had grudgingly installed.

Slim went to the bed and carefully turned back the faded coverlet. Maybe she had slept in it, but very possibly not; Mrs Koyper specialized in unironed sheets of such a ground-in gray that it wasn't easy to tell. Frowning, Slim put up the coverlet again and smoothed it.

Suddenly he struck his forehead, which yielded him a flash of pain from his injury. He ignored it. "The bag!"

It was under the bed, shoved there, not hidden there. He looked at it without touching it for a moment, so that it could be returned exactly. Then he hauled it out.

It was a black gladstone, neither new nor expensive, of that nondescript rusty color acquired by untended leatherette. It had a worn zipper closure and was not locked. Slim opened it. It contained a cardboard box, crisp and new, for a thousand virgin sheets of cheap white typewriter paper surrounded by a glossy bright blue band bearing a white diamond with the legend: *Nonpareil the writer's friend 15% cotton fiber trade mark registered.*

Slim lifted the paper out of the box, looked under it, riffled a thumbful of the sheets at the top and the same from the bottom, shook his head, replaced the paper, closed the box, put it back into the bag and restored everything precisely as he had found it. He paused again in the middle of the room, turning slowly once, but there was simply nothing else to look at. He let himself out, locked the door, and went silently back to his room.

He sat down on the edge of his bed and at last protested, "Nobody *lives* like that!"

His room was on the fourth and topmost floor of the old house. Anyone else would have called it the worst room in the place. It was small, dark, shabby and remote and it suited him beautifully.

Its door had a transom, the glass of which had many times been painted over. By standing on the foot of his bed, Slim could apply one eye to the peephole he had scratched in the

paint and look straight down the stairs to the third-floor
landing. On this landing, hanging to the stub of one of the
ancient gas jets, was a cloudy mirror surmounted by a dust-
mantled gilt eagle and surrounded by a great many rococo
carved flowers. By careful propping with folded cigarette
wrappers, innumerable tests and a great deal of silent
mileage up and down the stairs, Slim had arranged the exact
tilt necessary in the mirror so that it covered the second floor
landing as well. And just as a radar operator learns to
translate glowing pips and masses into aircraft and weather,
so Slim became expert at the interpretation of the fogged and
distant image it afforded him. Thus he had the comings and
goings of half the tenants under surveillance without having
to leave his room.

It was in this mirror, at twelve minutes past six, that he
saw Celia Sarton next, and as he watched her climb the
stairs, his eyes glowed.

The anonymity was gone. She came up the stairs two at a
time, with a gait like bounding. She reached the landing and
whirled into her corridor and was gone, and while a part of
Slim's mind listened for the way she opened her door
(hurriedly, rattling the key against the lock-plate, banging
the door open, slamming it shut), another part studied a
mental photograph of her face.

What raised its veil of the statistical ordinary was its set
purpose. Here were eyes only superficially interested in cars,
curbs, stairs, doors. It was as if she had projected every
important part of herself into that empty room of hers and
waited there impatiently for her body to catch up. There was
something in the room, or something she had to do there,
which she could not, would not, wait for. One goes this way
to a beloved after a long parting, or to a deathbed in the last,
precipitous moments. This was not the arrival of one who
wants, but of one who needs.

Slim buttoned his shirt, eased his door open and sidled
through it. He poised a moment on his landing like a great
moose sensing the air before descending to a waterhole, and
then moved downstairs.

Celia Sarton's only neighbor in the north corridor – the

spinster with the bottles – was settled for the evening; she was of very regular habits and Slim knew them well.

Completely confident that he would not be seen, he drifted to the girl's door and paused.

She was there, all right. He could see the light around the edge of the ill-fitting door, could sense that difference between an occupied room and an empty one, which exists however silent the occupant might be. And this one *was* silent. Whatever it was that had driven her into the room with such headlong urgency, whatever it was she was doing (*had* to do) was being done with no sound or motion that he could detect.

For a long time – six minutes, seven – Slim hung there, open-throated to conceal the sound of his breath. At last, shaking his head, he withdrew, climbed the stairs, let himself into his own room and lay down on the bed, frowning.

He could only wait. Yet he *could* wait. No one does any single thing for very long. Especially a thing not involving movement. In an hour, in two –

It was five. At half-past eleven, some faint sound from the floor below brought Slim, half-dozing, twisting up from the bed and to his high peephole in the transom. He saw the Sarton girl come out of the corridor slowly, and stop, and look around at nothing in particular, like someone confined too long in a ship's cabin who has emerged on deck, not so much for the lungs' sake, but for the eyes'. And when she went down the stairs, it was easily and without hurry, as if (again) the important part of her was in the room. But the something was finished with for now and what was ahead of her wasn't important and could wait.

Standing with his hand on his own doorknob, Slim decided that he, too, could wait. The temptation to go straight to her room was, of course, large, but caution also loomed. What he had tentatively established as her habit patterns did not include midnight exits. He could not know when she might come back and it would be foolish indeed to jeopardize his hobby – not only where it included her, but all of it – by being caught. He sighed, mixing resignation with anticipatory pleasure, and went to bed.

Less than fifteen minutes later, he congratulated himself

with a sleepy smile as he heard her slow footsteps mount the stairs below. He slept.

There was nothing in the closet, there was nothing in the ashtray, there was nothing in the medicine chest nor under the dresser scarf. The bed was made, the dresser drawers were empty, and under the bed was the cheap gladstone. In it was a box containing a thousand sheets of typing paper surrounded by a glossy blue band. Without disturbing this, Slim riffled the sheets, once at the top, once at the bottom. He grunted, shook his head and then proceeded, automatically but meticulously, to put everything back as he had found it.

"Whatever it is this girl does at night," he said glumly, "it leaves tracks like it makes noise."

He left.

The rest of the day was unusually busy for Slim. In the morning he had a doctor's appointment, and in the afternoon he spent hours with a company lawyer who seemed determined to (a) deny the existence of any head injury and (b) prove to Slim and the world that the injury must have occurred years ago. He got absolutely nowhere. If Slim had another characteristic as consuming and compulsive as his curiosity, it was his shyness; these two could stand on one another's shoulders, though, and still look upward at Slim's stubbornness. It served its purpose. It took hours, however, and it was after seven when he got home.

He paused at the third-floor landing and glanced down the corridor. Celia Sarton's room was occupied and silent. If she emerged around midnight, exhausted and relieved, then he would know she had again raced up the stairs to her urgent, motionless task, whatever it was . . . and here he checked himself. He had long ago learned the uselessness of cluttering up his busy head with conjectures. A thousand things might happen; in each case, only one would. He would wait, then, and could.

And again, some hours later, he saw her come out of her corridor. She looked about, but he knew she saw very little; her face was withdrawn and her eyes wide and unguarded. Then, instead of going out, she went back into her room.

He slipped downstairs half an hour later and listened at her door, and smiled. She was washing her lingerie at the handbasin. It was a small thing to learn, but he felt he was making progress. It did not explain why she lived as she did, but indicated how she could manage without so much as a spare handkerchief.

Oh, well, maybe in the morning.

In the morning, there was no maybe. He found it, he found it, though he could not know what it was he'd found. He laughed at first, not in triumph but wryly, calling himself a clown. Then he squatted on his heels in the middle of the floor (he would not sit on the bed, for fear of leaving wrinkles of his own on those Mrs Koyper supplied) and carefully lifted the box of paper out of the suitcase and put it on the floor in front of him.

Up to now, he had contented himself with a quick riffle of the blank paper, a little at the top, a little at the bottom. He had done just this again, without removing the box from the suitcase, but only taking the top off and tilting up the banded ream of *Non-pareil-the-writer's-friend*. And almost in spite of itself, his quick eye had caught the briefest flash of pale blue.

Gently, he removed the band, sliding it off the pack of paper, being careful not to slit the glossy finish. Now he could freely riffle the pages, and when he did, he discovered that all of them except a hundred or so, top and bottom, had the same rectangular cut-out, leaving only a narrow margin all the way around. In the hollow space thus formed, something was packed.

He could not tell what the something was, except that it was pale tan, with a tinge of pink, and felt like smooth untextured leather. There was a lot of it, neatly folded so that it exactly fitted the hole in the ream of paper.

He puzzled over it for some minutes without touching it again, and then, scrubbing his fingertips against his shirt until he felt that they were quite free of moisture and grease, he gently worked loose the top corner of the substance and unfolded a layer. All he found was more of the same.

He folded it down flat again to be sure he could, and then brought more of it out. He soon realized that the material was of an irregular shape and almost certainly of one piece, so that folding it into a tight rectangle required care and great skill. Therefore he proceeded very slowly, stopping every now and then to fold it up again, and it took him more than an hour to get enough of it out so that he could identify it.

Identify? It was completely unlike anything he had ever seen before.

It was a human skin, done in some substance very like the real thing. The first fold, the one which had been revealed at first, was an area of the back, which was why it showed no features. One might liken it to a balloon, except that a deflated balloon is smaller in every dimension than an inflated one. As far as Slim could judge, this was life-sized – a little over five feet long and proportioned accordingly. The hair was peculiar, looking exactly like the real thing until flexed, and then revealing itself to be one piece.

It had Celia Sarton's face.

Slim closed his eyes and opened them, and found that it was still true. He held his breath and put forth a careful, steady forefinger and gently pressed the left eyelid upward. There was an eye under it, all right, light blue and seemingly moist, but flat.

Slim released the breath, closed the eye and sat back on his heels. His feet were beginning to tingle from his having knelt on the floor for so long.

He looked all around the room once, to clear his head of strangeness, and then began to fold the thing up again. It took a while, but when he was finished, he knew he had it right. He replaced the typewriter paper in the box and the box in the bag, put the bag away and at last stood in the middle of the room in the suspension which overcame him when he was deep in thought.

After a moment of this, he began to inspect the ceiling. It was made of stamped tin, like those of many old-fashioned houses. It was grimy and flaked and stained; here and there, rust showed through, and in one or two places, edges of the tin sheets had sagged. Slim nodded to himself in profound satisfaction, listened for a while at the door, let himself out, locked it and went upstairs.

He stood in his own corridor for a minute, checking the position of doors, the hall window, and his accurate orientation of the same things on the floor below. Then he went into his own room.

His room, though smaller than most, was one of the few in the house which was blessed with a real closet instead of a rickety off-the-floor wardrobe. He went into it and knelt, and grunted in satisfaction when he found how loose the ancient, unpainted floorboards were. By removing the side baseboard, he found it possible to get to the air-space between the fourth floor and the third-floor ceiling.

He took out boards until he had an opening perhaps fourteen inches wide, and then, working in almost total silence, he began cleaning away dirt and old plaster. He did this meticulously, because when he finally pierced the tin sheeting, he wanted not one grain of dirt to fall into the room below. He took his time and it was late in the afternoon when he was satisfied with his preparations and began, with his knife, on the tin.

It was thinner and softer than he had dared to hope; he almost overcut on the first try. Carefully he squeezed the sharp steel into the little slot he had cut, lengthening it. When it was somewhat less than an inch long, he withdrew all but the point of the knife and twisted it slightly, moved it a sixteenth of an inch and twisted again, repeating this all down the cut until he had widened it enough for his purpose.

He checked the time, then returned to Celia Sarton's room for just long enough to check the appearance of his work from that side. He was very pleased with it. The little cut had come through a foot away from the wall over the bed and was a mere pencil line lost in the baroque design with which the tin was stamped and the dirt and rust that marred it. He returned to his room and sat down to wait.

He heard the old house coming to its evening surge of life, a voice here, a door there, footsteps on the stairs. He ignored them all as he sat on the edge of his bed, hands folded between his knees, eyes half closed, immobile like a machine fueled, oiled, tuned and ready, lacking only the right touch on the right control. And like that touch, the faint sound of Celia Sarton's footsteps moved him.

To use his new peephole, he had to lie on the floor half in and half out of the closet, with his head in the hole, actually below floor level. With this, he was perfectly content, any amount of discomfort being well worth his trouble – an attitude he shared with many another ardent hobbyist, mountain-climber or speleologist, duck-hunter or bird-watcher.

When she turned on the light, he could see her splendidly, as well as most of the floor, the lower third of the door and part of the washbasin in the bathroom.

She had come in hurriedly, with that same agonized haste he had observed before. At the same second she turned on the light, she had apparently flung her handbag toward the bed; it was in mid-air as the light appeared. She did not even glance its way, but hastily fumbled the old gladstone from under the bed, opened it, removed the box, opened it, took out the paper, slipped off the blue band and removed the blank sheets of paper which covered the hollowed-out ream.

She scooped out the thing hidden there, shaking it once like a grocery clerk with a folded paper sack, so that the long limp thing straightened itself out. She arranged it carefully on the worn linoleum of the floor, arms down at the side, legs slightly apart, face up, neck straight. Then she lay down on the floor, too, head-to-head with the deflated thing. She reached up over her head, took hold of the collapsed image of herself about the region of the ears, and for a moment did some sort of manipulation of it against the top of her own head.

Slim heard faintly a sharp, chitinous click, like the sound one makes by snapping the edge of a thumbnail against the edge of a fingernail.

Her hands slipped to the cheeks of the figure and she pulled at the empty head as if testing a connection. The head seemed now to have adhered to hers.

Then she assumed the same pose she had arranged for this other, letting her hands fall wearily to her sides on the floor, closing her eyes.

For a long while, nothing seemed to be happening, except for the odd way she was breathing, very deeply but very slowly, like the slow-motion picture of someone panting, gasping for breath after a long hard run. After perhaps ten minutes of this, the breathing became shallower and even slower, until, at the end of a half-hour, he could detect none at all.

Slim lay there immobile for more than an hour, until his body shrieked protest and his head ached from eyestrain. He hated to move, but move he must. Silently he backed out of the closet, stood up and stretched. It was a great luxury and he deeply enjoyed it. He felt moved to think over what he had just seen, but clearly and consciously decided not to – not yet, anyway.

When he was unkinked, again, he crept back into the closet, put his head in the hole and his eye to the slot.

Nothing had changed. She still lay quiet, utterly relaxed, so much so that her hands had turned palm upward.

Slim watched and he watched. Just as he was about to conclude that this was the way the girl spent her entire nights and that there would be nothing more to see, he saw a slight and sudden contraction about the region of her solar plexus, and then another. For a time, there was nothing more, and then the empty thing attached to the top of her head began to fill.

And Celia Sarton began to empty.

Slim stopped breathing until it hurt and watched in total astonishment.

Once it had started, the process progressed swiftly. It was as if something passed from the clothed body of the girl to this naked empty thing. The something, whatever it might be, had to be fluid, for nothing but a fluid would fill a flexible container in just this way, or make a flexible container slowly and evenly flatten out like this. Slim could see the fingers, which had been folded flat against the palms, inflate and move until they took on the normal relaxed curl of a normal hand. The elbows shifted a little to lie more normally against the body. And yes, it was a body now.

The other one was not a body any more. It lay foolishly limp in its garment, its sleeping face slightly distorted by its flattening. The fingers fell against the palms by their own limp weight. The shoes thumped quietly on their sides, heels together, toes pointing in opposite directions.

The exchange was done in less than ten minutes and then the newly filled body moved.

It flexed its hands tentatively, drew up its knees and stretched its legs out again, arched its back against the floor. Its eyes flickered open. It put up its arms and made some deft manipulation at the top of its head. Slim heard another version of the soft-hard click and the now-empty head fell flat to the floor.

The new Celia Sarton sat up and sighed and rubbed her hands lightly over her body, as if restoring circulation and sensation to a chilled skin. She stretched as comfortingly and luxuriously as Slim had a few minutes earlier. She looked rested and refreshed.

At the top of her head, Slim caught a glimpse of a slit through which a wet whiteness showed, but it seemed to be closing. In a brief time, nothing showed there but a small valley in the hair, like a normal parting.

She sighed again and got up. She took the clothed thing on the floor by the neck, raised it and shook it twice to make the clothes fall away. She tossed it to the bed and carefully picked up the clothes and deployed them about the room, the undergarments in the washbasin, the dress and slip on a hanger in the wardrobe.

Moving leisurely but with purpose, she went into the bathroom and, except from her shins down, out of Slim's range of vision. There he heard the same faint domestic sounds he had once detected outside her door, as she washed her underclothes. She emerged in due course, went to the wardrobe for some wire hangers and took them into the bathroom. Back she came with the underwear folded on the hangers, which she hooked to the top of the open wardrobe door. Then she took the deflated integument which lay crumpled on the bed, shook it again, rolled it up into a ball and took it into the bathroom.

Slim heard more water-running and sudsing noises, and, by ear, followed the operation through a soaping and two rinses. Then she came out again, shaking out the object, which had apparently just been wrung, pulled it through a wooden clothes-hanger, arranged it creaselessly suspending from the crossbar of the hanger with the bar about at its waistline, and hung it with the others on the wardrobe door.

Then she lay down on the bed, not to sleep or to read or even to rest – she seemed very rested – but merely to wait until it was time to do something else.

By now, Slim's bones were complaining again, so he wormed noiselessly backward out of his lookout point, got into his shoes and a jacket, and went out to get something to eat. When he came home an hour later and looked, her light was out and he could see nothing. He spread his overcoat carefully over the hole in the closet so no stray light from his room would appear in the little slot in the ceiling, closed the door, read a comic book for a while, and went to bed.

The next day, he followed her. What strange occupation she might have, what weird vampiric duties she might disclose, he did not speculate on. He was doggedly determined to gather information first and think later.

What he found out about her daytime activities was, if anything, more surprising than any wild surmise. She was a clerk in a small five-and-ten on the East Side. She ate in the store's lunch bar at lunchtime – a green salad and a surprising amount of milk – and in the evening she stopped at a hot-dog stand and drank a small container of milk, though she ate nothing.

Her steps were slowed by then and she moved wearily, speeding up only when she was close to the rooming house, and then apparently all but overcome with eagerness to get home and . . . into something more comfortable. She was watched in this process, and Slim, had he disbelieved his own eyes the first time, must believe them now.

So it went for a week, three days of which Slim spent in shadowing her, every evening in watching her make her strange toilet. Every twenty-four hours, she changed bodies, carefully washing, drying, folding and putting away the one she was not using.

Twice during the week, she went out for what was apparently a constitutional and nothing more – a half-hour around midnight, when she would stand on the walk in front of the rooming house, or wander around the block.

At work, she was silent but not unnaturally so; she spoke, when spoken to, in a small, unmusical voice. She seemed to have no friends; she maintained her aloofness by being uninteresting and by seeking no one out and by needing no one. She evinced no outside interests, never going to the movies or to the park. She had no dates, not even with girls. Slim thought she did not sleep, but lay quietly in the dark waiting for it to be time to get up and go to work.

And when he came to think about it, as ultimately he did, it occurred to Slim that within the anthill in which we all live and have our being, enough privacy can be exacted to allow for all sorts of strangeness in the members of society, providing the strangeness is not permitted to show. If it is a man's pleasure to sleep upside-down like a bat, and if he so arranges his life that no one ever sees him sleeping, or his sleeping-place, why, batlike he may sleep all the days of his life.

One need not, by these rules, even *be* a human being. Not if the mimicry is good enough. It is a measure of Slim's odd personality to report that Celia Sarton's ways did not frighten him. He was, if anything, less disturbed by her now than he'd been before he had begun to spy on her. He knew what she did in her room and how she lived. Before, he had not known. Now he did. This made him much happier.

He was, however, still curious.

His curiosity would never drive him to do what another man might – to speak to her on the stairs or on the street, get to know her and more about her. He was too shy for that. Nor was he moved to report to anyone the odd practice he watched each evening. It wasn't his business to report. She was doing no harm as far as he could see. In his cosmos, everybody had a right to live and make a buck if they could.

Yet his curiosity, its immediacy taken care of, did undergo a change. It was not in him to wonder what sort of being this was and whether its ancestors had grown up among human beings, living with them in caves and in tents, developing and evolving along with *homo sap* until it could assume the uniform of the smallest and most invisible of wage-workers.

He would never reach the conclusion that in the fight for survival, a species might discover that a most excellent characteristic for survival among human beings might be not to fight them but to join them.

No, Slim's curiosity was far simpler, more basic and less informed than any of these conjectures. He simply changed the field of his wonderment from *what* to *what if*?

So it was that on the eighth day of his survey, a Tuesday, he went again to her room, got the bag, opened it, removed the box, opened it, removed the ream of paper, slid the blue band off, removed the covering sheets, took out the second Celia Sarton, put her on the bed and then replaced paper, blue band, box-cover, box, and bag as he had found them. He put the folded thing under his shirt and went out, carefully locking the door behind him in his special way, and went upstairs to his room. He put his prize under the four clean shirts in his bottom drawer and sat down to await Celia Sarton's homecoming.

She was a little late that night – twenty minutes, perhaps. The delay seemed to have increased both her fatigue and her eagerness; she burst in feverishly, moved with the rapidity of near-panic. She looked drawn and pale and her hands shook. She fumbled the bag from under the bed, snatched out the box and opened it, contrary to her usual measured movements, by inverting it over the bed and dumping out its contents.

When she saw nothing there but sheets of paper, some with a wide rectangle cut from them and some without, she froze. She crouched over that bed without moving for an interminable two minutes. Then she straightened up slowly and glanced about the room. Once she fumbled through the paper, but resignedly, without hope. She made one sound, a high, sad whimper, and, from that moment on, was silent.

She went to the window slowly, her feet dragging, her shoulders slumped. For a long time, she stood looking out at the city, its growing darkness, its growing colonies of lights, each a symbol of life and life's usages. Then she drew down the blind and went back to the bed.

She stacked the papers there with loose uncaring fingers and put the heap of them on the dresser. She took off her shoes and placed them neatly side by side on the floor by the bed. She lay down in the same utterly relaxed pose she affected when she made her change, hands down and open, legs a little apart.

Her face looked like a death-mask, its tissues sunken and sagging. It was flushed and sick-looking. There was a little of the deep regular breathing, but only a little. There was a bit of the fluttering contractions at the midriff, but only a bit. Then – nothing.

Slim backed away from the peephole and sat up. He felt very bad about this. He had been only curious; he hadn't wanted her to get sick, to die. For he was sure she had died. How could he know what sort of sleep-surrogate an organism like this might require, or what might be the results of a delay in changing? What could he know of the chemistry of such a being? He had thought vaguely of slipping down the next day while she was out and returning her property. Just to see. Just to know *what if*. Just out of curiosity.

Should he call a doctor?

She hadn't. She hadn't even tried, though she must have known much better than he did how serious her predicament was. (Yet if a species depended for its existence on secrecy, it would be species-survival to let an individual die undetected.) Well, maybe not calling a doctor meant that she'd be all right, after all. Doctors would have a lot of silly questions to ask. She might even tell the doctor about her other skin, and if Slim was the one who had fetched the doctor, Slim might be questioned about that.

Slim didn't want to get involved with anything. He just wanted to know things.

He thought, "I'll take another look."

He crawled back into the closet and put his head in the hole. Celia Sarton, he knew instantly, would not survive this. Her face was swollen, her eyes protruded, and her purpled tongue lolled far – too far – from the corner of her mouth. Even as he watched, her face darkened still more and the skin of it crinkled until it looked like carbon paper which has been balled up tight and then smoothed out.

The very beginnings of an impulse to snatch the thing she needed out of his shirt drawer and rush it down to her died within him, for he saw a wisp of smoke emerge from her nostrils and then –

Slim cried out, snatched his head from the hole, bumping it cruelly, and clapped his hands over his eyes. Put the biggest size flash-bulb an inch from your nose, and fire it, and you might get a flare approaching the one he got through his little slot in the tin ceiling.

He sat grunting in pain and watching, on the insides of his eyelids, migrations of flaming worms. At last they faded and he tentatively opened his eyes. They hurt and the after-image of the slot hung before him, but at least he could see.

Feet pounded on the stairs. He smelled smoke and a burned, oily unpleasant something which he could not identify. Someone shouted. Someone hammered on the door. Then someone screamed and screamed.

It was in the papers next day. Mysterious, the story said. Charles Fort, in *Lo!*, had reported many such cases and there had been others since – people burned to a crisp by a fierce heat which had nevertheless not destroyed clothes or bedding, while leaving nothing for autopsy. This was, said the paper, either an unknown kind of heat or heat of such intensity and such brevity that it would do such a thing. No known relatives, it said. Police mystified – no clues or suspects.

Slim didn't say anything to anybody. He wasn't curious about the matter any more. He closed up the hole in the closet that same night, and next day, after he read the story, he used the newspaper to wrap up the thing in his shirt drawer. It smelled pretty bad and, even that early, was too far gone to be unfolded. He dropped it into a garbage can on the way to the lawyer's office on Wednesday.

They settled his lawsuit that afternoon and he moved.

RICHARD McKENNA

Casey Agonistes

The late Richard McKenna was probably best known in his lifetime as author of the fat and thoughtful bestselling mainstream novel *The Sand Pebbles* – later made into a big-budget but inferior (to the book) screen spectacular starring Steve McQueen – but during his short career, before his tragically early death in 1964, he also wrote a handful of powerful and elegant short science fiction stories that stand among the best work of the first half of the 1960s. The roster of them, alas, is short: the strange and wonderful novella "Fiddler's Green," "The Secret Place" – for which he won a posthumous Nebula Award – "The Night of Hoggy Darn," "Mine Own Ways," "Hunter, Come Home," "Bramble Bush." Many of them question the nature of reality, and investigate our flawed and prejudiced perceptions of it with a depth and complexity rivaled elsewhere at that time only by the work of Philip K. Dick. All of them reveal the sure touch of a master craftsman, and it is intriguing – if, of course, pointless – to wonder what kind of work McKenna would be turning out now, if fate had spared him.

The best of the McKenna stories, though, is the one that follows, "Casey Agonistes," one of the most powerful stories ever published in the genre – or out of it, for that matter. Amazingly, it was McKenna's first published story.

Almost all of McKenna's short fiction was collected in *Casey Agonistes and Other Science Fiction and Fantasy Stories*. A collection of his essays, *New Eyes For Old*, was published after his death.

You can't just plain die. You got to do it by the book.

That's how come I'm here in this TB ward with nine other recruits. Basic training to die.

You do it by stages. First a big ward, you walk around and go out and they call you mister. Then, if you got what it takes, a promotion to this isolation ward and they call you charles. You can't go nowhere, you meet the masks, and you get the feel of being dead.

Being dead is being weak and walled off. You hear car noises, and see little doll-people down on the sidewalks, but when they come to visit you they wear white masks and nightgowns and talk past you in the wrong voices. They're scared you'll rub some off on them. You would, too, if you knew how.

Nobody ever visits me. I had practice being dead before I come here. Maybe that's how I got to be charles so quick.

It's easy, playing dead here. You eat your pills, make out to sleep in the quiet hours and drink your milk like a good little charles. You grin at their phony joshing about how healthy you look and feel. You all know better, but them's the rules.

Sick call is when they really make you know it. It's a parade – the head doctor and nurse, the floor nurse Mary Howard and two interns, all in masks and nightgowns. Mary pushes the wheeled rack with our fever charts on it. The doc is a tall skinhead with wooden eyes and pinchnose glasses. The head nurse is fat, with little pig eyes and a deep voice.

The doc can't see, hear, smell or touch you. He looks at your reflection in the chart and talks about you like you was real, but it's Mary that pulls down the cover and opens your pajama coat, and the interns poke and look and listen and tell the doc what they see and hear. He asks them questions for you to answer. You tell them how good you feel and they tell him. He ain't supposed to get contaminated.

Mary's small, dark and sweet and the head nurse gives her a bad time. One intern is small and dark like Mary, but with soft black eyes and very gentle. The other one is pink and chubby.

The doc's voice is high and thin, like he ain't all there below decks. The head nurse snaps at Mary, snips at the interns, and puts a kind of dog wiggle in her voice when she talks to the doc.

I'm glad not to know what's under any of their masks, except maybe Mary's, because I can likely imagine better faces for them then God did. The head nurse makes rounds, writing the book. When she catches us out of line, like smoking or being up in a quiet hour, she gives Mary hell.

She gives us hell too, like we was babies. She kind of hints that if we ain't respectful to her and obey her rules maybe she won't let us die after all.

Christ, how I hate this hag! I hope I meet her in hell.

That's how it struck me, first day or two in isolation. I'd looked around for old shipmates, like a guy does, but didn't see any. On the third day one recognized me. I thought I knew that gravel voice, but even after he told me I couldn't hardly believe it was old Slop Chute Hewitt.

He was skin and bones and his blue eyes had a kind of puzzled look like I saw in them once years ago when a big limey sucker punched him in Nagasaki Joe's. When I remembered that, it made me know, all right.

He said glad to see me there and we both laughed. Some of the others shuffled over in striped bathrobes and all of a sudden I was in like Flynn, knowing Slop Chute. I found out they called the head doc Uncle Death. The fat nurse was Mama Death. The blond intern was Pink Waldo, the dark one Curly Waldo, and Mary was Mary. Knowing things like that is a kind of password.

They said Curly Waldo was sweet on Mary, but he was a poor Italian. Pink Waldo come of good family and was trying to beat him out. They were pulling for Curly Waldo.

When they left, Slop Chute and me talked over old times in China. I kept seeing him like he was on the *John D. Edwards*, sitting with a cup of coffee topside by the after fireroom hatch, while his snipes turned to down below. He wore bleached dungarees and shined shoes and he looked like a lord of the earth. His broad face and big belly. The way he stoked chow into himself in the guinea pullman – that's what give him his name. The way he took aboard beer and samshu in the Kongmoon Happiness Garden. The way he swung the little ne-sans dancing in the hotels on Skibby Hill. Now . . . Godalmighty! It made me know.

But he still had the big jack-lantern grin.

"Remember little Connie that danced at the Palais?" he asked.

I remember her, half Portygee, cute as hell.

"You know, Charley, now I'm headed for scrap, the

onliest one damn thing I'm sorry for is I didn't shack with her when I had the chance."

"She was nice," I said.

"She was green fire in the velvet, Charley. I had her a few times when I was on the *Monocacy*. She wanted to shack and I wouldn't never do it. Christ, Christ, I wish I did, now!"

"I ain't sorry for anything, that I can think of."

"You'll come to it, sailor. For every guy there's some one thing. Remember how Connie used to put her finger on her nose like a Jap girl?"

"Now, Mr Noble, you mustn't keep arthur awake in quiet hour. Lie down yourself, please."

It was Mama Death, sneaked up on us.

"Now rest like a good boy, charles, and we'll have you home before you know it," she told me on her way out.

I thought a thought at her.

The ward had green-gray linoleum, high, narrow windows, a sparcolor overhead, and five bunks on a side. My bunk was at one end next to the solarium. Slop Chute was across from me in the middle. Six of us was sailors, three soldiers, and there was one marine.

We got mucho sack time, training for the long sleep. The marine bunked next to me and I saw a lot of him.

He was a strange guy. Name of Carnahan, with a pointed nose and a short upper lip and a go-to-hell stare. He most always wore his radio earphones and he was all the time grinning and chuckling like he was in a private world from the rest of us.

It wasn't the program that made him grin, either, like I thought first. He'd do it even if some housewife was yapping about how to didify the dumplings. He carried on worst during sick call. Sometimes Uncle Death looked across almost like he could hear it direct.

I asked him about it and he put me off, but finally he told me. Seems he could hypnotize himself to see a big ape and then make the ape clown around. He told me I might could get to see it too. I wanted to try, so we did.

"He's there," Carnahan would say. "Sag your eyes, look out the corners. He won't be plain at first."

"Just *expect* him, he'll come. Don't want him to do anything. You just *feel*. He'll do what's natural," he kept telling me.

I got where I could see the ape – Casey, Carnahan called him – in flashes. Then one day Mama Death was chewing out Mary and I saw him plain. He come up behind Mama and – I busted right out laughing.

He looked like a bowlegged man in an ape suit covered with red-brown hair. He grinned and made faces with a mouth full of big yellow teeth and he was furnished like John Keeno himself. I roared.

"Put on your phones so you'll have an excuse for laughing," Carnahan whispered. "Only you and me can see him, you know."

Fixing to be dead, you're ready for God knows what, but Casey was sure something.

"Hell, no he ain't real," Carnahan said. "We ain't so real ourselves any more. That's why we can see him."

Carnahan told me okay to try and let Slop Chute in on it. It ended we cut the whole gang in, going slow so the masks wouldn't get suspicious.

It bothered Casey at first, us all looking at him. It was like we all had a string on him and he didn't know who to mind. He backed and filled and tacked and yawed all over the ward not able to steer himself. Only when Mama Death was there and Casey went after her, then it was like all the strings pulled the same way.

The more we watched him the plainer and stronger he got till finally he started being his own man. He came and went as he pleased and we never knew what he'd do next except that there'd be a laugh in it. Casey got more and more there for us, but he never made a sound.

He made a big difference. We all wore our earphones and giggled like idiots. Slop Chute wore his big sideways grin more often. Old Webster almost stopped griping.

There was a man filling in for a padre came to visitate us every week. Casey would sit on his knee and wiggle and drool, with one finger between those strong, yellow teeth.

The man said the radio was a Godsend to us patient spirits in our hour of trial. He stopped coming.

Casey made a real show out of sick call. He kissed Mama Death smack on her mask, danced with her and bit her on the rump. He rode piggy back on Uncle Death. He even took a hand in Mary's romance.

One Waldo always went in on each side of a bunk to look, listen and feel for Uncle. Mary could go on either side. We kept count of whose side she picked and how close she stood to him. That's how we figured Pink Waldo was ahead.

Well, Casey started to shoo her gently in by Curly Waldo and then crowd her closer to him. And, you know, the count began to change in Curly's favor. Casey had something.

If no masks were around to bedevil, Casey would dance and turn handsprings. He made us all feel good.

Uncle Death smelled a rat and had the radio turned off during sick call and quiet hours. But he couldn't cut off Casey.

Something went wrong with Roby, the cheerful black boy next to Slop Chute. The masks were all upset about it and finally Mary come told him on the sly. He wasn't going to make it. They were going to flunk him back to the big ward and maybe back to the world.

Mary's good that way. We never see her face, of course, but I always imagine for her a mouth like Venus has, in that picture you see her standing in the shell.

When Roby had to go, he come around to each bunk and said goodbye. Casey stayed right behind him with his tongue stuck out. Roby kept looking around for Casey, but of course he couldn't see him.

He turned around, just before he left the ward, and all of a sudden Casey was back in the middle and scowling at him. Roby stood looking at Casey with the saddest face I ever saw him wear. Then Casey grinned and waved a hand. Roby grinned back and tears run down his black face. He waved and shoved off.

Casey took to sleeping in Roby's bunk till another recruit come in.

One day two masked orderlies loaded old Webster the

whiner onto a go-to-Jesus cart and wheeled him off to X-ray. They said. But later one came back and wouldn't look at us and pushed Webster's locker out and we knew. The masks had him in a quiet room for the graduation exercises.

They always done that, Slop Chute told me, so's not to hurt the morale of the guys not able to make the grade yet. Trouble was, when a guy went to X-ray on a go-to-Jesus cart he never knew till he got back whether he was going to see the gang again.

Next morning when Uncle Death fell in for sick call, Casey come bouncing down the ward and hit him a haymaker plumb on the mask.

I swear the bald-headed bastard staggered. I know his glasses fell off and Pink Waldo caught them. He said something about a moment of vertigo, and made a quick job of sick call. Casey stayed right behind him and kicked his stern post every step he took.

Mary favored Curly Waldo's side that day without any help from Casey.

After that Mama Death really got ugly. She slobbered loving care all over us to keep us from knowing what we was there for. We got baths and back rubs we didn't want. Quiet hour had to start on the dot and be really quiet. She was always reading Mary off in whispers, like she knew it bothered us.

Casey followed her around aping her duck waddle and poking her behind now and again. We laughed and she thought it was at her and I guess it was. So she got Uncle Death to order the routine temperatures taken rectally, which she knew we hated. We stopped laughing and she knocked off the rectal temperatures. It was a kind of unspoken agreement. Casey give her a worse time than ever, but we saved our laughing till she was gone.

Poor Slop Chute couldn't do anything about his big, lopsided grin that was louder than a belly laugh. Mama give him a real bad time. She arthured the hell out of him.

He was coming along first rate, had another hemorrhage, and they started taking him to the clinic on a go-to-Jesus cart instead of in a chair. He was supposed to use ducks and a bedpan instead of going to the head, but he saved it up and after lights out we used to help him walk to the head. That made his reflection in the chart wrong and got him in deeper with Uncle Death.

I talked to him a lot, mostly about Connie. He said he dreamed about her pretty often now.

"I figure it means I'm near ready for the deep six, Charley."

"Figure you'll see Connie then?"

"No. Just hope I won't have to go on thinking about her then. I want it to be all night in and no reveille."

"Yeah," I said, "me too. What ever become of Connie?"

"I heard she ate poison right after the Reds took over Shanghai. I wonder if she ever dreamed about me?"

"I bet she did, Slop Chute," I said. "She likely used to wake up screaming and she ate the poison just to get rid of you."

He put on his big grin.

"You regret something too, Charley. You find it yet?"

"Well, maybe," I said. "Once on a stormy night at sea on the *Black Hawk* I had a chance to push King Brody over the side. I'm sorry now I didn't."

"Just come to you?"

"Hell, no, it come to me three days later when he give me a week's restriction in Tsingtao. I been sorry ever since."

"No. It'll smell you out, Charley. You wait."

Casey was shadow boxing down the middle of the ward as I shuffled back to my bunk.

It must've been spring because the days were longer. One night, right after the nurse come through, Casey and Carnahan and me helped Slop Chute walk to the head. While he was there he had another hemorrhage.

Carnahan started for help but Casey got in the way and motioned him back and we knew Slop Chute didn't want it.

We pulled Slop Chute's pajama top off and steadied him. He went on his knees in front of the bowl and the soft, bubbling cough went on for a long time. We kept flushing it. Casey opened the door and went out to keep away the nurse.

Finally it pretty well stopped. Slop Chute was too weak to stand. We cleaned him up and I put my pajama top on him, and we stood him up. If Casey hadn't took half the load, we'd'a never got him back to his bunk.

Godalmighty! I used to carry hundred-kilo sacks of cement like they was nothing.

We went back and cleaned up the head. I washed out the pajama top and draped it on the radiator. I was in a cold sweat and my face burned when I turned in.

Across the ward Casey was sitting like a statue beside Slop Chute's bunk.

Next day was Friday, because Pink Waldo made some crack about fish to Curly Waldo when they formed up for sick call. Mary moved closer to Curly Waldo and gave Pink Waldo a cold look. That was good.

Slop Chute looked waxy, and Uncle Death seemed to see it because a gleam come into his wooden eyes. Both Waldos listened all over Slop Chute and told Uncle what they heard in their secret language. Uncle nodded, and Casey thumbed his nose at him.

No doubt about it, the ways was greased for Slop Chute. Mama Death come back soon as she could and began to loosen the chocks. She slobbered arthurs all over Slop Chute and flittered around like women do when they smell a wedding. Casey give her extra special hell, and we all laughed right out and she hardly noticed.

That afternoon two orderly-masks come with a go-to-Jesus cart and wanted to take Slop Chute to X-ray. Casey climbed on the cart and scowled at them.

Slop Chute told 'em shove off, he wasn't going.

They got Mary and she told Slop Chute please go, it was doctor's orders.

Sorry, no, he said.

"Please, for me, Slop Chute," she begged.

She knows our right names – that's one reason we love her. But Slop Chute shook his head, and his big jaw bone stuck out.

Mary – she had to then – called Mama Death. Mama waddled in, and Casey spit in her mask.

"Now, arthur, what is this, arthur, you know we want to help you get well and go home, arthur," she arthured at Slop Chute. "Be a good boy now, arthur, and go along to the clinic."

She motioned the orderlies to pick him up anyway. Casey hit one in the mask and Slop Chute growled, "Sheer off, you bastards!"

The orderlies hesitated.

Mama's little eyes squinted and she wiggled her hands at them. "Let's not be naughty, arthur. Doctor knows best, arthur."

The orderlies looked at Slop Chute and at each other. Casey wrapped his arms around Mama Death and began chewing on her neck. He seemed to mix right into her, someway, and she broke and run out of the ward.

She came right back, though, trailing Uncle Death. Casey met him at the door and beat hell out of him all the way to Slop Chute's bunk. Mama sent Mary for the chart, and Uncle Death studied Slop Chute's reflection for a minute. He looked pale and swayed a little from Casey's beating.

He turned toward Slop Chute and breathed in deep and Casey was on him again. Casey wrapped his arms and legs around him and chewed at his mask with those big yellow teeth. Casey's hair bristled and his eyes were red as the flames of hell.

Uncle Death staggered back across the ward and fetched up against Carnahan's bunk. The other masks were scared spitless, looking all around, kind of knowing.

Casey pulled away, and Uncle Death said maybe he was wrong, schedule it for tomorrow. All the masks left in a hurry except Mary. She went back to Slop Chute and took his hand.

"I'm sorry, Slop Chute," she whispered.

"Bless you, Connie," he said, and grinned. It was the last thing I ever heard him say.

Slop Chute went to sleep, and Casey sat beside his bunk. He motioned me off when I wanted to help Slop Chute to the head after lights out. I turned in and went to sleep.

I don't know what woke me. Casey was moving around fidgety-like, but of course not making a sound. I could hear the others stirring and whispering in the dark too.

Then I heard a muffled noise – the bubbling cough again, and spitting. Slop Chute was having another hemorrhage and he had his head under the blankets to hide the sound. Carnahan started to get up. Casey waved him down.

I saw a deeper shadow high in the dark over Slop Chute's bunk. It came down ever so gently and Casey would push it back up again. The muffled coughing went on.

Casey had a harder time pushing back the shadow. Finally he climbed on the bunk straddle of Slop Chute and kept a steady push against it.

The blackness came down anyway, little by little. Casey strained and shifted his footing. I could hear him grunt and hear his joints crack.

I was breathing forced draft with my heart like to pull off its bed bolts. I heard other bedsprings creaking. Somebody across from me whimpered low, but it was sure never Slop Chute that done it.

Casey went to his knees, his hands forced almost level with his head. He swung his head back and forth and I saw his lips curled back from the big teeth clenched tight together. . . . Then he had the blackness on his shoulders like the weight of the whole world.

Casey went down on hands and knees with his back arched like a bridge. Almost I thought I heard him grunt . . . and he gained a little.

Then the blackness settled heavier, and I heard Casey's tendons pull out and his bones snap. Casey and Slop Chute disappeared under the blackness, and it overflowed from there over the whole bed . . . and more . . . and it seemed to fill the whole ward.

It wasn't like going to sleep, but I don't know anything it was like.

The masks must've towed off Slop Chute's hulk in the night, because it was gone when I woke up.

So was Casey.

Casey didn't show up for sick call and I knew then how much he meant to me. With him around to fight back I didn't feel as dead as they wanted me to. Without him I felt deader than ever. I even almost liked Mama Death when she charlesed me.

Mary came on duty that morning with a diamond on her third finger and a brighter sparkle in her eye. It was a little diamond, but it was Curly Waldo's and it kind of made up for Slop Chute.

I wished Casey was there to see it. He would've danced all around her and kissed her nice, the way he often did. Casey loved Mary.

It was Saturday, I know, because Mama Death come in and told some of us we could be wheeled to a special church hooraw before breakfast next morning if we wanted. We said no thanks. But it was a hell of a Saturday without Casey. Sharkey Brown said it for all of us – "With Casey gone, this place is like a morgue again."

Not even Carnahan could call him up.

"Sometimes I think I feel him stir, and then again I ain't sure," he said. "It beats hell where he's went to."

Going to sleep that night was as much like dying as it could be for men already dead.

Music from far off woke me up when it was just getting light. I was going to try to cork off again, when I saw Carnahan was awake.

"Casey's around somewhere," he whispered.

"Where?" I asked, looking around. "I don't see him."

"I feel him," Carnahan said. "He's around."

The others began to wake up and look around. It was like the night Casey and Slop Chute went under. Then something moved in the solarium . . .

It was Casey.

He come in the ward slow and bashful-like, jerking his head all around, with his eyes open wide, and looking scared we was going to throw something at him. He stopped in the middle of the ward.

"Yea, Casey!" Carnahan said in a low, clear voice.

Casey looked at him sharp.

"Yea, Casey!" we all said. "Come aboard, you hairy old bastard!"

Casey shook hands with himself over his head and went into his dance. He grinned . . . and I swear to God it was Slop Chute's big, lopsided grin he had on.

For the first time in my whole damn life I wanted to cry.

CORDWAINER SMITH
Mother Hitton's Littul Kittons

If, when I was a young would-be writer, struggling for a glimpse of the Light from out of the stifling provincial darkness of teenage life in a small New England factory town in the early 1960s, some supernatural agency had given me the chance to put on the saffron robe of an acolyte and sit at the feet of the writer of my choice, learning all that I could learn, I would have, without any hesitation, picked Cordwainer Smith as the Master at whose feet I would sit.

The late Cordwainer Smith – in "real" life Dr Paul M. A. Linebarger, scholar, statesman, and author of the definitive text (still taught from today) on the art of psychological warfare – was a writer of enormous talents who, from 1948 until his untimely death in 1966, produced a double-handful of some of the best short fiction this genre has ever seen – "Alpha Ralpha Boulevard," "A Planet Named Shayol," "On the Storm Planet," "The Ballad of Lost C'Mell," "The Dead Lady of Clown Town," "The Game of Rat and Dragon," "Drunkboat," "The Lady Who Sailed *The Soul*," "Under Old Earth," "Scanners Live in Vain" – as well as a large number of lesser, but still fascinating, stories, all twisted and blended and woven into an interrelated tapestry of incredible lushness and intricacy. Smith created a baroque cosmology unrivaled even today for its scope and complexity: a millennia-spanning Future History, logically outlandish and elegantly strange, set against a vivid, richly colored, mythically intense universe where animals assume the shape of men, vast planoform ships whisper through multi-dimensional space, immense sick sheep are the most valuable objects in the universe, immortality can be bought, and the mysterious Lords of the Instrumentality rule a hunted Earth too old for history . . .

It is a cosmology that looks as evocative and bizarre today in the 1990s as it did in the 1960s – certainly for sheer sweep and daring of conceptualization, in its vision of how different and *strange* the future will be, it rivals any contemporary vision conjured up by Young Turks such as Bruce Sterling and Greg Bear, and I suspect that it is timeless.

Here Smith takes us along on a thief's desperate quest to steal eternal life, with all the money in the world for forfeit, and only the childish-sounding "littul kittons" to bar the way . . .

Cordwainer Smith's books include the novel *Norstrilia* and the collections *Space Lords* – one of the landmark collections of the genre – *The Best of Cordwainer Smith*, *Quest of the Three Worlds*, *Stardreamer*, *You Will Never Be the Same*, and *The Instrumentality of Mankind*.

> Poor communications deter theft;
> good communications promote theft;
> perfect communications stop theft.
>
> *Van Braam*

1

The moon spun. The woman watched. Twenty-one facets had been polished at the moon's equator. Her function was to arm it. She was Mother Hitton, the Weapons Mistress of Old North Australia.

She was a ruddy-faced, cheerful blonde of indeterminate age. Her eyes were blue, her bosom heavy, her arms strong. She looked like a mother, but the only child she had ever had died many generations ago. Now she acted as mother to a planet, not to a person; the Norstrilians slept well because they knew she was watching. The weapons slept their long, sick sleep.

This night she glanced for the two-hundredth time at the warning bank. The bank was quiet. No danger lights shone. Yet she felt an enemy out somewhere in the universe – an enemy waiting to strike at her and her world, to snatch at the immeasurable wealth of the Norstrilians – and she snorted with impatience. *Come along, little man*, she thought. *Come along, little man, and die. Don't keep me waiting.*

She smiled when she recognized the absurdity of her own thought.

She waited for him.

And he did not know it.

He, the robber, was relaxed enough. He was Benjacomin Bozart, and was highly trained in the arts of relaxation.

No one at Sunvale, here on Ttiollé, could suspect that he was a Senior Warden of the Guild of Thieves, reared under the light of the starry-violet star. No one could smell the odor of Viola Siderea upon him. "Viola Siderea," the Lady Ru had said, "was once the most beautiful of worlds and it is now the most rotten. Its people were once models for mankind, and now they are thieves, liars and killers. You can smell their souls in the open day." The Lady Ru had died a long time ago. She was much respected, but she was wrong. The robber did not smell to others at all. He knew it. He was no more "wrong" than a shark approaching a school of cod. Life's nature is to live, and he had been nurtured to live as he had to live – by seeking prey.

How else could he live? Viola Siderea had gone bankrupt a long time ago, when the photonic sails had disappeared from space and the planoforming ships began to whisper their way between the stars. His ancestors had been left to die on an off-trail planet. They refused to die. Their ecology shifted and they became predators upon man, adapted by time and genetics to their deadly tasks. And he, the robber, was champion of all his people – the best of their best.

He was Benjacomin Bozart.

He had sworn to rob Old North Australia or to die in the attempt, and he had no intention of dying.

The beach at Sunvale was warm and lovely. Ttiollé was a free and casual transit planet. His weapons were luck and himself: he planned to play both well.

The Norstrilians could kill.

So could he.

At this moment, in this place, he was a happy tourist at a lovely beach. Elsewhere, elsewhen, he could become a ferret among conies, a hawk among doves.

Benjacomin Bozart, Thief and Warden. He did not know that someone was waiting for him. Someone who did not know his name was prepared to waken death, just for him. He was still serene.

Mother Hitton was not serene. She sensed him dimly but could not yet spot him.

One of her weapons snored. She turned it over.

A thousand stars away, Benjacomin Bozart smiled as he walked toward the beach.

2

Benjacomin felt like a tourist. His tanned face was tranquil. His proud, hooded eyes were calm. His handsome mouth, even without its charming smile, kept a suggestion of pleasantness at its corners. He looked attractive without seeming odd in the least. He looked much younger than he actually was. He walked with springy, happy steps along the beach of Sunvale.

The waves rolled in, white-crested, like the breakers of Mother Earth. The Sunvale people were proud of the way their world resembled Manhome itself. Few of them had even seen Manhome, but they had all heard a bit of history and most of them had a passing anxiety when they thought of the ancient government still wielding political power across the depth of space. They did not like the old Instrumentality of Earth, but they respected and feared it. The waves might remind them of the pretty side of Earth; they did not want to remember the not-so-pretty side.

This man was like the pretty side of old Earth. They could not sense the power within him. The Sunvale people smiled absently at him as he walked past them along the shoreline.

The atmosphere was quiet and everything around him serene. He turned his face to the sun. He closed his eyes. He let the warm sunlight beat through his eyelids, illuminating him with its comfort and its reassuring touch.

Benjacomin dreamed of the greatest theft that any man had ever planned. He dreamed of stealing a huge load of the wealth from the richest world that mankind had ever built. He thought of what would happen when he would finally bring riches back to the planet of Viola Siderea where he had been reared. Benjacomin turned his face away from the sun and languidly looked over the other people on the beach.

There were no Norstrilians in sight yet. They were easy enough to recognize. Big people with red complexions; superb athletes and yet, in their own way, innocent, young, and very tough. He had trained for this theft for two hundred years, his life prolonged for the purpose by the Guild of Thieves on Viola Siderea. He himself embodied the dreams of his own planet, a poor planet once a crossroads of commerce, now sunken to being a minor outpost for spoliation and pilferage.

He saw a Norstrilian woman come out from the hotel and go down to the beach. He waited, and he looked, and he dreamed. He had a question to ask and no adult Australian would answer it.

"Funny," thought he, "that I call them 'Australians' even now. That's the old, old Earth name for them – rich, brave, tough people. Fighting children standing on half the world . . . and now they are the tyrants of all mankind. They hold the wealth. They have the santaclara, and other people live or die depending upon the commerce they have with the Norstrilians. But I won't. And my people won't. We're men who are wolves to man."

Benjacomin waited gracefully. Tanned by the light of many suns, he looked forty though he was two hundred. He dressed casually, by the standards of a vacationer. He might have been an intercultural salesman, a senior gambler, an assistant starport manager. He might even have been a detective working along the commerce lanes. He wasn't. He was a thief. And he was so good a thief that people turned to him and put their property in his hands because he was reassuring, calm, gray-eyed, blond-haired. Benjacomin waited. The woman glanced at him, a quick glance full of open suspicion.

What she saw must have calmed her. She went on past. She called back over the dune, "Come on, Johnny, we can swim out here." A little boy, who looked eight or ten years old, came over the dune top, running toward his mother.

Benjacomin tensed like a cobra. His eyes became sharp, his eyelids narrowed.

This was the prey. Not too young, not too old. If the victim had been too young he wouldn't know the answer; if the victim were too old it was no use taking him on. Norstrilians were famed in combat; adults were mentally and physically too strong to warrant attack.

Benjacomin knew that every thief who had approached the planet of the Norstrilians – who had tried to raid the dream world of Old North Australia – had gotten out of contact with his people and had died. There was no word of any of them.

And yet he knew that hundreds of thousands of Norstrilians must know *the* secret. They now and then made jokes about it. He had heard these jokes when he was a young man, and now he was more than an old man without once coming near the answer. Life was expensive. He was well into his third lifetime and the lifetimes had been purchased honestly by his people. Good thieves all of them, paying out hard-stolen money to obtain the medicine to let their greatest thief remain living. Benjacomin didn't like violence. But when violence prepared the way to the greatest theft of all time, he was willing to use it.

The woman looked at him again. The mask of evil which had flashed across his face faded into benignity; he calmed. She caught him in that moment of relaxation. She liked him.

She smiled and, with that awkward hesitation so characteristic of the Norstrilians, she said, "Could you mind my boy a bit while I go in the water? I think we've seen each other here at the hotel."

"I don't mind," said he. "I'd be glad to. Come here, son."

Johnny walked across the sunlight dunes to his own death. He came within reach of his mother's enemy.

But the mother had already turned.

The trained hand of Benjacomin Bozart reached out. He seized the child by the shoulder. He turned the boy toward him, forcing him down. Before the child could cry out, Benjacomin had the needle into him with the truth drug.

All Johnny reacted to was pain, and then a hammerblow inside his own skull as the powerful drug took force.

Benjacomin looked out over the water. The mother was swimming. She seemed to be looking back at them. She was obviously unworried. To her, the child seemed to be looking at something the stranger was showing him in a relaxed, easy way.

"Now, sonny," said Benjacomin, "tell me, what's the outside defense?"

The boy didn't answer.

"What is the outer defense, sonny? What is the outer defense?" repeated Benjacomin. The boy still didn't answer.

Something close to horror ran over the skin of Benjacomin Bozart as he realized that he had gambled his safety on this planet, gambled the plans themselves for a chance to break the secret of the Norstrilians.

He had been stopped by simple, easy devices. The child had already been conditioned against attack. Any attempt to force knowledge out of the child brought on a conditioned reflex of total muteness. The boy was literally unable to talk.

Sunlight gleaming on her wet hair, the mother turned around and called back, "Are you all right, Johnny?"

Benjacomin waved to her instead. "I'm showing him my pictures, ma'am. He likes 'em. Take your time." The mother hesitated and then turned back to the water and swam slowly away.

Johnny, taken by the drug, sat lightly, like an invalid, on Benjacomin's lap.

Benjacomin said, "Johnny, you're going to die now and you will hurt terribly if you don't tell me what I want to know." The boy struggled weakly against his grasp. Benjacomin repeated. "I'm going to hurt you if you don't tell me what I want to know. What are the outer defenses? What are the outer defenses?"

The child struggled and Benjacomin realized that the boy was putting up a fight to comply with the orders, not a fight to get away. He let the child slip through his hands and the boy put out a finger and began writing on the wet sand. The letters stood out.

A man's shadow loomed behind them.

Benjacomin, alert, ready to spin, kill or run, slipped to the ground beside the child and said, "That's a jolly puzzle. That is a good one. Show me some more." He smiled up at the passing adult. The man was a stranger. The stranger gave him a very curious glance which became casual when he saw the pleasant face of Benjacomin, so tenderly and so agreeably playing with the child.

The fingers were still making the letters in the sand.

There stood the riddle in letters: MOTHER HITTON'S LITTUL KITTONS.

The woman was coming back from the sea, the mother with questions. Benjacomin stroked the sleeve of his coat and brought out his second needle, a shallow poison which it would take days or weeks of laboratory work to detect. He thrust it directly into the boy's brain, slipping the needle up behind the skin at the edge of the hairline. The hair shadowed the tiny prick. The incredibly hard needle slipped under the edge of the skull. The child was dead.

Murder was accomplished. Benjacomin casually erased the secret from the sand. The woman came nearer. He called to her, his voice full of pleasant concern, "Ma'am, you'd better come here, I think your son has fainted from the heat."

He gave the mother the body of her son. Her face changed to alarm. She looked frightened and alert. She didn't know how to meet this.

For a dreadful moment she looked into his eyes.

Two hundred years of training took effect. . . . She saw nothing. The murderer did not shine with murder. The hawk was hidden beneath the dove. The heart was masked by the trained face.

Benjacomin relaxed in professional assurance. He had been prepared to kill her too, although he was not sure that he could kill an adult, female Norstrilian. Very helpfully said he, "You stay here with him. I'll run to the hotel and get help. I'll hurry."

He turned and ran. A beach attendant saw him and ran toward him. "The child's sick," he shouted. He came to the mother in time to see blunt, puzzled tragedy on her face and with it, something more than tragedy: doubt.

"He's not sick," said she. "He's dead."

"He can't be." Benjacomin looked attentive. He felt attentive. He forced the sympathy to pour out of his posture, out of all the little muscles of his face. "He can't be. I was talking to him just a minute ago. We were doing little puzzles in the sand."

The mother spoke with a hollow, broken voice that sounded as though it would never find the right chords for human speech again, but would go on forever with the ill-attuned flats of unexpected grief. "He's dead," she said. "You saw him die and I guess I saw him die, too. I can't tell what's happened. The child was full of santaclara. He had a thousand years to live but now he's dead. What's your name?"

Benjacomin said, "Eldon. Eldon the salesman, ma'am. I live here lots of times."

3

"Mother Hitton's littul kittons. Mother Hitton's littul kittons."

The silly phrase ran in his mind. Who was Mother Hitton? Who was she the mother of? What were *kittons*? Were they a misspelling for "kittens"? Little cats? Or were they something else?

Had he killed a fool to get a fool's answer?

How many more days did he have to stay there with the doubtful, staggered woman? How many days did he have to watch and wait? He wanted to get back to Viola Siderea; to take the secret, bad as it was, for his people to study. Who was Mother Hitton?

He forced himself out of his room and went downstairs.

The pleasant monotony of a big hotel was such that the other guests looked interestedly at him. He was the man who had watched while the child died on the beach.

Some lobby-living scandalmongers that stayed there had made up fantastic stories that he had killed the child. Others attacked the stories, saying they knew perfectly well who Eldon was. He was Eldon the salesman. It was ridiculous.

People hadn't changed much, even though the ships with the Go-Captains sitting at their hearts whispered between the stars, even though people shuffled between worlds – when they had the money to pay their passage back and forth – like leaves falling in soft, playful winds. Benjacomin faced a tragic dilemma. He knew very well that any attempt to decode the answer would run directly into the protective devices set up by the Norstrilians.

Old North Australia was immensely wealthy. It was

known the length and breadth of all the stars that they had hired mercenaries, defensive spies, hidden agents and alerting devices.

Even Manhome – Mother Earth herself, whom no money could buy – was bribed by the drug of life. An ounce of the santaclara drug, reduced, crystalized and called "stroon," could give forty to sixty years of life. Stroon entered the rest of the Earth by ounces and pounds, but it was refined back on North Australia by the ton. With treasure like this, the Norstrilians owned an unimaginable world whose resources overreached all conceivable limits of money. They could buy anything. They could pay with other peoples' lives.

For hundreds of years they had given secret funds to buying foreigners' services to safeguard their own security.

Benjacomin stood there in the lobby: "Mother Hitton's littul kittons."

He had all the wisom and wealth of a thousand worlds stuck in his mind but he didn't dare ask anywhere as to what it meant.

Suddenly he brightened.

He looked like a man who had thought of a good game to play, a pleasant diversion to be welcomed, a companion to be remembered, a new food to be tasted. He had had a very happy thought.

There was one source that wouldn't talk. The library. He could at least check the obvious, simple things, and find out what there was already in the realm of public knowledge concerning the secret he had taken from the dying boy.

His own safety had not been wasted, Johnny's life had not been thrown away, if he could find any one of the four words as a key. *Mother* or *Hitton* or *Littul*, in its special meaning, or *Kitton*. He might yet break through to the loot of Norstrilia.

He swung jubilantly, turning on the ball of his right foot. He moved lightly and pleasantly toward the billiard room, beyond which lay the library. He went in.

This was a very expensive hotel and very old-fashioned. It even had books made out of paper, with genuine bindings. Benjacomin crossed the room. He saw that they had the *Galactic Encyclopedia* in two hundred volumes. He took down the volume headed "Hi-Hi." He opened it from the rear, looking for the name "Hitton" and there it was. "Hitton, Benjamin – pioneer of old North Australia. Said to be originator of part of the defense system. Lived AD 10719–17213." That was all. Benjacomin moved among the books. The word "kittons" in that peculiar spelling did not occur anywhere, neither in the encyclopedia nor in any other list maintained by the library. He walked out and upstairs, back to his room.

"Littul" had not appeared at all. It was probably the boy's own childish mistake.

He took a chance. The mother, half blind with bewilderment and worry, sat in a stiff-backed chair on the edge of the porch. The other women talked to her. They knew her husband was coming. Benjacomin went up to her and tried to pay his respects. She didn't see him.

"I'm leaving now, ma'am. I'm going to the next planet, but I'll be back in two or three subjective weeks. And if you need me for urgent questions, I'll leave my addresses with the police here."

Benjacomin left the weeping woman.

Benjacomin left the quiet hotel. He obtained a priority passage.

The easy-going Sunvale Police made no resistance to his demand for a sudden departure visa. After all, he had an identity, he had his own funds, and it was not the custom of Sunvale to contradict its guests. Benjacomin went on the ship and as he moved toward the cabin in which he could rest for a few hours, a man stepped up beside him. A youngish man, hair parted in the middle, short of stature, gray of eyes.

This man was the local agent of the Norstrilian secret police.

Benjacomin, trained thief that he was, did not recognize the policeman. It never occurred to him that the library itself had been attuned and that the word "kittons" in the peculiar Norstrilian spelling was itself an alert. Looking for that spelling had set off a minor alarm. He had touched the tripwire.

The stranger nodded. Benjacomin nodded back. "I'm a traveling man, waiting over between assignments. I haven't been doing very well. How are you making out?"

"Doesn't matter to me. I don't earn money; I'm a technician. Liverant is the name."

Benjacomin sized him up. The man was a technician all right. They shook hands perfunctorily. Liverant said, "I'll join you in the bar a little later. I think I'll rest a bit first."

They both lay down then and said very little while the momentary flash of planoform went through the ship. The flash passed. From books and lessons they knew that the ship was leaping forward in two dimensions while, somehow or other, the fury of space itself was fed into the computers – and that these in turn were managed by the Go-Captain who controlled the ship.

They knew these things but they could not feel them. All they felt was the sting of a slight pain.

The sedative was in the air itself, sprayed in the ventilation system. They both expected to become a little drunk.

The thief Benjacomin Bozart was trained to resist intoxication and bewilderment. Any sign whatever that a telepath had tried to read his mind would have been met with fierce animal resistance, implanted in his unconscious during early years of training. Bozart was not trained against deception by a technician; it never occurred to the Thieves' Guild back on Viola Siderea that it would be necessary for their own people to resist deceivers. Liverant had already been in touch with Norstrilia – Norstrilia whose money reached across the stars, Norstrilia who had alerted a hundred thousand worlds against the mere thought of trespass.

Liverant began to chatter. "I wish I could go further than this trip. I wish that I could go to Olympia. You can buy anything in Olympia."

"I've heard of it," said Bozart. "It's sort of a funny trading planet with not much chance for businessmen, isn't it?"

Liverant laughed and his laughter was merry and genuine. "Trading? They don't trade. They swap. They take all the stolen loot of a thousand worlds and sell it over again and they change and they paint it and they mark it. That's their business there. The people are blind. It's a strange world, and all you have to do is to go in there and you can have anything you want. Man," said Liverant, "what I could do in a year in that place! Everybody is blind except me and a couple of tourists. And there's all the wealth that everybody thought he's mislaid, half the wrecked ships, the forgotten colonies (they've all been cleaned out), and bang! it all goes to Olympia."

Olympia wasn't really that good and Liverant didn't know why it was his business to guide the killer there. All he knew was that he had a duty and the duty was to direct the trespasser.

Many years before either man was born the code word had been planted in directories, in books, in packing cases and invoices. *Kittons* misspelled. This was the cover name for the outer moon of Norstrilian defense. The use of the cover name brought a raging alert ready into action, with systemic nerves as hot and quick as incandescent tungsten wire.

By the time that they were ready to go to the bar and have refreshments, Benjacomin had half forgotten that it was his new acquaintance who had suggested Olympia rather than another place. He had to go to Viola Siderea to get the credits to make the flight to take the wealth, to win the world of Olympia.

4

At home on his native planet Bozart was the subject of a gentle but very sincere celebration.

The Elders of the Guild of Thieves welcomed him. They congratulated him. "Who else could have done what you've done, boy? You've made the opening move in a brand new game of chess. There has never been a gambit like this before. We have a name; we have an animal. We'll try it right here." The Thieves' Council turned to their own encyclopedia. They turned through the name "Hitton" and then found the reference "Kitton." None of them knew that a false lead had been planted there – by an agent in their world.

The agent, in his turn, had been seduced years before, debauched in the middle of his career, forced into temporary honesty, blackmailed and sent home. In all the years that he had waited for a dreaded countersign – a countersign which he himself never knew to be an extension of Norstrilian intelligence – he never dreamed that he could pay his debt to the outside world so simply. All they had done was to send him one page to add to the encyclopedia. He added it and then went home, weak with exhaustion. The years of fear and waiting were almost too much for the thief. He drank heavily for fear that he might otherwise kill himself. Meanwhile, the pages remained in order, including the new one, slightly altered for his colleagues. The encyclopedia indicated the change like any normal revision, though the whole entry was new and falsified:

> Beneath this passage one revision ready. Dated twenty-fourth year of second issue.
>
> The reported "Kittons" of Norstrilia are nothing more than the use of organic means to induce the disease in Earth-mutated sheep which produces a virus in its turn, refinable as the santaclara drug. The term "Kittons" enjoyed a temporary vogue as a reference term both to the disease and to the destructibility of the disease in the event of external attack. This is believed to have been connected with the career of Benjamin Hitton, one of the original pioneers of Norstrilia.

The Council of Thieves read it and the Chairman of the council said "I've got your papers ready. You can go try them now. Where do you want to go? Through Neuhamburg?"

"No," said Benjacomin. "I thought I'd try Olympia."

"Olympia's all right," said the Chairman. "Go easy. There's only one chance in a thousand you'll fail. But if you do, we might have to pay for it."

He smiled wryly and handed Benjacomin a blank mortgage against all the labor and all the property of Viola Siderea.

The Chairman laughed with a sort of snort. "It'd be pretty rough on us if you had to borrow enough on the trading planet to force us to become honest – and then lost out anyhow."

"No fear," said Benjacomin. "I can cover that."

There are some worlds where all dreams die, but square-clouded Olympia is not one of them. The eyes of men and women are bright on Olympia, for they see nothing.

"Brightness was the color of pain," said Nachtigall,

"when we could see. If thine eye offend thee, pluck thyself
out, for the fault lies not in the eye but in the soul."

Such talk was common in Olympia, where the settlers
went blind a long time ago and now think themselves
superior to sighted people. Radar wires tickle their living
brains; they can perceive radiation as well as can an animal-
type man with little aquariums hung in the middle of his
face. Their pictures are sharp, and they demand sharpness.
Their buildings soar at impossible angles. Their blind
children sing songs as the tailored climate proceeds according to the numbers, geometrical as a kaleidoscope.

There went the man, Bozart himself. Among the blind his
dreams soared, and he paid money for information which no
living person had ever seen.

Sharp-clouded and aqua-skied, Olympia swam past him
like another man's dream. He did not mean to tarry there,
because he had a rendezvous with death in the sticky, sparky
space around Norstrilia.

Once in Olympia, Benjacomin went about his arrangements for the attack on Old North Australia. On his second
day on the planet he had been very lucky. He met a man
named Lavender and he was sure he had heard the name
before. Not a member of his own Guild of Thieves, but a
daring rascal with a bad reputation among the stars.

It was no wonder that he had found Lavender. His pillow
had told him Lavender's story fifteen times during his sleep
in the past week. And, whenever he dreamed, he dreamed
dreams which had been planted in his mind by the
Norstrilian counterintelligence. They had beaten him in
getting to Olympia first and they were prepared to let him
have only that which he deserved. The Norstrilian Police
were not cruel, but they were out to defend their world. And
they were also out to avenge the murder of a child.

The last interview which Benjacomin had with Lavender in
striking a bargain before Lavender agreed was a dramatic one.

Lavender refused to move forward.

"I'm not going to jump off anywhere. I'm not going to raid
anything. I'm not going to steal anything. I've been rough, of
course I have. But I don't get myself killed and that's what
you're bloody well asking for."

"Think of what we'll have. The wealth. I tell you, there's more money here than anything else anybody's ever tried."

Lavender laughed. "You think I haven't heard that before? You're a crook and I'm a crook. I don't go anything that's speculation. I want my hard cash down. I'm a fighting man and you're a thief and I'm not going to ask you what you're up to . . . but I want my money first."

"I haven't got it," said Benjacomin.

Lavender stood up.

"Then you shouldn't have talked to me. Because it's going to cost you money to keep me quiet whether you hire me or not."

The bargaining process started.

Lavender looked ugly indeed. He was a soft, ordinary man who had gone to a lot of trouble to become evil. Sin is a lot of work. The sheer effort it requires often shows in the human face.

Bozart stared him down, smiling easily, not even contemptuously.

"Cover me while I get something from my pocket," said Bozart.

Lavender did not even acknowledge the comment. He did not show a weapon. His left thumb moved slowly across the outer edge of his hand. Benjacomin recognized the sign, but did not flinch.

"See," he said. "A planetary credit."

Lavender laughed. "I've heard that, too."

"Take it," said Bozart.

The adventurer took the laminated card. His eyes widened. "It's real," he breathed. "It is real." He looked up, incalculably more friendly. "I never even saw one of these before. What are your terms?"

Meanwhile the bright, vivid Olympians walked back and forth past them, their clothing all white and black in dramatic contrast. Unbelievable geometric designs shone on their cloaks and their hats. The two bargainers ignored the natives. They concentrated on their own negotiations.

Benjacomin felt fairly safe. He placed a pledge of one year's service of the entire planet of Viola Siderea in exchange for the full and unqualified services of Captain

Lavender, once of the Imperial Marines Internal Space Patrol. He handed over the mortgage. The year's guarantee was written in. Even on Olympia there were accounting machines which relayed the bargain back to Earth itself, making the mortgage a valid and binding commitment against the whole planet of thieves.

This, thought Lavender, was the first step of revenge. After the killer had disappeared, his people would have to pay with sheer honesty. Lavender looked at Benjacomin with a clinical sort of concern.

Benjacomin mistook his look for friendliness and Benjacomin smiled his slow, charming, easy smile. Momentarily happy, he reached out his right hand to give Lavender a brotherly solemnification of the bargain. The men shook hands, and Bozart never knew with what he shook hands.

5

"Gray lay the land oh. Gray grass from sky to sky. Not near the weir, dear. Not a mountain, low or high – only hills and gray gray. Watch the dappled, dimpled twinkles blooming on the star bar.

"That is Norstrilia.

"All the muddy gubbery is gone – all the work and the waiting and the pain.

"Beige-brown sheep lie on blue-gray grass while the clouds rush past, low overhead, like iron pipes ceilinging the world.

"Take your pick of sick sheep, man, it's the sick that pays. Sneeze me a planet, man, or cough me up a spot of immortality. If it's barmy there, where the noddies and the trolls like you live, it's too right here.

"That's the book, boy.

"If you haven't seen Norstrilia, you haven't seen it. If you did see it, you wouldn't believe it.

"Charts call it Old North Australia."

Here in the heart of the world was the farm which guarded the world. This was the Hitton place.

Towers surrounded it and wires hung between the towers,

some of them drooping crazily and some gleaming with the sheen not shown by any other metal made by men from Earth. Within the towers there was open land. And within the open land there were twelve thousand hectares of concrete. Radar reached down to within millimeter smoothness of the surface of the concrete and the other radar threw patterns back and forth, down through molecular thinness. The farm went on. In its center there was a group of buildings. That was where Katherine Hitton worked on the task which her family had accepted for the defense of her world.

No germ came in, no germ went out. All the food came in by space transmitter. Within this, there lived animals. The animals depended on her alone. Were she to die suddenly, by mischance or as a result of an attack by one of the animals, the authorities of her world had complete facsimiles of herself with which to train new animal tenders under hypnosis.

This was a place where the gray wind leapt forward released from the hills, where it raced across the gray concrete, where it blew past the radar towers. The polished, faceted, captive moon always hung due overhead. The wind hit the buildings, themselves gray, with the impact of a blow, before it raced over the open concrete beyond and whistled away into the hills.

Outside the buildings, the valley had not needed much camouflage. It looked like the rest of Norstrilia. The concrete itself was tinted very slightly to give the impression of poor, starved, natural soil. This was the farm, and this the woman. Together they were the outer defense of the richest world mankind had ever built.

Katherine Hitton looked out the window and thought to herself, "Forty-two days before I go to market and it's a welcome day that I get there and hear the jig of a music."

Oh, to walk on market day
And see my people proud and gay!

She breathed deeply of the air. She loved the gray hills – though in her youth she had seen many other worlds. And then she turned back into the building to the animals and the duties which awaited her. She was the only Mother Hitton and these were her littul kittons.

She moved among them. She and her father had bred them from Earth mink, from the fiercest, smallest, craziest little minks that had ever been shipped out from Manhome. Out of these minks they had made their lives to keep away other predators who might bother the sheep, on whom the stroon grew. But these minks were born mad.

Generations of them had been bred psychotic to the bone. They lived only to die and they died so that they could stay alive. These were the kittons of Norstrilia. Animals in whom fear, rage, hunger and sex were utterly intermixed; who could eat themselves or each other; who could eat their young, or people, or anything organic; animals who screamed with murder-lust when they felt love; animals born to loathe themselves with a fierce and livid hate and who survived only because their waking moments were spent on couches, strapped tight, claw by claw, so that they could not hurt each other or themselves. Mother Hitton let them waken only a few moments in each lifetime. They bred and killed. She wakened them only two at a time.

All that afternoon she moved from cage to cage. The sleeping animals slept well. The nourishment ran into their blood streams; they lived sometimes for years without awaking. She bred them when the males were only partly awakened and the females aroused only enough to accept her veterinary treatments. She herself had to pluck the young away from their mothers as the sleeping mothers begot them. Then she nourished the young through a few happy weeks of kittonhood, until their adult natures began to take, their eyes ran red with madness and heat and their emotions sounded in the sharp, hideous, little cries they uttered through the building; and the twisting of their neat, furry faces, the rolling of their crazy, bright eyes and the tightening of their sharp, sharp claws.

She woke none of them this time. Instead, she tightened them in their straps. She removed the nutrients. She gave them delayed stimulus medicine which would, when they were awakened, bring them suddenly full waking with no lulled stupor first.

Finally, she gave herself a heavy sedative, leaned back in a chair and waited for the call which would come.

When the shock came and the call came through, she would have to do what she had done thousands of times before.

She would ring an intolerable noise through the whole laboratory.

Hundreds of the mutated minks would awaken. In awakening, they would plunge into life with hunger, with hate, with rage and with sex; plunge against their straps; strive to kill each other, their young, themselves, her. They would fight everything and everywhere, and do everything they could to keep going.

She knew this.

In the middle of the room there was a tuner. The tuner was a direct, empathic relay, capable of picking up the simpler range of telepathic communications. Into this tuner went the concentrated emotions of Mother Hitton's littul kittons.

The rage, the hate, the hunger, the sex were all carried far beyond the limits of the tolerable, and then all were thereupon amplified. And then the waveband on which this telepathic control went out was amplified, right there beyond the studio, on the high towers that swept the mountain ridge, up and beyond the valley in which the laboratory lay. And Mother Hitton's moon, spinning geometrically, bounced the relay into a hollow englobement.

From the faceted moon, it went to the satellites – sixteen of them, apparently part of the weather control system. These blanketed not only space, but nearby subspace. The Norstrilians had thought of everything.

The short shocks of an alert came from Mother Hitton's transmitter bank.

A call came. Her thumb went numb.

The noise shrieked.

The mink wakened.

Immediately, the room was full of chattering, scraping, hissing, growling and howling.

Under the sound of animal voices, there was the other sound: a scratchy, snapping sound like hail falling on a frozen lake. It was the individual claws of hundreds of mink trying to tear their way through metal panels.

Mother Hitton heard a gurgle. One of the minks had succeeded in tearing its paw loose and had obviously started to work on its own throat. She recognized the tearing of fur, the ripping of veins.

She listened for the cessation of that individual voice, but she couldn't be sure. The others were making too much noise. One mink less.

Where she sat, she was partly shielded from the telepathic relay, but not altogether. She herself, old as she was, felt queer wild dreams go through her. She thrilled with hate as she thought of beings suffering out beyond her – suffering terribly, since they were not masked by the built-in defenses of the Norstrilian communications system.

She felt the wild throb of long-forgotten lust.

She hungered for things she had not known she remembered. She went through the spasms of fear that the hundreds of animals expressed.

Underneath this, her sane mind kept asking, "How much longer can I take it? How much longer must I take it? Lord God, be good to your people here on this world! Be good to poor old me."

The green light went on.

She pressed a button on the other side of her chair. The gas hissed in. As she passed into unconsciousness, she knew that her kittons passed into instant unconsciousness too.

She would waken before they did and then her duties would begin: checking the living ones, taking out the one that had clawed out its own throat, taking out those who had died of heart attacks, rearranging them, dressing their wounds, treating them alive and asleep – asleep and happy – breeding, living in their sleep – until the next call should come to waken them for the defense of the treasures which blessed and cursed her native world.

6

Everything had gone exactly right. Lavender had found an illegal planoform ship. This was no inconsequential accomplishment, since planoform ships were very strictly licensed and obtaining an illegal one was a chore on which a planet full of crooks could easily have worked a lifetime.

Lavender had been lavished with money – Benjacomin's money.

The honest wealth of the thieves' planet had gone in and had paid the falsifications and great debts, imaginary transactions that were fed to the computers for ships and cargoes and passengers that would be almost untraceably commingled in the commerce of ten thousand worlds.

"Let him pay for it," said Lavender, to one of his confederates, an apparent criminal who was also a Norstilian agent. "This is paying good money for bad. You better spend a lot of it."

Just before Benjacomin took off Lavender sent on an additional message.

He sent it directly through the Go-Captain, who usually did not carry messages. The Go-Captain was a relay commander of the Norstrilian fleet, but he had been carefully ordered not to look like it.

The message concerned the planoform license – another twenty-odd tablets of stroon which could mortgage Viola Siderea for hundreds upon hundreds of years. The Captain said: "I don't have to send that through. The answer is yes."

Benjacomin came into the control room. This was contrary to regulations, but he had hired the ship to violate regulations.

The Captain looked at him sharply. "You're a passenger, get out."

Benjacomin said: "You have my little yacht on board. I am the only man here outside of your people."

"Get out. There's a fine if you're caught here."

"It does not matter," Benjacomin said. "I'll pay it."

"You will, will you?" said the Captain. "You would not be paying twenty tablets of stroon. That's ridiculous. Nobody could get that much stroon."

Benjacomin laughed, thinking of the thousands of tablets he would soon have. All he had to do was to leave the planoform ship behind, strike once, go past the kittons and come back.

His power and his wealth came from the fact that he knew he could now reach it. The mortgage of twenty tablets of stroon against this planet was a low price to pay if it would pay off at thousands to one. The Captain replied: "It's not worth it, it just is not worth risking twenty tablets for your being here. But I can tell you how to get inside the Norstrilian communications net if that is worth twenty-seven tablets."

Benjacomin went tense.

For a moment he thought he might die. All this work, all this training – the dead boy on the beach, the gamble with the credit, and now this unsuspected antagonist!

He decided to face it out. "What do you know?" said Benjacomin.

"Nothing," said the Captain.

"You said 'Norstrilia.'"

"That I did," said the Captain.

"If you said Norstrilia, you must have guessed it. Who told you?"

"Where else would a man go if you look for infinite riches? If you get away with it. Twenty tablets is nothing to a man like you."

"It's two hundred years' worth of work from three hundred thousand people," said Benjacomin grimly.

"When you get away with it, you will have more than twenty tablets, and so will your people."

And Benjacomin thought of the thousands and thousands of tablets. "Yes, that I know."

"If you don't get away with it, you've got the card."

"That's right. All right. Get me inside the net. I'll pay the twenty-seven tablets."

"Give me the card."

Benjacomin refused. He was a trained thief, and he was alert to thievery. Then he thought again. This was the crisis of his life. He had to gamble a little on somebody.

He had to wager the card. "I'll mark it and then I'll give it back to you." Such was his excitement that Benjacomin did not notice that the card went into a duplicator, that the transaction was recorded, that the message went back to Olympic Center, that the loss and the mortgage against the planet of Viola Siderea should be credited to certain commercial agencies in Earth for three hundred years to come.

Benjacomin got the card back. He felt like an honest thief.

If he did die, the card would be lost and his people would not have to pay. If he won, he could pay that little bit out of his own pocket.

Benjacomin sat down. The Go-Captain signalled to his pinlighters. The ship lurched.

For half a subjective hour they moved, the Captain wearing a helmet of space upon his head, sensing and grasping and guessing his way, stepping to stepping stone, right back to his home. He had to fumble the passage, or else Benjacomin might guess that he was in the hands of double agents.

But the Captain was well trained. Just as well trained as Benjacomin.

Agents and thieves, they rode together.

They planoformed inside the communications net. Benjacomin shook hands with them. "You are allowed to materialize as soon as I call."

"Good luck, sir," said the Captain.

"Good luck to me," said Benjacomin.

He climbed into his space yacht. For less than a second in real space, the gray expanse of Norstrilia loomed up. The ship which looked like a simple warehouse disappeared into planoform, and the yacht was on its own.

The yacht dropped.

As it dropped, Benjacomin had a hideous moment of confusion and terror.

He never knew the woman down below but she sensed him plainly as he received the wrath of the much-amplified kittons. His conscious mind quivered under the blow. With a prolongation of subjective experience which made one or two seconds seem like months of hurt drunken bewilderment, Benjacomin Bozart swept beneath the tide of his own personality. The moon relay threw minkish minds against him. The synapses of his brain re-formed to conjure up might-have-beens, terrible things that never happened to any man. Then his knowing mind whited out in an overload of stress.

His subcortical personality lived on a little longer.

His body fought for several minutes. Mad with lust and

hunger, the body arched in the pilot's seat, the mouth bit deep into his own arm. Driven by lust, the left hand tore at his face, ripping out his left eyeball. He screeched with animal lust as he tried to devour himself . . . not entirely without success.

The overwhelming telepathic message of Mother Hitton's Littul Kittons ground into his brain.

The mutated minks were fully awake.

The relay satellites had poisoned all the space around him with the craziness to which the minks were bred.

Bozart's body did not live long. After a few minutes, the arteries were open, the head slumped forward and the yacht was dropping helplessly toward the warehouses which it had meant to raid. Norstrilian police picked it up.

The police themselves were ill. All of them were ill. All of them were white-faced. Some of them had vomited. They had gone through the edge of the mink defense. They had passed through the telepathic band at its thinnest and weakest point. This was enough to hurt them badly.

They did not want to know.

They wanted to forget.

One of the younger policemen looked at the body and said, "What on earth could do that to a man?"

"He picked the wrong job," said the police captain.

The young policeman said: "What's the wrong job?"

"The wrong job is trying to rob us, boy. We are defended, and we don't want to know how."

The young policeman, humiliated and on the verge of anger, looked almost as if he would defy his superior, while keeping his eyes away from the body of Benjacomin Bozart.

The older man said: "It's all right. He did not take long to die and this is the man who killed the boy Johnny, not very long ago."

"Oh, him? So soon?"

"We brought him." The old police officer nodded. "We let him find his death. That's how we live. Tough, isn't it?"

The ventilators whispered softly, gently. The animals slept again. A jet of air poured down on Mother Hitton. The telepathic relay was still on. She could feel herself, the sheds, the faceted moon, the little satellites. Of the robber there was no sign.

She stumbled to her feet. Her raiment was moist with perspiration. She needed a shower and fresh clothes. . . .

Back at Manhome, the Commercial Credit Circuit called shrilly for human attention. A junior subchief of the Instrumentality walked over to the machine and held out his hand.

The machine dropped a card neatly into his fingers.

He looked at the card.

"Debit Viola Siderea – credit Earth Contingency – subcredit Norstrilian account – four hundred million man megayears."

Though all alone, he whistled to himself in the empty room. "We'll all be dead, stroon or no stroon, before they finish paying that!" He went off to tell his friends the odd news.

The machine, not getting its card back, made another one.

JACK VANCE
The Moon Moth

I was talking to an academician a few years back, a fellow teaching an SF course on the college level, and found, to my astonishment, that he'd never heard of Jack Vance. This dismayed me, because Vance has not only produced some of the best work of the past forty years, he is an evolutionary figure of immense importance both to fantasy *and* science fiction.

Born in San Francisco in 1920, Vance served throughout World War II in the US Merchant Navy. Most of the individual stories that would later be melded into his first novel, *The Dying Earth*, were written while Vance was at sea – he was unable to sell them, a problem he would also have with the book itself, the market for fantasy being almost non-existent at the time. *The Dying Earth* was eventually published in an obscure edition in 1950 by a small semi-professional press, went out of print almost immediately, and remained out of print for more than a decade thereafter. Nevertheless, it became an underground cult classic, and its effect on future generations of writers is incalculable: for one example, out of many, *The Dying Earth* is one of the most recognizable influences on Gene Wolfe's *The Book of the New Sun* (Wolfe has said, for instance, that *The Book of Gold* which is mentioned by Severian is supposed to be *The Dying Earth*). Vance returned to this milieu in 1965, with a series of stories that would be melded into *The Eyes of the Overworld*, and, in the early '80s, returned yet again with *Cugel's Saga* and *Rhialto the Marvelous* – taken together, *The Dying Earth* stories represent one of the most impressive achievements in science-fantasy.

In science fiction itself, Vance would do some of his best early work for magazines such as *Thrilling Wonder Stories* and *Startling Stories* and the short-lived *Worlds Beyond* in the mid-'50s – "The Five Gold Bands," "Abercrombie Station," *The Houses of Iszm*, "The Kokod Warriors," "The New Prime" and the magazine version of "Big Planet," among others. (Vance also was appearing in *Astounding* from time to time, but most of his work for *Astounding* would be rather bland by Vance's standards, only one story there, the later novella "The Miracle Workers," being full-throated Vancian Future Baroque – a somewhat atypical style for *Astounding*, and I can't help but wonder if Campbell took the story mostly because it deals fairly centrally with psionics, a pet Campbellian topic of the time.)

By the late '50s and early '60s, Vance was doing some of his best work, and some of the best work of the period, most of it by this time for *Galaxy* and *F&SF* – the marvelous "The Dragon Masters," "The Men Return," the underrated *The Languages of Pao* (one of only a handful of books even today to deal with semantics as a science; Delany's *Babel 17* and Ian Watson's *The Embedding* are two later examples), the wonderful *The Star King* and *The Killing Machine* (two of the best hybrids of SF and the mystery/espionage novel ever written), "Green Magic," *The Blue World*, "The Last Castle".

And the story that follows, "The Moon Moth," a marvelous evocation of a complex and richly detailed alien milieu as well as a slyly satiric examination of how manners and morals and values change with fluid ease from society to society (a typical Vance motif), full of vivid color and moments of haunting strangeness, all laced with Vance's typical dour irony and deadpan humor.

Vance is reminiscent of R. A. Lafferty in that both men break all the supposed rules of writing, and get away with it. Both eschew naturalism, each using a mannered and highly idiosyncratic prose style (baroque and stiffly elegant in Vance's case, energetically informal and folksy in Laffety's), and both have their characters spout theatrical, deliberately nonnaturalistic, hieratic dialogue of a sort that never actually came out of anyone's mouth – if you were to film their work, no mumbling Method actors would need to apply; only someone with the flamboyant grandiloquence of a John Barrymore would do. Vance also – and here comes an even stranger comparison – reminds me of Philip K. Dick: each author relies heavily on a personal formula of his own, using the same basic frameworks, plots, and types of characters and situations again and again (what is important in each is not creating new motifs, but refining and developing variations on their obsessive themes); each man's style is limited in technical range, but, within that range, they are the best in the business at what they do well; both emphasize how manners and *mores* change from society to society; and, although neither is thought of as a humorist, the work of both is suffused with a dry, understated wit; Vance's humor is somewhat drier than Dick's, Dick's more surreal than Vance's, but both tend toward black humor, sly satire, a bitterly sardonic view of life and human nature, and to grotesque and macabrely ironic set-pieces. Both men have trouble ending novels, both frequently just letting the story peter away, as though they had gradually lost interest in what they were writing. And, with each, their impact on the field rests more on the aggregate effect of their work than on any particular story or novel – or, to adapt a remark of Thomas Disch's concerning Dick which is equally valid for Vance, their novels are more impressive collectively than each by each.

And, much as SF authors writing today about phenomenology or the nature of reality write inevitably in the shadow of Philip K. Dick, so writers describing distant worlds and alien societies with strange alien customs write in the shadow of Vance. No one in the history of the field has brought more intelligence, imagination, or inexhaustible fertility of invention to that theme than Vance; even ostensible potboilers such as his *Planet of Adventure* series are full of vivid and richly portrayed alien societies, and bizarre and often profoundly disturbing insights into the ways in which human psychology might be altered by immersion in alien values and cultural systems. No one is better than Vance is at delivering that quintessential "sense of wonder" that is at the heart of science fiction, and reading him has left me a legacy of evocative images that will stay with me forever.

Vance has won two Hugo Awards, a Nebula Award, two World Fantasy Awards (one the prestigious Life Achievement Award), and the Edgar Award for best mystery novel. His other books include *Emphyrio* (one of the best novels of the late '60s, up until the disappointing ending), *The Anome*, *The Palace of Love*, *The Face*, *The Book of Dreams*, *City of the Chasch*, *The Dirdir*, *The Pnume*, *The Brave Free Men*, *Lyonesse*, *The Green Pearl*, *Trullion: Alastor 2262*, *Wyst: Alastor 1716*, and *Araminta Station*, among many others. His short fiction has been collected in *Eight Fantasms and Magics*, *The Best of Jack Vance*, *Green Magic*, *Lost Moons*, *The Complete Magnus Ridolph*, *The World Between and Other Stories*, *The Dark Side of the Moon* and *The Narrow Land*.

The houseboat had been built to the most exacting standards of Sirenese craftmanship, which is to say, as close to the absolute as human eye could detect. The planking of waxy dark wood showed no joints, the fastenings were platinum rivets countersunk and polished flat. In style, the boat was massive, broad beamed, steady as the shore itself, without ponderosity or slackness of line. The bow bulged like a swan's breast, the stem rising high, then crooking forward to support an iron lantern. The doors were carved from slabs of a mottled black-green wood; the windows were many sectioned, paned with squares of mica, stained rose, blue, pale green and violet. The bow was given to service facilities and quarters for the slaves; amidships were a pair of sleeping cabins, a dining saloon and a parlor saloon, opening upon an observation deck at the stern.

Such was Edwer Thissell's houseboat, but ownership brought him neither pleasure nor pride. The houseboat had become shabby. The carpeting had lost its pile; the carved screens were chipped; the iron lantern at the bow sagged with rust. Seventy years ago the first owner, on accepting the boat, had honored the builder and had been likewise honored; the transaction (for the process represented a great deal more than simple giving and taking) had augmented the prestige of both. That time was far gone; the houseboat now commanded no prestige whatever. Edwer Thissell, resident on Sirene only three months, recognized the lack but could do nothing about it: this particular houseboat was the best he could get.

He sat on the rear deck practicing the *ganga*, a zitherlike instrument not much larger than his hand. A hundred yards inshore, surf defined a strip of white beach; beyond rose jungle, with the silhouette of craggy black hills against the sky. Mireille shone hazy and white overhead, as if through a tangle of spider web; the face of the ocean pooled and puddled with mother-of-pearl luster. The scene had become as familiar, though not as boring, as the *ganga*, at which he had worked two hours, twanging out the Sirenese scales, forming chords, traversing simple progressions. Now he put down the *ganga* for the *zachinko*, this a small sound-box studded with keys, played with the right hand. Pressure on the keys forced air through reeds in the keys themselves, producing a concertinalike tone. Thissel ran off a dozen quick scales, making very few mistakes. Of the six instruments he had set himself to learn, the *zachinko* had proved the least refractory (with the exception, of course, of the *hymerkin*, that clacking, slapping, clattering device of wood and stone used exclusively with the slaves).

Thissell practiced another ten minutes, then put aside the *zachinko*. He flexed his arms, wrung his aching fingers. Every waking moment since his arrival had been given to the instruments: the *hymerkin*, the *ganga*, the *zachinko*, the *kiv*, the *strapan*, the *gomapard*. He had practiced scales in nineteen keys and four modes, chords without number, intervals never imagined on the Home Planets. Trills, arpeggios, slurs, click-stops and nasalization; damping and augmentation of overtones; vibratos and wolf-tones; concavities and convexities. He practiced with a dogged, deadly diligence, in which his original concept of music as a source of pleasure had long become lost. Looking over the instruments Thissell resisted an urge to fling all six into the Titanic.

He rose to his feet, went forward through the parlor saloon, the dining saloon, along a corridor past the galley and came out on the foredeck. He bent over the rail, peered down into the underwater pens where Toby and Rex, the slaves, were harnessing the dray-fish for the weekly trip to Fan, eight miles north. The youngest fish, either playful or captious, ducked and plunged. Its streaming black muzzle broke water, and Thissell, looking into its face, felt a peculiar qualm: the fish wore no mask!

Thissell laughed uneasily, fingering his own mask, the Moon Moth. No question about it, he was becoming acclimated to Sirene! A significant stage had been reached when the naked face of a fish caused him shock!

The fish were finally harnessed; Toby and Rex climbed aboard, red bodies glistening, black cloth masks clinging to their faces. Ignoring Thissell they stowed the pen, hoisted anchor. The dray-fish strained, the harness tautened, the houseboat moved north.

Returning to the afterdeck, Thissell took up the *strapan* – this a circular sound-box eight inches in diameter. Forty-six wires radiated from a central hub to the circumference where they connected to either a bell or a tinkle-bar. When plucked, the bells rang, the bars chimed; when strummed, the instrument gave off a twanging, jingling sound. When played with competence, the pleasantly acid dissonances produced an expressive effect; in an unskilled hand, the results were less felicitous, and might even approach random noise. The *strapan* was Thissell's weakest instrument and he practiced with concentration during the entire trip north.

In due course the houseboat approached the floating city. The dray-fish were curbed, the houseboat warped to a mooring. Along the dock a line of idlers weighed and gauged every aspect of the houseboat, the slaves and Thissell himself, according to Sirenese habit. Thissell, not yet accustomed to such penetrating inspection, found the scrutiny unsettling, all the more so for the immobility of the masks. Self-consciously adjusting his own Moon Moth, he climbed the ladder to the dock.

A slave rose from where he had been squatting, touched knuckles to the black cloth at his forehead, and sang on a three-tone phrase of interrogation: "The Moon Moth before me possibly expresses the identity of Ser Edwer Thissell?"

Thissell tapped the *hymerkin* which hung at his belt and sang: "I am Ser Thissell."

"I have been honored by a trust," sang the slave. "Three days from dawn to dusk I have waited on the dock; three nights from dusk to dawn I have crouched on a raft below this same dock listening to the feet of the Night-men. At last I behold the mask of Ser Thissell."

Thissell evoked an impatient clatter from the *hymerkin*. "What is the nature of this trust?"

"I carry a message, Ser Thissell. It is intended for you."

Thissell held out his left hand, playing the *hymerkin* with his right. "Give me the message."

"Instantly, Ser Thissell."

The message bore a heavy superscription:

EMERGENCY COMMUNICATION! RUSH!

Thissell ripped open the envelope. The message was signed by Castel Cromartin, Chief Executive of the Inter-world Policies Board, and after the formal salutation read:

ABSOLUTELY URGENT the following orders be executed! Aboard *Carina Cruzeiro*, destination Fan, date of arrival January 10 UT, is notorious assassin, Haxo Angmark. Meet landing with adequate authority, effect detention and incarceration of this man. These instructions must be successfully implemented. Failure is unacceptable.

ATTENTION! Haxo Angmark is superlatively dangerous. Kill him without hesitation at any show of resistance.

Thissell considered the message with dismay. In coming to Fan as Consular Representative he had expected nothing like this; he felt neither inclination nor competence in the matter of dealing with dangerous assassins. Thoughtfully he rubbed the fuzzy gray cheek of his mask. The situation was not completely dark; Esteban Rolver, Director of the Spaceport, would doubtless cooperate, and perhaps furnish a platoon of slaves.

More hopefully, Thissell reread the message. January 10, Universal Time. He consulted a conversion calendar. Today, 40th in the Season of Bitter Nectar – Thissell ran his finger down the column, stopped. January 10. Today.

A distant rumble caught his attention. Dropping from the mist came a dull shape: the lighter returning from contact with the *Carina Cruzeiro*.

Thissell once more reread the note, raised his head, studied the descending lighter. Aboard would be Haxo Angmark. In five minutes he would emerge upon the soil of Sirene. Landing formalities would detain him possibly twenty minutes. The landing field lay a mile and a half distant, joined to Fan by a winding path through the hills.

Thissell turned to the slave. "When did this message arrive?"

The slave leaned forward uncomprehendingly. Thissell reiterated his question, singing to the clack of the *hymerkin*: "This message: you have enjoyed the honor of its custody how long?"

The slave sang: "Long days have I waited on the wharf, retreating only to the raft at the onset of dusk. Now my vigil is rewarded; I behold Ser Thissell."

Thissell turned away, walked furiously up the dock. Ineffective, inefficient Sirenese! Why had they not delivered the message to his houseboat? Twenty-five minutes – twenty-two now . . .

At the esplanade Thissell stopped, looked right, then left, hoping for a miracle: some sort of air-transport to wisk him to the spaceport, where, with Rolver's aid, Haxo Angmark might still be detained. Or better yet, a second message canceling the first. Something, anything. . . . But air-cars were not to be found on Sirene, and no second message appeared.

Across the esplanade rose a meager row of permanent structures, built of stone and iron and so proof against the efforts of the Night-men. A hostler occupied one of these structures, and as Thissell watched a man in a splendid pearl and silver mask emerged riding one of the lizardlike mounts of Sirene.

Thissell sprang forward. There was still time; with luck he might yet intercept Haxo Angmark. He hurried across the esplanade.

Before the line of stalls stood the hostler, inspecting his stock with solicitude, occasionally burnishing a scale or whisking away an insect. There were five of the beasts in prime condition, each as tall as a man's shoulder, with massive legs, thick bodies, heavy wedge-shaped heads. From their fore-fangs, which had been artificially lengthened and curved into near circles, gold rings depended; the scales of each had been stained in diaper-pattern; purple and green, orange and black, red and blue, brown and pink, yellow and silver.

Thissell came to a breathless halt in front of the hostler. He reached for his *kiv*[1], then hesitated. Could this be considered a casual personal encounter? The *zachinko* perhaps? But the statement of his needs hardly seemed to demand the formal approach. Better the *kiv* after all. He struck a chord, but by error found himself stroking the *ganga*. Beneath his mask Thissell grinned apologetically; his relationship with this hostler was by no means on an intimate basis. He hoped that the hostler was of sanguine disposition, and in any event the urgency of the occasion allowed no time to select an exactly appropriate instrument. He struck a second chord, and, playing as well as agitation, breathlessness and lack of skill allowed, sang out a request: "Ser

[1] *Kiv*: five banks of resilient metal strips, fourteen to the bank, played by touching, twisting, twanging.

Hostler, I have immediate need of a swift mount. Allow me to select from your herd."

The hostler wore a mask of considerable complexity which Thissell could not identify: a construction of varnished brown cloth, pleated gray leather and, high on the forehead, two large green and scarlet globes, minutely segmented like insect-eyes. He inspected Thissell a long moment, then, rather ostentatiously selecting his *stimic*[1], executed a brilliant progression of trills and rounds, of an import Thissell failed to grasp. The hostler sang, "Ser Moon Moth, I fear that my steeds are unsuitable to a person of your distinction."

Thissell earnestly twanged at the *ganga*. "By no means; they all seem adequate. I am in great haste and will gladly accept any of the group."

The hostler played a brittle cascading crescendo. "Ser Moon Moth," he sang, "the steeds are ill and dirty. I am flattered that you consider them adequate to your use. I cannot accept the merit you offer me. And" – here, switching instruments, he struck a cool tinkle from his *krodatch*[2] – "somehow I fail to recognize the boon companion and co-craftsman who accosts me so familiarly with his *ganga*."

The implication was clear. Thissell would receive no mount. He turned, set off at a run for the landing field. Behind him sounded a clatter of the hostler's *hymerkin* – whether directed toward the hostler's slaves or toward himself Thissell did not pause to learn.

The previous Consular Representative of the Home Planets on Sirene had been killed at Zundar. Masked as a Tavern Bravo he had accosted a girl beribboned for the Equinoctial Attitudes, a solecism for which he had been instantly beheaded by a Red Demiurge, a Sun Sprite and a Magic Hornet. Edwer Thissell, recently graduated from the Host-

---

[1] *Stimic*: three flutelike tubes equipped with plungers. Thumb and fore-finger squeeze a bag to force air across the mouthpieces; the second, third and fourth little fingers manipulate the slide. The *stimic* is an instrument well adapted to the sentiments of cool withdrawal, or even disapproval.

[2] *Krodatch*: a small square sound-box strung with resined gut. The musician scratches the strings with his fingernail, or strokes them with his fingertips, to produce a variety of quietly formal sounds. The *krodatch* is also used as an instrument of insult.

Institute, had been named his successor, and allowed three days to prepare himself. Normally of a contemplative, even cautious disposition, Thissell had regarded the appointment as a challenge. He learned the Sirenese language by sub-cerebral techniques, and found it uncomplicated. Then, in the *Journal of Universal Anthropology*, he read:

> The population of the Titanic littoral is highly individualistic, possibly in response to a bountiful environment which puts no premium upon group activity. The language, reflecting this trait, expresses the individual's mood, his emotional attitude toward a given situation. Factual information is regarded as a secondary concomitant. Moreover, the language is sung, characteristically to the accompaniment of a small instrument. As a result, there is great difficulty in ascertaining fact from a native of Fan, or the forbidden city Zundar. One will be regaled with elegant arias and demonstrations of astonishing virtuosity upon one or another of the numerous musical instruments. The visitor to this fascinating world, unless he cares to be treated with the most consummate contempt, must therefore learn to express himself after the approved local fashion.

Thissell made a note in his memorandum book: *Procure small musical instrument, together with directions as to use.* He read on.

> There is everywhere and at all times a plenitude, not to say superfluity, of food, and the climate is benign. With a fund of racial energy and a great deal of leisure time, the population occupies itself with intricacy. Intricacy in all things: intricate craftmanship, such as the carved panels which adorn the houseboats; intricate symbolism, as exemplified in the masks worn by everyone; the intricate half-musical language which admirably expresses subtle moods and emotions; and above all the fantastic intricacy of interpersonal relationships. Prestige, face, *mana*, repute, glory: the Sirenese word is *strakh*. Every man has his characteristic *strakh*, which determines whether, when he needs a houseboat, he will be urged to avail himself of a floating palace, rich with gems, alabaster lanterns, peacock faience and carved wood, or grudgingly permitted an abandoned shack on a raft. There is no medium of exchange on Sirene; the single and sole currency is *strakh* . . .

Thissell rubbed his chin and read further.

Masks are worn at all times, in accordance with the philosophy that a man should not be compelled to use a similitude foisted upon him by factors beyond his control; that he should be at liberty to choose that semblance most consonant with his *strakh*. In the civilized areas of Sirene – which is to say the Titanic littoral – a man literally never shows his face; it is his basic secret.

Gambling, by this token, is unknown on Sirene; it would be catastrophic to Sirenese self-respect to gain advantage by means other than the exercise of *strakh*. The word "luck" has no counterpart in the Sirenese language.

Thissell made another note: *Get mask. Museum? Drama guild?*

He finished the article, hastened forth to complete his preparations, and the next day embarked aboard the *Robert Astroguard* for the first leg of the passage to Sirene.

The lighter settled upon the Sirenese spaceport, a topaz disk isolated among the black, green and purple hills. The lighter grounded and Edwer Thissell stepped forth. He was met by Esteban Rolver, the local agent for Spaceways. Rolver threw up his hands, stepped back. "Your mask," he cried huskily. "Where is your mask?"

Thissell held it up rather self-consciously. "I wasn't sure –"

"Put it on," said Rolver, turning away. He himself wore a fabrication of dull green scales, blue-lacquered wood. Black quills protruded at the cheeks, and under his chin hung a black-and-white-checked pompom, the total effect creating a sense of sardonic supple personality.

Thissell adjusted the mask to his face, undecided whether to make a joke about the situation or to maintain a reserve suitable to the dignity of his post.

"Are you masked?" Rolver inquired over his shoulder.

Thissell replied in the affirmative and Rolver turned. The mask hid the expression on his face, but his hand unconsciously flicked a set of keys strapped to his thigh. The instrument sounded a trill of shock and polite consternation. "You can't wear that mask!" sang Rolver. "In fact – how, where, did you get it?"

"It's copied from a mask owned by the Polypolis museum," Thissell declared stiffly. "I'm sure it's authentic."

Rolver nodded, his own mask seeming more sardonic than ever. "It's authentic enough. It's a variant of the type known as the Sea Dragon Conqueror, and is worn on ceremonial occasions by persons of enormous prestige: princes, heroes, master craftsmen, great musicians."

"I wasn't aware –"

Rolver made a gesture of languid understanding. "It's something you'll learn in due course. Notice my mask. Today I'm wearing a Tarn Bird. Persons of minimal prestige – such as you, I, any other out-worlder – wear this sort of thing."

"Odd," said Thissell, as they started across the field toward a low concrete blockhouse. "I assumed that a person wore whatever he liked."

"Certainly," said Rolver. "Wear any mask you like – if you can make it stick. This Tarn Bird for instance. I wear it to indicate that I presume nothing. I make no claims to wisdom, ferocity, versatility, musicianship, truculence, or any of a dozen other Sirenese virtues."

"For the sake of argument," said Thissell, "What would happen if I walked through the streets of Zundar in this mask?"

Rolver laughed, a muffled sound behind his mask. "If you walked along the docks of Zundar – there are no streets – in any mask, you'd be killed within the hour. That's what happened to Benko, your predecessor. He didn't know how to act. None of us out-worlders know how to act. In Fan we're tolerated – so long as we keep our place. But you couldn't even walk around Fan in that regalia you're sporting now. Somebody wearing a Fire Snake or a Thunder Goblin – masks, you understand – would step up to you. He'd play his *krodatch*, and if you failed to challenge his audacity with a passage on the *skaranyi*[1], a devilish instrument, he'd play his *hymerkin* – the instrument we use

[1] *Skaranyi*: a miniature bagpipe, the sac squeezed between thumb and palm, the four fingers controlling the stops along four tubes.

with the slaves. That's the ultimate expression of contempt. Or he might ring his dueling-gong and attack you then and there."

"I had no idea that people here were quite so irascible," said Thissell in a subdued voice.

Rolver shrugged and swung open the massive steel door into his office. "Certain acts may not be committed on the Concourse at Polypolis without incurring criticism."

"Yes, that's quite true," said Thissell. He looked around the office. "Why the security? The concrete, the steel?"

"Protection against the savages," said Rolver. "They come down from the mountains at night, steal what's available, kill anyone they find ashore." He went to a closet, brought forth a mask. "Here. Use this Moon Moth; it won't get you in trouble."

Thissell unenthusiastically inspected the mask. It was constructed of mouse-colored fur; there was a tuft of hair at each side of the mouth-hole, a pair of featherlike antennae at the forehead. White lace flaps dangled beside the temples and under the eyes hung a series of red folds, creating an effect at once lugubrious and comic.

Thissell asked, "Does this mask signify any degree of prestige?"

"Not a great deal."

"After all, I'm Consular Representative," said Thissell. "I represent the Home Planets, a hundred billion people –"

"If the Home Planets want their representative to wear a Sea Dragon Conqueror mask, they'd better send out a Sea Dragon Conqueror type of man."

"I see," said Thissell in a subdued voice. "Well, if I must . . ."

Rolver politely averted his gaze while Thissell doffed the Sea Dragon Conqueror and slipped the more modest Moon Moth over his head. "I suppose I can find something just a bit more suitable in one of the shops," Thissell said. "I'm told a person simply goes in and takes what he needs, correct?"

Rolver surveyed Thissell critically. "That mask – temporarily, at least – is perfectly suitable. And it's rather important not to take anything from the shops until you know the *strakh* value of the article you want. The owner loses prestige if a person of low *strakh* makes free with his best work."

Thissell shook his head in exasperation. "Nothing of this was explained to me! I knew of the masks, of course, and the painstaking integrity of the craftsmen, but this insistence on prestige – *strakh*, whatever the word is . . ."

"No matter," said Rolver. "After a year or two you'll begin to learn your way around. I suppose you speak the language?"

"Oh, indeed. Certainly."

"And what instruments do you play?"

"Well – I was given to understand that any small instrument was adequate, or that I could merely sing."

"Very inaccurate. Only slaves sing without accompaniment. I suggest that you learn the following instruments as quickly as possible: The *hymerkin* for your slaves. The *ganga* for conversation between intimates or one a trifle lower than yourself in *strakh*. The *kiv* for casual polite intercourse. The *zachinko* for more formal dealings. The *strapan* or the *krodatch* for your social inferiors – in your case, should you wish to insult someone. The *gomapard*[1] or the double-*kamanthil*[2] for ceremonials." He considered a moment. "The *crebarin*, the water-lute and the *slobo* are highly useful also – but perhaps you'd better learn the other instruments first. They should provide at least a rudimentary means of communication."

"Aren't you exaggerating?" suggested Thissell. "Or joking?"

Rolver laughed his saturnine laugh. "Not at all. First of all, you'll need a houseboat. And then you'll want slaves."

Rolver took Thissell from the landing field to the docks of Fan, a walk of an hour and a half along a pleasant path under

---

[1] *Gomapard*: one of the few electric instruments used on Sirene. An oscillator produces an oboelike tone which is modulated, choked, vibrated, raised, and lowered in pitch by four keys.

[2] Double-*kamanthil*: an instrument similar to the *ganga*, except the tones are produced by twisting and inclining a disk of resined leather against one or more of the forty-six strings.

enormous trees loaded with fruit, cereal pods, sacs of sugary sap.

"At the moment," said Rolver, "there are only four out-worlders in Fan, counting yourself. I'll take you to Welibus, our Commercial Factor. I think he's got an old houseboat he might let you use."

Cornely Welibus had resided fifteen years in Fan, acquiring sufficient *strakh* to wear his South Wind mask with authority. This consisted of a blue disk inlaid with cabochons of lapis lazuli, surrounded by an aureole of shimmering snakeskin. Heavier and more cordial than Rolver, he not only provided Thissell with a houseboat, but also a score of various musical instruments and a pair of slaves.

Embarrassed by the largesse, Thissell stammered something about payment, but Welibus cut him off with an expansive gesture. "My dear fellow, this is Sirene. Such trifles cost nothing."

"But a houseboat —"

Welibus played a courtly little flourish on his *kiv*. "I'll be frank, Ser Thissell. The boat is old and a trifle shabby. I can't afford to use it; my status would suffer." A graceful melody accompanied his words. "Status as yet need not concern you. You require merely shelter, comfort, and safety from the Night-men."

" 'Night-men'?"

"The cannibals who roam the shore after dark."

"Oh, yes. Ser Rolver mentioned them."

"Horrible things. We won't discuss them." A shuddering little trill issued from his *kiv*. "Now, as to slaves." He tapped the blue disk of his mask with a thoughtful forefinger. "Rex and Toby should serve you well." He raised his voice, played a swift clatter on the *hymerkin*. "*Avan esx trobu!*"

A female slave appeared, wearing a dozen tight bands of pink cloth, and a dainty black mask sparkling with mother-of-pearl sequins.

"*Fascu etz Rex ae Toby.*"

Rex and Toby appeared, wearing loose masks of black cloth, russet jerkins. Welibus addressed them with a resonant clatter of *hymerkin*, enjoining them to the service of their new master, on pain of return to their native islands. They prostrated themselves, sang pledges of servitude to Thissell in soft husky voices. Thissell laughed nervously and essayed a sentence in the Sirenese language. "Go to the houseboat, clean it well, bring aboard food."

Toby and Rex stared blankly through the holes in their masks. Welibus repeated the orders with *hymerkin* accompaniment. The slaves bowed and departed.

Thissell surveyed the musical instruments with dismay. "I haven't the slightest idea how to go about learning these things."

Welibus turned to Rolver. "What about Kershaul? Could he be persuaded to give Ser Thissell some basic instruction?"

Rolver nodded judicially. "Kershaul might undertake the job."

Thissell asked, "Who is Kershaul?"

"The fourth of our little group of expatriates," replied Welibus; "an anthropologist. You've read *Zundar the Splendid? Rituals of Sirene? The Faceless Folk?* No? A pity. All excellent works. Kershaul is high in prestige and I believe visits Zundar from time to time. Wears a Cave Owl, sometimes a Star Wanderer, or even a Wise Arbiter."

"He's taken to an Equatorial Serpent," said Rolver. "The variant with the gilt tusks."

"Indeed!" marveled Welibus. "Well, I must say he's earned it. A fine fellow, good chap indeed." And he strummed his *zachinko* thoughtfully.

Three months passed. Under the tutelage of Mathew Kershaul, Thissell practiced the *hymerkin*, the *ganga*, the *strapan*, the *kiv*, the *gomapard* and the *zachinko*. The double-*kamanthil*, the *krodatch*, the *slobo*, the water-lute and a number of others could wait, said Kershaul, until Thissell had mastered the six basic instruments. He lent Thissell recordings of noteworthy Sirenese conversing in various moods and to various accompaniments, so that Thissell might learn the melodic conventions currently in vogue, and perfect himself in the niceties of intonation, the various rhythms, cross-rhythms, compound rhythms, implied rhythms and suppressed rhythms. Kershaul professed to find

Sirenese music a fascinating study, and Thissell admitted that it was a subject not readily exhausted. The quarter-tone tuning of the instruments admitted the use of twenty-four tonalities, which multiplied by the five modes in general use, resulted in one hundred and twenty separate scales. Kershaul, however, advised that Thissell primarily concentrate on learning each instrument in its fundamental tonality, using only two of the modes.

With no immediate business at Fan except the weekly visits to Mathew Kershaul, Thissell took his houseboat eight miles south and moored it in the lee of a rocky promontory. Here, if it had not been for the incessant practicing, Thissell lived an idyllic life. The sea was calm and crystal-clear; the beach, ringed by the gray, green and purple foliage of the forest, lay close at hand if he wanted to stretch his legs.

Toby and Rex occupied a pair of cubicles forward, Thissell had the after-cabins to himself. From time to time he toyed with the idea of a third slave, possibly a young female, to contribute an element of charm and gaiety to the ménage, but Kershaul advised against the step, fearing that the intensity of Thissell's concentration might somehow be diminished. Thissell acquiesced and devoted himself to the study of the six instruments.

The days passed quickly. Thissell never became bored with the pageantry of dawn and sunset; the white clouds and blue sea of noon; the night sky blazing with the twenty-nine stars of Cluster SI 1–715. The weekly trip to Fan broke the tedium: Toby and Rex foraged for food; Thissell visited the luxurious houseboat of Mathew Kershaul for instruction and advice. Then, three months after Thissell's arrival, came the message completely disorganizing the routine: Haxo Angmark, assassin, agent provocateur, ruthless and crafty criminal, had come to Sirene. *Effective detention and incarceration of this man!* read the orders. *Attention! Haxo Angmark superlatively dangerous. Kill without hesitation!*

Thissell was not in the best of condition. He trotted fifty yards until his breath came in gasps, then walked: through low hills crowned with white bamboo and black tree-ferns; across meadows yellow with grass-nuts; through orchards and wild vineyards. Twenty minutes passed, twenty-five minutes passed – twenty-five minutes!; with a heavy sensation in his stomach Thissell knew that he was too late. Haxo Angmark had landed, and might be traversing this very road toward Fan. But along the way Thissell met only four persons: a boy-child in a mock-fierce Alk Islander mask; two young women wearing the Red Bird and the Green Bird; a man masked as a Forest Goblin. Coming upon the man, Thissell stopped short. Could this be Angmark?

Thissell esayed a strategem. He went boldly to the man, stared into the hideous mask. "Angmark," he called in the language of the Home Planets, "you are under arrest!"

The Forest Goblin stared uncomprehendingly, then started forward along the track.

Thissell put himself in the way. He reached for his *ganga*, then recalling the hostler's reaction, instead struck a chord on the *zachinko*. "You travel the road from the spaceport," he sang. "What have you seen there?"

The Forest Goblin grasped his hand-bugle, an instrument used to deride opponents on the field of battle, to summon animals or occasionally to evince a rough and ready truculence. "Where I travel and what I see are the concern solely of myself. Stand back or I walk upon your face." He marched forward, and had not Thissell leaped aside the Forest Goblin might well have made good his threat.

Thissell stood gazing after the retreating back. Angmark? Not likely, with so sure a touch on the hand-bugle. Thissell hesitated, then turned and continued on his way.

Arriving at the spaceport, he went directly to the office. The heavy door stood ajar; as Thissell approached, a man appeared in the doorway. He wore a mask of dull green scales, mica plates, blue-lacquered wood and black quills – the Tarn Bird.

"Ser Rolver," Thissell called out anxiously, "who came down from the *Carina Cruzeiro*?"

Rolver studied Thissell a long moment. "Why do you ask?"

"Why do I ask?" demanded Thissell. "You must have seen the spacegram I received from Castel Cromartin!"

"Oh, yes," said Rolver. "Of course. Naturally."

"It was delivered only half an hour ago," said Thissell

bitterly. "I rushed out as fast as I could. Where is Angmark?"

"In Fan, I assume," said Rolver.

Thissell cursed softly. "Why didn't you hold him up, delay him in some way?"

Rolver shrugged. "I had neither authority, inclination nor the capability to stop him."

Thissell fought back his annoyance. In a voice of studied calm he said, "On the way I passed a man in rather a ghastly mask – saucer eyes, red wattles."

"A Forest Goblin," said Rolver. "Angmark brought the mask with him."

"But he played the hand-bugle," Thissell protested. "How could Angmark –"

"He's well acquainted with Sirene; he spent five years here in Fan."

Thissell grunted in annoyance. "Cromartin made no mention of this."

"It's common knowledge," said Rolver with a shrug. "He was Commercial Representative before Welibus took over."

"Were he and Welibus acquainted?"

Rolver laughed shortly. "Naturally. But don't suspect poor Welibus of anything more venal than juggling his accounts; I assure you he's no consort of assassins."

"Speaking of assassins," said Thissell, "do you have a weapon I might borrow?"

Rolver inspected him in wonder. "You came out here to take Angmark bare-handed?"

"I had no choice," said Thissell. "When Cromartin gives orders he expects results. In any event you were here with your slaves."

"Don't count on me for help," Rolver said testily. "I wear the Tarn Bird and make no pretensions of valor. But I can lend you a power pistol. I haven't used it recently; I won't guarantee its charge."

Rolver went into the office and a moment later returned with the gun. "What will you do now?"

Thissell shook his head wearily. "I'll try to find Angmark in Fan. Or might he head for Zundar?"

Rolver considered. "Angmark might be able to survive in

Zundar. But he'd want to brush up on his musicianship. I imagine he'll stay in Fan a few days."

"But how can I find him? Where should I look?"

"That I can't say," replied Rolver. "You might be safer not finding him. Angmark is a dangerous man."

Thissell returned to Fan the way he had come.

Where the path swung down from the hills into the esplanade a thick-walled *pisé de terre* building had been constructed. The door was carved from a solid black plank; the windows were guarded by enfoliated bands of iron. This was the office of Cornely Welibus, Commercial Factor, Importer and Exporter. Thissell found Welibus sitting at his ease on the tiled veranda, wearing a modest adaptation of the Waldemar mask. He seemed lost in thought, and might or might not have recognized Thissell's Moon Moth; in any event he gave no signal of greeting.

Thissell approached the porch. "Good morning, Ser Welibus."

Welibus nodded abstractedly and said in a flat voice, plucking at his *krodatch*, "Good morning."

Thissell was rather taken aback. This was hardly the instrument to use toward a friend and fellow out-worlder, even if he did wear the Moon Moth.

Thissell said coldly, "May I ask how long you have been sitting here?"

Welibus considered half a minute, and now when he spoke he acompanied himself on the more cordial *crebarin*. But the recollection of the *krodatch* chord still rankled in Thissell's mind.

"I've been here fifteen or twenty minutes. Why do you ask?"

"I wonder if you noticed a Forest Goblin pass?"

Welibus nodded. "He went on down the esplanade – turned into the first mask shop, I believe."

Thissell hissed between his teeth. This would naturally be Angmark's first move. "I'll never find him once he changes masks," he muttered.

"Who is this Forest Goblin?" asked Welibus, with no more than casual interest.

Thissell could see no reason to conceal the name. "A notorious criminal: Haxo Angmark."

"Haxo Angmark!" croaked Welibus, leaning back in his chair. "You're sure he's here?"

"Reasonably sure."

Welibus rubbed his shaking hands together. "This is bad news – bad news indeed! He's an unscrupulous scoundrel."

"You knew him well?"

"As well as anyone." Welibus was now accompanying himself with the *kiv*. "He held the post I now occupy. I came out as an inspector and found that he was embezzling four thousand UMIs a month. I'm sure he feels no great gratitude toward me." Welibus glanced nervously up the esplanade. "I hope you catch him."

"I'm doing my best. He went into the mask shop, you say?"

"I'm sure of it."

Thissell turned away. As he went down the path he heard the black plank door thud shut behind him.

He walked down the esplanade to the mask-maker's shop, paused outside as if admiring the display: a hundred miniature masks, carved from rare woods and minerals, dressed with emerald flakes, spider-web silk, wasp wings, petrified fish scales and the like. The shop was empty except for the mask-maker, a gnarled knotty man in a yellow robe, wearing a deceptively simple Universal Expert mask, fabricated from over two thousand bits of articulated wood.

Thissell considered what he would say, how he would accompany himself, then entered. The mask-maker, noting the Moon Moth and Thissell's diffident manner, continued with his work.

Thissell, selecting the easiest of his instruments, stroked his *strapan* – possibly not the most felicitous choice, for it conveyed a certain degree of condescension. Thissell tried to counteract his flavor by singing in warm, almost effusive, tones, shaking the *strapan* whimsically when he struck a wrong note: "A stranger is an interesting person to deal with; his habits are unfamiliar, he excites curiosity. Not twenty minutes ago a stranger entered this fascinating shop, to exchange his drab Forest Goblin for one of the remarkable and adventurous creations assembled on the premises."

The mask-maker turned Thissell a side-glance, and

without words played a progression of chords on an instrument Thissell had never seen before: a flexible sac gripped in the palm with three short tubes leading between the fingers. When the tubes were squeezed almost shut and air forced through the slit, an oboelike tone ensued. To Thissell's developing ear the instrument seemed difficult, the mask-maker expert, and the music conveyed a profound sense of disinterest.

Thissell tried again, laboriously manipulating the *strapan*. He sang, "To an out-worlder on a foreign planet, the voice of one from his home is like water to a wilting plant. A person who could unite two such persons might find satisfaction in such an act of mercy."

The mask-maker casually fingered his own *strapan*, and drew forth a set of rippling scales, his fingers moving faster than the eyes could follow. He sank in the formal style: "An artist values his moments of concentration; he does not care to spend time exchanging banalities with persons of at best average prestige." Thissell attempted to insert a counter melody, but the mask-maker struck a new set of complex chords whose portent evaded Thissell's understanding, and continued: "Into the shop comes a person who evidently has picked up for the first time an instrument of unparalleled complication, for the execution of his music is open to criticism. He sings of homesickness and longing for the sight of others like himself. He dissembles his enormous *strakh* behind a Moon Moth, for he plays the *strapan* to a Master Craftsman, and sings in a voice of contemptuous raillery. The refined and creative artist ignores the provocation. He plays a polite instrument, remains noncommittal, and trusts that the stranger will tire of his sport and depart."

Thissell took up his *kiv*. "The noble mask-maker completely misunderstands me —"

He was interrupted by staccato rasping of the mask-maker's *strapan*. "The stranger now sees fit to ridicule the artist's comprehension."

Thissell scratched furiously at his *strapan:* "To protect myself from the heat, I wander into a small and unpretentious mask shop. The artisan, though still distracted by the novelty of his tools, gives promise of development. He works zealously to perfect his skill, so much so that he refuses to converse with strangers, no matter what their need."

The mask-maker carefully laid down his carving tool. He rose to his feet, went behind a screen and shortly returned wearing a mask of gold and iron, with simulated flames licking up from the scalp. In one hand he carried a *skaranyi*, in the other a scimitar. He struck off a brilliant series of wild tones, and sang: "Even the most accomplished artist can augment his *strakh* by killing sea-monsters, Night-men and importunate idlers. Such an occasion is at hand. The artist delays his attack exactly ten seconds, because the offender wears a Moon Moth." He twirled his scimitar, spun it in the air.

Thissell desperately pounded the *strapan*. "Did a Forest Goblin enter the shop? Did he depart with a new mask?"

"Five seconds have lapsed," sang the mask-maker in steady ominous rhythm.

Thissell departed in frustrated rage. He crossed the square, stood looking up and down the esplanade. Hundreds of men and women sauntered along the docks, or stood on the decks of their houseboats, each wearing a mask chosen to express his mood, prestige and special attributes, and everywhere sounded the twitter of musical instruments.

Thissell stood at a loss. The Forest Goblin had disappeared. Haxo Angmark walked at liberty in Fan, and Thissell had failed the urgent instructions of Castel Cromartin.

Behind him sounded the casual notes of a *kiv*. "Ser Moon Moth Thissell, you stand engrossed in thought."

Thissell turned, to find beside him a Cave Owl, in a somber cloak of black and gray. Thissell recognized the mask, which symbolized erudition and patient exploration of abstract ideas; Mathew Kershaul had worn it on the occasion of their meeting a week before.

"Good morning, Ser Kershaul," muttered Thissell.

"And how are the studies coming? Have you mastered the C-Sharp Plus-scale on the *gomapard*? As I recall, you were finding those inverse intervals puzzling."

"I've worked on them," said Thissell, in a gloomy voice. "However, since I'll probably be recalled to Polypolis, it may be all time wasted."

"Eh? What's this?"

Thissell explained the situation in regard to Haxo Angmark. Kershaul nodded gravely. "I recall Angmark. Not a gracious personality, but an excellent musician, with quick fingers and a real talent for new instruments." Thoughtfully he twisted the goatee of his Cave Owl mask. "What are your plans?"

"They're non-existent," said Thissell, playing a doleful phrase on the *kiv*. "I haven't any idea what masks he'll be wearing and if I don't know what he looks like, how can I find him?"

Kershaul tugged at his goatee. "In the old days he favored the Exo Cambian Cycle, and I believe he used an entire set of Nether Denizens. Now of course his tastes may have changed."

"Exactly," Thissell complained. "He might be twenty feet away and I'd never know it." He glanced bitterly across the esplanade toward the mask-maker's shop. "No one will tell me anything; I doubt if they care that a murderer is walking their docks."

"Quite correct," Kershaul agreed. "Sirenese standards are different from ours."

"They have no sense of responsibility," declared Thissell. "I doubt if they'd throw a rope to a drowning man."

"It's true that they dislike interference," Kershaul agreed. "They emphasize individual responsibility and self-sufficency."

"Interesting," said Thissell, "but I'm still in the dark about Angmark."

Kershaul surveyed him gravely. "And should you locate Angmark, what will you do then?"

"I'll carry out the orders of my superior," said Thissell doggedly.

"Angmark is a dangerous man," mused Kerhsaul. "He's got a number of advantages over you."

"I can't take that into account. It's my duty to send him back to Polypolis. He's probably safe, since I haven't the remotest idea how to find him."

Kershaul reflected. "An out-worlder can't hide behind a mask, not from the Sirenes, at least. There are four of us here

at Fan – Rolver, Welibus, you and me. If another out-
worlder tries to set up housekeeping the news will get around
in short order."

"What if he heads for Zundar?"

Kershaul shrugged. "I doubt if he'd dare. On the other
hand –" Kershaul paused, then noting Thissell's sudden
inattention, turned to follow Thissell's gaze.

A man in a Forest Goblin mask came swaggering toward
them along the espanade. Kershaul laid a restraining hand
on Thissell's arm, but Thissell stepped out into the path of
the Forest Goblin, his borrowed gun ready. "Haxo
Angmark," he cried, "don't make a move, or I'll kill you.
You're under arrest."

"Are you sure this is Angmark?" asked Kershaul in a
worried voice.

"I'll find out," said Thissell. "Angmark, turn around,
hold up your hands."

The Forest Goblin stood rigid with surprise and puzzle-
ment. He reached to his *zachinko*, played an interrogatory
arpeggio, and sang, "Why do you molest me, Moon Moth?"

Kershaul stepped forward and played a placatory phrase
on his *slobo*. "I fear that a case of confused identity exists, Ser
Forest Goblin. Ser Moon Moth seeks an out-worlder in a
Forest Goblin mask."

The Forest Goblin's music became irritated, and he
suddenly switched to his *stimic*. "He asserts that I am an
out-worlder? Let him prove his case, or he has my retaliation
to face."

Kershaul glanced in embarrassment around the crowd
which had gathered and once more struck up an ingratiating
melody. "I am sure that Ser Moon Moth –"

The Forest Goblin interrupted with a fanfare of *skaranyi*
tones. "Let him demonstrate his case or prepare for the flow
of blood."

Thissell said, "Very well, I'll prove my case." He stepped
forward, grasped the Forest Goblin's mask. "Let's see your
face, that'll demonstrate your identity!"

The Forest Goblin sprang back in amazement. The crowd
gasped, then set up an ominous strumming and toning of
various instruments.

The Forest Goblin reached to the nape of his neck, jerked the cord to his duel-gong, and with his other hand snatched forth his scimitar.

Kershaul stepped forward, playing the *slobo* with great agitation. Thissell, now abashed, moved aside, conscious of the ugly sound of the crowd.

Kershaul sang explanations and apologies, the Forest Goblin answered; Kershaul spoke over his shoulder to Thissell: "Run for it, or you'll be killed! Hurry!"

Thissell hesitated; the Forest Goblin put up his hand to thrust Kershaul aside. "Run!" screamed Kershaul. "To Welibus' office, lock yourself in!"

Thissell took to his heels. The Forest Goblin pursued him a few yards, then stamped his feet, sent after him a set of raucous and derisive blasts of the hand-bugle, while the crowd produced a contemptuous counterpart of clacking *hymerkins*.

There was no further pursuit. Instead of taking refuge in the Import-Export office, Thissell turned aside and after cautious reconnaissance proceeded to the dock where his houseboat was moored.

The hour was not far short of dusk when he finally returned aboard. Toby and Rex squatted on the forward deck, surrounded by the provisions they had brought back: reed baskets of fruit and cereal, blue-glass jugs containing wine, oil and pungent sap, three young pigs in a wicker pen. They were cracking nuts between their teeth, spitting the shells over the side. They looked up at Thissell, and it seemed that they rose to their feet with a new casualness. Toby muttered something under his breath; Rex smothered a chuckle.

Thissell clacked his *hymerkin* angrily. He sang, "Take the boat offshore; tonight we remain at Fan."

In the privacy of his cabin he removed the Moon Moth, stared into a mirror at his almost unfamiliar features. He picked up the Moon Moth, examined the detested lineaments: the furry gray skin, the blue spines, the ridiculous lace flaps. Hardly a dignified presence for the Consular Representative of the Home Planets. If, in fact, he still held the position when Cromartin learned of Angmark's winning free!

Thissell flung himself into a chair, stared moodily into space. Today he'd suffered a series of setbacks, but he wasn't defeated yet; not by any means. Tomorrow he'd visit Mathew Kershaul; they'd discuss how best to locate Angmark. As Kershaul had pointed out, another out-world establishment could not be camouflaged; Haxo Angmark's identity would soon become evident. Also, tomorrow he must procure another mask. Nothing extreme or vain-glorious, but a mask which expressed a modicum of dignity and self-respect.

At this moment one of the slaves tapped on the door panel, and Thissell hastily pulled the hated Moon Moth back over his head.

Early next morning, before the dawn light had left the sky, the slaves sculled the houseboat back to that section of the dock set aside for the use of out-worlders. Neither Rolver nor Welibus nor Kershaul had yet arrived and Thissell waited impatiently. An hour passed, and Welibus brought his boat to the dock. Not wishing to speak to Welibus, Thissell remained inside his cabin.

A few moments later Rolver's boat likewise pulled in alongside the dock. Through the window Thissell saw Rolver, wearing his usual Tarn Bird, climb to the dock. Here he was met by a man in a yellow-tufted Sand Tiger mask, who played a formal accompaniment on his *gomapard* to whatever message he brought Rolver.

Rolver seemed surprised and disturbed. After a moment's thought he manipulated his own *gomapard*, and as he sang, he indicated Thissell's houseboat. Then, bowing, he went on his way.

The man in the Sand Tiger mask climbed with rather heavy dignity to the float and rapped on the bulwark of Thissell's houseboat.

Thissell presented himself. Sirenese etiquette did not demand that he invite a casual visitor aboard, so he merely struck an interrogation on his *zachinko*.

The Sand Tiger played his *gomapard* and sang, "Dawn over the bay of Fan is customarily a splendid occasion; the sky is white with yellow and green colors; when Mireille rises, the mists burn and writhe like flames. He who sings derives a greater enjoyment from the hour when the floating corpse of an out-worlder does not appear to mar the serenity of the view."

Thissell's *zachinko* gave off a startled interrogation almost of its own accord; the Sand Tiger bowed with dignity. "The singer acknowledges no peer in steadfastness of disposition; however, he does not care to be plagued by the antics of a dissatisfied ghost. He therefore has ordered his slaves to attach a thong to the ankle of the corpse, and while we have conversed they have linked the corpse to the stern of your houseboat. You will wish to administer whatever rites are prescribed in the out-world. He who sings wishes you a good morning and now departs."

Thissell rushed to the stern of his houseboat. There, near-naked and maskless, floated the body of a mature man, supported by air trapped in his pantaloons.

Thissell studied the dead face, which seemed characterless and vapid – perhaps in direct consequence of the mask-wearing habit. The body appeared of medium stature and weight, and Thissell estimated the age as between forty-five and fifty. The hair was nondescript brown, the features bloated by the water. There was nothing to indicate how the man had died.

This must be Haxo Angmark, thought Thissell. Who else could it be? Mathew Kershaul? Why not? Thissell asked himself uneasily. Rolver and Welibus had already disembarked and gone about their business. He searched across the bay to locate Kershaul's houseboat, and discovered it already tying up to the dock. Even as he watched, Kershaul jumped ashore, wearing his Cave Owl mask.

He seemed in an abstracted mood, for he passed Thissell's houseboat without lifting his eyes from the dock.

Thissell turned back to the corpse. Angmark, then, beyond a doubt. Had not three men disembarked from the houseboats of Rolver, Welibus and Kershaul, wearing masks characteristic of these men? Obviously, the corpse of Angmark. . . . The easy solution refused to sit quiet in Thissell's mind. Kershaul had pointed out that another out-worlder would be quickly identified. How else could Angmark maintain himself unless he . . . Thissell brushed the thought aside. The corpse was obviously Angmark.

And yet . . .

Thissell summoned his slaves, gave orders that a suitable container be brought to the dock, that the corpse be transferred therein, and conveyed to a suitable place of repose. The slaves showed no enthusiasm for the task and Thissell was compelled to thunder forcefully, if not skillfully, on the *hymerkin* to emphasize his orders.

He walked along the dock, turned up the esplanade, passed the office of Cornely Welibus and set out along the pleasant little lane to the landing field.

When he arrived, he found that Rolver had not yet made an appearance. An over-slave, given status by a yellow rosette on his black cloth mask, asked how he might be of service. Thissell stated that he wished to dispatch a message to Polypolis.

There was no difficulty here, declared the slave. If Thissell would set forth his message in clear block-print it would be dispatched immediately.

Thissell wrote:

> Out-worlder found dead, possibly Angmark. Age 48, medium physique, brown hair. Other means of identification lacking. Await acknowledgement and/or instructions.

He addressed the message to Castel Cromartin at Polypolis and handed it to the over-slave. A moment later he heard the characteristic sputter of trans-space discharge.

An hour passed. Rolver made no appearance. Thissell paced restlessly back and forth in front of the office. There was no telling how long he would have to wait: trans-space transmission time varied unpredictably. Sometimes the message snapped through in microseconds; sometimes it wandered through unknowable regions for hours; and there were several authenticated examples of messages being received before they had been transmitted.

Another half-hour passed, and Rolver finally arrived, wearing his customary Tarn Bird. Coincidentally Thissell heard the hiss of the incoming message.

Rolver seemed surprised to see Thissell. "What brings you out so early?"

Thissell explained. "It concerns the body which you

referred to me this morning. I'm communicating with my superiors about it."

Rolver raised his head and listened to the sound of the incoming message. "You seem to be getting an answer. I'd better attend to it."

"Why bother?" asked Thissell. "Your slave seems efficient."

"It's my job," declared Rolver. "I'm responsible for the accurate transmission and receipt of all spacegrams."

"I'll come with you," said Thissell. "I've always wanted to watch the operation of the equipment."

"I'm afraid that's irregular," said Rolver. He went to the door which led into the inner compartment. "I'll have your message in a moment."

Thissell protested, but Rolver ignored him and went into the inner office.

Five minutes later he reappeared, carrying a small yellow envelope. "Not too good news," he announced with unconvincing commiseration.

Thissell glumly opened the envelope. The message read:

Body not Angmark. Angmark has black hair. Why did you not meet landing? Serious infraction, highly dissatisfied. Return to Polypolis next opportunity.

Castel Cromartin

Thissell put the message in his pocket. "Incidentally, may I inquire the color of your hair?"

Rolver played a surprised little trill on his *kiv*. "I'm quite blond. Why do you ask?"

"Mere curiosity."

Rolver played another run on the *kiv*. "Now I understand. My dear fellow, what a suspicious nature you have! Look!" He turned and parted the folds of his mask at the nape of his neck. Thissell saw that Rolver was indeed blond.

"Are you reassured?" asked Rolver jocularly.

"Oh, indeed," said Thissell. "Incidentally, have you another mask you could lend me? I'm sick of this Moon Moth."

"I'm afraid not," said Rolver. "But you need merely go into a mask-maker's shop and make a selection."

"Yes, of course," said Thissell. He took his leave of Rolver and returned along the trail to Fan. Passing Welibus' office he hesitated, then turned in. Today Welibus wore a dazzling confection of green glass prisms and silver beads, a mask Thissell had never seen before.

Welibus greeted him cautiously to the accompaniment of a *kiv*. "Good morning, Ser Moon Moth."

"I won't take too much of your time," said Thissell, "but I have a rather personal question to put to you. What color is your hair?"

Welibus hesitated a fraction of a second, then turned his back, lifted the flap of his mask. Thissell saw heavy black ringlets. "Does that answer your question?" inquired Welibus.

"Completely," said Thissell. He crossed the esplanade, went out on the dock to Kershaul's houseboat. Kershaul greeted him without enthusiasm, and invited him aboard with a resigned wave of his hand.

"A question I'd like to ask," said Thissell; "what color is your hair?"

Kershaul laughed woefully. "What little remains is black. Why do you ask?"

"Curiosity."

"Come, come," said Kershaul with an unaccustomed bluffness. "There's more to it than that."

Thissell, feeling the need of counsel, admitted as much. "Here's the situation. A dead out-worlder was found in the harbor this morning. His hair was brown. I'm not entirely certain, but the chances are – let me see, yes – two out of three that Angmark's hair is black."

Kershaul pulled at the Cave Owl's goatee. "How do you arrive at that probability?"

"The information came to me through Rolver's hands. He has blond hair. If Angmark has assumed Rolver's identity, he would naturally alter the information which came to me this morning. Both you and Welibus admit to black hair."

"Hm," said Kershaul. "Let me see if I follow your line of reasoning. You feel that Haxo Angmark has killed either Rolver, Welibus or myself and assumed the dead man's identity. Right?"

Thissell looked at him in surprise. "You yourself emphasized that Angmark could not set up another out-world establishment without revealing himself! Don't you remember?"

"Oh, certainly. To continue. Rolver delivered a message to you stating that Angmark was dark, and announced himself to be blond."

"Yes. Can you verify this? I mean for the old Rolver?"

"No," said Kershaul sadly. "I've seen neither Rolver nor Welibus without their masks."

"If Rolver is not Angmark," Thissell mused, "if Angmark indeed has black hair, then both you and Welibus come under suspicion."

"Very interesting," said Kershaul. He examined Thissell warily. "For that matter, you yourself might be Angmark. What color is your hair?"

"Brown," said Thissell curtly. He lifted the gray fur of the Moon Moth mask at the back of his head.

"But you might be deceiving me as to the text of the message," Kershaul put forward.

"I'm not," said Thissell wearily. "You can check with Rolver if you care to."

Kershaul shook his head. "Unnecessary. I believe you. But another matter: what of voice? You've heard all of us before and after Angmark arrived. Isn't there some indication there?"

"No. I'm so alert for any evidence of change that you all sound rather different. And the masks muffle your voices."

Kershaul tugged the goatee. "I don't see any immediate solution to the problem." He chuckled. "In any event, need there be? Before Angmark's advent, there were Rolver, Welibus, Kershaul and Thissell. Now – for all practical purposes – there are still Rolver, Welibus, Kershaul and Thissell. Who is to say that the new member may not be an improvement upon the old?"

"An interesting thought," agreed Thissell, "but it so happens that I have a personal interest in identifying Angmark. My career is at stake."

"I see," murmured Kershaul. "The situation then becomes an issue between yourself and Angmark."

"You won't help me?"

"Not actively. I've become pervaded with Sirenese individualism. I think you'll find that Rolver and Welibus will respond similarly." He sighed. "All of us have been here too long."

Thissell stood deep in thought. Kershaul waited patiently a moment, then said, "Do you have any further questions?"

"No," said Thissell. "I have merely a favor to ask you."

"I'll oblige if I possibly can," Kershaul replied courteously.

"Give me, or lend me, one of your slaves, for a week or two."

Kershaul played an exclamation of amusement on the *ganga*. "I hardly like to part with my slaves; they know me and my ways —"

"As soon as I catch Angmark you'll have him back."

"Very well," said Kershaul. He rattled a summons on his *hymerkin*, and a slave appeared. "Anthony," sang Kershaul, "you are to go with Ser Thissell and serve him for a short period."

The slave bowed, without pleasure.

Thissell took Anthony to his houseboat, and questioned him at length, noting certain of the responses upon a chart. He then enjoined Anthony to say nothing of what had passed, and consigned him to the care of Toby and Rex. He gave further instructions to move the houseboat away from the dock and allow no one aboard until his return.

He set forth once more along the way to the landing field, and found Rolver at a lunch of spiced fish, shredded bark of the salad tree and a bowl of native currants. Rolver clapped an order on the *hymerkin*, and a slave set a place for Thissell. "And how are the investigations proceeding?"

"I'd hardly like to claim any progress," said Thissell. "I assume that I can count on your help?"

Rolver laughed briefly. "You have my good wishes."

"More concretely," said Thissell, "I'd like to borrow a slave from you. Temporarily."

Rolver paused in his eating. "Whatever for?"

"I'd rather not explain," said Thissell. "But you can be sure that I make no idle request."

Without graciousness Rolver summoned a slave and consigned him to Thissell's service.

On the way back to his houseboat, Thissell stopped at Welibus' office.

Welibus looked up from his work. "Good afternoon, Ser Thissell."

Thissell came directly to the point. "Ser Welibus, will you lend me a slave for a few days?"

Welibus hesitated, then shrugged. "Why not?" He clacked his *hymerkin*; a slave appeared. "Is he satisfactory? Or would you prefer a young female?" He chuckled rather offensively, to Thissell's way of thinking.

"He'll do very well. I'll return him in a few days."

"No hurry." Welibus made an easy gesture and returned to his work.

Thissell continued to his houseboat, where he separately interviewed each of his two new slaves and made notes upon his chart.

Dusk came soft over the Titanic Ocean. Toby and Rex sculled the houseboat away from the dock, out across the silken waters. Thissell sat on the deck listening to the sound of soft voices, the flutter and tinkle of musical instruments. Lights from the floating houseboats glowed yellow and wan watermelon-red. The shore was dark; the Night-men would presently come slinking to paw through refuse and stare jealously across the water.

In nine days the *Buenaventura* came past Sirene on its regular schedule; Thissell had his orders to return to Polypolis. In nine days, could he locate Haxo Angmark?

Nine days weren't too many, Thissell decided, but they might possibly be enough.

Two days passed, and three and four and five. Every day Thissell went ashore and at least once a day visited Rolver, Welibus and Kershaul.

Each reacted differently to his presence. Rolver was sardonic and irritable; Welibus formal and at least superficially affable; Kershaul mild and suave, but ostentatiously impersonal and detached in his conversation.

Thissell remained equally bland to Rolver's dour jibes,

Welibus' jocundity, Kershaul's withdrawal. And every day, returning to his houseboat he made marks on his chart.

The sixth, the seventh, the eighth day came and passed. Rolver, with rather brutal directness, inquired if Thissell wished to arrange for passage on the *Buenaventura*. Thissell considered, and said, "Yes, you had better reserve passage for one."

"Back to the world of faces." Rolver shuddered. "Faces! Everywhere pallid, fish-eyed faces. Mouths like pulp, noses knotted and punctured; flat, flabby faces. I don't think I could stand it after living here. Luckily you haven't become a real Sirenese."

"But I won't be going back," said Thissell.

"I thought you wanted me to reserve passage."

"I do. For Haxo Angmark. He'll be returning to Polypolis in the brig."

"Well, well," said Rolver. "So you've picked him out."

"Of course," said Thissell. "Haven't you?"

Rolver shrugged. "He's either Welibus or Kershaul, that's as close as I can make it. So long as he wears his mask and calls himself either Welibus or Kershaul, it means nothing to me."

"It means a great deal to me," said Thissell. "What time tomorrow does the lighter go up?"

"Eleven twenty-two sharp. If Haxo Angmark's leaving, tell him to be on time."

"He'll be here," said Thissell.

He made his usual call upon Welibus and Kershaul, then returning to his houseboat, put three final marks on his chart.

The evidence was here, plain and convincing. Not absolutely incontrovertible evidence, but enough to warrant a definite move. He checked over his gun. Tomorrow, the day of decision. He could afford no errors.

The day dawned bright white, the sky like the inside of an oyster shell; Mireille rose through iridescent mists. Toby and Rex sculled the houseboat to the dock. The remaining three out-world houseboats floated somnolently on the slow swells.

One boat Thissell watched in particular, that whose

owner Haxo Angmark had killed and dropped into the harbor. This boat presently moved toward the shore, and Haxo Angmark himself stood on the front deck, wearing a mask Thissell had never seen before: a construction of scarlet feathers, black glass and spiked green hair.

Thissell was forced to admire his poise. A clever scheme, cleverly planned and executed – but marred by an insurmountable difficulty.

Angmark returned within. The houseboat reached the dock. Slaves flung out mooring lines, lowered the gang-plank. Thissell, his gun ready in the pocket flap of his robes, walked down the dock, went aboard. He pushed open the door to the saloon. The man at the table raised his red, black and green mask in surprise.

Thissell said, "Angmark, please don't argue or make any –"

Something hard and heavy tackled him from behind; he was flung to the floor, his gun wrested expertly away.

Behind him the *hymerkin* clattered; a voice sang, "Bind the fool's arms."

The man sitting at the table rose to his feet, removed the red, black and green mask to reveal the black cloth of a slave. Thissell twisted his head. Over him stood Haxo Angmark, wearing a mask Thissell recognized as a Dragon Tamer, fabricated from black metal, with a knife-blade nose, socketed eyelids and three crests running back over the scalp.

The mask's expression was unreadable, but Angmark's voice was triumphant. "I trapped you very easily."

"So you did," said Thissell. The slave finished knotting his wrists together. A clatter of Angmark's *hymerkin* sent him away. "Get to your feet," said Angmark. "Sit in that chair."

"What are we waiting for?" inquired Thissell.

"Two of our fellows still remain out on the water. We won't need them for what I have in mind."

"Which is?"

"You'll learn in due course," said Angmark. "We have an hour or so on our hands."

Thissell tested his bonds. They were undoubtedly secure.

Angmark seated himself. "How did you fix on me? I admit

to being curious. . . . Come, come," he chided as Thissell sat silently. "Can't you recognize that I have defeated you? Don't make affairs unpleasant for youself."

Thissell shrugged. "I operated on a basic principle. A man can mask his face, but he can't mask his personality."

"Aha," said Angmark. "Interesting. Proceed."

"I borrowed a slave from you and the other two out-worlders, and I questioned them carefully. What masks had their masters worn during the month before your arrival? I prepared a chart and plotted their responses. Rolver wore the Tarn Bird about eighty percent of the time, the remaining twenty percent divided between the Sophist Abstraction and the Black Intricate. Welibus had a taste for the heroes of Kan Dachan Cycle. He wore the Chalekun, the Prince Intrepid, the Seavain most of the time: six days out of eight. The other two days he wore his South Wind or his Gay Companion. Kershaul, more conservative, preferred the Cave Owl, the Star Wanderer, and two or three other masks he wore at odd intervals.

"As I say, I acquired this information from possibly its most accurate source, the slaves. My next step was to keep watch upon the three of you. Every day I noted what masks you wore and compared it with my chart. Rolver wore his Tarn Bird six times, his Black Intricate twice. Kershaul wore his Cave Owl five times, his Star Wanderer once, his Quincunx once and his Ideal of Perfection once. Welibus wore the Emerald Mountain twice, the Triple Phoenix three times, the Prince Intrepid once and the Shark God twice."

Angmark nodded thoughtfully. "I see my error. I selected from Welibus' masks, but to my own taste – and as you point out, I revealed myself. But only to you." He rose and went to the window. "Kershaul and Rolver are now coming ashore; they'll soon be past and about their business – though I doubt if they'd interfere in any case; they've both become good Sirenese."

Thissell waited in silence. Ten minutes passed. Then Angmark reached to a shelf and picked up a knife. He looked at Thissell. "Stand up."

Thissell slowly rose to his feet. Angmark approached from the side, reached out, lifted the Moon Moth from Thissell's head. Thissell gasped and made a vain attempt to seize it. Too late; his face was bare and naked.

Angmark turned away, removed his own mask, donned the Moon Moth. He struck a call on his *hymerkin*. Two slaves entered, stopped in shock at the sight of Thissell.

Angmark played a brisk tattoo, sang, "Carry this man up to the dock."

"Angmark!" cried Thissell. "I'm maskless!"

The slaves seized him and in spite of Thissell's desperate struggles, conveyed him out on the dock, along the float and up on the dock.

Angmark fixed a rope around Thissell's neck. He said, "You are now Haxo Angmark, and I am Edwer Thissell. Welibus is dead, you shall soon be dead. I can handle your job without difficulty. I'll play musical instruments like a Night-man and sing like a crow. I'll wear the Moon Moth till it rots and then I'll get another. The report will go to Polypolis, Haxo Angmark is dead. Everything will be serene."

Thissell barely heard. "You can't do this," he whispered. "My mask, my face. . . ." A large woman in a blue and pink flower mask walked down the dock. She saw Thissell and emitted a piercing shriek, flung herself prone on the dock.

"Come along," said Angmark brightly. He tugged at the rope, and so pulled Thissell down the dock. A man in a Pirate Captain mask coming up from his houseboat stood rigid in amazement.

Angmark played the *zachinko* and sang, "Behold the notorious criminal Haxo Angmark. Through all the outerworlds his name is reviled; now he is captured and led in shame to his death. Behold Haxo Angmark!"

They turned into the esplanade. A child screamed in fright; a man called hoarsely. Thissell stumbled; tears tumbled from his eyes; he could see only disorganized shapes and colors. Angmark's voice belled out richly: "Everyone behold, the criminal of the out-worlds, Haxo Angmark! Approach and observe his execution!"

Thissell feebly cried out, "I'm not Angmark; I'm Edwer Thissell; he's Angmark." But no one listened to him; there were only cries of dismay, shock, disgust at the sight of his face. He called to Angmark, "Give me my mask, a slave-cloth . . ."

Angmark sang jubilantly, "In shame he lived, in maskless shame he dies."

A Forest Goblin stood before Angmark. "Moon Moth, we meet once more."

Angmark sang, "Stand aside, friend Goblin; I must execute this criminal. In shame he lived, in shame he dies!"

A crowd had formed around the group; masks stared in morbid titillation at Thissell.

The Forest Goblin jerked the rope from Angmark's hand, threw it to the ground. The crowd roared. Voices cried, "No duel, no duel! Execute the monster!"

A cloth was thrown over Thissell's head. Thissell awaited the thrust of a blade. But instead his bonds were cut. Hastily he adjusted the cloth, hiding his face, peering between the folds.

Four men clutched Haxo Angmark. The Forest Goblin confronted him, playing the *skaranyi*. "A week ago you reached to divest me of my mask; you have now achieved your perverse aim!"

"But he is a criminal," cried Angmark. "He is notorious, infamous!"

"What are his misdeeds?" sang the Forest Goblin.

"He has murdered, betrayed; he has wrecked ships; he has tortured, blackmailed, robbed, sold children into slavery; he has –"

The Forest Goblin stopped him. "Your religious differences are of no importance. We can vouch however for your present crimes!"

The hostler stepped forward. He sang fiercely, "This insolent Moon Moth nine days ago sought to preempt my choicest mount!"

Another man pushed close. He wore a Universal Expert, and sang, "I am a Master Mask-maker; I recognize this Moon Moth out-worlder! Only recently he entered my shop and derided my skill. He deserves death!"

"Death to the out-world monster!" cried the crowd. A wave of men surged forward. Steel blades rose and fell, the deed was done.

Thissell watched, unable to move. The Forest Goblin approached, and playing the *stimic* sang sternly, "For you we have pity, but also contempt. A true man would never suffer such indignities!"

Thissell took a deep breath. He reached to his belt and found his *zachinko*. He sang, "My friend, you malign me! Can you not appreciate true courage? Would you prefer to die in combat or walk maskless along the esplanade?"

The Forest Goblin sang, "There is only one answer. First I would die in combat; I could not bear such shame."

Thissell sang, "I had such a choice. I could fight with my hands tied, and so die – or I could suffer shame, and through this shame conquer my enemy. You admit that you lack sufficient *strakh* to achieve this deed. I have proved myself a hero of bravery! I ask, who here has courage to do what I have done?"

"Courage?" demanded the Forest Goblin. "I fear nothing, up to and beyond death at the hands of the Nightmen!"

"Then answer."

The Forest Goblin stood back. He played his double-*kamanthil*. "Bravery indeed, if such were your motives."

The hostler struck a series of subdued *gomapard* chords and sang, "Not a man among us would dare what this maskless man has done."

The crowd muttered approval.

The mask-maker approached Thissell, obsequiously stroking his double-*kamanthil*. "Pray Lord Hero, step into my nearby shop, exchange this vile rag for a mask befitting your quality."

Another mask-maker sang, "Before you choose, Lord Hero, examine my magnificent creations!"

A man in a Bright Sky Bird mask approached Thissell reverently.

"I have only just completed a sumptuous houseboat; seventeen years of toil have gone into its fabrication. Grant me the good fortune of accepting and using this splendid craft; aboard waiting to serve you are alert slaves and pleasant maidens; there is ample wine in storage and soft silken carpets on the decks."

"Thank you," said Thissell, striking the *zachinko* with vigor and confidence. "I accept with pleasure. But first a mask."

The mask-maker struck an interrogative trill on the *gomapard*. "Would the Lord Hero consider a Sea Dragon Conqueror beneath his dignity?"

"By no means," said Thissell. "I consider it suitable and satisfactory. We shall go now to examine it."

EDGAR PANGBORN
The Golden Horn

The late Edgar Pangborn is almost forgotten these days, and is rarely ever mentioned even in historical surveys of the '50s and '60s . . . which is a pity, since he had a depth and breadth of humanity that have rarely been matched inside the field or out. Although he was never a particularly prolific writer (five SF novels, one or two mainstream novels, and a baker's dozen or so of short pieces), he was nevertheless one of that select crew of underappreciated authors (one thinks of Cordwainer Smith, Fritz Leiber, Jack Vance, Avram Davidson, Richard McKenna) who have had an enormous underground effect on the field simply by impressing the hell out of other writers, and numerous authors-in-the-egg. Pangborn wrote about "little people" for the most part, only rarely focusing on the famous and powerful. He was one of only a handful of SF writers capable of writing about small-town or rural people with insight and sympathy (most SF is urban in orientation, written by city people *about* city people – or, when it *is* written by people from small towns, they are frequently kids who couldn't wait to get *out* of those small towns and off to the bright lights of the big city . . . which often amounts to the same thing, as far as sympathies are concerned), and he was also one of the few who could get inside the minds of both the very young and the very old with equal ease and compassion.

Pangborn's materpiece was *Davy*, which, in spite of a somewhat weak ending (or, at least, a final third that doesn't quite live up to the two-thirds that came before it), may well be the finest postholocaust novel ever written – in my opinion, it is seriously rivaled only by Walter M. Miller, Jr.'s *A Canticle for Leibowitz* and John Wyndham's *Re-birth*. In any fair world, *Davy* alone ought to be enough to guarantee Pangborn a distinguished place in the history of the genre, but there were also novels like *A Mirror for Observers* – his International Fantasy Award winner, somewhat dated now, but still powerful, in which alien observers from two opposing philosophical camps vie for the soul of a brilliant human boy – and *West of the Sun*, an underrated novel about the efforts of human castaways to survive on an alien world, as well as beautifuly crafted short work such as "A Master of Babylon," "Longtooth," "The World Is a Sphere," and "Angel's Egg."

The story that follows, "The Golden Horn," was probably Pangborn's best short work. Although it was later melded into the novel *Davy*, it stands well on its own, and its intelligence and wit, its eloquence and power and compassion, its evocation of moments of both raw beauty and raw horror, as well as its slyly satirical touches, make it as good a handling of its theme as has ever been seen in the genre.

Edgar Pangborn's other works include *The Judgment of Eve* and *The Company of Glory*, the mainstream novel *The Trial of Castilla Blake*, the collection *Good Neighbors and Other Strangers*, and the posthumously published collection *Still I Persist in Wondering*. After many years out of print. *Davy* was reissued this year, by Collier – go out and buy it at once, while you still have the chance.

Moha, where I was born, is mainly a nation of farms, grouped around their stockade village throughout the hill and lake and forest country. I grew up in Skoar, one of Moha's three cities, which lies in a cup of the hills near the Katskil border. Even there things moved with the seasons and the Corn Market trade; wilderness whispers at the city's borders, except where the two roads, the Northwest and the East, carry their double stream of men, mule-wagons, soldiers, tinkers, wanderers.

Farming's heartbreak work in Moha, same as everywhere. The stock give birth to as many mues as anywhere else, the labor's long sweat and toil and disappointment wearing a man down to old age in the thirties, few farmers ever able to afford a slave. But the people scrape along, as I've seen human beings do in places worse than Moha. I'm older, I've traveled, I've learned to write and read in spite of that mystery's being reserved to the priests. Looking back, I sometimes wonder if Moha wasn't the happiest land I ever knew.

The other cities – I've never visited them – are Moha City and Kanhar, both in the northwest on Moha Water. Their harbors can take big vessels up to thirty tons, the ships that trade with Levannon and the Katskil ports on the Hudson Sea. Moha City is the capital and Kanhar is the largest, twenty thousand population not counting slaves. Fifty miles south of Kanhar is Skoar, and there I was born squalling and redheaded in one of those houses that are licensed but still supposed not to exist. In such places they don't have time for kids, but since I was a well-formed chunk of humanity and not a mue, the policers took me from my mother, whoever she was, when I was weaned, and dumped me in the Skoar orphanage, where I stayed until I was nine, old enough to earn a living.

I'm thinking now of a day in middle March when I was past fourteen, and slipped away before dawn from the Bull and Iron where I worked as yardboy, bondservant of course, two dollars a week and board. I was merely goofing off. We'd gone through a tough winter with smallpox and flu, near-about everything except the lumpy plague, and a real snow in January almost an inch deep – I've never seen such a heavy fall of it before or since. There was even a frost in February; people called it unusual. In the stable loft where I slept I just thought it was damn cold. I remember looking out the loft window one January morning and seeing icicles on the sign over the inn door – a noble sign, painted for Old Jon Robson by some journeyman artist who likely got bed and a meal out of it along with the poverty talk that Old Jon saved for such occasions. A fine red bull with tremendous horns, tremendous everything, and for the iron there was a long spear sticking out of his neck and he not minding it a bit.

The wolves sharpnosed in close that winter. Mostly grays but a pack of blacks wiped out an entire farm family in Wilton Village near Skoar. Old Jon Robson would tell every new guest the particulars of the massacre, and he's probably doing it yet, along with tales about a crazy redheaded yardboy he had once. Well, Old Jon had connections in Wilton Village, knew the family the wolves killed and had to make a thing of it, clickety-yak. I never knew him to keep his mouth shut more than two minutes – one day when he was sick with a sore throat. He wouldn't shut it when he slept, either. He and Mam Robson had their bedroom across the wagonyard from my loft, and in midwinter with the windows shut tight I could still hear him sleep, like an ungreased wagonwheel.

Before sunup that March day I fed the mules and horses. I reasoned that somebody else ought to get his character strengthened by doing the shoveling. It was a Friday anyhow, so all work was sinful, unless you want to claim that shoveling is a work of necessity or piety, and I disagree. I crept into the main kitchen of the inn, where a yardboy wasn't supposed to appear. Safe enough. Everybody would be fasting before church – the comfortable way, in bed. The slave-man Judd who was boss of the kitchen wasn't up yet, and the worst he'd have done would have been to flap a rag and chase me ten steps on his gimp leg. I found a peach pie and surrounded it for breakfast. You see, I'd skipped fasting and church a good deal already – easy because who cares about a yardboy? – and the lightning hadn't located me yet. In the store room I collected a chunk of bacon and a loaf of oat bread, and started thinking. Why not run away for good?

Who'd be bothered? Maybe Jon Robson's daughter Emmia would, a little. Cry, and wish she'd been nicer to me. I worked on that as I stole out of the inn and down the long emptiness of Kurin Street, dawn still half an hour away. I worked on it hard. I had myself killed by black wolf, changed that to bandits, because black wolf wouldn't leave any bones. There ought to be bones for somebody to bring back. Somebody who'd say to Emmia: "Here's all that's left of poor redheaded Davy, except his Katskil knife. He did say he wanted for you to have that if anything happened to him." But bandits wouldn't have left the knife, rot them. I had a problem there.

Emmia was older than me, sixteen, big and soft like her papa only on her it looked good. How I did cherish and play with that rosy softness in the night – all in my fancy, dumb-virgin as a baby cockerel, alone in my loft.

I was gulping by the time I passed the town green, but as I neared the Corn Market, in North District and not far from the place where I knew I could climb the city stockade with no guard seeing me, most of that flapdoodle drained out of my head. I was thinking sharp and practical about running away for real, not just goofing off the way I'd done other times.

A bondservant, one grade better than a slave, I'd be breaking the law if I ran, and could be made a true slave for it, likely with a ten-year term. I told myself that morning what they could do with the law. I had the bacon and bread in a sack strapped across my shoulder. My Katskil knife hung in a sheath under my shirt, and all the money I'd saved during the winter, five dollars in silver, was knotted into my loin rag. Up in the woods on North Mountain where I'd found a cave in my lone wanderings the year before, other things lay hidden – ten dollars safely buried, an ash bow I'd made myself, brass-tipped arrows, fishlines with a couple of real steel hooks. Maybe I'd really do it, I thought. Maybe today.

I shinnied over the stockade without trouble and started up the mountain. I was being pulled two ways then. The Emmia who talked in my heart wasn't whimpering over bones. I was thinking about the real soft-lipped girl who'd probably want me to turn back, stick it out through my bond-period, get civilized, make something of myself. Who might not mind, might even like it, if I told her or showed her what I felt about her instead of just mooning at her through doorways like a stunned calf. The forest pulled the other way.

Climbing the steep ground from the city in the morning hush, I decided I'd merely stay lost a day or two as I'd done before. Other times it had usually been my proper monthly day off, not always. I'd risked trouble before and talked my way out of it. I'd stay this time, say until the bacon was gone, and spend that time polishing the fresh whopmagullion I'd have to tell, to celebrate my return and soften the action of Old Jon's leather strap on my rump. The decision itself perked me up. When I was well under cover of the woods and the time was right, I climbed a maple to watch the sunrise.

It was already beyond first-light, the fire not yet over the rim. I'd missed the earliest bird-calls, now their voices were rippling back and forth across the world. I heard a white-throat sparrow in a bush; robin and wood thrush, loveliest of all bird singers, were busy everywhere. A cardinal flew by me, a streak of flame, and a pair of smoky-white parrots broke out of a sycamore to skim over the tree-tops. In a sweet-gum nearby I caught sight of a pair of white-face monkeys who didn't mind me at all. When I looked away from them I saw the golden blaze begin.

For the first time that I can remember, I wanted to know, Where does it come from, the sun? What happens over there when it's set afire every morning? Why should God go to all that trouble to keep us warm?

Understand, at that time I had no learning at all. I'd scarcely heard of books except to know they were forbidden to all but the priests because they'd had something to do with the Sin of Man. I figured Old Jon was the smartest man in the world because he could keep accounts with the bead-board that hung in the taproom. I believed, as the Amran Church teaches everyone to believe, that the earth is a body of land three thousand miles square, once a garden and perfect, with God and the angels walking freely among men, until the time almost four hundred years ago when men sinned and spoiled everything; so now we're working out the penance until Abraham, the Spokesman of God, who died on the Wheel at Nuber in the year 37, returns to judge His people, saving the few elect and sending the rest to fry forever in the caverns of Hell. And on all sides of that lump of land spread the everlasting seas all the way to the rim of the world. The Book of Abraham, said the teacher-priests, doesn't tell how far away the rim is, because that's one of the things God does not wish men to know.

Doubts I did have. I thought it remarkable how the lightning never did arrive no matter how I sinned, even on Fridays. The doubts were small; young grass trying to work up through the brown old trash of winter.

I understood of course – all children far younger than fourteen understood it – that while you might get away with a lot of sinning on the sly, you agreed out loud with whatever the Church taught or else you didn't stay alive. I saw my first heretic-burning when I was nine, after I'd gone to work at the Bull and Iron. In Moha they were always conducted along with the Spring Festival. Children under nine weren't required to attend.

I watched the dawn from my maple, the birth and growing of the light. Surely I was not watching what happened in my mind, for the thought was living in me, and I not knowing how it could have come; the thought, What if someone traveled all the way to watch the firing of the sun?

Nowadays I understood that thoughts do not come to you. You make them, they grow in you until the time arrives when you must recognize them.

Down out of my maple then, up the long rise of the mountain in deep forest, where the heat of the day is always mild. I walked and climbed slowly, not wishing to raise a sweat, for the smell of it can drift a surprising distance, and black wolf and brown tiger may get interested. Against black wolf I had my knife. He dislikes steel. Brown tiger cares nothing for knives – a flip of his paw is sufficient – though he's said to respect arrows, thrown spears and fire, usually. I've heard tell of brown tiger leaping a fire-circle to make a meal of hunters. It could be true, for his hunger must be immense and compelling in a bad season when moose and deer and bison have gone scarce. I was not thinking much about those ancient enemies when I climbed North Mountain that morning. The question-thought was in me, saying, What if *I* were to go beyond the rim, where the sun is set afire . . . ?

My cave was a crack in a cliff, broadening inside to a room four feet wide, twenty deep. The cleft ran up into darkness, and must have broken through to the outside, for a small draft like the pull of a chimney kept the air fresh. Sometimes I wished the entrance was narrower – black wolf could have got in, maybe even tiger. I'd cleared out a few copperheads when I first found the cave, and had to be watchful against them too, or rattlers, slithering back to reclaim it. The approach was a ledge that widened in front of the cave, with enough earth to support a patch of grass, and the cave was located well around the east shoulder of the mountain, so that the city was shut away. I could safely build a fire at night behind the rocks at the cave entrance, and I always did. You need a sleep-fire for safety, and the knack of waking at the right moments to refresh it. I'd long ago lifted a flint-and-steel from the Bull and Iron kitchen where it didn't seem real decorative. I usually doused my fire before dawn. No sense painting smoke on bright sky to stir up the curious.

That morning I first made sure about my bow and arrows and fishing gear. They hadn't been disturbed. And yet I felt a strangeness. Not snakes and not intruders. Some eastern sunlight was entering; I could see as well as I needed to for safety but something nagged me. I stood a long time moving only my eyes. I moistened my nose, but caught no wrong scent.

When I found the trouble at last, far at the back on one of the cave walls where sunlight didn't reach, and where my glance must have touched it unknowingly while I was looking at my gear, I was no wiser. It was simply a small drawing made by the point of some softer, reddish rock. I goggled at it, trying to imagine it had been there always. No such thing. That cave was mine, the only place on earth I'd ever felt I owned, and I knew it like the skin of my body. This had been done since my last visit, in December before winter set in.

Two stick figures, circles for heads with no faces, single lines for legs and arms and bodies, both with male parts indicated. I'd heard of hunters' sign-messages. But what did this say that a hunter could want to know? The figures held nothing, did nothing, just stood there.

The one on my right was in human proportion, with slightly bent elbows and knees in the right places, all his fingers and toes. The other stood to the same height, but his legs were far too short without a knee-crook, and his arms too long, dangling below his crotch. He had only three toes for each foot, a big one and two squeezed-up little ones. His fingers were blunt stubs, though the artist had gone to a lot of trouble drawing good human fingers for the other jo.

No tracks in the cave or on the ledge. Nothing left behind.

I gave it up – nothing else to do. Somebody'd been here since December, and he was honest because he never touched my gear, and likely meant me no harm. Last year I'd brought a horse-shoe and slipped it into the jumble of rocks before the cave. Now I made certain it was still in place – it was; anyway I'd never heard of a trick like this being pulled by witches or spooks.

I worked awhile, gathering fresh balsam to sleep on, and a supply of firewood against the night. Then I shrugged off shirt and loin rag but not my knife, naturally – and lay out naked in the sunny grass, drowsing, daydreaming, not wondering much now about my visitor because I supposed he was long gone. I let other thoughts range wide, into the open sky and beyond the limits of the day.

I thought of journeying.

A patch of land three thousand miles square, and the everlasting seas. Hudson Sea, Moha Water, the Lorenta Sea, even the great Ontara Sea in the northwest – all of those, said the teacher-priests, are mere branches of the great sea, dividing the known world into islands. From travelers' talk – oh, I think all the best of my education up to fourteen came from evenings at the Bull and Iron when I was minding the fireplace in the taproom or lending a hand serving drinks with my ears flapping – I knew that in some places the Hudson Sea is only a few miles wide; small craft cross it readily in good weather. And I knew that some thirty-ton ships of Levannon sail coastwise through Moha Water to the Lorenta Sea, then south for trade with Nuin – Old City and Land's End, the easternmost part of the known world, except for a few of the outlying Cod Islands. Long, dangerous, roundabout, that northern passage, especially bad in the Lorenta Sea, where winds can be hellish or at other times fog may lie thick for days, hiding both shores – and as for the shores, wilderness on both sides, red bear and brown tiger country not meant for man. Yet that route was safer, travelers said, than the southern course down the Hudson Sea and along the Conicut coast, for at the end of that course the Cod Islands pirates with their devilish little scoon-rigged fighter craft were somehow able to smell out every third vessel worth the taking, and they couldn't be bothered with prisoners unless there were women abroad.

I thought, If thirty-tonners of Levannon make that northern passage for the sake of trade, why can't they sail farther, much farther? What's stopping them? Sure, I was ignorant. I'd never seen even the Hudson Sea, and couldn't picture it. Likely I'd never heard the word "navigation" at that time. I had no notion of the terror and the vastness of open sea when the land's gone and there's no mark to steer by unless someone aboard knows the mystery of guessing position from the pattern of the stars. But an ignorant boy can think. And I thought, if nobody dares sail beyond sight of land, and if the Book of Abraham doesn't say, how can anyone, even the priests, claim to *know* what's out there? Can't there be other lands before you come to the rim?

I thought, How do they even know there is a rim? If it goes on forever –

And I thought, If *I* were to sail east toward the place of sunrise –

Nay, but suppose I traveled at least to Levannon, where a young man might sign aboard one of those thirty-tonners. Suppose I started this morning . . .

I thought of Emmia.

I'd glimpsed her once at her window, birth-naked for bed-time, prettier than any flower. That was the year before. I'd sneaked out of my loft sore and angry from a licking Old Jon gave me – a mule got loose in the vegetable patch, not my fault but he wouldn't hear of it. That night I swore I'd run away and the hell with all of them. But from the street my eye caught the glow of candlelight at a window at the side of the inn on the second floor, that I knew was Emmia's. A thick-stemmed jinny-creeper vine ran up that side of the building, spreading leaf patterns over many of the windows, and hers was one, and behind the ghostly dark patches of the pointed leaves her sweet body was moving. I saw her let free red-brown hair to tumble over her shoulders, and she combed it, watching herself no doubt in a mirror I couldn't see. Then she must have suddenly noticed the curtain was still open, for she came to close it. Not in any hurry. She couldn't have seen me, my skinny carcass squinched into the shadow of the next building. She stood gazing out into the dark a short while, long enough to bewitch me as if I'd never seen her before, the slow grace of her motion, her round lifted arm, deep-curved waist and the warm triangle and the division between her big breasts a line of tender darkness.

Naked women weren't news to me, though I'd never had one. Skoar had peep-shows like any civilized city, including penny-a-look ones that I could afford. But this was Emmia, whom I saw every day in her smock or slack-pants, busy at a hundred tasks around the inn and scolded by her ma for laziness half the time, candle-making, mending, dusting, overseeing the slave help when Mam Robson was sick, waiting on table, coming out to the barn and stable sometimes to help me collect hens' eggs, even lend a hand feeding the critters and milking the goats. This was Emmia, and like sudden music I loved her.

I couldn't run away then, nor think of it. She drew the curtain, her candle died, I stole back to my loft forgetting Old Jon's beating and all my wrath. I fell asleep that night imagining the pressure and savor of her beside me on my pallet in the hay-well and part of the time I had myself inheriting the inn and Old Jon's fortune, and Old Jon's dying speech with a blessing on the marriage would have made a skunk weep and forgive all his enemies. Though many times later I risked going out to stare at that window after dark, it never happened again. But the image lived in me, was with me on my ledge before the cave as morning glided toward noon.

My ears must have caught the knowledge first, then my right hand firming on my knife while my mind was still beclouded by love and fancy. Then everything in me said, Look out! Wake up! I opened my eyes and turned my head slowly enough like a creature rousing in the natural way.

My visitor was there, a short way up the ledge, and he smiled.

Anyway I think he smiled, or wanted to. His mouth was a poor gash no longer than the mid-joint of my forefinger, in a broad flat hairless face. Monstrously dirty he was, and fat, with a heavy swaying paunch. Seeing his huge long arms and little stub legs, I thought I knew who he was.

He did have knees but they scarcely showed, for his lower legs were as big around as his thighs, blocky columns with fat-rolls drooping from the thigh sections. Baldheaded as a pink snake, hairless to the middle, but there at his navel a great thatch of twisty black hair began and ran all the way down his legs to his stubby three-toed feet. He wore nothing at all, poor jo, and it didn't matter. So thick was that frowsy hair I had to look twice before I was sure he was male. He had no ears, just small openings where they should have been. And he had no nose – none at all, you understand? Simply a pair of slits below the little sorrowful black eyes that were meeting my stare bravely enough. He said: "I go away?"

I'd been about to draw my knife and shriek at him to go away. I didn't. I tried to move slowly, getting on my feet. Whatever my face was doing, it made him no more frightened than he was already.

In spite of those legs he stood tall as I, maybe five feet five. He was grief and loneliness standing in the sun, ugly as unwanted death.

A mue.

In Moha, and all countries I've since known, the law of church and state says flat and plain: A *mue born of woman or beast shall not live*.

Well, law is what men make it, and you heard tales. A woman with a devil's aid might bribe a priest to help conceal a mue-birth, hoping (always a vain hope according to the tales) that the mue might outgrow its evil and appear human instead of devil-begotten. I think, by the way, that Nuin and Katskil are the only countries which require that the mother of a mue must be killed. In Moha, I know, the law explains that a demon bent on planting mue-seed is well known to enter women in their sleep and without their knowledge, therefore they aren't to blame unless witnesses can prove the contrary, that they performed the act with the demon awake and knowingly. At the Bull and Iron I'd heard plenty of such tales about mues born in secret – single-eyed, tailed, purple-skinned, monkey-sized, four-armed, or anything else the storyteller cared to imagine, I guess – growing up in secret and finally taking to the wilderness, where it was the duty of any decent citizen to kill them on sight – a dangerous undertaking even if they seemed defenseless, for the stories claimed that the demon who fathered the mue was likely enough to be watching over his offspring, perhaps in the shape of an animal, a snake or wolf or tiger.

He said again: "I go away?"

His voice was deep, slow, blurred, hard to understand. He didn't move except for an idle swinging of his arms. Sprouting huge out of his soggy body – why, those arms could have torn a bull in quarters.

"No, don't go."

"Man," he said. "Boy-man. Beautiful."

I'm not, of course. I'm puggy-nosed, freckled, knotty-muscled, small but limber. It didn't occur to me at first that he meant me, but he was studying me sharply with those sad little pouch eyes, as I stood there with nothing on but my knife-belt, and there was nothing else he could have meant. I suppose I understand now that anything in the natural human shape would have looked beautiful to him. I knew he could see the bumpy racing of my heart; glancing down, I could see it myself, a crazy bird's-wing flutter below the flare of my bottom ribs. Out of the uproar in my head I could find nothing to say except: "Thanks for the picture. I like it." I saw he didn't know the word "picture". "Lines," I said, and pointed to the cave. "Good."

He understood then; smiled and chuckled and gobbled. "You come me," he said. "I show you good things, I."

Go with him? Father Abraham, no! And maybe meet his father? I should – but I couldn't think. I pulled on my shirt and loin rag, trying to watch not only the mue but the ledge behind him, and the region behind my back too. I said: "W-w-wait!" and I stepped into my cave.

Out of his sight, I was taken with a fit of trembling, sick and silly. Then I had my knife out and was hacking away a good half of that loaf of oat bread. I know I had some notion of buying him off. I recall thinking that if his father was in wolf-shape, maybe the bacon would do some good. But I didn't take it; I set it, and the rest of the loaf, back on the rock ledge with my bow and arrows, and my fingers were reaching for the luck charm at my neck. It wasn't there. I remembered I'd dropped it in my sack because the string had broken the day before and I couldn't find another. Now I slid the sack over my shoulder, and took some comfort from feeling the charm, the little male-female god-thing, lumpy through the cloth of the sack.

A clay trifle. I've learned since then that they carve such

trash down in Penn, to sell to travelers for souvenirs, and likely it came from there. It was given me by my mother, or by somebody in the house where I was born, for I'm told it was on a string around my neck when I was taken to the orphanage, and there they laughed at it some but let me keep it. Emmia was often curious about it — such things aren't common in Moha. Once, when we were looking for hens' eggs in the barn loft, she caught hold of it and asked me, a bit red-faced and whispery, if I knew what it meant. I was thirteen; it was before I'd seen her in her window. I knew and didn't know what *she* meant, was scared of the difference in her face and of the queer sweet-smelling warmth that reached me from her nearness, and so nothing came of what might have been a lively hour if my thoughts had grown a little closer toward those of a man. Oh, I don't believe in luck-charms nowadays. Luck, good or bad, simply happens; you can't make it, or push it around with charms and words and all that jibberty-mumble. But in those days I more than half believed in it. And since I did, it helped to stop my trembling, as I carried out that half-loaf to – him. Carried it out, knowing with not a trace of doubt what I ought to do, meant to do, what the law said I must do.

He didn't reach for it. Those nostril-slits flared, though, and his gaze followed my fingers like a dog's when I broke off a small piece of the bread and ate it myself. I held out the rest to him and he accepted it, carried it to his pitiful mouth. I got a glimpse of his teeth, brownish, small, close-set, weak-looking. He gnawed awkwardly. His eyes never left me as he munched, and snuffled, and slobbered. He kept grunting, "Good, good!" and trying to smile with his mouth full. Merciful winds, it was nothing but common oat bread! And with all that fat, he couldn't have been going hungry.

At fourteen I couldn't understand that it wasn't bread he was starved for. I know it now.

The bread gone, he gave his wet mouth a swipe and said: "You come me now? Good things. Show good things, I." He walked a few steps up the ledge, looking back. Like a dog.

Yes, I followed him.

He walked better than I expected. His knees could bend

only a few inches, but the stub legs were powerful to hold up all that weight, and they could pump along at surprising speed. On the level, it was a stiff-legged waddle. But on the steep ground, as we climbed around toward the northern side of the mountain, his arms would swing forward touching the earth, a four-legged scramble that carried him up the rises about as fast as I cared to walk. And he was quiet, in the same way I'd learned to go quiet in the woods. He knew this country, got his living out of it, must have known it a good while. I couldn't guess his age, however, and hardly tried to.

North Mountain mue, I've got no other name for him. He would never have owned one. What the hell, like other orphanage kids I never had a last name myself, and don't miss it. I'm just Davy.

Don't think my kindness – if it was kindness, that business with the bread – came from anything good in me. It didn't. It came partly from fear, partly from an ugly sort of planning. From the year of teaching by the priests that every child in Moha is required to sweat out before he's twelve, and from the Bull and Iron tales, I knew that mues weren't in the same class with demons or ghosts or elves, but solid flesh in spite of being the get of devils. They couldn't vanish or float through walls; they didn't have the evil eye. If you got near one you'd see and smell him, he couldn't use spells or witch-signs (though his father might) because God wouldn't allow that to a miserable mue, and he would die for good when you put a knife in him. The law said when, not if. It said you must if you could; if you couldn't, you must notify the Church at once, so that he could be hunted down by men properly equipped and with the protection of a priest.

I walked on behind him, up through the deeper forest on the north side of the mountain, and more and more I hated and resented him, cursing the luck that made me the one to find him, imagining his demon father behind every tree, and sickened the way anyone might be sickened by ugliness, terror, strangeness and a foul smell.

We reached a level area, a flanking ridge of the mountain's north side where the trees stood great and old, spaced well apart but casting thick shade from interlacing branches.

Most of them were pines, that through the years had built a heavy carpet; here anyone could walk soft as a breeze. My ears, and they are keen, could barely hear the mue a few steps ahead of me as his blobby feet pressed the pine needles. I myself moved more quietly than that. I felt that he didn't like it here. He could shamble along faster on sloping ground. In this place anything could overtake him. He padded on at his best poor speed, with constant glances to left and right – truly like someone who knew nothing more about the shadows than I did.

The stories didn't say there was *always* a demon attending a mue.

It would be easiest, and I knew it, here on the level. Six inches of double-edge Katskil steel, honed to the limit as mine always was, will go through anything made of flesh. I was watching the best spot, below his last rib on the left side. If a no-way human thing, or being, was observing us, he or it might read my thought. It might not be in animal shape at all. But as for the mue – well, if I failed to kill at the first stab, at least I'd have time to dodge his frightful arms, and run faster than he could hope to do, while the blood drained out of him. Mue blood. Devil-fathered blood.

I slid my knife free. I lowered it quickly out of sight inside the mouth of my sack, afraid he might turn suddenly before I was ready, afraid of other eyes. I lessened the distance between us, calculating angles, arm length, the lie of the ground. It would be best if I stooped slightly and drove my knife upward.

He coughed slightly, a little throat-clearing, a completely human sound. It hurt me somehow, angered me too, for surely he had no right to do things in the human way. Anyhow there was no hurry; plenty more of this partly open area where it would be safest to do it. I saw no change in the tree-pattern up ahead. I told myself to wait till I felt more ready. I told myself how easy it would be. Just wait a minute . . .

I saw myself back at the Bull and Iron telling my true-tale. I wouldn't brag, nay, I'd speak with a noble calm. I could afford it. I'd be the Yardboy Who Killed A Mue.

They would send out a mission, priests, hunters and

soldiers, to find the body and verify my story. I'd go along, and they'd find it. A skeleton, with those awful leg-bones, would be enough – and that's all it would be, for in the time it took the mission to argue and get going, the carrion-ants would finish what other scavengers began, the old necessary wilderness housecleaning. The skeleton would do. They'd set out doubting me, snickering behind their hands. Then the laughers would look sick, and I'd be a hero.

It came to me that this was no gaudy daydream of the kind that had filled my head with rosy mists at other times. This was what would happen in sober fact. I'd be questioned and examined afterward by the priests, maybe the Bishop of Skoar, the Mayor, even the Colonel of the army garrison. Why, possibly the Kurin family, absolute tops in the Skoar aristocracy, would hear of me and want to learn more. If they liked me, I'd be a bondservant no longer. With them for my patrons I'd be the same as rich.

I would go to Levannon, on a roan horse. Two attendants – no, three, one to ride ahead and make sure of a room for me at the next inn, never mind who had to be tossed out; and a maid-servant to bathe me and keep the bed warm. In Levannon I would *buy* me a ship, a thirty-tonner. And wouldn't I wear a green hat with a hawk's feather, a red shirt of Penn silk, my loin cloth silken too, none of your damned scratchy linsey rags, maybe white with small golden stars and crosses! Real leather moccasins with ornaments of brass.

I saw Old Jon Robson ashamed of past unkindness but quick to get in on the glory. I'd let him. It would suit my dignity. Clickety-yak, he knew all along the boy had wonderful stuff in him, only needed an opportunity to bring it out, what he'd always said, clickety-clickety, and me looking calm, friendly, a little bit bored. Poor Old Jon!

And Emmia: "Davy, weren't you *terrified*? O Davy darling, what if *he'd* killed *you*?" Maybe not just "darling"; maybe she'd call me "Spice," which girls didn't say in my native city unless they meant come-take-it. "Davy, Spice, what if I'd lost you?" "Nay, Emmia, it wasn't anything. I had to do it." So, since she'd called me that, it wasn't the taproom where she spoke, but her bedroom, and she'd let down her lovely hair to cover the front of her in make-believe modesty, but I

put my hands below her chin – you know, gentle, nevertheless the hands that had killed a mue – parting that flowing
softness to let the pink flower-tips peep through . . .

The mue halted and turned to me. "Bad place," he said,
pointing at some of the enormous trees, to remind me how
anything might lurk behind them. "No fear, boy-man. Bad
thing come, I help, I." He tapped the bulges of his right arm.
"Fight big, you, I. You, I – word? – fra – fre –"

"Friends," I said, or my voice said it for me.

"Friends." He nodded, satisfied, turned his broad back to
me and went on.

I pushed my knife into its sheath and did not draw it again
that day.

The big-tree region ended. For a while our course slanted
downhill through smaller growth; now and then a gap in the
tree cover let me glance out across rolling land to the north
and east. Then we came to a place where the master growth
was no longer trees but the wild grape. Monstrous vines
looped and clung in their slow violence throughout a stand of
maple and oak, the trees twisted into tortured attitudes by
the ceaseless pressure. Many of the trees were dead but still
provided firm columns to uphold their murderers. In the
upper shadows I saw flashes of brilliance, not birds but the
flowers called orchids whose roots grow on the branches
never touching earth. Moss hung there too, a gray-green
strangeness; I had never seen more than a little of it on the
Skoar side of the mountain, but here it grew dense, making
me think of dusty curtains swaying to a breeze I could not
feel.

In this man-forgotten place, the mue stopped, glanced up
into the vine-bound branches and studied my legs and arms,
bothered. "You can't," he said, and showed me what he
meant by catching a loop of vine and swarming up hand over
hand till in a moment he was thirty feet above ground. There
he swung, and launched his great bulk across a gap, catching
another loop, and another. A hundred feet away, he shifted
his arms so quickly I could not follow the motion, and came
swinging back above me. Now I'm clever in the trees, but my
arms are merely human, not that good. He called down

softly: "You go ground? Not far. Bad thing come, I help quick."

So I went ground. It was nasty walking – thicket, groundvines, fallen branches, dead logs where fire-ants would be living. The fat black-and-gold orb-spiders liked this place and had their dainty-looking homes everywere; their bite can't kill, but will make you wish it would. I had to think of snake and scorpion too, and listen for any noise in the brush that wasn't my own. I struggled through maybe a quarter-mile of that stuff, knowing the mue was near me but often unable to see or hear him, before I came up against a network of cat-brier, and there I was stopped.

Ten-foot elastic stems, tougher than moose-tendon and barbed every inch, growing so close they'd built a sort of basket-weave. Brown tiger himself, with his shoe-leather hide and three inches of fur, would never try it. Then beyond that barricade I saw what could have been the tallest tree in Moha.

A tulip tree twelve feet through at the base and I'm not lying. The wild grape had found it long ago and gone rioting up into the sunshine, but might not kill the giant for another hundred years. My mue was up there, calling, pointing out a place on my side where a stem of the vine thick as my wrist grew up straight for thirty feet and connected with the strands around the tulip tree. Well, that I could manage. I shinnied up, and worked over to the great tree along a dizzy-sagging horizontal vine. The mue grasped my foot and set it gently on a solid branch.

As soon as he was sure of my safety he began climbing, and I followed – I don't know how far up, call it sixty feet more. It was easy enough, like a ladder. The side-branches had become smaller, the vine-leaves thicker in the increase of sunshine, when we reached an obstruction of crossed sticks and interwoven vine. No eagle's nest as I foolishly thought at first – no bird ever moved sticks of that size.

The mue walked out on the branch below this structure and hoisted himself to the next limb. Up beside him, I could understand it. A nest, yes, five feet across, built on a double crotch, woven as shrewdly as any willow basket I ever saw in the Corn Market, and thickly lined with gray moss. He let

himself down into his home and his sad mouth grinned. I
grinned back – I couldn't help it – and followed, with more
caution than I needed, for the thing was solid as a house. It
was a house.

He talked to me.

I felt no sense of dreaming, as people sometimes say they
do in a time of strangeness. But didn't you, in childhood,
play the game of imaginary countries? Promise yourself, say,
that if you passed through the gap of a forked tree-trunk
you'd be in a different world? Then if you did in the flesh step
through such a tree, you learned that you must still rely on
make-believe, didn't you? And that hurt, some. It cut a few
of the threads of your fancy. But suppose that after passing
through your tree-fork, you had been met in solid truth by –
oh, a gnome, dragon, fairy-tale princess. . . . But time moved
curiously for me there in the mue's nest, and all the inner life
of me – thought, vision, ignorance, wonder – was the life of
someone who had not existed before that day. I think we
never do know yesterday any better than we know
tomorrow.

He was fingering my shirt. "Cloth?" he said, and I
nodded. "Is beautiful." A rarely dirty old shirt, I'd patched
it myself a dozen times. But he liked that word "beautiful"
and to him I suppose it meant many things it wouldn't to you
or me. "See you before," he told me. "Times ago."

He must have meant he'd watched me secretly on my
other visits to North Mountain, from high in a tree or rock-
still in a thicket. To guess it would have scared me gutless;
learning of it now I only felt silly, me with my sharp eyes and
ears and nose – studied all this time and never a hint of it.

Then he was telling me about his life. I won't try to record
much of his actual talk, the jumbled half-swallowed words,
pauses when he could find no word at all. Some of it I
couldn't understand, gaps that caught no light from my few
clumsy questions.

He was born somewhere in the northeast. He waved that
way; from our height, it was all a green sea under sunshine.
He said "ten sleeps," but I don't know what distance he
could have covered in a day at the time he left his birthplace.

His mother, evidently a farm woman, had born him secretly in a cave in the woods. "Mother's man die before that" – I think he was speaking of his father, or should I say the man who would have been his father if he had not been devil-begotten?

Describing his mother, all he could say was "Big, good." I could piece it out from Bull and Iron tales. She must have been some strapping stout woman who'd been able to hide her pregnancy in the early months. The law says every pregnancy must be reported to the authorities at once, no pregnant woman may ever be left alone after the fifth month, and a priest must always be present at the birth to do what's necessary if the birth should be a mue. She evaded that somehow – maybe the death of her husband made it simpler – and bore him and nursed him in secret, raised him to some age between eight and ten with no help except that of a great dog.

The dog was probably one of the tall gray wolfhounds that farm families need if they live outside the village stockade. The bitch guarded the baby constantly while his mother could not be with him, and grew old while he grew up, his closest companion, nurse, friend.

His mother taught him speech, what he had of it, weakened now by years of disuse. Above all, she taught him that he was different, that he must live always in the woods and forever avoid human beings because they would kill him if they found him. She taught him to get a living from the wilderness, hunting, snaring, learning the edible plants and avoiding the poisonous; how to stalk; more important, how to hide. Then, some time between his eighth and tenth year as I understood it – "she come no more."

He waited a long while. The dog stayed with him of course, hunted with him and for him, never let him out of her sight until – grown old no doubt but unchanging in devotion because the gray wolfhounds are like that – she was killed fighting off a wild boar.

After that he knew or felt that his mother must have died too, and he had to go away. He couldn't explain the need – "I must go, I." So he made his journey of ten sleeps. I tried to ask him about years. He knew the world dimly, but had never thought of counting the times when the world cooled into the winter rains. Looking back, guessing, I believe he wasn't much more than twenty-five.

During the journey of ten sleeps a hunter had sighted him, shot an arrow into his back, loosed a dog at him. "I must kill the dog, I." He lifted his stub hands with the fingers curling tightly inward to show me how it had been done. A harsh lesson, and it hurt him to remember it, that proof of his mother's teaching, that dogs can sometimes be almost as dangerous as men. "Then man come for me with sharp-end stick, man beautiful." That word again. And again his hands came up, the fingers squeezing life out of a remembered throat. After which he trembled and covered his face, but was watching me I think through a slit between those same curious fingers.

I said: "I would not kill you."

When his hands fell I thought he looked puzzled, as though he had known that all along, no cause for me to say it.

"I show you good thing." He was solemn, lifting himself from the nest and climbing down the tree, this time all the way to the ground. Here a floor of smallish rocks made a circle spreading five or six feet from the base of the tree to the edge of the complete cat-brier barrier, a little fortress. The rocks were all about a foot in diameter, most of them with a flattened part, overlapping so that the brier had no chance to force its way through them. Nature never builds a rock-pile like that; I knew who had – and what a labor, searching out the size and kind he wanted, hundreds of them, transporting them up and down his grape-vine path!

He was watching me more intently, maybe not so trustingly. He said: "Wait here." He stumped off to the other side of the great tree, and I heard the noise of rocks being carefully moved. His body stayed out of sight, but his hands appeared beyond the trunk at my left and set down a slab of stone the size of my head – dull reddish, and I noticed the glint of an embedded quartz pebble. Not then with any ugly intent, just thinking ahead of his poor limited mind the way anyone might, I guessed that would be the marker-stone of some hidey-hole. A moment later he returned to me, carrying a thing whose like I have never seen elsewhere in the world.

Not even in Old City of Nuin, where I later lived awhile, and learned writing and reading, and more about Old Time than it's safe for a man to know.

I thought when I first saw the golden shining of it in his dirty hands that it must be a horn such as hunters and cavalry soldiers use, or one of the screechy brass things – cornets they're called – that I'd heard a few times when Rambler gangs passed through Skoar and gave us their gaudy entertainments in the town green. But this was none of those poor noisemakers.

The large flared end a foot across, the two round coils and straight sections of the pipe between bell and mouthpiece, the three movable pegs (I call them pegs though it doesn't quite rightly describe them) built with impossible smoothness and perfection into the pipe – all these things, and the heavy firmness of the metal, the unbelievable soft gleaming of it, made this a marvel that no one of our world could build.

Ancient coins, knives, spoons, kitchenware that won't rust – such objects of Old-Time magic metal are upturned in plowing now and then, even today. I knew about them. If the thing is simple and has an obvious use, the rule in Moha is finders keepers, if the finder can pay the priest for his trouble in exorcising the bad influence. Mam Robson had a treasure like that, a skillet-thing four inches deep, of shiny gray metal light and very hard that never took a spot of rust. It had been found in plowing by her grandfather, and handed down to her when she married Old Jon. She never used it, but liked to bring it from her bedroom now and then to show the guests, and tell how her mother did use it for cooking and took no harm. Then Old Jon would crash in with the story of how it was found as if he'd been there, clicket-clickety, the Mam watching sidelong and her gloomy horse-face saying *he* wasn't a man who'd ever find her such a thing, not him, miracle if he ever got up off his ass except to scratch. Well, and if the Old-Time object is something for which no reasonable man can imagine a use – a good many are said to be like that – naturally the priest will keep it, and bury it where it can work no damage, men suppose.

Ignorant as I was, I knew before the mue let me take it in my hands that I was looking on a work of ancient days that might be not for any man to touch. It is not gold of course, but as I've said, a metal of Old Time that has no name in our day. I've seen true gold in Old City; its weight is much greater, the feel of it altogether different. But I still call this a golden horn, because I thought of it so for a long time, and now that I know better the name still seems to me somehow true.

"Mother's man's thing," the mue said, and at length passed it to me. He was not happy while, dazed and afraid and wondering, I turned it about in my hands. It gathered light from this shady place and made itself a sun. "She bring me. I little, I. I to keep. She said, I to keep, I." He started once or twice to take it back, the motion uncompleted, and I was too deep in bewilderment to let it go. Then he said: "You blow." So he knew at least that it was a thing for music.

I puffed my cheeks and blew, and nothing happened – a breath-noise and a mutter. The mue laughed, really laughed. Expecting it. He took it from me hastily. "Now I blow, I."

His miserable mouth almost disappeared in the cup, and he did something with his cheeks, not puffing them at all but tightening them till his flat face altered with carven lines. And I heard it speak.

There is no other voice like that on earth. Have you seen an icicle breaking sunshine to a thousand jewels of colored light, and can you in a waking dream imagine that icicle entering your heart with no common pain but with a transfiguration so that the light lives within you, not to die until your own time of dying? You see, it is foolish – I have learned something of music since my childhood, even a great deal as such things are measured, but words will not give you what I know. I've heard the viols they make in Old City that are said to follow a design of Old Time. I've heard singers, a few of them with such voices as men imagine for angels. But there's no other voice like that of the golden horn. And the more I know of music, the less able am I to speak anything of it except in music's own language. Words! Can you talk of color to a man blind from birth? Could I know anything of the ocean until the day came when I stood on the beach and my own eyes saw the blue and gold, the white of foam, the green depth and the gray of distance, and I heard the sigh and thunder, the joy and the lamentation of wave on sand and wind on wave?

The one long note the mue first played – soft, loud, soft, low in pitch – shook me with unbelief. As you might be shaken if the curtain of stars and night were swept aside, and you saw – how should I know what you would see? He pressed one of the pegs, and blew another note. Another peg, another note. Two pegs at once, another. All pure, all clear and strong, changing, fading and swelling and dying out. A single note to each breath – he had no thought of combining them, no notion of melody; I think he never even moved one of the pegs while he blew. I understood presently, in spite of my own thick ignorance, that he, poor jo, had no knowledge at all of the thing he held in his hands. How could he?

Mother's man's thing – had his father known more? A miracle of Old Time, found – where? Hidden away – how? Hidden away surely, I thought, for how could a man play this horn where others heard and not be known at once for a possessor of magic, brought before priests and princes to tell of it, and play it, and no doubt lose it to their itching hands? A miracle of Old Time, carried off to be a toy for a mue-child in the wilderness . . .

"She said, I to keep, I. Good?"

"Good. Yes, good."

He asked, not happily: "You blow now?"

"I daren't."

He seemed relieved by that. He chuckled, and padded away behind the tree hugging the horn. I stayed where I was, hot and cold within. I watched the slab of reddish rock till his hands reached out for it. I heard the chink as it was set in place, and I knew the golden horn had to be mine.

It had to be mine.

He came back smiling and rubbing his lips, no longer concerned about his treasure, while I could think of nothing else. But a mean sort of caution kept me from saying anything more about it. And there was meanness, calculation, in the friendliness I showed him from then on. Almost certain what I meant to do, pushed toward it (so I excused myself) as if by a force outside of me, I acted a part. I grinned, nodded, made noises like his, stared around me as though his dwelling-place were a wonder of the world, while inside me I could think of nothing except how to get at that rock-pile in his absence.

For one thing I will give myself a small trace of honor. I did not again plan to kill him. The power had burned out of that. The idea was there, yes – was painfully strong at moments when he trustingly turned his back or looked away from me. and I remembered how fast my hand was, how quickly I could run, and how I would be praised and honored, not punished, for destroying him. Maybe I understood, without reasoning it through, that I just don't have it in me to kill another being for any reason except hunger or self-defense – anyway I never have, and I've been tempted to it a few times in my travels since that day. Whatever the reason, I did reject the thought of killing him, not purely from cowardice, so for what it's worth, that's my scrap of virtue.

All the same I'm not going to enjoy writing the next page or two. I could lie about what happened – how would you know the difference? Anybody can lie about himself; we all do it every day, trying like sin to show the world an image with all the warts rubbed off. Writing this story for you, some-way I don't want to lie. Merely writing it seems to make the warts your business, so I won't draw myself as a saint or a hero or a wise man. Better just remember, friends, that a lot of the time I've acted almost as bad as you do, and be damned to it.

We climbed up from the cat-brier fortress into the tulip-tree, and I got clever. I asked: "Where is water?"

He pointed off into the jungle. "You want drink? I show you, I."

"Wash too," I said, hoping to get him interested in a brand-new idea. You can see how clever it was – if he ever got serious about washing himself, he had a long project ahead of him. "Washing is good," I said, and touched my arms and face, which happened to be pretty clean. "Dirt comes off in water. Is good, good. Wash."

I think he'd known the word once, though obviously it wasn't one of his favorites. He worked on it, studying my crazy gestures, frowning and mumbling. Then he studied his own skin, what you could see of it through the crust, and all of a sudden the great idea got to him. "Wash!" he said, and chuckled till he drooled, and wiped that away among the other smears. "Wash! I wash *all* me, be like you!"

Well . . . I did have the decency to feel sick. I'm sure he imagined, for a while at least, that I knew how to work some magic with water which would take away his ugliness and make him man-beautiful. I'd never intended that, and now I didn't see how to change the idea or explain it.

And he couldn't wait. He practically pushed me along the grape-vine route, down outside the cat-briers and off through the woods. This time he stayed with me on the ground instead of swinging ahead above me. I think he wanted to keep close, so that he could go on reminding me with grins and mumbles about our wonderful project.

We walked mostly downhill as I'd expected, and it was bad going until he turned off to follow a deer-trail out of the wild-grape area and into a clearer space, which suited me fine. I wanted distance from his home, lots of it. The trees had become well spaced, no more vines overhead, the ground reasonably clear. In country like this I could run like a bird before the wind. Not too soon, we reached the brook he had in mind, and traveled a comfortable distance further before arriving at a pool big enough for bathing, a quiet and lovely place of filtered sunlight and the muttering of cool water. We both studied the tracks of animals who had come to drink here, and found no record of danger, only deer, fox, wildcat, porcupine, whiteface monkey. I dropped my clothes on the bank and slipped into the water, slow and noiseless the way I like to go, while he watched me, scared and doubtful, not quite believing anyone could really do a thing like that.

I beckoned to him with grins and simple words, made a show of scrubbing myself to show him how it was done. At last he ventured in, the big baby, an inch at a time. The pool was narrow but long, nowhere deeper than three feet. I'm glad to remember I didn't try to persuade him to try

swimming – with his poor legs he'd probably have drowned.
But I showed him he could walk or stand in the water and
still have his head well above it. Gradually he caught on,
found himself all the way in and began to love it.

I frolicked around, burning and impatient inside, my head
full of just one thing. When I was sure he was really enjoying
himself and wanted to go on with the great washing thing, I
let him see me look suddenly and anxiously toward the
afternoon sun. He understood I was thinking about time and
the approach of the evening. I said: "I must go back. You
stay here, finish wash. I must go fast. You stay."

He understood but didn't like it. When I'd nipped out on
the bank he started to follow, very slow, clumsy, timid in the
water. "No," I said, "you finish wash." I pointed to the
plentiful dirt still on him, made motions of sloshing water on
my back. "All dirt bad. Washing good, good. You finish
wash. I will come back."

"I finish wash, then I be – "

"Finish wash," I said, cutting that off – so I'll never know,
and didn't want to know, whether he really imagined that
washing would make him man-beautiful. "I must go now
before sun go down."

"To smoke-place, big sticks?" He meant Skoar and its
stockade.

"Yes." And I said again, as plain and friendly (and
treacherous) as I could: "I will come back . . ."

I don't know if he watched me out of sight, for I couldn't
look behind me. Presently I was running, as quickly and
surely as I had ever done in my life, remembering all the
landmarks without thinking of them. Up across the easy
ground, that was hard for him, and into the grapevine
jungle, pulled accurately and fast as if I were bound to the
golden horn by a tightening cord.

Up the grapevine into the tulip tree, and down inside the
brier fortress, finding that red rock at once and lifting it
aside. The horn lay there wrapped in gray-green moss that
was like a cloth, and with hardly a glance to delay me I
shoved it still wrapped into my sack, and was up over the
grapevine, and out, and gone. If the mue had followed me at
his best speed, and I'm sure he didn't follow at all, I would

still have been gone on my way before ever he came in sight
of his home. Yes, I was very clever.

And now, in no danger from him at all, I was running
faster than ever. Like a crazed hunted animal without sense
or caution. Wolf or tiger could have taken me then with no
trouble – but you need to be strangely alive in order to write
words on paper; you notice I'm still living. I couldn't escape
that driving need to run until I had gone all the way around
the east side of the mountain, past the ledge that led to my
cave, and had caught sight of the Skoar church-spires. Then
I collapsed on a fallen log gulping for air.

The skin of my belly hurt horribly. I twitched my shirt
aside and found red-burning skin and the puncture mark.
Why, somewhere, during my mad running after I had stolen
the horn, I must have blundered through an orb-spider's
web, the thing had bitten me, and I hadn't even known it
until now.

It wouldn't kill me. I'd had a bite from one of them before,
on the arm. Needles were doing a jerking jig all over me, and
my guts ached. I wouldn't sleep much, I knew. Tomorrow it
would become an infernal itch for a while, and then stop
hurting.

I wondered, as if someone had spoken aloud to stab me
with the thought, whether I'd ever sleep well again.

I took out the horn with wobbling hands, unwrapping it
from the moss. Oh, the clear splendor, and the shining!
Forest daylight flowed into it and was itself a silent music.
And the horn was mine. Wasn't it?

I raised it to my lips, trembling but compelled. It amazed
me – still does – how naturally the body of the horn rests
against my body, and my right hand moves without
guidance of thought over those three pegs. Did the faraway
makers of the horn leave in it some Old-Time magic that
even now tells the holder of the horn what he must do? – oh,
foolishness; they simply remembered the shape and the
needs of a human body, the way the maker of a simple knife-
hilt will remember the natural shape of a human hand. But
still, still – that kind of thinking and remembering, planning
for necessity but also dreaming your way into the impossible
until it changes and becomes true and real in your hand, isn't

that a kind of magic? And so, many of us are magicians but have never noticed it; anyway I give you the thought if you'll have it.

I did not dare blow into the horn; then I did so in spite of myself, not puffing or straining but breathing gently and, by accident I think, firming my lips and cheeks in what happened to be the right way. It spoke to me.

It was mine.

Only one note, and soft, so light was the breath I dared to use. But it was clear and perfect, the sunlight and the shining transformed to sound, and I knew then there was music hidden here that not the mue, maybe not anyone since the days of Old Time, had ever dreamed of until it came into my hands. And, sick and scared and miserable though I was, I knew it was for me to bring forth that music, or die.

Then I shook with common fright, for what if even that small sound of the horn could travel by some magic around the mountain where the true owner –

But *I* was the true owner. It was mine.

I returned it to the sack and stumbled on down the mountain toward the city. The spider-bite was making me dizzy and slow, a bit feverish. Once I had to stop and heave, all blackness surging around me – any hunting beast could have had me for nothing. That cleared, and I went on. Near the edge of the forest, a hundred yards or so from the stockade, I holed up in a thicket, enough sense left in me to know I must wait for dark and the stockade guards' supper-time.

That was a bad hour. I crouched hugging the horn against my middle where the spider-bite jabbed me with fire-lances. I vomited again once or twice. I couldn't stand it to think of the mue, his friendliness, his human ways, for that would start me wondering what sort of thing *I* was.

There are tales of brain-mues. The most frightful kind of all, for they grow up in the natural human shape, and no one knows they are devil-begotten until, perhaps when they are full-grown, they go through a change that is called madness, behaving like wild beasts, or sometimes forgetting who or where they are, seeing and believing all manner of out-rageous things until their infernal origin becomes known to

everyone and they must be given over to the priests. What if
I –

I could not examine nor tolerate the thought then. It
stayed, at the fringes of my mind, a black wolf waiting.

Yes, a bad hour. Maybe it was also the hour when I
started changing into a man.

The spider-bite was still a blazing misery under my shirt
when it grew dark enough for me to move. All I remember
about the agony of climbing the stockade is that when I
reached the top of it I had to scrounge back out of sight and
wait for a patrolling guard to walk on, and then waste my
strength cussing his lights and gizzard when he met another
guard and they spent ten minutes beating their gums. But
that ended, I was in the city, the heavy burden in my sack
unharmed, and I sneaked along easily enough to the Bull
and Iron, keeping close in the shadow of the buildings.

I saw a light in Emmia's window, though it wasn't late
enough for her bedtime, and when I crept into the stable she
was there, doing my work for me with a lantern. She'd just
done watering the mule team an hour late, and turned to me
quick and sore with a finger at her lips. "They think I'm in
my room. I swear this is the last time I cover up for you,
Davy. What are we going to *do* about you? Don't you live
here any more, Mr Independent?" I couldn't answer. It took
all I had merely to look at her and try to appear human while
I squirmed my sack off and set it on the table floor. I wished
there was more shadow. I pulled my shirt open, and even in
the dim lantern light she noticed the red patch on my belly.
"Davy darling, what happened?" She dropped the water
bucket and hurried to me, with no more thought of scolding,
or of anything except helping me. "What is it?"

"Orb-spider."

"Davy, *boy!* You silly jerk, the way you go wandering off
where all those awful things are, I swear if you was only
small enough to turn over my knee –" and she went on so,
quite a while, the warm soft-mother kind of scolding that
doesn't mean a thing.

"I didn't goof off, Emmia, I thought it was my regular day
off –"

"Oh, *shed* up, Davy, you didn't think never any such thing, why've you got to lie to me? But I won't tell, I said I'd covered up for you, only more fool me if ever I do it again, and you're lucky it's Friday, you wasn't missed. Now look, you go straight up to your bed and I'll bring you a mint-leaf poultice for that nasty bite. The things you get into! Here, take my lantern up with you, I won't need it. Now you –"

"Kay," I said. There was that about Emmia – she was sweet as all summertime, but if you wanted to say anything to her, you had to work a mite fast to get it in. I tried to scoop up my sack without her noticing, but she could be sharp too sometimes, and I was clumsy with the lantern and all.

"Davy, merciful winds, whatever have you got *there*?"

"Nothing."

"Nothing! There you go again, and the thing as big as a house. Davy, if you've gone and taken something you shouldn't –"

"It's nothing!" I was yelling at her, and hurrying for the loft ladder. "If you got to know, it's some special wood I picked up, to carve something for – for your name day, if you *got* to know."

"Davy! Little Spice!" So here she comes for me all in a warm rush. I swung the sack around behind me before a kiss landed – not on my mouth, where I wanted it, because I ducked, but on my eyebrow anyhow, and anyhow a kiss. Well, "little Spice" doesn't mean the same or even half as much as just "Spice." "Please forgive me, Davy, I'm *sorry!* Me scolding you, and all the time you're sick with that awful bite. Here!" I looked up, and she kissed me again, sudden-sweet, full on the mouth.

When my arms tightened around her she pulled away, staring at me deep, her eyes swimming in the lantern-light. She looked surprised, as if nothing like that had ever crossed her mind. "Why, Davy!" she said, dreamy-voiced. "Why, Davy boy. . . ." But then she pulled her wits together. "Now then, straight up to bed with you, and I'll bring you that poultice soon as I can sneak the stuff and slip away with it. I'm not supposed to be here, you know."

I climbed to the loft, not too easily. I was thinking of other things she'd be bringing me, up that ladder. I couldn't make it seem real, yet my heart went to racing and thundering for other reasons than sickness from the bite and memory of what I'd done to a friend.

I hid the sack in the hay near my pallet, carelessly because dizziness and fever from the spider's poison had grown worse. Besides, I had a half-desire to show someone that horn and tell my story. Who but Emmia? Of all the South District boys I knew – few enough, for I never ran with the street gangs – there wasn't a one that I thought would understand or keep quiet about it. I could picture myself being called yellow for not killing the mue and wicked for not reporting it . . .

A chill shook me as I slipped off my loin rag. I kept my shirt on as I crawled under my blanket, and there's a kind of blank stretch when my wits were truly wandering. I know I was trying to fold the blanket double for warmth and making a slithery mess of it when a second blanket was spread over me. Emmia had come back so softly that in sickness and confusion I hadn't seen or heard her. The blanket was wool-soft, full of the special girl-scent of her. From her own bed, and me a dirty yardboy, and a thief. "Emmia –"

"Hush! You're a bit fevery, Davy. Be a good boy now and let me put on this poultice, ha?" Well, I wouldn't stop her, her hands gentle as moth wings easing down the blankets, pressing the cloth with some cool minty stuff where my flesh was burning. "Davy, what was you raving about? Something about where the sun rises – but it's only evening." She brought the blanket back up to my chin, and pushed my arms under it, and I let her, like a baby. "You was talking about going somewhere, and where the sun rises, and funny stuff. You're real light in the head, Davy. You better get to sleep."

I said: "What if a man could go where the sun rises, and see for himself?" Yes, maybe I was light in the head, but it was clearing. I knew where I was, and knew I wanted to tell her and ask her a thousand things. "You go to church better than I do, Emmia, I guess you never miss – is there anything says a man can't go looking, maybe for other lands, go out to sea, maybe a long way?" I believe I went on that way quite a while.

There was no harm in it. She blamed most of it on the fever, which I wasn't feeling any more, and the rest on a boy's wildheadedness. She sat by me with a hand resting light on the blanket over my chest, and now and then said little things like "You're all right, Davy boy," and "It must be nice to travel a bit. I always wished I could . . ."

I felt better merely from the talk. When I quit, the fever from the bite was gone. Leaving the other fever, which I understood fairly well for fourteen, enough to realize that something was wrong with it.

I knew what men did with women. Any South District kid knows that. I knew it was what I wanted with Emmia. I knew she knew it, and wasn't angry. My trouble was fear, cold shadow-fear. Not of Emmia surely – who'd be afraid of Emmia, gentle as spring night, and her face in the dim glow of the lantern a little rose? "Are you warm enough now, Davy?"

"I'm warm, I wish – I wish –

"What, Davy?"

"I wish you was always with me."

She moved quickly, startling me, and was lying beside me, the blankets between us, lying on my right arm so that it couldn't slide around her, and when my other arm tried to she caught my wrist and held it awhile. But her lips were on my forehead and I could feel her breathing hard.

"Davy, Spice, I oughtn't to do this, mustn't. Little Davy. . . ." She let go my wrist. Our hands would wander then, and mine didn't dare. Hers did, straying over the blanket, resting here and there light and warm.

And nothing happened. I knew what ought to happen. It was almost as if someone in deepest shadow was muttering over and over: "I show you good things, I."

And I thought, What if she rolls over and bumps against that horn? – it's right behind her. And, what if Mam Robson, or Judd, or Old Jon –

She sat up brushing a wisp of hay out of her hair and looking angry, but not at me. "I'm sorry, Davy. I'm being foolish."

"We didn't do anything, S-s –"

"What?"

"We didn't do anything, Spice."

"You mustn't call me that. It's my fault, Davy."

"We haven't done anything."

"I don't know what got into me."

"I wanted you to."

"I know, but. . . . We must forget about it." Her voice was different, higher, too controlled, scared. "They'd all be after us."

"Let's run away, you and me."

"Now you're really talking wild." But at least she didn't laugh. No, she sat quiet three feet away from me, her smock tucked neat and careful over her knees, and talked to me awhile sweet and serious. About how I was a good, dear boy except for my wildness, and was going to be a good man, only I must prove myself, and remember that being a man wasn't all fun and freedom, it was hard work too, and responsibility, minding what people said and she meant not only the priests but everybody who lived respectable, learning how to do things the right way, and not dreaming and goofing off. I must work out my bond-period, and save money, and then I'd be free and I could go apprentice and learn a good trade, like for instance inn-keeping, and then some time – why, maybe some time – but right now, she said, why didn't I set myself something sort of difficult to do, a real task, to prove myself, and stay right with it? Not goofing off.

"Like what for instance?"

"Like – oh, I don't know, Davy dear. You should pick it yourself. It should be something – you know, difficult but not impossible, and – and good and honest of course. Then I'll be proud of you. I know I'm right, Davy, you'll see. Now I'm going to say good night, and you go straight to sleep, you hear? And we won't talk about any of this in the morning, either. I wasn't here, understand? You was here all day, and fed the stock yourself." She took up the lantern. "Good night, Davy."

"Good night," I said, and could have tried for another kiss, but instead I lay there like a boy wondering if she'd give me one, which she didn't. She left the lantern by the top of the ladder, blew it out, and was gone.

*

I slept, and I woke in a place full of the black dark of horror. The loft, yes – gradually I knew that, as a dream drained away from me. Some of me, though, was still running mush-footed through a house something like the Bull and Iron but with ten thousand rooms, and the black wolf followed me, slow as I was because he could wait, and snuffling in noises like words: "Look at me, look at me, look at me!" If I looked, he would have me, so I went on, opening doors, every new room strange but with no window, no sunrise-place. Not one of the doors would latch. Sometimes I leaned my back against one, hearing him slobber and whisper at the crack: "Look at me!" He could open it as soon as I took my weight away, and anyway I must go on to the next door, and the next. . . . When I knew I was awake, when I heard my own rustling against the hay and recognized the feel of my pallet, my own voice broke loose in a whimper: "I'm not a brain-mue. I'll prove it, I'll prove it!"

I did get myself in hand. By the time I thought I had courage enough to fumble after the lantern and my flint-and-steel, I no longer needed the light. It was just the loft, with even a trace of moonlight in the one high window. I could wipe the sweat from my body (remembering too late that it was Emmia's blanket) and think awhile.

Something difficult, and good, and honest. I knew soon enough what that had to be. Then it hardly even troubled me that I couldn't tell Emmia of it afterward, for there was much about it that wouldn't seem right to her and so couldn't be explained. I understood there would always be many things I would not be telling to Emmia . . .

When the square of moonlight began to change to a different gray I was dressed and ready, the sack with the horn over my shoulder. Nothing remained of the spider-bite but a nasty itch, and that was fading out.

I went down the ladder, out and away, across the city in the still heavy dark, over the stockade and up the mountain with barely enough light to be sure of my course. I traveled slowly, but I was passing my cave (not pausing even to see if the ants had got after my bacon) when the first-light glory told me that sunrise would arrive within the hour. I didn't see it – when it happened I was passing through that solemn big-tree region where yesterday I might have killed the mue. If I were the killing kind.

In the tangled ugly passage where the grapevines thickened overhead, I caught a wrong smell. Wolf smell.

My knife came out, and was steady in my fingers. My back chilled and tingled, but I think I was more angry than anything else. Angry that I must be halted or threatened by a danger that had nothing to do (I thought) with my errand. I didn't stop, just worked on through the bad undergrowth watching everywhere, sniffing, as nearly ready as I could be, seeing that no one is ever quite ready to die. All the way to the cat-briers.

The black wolf was directly below the strand of grape-vine that hung down outside the mue's tulip-tree, and she was dead. I stepped up to the huge carcass and prodded it with my knife. She stretched maybe six feet from nose to tail-tip, an old one, scarred, dingy black, foul. Her neck was broken. I proved to myself, lifting and prodding, that her neck was broken – if you don't believe it, remember you never saw my North Mountain mue, and his arms. The patches and spatters of blood on the rocks, the ground, the dangling grape-stem, were not hers.

Her body was beginning to stiffen, and cold. It must have happened yesterday, maybe when he came back from the pool, careless perhaps, wondering why he hadn't started changing to man-beautiful.

I set down my sack and climbed the tulip-tree. I called to him a few times. It troubled me that I hadn't any name for him. I called: "Friend? I'm coming up, friend. I brought something back to you." He didn't answer. I knew why, before I reached the branch above his nest and looked down. The carrion ants were already at work, earning their living. I said: "I brought it back. I did steal it, friend, but I brought it back."

I don't remember how many other things I said that would never be answered.

I went back through the forest to my cave, with my golden horn, and the day passed over me. Much of the time I wasn't thinking at all, but in other hours I was. About the thirty-tonners that sail out of Levannon for the northern passage, and then eastward – for the safe Nuin harbors, yes, but eastward, toward the place where the sun is set afire for the day. And I would not go to Levannon on a roan horse, with the blessing and the money of the Kurin family and three attendants, and a serving-maid to warm the bed for me in the next inn. But I would go.

In the afternoon, in the strong light on my ledge, I took out my golden horn, and learned a little. Not a great deal – that day I touched only the fringes of it, but I did discover many notes that the mue had not shown me, and when I ceased to be afraid, the cliff rang, and the voice was clearer than any fancied voice of angels, and it was mine.

Late in the day, I did something like what my poor mue had done. I went up the mountainside well away from my ledge, and with a flat rock I scooped out a pocket in the ground, scattering the earth and wiping out my traces, leaving my golden horn with nothing to mark the place except what was written in my memory. My sack, as well as the mue's gray moss, was wrapped around it, for I knew it was only a little while before I would be coming back for it. In the meantime there was a need.

I waited a long time outside the stockade that night. It must have been midnight, or past, when I climbed it, and crossed the city once more, and stood a foolish while in the darkness watching Emmia's dark window, and the jinny-creeper vine, and hearing the city's last noises dwindle away into nothing. I remember being astonished, so changed was the world (or if you like, myself), that I had never before even dreamed of climbing that vine to her window.

Now it seemed to me that I was afraid of nothing, I was only waiting for a little deeper quiet, a heavier sleep in the old grimy city that had nothing to do with me. Then my hands were on the vine, and I was climbing up through a harmless whisper of leaves, and opening her window all the way, and crossing the sweet-smelling room where I'd never entered before – but her soft breathing told me where she was, and that she slept.

I would have liked to stand there by her bed a long time, feeling her nearness without touching her, just able to make out a little of her face and her arm in the hint of moonlight. I leaned down and spoke her name a few times softly before I kissed her, and she came awake quickly, like a child. "Emmia, it's just me, Davy. Don't be afraid of anything. I'm going away, Emmia."

"No. What – how – what are you doing here? What –"

I closed her mouth, awhile, the best way. Then I said: "I did something difficult, Emmia, and I think it was good and honest too, but I can't ever tell you what it was, so please – please – don't ever ask me."

And so, of course, she asked me, fluttery and troubled and scared but not angry, not pulling away from me. I knew what to do, and words were no part of it, except that many times, after our first plunge into the rainbow, she called me Spice. Other words came later, maybe an hour later: "Davy, you're not going away for true, are you? Don't ever go away, Davy."

"Why, Emmia," I said, "love package, honey spice, what nonsense! Of course I'll never go away."

I think and hope she knew as well as I did that for love's sake I was lying.

KEITH ROBERTS
The Lady Margaret

The year 1968 was one of the best years for SF novels in recent history, seeing the publication of memorable work such as Philip K. Dick's *Do Androids Dream of Electric Sheep?*, R. A. Lafferty's *Past Master*, John Brunner's *Stand on Zanzibar*, Joanna Russ's *Picnic on Paradise*, James Blish's *Black Easter* and Samuel R. Delany's *Nova*, among others. Even in this august company, however, Keith Robert's *Pavane* was a standout: a lyrically written and evocative book with a sweeping historical perspective across several generations, somberly beautiful, full of inventive detail, psychologically complex human characters, and a tragic vision of ordinary men and women doing the best they can against the immense, blank, grinding forces of history; it struck me with enormous force. It holds up just as well in retrospect, more than twenty years later – it is clearly one of the best books of the '60s, and one of the best alternate history novels ever written, rivaled only by books such as L. Sprague de Camp's *Lest Darkness Fall*, Ward Moore's *Bring the Jubilee*, and Philip K. Dick's *The Man in the High Castle*. I have little doubt that it will turn out to be one of the enduring classics of the genre.

"The Lady Margaret" is probably the best of the stories that would later be melded into *Pavane*. In it, he takes us sideways in time to an alternate England where Queen Elizabeth was cut down by an assassin's bullet, and England itself fell to the Spanish Armada – a twentieth-century England where the deep shadow of the Church Militant stretches across a still-medieval land of forests and castles and little huddled towns; an England where travelers alone by night on the desolate, windswept expanses of the heath fear the sudden lantern gleam ahead in the darkness that signals an attack by the remorseless brigands known as *routiers* . . .

Pavane was the first work by Roberts to come to my attention, but he was already an important figure behind the scenes in

Britain by the time of its American publication. Trained as an illustrator – he did work extensively as an illustrator and cover artist in the British SF world of the '60s – Roberts made his first sale to *Science Fantasy* in 1964. Later, he took over the editorship of *Science Fantasy*, by then called *SF Impulse*, as well as providing many of the magazine's striking covers; the *Pavane* stories originally appeared there, in 1966. Roberts's somewhat weak first novel, *The Furies*, appeared in 1966 as well.

By the mid-70s, Roberts was producing some of the best short work in the genre: the brilliant "Weihnachtsabend," "The Grain Kings," "Coranda," "The Big Fans," "I Lose Medea," "The Lake of Tuonela," "The God House," but most of them were underappreciated, and some simply ignored, perhaps because of backlash against the British New Wave movement with which they were associated, although the majority of them are not experimental pieces, but work solidly in the central traditions of the field. "The God House" and a number of other linked stories were melded into *The Chalk Giants*, another marvelously evocative story-cycle, but that book was little noticed in America, perhaps because only a mutilated version of it was ever published in the United States. In fact, in America at least, Roberts's reputation would fade throughout the late '70s and '80s, until, by the beginning of the '90s, he was known only to a small group of insiders and *cognoscenti*. He remains somewhat better known in Britain, although, shamefully, most of his recent books have found no British trade editions either, appearing instead in small-press editions; most of them have had no American publication at all.

Roberts did attract some attention on both sides of the Atlantic, though, with his recent *Kiteworld*. He is still producing first-rate short fiction, and it's one of my foremost hopes for the '90s that this brilliant and severely underappreciated author, one of the most powerful talents to enter the field in the last thirty years, will at last receive some of the attention and acclaim that he deserves.

Roberts's other books include *The Boat of Fate*, one of my favorite historical novels, *The Inner Wheel*, *Molly Zero*, and *Grainne*, and the collections *Machines and Men*, *The Grain Kings*, *The Passing of the Dragons*, *Ladies from Hell*, and *The Lordly Ones*.

Durnovaria, England, 1968.
The appointed morning came, and they buried Eli Strange. The coffin, black and purple drapes twitched aside, eased down into the

grave; the white webbings slid through the hands of the bearers in nomine Patris, et Fili, et Spiritus Sancti. . . . *The earth took back her own. And miles away* Iron Margaret *cried cold and wreathed with steam, drove her great sea-voice across the hills.*

At three in the afternoon the engine sheds were already gloomy with the coming night. Light, blue and vague, filtered through the long strips of the skylights, showing the roof ties stark like angular metal bones. Beneath, the locomotives waited brooding, hulks twice the height of a man, their canopies brushing the rafters. The light gleamed in dull spindle shapes, here from the strappings of a boiler, there from the starred boss of a flywheel. The massive road wheels stood in pools of shadow.

Through the half-dark a man came walking. He moved steadily, whistling between his teeth, boot studs rasping on the worn brick floor. He wore the jeans and heavy reefer jacket of a haulier; the collar of the jacket was turned up against the cold. On his head was a woolen cap, once red, stained now with dirt and oil. The hair that showed beneath it was thickly black. A lamp swung in his hand, sending cusps of light flicking across the maroon livery of the engines.

He stopped by the last locomotive in line and reached up to hang the lamp from her hornplate. He stood a moment gazing at the big shapes of the engines, chafing his hands unconsciously, sensing the faint ever-present stink of smoke and oil. Then he swung onto the footplate of the loco and opened the firebox doors. He crouched, working methodically. The rake scraped against the fire bars; his breath jetted from him, rising in wisps over his shoulder. He laid the fire carefully, wadding paper, adding a crisscrossing of sticks, shoveling coal from the tender with rhythmic swings of his arms. Not too much fire to begin with, not under a cold boiler. Sudden heat meant sudden expansion and that meant cracking, leaks round the fire tube joints, endless trouble. For all their power the locos had to be cosseted like children, coaxed and persuaded to give of their best.

The haulier laid the shovel aside and reached into the firebox mouth to sprinkle paraffin from a can. Then a soaked rag, a match . . . The lucifer flared brightly, sputtering. The

oil caught with a faint *whoomph*. He closed the doors, opened
the damper handles for draught. He straightened up, wiped
his hands on cotton waste, then dropped from the footplate
and began mechanically rubbing the brightwork of the
engine. Over his head, long nameboards carried the style of
the firm in swaggering, curlicued letters: *Strange and Sons of
Dorset, Hauliers*. Lower, on the side of the great boiler, was the
name of the engine herself. The *Lady Margaret*. The hulk of
rag paused when it reached the brass plate; then it polished it
slowly, with loving care.

The *Margaret* hissed softly to herself, cracks of flame light
showing round her ash pan. The shed foreman had filled her
boiler and the belly and tender tanks that afternoon; her
train was linked up across the yard, waiting by the
warehouse loading bays. The haulier added more fuel to the
fire, watched the pressure building slowly toward working
head; lifted the heavy oak wheel scotches, stowed them in the
steamer alongside the packaged water gauge glasses. The
barrel of the loco was warming now, giving out a faint heat
that radiated toward the cab.

The driver looked above him broodingly at the skylights.
Mid-December; and it seemed as always God was stinting
the light itself so the days came and vanished like the
blinking of a dim gray eye. The frost would come down hard
as well, later on. It was freezing already; in the yard the
puddles had crashed and tinkled under his boots, the skin of
ice from the night before barely thinned. Bad weather for the
hauliers, many of them had packed up already. This was the
time for the wolves to leave their shelter, what wolves there
were left. And the *routiers* . . . this was their season right
enough, ideal for quick raids and swoopings, rich hauls from
the last road trains of the winter. The man shrugged under
his coat. This would be the last run to the coast for a month
or so at least, unless that old goat Serjeantson across the way
tried a quick dash with his vaunted Fowler triple compound.
In that case the *Margaret* would go out again; because
Strange and Sons made the last run to the coast. Always had,
always would . . .

Working head, a hundred and fifty pounds to the inch.
The driver hooked the hand lamp over the push pole bracket

on the front of the smokebox, climbed back to the footplate, checked gear for neutral, opened the cylinder cocks, inched the regulator across. The *Lady Margaret* woke up, pistons thumping, crossheads sliding in their guides, exhaust beating sudden thunder under the low roof. Steam whirled back and smoke, thick and cindery, catching at the throat. The driver grinned faintly and without humor. The starting drill was a part of him, burned on his mind. Gear check, cylinder cocks, regulator. . . . He'd missed out just once, years back when he was a boy, opened up a four-horse Roby traction with her cocks shut, let the condensed water in front of the piston knock the end out of the bore. His heart had broken with the cracking iron; but old Eli had still taken a studded belt, and whipped him till he thought he was going to die.

He closed the cocks, moved the reversing lever to forward full, and opened the regulator again. Old Dickon the yard foreman had materialized in the gloom of the shed; he hauled back on the heavy doors as the *Margaret*, jetting steam, rumbled into the open air, swung across the yard to where her train was parked.

Dickon, coatless despite the cold, snapped the linkage onto the *Lady Margaret*'s drawbar, clicked the brake unions into place. Three waggons, and the water tender; a light enough haul this time. The foreman stood, hands on hips, in breeches and grubby, ruffed shirt, grizzled hair curling over his collar. "Best let I come with 'ee, Master Jesse . . ."

Jesse shook his head somberly, jaw set. They'd been through this before. His father had never believed in overstaffing; he'd worked his few men hard for the wages he paid, and got his money's worth out of them. Though how long that would go on was anybody's guess with the Guild of Mechanics stiffening its attitude all the time. Eli had stayed on the road himself up until a few days before his death; Jesse had steered for him not much more than a week before, taking the *Margaret* round the hill villages topside of Bridport to pick up serge and worsted from the combers there; part of the load that was now outward bound for Poole. There'd been no sitting back in an office chair for old Strange, and his death had left the firm badly shorthanded; pointless taking on fresh drivers now, with the end of the season only days away. Jesse gripped Dickon's shoulder. "We can't spare thee, Dick. Run the yard, see my mother's all right. That's what he'd have wanted." He grimaced briefly. "If I can't take *Margaret* out by now, 'tis time I learned."

He walked back along the train pulling at the lashings of the tarps. The tender and numbers one and two were shipshape, all fast. No need to check the trail load; he'd packed it himself the day before, taken hours over it. He checked it all the same, saw the tail lights and number plate lamp were burning before taking the cargo manifest from Dickon. He climbed back to the footplate, working his hands into the heavy driver's mitts with their leather-padded palms.

The foreman watched him stolidly. "Take care for the *routiers*. Norman bastards . . ."

Jesse grunted. "Let 'em take care for themselves. See to things, Dickon. Expect me tomorrow."

"God be with 'ee . . ."

Jesse eased the regulator forward, raised an arm as the stocky figure fell behind. The *Margaret* and her train clattered under the arch of the yard gate and into the rutted streets of Durnovaria.

Jesse had a lot to occupy his mind as he steered his load into the town; for the moment, the *routiers* were the least of his worries. Now, with the first keen grief just starting to lose its edge, he was beginning to realize how much they'd all miss Eli. The firm was a heavy weight to have hung round his neck without warning; and it could be there were awkward times ahead. With the Church openly backing the clamor of the Guilds for shorter hours and higher pay it looked as if the haulage companies were going to have to tighten their belts again, though God knew profit margins were thin enough already. And there were rumors of more restrictions on the road trains themselves; a maximum of six trailers it would be this time, and a water cart. Reason given had been the increasing congestion round the big towns. That, and the state of the roads; but what else could you expect, Jesse asked himself sourly, when half the tax levied in the country went to buy gold plate for its churches? Maybe though this was just the start of a new trade recession like the one engineered a couple of centuries back by Gisevius. The memory of that still rankled in the West at least. The economy of England was stable now, for the first time in years; stability meant wealth, gold reserves. And gold, stacked anywhere but in the half-legendary coffers of the Vatican, meant danger . . .

Months back Eli, swearing blue fire, had set about getting round the new regulations. He'd had a dozen trailers modified to carry fifty gallons of water in a galvanized tank just abaft the drawbar. The tanks took up next to no space and left the rest of the bed for payload; but they'd be enough to satisfy the sheriff's dignity. Jesse could imagine the old devil cackling at his victory; only he hadn't lived to see it. His thoughts slid back to his father, as irrevocably as the coffin had slid into the earth. He remembered his last sight of him, the grey wax nose peeping above the drapes as the visitors, Eli's drivers among them, filed through the morning room of the old house. Death hadn't softened Eli Strange; it had ravaged the face but left it strong, like the side of a quarried hill.

Queer how when you were driving you seemed to have more time to think. Even driving on your own when you had to watch the boiler gauge, steam head, fire. . . . Jesse's hands felt the familiar thrilling in the wheel rim, the little stresses that on a long run would build and build till countering them brought burning aches to the shoulders and back. Only this was no long run; twenty, twenty-two miles, across to Wool then over the Great Heath to Poole. An easy trip for the *Lady Margaret*, with an easy load; thirty tons at the back of her, and flat ground most of the way. The loco had only two gears; Jesse had started off in high, and that was where he meant to stay. The *Margaret*'s nominal horsepower was ten, but that was on the old rating; one horsepower to be deemed equal of ten circular inches of piston area. Pulling against the brake the Burrell would clock seventy, eighty horse; enough to shift a rolling load of a hundred and thirty tons, old Eli had pulled a train that heavy once for a wager. And won . . .

Jesse checked the pressure gauge, eyes performing their work nearly automatically. Ten pounds under max. All right for a while; he could stoke on the move, he'd done it times enough before, but as yet there was no need. He reached the

first crossroads, glanced right and left and wound at the
wheel, looking behind him to see each waggon of the train
turning sweetly at the same spot. Good; Eli would have liked
that turn. The trail load would pull across the road crown he
knew, but that wasn't his concern. His lamps were burning,
and any drivers who couldn't see the bulk of *Margaret* and her
load deserved the smashing they would get. Forty-odd tons,
rolling and thundering; bad luck on any butterfly cars that
got too close.

Jesse had all the hauliers' ingrained contempt for internal
combustion, though he'd followed the arguments for and
against it keenly enough. Maybe one day petrol propulsion
might amount to something and there was that other system,
what did they call it, *diesel.* . . . But the hand of the Church
would have to be lifted first. The Bull of 1910, *Petroleum Veto*,
had limited the capacity of IC engines to 150 cc, and since
then the hauliers had had no real competition. Petrol
vehicles had been forced to fit gaudy sails to help tow
themselves along; load hauling was a singularly bad joke.

Mother of God, but it was cold! Jesse shrugged himself
deeper into his jacket. The *Lady Margaret* carried no spectacle
plate; a lot of other steamers had installed them now, even
one or two in the Strange fleet, but Eli had sworn not the
Margaret, not on the *Margaret.* . . . She was a work of art,
perfect in herself; as her makers had built her, so she would
stay. Decking her out with gewgaws, the old man had been
half sick at the thought. It would make her look like one of
the railway engines Eli so despised. Jesse narrowed his eyes,
forcing them to see against the searing bite of the wind. He
glanced down at the tachometer. Road speed fifteen miles an
hour, revs one fifty. One gloved hand pulled back on the
reversing lever. Ten was the limit through towns, fixed by
the laws of the realm; and Jesse had no intention of being run
in for exceeding it. The firm of Strange had always kept well
in with the JPs and serjeants of police; it partially accounted
for their success.

Entering the long High Street, he cut his revs again. The
Margaret, balked, made a frustrated thunder; the sound
echoed back, clapping from the fronts of the gray stone
buildings. Jesse felt through his boot soles the slackening

pull on the drawbar and spun the brake wheel; a jack-knifed train was about the worst blot on a driver's record. Reflectors behind the tail lamp flames clicked upward, momentarily doubling their glare. The brakes bit; compensators pulled the trail load first, straightening the waggons. He eased back another notch on the reversing lever; steam admitted in front of the pistons checked *Margaret*'s speed. Ahead were the gas lamps of town centre, high on their standards; beyond, the walls and the East Gate.

The serjeant on duty saluted easily with his halberd, waving the Burrell forward. Jesse shoved at the lever, wound the brakes away from the wheels. Too much stress on the shoes and there could be a fire somewhere in the train; that would be bad, most of the load was inflammable this time.

He ran through the manifest in his mind. The *Margaret* was carrying bale on bale of serge; bulkwise it accounted for most of her cargo. English woolens were famous on the Continent; correspondingly, the serge combers were among the most powerful industrial groups in the Southwest. Their manufactories and storing sheds dotted the villages for miles around; monopoly of the trade had helped keep old Eli out ahead of his rivals. Then there were dyed silks from Anthony Harcourt at Mells; Harcourt shifts were sought after as far abroad as Paris. And crate after crate of turned ware, products of the local bodgers, Erasmus Cox and Jed Roberts of Durnovaria, Jermiah Stringer out of Martinstown. Specie, under the county lieutenant's seal; the last of the season's levies, outward bound for Rome. And machine parts, high grade cheeses, all kinds of oddments. Clay pipes, horn buttons, ribbons and tape; even a shipment of cherrywood Madonnas from that Newworld-financed firm over at Beaminster. What did they call themselves, *Calmers of the Soul, Inc. . . ?* Woolens and worsteds atop the water tender and in waggon number one, turned goods and the rest in number two. The trail load needed no consideration. That would look after itself.

The East Gate showed ahead, and the dark bulk of the wall. Jesse slowed in readiness. There was no need; the odd butterfly cars that were still braving the elements on this bitter night were already stopped, held back out of harm's

way by the signals of the halberdiers. The *Margaret* hooted,
left behind a cloud of steam that hung glowing against the
evening sky. Passed through the ramparts to the heath and
hills beyond.

Jesse reached down to twirl the control of the injector
valve. Water, preheated by its passage through an extension
of the smokebox, swirled into the boiler. He allowed the
engine to build up speed. Durnovaria vanished, lost in the
gloom astern; the light was fading fast now. To right and left
the land was featureless, dark; in front of him was the half-
seen whirling of the crankshaft, the big thunder of the
engine. The haulier grinned, still exhilarated by the physical
act of driving. Flame light striking round the firebox doors
showed the side, hard jaw, the deep-set eyes under brows
that were level and thickly black. Just let old Serjeantson try
and sneak in a last trip. The *Margaret* would take his Fowler,
uphill or down; and Eli would churn with glee in his fresh-
made grave . . .

The *Lady Margaret*. A scene came unasked into Jesse's
mind. He saw himself as a boy, voice half broken. How long
ago was that, eight seasons, ten? The years had a way of
piling themselves one atop the next, unnoticed and un-
counted; that was how young men turned into old ones. He
remembered the morning the *Margaret* first arrived in the
yard. She'd come snorting and plunging through
Durnovaria, fresh from Burrell's works in far-off Thetford,
paintwork gleaming, whistle sounding, brasswork a-twinkle
in the sun; a compound locomotive of ten NHP, all her
details specified from flywheel decoration to static discharge
chains. Spud pan, belly pan, water lifts; Eli had got what he
wanted all right, one of the finest steamers in the West. He'd
fetched her himself, making the awkward journey across
many counties to Norfork; nobody else had been trusted to
bring back the pride of the fleet. And she'd been his steamer
ever since; if the old granite shell that had called itself Eli
Strange ever loved anything on earth, it had been the huge
Burrell.

Jesse had been there to meet her, and his kid brother Tim
and the others; James and Micah, dead now – God rest their
souls – of the Plague that had taken them both that time in

Bristol. He remembered how his father had swung off the footplate, looked up at the loco standing shaking like a live thing still and spewing steam. The firm's name had been painted there already, the letters glowing along the canopy edge, but as yet the Burrell had no name of her own. "What be 'ee g'wine call 'en?" his mother had shouted, over the noise of her idling; and Eli had rumpled his hair, pucked his red face. "Danged if I knows. . . ." They had *Thunderer* already and *Apocalypse*, *Oberon* and *Ballard Down* and *Western Strength*; big-sounding names, right for the machines that carried them. "Danged if I *knows*," said old Eli, grinning; and Jesse's voice had spoken without his permission, faltering up in its adolescent yodel. "The *Lady Margaret*, sir . . . *Lady Margaret*. . . ."

A bad thing that, speaking without being addressed. Eli had glared, shoved up his cap, scrubbed at his hair again and burst into a roar of laughter. "I *like* en . . . bugger me if I *don't* like en. . . ." And the *Lady Margaret* she had become, over the protests of his drivers, even over old Dickon's head. He claimed it "were downright luck" to call a loco after "some bloody 'oman. . . ." Jesse remembered his ears burning, he couldn't tell whether with shame or pride. He'd unwished the name a thousand times, but it had stuck. Eli liked it; and nobody crossed old Strange, not in the days of his strength.

So Eli was dead. There'd been no warning; just the coughing, the hands gripping the chair arms, the face that suddenly wasn't his father's face, staring. Quick dark spattering of blood, the lungs sighing and bubbling; and a clay-colored old man lying abed, one lamp burning, the priest in attendance, Jesse's mother watching empty-faced. Father Thomas had been cold, disapproving of the old sinner; the wind had soughed round the house vicious with frost while the priest's lips absolved and mechanically blessed . . . but that hadn't been death. A death was more than an ending; it was like pulling a thread from a richly patterned cloth. Eli had been a part of Jesse's life, as much part as his bedroom under the eaves of the old house. Death disrupted the processes of memory, jangled old chords that were maybe best left alone. It took so little imagination for Jesse to see his father still, the craggy face, weathered hands, haulier's greasy buckled cap pulled low over his eyes. The knotted muffler, ends anchored round the braces, the greatcoat, old thick working corduroys. It was here he missed him, in the clanking and the darkness, with the hot smell of oil, smoke blowing back from the tall stack to burn his eyes. This was how he'd known it would be. Maybe this was what he'd wanted.

Time to feed the brute. Jesse took a quick look at the road stretching out straight in front of him. The steamer would hold her course, the worm steering couldn't kick back. He opened the firebox doors, grabbed the shovel. He stoked the fire quickly and efficiently, keeping it dished for maximum heat. Swung the doors shut, straightened up again. The steady thunder of the loco was part of him already, in his bloodstream. Heat struck up from the metal of the footplate, working through his boots; the warmth from the firebox blew back, breathed against his face. Time later for the frost to reach him, nibbling at his bones.

Jesse had been born in the old house on the outskirts of Durnovaria soon after his father started up in business there with a couple of plowing engines, a thresher, and an Aveling and Porter tractor. The third of four brothers, he'd never seriously expected to own the fortunes of Strange and Sons. But God's ways were as inscrutable as the hills; two Strange boys had gone black-faced to Abraham's bosom, now Eli himself. . . . Jesse thought back to long summers spent at home, summers when the engine sheds were boiling hot and reeking of smoke and oil. He'd spend his days there, watching the trains come in and leave, helping unload on the warehouse steps, climbing over the endless stacks of crates and bales. There too were scents; richness of dried fruits in their boxes, apricots and figs and raisins; sweetness of fresh pine and deal, fragrance of cedarwood, thick headiness of twist tobacco cured in rum. Champagne and Oporto for the luxury trade, cognac, French lace; tangerines and pine-apples, rubber and saltpetre, jute and hemp. . . .

Sometimes he'd cadge rides on the locos, down to Poole or Bourne Mouth, across to Bridport, Wey Mouth; or west down to Isca, Lindinis. He went to Londinium once, and northeast again to Camulodunum. The Burrells and

Claytons and Fodens ate miles; it was good to sit on the trail load of one of those old trains, the engine looking half a mile away, hooting and jetting steam. Jesse would pant on ahead to pay the toll keepers, stay behind to help them close the gates with their long white and red striped bars. He remembered the rumbling of the many wheels, the thick rising of dust from the rutted trackways. The dust lay on the verges and hedges, making the roads look like white scars crossing the land. Odd nights he'd spend away from home, squatting in some corner of a tavern bar while his father caroused. Sometimes Eli would turn morose, and cuff Jesse upstairs to bed; at others he'd get expansive and sit and spin tall tales about when he himself was a boy, when the locos had shafts in front of their boilers and horses between them to steer. Jesse had been a brakeboy at eight, a steersman at ten for some of the shorter runs. It had been a wrench when he'd been sent away to school.

He wondered what had been in Eli's mind. "Get some bliddy eddycation" was all the old man had said. "That's what counts, lad. . . ." Jesse remembered how he'd felt; how he'd wandered in the orchards behind the house, seeing the cherry plums hanging thick on the old trees that were craggy and leaning, just right to climb. The apples, Bramleys and Lanes and Haley's Orange; Commodore pears hanging like rough-skinned bombs against walls mellow with September sunlight. Always before, Jesse had helped bring in the crop; but not this year, not any more. His brothers had learned to write and read and figure in the little village school, and that was all; but Jesse had gone to Sherborne, and stayed on to college in the old university town. He'd worked hard at his languages and sciences, and done well; only there had been something wrong. It had taken him years to realize his hands were missing the touch of oiled steel, his nostrils needed the scent of steam. He'd packed up and come home and started work like any other haulier; and Eli had said not a word. No praise, no condemnation. Jesse shook his head. Deep down he'd always known without any possibility of doubt just what he was going to do. At heart, he was a haulier; like Tim, like Dickon, like old Eli. That was all; and it would have to be enough.

The *Margaret* topped a rise and rumbled onto a down-slope. Jesse glanced at the long gauge glass by his knee and instinct more than vision made him open the injectors, valve water into the boiler. The loco had a long chassis; that meant caution descending hills. Too little water in her barrel and the forward tilt would uncover the firebox crown, melt the fusable plug there. All the steamers carried spares, but fitting one was a job to avoid. It meant drawing the fire, a crawl into a baking-hot firebox, an eternity of wrestling overhead in darkness. Jesse had burned his quota of plugs in his time, like any other tyro; it had taught him to keep his firebox covered. Too high a level on the other hand meant water reaching the steam outlets, descending from the stack in a scalding cloud. He'd had that happen too.

He spun the valve and the hissing of the injectors stopped. The *Margaret* lumbered at the slope, increasing her speed. Jesse pulled back on the reversing lever, screwed the brakes on to check the train; heard the altered beat as the loco felt the rising gradient, and gave her back her steam. Light or dark, he knew every foot of the road; a good driver had to.

A solitary gleam ahead of him told him he was nearing Wool. The *Margaret* shrieked a warning to the village, rumbled through between the shuttered cottages. A straight run now, across the heath to Poole. An hour to the town gates, say another half to get down to the quay. If the traffic holdups weren't too bad. . . . Jesse chafed his hands, worked his shoulders inside his coat. The cold was getting to him now, he could feel it settling in his joints.

He looked out to either side of the road. It was full night, and the Great Heath was pitch black. Far off he saw or thought he saw the glimmer of a will-o'-the wisp, haunting some stinking bog. A chilling wind moaned in from the emptiness. Jesse listened to the steady pounding of the Burrell and as often before the image of a ship came to him. The *Lady Margaret*, a speck of light and warmth, forged through the waste like some vessel crossing a vast and inimical ocean.

This was the twentieth century, the age of reason; but the heath was still the home of superstitious fears. The haunt of wolves and witches, were-things and Fairies; and the *routiers*. . . . Jesse curled his lip. "Norman bastards" Dickon had called them. It was as accurate a description as any. True, they claimed Norman descent; but in this Catholic England of more than a thousand years after the Conquest, bloodlines of Norman, Saxon, and original Celt were hopelessly mixed. What distinctions existed were more or less arbitrary, reintroduced in accordance with the racial theories of Gisevius the Great a couple of centuries ago. Most people had at least a smattering of the five tongues of the land: the Norman French of the ruling classes, Latin of the Church, Modern English of commerce and trade, the outdated Middle English and Celtic of the churls. There were other languages of course: Gaelic, Cornish, and Welsh, all fostered by the Church, kept alive centuries after their use had worn thin. But it was good to chop a land piecemeal, set up barriers of language as well as class. "Divide and rule" had long been the policy, unofficially at least, of Rome.

The *routiers* themselves were surrounded by a mass of legend. There had always been gangs of footpads in the Southwest, probably always would be; they smuggled, they stole, they looted the road trains. Usually, but not invariably, they stopped short at murder. Some years the hauliers suffered worse than others; Jesse could remember the *Lady Margaret* limping home one black night with her steersman dead from a crossbow quarrel, half her train ablaze and old Eli swearing death and destruction. Troops from as far off as Sorviodunum had combed the heath for days, but it had been useless. The gang had dispersed; gone to their homes if Eli's theories had been correct, turned back into honest God-fearing citizens. There'd been nothing on the heath to find; the rumoured strongholds of the outlaws just didn't exist.

Jesse stoked again, shivering inside his coat. The *Margaret* carried no guns; you didn't fight the *routiers* if they came, not if you wanted to stay alive. At least not by conventional methods; Eli had had his own ideas on the matter though he hadn't lived long enough to see them carried out. Jesse set his mouth. If they came, they came; but all they'd get from the firm of Strange they'd be welcome to keep. The business hadn't been built on softness; in this England, haulage wasn't a soft trade.

A mile or so ahead a brook, a tributary of the Frome, crossed the road. On this run the hauliers usually stopped there to replenish their tanks. There were no waterholes on the heath, the cost of making them would be prohibitive. Water standing in earth hollows would turn brackish and foul, unsafe for the boilers: the splashes would have to be concrete lined, and a job like that would set somebody back half a year's profits. Cement manufacture was controlled rigidly by Rome, its price prohibitive. The embargo was deliberate of course; the stuff was far too handy for the erection of quick strong-points. Over the years there had been enough revolts in the country to teach caution even to the Popes.

Jesse, watching ahead, saw the sheen of water or ice. His hand went to the reversing lever and the train brakes. The *Margaret* stopped on the crown of a little bridge. Its parapets bore solemn warnings about "ponderous carriages" but few of the hauliers paid much attention to them after dark at least. He swung down and unstrapped the heavy armored hose from the side of the boiler, slung its end over the bridge. Ice broke with a clatter. The water lifts hissed noisily, steam pouring from their vents. A few minutes and the job was done. The *Margaret* would have made Poole and beyond without trouble; but no haulier worth his salt ever felt truly secure with his tanks less than brimming full. Specially after dark, with the ever-present chance of attack. The steamer was ready now if needs be for a long, hard flight.

Jesse recoiled the hose and took the running lamps out of the tender. Four of them, one for each side of the boiler, two for the front axle. He hung them in place, turning the valves over the carbide, lifting the front glasses to sniff for acetylene. The lamps threw clear white fans of light ahead and to each side, making the frost crystals on the road surface sparkle. Jesse moved off again. The cold was bitter; he guessed several degrees of frost already, and the worst of the night was still to come. This was the part of the journey where you started to think of the cold as a personal enemy. It caught at your throat, drove glassy claws into your back; it was a thing to be fought, continuously, with the body and brain. Cold could stun a man, freeze him on the footplate till his fire burned low and he lost steam and hadn't the sense to stoke. It had happened before; more than one haulier had lost his life like that out on the road. It would happen again.

The *Lady Margaret* bellowed steadily; the wind moaned in across the heath.

On the landward side, the houses and cottages of Poole huddled behind a massive rampart and ditch. Along the fortifications, cressets burned; their light was visible for miles across the waste ground. The *Margaret* raised the line of twinkling sparks, closed with them slowly. In sight of the West Gate Jesse spun the brake wheel and swore. Stretching out from the walls, dimly visible in torchlight, was a confusion of traffic; Burrows, Avelings, Claytons, Fowlers, each loco with a massive train. Officials scurried about; steam plumed into the air; the many engines made a muted thundering. The *Lady Margaret* slowed, jetting white clouds like exhaled breath, edged into the turmoil alongside a ten horse Fowler liveried in the colors of the Merchant Adventurers.

Jesse was fifty yards from the gates, and the jam looked like taking an hour or better to sort out. The air was full of din; the noise of the engines; shouts from the steersmen and drivers, the bawling of town marshalls and traffic wardens. Bands of Pope's Angels wound between the massive wheels, chanting carols and holding up their cups for offerings. Jesse hailed a harassed-looking peeler. The Serjeant grounded his halberd, looked back at the *Lady Margaret*'s load and grinned.

"Bishop Blaize's benison again, friend?"

Jesse grunted an affirmative; alongside, the Fowler let fly by a deafening series of hoots.

"Belay that," roared the policeman. "What've ye got up there, that needs so much hurry?"

The driver, a little sparrow of a man muffled in scarf and greatcoat, spat a cigarette butt overboard. "Shellfish for 'Is 'Oliness," he quipped. "They're burning Rome tonight. . . ." The story of Pope Orlando dining on oysters while his mercenaries sacked Florence had already passed into legend.

"Any more of that," shouted the Serjeant furiously, "and

you'll find the gates shut in your face. You'll lie on the heath all night, and the *routiers* can have their pick of you. Now roll that pile of junk, *roll* it I say. . . ."

A gap had opened ahead; the Fowler thundered contemptuously and moved into it. Jesse followed. An age of shunting and hooting and he was finally past the bottleneck, guiding his train down the long main street of Poole.

Strange and Sons maintained a bonded store on the quay, not far from the old customs house. The *Margaret* threaded her way to it, inching between piles of merchandise that had overflowed from loading bays. The docks were busy for so late in the season; Jesse passed a Scottish collier, a big German freighter, a Frenchman; a Newworlder, an ex-slaver by her raking lines, a handsome Swedish clipper still defiantly under sail; and an old Dutch tramp, the *Groningen*, that he knew to be still equipped with the antiquated and curious mercury boilers. He swung his train eventually into the company warehouse, nearly an hour overdue.

The return load had already been made up; Jesse ditched the down-waggons thankfully, handed over the manifest to the firm's agent and backed onto the new haul. He saw again to the securing of the trail load, built steam, and headed out. The cold was deep inside him now, the windows of the waterfront pubs tempting with their promise of warmth, drink, and hot food; but tonight the *Margaret* wouldn't lie in Poole. It was nearly eight of the clock by the time she reached the ramparts, and the press of traffic was gone. The gates were opened by a surly-faced Serjeant; Jesse guided his train through to the open road. The moon was high now, riding a clear sky, and the cold was intense.

A long drag southwest, across the top of Poole harbour to where the Wareham turn branched left from the road to Durnovaria. Jesse coaxed the waggons round it. He gave the *Margaret* her head, clocking twenty miles an hour on the open road. Then into Wareham, the awkward bend by the railway crossing; past the Black Bear with its monstrous carved sign and over the Frome where it ran into the sea, limning the northern boundary of Purbeck Island. After that the heaths again; Stoborough, Slepe, Middlebere, Norden, empty and vast, full of droning wind. Finally a twinkle of light showed ahead, high off the road and to the right; the *Margaret* thundered into Corvesgeat, the ancient pass through the Purbeck hills. Foursquare in the cutting and commanding the road, the great castle of Corfe squatted atop its mound, windows blazing light like eyes. My Lord of Purbeck must be in residence then, receiving his guests for Christmas.

The steamer circled the high flanks of the *motte*, climbed to the village beyond. She crossed the square, wheels and engine reflecting a hollow clamour from the front of the Greyhound Inn, climbed again through the long main street to where the heath was waiting once more, flat and desolate, haunted by wind and stars.

The Swanage road. Jesse, doped by the cold, fought the idea that the *Margaret* had been running through this void fuming her breath away into blackness like some spirit cursed and bound in a frozen hell. He would have welcomed any sign of life, even of the *routiers*; but there was nothing. Just the endless bitterness of the wind, the darkness stretching out each side of the road. He swung his mittened hands, stamping on the footplate, turning to see the tall shoulders of the load swaying against the night, way back the faint reflection of the tail lamps. He'd long since given up cursing himself for an idiot. He should have laid up at Poole, moved out again with the dawn; he knew that well enough. But tonight he felt obscurely that he was not driving but being driven.

He valved water through the preheater, stoked, valved again. One day they'd swap these solid-burners for oil-fueled machines. The units had been available for years now; but oil firing was still a theory in limbo, awaiting the Papal verdict. Might be a decision next year, or the year after, or maybe not at all. The ways of Mother Church were devious, not to be questioned by the herd.

Old Eli would have fitted oil burners and damned the priests black to their faces, but his drivers and steersmen would have balked at the excommunication that would certainly have followed. Strange and Sons had bowed the knee there, not for the first time and not for the last. Jesse found himself thinking about his father again while the *Margaret* slogged upwards, back into the hills. It was odd;

but *now* he felt he could talk to the old man. *Now* he could explain his hopes, his fears. . . . Only now was too late; because Eli was dead and gone, six foot of Dorset muck on his chest. Was that the way of the world? Did people always feel they could talk, and talk, when it was just that bit too late?

The big mason's yard outside Long Tun Matravers. The piles of stone thrust up, dimly visible in the light of the steamer's lamps, breaking at last the deadly emptiness of the heath. Jesse hooted a warning; the voice of the Burrell rushed across the housetops, mournful and huge. The place was deserted, like a town of the dead. On the right the King's Head showed dim lights; its sign creaked uneasily, rocking in the wind. The *Margaret*'s wheels hit cobbles, slewed; Jesse spun the brakes on, snapping back the reversing lever to cut the power from the pistons. The frost had gathered thickly here, in places the road was like glass. At the crest of the hill into Swanage he twisted the control that locked his differentials. The loco steadied and edged down, groping for her haven. The wind skirled, lifting a spray of snow crystals across her headlights.

The roofs of the little town seemed to cluster under their mantel of frost. Jesse hooted again, the sound enormous between the houses. A gang of kids appeared from somewhere, ran yelling alongside the train. Ahead was a crossroads, and the yellow lamps on the front of the George Hotel. Jesse aimed the loco for the yard entrance, edged forward. The smokestack brushed the passageway overhead. Here was where he needed a mate; the steam from the Burrell, blowing back in the confined space, obscured his vision. The children had vanished; he gentled the reversing lever, easing in. The exhaust beats thrashed back from the walls, then the *Margaret* was clear, rumbling across the yard. The place had been enlarged years back to take the road trains; Jesse pulled across between a Garrett and a six-horse Clayton and Shuttleworth, neutralized the reversing lever and closed the regulator. The pounding stopped at last.

The haulier rubbed his face and stretched. The shoulders of his coat were beaded with ice; he brushed at it and got down stiffly, shoved the scotches under the engine's wheels, valved off her lamps. The hotel yard was deserted, the wind booming in the surrounding roofs; the boiler of the loco seethed gently. Jesse blew her excess steam, banked his fire and shut the dampers, stood on the front axle to set a bucket upside down atop the chimney. The *Margaret* would lie the night now safely. He stood back and looked at the bulk of her still radiating warmth, the faint glint of light from round the ash pan. He took his haversack from the cab and walked to the George to check in.

They showed him his room and left him. He used the loo, washed his face and hands, and left the hotel. A few yards down the street the windows of a pub glowed crimson, light seeping through the drawn curtains. Its sign proclaimed it the Mermaid Inn. He trudged down the alley that ran alongside the bars. The back room was full of talk, the air thick with the fumes of tobacco. The Mermaid was a hauliers' pub; Jesse saw half a score of men he knew, Tom Skinner from Powerstock, Jeff Holroyd from Wey Mouth, two of old Serjeantson's boys. On the road, news travels fast; they crowded round him, talking against each other. He grunted answers, pushing his way to the bar. Yes, his father had had a sudden hemorrhage; no, he hadn't lived long after it. Five of the clock the next afternoon. . . . He pulled his coat open to reach his wallet, gave his order, took the pint and the double Scotch. A poker, thrust glowing into the tankard, mulled the ale; creamy froth spilled down the sides of the pot. The spirit burned Jesse's throat, made his eyes sting. He was fresh off the road; the others made room for him as he crouched knees apart in front of the fire. He swigged at the pint feeling heat invade his crotch, move into his stomach. Somehow his mind could still hear the pounding of the Burrell, the vibration of her wheel was still in his fingers. Time later for talk and questioning; first the warmth. A man had to be warm.

She managed somehow to cross and stand behind him, spoke before he knew she was there. He stopped chafing his hands and straightened awkwardly, conscious now of his height and bulk.

"Hello, Jesse . . ."

Did she know? The thought always came. All those years back when he'd named the Burrell; she'd been a gawky stripling then, all legs and eyes, but she was the Lady he'd meant. She'd been the ghost that haunted him those hot, adolescent nights, trailing her scent among the scents of the garden flowers. He'd been on the steamer when Eli took that monstrous bet, sat and cried like a fool because when the Burrell breasted the last slope she wasn't winning fifty golden guineas for his father, she was panting out the glory of Margaret. But Margaret wasn't a stripling now, not any more; the lamps put bright highlights on her brown hair, her eyes flickered at him, the mouth quirked . . .

He grunted at her. "Evenin', Margaret . . ."

She brought him his meal, set a corner table, sat with him awhile as he ate. That made his breath tighten in his throat; he had to force himself to remember it meant nothing. After all you don't have a father die every week of your life. She wore a chunky costume ring with a bright blue stone; she had a habit of turning it restlessly between her fingers as she talked. The fingers were thin with flat, polished nails, the hands wide across the knuckles like the hands of a boy. He watched her hands now touching her hair, drumming at the table, stroking the ash of a cigarette sideways into a saucer. He could imagine them sweeping, dusting, cleaning, as well as doing the other things, the secret things women must do to themselves.

She asked him what he'd brought down. She always asked that. He said "Lady" briefly, using the jargon of the hauliers. Wondering again if she ever watched the Burrell, if she knew she was the Lady *Margaret*; and whether it would matter to her if she did. Then she brought him another drink and said it was on the house, told him she must go back to the bar now and that she'd see him again.

He watched her through the smoke, laughing with the men. She had an odd laugh, a kind of flat chortle that drew back the top lip and showed the teeth while the eyes watched and mocked. She was a good barmaid, was Margaret; her father was an old haulier, he'd run the house this twenty years. His wife had died a couple of seasons back, the other daughters had married and moved out but Margaret had stayed. She knew a soft touch when she saw one; leastways that was the talk among the hauliers. But that was crazy, running a pub wasn't an easy life. The long hours seven days a week, the polishing and scrubbing, mending and sewing and cooking . . . though they did have a woman in the mornings for the rough work. Jesse knew that like he knew most other things about his Margaret. He knew her shoe size, and that her birthday was in May; he knew she was twenty-four inches round the waist and that she liked Chanel and had a dog called Joe. And he knew she'd sworn never to marry; she'd said running the Mermaid had taught her as much about men as she wanted to learn, five thousand down on the counter would buy her services but nothing else. She'd never met anybody that could raise the half of that, the ban was impossible. But maybe she hadn't said it at all; the village air swam with gossip, and amongst themselves the hauliers yacked like washerwomen.

Jesse pushed his plate away. Abruptly he felt the rising of a black self-contempt. Margaret was the reason for nearly everything; she was why he'd detoured miles out of his way, pulled his train to Swanage for a couple of boxes of *iced* fish that wouldn't repay the hauling back. Well, he'd wanted to see her and he'd seen her. She'd talked to him, sat by him; she wouldn't come to him again. Now he could go. He remembered again the raw sides of a grave, the spattering of earth on Eli's coffin. That was what waited for him, for all God's so-called children; only he'd wait for his death alone. He wanted to drink now, wash out the image in a warm brown haze of alcohol. But not here, not here. . . . He headed for the door.

He collided with the stranger, growled an apology, walked on. He felt his arm caught; he turned back, stared into liquid brown eyes set in a straight-nosed, rakishly handsome face. "No." said the newcomer. "No, I don't believe it. By all tha's unholy, *Jesse Strange* . . ."

For a moment the other's jaunty fringe of a beard baffled him; then Jesse started to grin in spite of himself. "Colin," he said slowly. "Col de la Haye . . ."

Col brought his other arm round to grip Jesse's biceps. "Well, hell," he said. "Jesse, you're lookin' well. This calls f'r a drink, ol' boy. What you bin doin' with yourself? Hell, you're lookin' well . . ."

They leaned in a corner of the bar, full pints in front of them. "God damn, Jesse, that's lousy luck. Los' your ol' man, eh? Tha's rotten. . . ." He lifted his tankard. "To you, ol' Jesse. Happier days . . ."

At college in Sherborne Jesse and Col had been fast friends. It had been the attraction of opposites; Jesse slow-talking, studious, and quiet, de la Haye the rake, the man-about-town. Col was the son of a west country businessman, a feminist and rogue at large; his tutors had always sworn that like the Fielding character he'd been born to be hanged. After college Jesse had lost touch with him. He'd heard vaguely Col had given up the family business; importing and warehousing just hadn't been fast enough for him. He'd apparently spent a time as a strolling *jongleur*, working on a book of ballads that had never got written, had six months on the boards in Londinium before being invalided home the victim of a brawl in a brothel. "A'd show you the scar," said Col, grinning hideously, "but it's a bit bloody awkward in mixed comp'ny, ol' boy. . . ." He'd later become, of all things, a haulier for a firm in Isca. That hadn't lasted long; halfway through his first week he'd howled into Bristol with an eight-horse Clayton and Shuttleworth, unreeled his hose and drained the corporation horse trough in the town center before the peelers ran him in. The Clayton hadn't quite exploded but it had been a near go. He'd tried again, up in Aquae Sulis where he wasn't so well known; that time he lasted six months before a broken gauge glass stripped most of the skin from his ankles. De la Haye had moved on, seeking as he put it "less lethal employment." Jesse chuckled and shook his head. "So what be 'ee doin' now?"

The insolent eyes laughed back at him. "A' trade," said Col breezily. "A' take what comes; a li'l there. . . . Times are hard, we must all live how we can. Drink up, ol' Jesse, the next one's mine. . . ."

They chewed over old times while Margaret served up pints and took the money, raising her eyebrows at Col. The night de la Haye, pot-valiant, had sworn to strip his professor's cherished walnut tree. . . . "A' remember that like it was yes'day," said Col happily. "Lovely ol' moon there was, bright as day. . . ." Jesse had held the ladder while Col climbed; but before he reached the branches the tree was shaken as if by a hurricane. "Nuts comin' down like bloody hailstones," chortled Col. "Y' remember, Jesse, y'must remember. . . . An' there was that . . . that bloody ol' rogue of a peeler Toby Warrilow sittin' up there with his big ol' boots stuck out, shakin' the hell out of that bloody tree. . . ." For weeks after that, even de la Haye had been able to do nothing wrong in the eyes of the law; and a whole dormitory had gorged themselves on walnuts for nearly a month.

There'd been the business of the two nuns stolen from Sherborne Convent; they'd tried to pin that on de la Haye and hadn't quite managed it, but it had been an open secret who was responsible. Girls in Holy Orders had been removed odd times before, but only Col would have taken two at once. And the affair of the Poet and Peasant. The landlord of that inn, thanks to some personal quirk, kept a large ape chained in the stables; Col, evicted after a singularly rowdy night, had managed to slit the creature's collar. The Godforsaken animal caused troubles and panics for a month; men went armed, women stayed indoors. The thing had finally been shot by a militiaman who caught it in his room drinking a bowl of soup.

"So what you goin' to do now?" asked de la Haye, swigging back his sixth or seventh beer. "Is your firm now, no?"

"Aye." Jesse brooded, hands clasped, chin touching his knuckles. "Goin' to run it, I guess . . ."

Col draped an arm round his shoulders. "You be okay," he said. "You be okay pal, why so sad? Hey, tell you what. You get a li'l girl now, you be all right then. Tha's what you need, ol' Jesse; a' know the signs." He punched his friend in the ribs and roared with laughter. "Keep you warm nights better'n a stack of extra blankets. An' stop you getting fat, no?"

Jesse looked faintly startled. "Dunno 'bout *that* . . ."

"Ah, hell," said de la Haye. "Tha's the thing though. Ah, there's nothin' like it. *Mmmmyowwhh.* . . ." He wagged his hips, shut his eyes, drew shapes with his hands, contrived to look rapturous and lascivious at the same time. "Is no trouble now, ol' Jesse," he said, "You loaded now, you know that? Hell, man, you're *eligible*. . . . They come runnin' when they hear, you have to fight 'em off with a . . . a pushpole couplin', no?" He dissolved again in merriment.

Eleven of the clock came round far too quickly. Jesse struggled into his coat, followed Col up the alley beside the pub. It was only when the cold air hit him he realized how stoned he was. He stumbled against de la Haye, then ran into the wall. They reeled along the street laughing, parted company finally at the George. Col, roaring out promises, vanished into the night.

Jesse leaned against the *Margaret*'s rear wheel, head laid back on its struts, and felt the beer fume in his brain. When he closed his eyes a slow movement began; the ground seemed to tilt forward and back under his feet. Man, but that last hour had been good. It had been college all over again; he chuckled helplessly, wiped his forehead with the back of his hand. De la Haye was a no-good bastard all right but a nice guy, nice guy. . . . Jesse opened his eyes blearily, looked up at the road train. Then he moved carefully, hand over hand along the engine, to test her boiler temperature with his palm. He hauled himself to the footplate, opened the firebox doors, spread coal, checked the dampers and water gauge. Everything secure. He tacked across the yard, feeling the odd snow crystals sting his face.

He fiddled with his key in the lock, swung the door open. His room was black and icily cold. He lit the single lantern, left its glass ajar. The candle flame shivered in a draught. He dropped across the bed heavily, lay watching the one point of yellow light sway forward and back. Best get some sleep, make an early start tomorrow. . . . His haversack lay where he'd slung it on the chair but he lacked the strength of will to unpack it now. He shut his eyes.

Almost instantly the images began to swirl. Somewhere in his head the Burrell was pounding; he flexed his hands, feeling the wheel rim thrill between them. That was how the locos got you, after a while; throbbing and throbbing hour on hour till the noise became a part of you, got in the blood and brain so you couldn't live without it. Up at dawn, out on the road, driving till you couldn't stop; Londinium, Aquae Sulis, Isca; stone from the Purbeck quarries, coal from Kimmeridge, wool and grain and worsted, flour and wine, candlesticks, Madonnas, shovels, butter scoops, powder and shot, gold, lead, tin; out on contract to the Army, the Church. . . . Cylinder cocks, dampers, regulator, reversing lever; the high iron shaking of the footplate . . .

He moved restlessly, muttering. The colors in his brain grew sharper. Maroon and gold of livery, red saliva on his father's chin, flowers bright against fresh earth; steam and lamplight, flames, the hard sky clamped against the hills.

His mind toyed with memories of Col, hearing sentences, hearing him laugh; the little intake of breath, squeaky and distinctive, then the sharp machine gun barking while he screwed his eyes shut and hunched his shoulders, pounded with his fist on the counter. Col had promised to look him up in Durnovaria, reeled away shouting he wouldn't forget. But he would forget; he'd lose himself, get involved with some woman, forget the whole business, forget the meeting. Because Col wasn't like Jesse. No planning and waiting for de la Haye, no careful working out of odds; he lived for the moment, vividly. He would never change.

The locos thundered, cranks whirling, crossheads dipping, brass gleaming and tinkling in the wind.

Jesse half sat up, shaking his head. The lamp burned steady now, its flame thin and tall, just vibrating slightly at the tip. The wind boomed, carrying with it the striking of a church clock. He listened, counting. Twelve strokes. He frowned. He'd slept, and dreamed; he'd thought it was nearly dawn. But the long, hard night had barely begun. He lay back with a grunt, feeling drunk but queerly wide awake. He couldn't take his beer any more; he'd had the horrors. Maybe there were more to come.

He started revolving idly the things de la Haye had said. The crack about getting a woman. That was crazy, typical of Col. No trouble maybe for him, but for Jesse there had only ever been one little girl. And she was out of reach.

His mind, spinning, seemed to check and stop quite still. Now, he told himself irritably, forget it. You've got troubles enough, let it go . . . but a part of him stubbornly refused to obey. It turned the pages of mental ledgers, added, subtracted, thrust the totals insistently into his consciousness. He swore, damning de la Haye. The idea, once implanted, wouldn't leave him. It would haunt him now for weeks, maybe years.

He gave himself up, luxuriously, to dreaming. She knew all about him, that was certain; women knew such things unfailingly. He'd given himself away a hundred times, a thousand; little things, a look, a gesture, a word, were all it needed. He'd kissed her once, years back. Only the one time; that was maybe why it had stayed so sharp and bright in his mind, why he could still relive it. It had been a nearly accidental thing; a New Year's Eve, the pub bright and noisy, a score or more of locals seeing the new season in. The church clock striking, the same clock that marked the hours now, doors in the village street popping undone, folk eating mince pies and drinking wine, shouting to each other across the dark, kissing; and she'd put down the tray she was holding, watching him. "Let's not be left out, Jesse," she said. "Us too . . ."

He remembered the sudden thumping of his heart, like the fussing of a loco when her driver gives her steam. She'd turned her face up to him, he'd seen the lips parting; then she was pushing hard, using her tongue, making a little noise deep in her throat. He wondered if she made the sound every time automatically, like a cat purring when you rubbed its fur. And somehow too she'd guided his hand to her breast; it lay cupped there, hot under her dress, burning his palm. He'd tightened his arm across her back then, pulling her onto her toes till she wriggled away gasping. "*Whoosh*," she said. "Well done, Jesse. *Ouch* . . . well done. . . ." Laughing at him again, patting her hair; and all past dreams and future visions had met in one melting point of Time.

He remembered how he'd stoked the loco all the long haul back, tireless, while the wind sang and her wheels crashed through a glowing landscape of jewels. The images were back now; he saw Margaret at a thousand sweet moments, patting, touching, undressing, laughing. And he remembered, suddenly, a hauliers' wedding; the ill-fated marriage of his brother Micah to a girl from Sturminster Newton. The engines burnished to their canopies, beribboned and flag draped, each separate plank of their flatbed trailers gleaming white and scoured; drifts of confetti like bright-coloured snow, the priest standing laughing with his glass of wine, old Eli, hair plastered miraculously flat, incongruous white collar clamped round his neck, beaming and red-faced, waving from the *Margaret*'s footplate a quart of beer. Then, equally abruptly, the scene was gone; and Eli, in his Sunday suit, with his pewter mug and his polished hair, was whirled away into a dark space of wind.

"*Father . . . !*"

Jesse sat up, panting. The little room showed dim, shadows flicking as the candle flame guttered. Outside, the clock chimed for twelve-thirty. He stayed still, squatting on the edge of the bed with his head in his hands. No weddings for him, no gayness. Tomorrow he must go back to a dark and still mourning house; to his father's unsolved worries and the family business and the same ancient, dreary round . . .

In the darkness, the image of Margaret danced like a solitary spark.

He was horrified at what his body was doing. His feet found the flight of wooden stairs, stumbled down them. He felt the cold air in the yard bite at his face. He tried to reason with himself but it seemed his legs would no longer obey him. He felt a sudden gladness, a lightening. You didn't stand the pain of an aching tooth forever; you took yourself to the barber, changed the nagging for a worse quick agony and then for blessed peace. He'd stood this long enough; now it too was to be finished. Instantly, with no more waiting. He told himself ten years of hoping and dreaming, of wanting dumbly like an animal, that has to count. He asked himself, what had he expected her to do? She wouldn't come running to him pleading, throw herself across his feet, women weren't made like that, she had her dignity too. . . . He tried to remember when the gulf between him and Margaret had been fixed. He told himself, never; by no token, no word. . . . He'd never given her a chance, what if she'd been waiting too all these years? Just waiting to be *asked*. . . . It had to be true. He knew, glowingly, it was true. As he tacked along the street, he started to sing.

The watchman loomed from a doorway, a darker shadow, gripping a halberd short.

"You all right, sir?"

The voice, penetrating as if from a distance, brought Jesse up short. He gulped, nodded, grinned. "Yeah. Yeah, sure. . . ." He jerked a thumb behind him. "Brought a . . . train down. Strange, Durnovaria . . ."

The man stood back. His attitude said plainly enough "One o' they beggars. . . ." He said gruffly, "Best get along then, sir, don't want to have to run 'ee in. 'Tis well past twelve o' the clock, y'know . . ."

"On m'way, officer," said Jesse. "On m'way. . . ." A dozen steps along the street he turned back. "Officer . . . you m-married?"

The voice was uncompromising. "Get along now, sir. . . ." Its owner vanished in blackness.

The little town, asleep. Frost glinting on the rooftops, puddles in the road ruts frozen to iron, houses shuttered blind. Somewhere an owl called; or was it the noise of a far-off engine, out there somewhere on the road. . . . The Mermaid was silent, no lights showing. Jesse hammered at the door. Nothing. He knocked louder. A light flickered on across the street. He started to sob for breath. He'd done it all wrong, she wouldn't open. They'd call the watch instead. . . . But she'd know, she'd know who was knocking, women always knew. He beat at the wood, terrified. "*Margaret* . . ."

A shifting glint of yellow; then the door opened with a suddenness that sent him sprawling. He straightened up still breathing hard, trying to focus his eyes. She was standing holding a wrap across her throat, hair tousled. She held a lamp high; then, "*You* . . . *!*" She shut the door with a thump, snatched the bolt across and turned to face him. She said in a low, furious voice, "What the devil do you think you're doing?"

He backed up. "I . . ." he said, "I . . ." He saw her face change. "Jesse," she said, "what's wrong? Are you hurt, what happened?"

"I . . . sorry," he said. "Had to see you, Margaret. Couldn't leave it no more. . . ."

"Hush," she said. Hissed. "You'll wake my father, if you haven't done it already. *What are you talking about?*"

He leaned on the wall, trying to stop the spinning in his head. "Five thousand," he said thickly. "It's . . . nothing, Margaret. Not any more. Margaret, I'm . . . rich, God help me. It don't matter no more. . . ."

"*What?*"

"On the roads," he said desperately. "The . . . hauliers' talk. They said you wanted five thousand. Margaret, I can do ten . . ."

A dawning comprehension. And for God's sake, she was starting to laugh. "Jesse Strange," she said, shaking her head. "What are you trying to say?"

And it was out, at last. "I love you, Margaret," he said simply. "Reckon I always have. And I . . . want you to be my wife."

She stopped smiling then, stood quite still and let her eyes close as if suddenly she was very tired. Then she reached forward quietly and took his hand. "Come on," she said. "Just for a little while. Come and sit down."

In the back bar the firelight was dying. She sat by the hearth curled like a cat, watching him, her eyes big in the dimness; and Jesse talked. He told her everything he'd never imagined himself speaking. How he'd wanted her, and hoped, and known it was no use; how he'd waited so many years he'd nearly forgotten a time when she hadn't filled his mind. She stayed still, holding his fingers, stroking the back of his hand with her thumb, thinking and brooding. He told her how she'd be mistress of the house and have the gardens, the orchards of cherry plums, the rose terraces, the servants, her drawing account in the bank; how she'd have nothing to do any more ever but be Margaret Strange, his wife.

The silence lengthened when he'd finished, till the ticking of the big bar clock sounded loud. She stirred her foot in the warmth of the ashes, wriggling her toes; he gripped her instep softly, spanning it with finger and thumb. "I do love you, Margaret," he said. "I truly do . . ."

She still stayed quiet, staring at nothing visible, eyes opaque. She'd let the shawl fall off her shoulders; he could see her breasts, the nipples pushing against the flimsiness of the nightdress. She frowned, pursed her mouth, looked back at him. "Jesse," she said, "when I've finished talking, will you do something for me? Will you promise?"

Quite suddenly, he was no longer drunk. The whirling and the warmth faded, leaving him shivering. Somewhere he was sure the loco hooted again. "Yes, Margaret," he said. "If that's what you want."

She came and sat by him. "Move up," she whispered. "You're taking all the room." She saw the shivering; she put her hand inside his jacket, rubbed softly. "Stop it," she said. "Don't do that, Jesse. Please . . ."

The spasm passed; she pulled her arm back, flicked at the shawl, gathered her dress round her knees. "When I've said what I'm going to, will you promise to go away? Very quietly, and not . . . make trouble for me? Please, Jesse. I did let you in . . ."

"That's all right," he said. "Don't worry, Margaret, that's all right." His voice, talking, sounded like the voice of a stranger. He didn't want to hear what she had to say; but listening to it meant he could stay close just a little longer. He felt suddenly he knew what it would be like to be given a cigarette just before you were hanged; how every puff would mean another second's life.

She twined her fingers together, looked down at the carpet. "I . . . want to get this just right," she said. "I want to . . . say it properly, Jesse, because I don't want to hurt you. I . . . like you too much for that.

"I . . . knew about it of course, I've known all the time. That was why I let you in. Because I . . . like you very much, Jesse, and didn't want to hurt. And now you see I've . . . trusted you, so you mustn't let me down. I can't marry you, Jesse, because I don't love you. I never will. Can you understand that? It's terribly hard knowing . . . well, how you felt and all that and still having to say it to you but I've got to because it just wouldn't work. I . . . knew this was going to happen sometime, I used to lie awake at night thinking about it, thinking all about you, honestly I did, but it wasn't any good. It just . . . wouldn't work, that's all. So . . . no. I'm terribly sorry but . . . no."

How can a man balance his life on a dream, how can he be such a fool? How can he live, when the dream gets knocked apart. . . ?

She saw his face alter and reached for his hand again. "Jesse, *please* . . . I . . . think you've been terribly sweet waiting all this time and I . . . know about the money, I know why you said that, I know you just wanted to give me a . . . good life. It was terribly sweet of you to think like that about me and I . . . know you'd do it. But it just wouldn't work . . . Oh God, isn't this awful . . ."

You try to wake from what you know is a dream, and you can't. Because you're awake already, this is the dream they call life. You move in the dream and talk, even when something inside you wants to twist and die.

He rubbed her knee, feeling the firm smoothness. "Margaret," he said. "I don't want you to rush into anything. Look, in a couple of months I shall be comin' back through . . ."

She bit her lip. "I knew you were . . . going to say that as well. But . . . no, Jesse. It isn't any use thinking about it, I've tried to and it wouldn't work. I don't want to . . . have to go through this again and hurt you all over another time. Please don't ask me again. Ever."

He thought dully, he couldn't buy her. Couldn't win her, and couldn't buy. Because he wasn't man enough, and that was the simple truth. Just not quite what she wanted. That was what he'd known all along, deep down, but he'd never faced it; he'd kissed his pillows nights, and whispered love for Margaret, because he hadn't dared bring the truth into the light. And now he'd got the rest of time to try and forget . . . this.

She was still watching him. She said, "Please understand . . ."

And he felt better. God preserve him, some weight seemed to shift suddenly and let him talk. "Margaret," he said, "this sounds damn stupid, don't know how to say it . . ."

"Try . . ."

He said, "I don't want to . . . hold you down. It's . . . selfish, like somehow having a . . . bird in a cage, owning it. . . . Only I didn't think on it that way before. Reckon I . . . really love you because I don't want that to happen to you. I wouldn't do anything to hurt. Don't you worry, Margaret, it'll be all right. It'll be all right now. Reckon I'll just . . . well, get out o' your way like . . ."

She put a hand to her head. "God this is awful, I knew it would happen. . . . Jesse don't just . . . well, vanish. You know, go off an' . . . never come back. You see I . . . like you so very much, as a friend, I should feel terrible if you did that. Can't things be like they . . . were before, I mean can't you just sort of . . . come in and see me, like you used to? Don't go right away, please. . . ."

Even that, he thought. *God, I'll do even that.*

She stood up. "And now go. Please . . ."

He nodded dumbly. "It'll be all right. . . ."

"Jesse," she said. "I don't want to . . . get in any deeper. But –" She kissed him, quickly. There was no feeling there this time. No fire. He stood until she let him go; then he walked quickly to the door.

He heard, dimly, his boots ringing on the street. Somewhere a long way off from him was a vague sighing, a susurration; could have been the blood in his ears, could have been the sea. The house doorways and the dark-socketed windows seemed to lurch toward him of their own accord, fall away behind. He felt as a ghost might feel grappling with the concept of death, trying to assimilate an idea too big for its consciousness. There was no Margaret now, not any more. No Margaret. Now he must leave the grown-up world where people married and loved and mated and mattered to each other, go back for all time to his child's universe of oil and steel. And the days would come, and the days would go, till on one of them he would die.

He crossed the road outside the George; then he was walking under the yard entrance, climbing the stairs, opening again the door of his room. Putting out the light, smelling Goody Thompson's fresh-sour sheets.

The bed felt cold as a tomb.

The fishwives woke him, hawking their wares through the streets. Somewhere there was a clanking of milk churns; voices crisped in the cold air of the yard. He lay still, face down, and there was an empty time before the cold new fall of grief. He remembered he was dead; he got up and dressed, not feeling the icy air on his body. He washed, shaved the blue-chinned face of a stranger, went out to the Burrell. Her livery glowed in weak sunlight, topped by a thin bright icing of snow. He opened her firebox, raked the embers of the fire and fed it. He felt no desire to eat; he went down to the quay instead, haggled absentmindedly for the fish he was going to buy, arranged for its delivery to the George. He saw the boxes stowed in time for late service at the church, stayed on for confession. He didn't go near the Mermaid; he wanted nothing now but to leave, get back on the road. He checked the *Lady Margaret* again, polished her nameplates, hubs, flywheel boss. Then he remembered seeing something in a shop window, something he'd intended to buy; a little tableau, the Virgin, Joseph, the Shepherds kneeling, the Christ-child in the manger. He knocked up the storekeeper, bought it and had it packed; his mother set great store by such things, and it would look well on the sideboard over Christmas.

By then it was lunchtime. He made himself eat, swallowing food that tasted like string. He nearly paid his bill before he remembered. Now, it went on account; the account of Strange and Sons of Dorset. After the meal he went to one of the bars of the George, drank to try and wash the sour taste from his mouth. Subconsciously, he found himself waiting; for footsteps, a remembered voice, some message from Margaret to tell him not to go, she'd changed her mind. It was a bad state of mind to get into but he couldn't help himself. No message came.

It was nearly three of the clock before he walked out to the Burrell and built steam. He uncoupled the *Margaret* and turned her, shackled the load to the push pole lug and backed it into the road. A difficult feat but he did it without thinking. He disconnected the loco, brought her round again, hooked on, shoved the reversing lever forward and inched open on the regulator. The rumbling of the wheels started at last. He knew once clear of Purbeck he wouldn't come back. Couldn't, despite his promise. He'd send Tim or one of the others; the thing he had inside him wouldn't stay dead, if he saw her again it would have to be killed all over. And once was more than enough.

He had to pass the pub. The chimney smoked but there was no other sign of life. The train crashed behind him, thunderously obedient. Fifty yards on he used the whistle, over and again, waking *Margaret*'s huge iron voice, filling the street with steam. Childish, but he couldn't stop himself. Then he was clear. Swanage dropping away behind as he climbed toward the heath. He built up speed. He was late; in that other world he seemed to have left so long ago, a man called Dickon would be worrying.

Way off on the left a semaphore stood stark against the sky. He hooted to it, the two pips followed by the long call that all the hauliers used. For a moment the thing stayed dead; then he saw the arms flip an acknowledgement. Out there he knew Zeiss glasses would be trained on the Burrell. The Guildsmen had answered; soon a message would be streaking north along the little local towers. *The* Lady Margaret, *locomotive, Strange and Sons, Durnovaria; out of Swanage routed for Corvesgat, fifteen thirty hours. All well . . .*

Night came quickly; night and the burning frost. Jesse swung west well before Wareham, cutting straight across the heath. The Burrell thundered steadily, gripping the road with her seven-foot drive wheels, leaving thin wraiths of steam behind her in the dark. He stopped once, to fill his tanks and light the lamps, then pushed on again into the heathland. A light mist or frost smoke was forming now; it clung to the hollows of the rough ground, glowing oddly in the light from the side lamps. The wind soughed and threatened. North of the Purbecks, off the narrow coastal strip, the winter could strike quick and hard; come morning the heath could be impassable, the trackways lost under two feet or more of snow.

An hour out from Swanage, and the *Margaret* still singing her tireless song of power. Jesse thought, blearily, that she at least kept faith. The semaphores had lost her now in the dark; there would be no more messages till she made her base. He could imagine old Dickon standing at the yard gate under the flaring cressets, worried, cocking his head to catch the beating of an exhaust miles away. The loco passed through Wool. Soon be home, now; home, to whatever comfort remained . . .

The boarder took him nearly by surprise. The train had
slowed near the crest of a rise when the man ran alongside,
lunged for the footplate step. Jesse heard the scrape of a shoe
on the road; some sixth sense warned him of movement in
the darkness. The shovel was up, swinging for the stranger's
head, before it was checked by an agonized yelp. "Hey ol'
boy, don' you know your friends?"

Jesse, half off balance, grunted and grabbled at the
steering. "*Col.* . . . What the hell are you doin' here?"

De la Haye, still breathing hard, grinned at him in the
reflection of the sidelights. "Jus' a fellow traveler, my friend.
Happy to see you come along there, I tell you. Had a li'l bit of
trouble, thought a'd have to spend the night on the bloody
heath . . ."

"What trouble?"

"Oh, I was ridin' out to a place a' know," said de la Haye.
"Place out by Culliford, li'l farm. Christmas with friends.
Nice daughters. Hey. Jesse, you know?" He punched Jesse's
arm, started to laugh. Jesse set his mouth. "What happened
to your horse?"

"Bloody thing foundered, broke its leg."

"Where?"

"On the road back there," said de la Haye carelessly. "A'
cut its throat an' rolled it in a ditch. Din' want the damn
routiers spottin' it, gettin' on my tail. . . ." He blew his hands,
held them out to the firebox, shivered dramatically inside his
sheepskin coat. "Damn cold, Jesse, cold as a bitch. . . . How
far you go?"

"Home. Durnovaria."

De la Haye peered at him. "Hey, you don' sound good.
You sick, ol' Jesse?"

"No."

Col shook his arm insistently. "Whassamatter, ol' pal?
Anythin' a friend can do to help?"

Jesse ignored him, eyes searching the road ahead. De la
Haye bellowed suddenly with laughter. "Was the beer. The
beer, no? Ol' Jesse, your stomach has shrunk!" He held up a
clenched fist. "Like the stomach of a li'l baby, no? Not the old
Jesse any more; ah, life is hell . . ."

Jesse glanced down at the gauge, turned the belly tank

cocks, heard water splash on the road, touched the injector controls, saw the burst of steam as the lifts fed the boiler. The pounding didn't change its beat. He said steadily, "Reckon it must have bin the beer that done it. Reckon I might go on the waggon. Gettin' old."

De la Haye peered at him again, intently. "Jesse," he said. "You got problems, my son. You got troubles. What gives? C'mon, spill . . ."

That damnable intuition hadn't left him then. He'd had it right through college; seemed somehow to know what you were thinking nearly as soon as it came into your head. It was Col's big weapon; he used it to have his way with women. Jesse laughed bitterly; and suddenly the story was coming out. He didn't want to tell it; but he did, down to the last word. Once started, he couldn't stop.

Col heard him in silence; then he started to shake. The shaking was laughter. He leaned back against the cab side, holding onto a stanchion. "Jesse, Jesse, you are a lad. Christ, you never change. . . . Oh, you bloody Saxon. . . ." He went off into fresh peals, wiped his eyes. "So . . . so she show you her pretty li'l scut, he? Jesse, you are a lad; when will you learn? What, you go to her with . . . with this. . . ." He banged the *Margaret*'s hornplate. "An' your face so earnest an' black, oh, Jesse, a' can see that face of yours. Man, she don' want your great iron *destrier*. Christ above, no. . . . But a' . . . a' tell you what you do . . ."

Jesse turned down the corners of his lips. "Why don't you just *shut up* . . ."

De la Haye shook his arm. "Nah, listen. Don' get mad, listen. You . . . woo her, Jesse; she like that, that one. You know? Get the ol' glad rags on, man, get a butterfly car, mak' its wings of cloth of gold. She like that. . . . Only don' stand no shovin', ol' Jesse. An' don' ask her nothin', not no more. You tell her what you want, say you goin' to get it. . . . Pay for your beer with a golden guinea, tell her you'll tak' the change upstairs, no? She's worth it, Jesse, she's worth havin' is that one. Oh but she's nice . . ."

"Go to hell . . ."

"You don' want her?" De la Haye looked hurt. "A' jus' try to help, ol' pal. . . . You los' interest now?"

"Yeah," said Jesse. "I lost interest."

"Ahhh . . ." Col sighed. "Ah, but is a shame. Young love all blighted. . . . Tell you what though." He brightened. "You given me a great idea, ol' Jesse. You don' want her, a' have her myself. Okay?"

When you hear the wail that means your father's dead your hands go on wiping down a crosshead guide. When the world turns red and flashes, and drums roll inside your skull, your eyes watch ahead at the road, your fingers stay quiet on the wheel. Jesse heard his own voice speak dryly. "You're a lying bastard, Col, you always were. She wouldn't fall for you . . ."

Col snapped his fingers, danced on the footplate. "Man, a' got it halfway made. Oh but she's nice. . . . Those li'l eyes, they were flashin' a bit las' night, no? Is easy, man, easy. . . . A' tell you what, a' bet she be sadistic in bed. But nice, ahhh, *nice*. . . ." His gestures somehow suggested rapture. "I tak' her five ways in a night," he said. "An' send you proof. Okay?"

Maybe he doesn't mean it. Maybe he's lying. But he isn't. I know Col; and Col doesn't lie. Not about this. What he says he'll do, he'll do . . . Jesse grinned, just with his teeth. "You do that, Col. Break her in. Then I take her off you. Okay?"

De la Haye laughed and gripped his shoulder. "Jesse, you are a lad. Eh . . . ? Eh . . . ?"

A light flashed briefly, ahead and to the right, way out on the heathland. Col spun round, stared at where it had been, looked back to Jesse. "You see that?"

Grimly. "I saw."

De la Haye looked round the footplate nervously. "You got a gun?"

"Why?"

"The bloody light. The *routiers* . . ."

"You don't fight the *routiers* with a gun."

Col shook his head. "Man, I hope you know what you're doin' . . ."

Jesse wrenched at the firebox doors, letting out a blaze of light and heat. "Stoke . . ."

"What?"

"*Stoke!*"

"Okay, man," said de la Haye. "All right, Okay. . . ." He

swung the shovel, building the fire. Kicked the doors shut, straightened up. "A' love you an' leave you soon," he said. "When we pass the light. If we pass the light . . ."

The signal, if it had been a signal, was not repeated. The heath stretched out empty and black. Ahead was a long series of ridges; the *Lady Margaret* bellowed heavily, breasting the first of them. Col stared round again uneasily, hung out the cab to look back along the train. The high shoulders of the tarps were vaguely visible in the night. "What you carryin', Jesse?" he asked. "You got the goods?"

Jesse shrugged. "Bulk stuff. Cattle cake, sugar, dried fruit. Not worth their trouble."

De la Haye nodded worriedly. "Wha's in the trail load?"

"Brandy, some silks. Bit of tobacco. Veterinary supply. Animal castrators." He glanced sideways. "Cord grip. Bloodless."

Col looked startled again, then started to laugh. "Jesse, you are a lad. A right bloody lad. . . . But tha's a good load, ol' pal. Nice pickings . . ."

Jesse nodded, feeling empty. "Ten thousand quids' worth. Give or take a few hundred."

De la Haye whistled. "Yeah. Tha's a good load . . ."

They passed the point where the light had appeared, left it behind. Nearly two hours out now, not much longer to run. The *Margaret* came off the down-slope, hit the second rise. The moon slid clear of a cloud, showed the long ribbon of road stretching ahead. They were almost off the heath now, Durnovaria just over the horizon. Jesse saw a track running away to the left before the moon, veiling itself, gave the road back to darkness.

De la Haye gripped his shoulder. "You be fine now," he said. "We passed the bastards. . . . You be all right. I drop off now, ol' pal; thanks for th' ride. An' remember, 'bout the li'l girl. You get in there punchin', you do what a' say. Okay, ol' Jesse?"

Jesse turned to stare at him. "Look after yourself, Col," he said.

The other swung onto the step. "A' be okay. A' be great." He let go, vanished in the night.

He'd misjudged the speed of the Burrell. He rolled

forward, somersaulted on rough grass, sat up grinning. The lights on the steamer's trail load were already fading down the road. There were noises round him; six mounted men showed dark against the sky. They were leading a seventh horse, its saddle empty. Col saw the quick gleam of a gun barrel, the bulky shape of a crossbow. *Routiers.* . . . He got up still laughing, swung onto the spare mount. Ahead the train was losing itself in the low fogbanks. De la Haye raised his arm. "The last waggon. . . ." He rammed his heels into the flanks of his horse, and set off at a flat gallop.

Jesse watched his gauges. Full head, a hundred and fifty pounds in the boiler. His mouth was still grim. It wouldn't be enough; down this next slope, halfway up the long rise beyond, that was where they would take him. He moved the regulator to its farthest position; the *Lady Margaret* started to build speed again, swaying as her wheels found the ruts. She hit the bottom of the slope at twenty-five, slowed as her engine felt the dead pull of the train.

Something struck the nearside hornplate with a ringing crash. An arrow roared overhead, lighting the sky as it went. Jesse smiled, because nothing mattered any more. The *Margaret* seethed and bellowed; he could see the horsemen now, galloping to either side. A pale gleam that could have been the edge of a sheepskin coat. Another concussion, and he tensed himself for the iron shock of a crossbow bolt in his back. It never came. But that was typical of Col de la Haye; he'd steal your woman but not your dignity, he'd take your trail load but not your life. Arrows flew again, but not at the loco. Jesse, craning back past the shoulders of the waggons, saw flames running across the sides of the last tarp.

Halfway up the rise; the *Lady Margaret* labouring, panting with rage. The fire took hold fast, tongues of flame licking forward. Soon they would catch the next trailer in line. Jesse reached down. His hand closed slowly, regretfully, round the emergency release. He eased upward, felt the catch disengage, heard the engine beat slacken as the load came clear. The burning truck slowed, faltered, and began to roll back away from the rest of the train. The horsemen galloped after it as it gathered speed down the slope, clustered round it in a knot of whooping and beating upward with their cloaks at the fire. Col passed them at the run, swung from the saddle and leaped. A scramble, a shout; and the *routiers* bellowed their laughter. Poised on top of the moving load, gesticulating with his one free hand, their leader was pissing valiantly onto the flames.

The *Lady Margaret* had topped the rise when the cloud scud overhead lit with a white glare. The explosion cracked like a monstrous whip; the shock wave slapped at the trailers, skewed the steamer off course. Jesse fought her straight, hearing echoes growl back from distant hills. He leaned out from the footplate, stared down past the shoulders of the load. Behind him twinkled spots of fire where the hell-burner, two score kegs of fine-grain powder packed round with bricks and scrap iron, had scythed the valley clear of life.

Water was low. He worked the injectors, checked the gauge. "We must live how we can," he said, not hearing the words. "We must all live how we can." The firm of Strange had not been built on softness; what you stole from it, you were welcome to keep.

Somewhere a semaphore clacked to Emergency Attention, torches lighting its arms. The *Lady Margaret*, with her train behind her, fled to Durnovaria, huddled ahead in the dim silver elbow of the Frome.

ROGER ZELAZNY

This Moment of the Storm

Like a number of other writers, Roger Zelazny began publishing in 1962 in the pages of Cele Goldsmith's *Amazing*. This was the so-called "Class of '62," whose membership also included Thomas M. Disch, Keith Laumer and Ursula K. Le Guin. Everyone in that "class" would eventually achieve prominence, but some of them would achieve it faster than others, and Zelazny's subsequent career would be one of the most meteoric in the history of SF. The first Zelazny story to attract wide notice was "A Rose for Ecclesiastes," published in 1963. (It was later selected by vote of the SFWA membership to have been one of the best SF stories of all time.) By the end of that decade, he had won two Nebula Awards and two Hugo Awards and was widely regarded as one of the two most important American SF writers of the '60s (the other was Samuel R. Delany).

Zelazny's early novels were, on the whole, well-received (the first half of *This Immortal*, before the giant pigs and giant dogs come out, is excellent), but it was the strong and stylish short work he published in magazines like *F&SF* and *Amazing* and *Worlds of If* throughout the middle years of the decade that electrified the genre. It was these early stories – stories like "The Doors of His Face, the Lamps of His Mouth," "The Graveyard Heart," "He Who Shapes," "The Keys to December," "For a Breath I Tarry," and "This Mortal Mountain" – that established Zelazny as a giant of the field, and that many still consider to be his best work. These stories are still amazing for their invention and elegance and verve, for their good-natured effrontery and easy ostentation, for the risks Zelazny took in pursuit of eloquence without ruffling a hair, the grace and nerve he displayed as he switched from high-flown pseudo-Spenserian to wisecracking Chandlerian slang to vivid prose-poetry to Hemingwayesque starkness in the course of only a few lines – and for the way he made it all look easy and effortless, the same kind of illusion Fred Astaire used to generate when he danced.

The story that follows is Zelazny at the top of his form, writing about the indifference of the universe and the inevitability of time, with unruffled elegance and grace, all wrapped in vivid and atmospheric prose.

After a string of weak books in the '70s, the critics, whose darling he had always been until then, would turn sharply on Zelazny, but he remained popular with the readership. By the end of the '70s, his long series of novels about the enchanted land of Amber – beginning with *Nine Princes in Amber* – had made him one of the best-selling SF and fantasy writers of our time, and inspired the founding of worldwide fan clubs and fanzines. He won Nebula and Hugo Awards in 1976 for his novella "Home Is the Hangman," and another Hugo in 1986 for his novella "24 Views of Mt Fugi, by Hosiki." His books include the novels *This Immortal*, *The Dream Master*, *Lord of Light*, *Isle of the Dead* and *Roadmaps*, and the collections *The Doors of His Face, the Lamps of His Mouth and Other Stories*, and *Frost and Fire*. His most recent novel is *Sign of Chaos*. He lives with his family in Santa Fe, New Mexico.

Back on Earth, my old philosophy prof – possibly because he'd misplaced his lecture notes – came into the classroom one day and scrutinized his sixteen victims for the space of half a minute. Satisfied then, that a sufficiently profound tone had been established, he asked:

"What is a man?"

He had known exactly what he was doing. He'd had an hour and a half to kill, and eleven of the sixteen were coeds (nine of them in liberal arts, and the other two stuck with an Area Requirement).

One of the other two, who was in the pre-med program, proceeded to provide a strict biological classification.

The prof (McNitt was his name, I suddenly recall) nodded then, and asked:

"Is that all?"

And there was his hour and a half.

I learned that Man is the Reasoning Animal, Man is the One Who Laughs, Man is greater than beasts but less than angels, Man is the one who watches himself watch himself doing things he knows are absurd (this from a Comparative Lit gal), Man is the culture-transmitting animal, Man is the spirit which aspires, affirms, loves, the one who uses tools, buries his dead, devises religions, and the one who tries to define himself. (That last from Paul Schwartz, my roommate – which I thought pretty good, on the spur of the moment. Wonder whatever became of Paul?)

Anyhow, to most of these I say "perhaps" or "partly, but –" or just plain "crap!" I still think mine was the best, because I had a chance to try it out, on Tierra del Cygnus, Land of the Swan . . .

I'd said, "Man is the sum total of everything he has done, wishes to do or not to do, and wishes he had done, or hadn't."

Stop and think about it for a minute. It's purposely as general as the others, but it's got room in it for the biology and the laughing and the aspiring, as well as the culture-transmitting, the love, and the room full of mirrors, and the defining. I even left the door open for religion, you'll note. But it's limiting too. Ever met an oyster to whom the final phrases apply?

Tierra del Cygnus, Land of the Swan – delightful name.

Delightful place too, for quite awhile . . .

It was there that I saw Man's definitions, one by one, wiped from off the big blackboard, until only mine was left.

. . . My radio had been playing more static than usual. That's all.

For several hours there was no other indication of what was to come.

My hundred-thirty eyes had watched Betty all morning, on that clear, cool spring day with the sun pouring down its honey and lightning upon the amber fields, flowing through the streets, invading western store-fronts, drying curbstones, and washing the olive and umber buds that spread the skin of the trees there by the roadway; and the light that wrung the blue from the flag before Town Hall made orange mirrors out of windows, chased purple and violet patches across the shoulders of Saint Stephen's Range, some thirty miles distant, and came down upon the forest at its feet like some supernatural madman with a million buckets of paint – each of a different shade of green, yellow, orange, blue and red – to daub with miles-wide brushes at its heaving sea of growth.

Mornings the sky is cobalt, midday is turquoise, and sunset is emeralds and rubies, hard and flashing. It was halfway between cobalt and seamist at eleven hundred hours, when I watched Betty with my hundred-thirty eyes and saw nothing to indicate what was about to be. There was only that persistent piece of static, accompanying the piano and strings within my portable.

It's funny how the mind personifies, engenders. Ships are always women: You say, "She's a good old tub," or, "She's a fast, tough number, this one," slapping a bulwark and feeling the aura of feminity that clings to the vessel's curves; or, conversely, "He's a bastard to start, that little Sam!" as you kick the auxiliary engine in an inland transport-vehicle; and hurricanes are always women, and moons, and seas. Cities, though, are different. Generally, they're neuter. Nobody calls New York or San Francisco "he" or "she." Usually, cities are just "it."

Sometimes, however, they do come to take on the attributes of sex. Usually, this is in the case of small cities near to the Mediterranean, back on Earth. Perhaps this is because of the sex-ridden nouns of the languages which prevail in that vicinity, in which case it tells us more about the inhabitants than it does about the habitations. But I feel that it goes deeper than that.

Betty was Beta Station for less than ten years. After two decades she was Betty officially, by act of Town Council. Why? Well, I felt at the time (ninety-some years ago), and still feel, that it was because she was what she was – a place of rest and repair, of surface-cooked meals and of new voices, new faces, of landscapes, weather, and natural light again, after that long haul through the big night, with its casting away of so much. She is not home, she is seldom destination, but she is like unto both. When you come upon light and warmth and music after darkness and cold silence, it is Woman. The old-time Mediterranean sailor must have felt it when he first spied port at the end of a voyage. *I* felt it when I first saw Beta Station – Betty – and the second time I saw her, also.

I am her Hell Cop.

. . . When six or seven of my hundred-thirty eyes flickered, then saw again, and the music was suddenly washed away by a wave of static, it was then that I began to feel uneasy.

I called Weather Central for a report, and the recorded girlvoice told me that seasonal rains were expected in the afternoon or early evening. I hung up and switched an eye from ventral to dorsal-vision.

Not a cloud. Not a ripple. Only a formation of green-winged skytoads, heading north, crossed the field of the lens.

I switched it back, and I watched the traffic flow, slowly, and without congestion, along Betty's prim, well-tended streets. Three men were leaving the bank and two more were entering. I recognized the three who were leaving, and in my mind I waved as I passed by. All was still at the post office, and patterns of normal activity lay upon the steel mills, the stockyard, the plast-synth plants, the airport, the spacer pads, and the surfaces of all the shopping complexes; vehicles came and went at the Inland Transport-Vehicle garages crawling from the rainbow forest and the mountains beyond like dark slugs, leaving tread-trails to mark their comings and goings through wilderness; and the fields of the countryside were still yellow and brown, with occasional patches of green and pink; the country houses, mainly simple, A-frame affairs, were chisel blade, spike-tooth, spire and steeple, each with a big lightning rod and dipped in many colors and scooped up in the cups of my seeing and dumped out again, as I sent my eyes on their rounds and tended my gallery of one hundred-thirty changing pictures, on the big wall of the Trouble Center, there atop the Watch Tower of Town Hall.

The static came and went until I had to shut off the radio. Fragments of music are worse than no music at all.

My eyes, coasting weightless along magnetic lines, began to blink.

I knew then that we were in for something.

I sent an eye scurrying off toward Saint Stephen's at full speed, which meant a wait of about twenty minutes until it topped the range. Another, I sent straight up, skywards, which meant perhaps ten minutes for a long shot of the same scene. Then I put the auto-scan in full charge of operations and went downstairs for a cup of coffee.

*

I entered the Mayor's outer office, winked at Lottie, the receptionist, and glanced at the inner door.

"Mayor in?" I asked.

I got an occasional smile from Lottie, a slightly heavy, but well-rounded girl of indeterminate age and intermittent acne, but this wasn't one of the occasions.

"Yes," she said, returning to the papers on her desk.

"Alone?"

She nodded, and her earrings danced. Dark eyes and dark complexion, she could have been kind of sharp, if only she'd fix her hair and use more makeup. Well . . .

I crossed to the door and knocked.

"Who?" asked the Mayor.

"Me," I said, opening it, "Godfrey Justin Holmes – 'God' for short. I want someone to drink coffee with, and you're elected."

She turned in her swivel chair, away from the window she had been studying, and her blonde-hair-white-hair-fused, short and parted in the middle, gave a little stir as she turned – like a sunshot snowdrift struck by sudden winds.

She smiled and said, "I'm busy."

Eyes green, chin small, cute little ears – I love them all – from an anonymous Valentine I'd sent her two months previous, and true.

". . . But not too busy to have coffee with God," she stated. "Have a throne, and I'll make us some instant."

I did, and she did.

While she was doing it, I leaned back, lit a cigarette I'd borrowed from her canister, and remarked, "Looks like rain."

"Uh-huh," she said.

"Not just making conversation," I told her. "There's a bad storm brewing somewhere – over Saint Stephen's, I think. I'll know real soon."

"Yes, grandfather," she said, bringing me my coffee. "You old-timers with all your aches and pains are often better than Weather Central, it's an established fact. I won't argue."

She smiled, frowned, then smiled again.

I set my cup on the edge of her desk.

"Just wait and see," I said. "If it makes it over the mountains, it'll be a nasty high-voltage job. It's already jazzing up reception."

Big-bowed white blouse, and black skirt around a well-kept figure. She'd be forty in the fall, but she'd never completely tamed her facial reflexes – which was most engaging, so far as I was concerned. Spontaneity of expression so often vanishes so soon. I could see the sort of child she'd been by looking at her, listening to her now. The thought of being forty was bothering her again, too, I could tell. She always kids me about age when age is bothering her.

See, I'm around thirty-five, actually, which makes me her junior by a bit, but she'd heard her grandfather speak of me when she was a kid, before I came back again this last time. I'd filled out the balance of his two-year term, back when Betty-Beta's first mayor, Wyeth, had died after two months in office. I was born five hundred ninety-seven years ago, on Earth, but I spent about five hundred sixty-two of those years sleeping, during my long jaunts between the stars. I've made a few more trips than a few others; consequently, I am an anachronism. I am really, of course, only as old as I look – but still, people always seem to feel that I've cheated somehow, especially women in their middle years. Sometimes it is most disconcerting . . .

"Eleanor," said I, "your term will be up in November. Are you still thinking of running again?"

She took off her narrow, elegantly trimmed glasses and brushed her eyelids with thumb and forefinger. Then she took a sip of coffee.

"I haven't made up my mind."

"I ask not for press-release purposes," I said, "but for my own."

"Really, I haven't decided," she told me. "I don't know . . ."

"Okay, just checking. Let me know if you do."

I drank some coffee.

After a time, she said, "Dinner Saturday? As usual?"

"Yes, good."

"I'll tell you then."

"Fine – capital."

As she looked down into her coffee, I saw a little girl staring into a pool, waiting for it to clear, to see her reflection or to see the bottom of the pool, or perhaps both.

She smiled at whatever it was she finally saw.

"A bad storm?" she asked me.

"Yep. Feel it in my bones."

"Tell it to go away?"

"Tried. Don't think it will, though."

"Better batten some hatches, then."

"It wouldn't hurt and it might help."

"The weather satellite will be overhead in another half hour. You'll have something sooner?"

"Think so. Probably any minute."

I finished my coffee, washed out the cup.

"Let me know right away what it is."

"Check. Thanks for the coffee."

Lottie was still working and did not look up as I passed.

Upstairs again, my highest eye was now high enough. I stood it on its tail and collected a view of the distance: Fleecy mobs of clouds boiled and frothed on the other side of Saint Stephen's. The mountain range seemed a breakwall, a dam, a ricky shoreline. Beyond it, the waters were troubled.

My other eye was almost in position. I waited the space of half a cigarette, then it delivered me a sight:

Gray, and wet and impenetrable, a curtain across the countryside, that's what I saw.

. . . And advancing.

I called Eleanor.

"It's gonna rain, chillun," I said.

"Worth some sandbags?"

"Possibly."

"Better be ready then. Okay. Thanks."

I returned to my watching.

Tierra del Cygnus, Land of the Swan – delightful name. It refers to both the planet and its sole continent.

How to describe the world, like quick? Well, roughly Earth-size; actually, a bit smaller, and more watery. As for the main land-mass, first hold a mirror up to South America, to get the big bump from the right side over to the left, then rotate it ninety degrees in a counter-clockwise direction and push it up into the northern hemisphere. Got that? Good. Now grab it by the tail and pull. Stretch it another six or seven hundred miles, slimming down the middle as you do, and let the last five or six hundred fall across the equator. There you have Cygnus, its big gulf partly in the tropics, partly not. Just for the sake of thoroughness, while you're about it, break Australia into eight pieces and drop them about at random down in the southern hemisphere, calling them after the first eight letters in the Greek alphabet. Put a big scoop of vanilla at each pole, and don't forget to tilt the globe about eighteen degrees before you leave. Thanks.

I recalled my wandering eyes, and I kept a few of the others turned toward Saint Stephen's until the cloudbanks breasted the range about an hour later. By then, though, the weather satellite had passed over and picked the thing up also. It reported quite an extensive cloud cover on the other side. The storm had sprung up quickly, as they often do here on Cygnus. Often, too, they disperse just as quickly, after an hour or so of heaven's artillery. But then there are the bad ones – sometimes lingering and lingering, and bearing more thunderbolts in their quivers than any Earth storm.

Betty's position, too, is occasionally precarious, though its advantages, in general, offset its liabilities. We are located on the gulf about twenty miles inland, and are approximately three miles removed (in the main) from a major river, the Noble; part of Betty does extend down to its banks, but this is a smaller part. We are almost a strip city, falling mainly into an area some seven miles in length and two miles wide, stretching inland, east from the river, and running roughly parallel to the distant seacoast. Around eighty percent of the one hundred thousand population is concentrated about the business district, five miles in from the river.

We are not the lowest land about, but we are far from being the highest. We are certainly the most level in the area. This latter feature, as well as our nearness to the equator, was a deciding factor in the establishment of Beta Station. Some other things were our proximity both to the ocean and to a large river. There are nine other cities on the continent, all of them younger and smaller, and three of them located upriver from us. We are the potential capital of a potential country.

We're a good, smooth, easy landing site for drop-boats from orbiting interstellar vehicles, and we have major assets for future growth and coordination when it comes to expanding across the continent. Our original *raison d'être*, though, was Stopover, repair-point, supply depot, and refreshment stand, physical and psychological, on the way out to other, more settled worlds, further along the line. Cyg was discovered later than many others – it just happened that way – and the others got off to earlier starts. Hence, the others generally attract more colonists. We are still quite primitive. Self-sufficiency, in order to work on our population:land scale, demanded a society on the order of that of the mid-nineteenth century in the American southwest – at least for purposes of getting started. Even now, Cyg is still partly on a natural economy system, although Earth Central technically determines the coin of the realm.

Why Stopover, if you sleep most of the time between the stars?

Think about it awhile, and I'll tell you later if you're right.

The thunderheads rose in the east, sending billows and streamers this way and that, until it seemed from the formations that Saint Stephen's was a balcony full of monsters, leaning and craning their necks over the rail in the direction of the stage; us. Cloud piled upon slate-colored cloud, and then the wall slowly began to topple.

I heard the first rumbles of thunder almost half an hour after lunch, so I knew it wasn't my stomach.

Despite all my eyes, I moved to a window to watch. It was like a big, gray, aerial glacier plowing the sky.

There was a wind now, for I saw the trees suddenly quiver and bow down. This would be our first storm of the season. The turquoise fell back before it, and finally it smothered the sun itself. Then there were drops upon the windowpane, then rivulets.

Flint-like, the highest peaks of Saint Stephen's scraped its belly and were showered with sparks. After a moment it bumped into something with a terrible crash, and the rivulets on the quartz panes turned into rivers.

I went back to my gallery, to smile at dozens of views of people scurrying for shelter. A smart few had umbrellas and raincoats. The rest ran like blazes. People never pay attention to weather reports; this, I believe, is a constant factor in man's psychological makeup, stemming probably from an ancient tribal distrust of the shaman. You want them to be wrong. If they're right, then they're somehow superior, and this is even more uncomfortable than getting wet.

I remembered then that I had forgotten my raincoat, umbrella and rubbers. But it *had* been a beautiful morning, and WC *could* have been wrong . . .

Well, I had another cigarette and leaned back in my big chair. No storm in the world could knock my eyes out of the sky.

I switched on the filters and sat and watched the rain pour past.

Five hours later it was still raining, and rumbling and dark.

I'd had hopes that it would let up by quitting time, but when Chuck Fuller came around the picture still hadn't changed any. Chuck was my relief that night, the evening Hell Cop.

He seated himself beside my desk.

"You're early," I said. "They don't start paying you for another hour."

"Too wet to do anything but sit. Rather sit here than at home."

"Leaky roof?"

He shook his head.

"Mother-in-law. Visiting again."

I nodded.

"One of the disadvantages of a small world."

He clasped his hands behind his neck and leaned back in the chair, staring off in the direction of the window. I could feel one of his outbursts coming.

"You know how old I am?" he asked, after awhile.

"No," I said, which was a lie. He was twenty-nine.

"Twenty-seven," he told me, "and going to be twenty-eight soon. Know where I've been?"

"No."

"No place, that's where! I was born and raised on this crummy world! And I married and I settled down here – and I've never been off it! Never could afford it when I was younger. Now I've got a family . . ."

He leaned forward again, rested his elbows on his knees, like a kid. Chuck would look like a kid when he was fifty – blond hair, close-cropped, pug nose, kind of scrawny, takes a suntan quickly, and well. Maybe he'd act like a kid at fifty, too. I'll never know.

I didn't say anything because I didn't have anything to say.

He was quiet for a long while again.

Then he said, "*You've* been around."

After a minute, he went on:

"You were born on Earth. Earth! And you visited lots of other worlds too, before I was even born. Earth is only a name to me. And pictures. And all the others – they're the same! Pictures. Names . . ."

I waited, then after I grew tired of waiting I said, "'Miniver Cheevy, child of scorn . . .'"

"What does that mean?"

"It's the beginning to an ancient poem. It's an ancient poem now, but it wasn't really ancient when I was a boy. Just old. *I* had friends, relatives, even in-laws, once myself. They are not just bones now. They are dust. Real dust, not metaphorical dust. The past fifteen years seem fifteen years to me, the same as to you, but they're not. They are already many chapters back in the history books. Whenever you travel between the stars you automatically bury the past. The world you leave will be filled with strangers if you ever return – or caricatures of your friends, your relatives, even yourself. It's no great trick to be a grandfather at sixty, a great-grandfather at seventy-five or eighty – but go away for three hundred years, and then come back and meet your great-great-great-great-great-great-great-great-great-great-great-great-grandson, who happens to be fifty-five years old, and puzzled, when you look him up. It shows you just how alone you really are. You are not simply a man without a country or without a world. You are a man without a time.

You and the centuries do not belong to each other. You are like the rubbish that drifts between the stars."

"It would be worth it," he said.

I laughed. I'd had to listen to his gripes every month or two for over a year and a half. It had never bothered me so much before, so I guess it was a cumulative effect that day – the rain, and Saturday night next, and my recent library visits, *and* his complaining, that had set me off.

His last comment had been too much. "It would be worth it." What could I say to that?

I laughed.

He turned bright red.

"You're laughing at me!"

He stood up and glared down.

"No I'm not," I said, "I'm laughing at me. I shouldn't have been bothered by what you said, but I was. That tells me something funny about me."

"What?"

"I'm getting sentimental in my old age, and that's funny."

"Oh." He turned his back on me and walked over to the window and stared out. Then he jammed his hands into his pockets and turned around and looked at me.

"Aren't you happy?" he asked. "Really, I mean? You've got money, and no strings on you. You could pick up and leave on the next I-V that passes, if you wanted to."

"Sure I'm happy," I told him. "My coffee was cold. Forget it."

"Oh," again. He turned back to the window in time to catch a bright flash full in the face, and to have to compete with thunder to get his next words out. "I'm sorry," I heard him say, as in the distance. "It just seems to me that you should be one of the happiest guys around . . ."

"I am. It's the weather today. It's got everybody down in the mouth, yourself included."

"Yeah, you're right," he said. "Look at it rain, will you? Haven't seen any rain in months . . ."

"They've been saving it all up for today."

He chuckled.

"I'm going down for a cup of coffee and a sandwich before I sign on. Can I bring you anything?"

"No, thanks."

"Okay. See you in a little while."

He walked out whistling. He never stays depressed. Like a kid's moods, his moods, up and down, up and down. . . . And he's a Hell Cop. Probably the worst possible job for him, having to keep his attention in one place for so long. They say the job title comes from the name of an antique flying vehicle – a hellcopper, I think. We send our eyes on their appointed rounds, and they can hover or soar or back up, just like those old machines could. We patrol the city and the adjacent countryside. Law enforcement isn't much of a problem on Cyg. We never peek in windows or send an eye into a building without an invitation. Our testimony is admissible in court – or, if we're fast enough to press a couple buttons, the tape that we make does an even better job – and we can dispatch live or robot cops in a hurry, depending on which will do a better job.

There isn't much crime on Cyg, though, despite the fact that everybody carries a sidearm of some kind, even little kids. Everybody knows pretty much what their neighbors are up to, and there aren't too many places for a fugitive to run. We're mainly aerial traffic cops, with an eye out for local wildlife (which is the reason for all the sidearms).

SPCU is what we call the latter function – Society for the Prevention of Cruelty to Us – which is the reason each of my hundred-thirty eyes has six forty-five caliber eyelashes.

There are things like the cute little panda-puppy – oh, about three feet high at the shoulder when it sits down on its rear like a teddy bear, and with big, square, silky ears, a curly pinto coat, large, limpid, brown eyes, pink tongue, button nose, powder puff tail, sharp little white teeth more poisonous than a Quemeda Island viper's, and possessed of a way with mammal entrails like unto the way of an imaginative cat with a rope of catnip.

Then there's a *snapper*, which *looks* as mean as it sounds: a feathered reptile, with three horns on its armored head – one beneath each eye, like a tusk, and one curving skyward from the top of its nose – legs about eighteen inches long, and a four-foot tail which it raises straight into the air whenever it jogs along at greyhound speed, and which it swings like a sandbag – and a mouth full of long, sharp teeth.

Also, there are amphibious things which come from the ocean by way of the river on occasion. I'd rather not speak of them. They're kind of ugly and vicious.

Anyway, those are some of the reasons why there are Hell Cops – not just on Cyg, but on many, many frontier worlds. I've been employed in that capacity on several of them, and I've found that an experienced HC can always find a job Out Here. It's like being a professional clerk back home.

Chuck took longer than I thought he would, came back after I was technically off duty, looked happy though, so I didn't say anything. There was some pale lipstick on his collar and a grin on his face, so I bade him good morrow, picked up my cane, and departed in the direction of the big washing machine.

It was coming down too hard for me to go the two blocks to my car on foot.

I called a cab and waited another fifteen minutes. Eleanor had decided to keep Mayor's Hours, and she'd departed shortly after lunch; and almost the entire staff had been released an hour early because of the weather. Consequently, Town Hall was full of dark offices and echoes. I waited in the hallway behind the main door, listening to the purr of the rain as it fell, and hearing its gurgle as it found its way into the gutters. It beat the street and shook the windowpanes and made the windows cold to touch.

I'd planned on spending the evening at the library, but I changed my plans as I watched the weather happen – tomorrow, or the next day, I decided. It was an evening for a good meal, a hot bath, my own books and brandy, and early to bed. It was good sleeping weather, if nothing else. A cab pulled up in front of the Hall and blew its horn.

I ran.

The next day the rain let up for perhaps an hour in the morning. Then a slow drizzle began; and it did not stop again.

It went on to become a steady downpour by afternoon.

The following day was Friday, which I always have off, and I was glad that it was.

Put dittoes under Thursday's weather report. That's Friday.

But I decided to do something anyway.

I lived down in that section of town near the river. The Noble was swollen, and the rains kept adding to it. Sewers had begun to clog and back up; water ran in the streets. The rain kept coming down and widening the puddles and lakelets, and it was accompanied by drum solos in the sky and the falling of bright forks and sawblades. Dead skytoads were washed along the gutters, like burnt-out fireworks. Ball lightning drifted across Town Square; Saint Elmo's Fire clung to the flag pole, the Watch Tower, and the big statue of Wyeth trying to look heroic.

I headed uptown to the library, pushing my car slowly through the countless beaded curtains. The big furniture movers in the sky were obviously non-union, because they weren't taking any coffee breaks. Finally, I found a parking place and I umbrellaed my way to the library and entered.

I have become something of a bibliophile in recent years. It is not so much that I hunger and thirst after knowledge, but that I am news-starved.

It all goes back to my position in the big mixmaster. Admitted, there are *some* things faster than light, like the phase velocities of radio waves in ion plasma, or the tips of the ion-modulated light-beams of Duckbill, the comm-setup back in Sol System, whenever the hinges of the beak snap shut on Earth – but these are highly restricted instances, with no application whatsoever to the passage of shiploads of people and objects between the stars. You can't exceed lightspeed when it comes to the movement of matter. You can edge up pretty close, but that's about it.

Life can be suspended though, that's easy – it can be switched off and switched back on again with no trouble at all. This is why *I* have lasted so long. If we can't speed up the ships, we *can* slow down the people – slow them until they stop – and *let* the vessel, moving at near-lightspeed, take half a century, or more if it needs it, to convey its passengers to where they are going. This is why I am very alone. Each little death means resurrection into both another land and another time. I have had several, and *this* is why I have become a bibliophile: news travels slowly, as slowly as the ships and the people. Buy a newspaper before you hop aboard ship and it will still be a newspaper when you reach your destination – but back where you bought it, it would be considered an historical document. Send a letter back to Earth and your correspondent's grandson may be able to get an answer back to your great-grandson, if the message makes real good connections and both kids live long enough.

All the little libraries Out Here are full of rare books – first editions of best sellers which people pick up before they leave Someplace Else, and which they often donate after they've finished. We assume that these books have entered the public domain by the time they reach here, and we reproduce them and circulate our own editions. No author has ever sued, and no reproducer has ever been around to *be* sued by representatives, designates, or assigns.

We are completely autonomous and are always behind the times, because there is a transit-lag which cannot be overcome. Earth Central, therefore, exercises about as much control over us as a boy jiggling a broken string while looking up at his kite.

Perhaps Yeats had something like this in mind when he wrote that fine line, "Things fall apart; the center cannot hold." I doubt it, but I still have to go to the library to read the news.

The day melted around me.

The words flowed across the screen in my booth as I read newspapers and magazines, untouched by human hands, and the waters flowed across Betty's acres, pouring down from the mountains now, washing the floors of the forest, churning our fields to peanut-butter, flooding basements, soaking its way through everything, and tracking our streets with mud.

I hit the library cafeteria for lunch, where I learned from a girl in a green apron and yellow skirts (which swished pleasantly) that the sandbag crews were now hard at work and that there was no eastbound traffic past Town Square.

After lunch I put on my slicker and boots and walked up that way.

Sure enough, the sandbag wall was already waist high across Main Street; but then, the water *was* swirling around at ankle level, and more of it falling every minute.

I looked up at old Wyeth's statue. His halo had gone away now, which was sort of to be expected. It had made an honest mistake and realized it after a short time.

He was holding a pair of glasses in his left hand and sort of glancing down at me, as though a bit apprehensive, wondering perhaps, there inside all that bronze, if I would tell on him now and ruin his hard, wet, greenish splendor. Tell. . . ? I guess I was the only one left around who really remembered the man. He had wanted to be the father of this great new country, literally, and he'd tried awfully hard. Three months in office and I'd had to fill out the rest of the two-year term. The death certificate gave the cause as "heart stoppage," but it didn't mention the piece of lead which had helped slow things down a bit. Everybody involved is gone now: the irate husband, the frightened wife, the coroner. All but me. And I won't tell anybody if Wyeth's statue won't, because he's a hero now, and we need heroes' statues Out Here even more than we do heroes. He *did* engineer a nice piece of relief work during the Butler Township floods, and he may as well be remembered for that.

I winked at my old boss, and the rain dripped from his nose and fell into the puddle at my feet.

I walked back to the library through loud sounds and bright flashes, hearing the splashing and the curses of the work crew as the men began to block off another street. Black, overhead, an eye drifted past. I waved, and the filter snapped up and back down again. I think H. C. John Keams was tending shop that afternoon, but I'm not sure.

Suddenly the heavens opened up and it was like standing under a waterfall.

I reached for a wall and there wasn't one, slipped then, and managed to catch myself with my cane before I flopped. I found a doorway and huddled.

Ten minutes of lightning and thunder followed. Then, after the blindness and the deafness passed away and the rains had eased a bit, I saw that the street (Second Avenue) had become a river. Bearing all sorts of garbage, papers, hats, sticks, mud, it sloshed past my niche, gurgling nastily. It looked to be over my boot tops, so I waited for it to subside.

It didn't.

It got right up in there with me and started to play footsie.

So, then seemed as good a time as any. Things certainly weren't getting any better.

I tried to run, but with filled boots the best you can manage is a fast wade, and my boots were filled after three steps.

That shot the afternoon. How can you concentrate on anything with wet feet? I made it back to the parking lot, then churned my way homeward, feeling like a riverboat captain who really wanted to be a camel driver.

It seemed more like evening than afternoon when I pulled up into my damp but unflooded garage. It seemed more like night than evening in the alley I cut through on the way to my apartment's back entrance. I hadn't seen the sun for several days, and it's funny how much you can miss it when it takes a vacation. The sky was a sable dome, and the high brick walls of the alley were cleaner then I'd ever seen them, despite the shadows.

I stayed close to the lefthand wall, in order to miss some of the rain. As I had driven along the river I'd noticed that it was already reaching after the high water marks on the sides of the piers. The Noble was a big, spoiled, blood sausage, ready to burst its skin. A lightning flash showed me the whole alley, and I slowed in order to avoid puddles.

I moved ahead, thinking of dry socks and dry martinis, turned a corner to the right, and it struck at me: an org.

Half of its segmented body was reared at a forty-five-degree angle above the pavement, which placed its wide head with the traffic-signed eyes saying "Stop" about three and a half feet off the ground, as it rolled toward me on all its pale little legs, with its mouthful of death aimed at my middle.

I pause now in my narrative for a long digression concerning my childhood, which, if you will but consider the circumstances, I was obviously quite fresh on in an instant:

Born, raised, educated on Earth, I had worked two summers in a stockyard while going to college. I still remember the smells and the noises of the cattle; I used to prod them out of the pens and on their way up the last mile. And I remember the smells and noises of the university: the formaldehyde in the Bio labs, the sounds of Freshmen slaughtering French verbs, the overpowering aroma of coffee mixed with cigarette smoke in the Student Union, the splash of the newly pinned frat man as his brothers tossed him into the lagoon down in front of the Art Museum, the sounds of ignored chapel bells and class bells, the smell of the lawn after the year's first mowing (with big, black Andy perched on his grass-chewing monster, baseball cap down to his eyebrows, cigarette somehow not burning his left cheek), and always, always, the *tick-tick-snick-stamp!* as I moved up or down the strip. I had not wanted to take General Physical Education, but four semesters of it were required. The only out was to take a class in a special sport. I picked fencing because tennis, basketball, boxing, wrestling, handball, judo, all sounded too strenuous, and I couldn't afford a set of golf clubs. Little did I suspect what would follow this choice. It was as strenuous as any of the others, and more than several. But I liked it. So I tried out for the team in my Sophomore year, made it on the épée squad, and picked up three varsity letters, because I stuck with it through my Senior year. Which all goes to show: cattle who persevere in looking for an easy way out still wind up in the abattoir, but they may enjoy the trip a little more.

When I came out here on the raw frontier where people all carry weapons, I had my cane made. It combines the better features of the épée and the cattle prod. Only, it is the kind of prod which, if you were to prod cattle with, they would never move again.

Over eight hundred volts, max, when the tip touches, if the stud in the handle is depressed properly . . .

My arm shot out and up and my fingers depressed the stud properly as it moved.

That was it for the org.

A noise came from between the rows of razor blades in its mouth as I scored a touch on its soft underbelly and whipped my arm away to the side – a noise halfway between an exhalation and "peep" – and that was it for the org (short for "organism-with-a-long-name-which-I-can't-remember").

I switched off my cane and walked around it. It was one of those things which sometimes come out of the river. I remember that I looked back at it three times, then I switched the cane on again at max and kept it that way till I was inside my apartment with the door locked behind me and all the lights burning.

Then I permitted myself to tremble, and after awhile I changed my socks and mixed my drink.

May your alleys be safe from orgs.

Saturday.

More rain.

Wetness was all.

The entire east side had been shored with sand bags. In some places they served only to create sandy waterfalls, where otherwise the streams would have flowed more evenly and perhaps a trifle more clearly. In other places they held it back, for awhile.

By then, there were six deaths as a direct result of the rains.

By then, there had been fires caused by the lightning, accidents by the water, sicknesses by the dampness, the cold.

By then, property damages were beginning to mount pretty high.

Everyone was tired and angry and miserable and wet, by then. This included me.

Though Saturday was Saturday, I went to work. I worked in Eleanor's office, with her. We had the big relief map spread on a table, and six mobile eyescreens were lined against one wall. Six eyes hovered above the half-dozen emergency points and kept us abreast of the actions taken upon them. Several new telephones and a big radio set stood on the desk. Five ashtrays looked as if they wanted to be empty, and the coffeepot chuckled cynically at human activity.

The Noble had almost reached its high-water mark. We were not an isolated storm center by any means. Upriver, Butler Township was hurting, Swan's Nest was a-drip, Laurie was weeping into the river, and the wilderness in between was shaking and sreaming.

Even though we were in direct contact we went into the field on three occasions that morning – once, when the north-south bridge over the Lance River collapsed and was washed down toward the Noble as far as the bend by the Mack steel mill; again, when the Wildwood Cemetery, set up on a storm-gouged hill to the east, was plowed deeply, graves opened, and several coffins set awash; and finally, when three houses full of people toppled, far to the east. Eleanor's small flyer was buffeted by the winds as we fought our way through to these sites for on-the-spot supervision; I navigated almost completely by instruments. Downtown proper was accommodating evacuees left and right by then. I took three showers that morning and changed clothes twice.

Things slowed down a bit in the afternoon, including the rain. The cloud cover didn't break, but a drizzle-point was reached which permitted us to gain a little on the waters. Retaining walls were reinforced, evacuees were fed and dried, some of the rubbish was cleaned up. Four of the six eyes were returned to their patrols, because four of the emergency points were no longer emergency points.

. . . And we wanted all of the eyes for the org patrol.

Inhabitants of the drenched forest were also on the move. Seven *snappers* and a horde of panda-puppies were shot that day, as well as a few crawly things from the troubled waters of the Noble – not to mention assorted branch-snakes, stingbats, borers, and land-eels.

By nineteen hundred hours it seemed that a stalemate had been achieved. Eleanor and I climbed into her flyer and drifted skyward.

We kept rising. Finally, there was a hiss as the cabin began to pressurize itself. The night was all around us. Eleanor's face, in the light from the instrument panel, was a mask of weariness. She raised her hands to her temples as if to remove it, and then when I looked back again it appeared that she had. A faint smile lay across her lips now and her eyes sparkled. A stray strand of hair shadowed her brow.

"Where are you taking me?" she asked.

"Up high," said I, "above the storm."

"Why?"

"It's been many days," I said, "since we have seen an uncluttered sky."

"True," she agreed, and as she leaned forward to light a

cigarette I noticed that the part in her hair had gone all askew. I wanted to reach out and straighten it for her, but I didn't.

We plunged into the sea of clouds.

Dark was the sky, moonless. The stars shone like broken diamonds. The clouds were a floor of lava.

We drifted. We stared up into the heavens. I "anchored" the flyer, like an eye set to hover, and lit a cigarette myself.

"You are older than I am," she finally said, "really. You know?"

"No."

"There is a certain wisdom, a certain strength, something like the essence of the time that passes – that seeps into a man as he sleeps between the stars. I know, because I can feel it when I'm around you."

"No," I said.

"Then maybe it's people expecting you to have the strength of centuries that gives you something like it. It was probably there to begin with."

"No."

She chuckled.

"It isn't exactly a positive sort of thing either."

I laughed.

"You asked me if I was going to run for office again this fall. The answer is no. I'm planning on retiring. I want to settle down."

"With anyone special?"

"Yes, very special, Juss," she said, and she smiled at me and I kissed her, but not for too long, because the ash was about to fall off her cigarette and down the back of my neck.

So we put both cigarettes out and drifted above the invisible city, beneath a sky without a moon.

I mentioned earlier that I would tell you about Stopovers. If you are going a distance of a hundred-forty-five light years and are taking maybe a hundred-fifty actual years to do it, why stop and stretch your legs?

Well, first of all and mainly, almost nobody sleeps out the whole jaunt. There are lots of little gadgets which require human monitoring at all times. No one is going to sit there for a hundred-fifty years and watch them, all by himself. So everyone takes a turn or two, passengers included. They are all briefed on what to do till the doctor comes, and who to awaken and how to go about it, should troubles crop up. Then everyone takes a turn at guard mount for a month or so, along with a few companions. There are always hundreds of people aboard, and after you've worked down through the role you take it again from the top. All sorts of mechanical agents are backing them up, many of which they are unaware of (to protect *against* them, as well as *with* them – in the improbable instance of several oddballs getting together and deciding to open a window, change course, murder passengers, or things like that), and the people are well-screened and carefully matched up, so as to check and balance each other as well as the machinery. All of this because gadgets and people both bear watching.

After several turns at ship's guard, interspersed with periods of cold sleep, you tend to grow claustrophobic and somewhat depressed. Hence, when there is an available Stopover, it is utilized to restore mental equilibrium and to rearouse flagging animal spirits. This also serves the purpose of enriching the life and economy of the Stopover world, by whatever information and activities you may have in you.

Stopover, therefore, has become a traditional holiday on many worlds, characterized by festivals and celebrations on some of the smaller ones, and often by parades and world-wide broadcast interviews and press conferences on those with greater populations. I understand that it is now pretty much the same on Earth, too, whenever colonial visitors stop by. In fact, one fairly unsuccessful young starlet, Marilyn Austin, made a long voyage Out, stayed a few months, and returned on the next vessel headed back. After appearing on tri-dee a couple times, sounding off about interstellar culture, and flashing her white, white teeth, she picked up a flush contract, a third husband, and her first big part in tapes. All of which goes to show the value of Stopovers.

I landed us atop Helix, Betty's largest apartment-complex, wherein Eleanor had her double-balconied corner suite, affording views both of the distant Noble and of the lights of Posh Valley, Betty's residential section.

Eleanor prepared steaks, with baked potatoes, cooked corn, beer – everything I liked. I was happy and sated and such, and I stayed till around midnight, making plans for our future. Then I took a cab back to Town Square, where I was parked.

When I arrived, I thought I'd check with the Trouble Center just to see how things were going. So I entered the Hall, stamped my feet, brushed off excess waters, hung my coat, and proceeded up the empty hallway to the elevator.

The elevator was too quiet. They're supposed to rattle, you know? They shouldn't sigh softly and have doors that open and close without a sound. So I walked around an embarrassing corner on my way to the Trouble Center.

It was a pose Rodin might have enjoyed working with. All I can say is that it's a good thing I stopped by when I did, rather than five or ten minutes later.

Chuck Fuller and Lottie, Eleanor's secretary, were practicing mouth to mouth resuscitation and keeping the victim warm techniques, there on the couch in the little alcove off to the side of the big door to TC.

Chuck's back was to me, but Lottie spotted me over his shoulder, and her eyes widened and she pushed him away. He turned his head quickly.

"Juss . . ." he said.

I nodded.

"Just passing by," I told him. "Thought I'd stop in to say hello and take a look at the eyes."

"Uh – everything's going real well," he said, stepping back into the hallway. "It's on auto right now, and I'm on my – uh, coffee break. Lottie is on night duty, and she came by to – to see if we had any reports we needed typed. She had a dizzy spell, so we came out here where the couch . . ."

"Yeah, she looks a little – peaked," I said. "There are smelling salts and aspirins in the medicine chest."

I walked on by into the Center, feeling awkward.

Chuck followed me after a couple of minutes. I was watching the screens when he came up beside me. Things appeared to be somewhat in hand, though the rains were still moistening the one hundred thirty views of Betty.

"Uh, Juss," he said, "I didn't know you were coming by . . ."

"Obviously."

"What I'm getting at is – you won't report me, will you?"

"No, I won't report you."

". . . And you wouldn't mention it to Cynthia, would you?"

"Your extracurricular activities," I said, "are your own business. As a friend, I suggest you do them on your own time and in a more propitious location. But it's already beginning to slip my mind. I'm sure I'll forget the whole thing in another minute."

"Thanks, Juss," he said.

I nodded.

"What's Weather Central have to say these days?" I asked, raising the phone.

He shook his head, so I dialed and listened.

"Bad," I said, hanging up. "More wet to come."

"Damn," he announced and lit a cigarette, his hands shaking. "This weather's getting me down."

"Me too," said I. "I'm going to run now, because I want to get home before it starts in bad again. I'll probably be around tomorrow. See you."

"Night."

I elevated back down, fetched my coat, and left. I didn't see Lottie anywhere about, but she probably was, waiting for me to go.

I got to my car and was halfway home before the faucets came on full again. The sky was torn open with lightnings, and a sizzlecloud stalked the city like a long-legged arachnid, forking down bright limbs and leaving tracks of fire where it went. I made it home in another fifteen minutes, and the phenomenon was still in progress as I entered the garage. As I walked up the alley (cane switched on) I could hear the distant sizzle and the rumble, and a steady half-light filled the spaces between the buildings, from its *flash-burn-flash-burn* striding.

Inside, I listened to the thunder and the rain, and I watched the apocalypse off in the distance.

Delirium of a city under storm –

The buildings across the way were quite clear in the pulsing light of the thing. The lamps were turned off in my apartment so that I could better appreciate the vision. All of the shadows seemed incredibly black and inky, lying right beside glowing stairways, pediments, windowsills, balconies; and all of that which was illuminated seemed to burn as though with an internal light. Overhead, the living/not living insect-thing of fire stalked, and an eye wearing a blue halo was moving across the tops of nearby buildings. The fires pulsed and the clouds burnt like the hills of Gehenna; the thunders burbled and banged; and the white rain drilled into the roadway which had erupted into a steaming lather. Then a *snapper*, tri-horned, wet feathered, demon-faced, sword-tailed, and green, raced from around a corner, a moment after I heard a sound which I had thought to be a part of the thunder. The creature ran, at an incredible speed, along the smoky pavement. The eye swooped after it, adding a hail of lead to the falling raindrops. Both vanished up another street. It had taken but an instant, but in that instant it had resolved a question in my mind as to who should do the painting. Not El Greco, not Blake; no: Bosch. Without any question, Bosch – with his nightmare visions of the streets of Hell. He would be the one to do justice to this moment of the storm.

I watched until the sizzlecloud drew its legs up into itself, hung like a burning cocoon, then died like an ember retreating into ash. Suddenly, it was very dark and there was only the rain.

Sunday was the day of chaos.

Candles burned, churches burned, people drowned, beasts ran wild in the streets (or swam there), houses were torn up by the roots and bounced like paper boats along the waterways, the great wind came down upon us, and after than the madness.

I was not able to drive to Town Hall, so Eleanor sent her flyer after me.

The basement was filled with water, and the ground floor was like Neptune's waiting room. All previous high water marks had been passed.

We were in the middle of the worst storm in Betty's history.

Operations had been transferred up onto the third floor. There was no way to stop things now. It was just a matter of riding it out and giving what relief we could. I sat before my gallery and watched.

It rained buckets, it rained vats; it rained swimming pools and lakes and rivers. For awhile it seemed that it rained oceans upon us. This was partly because of the wind which came in from the gulf and suddenly made it seem to rain sideways with the force of its blasts. It began at about noon and was gone in a few hours, but when it left our town was broken and bleeding. Wyeth lay on his bronze side, the flagpole was gone, there was no building without broken windows and water inside, we were suddenly suffering lapses of electrical power, and one of my eyes showed three panda-puppies devouring a dead child. Cursing, I killed them across the rain and the distance. Eleanor wept at my side. There was a report later of a pregnant woman who could only deliver by Caesarean section, trapped on a hilltop with her family, and in labor. We were still trying to get through to her with a flyer, but the winds. . . . I saw burning buildings and the corpses of people and animals. I saw half-buried cars and splintered homes. I saw waterfalls where there had been no waterfalls before. I fired many rounds that day, and not just at beasts from the forest. Sixteen of my eyes had been shot out by looters. I hope that I never again see some of the films I made that day.

When the worst Sunday night in my life began, and the rains did not cease, I knew the meaning of despair for the third time in my life.

Eleanor and I were in the Trouble Center. The lights had just gone out for the eighth time. The rest of the staff was down on the third floor. We sat there in the dark without moving, without being able to do a single thing to halt the course of chaos. We couldn't even watch it until the power came back on.

So we talked.

Whether it was for five minutes or an hour, I don't really know. I remember telling her, though, about the girl buried on another world, whose death had set me to running. Two trips to two worlds and I had broken my bond with the times. But a hundred years of travel do not bring a century of forgetfulness – not when you cheat time with the *petite mort* of the cold sleep. Times's vengeance is memory, and though for an age you plunder the eye of seeing and empty the ear of sound, when you awaken your past is still with you. The worst thing to do then is to return to visit your wife's nameless grave in a changed land, to come back as a stranger to the place you had made your home. You run again then, and after a time you *do* forget, some, because a certain amount of actual time must pass for you also. But by then you are alone, all by yourself: completely alone. That was the *first* time in my life that I knew the meaning of despair. I read, I worked, I drank, I whored, but came the morning after and I was always me, by myself. I jumped from world to world, hoping things would be different, but with each change I was further away from all the things I had known.

Then another feeling gradually came upon me, and a really terrible feeling it was: There *must* be a time and a place best suited for each person who has ever lived. After the worst of my grief had left me and I had come to terms with the vanished past, I wondered about a man's place in time and in space. Where, and *when* in the cosmos would I most like to live out the balance of my days – to live at my fullest potential? The past *was* dead, but perhaps a better time waited on some as yet undiscovered world, waited at one yet-to-be-recorded moment in its history. How could I *ever* know? How could I ever be sure that my Golden Age did not lay but one more world away, and that I might be struggling in a Dark Era, while the Renaissance of my days was but a ticket, a visa and a diary-page removed? That was my *second* despair. I did not know the answer until I came to the Land of the Swan. I do not know why I loved you, Eleanor, but I did, and that was my answer. Then the rains came.

When the lights returned we sat there and smoked. She had told me of her husband, who had died a hero's death in time to save him from the delirium tremens which would have ended his days. Died as the bravest die – not knowing why – because of a reflex, which after all had been a part of

him, a reflex which had made him cast himself into the path
of a pack of wolf-like creatures attacking the exploring party
he was with – off in that forest at the foot of Saint Stephen's –
to fight them with a machete and to be torn apart by them
while his companions fled to the camp, where they made a
stand and saved themselves. Such is the essence of valor: an
unthinking moment, a spark along the spinal nerves,
predetermined by the sum total of everything you have ever
done, wished to do or not to do, and wish you had done, or
hadn't, and then comes the pain.

We watched the gallery on the wall. Man is the reasoning
animal? Greater than beasts but less than angels? Not the
murderer I shot that night. He wasn't even the one who uses
tools or buries his dead. Laughs, aspires, affirms? I didn't see
any of those going on. Watches himself watch himself doing
what he knows is absurd? Too sophisticated. He just did the
absurd without watching. Like running back into a burning
house after his favorite pipe and a can of tobacco. Devises
religions? I saw people praying, but they weren't devising.
They were making last-ditch efforts at saving themselves, after
they'd exhausted everything else they knew to do. Reflex.

The creature who loves?

That's the only one I might not be able to gainsay.

I saw a mother holding her daughter up on her shoulders
while the water swirled about her armpits, and the little girl
was holding her doll up above *her* shoulders, in the same way.
But isn't that – the love – a part of the total? Of everything
you have ever done, or wished? Positive or neg? I know that it
is what made me leave my post, running, and what made me
climb into Eleanor's flyer and what made me fight my way
through the storm and out to that particular scene.

I didn't get there in time.

I shall never forget how glad I was that someone else did.
Johnny Keams blinked his lights above me as he rose, and he
radioed down:

"It's all right. They're okay. Even the doll."

"Good," I said, and headed back.

As I set the ship down on its balcony landing, one figure
came toward me. As I stepped down a gun appeared in
Chuck's hand.

"I wouldn't kill you, Juss," he began, "but I'd wound you. Face that wall. I'm taking the flyer."

"Are you crazy?" I asked him.

"I know what I'm doing. I need it, Juss."

"Well, if you need it, there it is. You don't have to point a gun at me. I just got through needing it myself. Take it."

"Lottie and I both need it," he said. "Turn around!"

I turned toward the wall.

"What do you mean?" I asked.

"We're going away, together – now!"

"You *are* crazy," I said. "This is no time . . ."

"C'mon, Lottie," he called, and there was a rush of feet behind me and I heard the flyer's door open.

"Chuck!" I said. "We need you now! You can settle this thing peacefully, in a week, in a month, after some order has been restored. There *are* such things as divorces, you know."

"That won't get me off this world, Juss."

"So how is *this* going to?"

I turned, and I saw that he had picked up a large canvas bag from somewhere and had slung it over his left shoulder, like Santa Claus.

"Turn back around! I don't want to shoot you," he warned.

The suspicion came, grew stronger.

"Chuck, have you been looting?" I asked him.

"Turn around!"

"All right, I'll turn around. How far do you think you'll get?"

"Far enough," he said. "Far enough so that no one will find us – and when the time comes, we'll leave this world."

"No," I said. "I don't think you will, because I know you."

"We'll see." His voice was further away then.

I heard three rapid footsteps and the slamming of a door. I turned then, in time to see the flyer rising from the balcony.

I watched it go. I never saw either of them again.

Inside, two men were unconscious on the floor. It turned out that they were not seriously hurt. After I saw them cared for, I rejoined Eleanor in the Tower.

All that night did we wait, emptied, for morning.

Somehow, it came.

We sat and watched the light flow through the rain. So much had happened so quickly. So many things had occurred during the past week that we were unprepared for morning.

It brought an end to the rains.

A good wind came from out of the north and fought with the clouds, like En-ki with the serpent Tiamat. Suddenly, there was a canyon of cobalt.

A cloudquake shook the heavens and chasms of light opened across its dark landscape.

It was coming apart as we watched.

I heard a cheer, and I croaked in unison with it as the sun appeared.

The good, warm, drying, beneficent sun drew the highest peak of Saint Stephen's to its face and kissed both its cheeks.

There was a crowd before each window. I joined one and stared, perhaps for ten minutes.

When you awaken from a nightmare you do not normally find its ruins lying about your bedroom. This is one way of telling whether or not something was only a bad dream, or whether or not you are really awake.

We walked the streets in great boots. Mud was everywhere. It was in basements and in machinery and in sewers and in living room clothes closets. It was on buildings and on cars and on people and on the branches of trees. It was broken brown blisters drying and waiting to be peeled off from clean tissue. Swarms of skytoads rose into the air when we approached, hovered like dragonflies, returned to spoiling food stores after we had passed. Insects were having a heyday, too. Betty would have to be deloused. So many things were overturned or fallen down, and half-buried in the brown Sargassos of the streets. The dead had not yet been numbered. The water still ran by, but sluggish and foul. A stench was beginning to rise across the city. There were smashed-in store fronts and there was glass everywhere, and bridges fallen down and holes in the streets. . . . But why go on? If you don't get the picture by now, you never will. It was the big morning after, following a drunken party by the gods. It is the lot of mortal man always to clean up their leavings or to be buried beneath them.

So clean we did, but by noon Eleanor could no longer stand. So I took her home with me, because we were working down near the harbor section and my place was nearer.

That's almost the whole story – light to darkness to light – except for the end, which I don't really know. I'll tell you of its beginning, though . . .

I dropped her off at the head of the alleyway, and she went on toward my apartment while I parked the car. Why didn't I keep her with me? I don't know. Unless it was because the morning sun made the world seem at peace, despite its filth. Unless it was because I was in love and the darkness was over, and the spirit of the night had surely departed.

I parked the car and started up the alley. I was halfway before the corner where I had met the org when I heard her cry out.

I ran. Fear gave me speed and strength and I ran to the corner and turned it.

The man had a bag, not unlike the one Chuck had carried away with him, lying beside the puddle in which he stood. He was going through Eleanor's purse, and she lay on the ground – so still! – with blood on the side of her head.

I cursed him and ran toward him, switching on my cane as I went. He turned, dropped her purse, and reached for the gun in his belt.

We were about thirty feet apart, so I threw my cane.

He drew his gun, pointed it at me, and my cane fell into the puddle in which he stood.

Flights of angels sang him to his rest, perhaps.

She was breathing, so I got her inside and got hold of a doctor – I don't remember how, not too clearly, anyway – and I waited and waited.

She lived for another twelve hours and then she died. She recovered consciousness twice before they operated on her, and not again after. She didn't say anything. She smiled at me once, and went to sleep again.

I don't know.

Anything, really.

It happened again that I became Betty's mayor, to fill in until November, to oversee the rebuilding. I worked, I worked my head off, and I left her bright and shiny, as I had found her. I think I could have won if I had run for the job that fall, but I did not want it.

The Town Council overrode my objections and voted to erect a statue of Godfrey Justin Holmes beside the statue of Eleanor Schirer which was to stand in the Square across from cleaned-up Wyeth. I guess it's out there now.

I said that I would never return, but who knows? In a couple of years, after some more history has passed, I may revisit a Betty full of strangers, if only to place a wreath at the foot of the one statue. Who knows but that the entire continent may be steaming and clanking and whirring with automation by then, and filled with people from shore to shining shore?

There was a Stopover at the end of the year and I waved goodbye and climbed aboard and went away, anywhere.

I went aboard and went away, to sleep again the cold sleep.

Delirium of ship among stars –

Years have passed, I suppose. I'm not really counting them any more. But I think of this thing often: Perhaps there *is* a Golden Age someplace, a Renaissance for me sometime, a special time somewhere, somewhere but a ticket, a visa, a diary-page away. I don't know where or when. Who does? Where are all the rains of yesterday?

In the invisible city?

Inside me?

It is cold and quiet outside and the horizon is infinity. There is no sense of movement.

There is no moon, and the stars are very bright, like broken diamonds, all.

R. A. LAFFERTY
Narrow Valley

R. A. Lafferty is not usually listed as one of the major authors of the New Wave era, and yet, for me, the stories he published in the magazines and anthologies of the mid-'60s had as much to do with establishing the special excitement of that era as anything by Delany or Zelazny or Disch. Certainly they were, in their own quirky way, just as radical and revolutionary, and every bit as effective in shattering worn-out old molds and letting us suddenly see wild new possibilities in what could be done with the science fiction short story. If nothing else, the sheer wonderful brass it took to give characters names like Aloysius Shiplap, Willy McGilly, Diogenes Pontifex, or Basil Bagelbaker, and get *away* with it, was admirable.

Lafferty has published memorable novels that stand up quite well today – among the best of them are *Past Master*, *The Devil Is Dead*, *The Reefs of Earth*, the historical novel *Okla Hannali*, and the totally unclassifiable (a fantasy novel *disguised as* a non-fiction historical study, perhaps?) *The Fall of Rome* – but it was the prolific stream of short stories he began publishing in 1960 that would eventually establish his reputation. Stories like "Slow Tuesday Night," "Thus We Frustrate Charlemagne," "Hog-Belly Honey," "The Hole on the Corner," "All Pieces of a River Shore," "Among the Hairy Earthmen," "Seven Day Teror," "Continued on Next Rock," "The Configuration of the Northern Shore," "All But the Words" and many others, are among the freshest and funniest SF ever written. At his best, Lafferty possessed one of the most outlandish imaginations in all of SF, a store of offbeat erudition matched only by Avram Davidson, and a strong, shaggy sense of humor unrivaled by anyone. His stories have been gathered in the landmark collection *Nine Hundred Grandmothers*, as well as in *Strange Doings*, *Does Anyone Else Have Something Further to Add?* and *Ringing the Changes*.

Outlandish and richly strange, "Narrow Valley" is one of

Lafferty's best, and is wildly imaginative even by *his* standards. It is also very funny.

Lafferty retired from writing in 1987, at age seventy. Much of his work in the decade of the '80s – like the very strange novel *Archipelago* – is available only in small press editions or as chapbooks. His novel *My Heart Leaps Up* is being serialized as a series of chapbooks, three chapters at a time, a project that could take years to complete. But his other books in trade editions include *The Flame Is Green, Arrive at Easterwine, Space Chantey,* and *Fourth Mansions.* Lafferty won the Hugo Award in 1973 for his story "Eurema's Dam," and in 1990 received a World Fantasy Award, the prestigious Life Achievement Award. He lives in Oklahoma.

In the year 1893, land allotments in severalty were made to the remaining eight hundred and twenty-one Pawnee Indians. Each would receive one hundred and sixty acres of land and no more, and thereafter the Pawnees would be expected to pay taxes on their land, the same as the White-Eyes did.

"Kitkehahke!" Clarence Big-Saddle cussed. "You can't kick a dog around proper on a hundred and sixty acres. And I sure am not hear before about this pay taxes on land."

Clarence Big-Saddle selected a nice green valley for his allotment. It was one of the half-dozen plots he had always regarded as his own. He sodded around the summer lodge that he had there and made it an all-season home. But he sure didn't intend to pay taxes on it.

So he burned leaves and bark and made a speech:

"That my valley be always wide and flourish and green and such stuff as that!" he orated in Pawnee chant style. "But that it be narrow if an intruder come."

He didn't have any balsam bark to burn. He threw on a little cedar bark instead. He didn't have any elder leaves. He used a handful of jack-oak leaves. And he forgot the word. How you going to work it if you forget the word?

"Petahauerat!" he howled out with the confidence he hoped would fool the fates.

"That's the same long of a word," he said in a low aside to himself. But he was doubtful. "What am I, a White Man, a burr-tailed jack, a new kind of nut to think it will work?" he asked. "I have to laugh at me. Oh well, we see."

He threw the rest of the bark and the leaves on the fire, and he hollered the wrong word out again.

And he was answered by a dazzling sheet of summer lightning.

"Skidi!" Clarence Big-Saddle swore. "It worked. I didn't think it would."

Clarence Big-Saddle lived on his land for many years, and he paid no taxes. Intruders were unable to come down to his place. The land was sold for taxes three times, but nobody ever came down to claim it. Finally, it was carried as open land on the books. Homesteaders filed on it several times, but none of them fulfilled the qualification of living on the land.

Half a century went by. Clarence Big-Saddle called his son.

"I've had it, boy," he said. "I think I'll just go in the house and die."

"Okay, Dad," the son Clarence Little-Saddle said. "I'm going in to town to shoot a few games of pool with the boys. I'll bury you when I get back this evening."

So the son Clarence Little-Saddle inherited. He also lived on the land for many years without paying taxes.

There was a disturbance in the courthouse one day. The place seemed to be invaded in force, but actually there were but one man, one woman, and five children. "I'm Robert Rampart," said the man, "and we want the Land Office."

"I'm Robert Rampart Junior," said a nine-year-old gangler, "and we want it pretty blamed quick."

"I don't think we have anything like that," the girl at the desk said. "Isn't that something they had a long time ago?"

"Ignorance is no excuse for inefficiency, my dear," said Mary Mabel Rampart, an eight-year-old who could easily pass for eight and a half. "After I make my report, I wonder who will be sitting at your desk tomorrow."

"You people are either in the wrong state or the wrong century," the girl said.

"The Homestead Act still obtains," Robert Rampart insisted. "There is one tract of land carried as open in this county. I want to file on it."

Cecilia Rampart answered the knowing wink of a beefy man at the distant desk. "Hi," she breathed as she slinked over. "I'm Cecilia Rampart, but my stage name is Cecilia San Juan. Do you think that seven is too young to play ingenue roles?"

"Not for you," the man said. "Tell your folks to come over here."

"Do you know where the Land Office is?" Cecilia asked.

"Sure. It's the fourth left-hand drawer of my desk. The smallest office we got in the whole courthouse. We don't use it much any more."

The Ramparts gathered around. The beefy man started to make out the papers.

"This is the land description," Robert Rampart began. "Why, you've got it down already. How did you know?"

"I've been around here a long time," the man answered.

They did the paper work, and Robert Rampart filed on the land.

"You won't be able to come onto the land itself, though," the man said.

"Why won't I?" Rampart demanded. "Isn't the land description accurate?"

"Oh, I suppose so. But nobody's ever been able to get to the land. It's become a sort of joke."

"Well, I intend to get to the bottom of that joke," Rampart insisted. "I will occupy the land, or I will find out why not."

"I'm not sure about that," the beefy man said. "The last man to file on the land, about a dozen years ago, wasn't able to occupy the land. And he wasn't able to say why he couldn't. It's kind of interesting, the look on their faces after they try it for a day or two, and then give it up."

The Ramparts left the courthouse, loaded into their camper, and drove out to find their land. They stopped at the house of a cattle and wheat farmer named Charley Dublin. Dublin met them with a grin which indicated he had been tipped off.

"Come along if you want to, folks," Dublin said. "The easiest way is on foot across my short pasture here. Your land's directly west of mine."

They walked the short distance to the border.

"My name is Tom Rampart, Mr Dublin." Six-year-old Tom made conversation as they walked. "But my name is really Ramires, and not Tom. I am the issue of an indiscretion of my mother in Mexico several years ago."

"The boy is a kidder, Mr Dublin," said the mother Nina Rampart, defending herself. "I have never been in Mexico, but sometimes I have the urge to disappear there forever."

"Ah yes, Mrs Rampart. And what is the name of the youngest boy here?" Charley Dublin asked.

"Fatty," said Fatty Rampart.

"But surely that is not your given name?"

"Audifax," said five-year-old Fatty.

"Ah well, Audifax, Fatty, are you a kidder too?"

"He's getting better at it, Mr Dublin," Mary Mabel said. "He was a twin till last week. His twin was named Skinny. Mama left Skinny unguarded while she was out tippling, and there were wild dogs in the neighborhood. When Mama got back, do you know what was left of Skinny? Two neck bones and an ankle bone. That was all."

"Poor Skinny," Dublin said. "Well, Rampart, this is the fence and the end of my land. Yours is just beyond."

"Is that ditch on my land?" Rampart asked.

"That ditch *is* your land."

"I'll have it filled in. It's a dangerous deep cut even if it is narrow. And the other fence looks like a good one, and I sure have a pretty plot of land beyond it."

"No, Rampart, the land beyond the second fence belongs to Holister Hyde," Charley Dublin said. "That second fence is the *end* of your land."

"Now, just wait a minute, Dublin! There's something wrong here. My land is one hundred and sixty acres, which would be a half mile on a side. Where's my half-mile width?"

"Between the two fences."

"That's not eight feet."

"Doesn't look like it, does it, Rampart? Tell you what – there's plenty of throwing-sized rocks around. Try to throw one across it."

"I'm not interested in any such boys' games," Rampart exploded. "I want my land."

But the Rampart children *were* interested in such games.

They got with it with those throwing rocks. They winged them out over the little gully. The stones acted funny. They hung in the air, as it were, and diminished in size. And they were small as pebbles when they dropped down, down into the gully. None of them could throw a stone across that ditch, and they were throwing kids.

"You and your neighbor have conspired to fence open land for your own use," Rampart charged.

"No such thing, Rampart," Dublin said cheerfully. "My land checks perfectly. So does Hyde's. So does yours, if we knew how to check it. It's like one of those trick topological drawings. It really is half a mile from here to there, but the eye gets lost somewhere. It's your land. Crawl through the fence and figure it out."

Rampart crawled through the fence, and drew himself up to jump the gully. Then he hesitated. He got a glimpse of just how deep that gully was. Still, it wasn't five feet across.

There was a heavy fence post on the ground, designed for use as a corner post. Rampart up-ended it with some effort. Then he shoved it to fall and bridge the gully. But it fell short, and it shouldn't have. An eight-foot post should bridge a five-foot gully.

The post fell into the gully, and rolled and rolled and rolled. It spun as though it were rolling outward, but it made no progress except vertically. The post came to rest on a ledge of the gully, so close that Rampart could almost reach out and touch it, but it now appeared no bigger than a match stick.

"There is something wrong with that fence post, or with the world, or with my eyes," Robert Rampart said. "I wish I felt dizzy so I could blame it on that."

"There's a little game that I sometimes play with my neighbor Hyde when we're both out," Dublin said. "I've a heavy rifle and I train it on the middle of his forehead as he stands on the other side of the ditch apparently eight feet away. I fire it off then (I'm a good shot), and I hear it whine across. It'd kill him dead if things were as they seem. But Hyde's in no danger. The shot always bangs into that little scuff of rocks and boulders about thirty feet below him. I can see it kick up the rock dust there, and the sound of it rattling into those little boulders comes back to me in about two and a half seconds."

A bull-bat (poor people call it the night-hawk) raveled around in the air and zoomed out over the narrow ditch, but it did not reach the other side. The bird dropped below ground level and could be seen against the background of the other side of the ditch. It grew smaller and hazier as though at a distance of three or four hundred yards. The white bars on its wings could no longer be discerned; then the bird itself could hardly be discerned; but it was far short of the other side of the five-foot ditch.

A man identified by Charley Dublin as the neighbor Hollister Hyde had appeared on the other side of the little ditch. Hyde grinned and waved. He shouted something, but could not be heard.

"Hyde and I both read mouths," Dublin said, "so we can talk across the ditch easy enough. Which kid wants to play chicken? Hyde will barrel a good-sized rock right at your head, and if you duck or flinch you're chicken."

"Me! Me!" Audifax Rampart challenged. And Hyde, a big man with big hands, did barrel a fearsome jagged rock right at the head of the boy. It would have killed him if things had been as they appeared. But the rock diminished to nothing and disappeared into the ditch. Here was a phenomenon: things seemed real-sized on either side of the ditch, but they diminished coming out over the ditch either way.

"Everybody game for it?" Robert Rampart Junior asked.

"We won't get down there by standing here," Mary Mabel said.

"Nothing wenchered, nothing gained," said Cecilia. "I got that from an ad for a sex comedy."

Then the five Rampart kids ran down into the gully. Ran *down* is right. It was almost as if they ran down the vertical face of a cliff. They couldn't do that. The gully was no wider than the stride of the biggest kids. But the gully diminished those children, it ate them alive. They were doll-sized. They were acorn-sized. They were running for minute after minute across a ditch that was only five feet across. They were going, deeper in it, and getting smaller. Robert Rampart was roaring his alarm, and his wife Nina was screaming. Then she stopped. "What am I carrying on so loud about?" she asked herself. "It looks like fun. I'll do it too."

She plunged into the gully, diminished in size as the children had done, and ran at a pace to carry her a hundred yards away across a gully only five feet wide.

That Robert Rampart stirred things up for a while then. He got the sheriff there, and the highway patrolmen. A ditch had stolen his wife and five children, he said, and maybe had killed them. And if anybody laughs, there may be another killing. He got the colonel of the State National Guard there, and a command post set up. He got a couple of airplane pilots. Robert Rampart had one quality: when he hollered, people came.

He got the newsmen out from T-Town, and the eminent scientists, Dr Velikof Vonk, Arpad Arkabaranan, and Willy McGilly. That bunch turns up every time you get on a good one. They just happen to be in that part of the country where something interesting is going on.

They attacked the thing from all four sides and the top, and by inner and outer theory. If a thing measures half a mile on each side, and the sides are straight, there just has to be something in the middle of it. They took pictures from the air, and they turned out perfect. They proved that Robert Rampart had the prettiest hundred and sixty acres in the country, the larger part of it being a lush green valley, and all of it being half a mile on a side, and situated just where it should be. They took ground-level photos then, and it showed a beautiful half-mile stretch of land between the boundaries of Charley Dublin and Hollister Hyde. But a man isn't a camera. None of them could see that beautiful spread with the eyes in their heads. Where was it?

Down in the valley itself everything was normal. It really was half a mile wide and no more than eighty feet deep with a very gentle slope. It was warm and sweet, and beautiful with grass and grain.

Nina and the kids loved it, and they rushed to see what squatter had built that little house on their land. A house, or a shack. It had never known paint, but paint would have spoiled it. It was built of split timbers dressed near smooth with ax and draw knife, chinked with white clay, and sodded up to about half its height. And there was an interloper standing by the little lodge.

"Here, here what are you doing on our land?" Robert Rampart Junior demanded of the man. "Now you just shamble off again wherever you came from. I'll bet you're a thief too, and those cattle are stolen."

"Only the black-and-white calf," Clarence Little-Saddle said. "I couldn't resist him, but the rest are mine. I guess I'll just stay around and see that you folks get settled all right."

"Is there any wild Indians around here?" Fatty Rampart asked.

"No, not really. I go on a bender about every three months and get a little bit wild, and there's a couple Osage boys from Gray Horse that get noisy sometimes, but that's about all," Clarence Little-Saddle said.

"You certainly don't intend to palm yourself off on us as an Indian," Mary Mabel challenged. "You'll find us a little too knowledgeable for that."

"Little girl, you might as well tell this cow there's no room for her to be a cow since you're so knowledgeable. She thinks she's a short-horn cow named Sweet Virginia. I think I'm a Pawnee Indian named Clarence. Break it to us real gentle if we're not."

"If you're an Indian where's your war bonnet? There's not a feather on you anywhere."

"How you be sure? There's a story that we got feathers instead of hair on – Aw, I can't tell a joke like that to a little girl! How come you're not wearing the Iron Crown of Lombardy if you're a white girl? How you expect me to believe you're a little white girl and your folks came from Europe a couple hundred years ago if you don't wear it? There are six hundred tribes, and only one of them, the Oglala Sioux, had the war bonnet, and only the big leaders, never more than two or three of them alive at one time, wore it."

"Your analogy is a little strained," Mary Mabel said. "Those Indians we saw in Florida and the ones at Atlantic City had war bonnets, and they couldn't very well have been the kind of Sioux you said. And just last night on the TV in the motel, those Massachusetts Indians put a war bonnet on the President and called him the Great White Father. You mean to tell me that they were all phonies? Hey, who's laughing at who here?"

"If you're an Indian where's your bow and arrow?" Tom Rampart interrupted. "I bet you can't even shoot one."

"You're sure right there," Clarence admitted. "I never shot one of those things but once in my life. They used to have an archery range in Boulder Park over in T-Town, and you could rent the things and shoot at targets tied to hay bales. Hey, I barked my whole forearm and nearly broke my thumb when the bow-string thwacked home. I couldn't shoot that thing at all. I don't see how anybody ever could shoot one of them."

"Okay, kids," Nina Rampart called to her brood. "Let's start pitching this junk out of the shack so we can move in. Is there any way we can drive our camper down here, Clarence?"

"Sure, there's a pretty good dirt road, and it's a lot wider than it looks from the top. I got a bunch of green bills in an old night charley in the shack. Let me get them, and then I'll clear out for a while. The shack hasn't been cleaned out for seven years, since the last time this happened. I'll show you the road to the top, and you can bring your car down it."

"Hey, you old Indian, you lied!" Cecilia Rampart shrilled from the doorway of the shack. "You *do* have a war bonnet. Can I have it?"

"I didn't mean to lie, I forgot about that thing," Clarence Little-Saddle said. "My son Clarence Bare-Back sent that to me from Japan for a joke a long time ago. Sure, you can have it."

All the children were assigned tasks carrying the junk out of the shack and setting fire to it. Nina Rampart and Clarence Little-Saddle ambled up to the rim of the valley by the vehicle road that was wider than it looked from the top.

"Nina, you're back! I thought you were gone forever," Robert Rampart jittered at seeing her again. "What – where are the children?"

"Why, I left them down in the valley, Robert. That is, ah, down in that little ditch right there. Now you've got me worried again. I'm going to drive the camper down there and unload it. You'd better go on down and lend a hand too, Robert, and quit talking to all these funny-looking men here."

And Nina went back to Dublin's place for the camper.

"It would be easier for a camel to go through the eye of a needle than for that intrepid woman to drive a car down into that narrow ditch," the eminent scientist Dr Velikof Vonk said.

"You know how that camel does it?" Clarence Little-Saddle offered, appearing of a sudden from nowhere. "He just closes one of his own eyes and flops back his ears and plunges right through. A camel is mighty narrow when he closes one eye and flops back his ears. Besides, they use a big-eyed needle in the act."

"Where'd this crazy man come from?" Robert Rampart demanded, jumping three feet in the air. "Things are coming out of the ground now. I want my land! I want my children! I want my wife! Whoops, here she comes driving it. Nina, you can't drive a loaded camper into a little ditch like that! You'll be killed or collapsed!"

Nina Rampart drove the loaded camper into the little ditch at a pretty good rate of speed. The best of belief is that she just closed one eye and plunged right through. The car diminished and dropped, and it was smaller than a toy car. But it raised a pretty good cloud of dust as it bumped for several hundred yards across a ditch that was only five feet wide.

"Rampart, it's akin to the phenomenon known as looming, only in reverse," the eminent scientist Arpad Arkabaranan explained as he attempted to throw a rock across the narrow ditch. The rock rose very high in the air, seemed to hang at its apex while it diminished to the size of a grain of sand, and then fell into the ditch not six inches of the way across. There isn't anybody going to throw across a half-mile valley even if it looks five feet. "Look at a rising moon sometimes, Rampart. It appears very large, as though covering a great sector of the horizon, but it only covers one-half of a degree. It is hard to believe that you could set seven hundred and twenty of such large moons side by side around the horizon, or that it would take one hundred and eighty of the big things to reach from the horizon to a point overhead. It is also hard to believe that your valley is five hundred times as wide as it appears, but it has been surveyed, and it is."

"I want my land. I want my children. I want my wife," Robert chanted dully. "Damn, I let her get away again."

"I tell you, Rampy," Clarence Little-Saddle squared on him, "a man that lets his wife get away twice doesn't deserve to keep her. I give you till nightfall; then you forfeit. I've taken a liking to the brood. One of us is going to be down there tonight."

After a while a bunch of them were off in that little tavern on the road between Cleveland and Osage. It was only half a mile away. If the valley had run in the other direction, it would have been only six feet away.

"It is a psychic nexus in the form of an elongated dome," said the eminent scientist Dr Velikof Vonk. "It is maintained subconsciously by the concatenation of at least two minds, the stronger of them belonging to a man dead for many years. It has apparently existed for a little less than a hundred years, and in another hundred years it will be considerably weakened. We know from our checking out folk tales of Europe as well as Cambodia that these ensorceled areas seldom survive for more than two hundred and fifty years. The person who first set such a thing in being will usually lose interest in it, and in all worldly things, within a hundred years of his own death. This is a simple thanato-psychic limitation. As a short-term device, the thing has been used several times as a military tactic.

"This psychic nexus, as long as it maintains itself, causes group illusion, but it is really a simple thing. It doesn't fool birds or rabbits or cattle or cameras, only humans. There is nothing meteorological about it. It is strictly psychological. I'm glad I was able to give a scientific explanation to it or it would have worried me."

"It is a continental fault coinciding with a noospheric fault," said the eminent scientist Arpad Arkabaranan. "The valley really is half a mile wide, and at the same time it really is only five feet wide. If we measured correctly, we would get these dual measurements. Of course it is meteorological! Everything including dreams is meteorological. It is the animals and cameras which are fooled, as lacking a true dimension; it is only humans who see the true duality. The phenomenon should be common along the whole continental fault where the Earth gains or loses half a mile that has to go somewhere. Likely it extends through the whole sweep of the Cross Timbers. Many of those trees appear twice, and many do not appear at all. A man in the proper state of mind could farm that land or raise cattle on it, but it doesn't really exist. There is a clear parallel in the Luftspiegelungthal sector in the Black Forest of Germany which exists, or does not exist, according to the circumstances and to the attitude of the beholder. Then we have the case of Mad Mountain in Morgan County, Tennessee, which isn't there all the time, and also the Little Lobo Mirage south of Presidio, Texas, from which twenty thousand barrels of water were pumped in one two-and-a-half-year period before the mirage reverted to mirage status. I'm glad I was able to give a scientific explanation to this or it would have worried me."

"I just don't understand how he worked it," said the eminent scientist Willy McGilly. "Cedar bark, jack-oak leaves, and the world 'Petahauerat'. The thing's impossible! When I was a boy and we wanted to make a hideout, we used bark from the skunk-spruce tree, the leaves of a box-elder, and the word was 'Boadicea'. All three elements are wrong here. I cannot find a scientific explanation for it, and it does worry me."

They went back to Narrow Valley. Robert Rampart was still chanting dully: "I want my land. I want my children. I want my wife."

Nina Rampart came chugging up out of the narrow ditch in the camper and emerged through that little gate a few yards down the fence row.

"Supper's ready and we're tired of waiting for you, Robert," she said. "A fine homesteader you are! Afraid to come onto your own land! Come along now; I'm tired of waiting for you."

"I want my land! I want my children! I want my wife!" Robert Rampart still chanted. "Oh, there you are, Nina. You stay here this time. I want my land! I want my children! I want an answer to this terrible thing."

"It is time we decided who wears the pants in this family," Nina said stoutly. She picked up her husband, slung him over her shoulder, carried him to the camper and dumped him in, slammed (as it seemed) a dozen doors at once, and drove furiously down into the Narrow Valley, which already seemed wider.

Why, that place was getting normaler and normaler by the minute! Pretty soon it looked almost as wide as it was supposed to be. The psychic nexus in the form of an elongated dome had collapsed. The continental fault that coincided with the noospheric fault had faced facts and decided to conform. The Ramparts were in effective possession of their homestead, and Narrow Valley was as normal as any place anywhere.

"I have lost my land," Clarence Little-Saddle moaned. "It was the land of my father Clarence Big-Saddle, and I meant it to be the land of my son Clarence Bare-Back. It looked so narrow that people did not notice how wide it was, and people did not try to enter it. Now I have lost it."

Clarence Little-Saddle and the eminent scientist Willy McGilly were standing on the edge of Narrow Valley, which now appeared its true half-mile extent. The moon was just rising, so big that it filled a third of the sky. Who would have imagined that it would take a hundred and eight of such monstrous things to reach from the horizon to a point overhead, and yet you could sight it with sighters and figure it so.

"I had a little bear-cat by the tail and I let go," Clarence groaned. "I had a fine valley for free, and I have lost it. I am like that hard-luck guy in the funny-paper or Job in the Bible. Destitution is my lot."

Willy McGilly looked around furtively. They were alone on the edge of the half-mile-wide valley.

"Let's give it a booster shot," Willy McGilly said.

Hey, those two got with it! They started a snapping fire and began to throw the stuff onto it. Bark from the dog-elm tree – how do you know it won't work?

It *was* working! Already the other side of the valley seemed a hundred yards closer, and there were alarmed noises coming up from the people in the valley.

Leaves from a black locust tree – and the valley narrowed still more! There was, moreover, terrified screaming of both children and big people from the depths of Narrow Valley, and the happy voice of Mary Mabel Rampart chanting, "Earthquake! Earthquake!"

"That my valley be always wide and flourish and such stuff, and green with money and grass!" Clarence Little-Saddle orated in Pawnee chant style, "but that it be narrow if intruders come, smash them like bugs!"

People, that valley wasn't over a hundred feet wide now, and the screaming of the people in the bottom of the valley had been joined by the hysterical coughing of the camper car starting up.

Willy and Clarence threw everything that was left on the fire. But the word? The word? Who remembers the word?

"Corsicanatexas!" Clarence Little-Saddle howled out with confidence he hoped would fool the fates.

He was answered not only by a dazzling sheet of summer lightning, but also by thunder and raindrops.

"Chahiksi!" Clarence Little-Saddle swore. "It worked. I didn't think it would. It will be all right now. I can use the rain."

The valley was again a ditch only five feet wide.

The camper car struggled out of Narrow Valley through the little gate. It was smashed flat as a sheet of paper, and the screaming kids and people in it had only one dimension.

"It's closing in! It's closing in!" Robert Rampart roared, and he was no thicker than if he had been made out of cardboard.

"We're smashed like bugs," the Rampart boys intoned. "We're thin like paper."

"*Mort, ruine, écrasement!*" spoke-acted Cecilia Rampart like the great tragedienne she was.

"Help! Help!" Nina Rampart croaked, but she winked at Willy and Clarence as they rolled by. "This homesteading jag always did leave me a little flat."

"Don't throw those paper dolls away. They might be the Ramparts," Mary Mabel called.

The camper car coughed again and bumped along on level ground. This couldn't last forever. The car was widening out as it bumped along.

"Did we overdo it, Clarence?" Willy McGilly asked. "What did one flat-lander say to the other?"

"Dimension of us never got around," Clarence said. "No, I don't think we overdid it, Willy. That car must be eighteen inches wide already, and they all ought to be normal by the time they reach the main road. The next time I do it, I think I'll throw wood-grain plastic on the fire to see who's kidding who."

SAMUEL R. DELANY
Driftglass

I picked up Samuel R. Delany's first published novel, *The Jewels of Aptor*, in 1962, as soon as it hit the newsstands (I even remember *which* newsstand, one on the platform in a subway station under what had once been Scolley Square, in Boston; memory is a funny thing), and, although it was packaged no differently than dozens of other Ace Doubles I'd read with only low-key interest in other years – same garish and ugly pulp cover, same overheated pulp blurbs – I felt a thrill of excitement with the very first page, an almost physical tingle, as though a small electric current was passing through the paper, and I knew at once that I was in contact with a very uncommon talent indeed.

Throughout the early years of the '60s, I bought every Delany book as it appeared, and with each book that feeling was sharper, and my conviction grew that here was a Master of the form. It was a conviction shared by just about no one else in those days, perhaps because Delany's books *were* published, with maximum obscurity, as garish and pulpy-looking Ace Doubles, the bottom of the novel market, and perhaps because a hurried and unsympathetic look at the plot-synopsis teasers on the inside page – or even a dip inside, if your glance happened to fall on, for instance, a character named "Comet Jo" – would lead you to assume that this was standard, lowest-common-denominator space opera of the most fundamental kind.

Well, it *was* space opera – and it wasn't. That was one of the things I loved about Delany, his ability to mix the most outrageous of space opera *shticks* (including some as wild and cosmic as anything seen since the "superscience" era of the '30s) with the most subtle of philosophies and metaphysics. As his talent grew throughout the first half of the decade, so did my admiration for the intensity and clotted eloquence of his prose, for his psychologically complex characterizations, for his radical insight into the workings of social systems, and also for the feeling I got from him – growing more powerful with every book – that here was the authentic view from *the other side*, a perspective from beyond the confining provincial world whose boundaries and sharply limited vistas I chafed against. (By the mid-'60s, Delany's talent had deepened so that I imagined him to be some white-bearded sage – perhaps even forty! – steeped in years and wisdom; when I found out instead that he was only a few years older than I was – having started selling novels when he was nineteen – the shock was considerable.)

So I went around for a few years pushing copies of Delany novels on friends, who pushed them away with indifference, until he hit big with 1966's *Babel 17*, and everyone else went galloping retrospectively back through his earlier work, while I stood by smiling smugly. (I had the identical experience, at just about the same time, with Le Guin's work – it frequently pays to keep your eye on what's happening on the bottom of the heap.)

Delany went on to become one of the two most critically acclaimed new American SF writers of the '60s (the other being Roger Zelazny). He won the Nebula Award in 1966 for *Babel 17*, won two more Nebulas in 1967, for *The Einstein Intersection* and for his first short story, "Aye, and Gomorrah . . ." and his 1968 novella "Time Considered as a Helix of Semi-Precious Stones" won both the Nebula Award and the Hugo Award. His monumental novel *Nova* was, in my opinion, one of the best SF novels of the '60s, and its appearance prompted critic Algis Budrys to hail him as "the best science-fiction writer in the world" – an opinion it would have been possible to find a great deal of support for by the end of the decade, at least on the American side of the Atlantic.

Delany only ever wrote a handful of short stories – unlike Zelazny, he made his biggest impact on the field with his novels – but they deserve to be numbered among the best short work of the '60s. Aside from the stories already named – and the one that follows – they include the marvellous novella "The Star Pit," the ornately titled "We, in Some Strange Power's Employ, Move on a Rigorous Line," "Corona," and "Dog in a Fisherman's Net." Almost all of his short fiction was assembled in the landmark collection *Driftglass*.

Here he gives us an evocative, richly colored glimpse of a vividly realized future world, one complexly in flux . . . and elementally unchanged.

After *Nova*, Delany fell silent for seven years, and when he did return, it was with work that no longer had as broad an appeal within the genre, like the immense, surreal *Dhalgren* . . . which did, however, become a bestseller outside of the usual genre boundaries, and help gain him wide new audiences. Although he continued to publish a series of ornate and somewhat abstract intellectual fantasy novels throughout the rest of the '70s and the '80s, his most direct subsequent impact on SF has probably been as a critic. But it is evident that his '60s work was one of the most powerful direct influences on the Cyberpunk movement of the mid-80s. (Delany once told me that as a young writer he was trying "to do Bester for the '60s, to write a book that would be as exciting to a twenty-five-year-old as Bester's *The Stars My Destination* had been to me when I was fourteen" – and William Gibson once admitted to me that at least part of what *he* was trying to accomplish with his work was "to do Delany for the '80s".)

Delany's other works include the novels *Triton, Stars in My Pocket Like Grains of Sand, The Fall of the Towers, The Ballad of Beta 2, Empire Star, Flight from Neveryon, The Bridge of Lost Desire, Tales of Neveryon,* and the critical works *The Jewel-Hinged Jaw, The Straits of Messina, Starboard Wine,* and *The American Shore.*

1

Sometimes I go down to the port, splashing sand with my stiff foot at the end of my stiff leg locked in my stiff hip, with the useless arm a-swinging, to get wet all over again, drink in the dives with cronies ashore, feeling old, broken, sorry for myself, laughing louder and louder. The third of my face that was burned away in the accident was patched with skingrafts from my chest, so what's left of my mouth distorts all loud sounds; sloppy sartorial reconstruction. Also I have a hairy chest. Chest hair does not look like beard hair, and it grows all up under my right eye. And: my beard is red, my chest hair brown, while the thatch curling down over neck and ears is sun-streaked to white here, darkened to bronze there, midst general blondness.

By reason of my being a walking (I suppose my gait could be called headlong limping) horror show, plus a general inclination to sulk, I spend most of the time up in the wood and glass and aluminum house on the surf-sloughed point that the Aquatic Corp ceded me along with my pension.

Rugs from Turkey there, copper pots, my tenor recorder which I can no longer play, and my books.

But sometimes, when the gold fog blurs the morning, I go down to the beach and tromp barefoot in the wet edging of the sea, searching for driftglass.

It was foggy that morning, and the sun across the water moiled the mists like a brass ladle. I lurched to the top of the rocks, looked down through the tall grasses into the frothing inlet where she lay, and blinked.

She sat up, long gills closing down her neck and the secondary slits along her back just visible at their tips because of much hair, wet and curling copper, falling there. She saw me. "What are you doing here, huh?" She narrowed blue eyes.

"Looking for driftglass."

"What?"

"There's a piece." I pointed near her and came down the rocks like a crab with one stiff leg.

"Where?" She turned over, half in, half out of the water, the webs of her fingers cupping nodules of black stone.

While the water made cold overtures between my toes, I picked up the milky fragment by her elbow where she wasn't looking. She jumped, because she obviously had thought it was somewhere else.

"See?"

"What . . . what is it?" She raised her cool hand to mine. For a moment the light through the milky gem and the pale film of my own webs pearled the screen of her palms. (Details like that. Yes, they are the important things, the points from which we suspend later pain.) A moment later wet fingers closed to the backs of mine.

"Driftglass," I said. "You know all the Coca-Cola bottles and cut-crystal punch bowls and industrial silicon slag that goes into the sea?"

"I know the Coca-Cola bottles."

"They break, and the tide pulls the pieces back and forth over the sandy bottom, wearing the edges, changing their shape. Sometimes chemicals in the glass react with chemicals in the ocean to change the color. Sometimes veins work their way through in patterns like snowflakes, regular and geometric; others, irregular and angled like coral. When the pieces dry, they're milky. Put them in water and they become transparent again."

"Ohhh!" she breathed as the beauty of the blunted triangular fragment in my palm assailed her like perfume. Then she looked at my face, blinking the third, aqueous-filled lid that we use as a correction lens for underwater vision.

She watched the ruin calmly.

Then her hand went to my foot where the webs had been torn back in the accident. She began to take in who I was. I looked for horror, but saw only a little sadness.

The insignia on her buckle – her stomach was making little jerks the way you always do during the first few minutes when you go from breathing water to air – told me she was a Biological Technican. (Back up at the house there was a similar uniform of simulated scales folded in the bottom drawer of the dresser and the belt insignia said Depth Gauger.) I was wearing some very frayed jeans and a red cotton shirt with no buttons.

She reached for my neck, pushed my collar back from my shoulders and touched the tender slits of my gills, outlining them with cool fingers. "Who are you?" Finally.

"Cal Svenson."

She slid back down in the water. "You're the one who had the terrible . . . but that was years ago! They still talk about it, down. . . ." She stopped.

As the sea softens the surface of a piece of glass, so it blurs the souls and sensibilities of the people who toil beneath her. And according to the last report of the Marine Reclamation Division there are to date seven hundred and fifty thousand who have been given gills and webs and sent under the foam where there are no storms up and down the American coast.

"You live on shore? I mean around here? But so long ago . . ."

"How old are you?"

"Sixteen."

"I was two years older than you when the accident happened."

"You were eighteen?"

"I'm twice that now. Which means it happened almost twenty years ago. It is a long time."

"They still talk about it."

"I've almost forgotten," I said. "I really have. Say, do you play the recorder?"

"I used to."

"Good! Come up to my place and look at my tenor recorder. And I'll make some tea. Perhaps you can stay for lunch –"

"I have to report back to Marine Headquarters by three. Tork is going over the briefing to lay the cable for the big dive, with Jonni and the crew." She paused, smiled. "But I can catch the undertow and be there in half an hour if I leave by two-thirty."

On the walk up I learned her name was Ariel. She thought the patio was charming and the mosaic evoked, "Oh look!" and "Did you do this yourself?" a half-dozen times. (I had done it, in the first lonely years.) She picked out the squid and the whale in battle, the wounded shark and the diver. She told me she didn't get time to read much, but she was impressed by all the books. She listened to me reminisce. She talked a lot to me about her work, husbanding the deep-down creatures they were scaring up. Then she sat on the kitchen stool, playing a Lukas Foss serenade on my recorder, while I put rock salt in the bottom of the broiler tray for two dozen Oysters Rockefeller, and the tea water whistled. I'm a comparatively lonely guy. I like being followed by beautiful young girls.

2

"Hey, Juao!" I bawled across the jetty.

He nodded to me from the center of his nets, sun glistening on polished shoulders, sun lost in rough hair. I walked across to where he sat, sewing like a spider. He pulled another section up over his horny toes, then grinned at me with his mosaic smile: gold, white, black gap below, crooked yellow; white, gold, white. Shoving my bad leg in front I squatted.

"I fished out over the coral where you told me." He filled

his cheek with his tongue and nodded. "You come up to the house for a drink, eh?"

"Fine."

"Just – a moment more."

There's a certain sort of Brazilian you find along the shore in the fishing villages, old yet ageless. See one of their men and you think he could be fifty, he could be sixty – will probably look the same when he's eighty-five. Such was Juao. We once figured it out. He's seven hours older than I am.

We became friends some time before the accident when I got tangled in his nets working high lines in the Vorea Current. A lot of guys would have taken their knife and hacked their way out of the situation, ruining fifty-five, sixty dollars' worth of nets. That's an average fisherman's monthly income down here. But I surfaced and sat around in his boat while we untied me. Then we came in and got plastered. Since I cost him a day's fishing, I've been giving him hints on where to fish ever since. He buys me drinks when I come up with something.

This has been going on for twenty years. During that time my life has been smashed up and land-bound. In the same time Juao has married off his five sisters, got married himself and has two children. (Oh, those *bolitos* and *teneros asados* that Amalia – her braids swung out, her brown breasts shook so when she turned to laugh – would make for Sunday dinner/supper/Monday breakfast.) I rode with them in the ambulance 'copter all the way into Brasilia; in the hospital hall Juao and I stood together, both still barefoot, he tattered with fish scales in his hair, me just tattered, and I held him while he cried and I tried to explain to him how a world that could take a pubescent child and with a week of operations make an amphibious creature that can exist for a month on either side of the sea's foam-fraught surface could still be helpless before certain rampant endocrine cancers coupled with massive renal deterioration. Juao and I returned to the village alone, by bus, three days before our birthday – back when I was twenty-three and Juao was twenty-three and seven hours old.

"This morning," Juao said. (The shuttle danced in the web at the end of the orange line.) "I got a letter for you to read me. It's about the children. Come on, we go up and drink." The shuttle paused, backtracked twice, and he yanked the knot tight. We walked along the port toward the square. "Do you think the letter says that the children are accepted?"

"If it's from the Aquatic Corp. They just send postcards when they reject someone. The question is, how do *you* feel about it?"

"You are a good man. If they grow up like you, then it will be fine."

"But you're still worried." I'd been prodding Juao to get the kids into the International Aquatic Corp nigh on since I became their godfather. The operations had to be performed near puberty. It would mean much time away from the village during their training period – and they might eventually be stationed in any ocean in the world. But two motherless children had not been easy on Juao or his sisters. The Corp would mean education, travel, interesting work, the things that make up one kind of good life. They wouldn't look twice their age when they were thirty-five; and not too many amphimen look like me.

"Worry is part of life. But the work is dangerous. Did you know there is an amphiman going to try and lay cable down in the Slash?"

I frowned. "Again?"

"Yes. And that is what you tried to do when the sea broke you to pieces and burned the parts, eh?"

"Must you be so damned picturesque?" I asked. "Who's going to beard the lion this time?"

"A young amphiman named Tork. They speak of him down at the docks as a brave man."

"Why the hell are they still trying to· lay the cable there? They've gotten by this long without a line through the Slash."

"Because of the fish," Juao said. "You told me why twenty years ago. The fish are still there, and we fishermen who cannot live below are still here. If the children go for the operations, then there will be less fishermen. But today. . . ." He shrugged. "They must either lay the line across the fish paths or down in the Slash." Juao shook his head.

Funny things, the great power cables the Aquatic Corp has been strewing across the ocean floor to bring power to their undersea mines and farms, to run their oil wells – and how many flaming wells have I capped down there – for their herds of whale, and chemical distillation plants. They carry two-hundred-sixty-cycle current. Over certain sections of the ocean floor, or in sections of the water with certain mineral contents, this sets up inductance in the water itself which sometimes – and you will probably get a Nobel Prize if you can detail exactly why it isn't always – drive the fish away over areas up to twenty-five and thirty miles, unless the lines are laid in the bottom of those canyons that delve into the ocean floor.

"This Tork thinks of the fishermen. He is a good man too."

I raised my eyebrows – the one that's left, anyway – and tried to remember what my little Undine had said about him that morning. And remembered not much.

"I wish him luck," I said.

"What do you feel about this young man going down into the coral-rimmed jaws to the Slash?"

I thought for a moment. "I think I hate him."

Juao looked up.

"He is an image in a mirror where I look and am forced to regard what I was," I went on. "I envy him the chance to succeed where I failed, and I can come on just as quaint as you can. I hope he makes it."

Juao twisted his shoulders in a complicated shrug (once I could do that) which is coastal Brazilian for, "I didn't know things had progressed to that point, but seeing that they have, there is little to be done."

"The sea is that sort of mirror," I said.

"Yes." Juao nodded.

Behind us I heard the slapping of sandals on concrete. I turned in time to catch my goddaughter in my good arm. My godson had grabbed hold of the bad one and was swinging on it.

"Tio Cal –"

"Hey, Tio Cal, what did you bring us?"

"You will pull him over," Juao reprimanded them. "Let go."

And, bless them, they ignored their father.

"What did you bring us?"

"What did you bring us, Tio Cal?"

"If you let me, I'll show you." So they stepped back dark-eyed and quivering. I watched Juao watching: brown pupils on ivory balls, and in the left eye a vein had broken in a jagged smear. He was loving his children, who would soon be as alien to him as the fish he netted. He was also looking at the terrible thing that was me and wondering what would come to his own spawn. And he was watching the world turn and grow older, clocked by the waves, reflected in that mirror.

It's impossible for me to see what the population explosion and the budding colonies on Luan and Mars and the flowering beneath the ocean really look like from the disrupted cultural melange of a coastal fishing town. But I come closer than many others, and I know what I don't understand.

I pushed around in my pocket and fetched out the milky fragment I had brought from the beach. "Here. Do you like this one?" And they bent above my webbed and alien fingers.

In the supermarket, which is the biggest building in the village, Juao bought a lot of cake mixes. "That moist, delicate texture," whispered the box when you lifted it from the shelf, "with that deep flavor, deeper than chocolate!"

I'd just read an article about the new vocal packaging in a U.S. magazine that had gotten down last week, so I was prepared and stayed in the fresh vegetable section to avoid temptation. Then we went up to Juao's house. The letter proved to be what I'd expected. The kids had to take the bus into Brasilia tomorrow. My godchildren were on their way to becoming fish.

We sat on the front steps and drank and watched the donkeys and the motorbikes and the men in baggy trousers, the women in yellow scarves and bright skirts with wreaths of garlic and sacks of onions. As well, a few people glittered in the green scales of amphimen uniforms.

Finally Juao got tired and went in to take a nap. Most of my life has been spent on the coast of countries accustomed to siestas, but those first formative ten were passed on a Danish collective farm and the idea never really took. So I stepped over my goddaughter, who had fallen asleep on her fists on the bottom step and walked back through the town toward the beach.

3

At midnight Ariel came out of the sea, climbed the rocks, and clicked her nails aganst my glass wall so the droplets ran, pealed by the gibbous moon.

Earlier I had stretched in front of the fireplace on the sheepskin throw to read, then dozed off. The conscientious timer had asked me if there was anything I wanted, and getting no answer had turned off the Dvorak *Cello Concerto* that was on its second time around, extinguished the reading lamp, and stopped dropping logs onto the flame so that now, as I woke, the grate was carpeted with coals.

She clicked again, and I raised my head from the cushion. The green uniform, her amber hair – all color was lost under the silver light outside. I lurched across the rug, touched the button, and the glass slid into the floor. The breeze came to my face, as the barrier fell.

"What do you want?" I asked. "What time is it, anyway?"

"Tork is on the beach, waiting for you."

The night was warm but windy. Below the rocks silver flakes chased each other in to shore. The tide lay full.

I rubbed my face. "The new boss man? Why didn't you bring him up to the house? What does he want to see me about?"

She touched my arm. "Come. They are all down on the beach."

"Who all?"

"Tork and the others."

She led me across the patio and to the path that wound to the sand. The sea roared in the moonlight. Down the beach people stood around a driftwood fire that whipped the night. Ariel walked beside me.

Two of the fishermen from town were crowding each other on the bottom of the overturned washtub, playing guitars.

The singing, raucous and rhythmic, jarred across the paled sand. Shark's teeth on the necklace of an old woman dancing. Others were sitting on an overturned dinghy, eating.

Over one part of the fire on a skillet two feet across, oil frothed through pink islands of shrimp. One woman ladled them in, another ladled them out.

"Tio Cal!"

"Look, Tio Cal is here!"

"Hey, what are you two doing up?" I asked. "Shouldn't you be home in bed?"

"Poppa Juao said we could come. He'll be here, too, soon."

I turned to Ariel. "Why are they all gathering?"

"Because of the laying of the cable tomorrow at dawn."

Someone was running up the beach, waving a bottle in each hand.

"They didn't want to tell you about the party. They thought that it might hurt your pride."

"My what. . . ?"

If you knew they were making so big a thing of the job you had failed at –"

"But –"

"– and that had hurt you so in failure. They did not want you to be sad. But Tork wants to see you. I said you would not be sad. So I went to bring you down from the rocks."

"Thanks, I guess."

"Tio Cal?"

But the voice was bigger and deeper than a child's.

He sat on a log back from the fire, eating a sweet potato. The flame flickered on his dark cheekbones, in his hair, wet and black. He stood, came to me, held up his hand. I held up mine and we slapped palms. "Good." He was smiling. "Ariel told me you would come. I will lay the power line down through the Slash tomorrow." His uniform scales glittered down his arms. He was very strong. But standing still, he still moved. The light on the cloth told me that. "I. . . ." He paused. I thought of a nervous, happy dancer. "I wanted to talk to you about the cable." I thought of an eagle, I thought of a shark. "And about the . . . accident. If you would."

"Sure," I said. "If there's anything I could tell you that would help."

"See, Tork," Ariel said. "I told you he would talk to you about it."

I could hear his breathing change. "It really doesn't bother you to talk about the accident?"

I shook my head and realized something about that voice. It was a boy's voice that could imitate a man's. Tork was not over nineteen.

"We're going fishing soon," Tork told me. "Will you come?"

"If I'm not in the way."

A bottle went from the woman at the shrimp crate to one of the guitarists, down to Ariel, to me, then to Tork. (The liquor, made in a cave seven miles inland, was almost rum. The too tight skin across the left side of my mouth makes the manful swig a little difficult to bring off. I got "rum" down my chin.)

He drank, wiped his mouth, passed the bottle on and put his hand on my shoulder. "Come down to the water."

We walked away from the fire. Some of the fishermen stared after us. A few of the amphimen glanced, and glanced away.

"Do all the young people of the village call you Tio Cal?"

"No. Only my godchildren. Their father and I have been friends since I was your age."

"Oh, I thought perhaps it was a nickname. That's why I called you that."

We reached wet sand where orange light cavorted at our feet. The broken shell of a lifeboat rocked in moonlight. Tork sat down on the shell's rim. I sat beside him. The water splashed to our knees.

"There's no other place to lay the power cable?" I asked. "There is no other way to take it except through the Slash?"

"I was going to ask you what you thought of the whole business. But I guess I don't really have to." He shrugged and clapped his hands together a few times. "All the projects this side of the bay have grown huge and cry for power. The new operations tax the old lines unmercifully. There was a power failure last July in Cayine down the shelf below the twilight level. The whole village was without light for two days, and twelve amphimen died of over-exposure to the cold currents coming up from the depths. If we laid the cables farther up, we chance disrupting our own fishing operations as well as those of the fishermen on shore."

I nodded.

"Cal, what happened to you in the Slash?"

Eager, scared Tork. I was remembering now, not the accident, but the midnight before, pacing the beach, guts clamped with fists of fear and anticipation. Some of the Indians back where they make the liquor still send messages by tying knots in palm fibers. One could have spread my entrails then, or Tork's tonight, to read our respective horospecs.

Juao's mother knew the knot language, but he and his sisters never bothered to learn because they wanted to be modern, and, as children, still confused with modernity the new ignorances, lacking modern knowledge.

"When I was a boy," Tork said, "we would dare each other to walk the boards along the edge of the ferry slip. The sun would be hot and the boards would rock in the water, and if the boats were in and you fell down between the boats and the piling, you could get killed" He shook his head. "The crazy things kids will do. That was back when I was eight or nine, before I became a waterbaby."

"Where was it?"

Tork looked up. "Oh. Manila. I'm Filipino."

The sea licked our knees, and the gunwale sagged under us.

"What happened in the Slash?"

"There's a volcanic flaw near the base of the Slash."

"I know."

"And the sea is hypersensitive down there. You don't insult her fashion or her figure. We had an avalanche. The cable broke. The sparks were so hot and bright they made gouts of foam fifty feet high on the surface, so they tell me."

"What caused the avalanche?"

I shrugged. "It could have been just a goddamned coincidence. There are rock falls down there all the time. It could have been the noise from the machines – though we masked them pretty well. It could have been something to do with the inductance from the smaller cables power. Or maybe somebody just kicked out the wrong stone that was holding everything up."

One webbed hand became a fist, sank into the other, and hung.

Calling, "Cal!"

I looked up. Juao, pants rolled to his knees, shirt sailing in the sea wind, stood in the weave of white water. The wind lifted Tork's hair from his neck; and the fire roared on the beach.

Tork looked up too.

"They're getting ready to catch a big fish!" Juao called.

Men were already pushing their boats out. Tork clapped my shoulder. "Come, Cal. We fish now." We waded back to the shore.

Juao caught me as I reached dry sand. "You ride in my boat, Cal!"

Someone came with the acrid flares that hissed. The water slapped around the bottom of the boats as we wobbled into the swell.

Juao vaulted in and took up the oars. Around us green amphimen walked into the sea, struck forward, and were gone.

Juao pulled, leaned, pulled. The moonlight slid down his arms. The fire diminished on the beach.

Then among the boats, there was a splash, an explosion, and the red flare bloomed in the sky: the amphimen had sighted a big fish.

The flare hovered, pulsed once, twice, three times, four times (twenty, forty, sixty, eighty stone they estimated its weight to be), then fell.

Suddenly I shrugged out of my shirt, pulled at my belt buckle. "I'm going over the side, Juao!"

He leaned, he pulled, he leaned. "Take the rope."

"Yeah. Sure." It was tied to the back of the boat. I made a loop in the other end, slipped it around my shoulder. I swung my bad leg over the side, flung myself on the black water –

– mother-of-pearl shattered over me. That was the moon, blocked by the shadow of Juao's boat ten feet overhead. I turned below the rippling wounds Juao's oars made stroking the sea.

One hand and one foot with torn webs, I rolled over and looked down. The rope snaked to its end, and I felt Juao's strokes pulling me through the water.

They fanned below with underwater flares. Light undulated on their backs and heels. They circled, they closed, like those deep-sea fish who carry their own illumination. I saw the prey, glistening as it neared a flare.

You chase a fish with one spear among you. And that spear would be Tork's tonight. The rest have ropes to bind him that go up to the fishermen's boats.

There was a sudden confusion of lights below. The spear had been shot!

The fish, long as a tall and short man together, rose through the ropes. He turned out to sea, trailing his pursuers. But others waited there tried to loop him. Once I had flung those ropes, treated with tar and lime to dissolve the slime of the fish's body and hold to the beast. The looped ropes caught, and by the movement of the flares, I saw them jerked from their paths. The fish turned, rose again, this time toward me.

He pulled around when one line ran out (and somewhere on the surface the prow of a boat doffed deep) but turned back and came on.

Of a sudden, amphimen were flicking about me as the fray's center drifted by. Tork, his spear dug deep, forward and left of the marlin's dorsal, had hauled himself astride the beast.

The fish tried to shake him, then dropped his tail and rose straight. Everybody started pulling toward the surface. I broke foam and grabbed Juao's gunwale.

Tork and the fish exploded up among the boats. They twisted in air, in moonlight, in froth. The fish danced across the water on its tail, fell.

Juao stood up in the boat and shouted. The other fishermen shouted too, and somebody perched on the prow of a boat flung a rope and someone in the water caught it.

Then fish and Tork and me and a dozen amphimen all went underwater at once.

They dropped in a corona of bubbles. The fish struck the end of another line, and shook himself. Tork was thrown free, but he doubled back.

Then the lines began to haul up again, quivering, whipping, quivering again.

Six lines from six boats had him. For one moment he was still in the submarine moonlight. I could see his wound tossing scarves of blood.

When he (and we) broke surface, he was thrashing again, near Juao's boat. I was holding onto the side when suddenly Tork, glistening, came out of the water beside me and went over into the dinghy.

"Here you go," he said, turning to kneel at the bobbing rim, and pulled me up while Juao leaned against the far side to keep balance.

Wet rope slopped on the prow. "Hey, Cal!" Tork laughed grabbed it up, and began to haul.

The fish prised wave from white wave in the white water.

The boats came together. The amphimen had all climbed up. Ariel was across from us, holding a flare that drooled smoke down her arm. She peered by the hip of the fisherman who was standing in front of her.

Juao and Tork were hauling the rope. Behind them I was coiling it with one hand as it came back to me.

The fish came up and was flopped into Ariel's boat, tail out, head up, chewing air.

I had just finished pulling on my trousers when Tork fell down on the seat behind me and grabbed me around the shoulders with his wet arms. "Look at our fish, Tio Cal! Look!" He gasped air, laughing, his dark face diamonded beside the flares. "Look at our fish there, Cal!"

Juao, grinning white and gold, pulled us back into shore. The fire, the singing, hands beating hands – and my godson had put pebbles in the empty rum bottles and was shaking them to the music – the guitars spiraled around us as we carried the fish up the sand and the men brought the spit.

"Watch it!" Tork said, grasping the pointed end of the great stick that was thicker than his wrist.

We turned the fish over.

"Here, Cal?"

He prodded two fingers into the white flesh six inches back from the bony lip.

"Fine."

Tork jammed the spit in.

We worked it through the body. By the time we carried it to the fire, they had brought more rum.

"Hey, Tork. Are you going to get some sleep before you go down in the morning?" I asked.

He shook his head. "Slept all afternoon." He pointed toward the roasting fish with his elbow. "That's my breakfast."

But when the dancing grew violent a few hours later, just before the fish was to come off the fire, and the kids were pushing the last of the sweet potatoes from the ashes with sticks, I walked back to the lifeboat shell we had sat on earlier. It was three-quarters flooded.

Curled below still water, Tork slept, fist loose before his mouth, the gills at the back of his neck pulsing rhythmically. Only his shoulder and hip made islands in the floated boat.

"Where's Tork?" Ariel asked me at the fire. They were swinging up the sizzling fish.

"Taking a nap."

"Oh, he wanted to cut the fish!"

"He's got a lot of work coming up. Sure you want to wake him up?"

"No, I'll let him sleep."

But Tork was coming up from the water, brushing his dripping hair back from his forehead.

He grinned at us, then went to carve. I remember him standing on the table, astraddle the meat, arm going up and down with the big knife (details, yes, those are the things you remember), stopping to hand down the portions, then hauling his arm back to cut again.

That night, with music and stomping on the sand and shouting back and forth over the fire, we made more noise than the sea.

4

The eight-thirty bus was more or less on time.

"I don't think they want to go," Juao's sister said. She was accompanying the children to the Aquatic Corp Headquarters in Brasilia.

"They are just tired," Juao said. "They should not have stayed up so late last night. Get on the bus now. Say goodbye to Tio Cal."

"Goodbye."

"Goodbye."

Kids are never their most creative in that sort of situation. And I suspect that my godchildren may have just been suffering their first (or one of their first) hangovers. They had been very quiet all morning.

I bent down and gave them a clumsy hug. "When you come back on your first weekend off, I'll take you exploring down below at the point. You'll be able to gather your own coral now."

Juao's sister got teary, cuddled the children, cuddled me, Juao, then got on the bus.

Someone was shouting out the bus window for someone at the bus stop not to forget something. They trundled around the square and then toward the highway. We walked back across the street where the café owners were putting out canvas chairs.

"I will miss them," he said, like a long-considered admission.

"You and me both." At the docks near the hydrofoil wharf where the submarine launches went out to the undersea cities, we saw a crowd. "I wonder if they had any trouble laying the –"

A woman screamed in the crowd. She pushed from the others, dropping eggs and onions. She began to pull her hair and shriek. (Remember the skillet of shrimp? She had been the woman ladling them out.) A few people moved to help her.

A clutch of men broke off and ran into a side street. I grabbed a running amphiman, who whirled to face me.

"What in hell is going on?"

For a moment his mouth worked on his words for all the trite world like a beached fish.

"From the explosion . . ." he began. "They just brought them back from the explosion at the Slash!"

I grabbed his other shoulder. "What happened!"

"About two hours ago. They were just a quarter of the way through, when the whole fault gave way. They had a goddamn underwater volcano for half an hour. They're still getting seismic disturbances."

Juao was running toward the launch. I pushed the guy away and limped after him, struck the crowd and jostled through calico, canvas, and green scales.

They were carrying the corpses out of the hatch of the submarine and laying them on a canvas spread across the dock. They still return bodies to the countries of birth for the family to decide the method of burial. When the fault had given, the hot slag that had belched into the steaming sea was mostly molten silicon.

Three of the bodies were only slightly burned here and there; from their bloated faces (one still bled from the ear) I guessed they had died from sonic concussion. But several of the bodies were almost totally encased in dull, black glass.

"Tork – " I kept asking. "Is one of them Tork?"

It took me forty-five minutes, asking first the guys who were carrying the bodies, then going into the launch and asking some guy with a clipboard, and then going back on the dock and into the office to find out that one of the more unrecognizable bodies was, yes, Tork.

Juao brought me a glass of buttermilk in a café on the square. He sat still a long time, then finally rubbed away his white moustache, released the chair rung with his toes, put his hands on his knees.

"What are you thinking about?"

"That it's time to go fix nets. Tomorrow morning I will fish." He regarded me a moment. "Where should I fish tomorrow, Cal?"

"Are you wondering about . . . well, sending the kids off today?"

He shrugged. "Fishermen from this village have drowned. Still it is a village of fishermen. Where should I fish?"

I finished my buttermilk. "The mineral content over the Slash should be high as the devil. Lots of algae will gather tonight. Lots of small fish down deep. Big fish hovering over."

He nodded. "Good. I will take the boat out there tomorrow."

We got up.

"See you, Juao."

I limped back to the beach.

5

The fog had unsheathed the sand by ten. I walked around, poking clumps of weeds with a stick, banging the same stick on my numb leg. When I lurched up to the top of the rocks, I stopped in the still grass. "Ariel?"

She was keeling in the water, head down, red hair breaking over sealed gills. Her shoulders shook, stopped, shook again.

"Ariel?" I came down over the blistered stones.

She turned away to look at the ocean.

The attachments of children are so important and so brittle. "How long have you been sitting here?"

She looked at me now, the varied waters of her face stilled on drawn cheeks. And her face was exhausted. She shook her head.

Sixteen? Seventeen? Who was the psychologist, back in the seventies, who decided that "adolescents" were just physical and mental adults with no useful work? "You want to come up to the house?"

The head-shaking got faster, then stopped.

After a while I said, "I guess they'll be sending Tork's body back to Manila."

"He didn't have a family," she explained. "He'll be buried here, at sea."

"Oh," I said.

And the rough volcanic glass, pulled across the ocean's sands, changing shape, dulling –

"You were – you liked Tork a lot, didn't you? You kids looked like you were pretty fond of each other."

"Yes. He was an awfully nice –" then she caught my meaning and blinked. "No," she said. "Oh, no. I was – I was engaged to Jonni . . . the brown-haired boy from California? Did you meet him at the party last night? We're both from Los Angeles, but we only met down here. And now . . . they're sending his body back this evening." Her eyes got very wide, then closed.

"I'm sorry, Ariel."

I'm a clumsy cripple, I step all over everybody's emotions. In that mirror I guess I'm too busy looking at what might have been.

"I'm sorry, Ariel."

She opened her eyes and began to look around her.

"Come on up to the house and have an avocado. I mean, they have avocados in now, not at the supermarket, but at the old town market on the other side. And they're better than any they grow in California."

She kept looking around.

"None of the amphimen get over there. It's a shame, because soon the market will probably close, and some of their fresh foods are really great. Oil and vinegar is all you need on them." I leaned back on the rocks. "Or a cup of tea?"

"Okay." She remembered to smile. I know the poor kid didn't feel like it. "Thank you. I won't be able to stay long, though."

We walked back up the rocks toward the house, the sea on our left. Just as we reached the patio, she turned and looked back. "Cal?"

"Yes? What is it?"

"Those clouds over there, across the water. Those are the only ones in the sky. Are they from the eruption in the Slash?"

I squinted. "I think so. Come on inside."

BRIAN W. ALDISS

The Worm That Flies

In many ways, Brian W. Aldiss was the *enfant terrible* of the late-
'50s, exploding into the science fiction world and shaking it up
with the ferocious verve and pyrotechnic verbal brilliance of
stories like "Poor Little Warrior," "Outside," "The New Father
Christmas," "Who Can Replace a Man?", "A Kind of
Artistry," and "Old Hundredth," and with the somber beauty
and unsettling poetic vision – in the main, of a world where
Mankind signally has *not* triumphantly conquered the universe,
as the Campbellian dogma of the time insisted that he would –
of his classic novels *Starship* and *The Long Afternoon of Earth* (*Non-
Stop* and *Hothouse*, respectively, in Britain). All this made him
one of the most controversial writers of the day . . . and, some
years later, he'd be one of the most controversial figures of the
New Wave era as well, shaking up the SF world of the mid-'60s
in an even more dramatic and drastic fashion with the
ferociously Joycean "acidhead war" stories that would be
melded into *Barefoot in the Head*, with the irreverent *Cryptozoic!*,
and with his surrealistic anti-novel *Report on Probability A*.

But Aldiss has never been willing to work any one patch of
ground for very long. By 1976, he had worked his way through
two controversial British mainstream bestsellers – *The Hand-
Reared Boy* and *A Soldier Erect* – and the strange transmuted
Gothic of *Frankenstein Unbound*, and gone on to produce a lyrical
masterpiece of science-fantasy, *The Malacia Tapestry*, perhaps his
best book, and certainly one of the best novels of the '70s.
Ahead, in the decade of the '80s, was the monumental
accomplishment of his *Helliconia* trilogy – *Helliconia Spring*,
Helliconia Summer and *Helliconia Winter* – and by the end of that
decade only the grumpiest of reactionary critics could deny that
Aldiss was one of the true giants of the field, a figure of artistic
complexity and amazing vigor, as much on the Cutting Edge in
the '90s as he had been in the '50s.

Few SF writers have ever had the imagination, poetic skills

and visionary scope to write convincingly about the *really* far future – once you have mentioned Olaf Stapledon, Clark Ashton Smith, Jack Vance, Gene Wolfe, Cordwainer Smith, Michael Moorcock, and M. John Harrison, you have almost exhausted the roster of authors who have handled the theme with any kind of evocativeness or complexity – but Aldiss has almost made a specialty of it. *The Long Afternoon of Earth* remains one of the classic visions of the distant future of Earth, and Aldiss has also handled the theme with grace and a wealth of poetic imagination in stories like "Old Hundredth" and "Full Sun." Never more vividly than here, though, as he takes us to a remote and terrible future to unravel the dread mystery of "The Worm That Flies."

The Long Afternoon of Earth won a Hugo Award in 1962. "The Saliva Tree" won a Nebula Award in 1965, and his novel *Starship* won the Prix Jules Verne in 1977. He took another Hugo Award in 1987 for his critical study of science fiction, *Trillion Year Spree*, written with David Wingrove. His other books include *An Island Called Moreau, Greybeard, Enemies of the System, A Rude Awakening, Life in the West,* and *Forgotten Life.* His short fiction has been collected in *Space, Time, and Nathaniel, Who Can Replace a Man?, New Arrivals, Old Encounters, Galaxies Like Grains of Sand,* and *Seasons in Flight.* His many anthologies include *Space Opera, Space Odysseys, Evil Earths, The Penguin Science Fiction Omnibus,* and, with Harry Harrison, *Decade: the 1940s, Decade: the 1950s,* and *Decade: the 1960s.* His latest books are *Dracula Unbound,* a novel, and *Bury My Heart at W. H. Smith's,* a memoir. He lives with his family in Oxford.

When the snow began to fall, the traveler was too absorbed in his reveries to notice. He walked slowly, his stiff and elaborate garments, fold over fold, ornament over ornament, standing out from his body like a wizard's tent.

The road along which he walked had been falling into a great valley, and was increasingly hemmed in by walls of mountain. On several occasions it had seemed that a way out of these huge accumulations of earth matter could not be found, that the geological puzzle was insoluble, the chthonian arrangement of discord irresolvable: And then vale and rumlin created between them a new direction, a surprise, an escape, and the way took fresh heart and plunged recklessly still deeper into the encompassing up-heaval.

The traveler, whose name to his wife was Tapmar and to the rest of the world Argustal, followed this natural harmony in complete paraesthesia, so close was he in spirit to the atmosphere presiding here. So strong was this bond, that the freak snowfall merely heightened his rapport.

Though the hour was only midday, the sky became the intense blue-gray of dusk. The Forces were nesting in the sun again, obscuring its light. Consequently, Argustal was scarcely able to detect when the layered and fractured bulwark of rock on his left side, the top of which stood unseen perhaps a mile above his head, became patched by artificial means, and he entered the domain of the Tree-men of Or.

As the way made another turn, he saw a wayfarer before him, heading in his direction. It was a great pine, immobile until warmth entered the world again and sap stirred enough in its wooden sinews for it to progress slowly forward once more. He brushed by its green skirts, apologetic but not speaking.

This encounter was sufficient to raise his consciousness above its trance level. His extended mind, which had reached out to embrace the splendid terrestrial discord hereabouts, now shrank to concentrate again on the particularities of his situation, and he saw that he had arrived at Or.

The way bisected itself, unable to choose between two equally unpromising ravines; Argustal saw a group of humans standing statuesque in the left-hand fork. He went toward them, and stood there silent until they should recognize his presence. Behind him, the wet snow crept into his footprints.

These humans were well advanced into the New Form, even as Argustal had been warned they would be. There were five of them standing here, their great brachial extensions bearing some tender brownish foliage, and one of them attenuated to a height of almost twenty feet. The snow lodged in their branches and in their hair.

Argustal waited for a long span of time, until he judged the afternoon to be well advanced, before growing impatient. Putting his hands to his mouth, he shouted fierecely at them,

"Ho then, Tree-men of Or, wake you from your arboreal sleep and converse with me. My name is Argustal to the world, and I travel to my home in far Talembil, where the seas run pink with the spring plankton. I need from you a component for my parapatterner, so rustle yourselves and speak, I beg!"

Now the snow had gone; a scorching rain had driven away its traces. The sun shone again, but its disfigured eye never looked down into the bottom of this ravine. One of the humans shook a branch, scattering water drops all around, and made preparation for speech.

This was a small human, no more than ten feet high, and the old primate form which it had begun to abandon, perhaps a couple of million years ago, was still in evidence. Among the gnarls and whorls of its naked flesh, its mouth was discernible; this it opened and said, "We speak to you, Argustal-to-the-world. You are the first ape-human to fare this way in a great time. Thus you are welcome, although you interrupt our search for new ideas."

"Have you found any new ideas?" Argustal asked, with his customary boldness. "I heard there were none on all Yzazys."

"Indeed. But it is better for our senior to tell you of them, if he so judges good."

It was by no means clear to Argustal whether he wished to hear what the new ideas were, for the Tree-men were known for their deviations into incomprehensibility. But there was a minor furore among the five, as if private winds stirred in their branches, and he settled himself on a boulder, preparing to wait. His own quest was so important that all impediments to its fulfillment seemed negligible.

Hunger overtook him before the senior spoke. He hunted about and caught slow-galloping grubs under logs, and snatched a brace of tiny fish from the stream, and a handful of nuts from a bush that grew by the stream.

Night fell before the senior spoke. As he raspingly cleared his gnarled throat, one faded star lit in the sky. That was Hrt, the flaming stone. It and Yzazys' sun burned alone on the very brink of the cataract of fire that was the universe. All the rest of the night sky in this hemisphere was filled with the unlimited terror of vacancy, a towering nothingness that continued without end or beginning.

Hrt had no worlds attending it. It was the last thing in the universe. And, by the way its light flickered, the denizens of Yzazys knew that it was already infested by the Forces which had swarmed outward from their eyries in the heart of the dying galaxy.

The eye of Hrt winked many times in the empty skull of space before the senior of the Tree-men of Or wound himself up to address Argustal.

Tall and knotty, his vocal chords were clamped within his gnarled body, and he spoke by curving his branches until his finest twigs, set against his mouth, could be blown through to give a slender and whispering version of language. The gesture made him seem curiously like a maiden who spoke with her finger cautiously to her lips.

"Indeed we have a new idea, oh Argustal-to-the-world, though it may be beyond your grasping or our expressing. We have perceived that there is a dimension called time, and from this we have drawn a deduction.

"We will explain dimensional time simply to you like this. We know that all things have lived so long on Yzazys that their origins are forgotten. What we can remember carries from that lost-in-the-mist thing up to this present moment; it is the time we inhabit, and we are used to thinking of it as all the time there is. But we men of Or have reasoned that this is not so."

"There must be other past times in the lost distances of time," said Argustal, "but they are nothing to us because we cannot touch them as we can our own pasts."

As if this remark had never been, the silvery whisper continued, "As one mountain looks small when viewed from another, so the things that we remember in our past look small from the present. But suppose we moved back to that past to look at this present! We could not see it – yet we know it exists. And from this we reason that there is still more time in the future, although we cannot see it."

For a long while, the night was allowed to exist in silence, and then Argustal said, "Well, I don't see that as being very wonderful reasoning. We know that, if the Forces permit, the sun will shine again tomorrow, don't we?"

The small Tree-man who had first spoken said, "but 'tomorrow' is expressional time. We have discovered that tomorrow exists in dimensional time also. It is real already, as real as yesterday."

Holy spirits! thought Argustal to himself, *why did I get myself involved in philosophy?* Aloud he said, "Tell me of the deduction you have drawn from this."

Again the silence, until the senior drew his branches together and whispered from a bower of twiggy fingers, "We have proved that tomorrow is no surprise. It is as unaltered as today or yesterday, merely another yard of the path of time. But we comprehend that things change, don't we? You comprehend that, don't you?"

"Of course. You yourselves are changing, are you not?"

"It is as you say, although we no longer recall what we were before, for that thing is become too small back in time. So: if time is all of the same quality, then it has no change, and thus cannot force change. So: there is another unknown element in the world that forces change!"

Thus in their fragmentary whispers they reintroduced sin into the world.

Because of the darkness, a need for sleep was induced in Argustal. With the senior Tree-man's permission, he climbed up into his branches and remained fast asleep until dawn returned to the fragment of sky above the mountains and filtered down to their retreat. Argustal swung to the ground, removed his outer garments, and performed his customary exercises. Then he spoke to the five beings again, telling them of his parapatterner, and asked for certain stones.

Although it was doubtful whether they understood what he was about, they gave him permission, and he moved round about the area, searching for a necessary stone; his senses blowing into nooks and crannies for it like a breeze.

The ravine was blocked at its far end by a rock fall, but the stream managed to pour through the interstices of the detritus into a yet lower defile. Climbing painfully, Argustal scrambled over the mass of broken rock to find himself in a cold and moist passage, a mere cavity between two great thighs of mountain. Here the light was dim, and the sky could hardly be seen, so far did the rocks overhang on the many shelves of strata overhead. But Argustal scarcely looked up. He followed the stream where it flowed into the rock itself, to vanish forever from human view.

He had been so long at his business, trained himself over so many millennia, that the stones almost spoke to him. And he became more certain than ever that he would find a stone to fit in with his grand design.

It was there. It lay just above the water, the upper part of it polished. When he had prized it out from the surrounding pebbles and gravel, he lifted it and could see that underneath it was slightly jagged, as if a smooth gum grew black teeth. He was surprised, but as he squatted to examine it, he began to see that what was necessary to the design of his parapatterner was precisely some such roughness. At once, the next step of the design revealed itself, and he saw for the first time the whole thing as it would be in its entirety. The vision disturbed and excited him.

He sat where he was, his blunt fingers around the rough-smooth stone, and for some reason he began to think about his wife Pamitar. Warm feelings of love ran through him, so that he smiled to himself and twitched his brows.

By the time he stood up and climbed out of the defile, he knew much about the new stone. His nose-for-stones sniffed it back to times when it was a much larger affair, when it occupied a grand position on a mountain, when it was engulfed in the bowels of the mountain, when it had been cast up and shattered down, when it had been a component of a bed of rock, when that rock had been ooze, when it had been a gentle rain of volcanic sediment, showering through an unbreathable atmosphere and filtering down through warm seas in an early and unknown place.

With tender respect, he tucked the stone away in a large pocket and scrambled back along the way he had come. He made no farewell to the five of Or. They stood mute together, branch-limbs interlocked, dreaming of the dark sin of change.

Now he made haste for home, traveling first through the borderlands of Old Crotheria and then through the region of Tamia, where there was only mud. Legends had it that

Tamia had once known fertility, and that speckled fish had swum in streams between forests; but now mud conquered everything, and the few villages were of baked mud, while the roads were dried mud, the sky was the color of mud, and the few mud-colored humans, who chose for their own mud-stained reasons to live here, had scarcely any antlers growing from their shoulders and seemed about to deliquesce into mud. There wasn't a decent stone anywhere about the place. Argustal met a tree called David-by-the-moat-that-dries that was moving into his own home region. Depressed by the everlasting brownness of Tamia he begged a ride from it, and climbed into its branches. It was old and gnarled, its branches and roots equally hunched, and it spoke in grating syllables of its few ambitions.

As he listened, taking pains to recall each syllable while he waited long for the next, Argustal saw that David spoke by much the same means as the people of Or had done, stuffing whistling twigs to an orifice in its trunk; but whereas it seemed that the Tree-men were losing the use of their vocal chords, the man-tree was developing some from the stringy integuments of its fibers, so that it became a nice problem as to which was inspired by which, which copied which, or whether – for both sides seemed so self-absorbed that this also was a possibility – they had come on a mirror-image of perversity independently.

"Motion is the prime beauty," said David-by-the-moat-that-dries, and took many degrees of the sun across the muddy sky to say it. "Motion is in me. There is no motion in the ground. In the ground there is not motion. All that the ground contains is without motion. The ground lies in quiet and to lie in the ground is not to be. Beauty is not in the ground. Beyond the ground is the air. Air and ground make all there is and I would be of the ground and air. I was of the ground and of the air but I will be of the air alone. If there is ground, there is another ground. The leaves fly in the air and my longing goes with them but they are only part of me because I am of wood. Oh, Argustal, you know not the pains of wood!"

Argustal did not indeed, for long before this gnarled speech was spent, the moon had risen and the silent muddy night had fallen with Hrt flickering overhead, and he was curled asleep in David's distorted branches, the stone in his deep pocket.

Twice more he slept, twice more watched their painful progress along the unswept tracks, twice more joined converse with the melancholy tree – and when he woke again, all the heavens were stacked with fleecy clouds that showed blue between, and low hills lay ahead. He jumped down. Grass grew here. Pebbles littered the track. He howled and shouted with pleasure. The mud had gone.

Crying his thanks, he set off across the heath.

". . . growth . . ." said David-by-the-moat-that-dries.

The heath collapsed and gave way to sand, fringed by sharp grass that scythed at Argustal's skirts as he went by. He plowed across the sand. This was his own country, and he rejoiced, taking his bearing from the occasional cairn that pointed a finger of shade across the sand. Once one of the Forces flew over, so that for a moment of terror the world was plunged in night, thunder growled, and a paltry hundred drops of rain spattered down; then it was already on the far confines of the sun's domain, plunging away – no matter where!

Few animals, fewer birds, still survived. In the sweet deserts of Outer Talembil, they were especially rare. Yet Argustal passed a bird sitting on a cairn, its hooded eye bleared with a million years of danger. It clattered one wing at sight of him, in tribute to old reflexes, but he respected the hunger in his belly too much to try to dine on sinews and feathers, and the bird appeared to recognize the fact.

He was nearing home. The memory of Pamitar was sharp before him, so that he could follow it like a scent. He passed another of his kind, an old ape wearing a red mask hanging almost to the ground; they barely gave each other a nod of recognition. Soon on the idle skyline he saw the blocks that marked Gornilo, the first town of Talembil.

The ulcerated sun traveled across the sky. Stoically, Argustal traveled across the intervening dunes, and arrived in the shadow of the white blocks of Gornilo.

No one could recollect now – recollection was one of the lost things that many felt privileged to lose – what factors had determined certain features of Gornilo's architecture. This was an ape-human town, and perhaps in order to construct a memorial to yet more distant and dreadful things, the first inhabitants of the town had made slaves of themselves and of the other creatures that were now no more, and erected these great cubes that now showed signs of weathering, as if they tired at last of swinging their shadows every day about their bases. The ape-humans who lived here were the same ape-humans who had always lived here; they sat as untiringly under their mighty memorial blocks as they had always done – calling now to Argustal as he passed as languidly as one flicks stones across the surface of a lake – but they could recollect no longer if or how they had shifted the blocks across the desert; it might be that that forgetfulness formed an integral part of being as permanent as the granite of the blocks.

Beyond the blocks stood the town. Some of the trees here were visitors, bent on becoming as David-by-the-moat-that-dries was, but most grew in the old way, content with ground and indifferent to motion. They knotted their branches this way and slatted their twigs that way, and humped their trunks the other way, and thus schemed up ingenious and ever-changing homes for the tree-going inhabitants of Gornio.

At last Argustal came to his home, on the far side of the town.

The name of his home was Cormok. He pawed and patted and licked it first before running lightly up its trunk to the living room.

Pamitar was not there.

He was not surprised at this, hardly even disappointed, so serene was his mood. He walked slowly about the room, sometimes swinging up to the ceiling in order to view it better, licking and sniffing as he went, chasing the after-images of his wife's presence. Finally, he laughed and fell into the middle of the floor.

"Settle down, boy!" he said.

Sitting where he had dropped, he unloaded his pockets, taking out the five stones he had acquired in his travels and laying them aside from his other possessions. Still sitting, he disrobed, enjoying doing it inefficiently. Then he climbed into the sand bath.

While Argustal lay there, a great howling wind sprang up, and in a moment the room was plunged into sickly grayness. A prayer went up outside, a prayer flung by the people at the unheeding Forces not to destroy the sun. His lower lip moved in a gesture at once of contentment and contempt; he had forgotten the prayers of Talembil. This was a religious city. Many of the Unclassified congregated here from the waste miles, people or animals whose minds had dragged them aslant from what they were into rococo forms that more exactly defined their inherent qualities, until they resembled forgotten or extinct forms, or forms that had no being till now, and acknowledged no common cause with any other living thing – except in this desire to preserve the festering sunlight from further ruin.

Under the fragrant grains of the bath, submerged all but for head and a knee and hand, Argustal opened wide his perceptions to all that might come: And finally thought only what he had often thought while lying there – for the armories of cerebration had long since been emptied of all new ammunition, whatever the Tree-men of Or might claim – that in such baths, under such an unpredictable wind, the major life forms of Yzazys, men and trees, had probably first come at their impetus to change. But change itself . . . had there been a much older thing blowing about the world that everyone had forgotten?

For some reason, that question aroused discomfort in him. He felt dimly that there was another side of life than contentment and happiness; all beings felt contentment and happiness; but were those qualities a unity, or were they not perhaps one side only of a – of a shield?

He growled. Start thinking gibberish like that and you ended up human with antlers on your shoulders!

Brushing off the sand, he climbed from the bath, moving more swiftly than he had done in countless time, sliding out of his home, down to the ground, without bothering to put on his clothes.

He knew where to find Pamitar. She would be beyond the

town, guarding the parapatterner from the tattered angry beggars of Talembil.

The cold wind blew, with an occasional slushy thing in it that made a being blink and wonder about going on. As he strode through the green and swishing heart of Gornilo, treading among the howlers who knelt casually everywhere in rude prayer, Argustal looked up at the sun. It was visible by fragments, torn through tree and cloud. Its face was blotched and pimpled, sometimes obscured altogether for an instant at a time, then blazing forth again. It sparked like a blazing blind eye. A wind seemed to blow from it that blistered the skin and chilled the blood.

So Argustal came to his own patch of land, clear of the green town, out in the stirring desert, and his wife Pamitar, to the rest of the world called Miram. She squatted with her back to the wind, the sharply flying grains of sand cutting about her hairy ankles. A few paces away, one of the beggars pranced among Argustal's stones.

Pamitar stood up slowly, removing the head shawl from her head.

"Tapmar!" she said.

Into his arms he wrapped her, burying his face in her shoulder. They chirped and clucked at each other, so engrossed that they made no note of when the breeze died and the desert lost its motion and the sun's light improved.

When she felt him tense, she held him more loosely. At a hidden signal, he jumped away from her, jumping almost over her shoulder, springing ragingly forth, bowling over the lurking beggar into the sand.

The creature sprawled, two-sided and misshapen, extra arms growing from arms, head like a wolf, back legs bowed like a gorilla, clothed in a hundred textures, yet not unlovely. It laughed as it rolled and called in a high clucking voice, "Three men sprawling under a lilac tree and none to hear the first one say, 'Ere the crops crawl, blows fall,' and the second abed at night with mooncalves, answer me what's the name of the third, feller?"

"Be off with you, you mad old crow!"

And as the old crow ran away, it called out its answer,

laughing, "Why Tapmar, for he talks to nowhere!" confusing the words as it tumbled over the dunes and made its escape.

Argustal and Pamitar turned back to each other, vying with the strong sunlight to search out each other's faces, for both had forgotten when they were last together, so long was time, so dim was memory. But there were memories, and as he searched they came back. The flatness of her nose, the softness of her nostrils, the roundness of her eyes and their brownness, the curve of the rim of her lips: All these, because they were dear, became remembered, thus taking on more than beauty.

They talked gently to each other, all the while looking. And slowly something of that other thing he suspected on the dark side of the shield entered him – for her beloved countenance was not as it had been. Around her eyes, particularly under them, were shadows, and faint lines creased from the sides of her mouth. In her stance too, did not the lines flow more downward than heretofore?

The discomfort growing too great, he was forced to speak to Pamitar of these things, but there was no proper way to express them. She seemed not to understand, unless she understood and did not know it, for her manner grew agitated, so that he soon forwent questioning, and turned to the parapatterner to hide his unease.

It stretched over a mile of sand, and rose several feet into the air. From each of his long expeditions, he brought back no more than five stones, yet there were assembled here many hundreds of thousands of stones, perhaps millions, all painstakingly arranged, so that no being could take in the arrangement from any one position, not even Argustal. Many were supported in the air at various heights by stakes or poles, more lay on the ground, where Pamitar always kept the dust and the wild men from encroaching them; and of these on the ground, some stood isolated, while others lay in profusion, but all in a pattern that was ever apparent only to Argustal – and he feared that it would take him until the next Sunset to have that pattern clear in his head again. Yet already it started to come clearer, and he recalled with wonder the devious and fugal course he had taken, walking down to the ravine of the Tree-men of Or, and knew that he still contained the skill to place the new stones he had brought within the general pattern with reference to that natural harmony – so completing the parapatterner.

And the lines on his wife's face: Would they too have a place within the pattern?

Was there sense in what the crow beggar had cried, that he talked to nowhere? And . . . and . . . the terrible and, would nowhere answer him?

Bowed, he took his wife's arm, and scurried back with her to their home high in the leafless tree.

"My Tapmar," she said that evening as they ate a dish of fruit, "it is good that you come back to Gornilo, for the town sedges up with dreams like an old river bed, and I am afraid."

At this he was secretly alarmed, for the figure of speech she used seemed to him an apt one for the newly observed lines on her face; so that he asked her what the dreams were in a voice more timid than he meant to use.

Looking at him strangely, she said, "The dreams are as thick as fur, so thick that they congeal my throat to tell you of them. Last night, I dreamed I walked in a landscape that seemed to be clad in fur all around the distant horizons, fur that branched and sprouted and had somber tones of russet and dun and black and a lustrous black-blue. I tried to resolve this strange material into the more familiar shapes of hedges and old distorted trees, but it stayed as it was, and I became . . . well, I had the word in my dream that I became a *child*."

Argustal looked aslant over the crowded vegetation of the town and said, "These dreams may not be of Gornilo but of you only, Pamitar. What is *child?*"

"There's no such thing in reality, to my knowledge, but in the dream the child that was I was small and fresh and in its actions at once nimble and clumsy. It was alien from me, its motions and ideas never mine – and yet it was all familiar to me. I was it, Tapmar, I was that child. And now that I wake, I become sure that I once was such a thing as a *child*."

He tapped his fingers on his knees, shaking his head and blinking in a sudden anger. "This is your bad secret, Pamitar! I knew you had one the moment I saw you! I read it in your face which has chanted in an evil way! You know you were never anything but Pamitar in all the millions of years of your life, and that *child* must be an evil phantom that possesses you. Perhaps you will now be turned into *child!*"

She cried out and hurled a green fruit into which she had bitten. Deftly, he caught it before it struck him.

They made a provisional peace before settling for sleep. That night, Argustal dreamed that he also was small and vulnerable and hardly able to manage the language; his intentions were like an arrow and his direction clear.

Waking, he sweated and trembled, for he knew that as he had been *child* in his dream, so he had been *child* once in life. And this went deeper than sickness. When his pained looks directed themselves outside, he saw the night was like shot silk, with a dappled effect of light and shadow in the dark blue dome of the sky, which signified that the Forces were making merry with the sun while it journeyed through Yzazys; and Argustal thought of his journeys across the face of Yzazys, and of his visit to Or, when the Tree-men had whispered of an unknown element that forces change.

"They prepared me for this dream!" he muttered. He knew now that change had worked in his very foundations; once, he had been this thin tiny alien thing called *child*, and his wife had been too, and possibly others. He thought of that little apparition again, with its spindly legs and piping voice; the horror of it chilled his heart; he broke into prolonged groans that all Pamitar's comforting took a long part of the dark to silence.

He left her sad and pale. He carried with him the stones he had gathered on his journey, the odd-shaped one from the ravine and the ones he had acquired before that. Holding them tightly to him, Argustal made his way through the town to his spatial arrangement. For so long, it had been his chief preoccupation; today, the long project would come to completion; yet because he could not even say why it had so preoccupied him, his feelings inside lay flat and wretched. Something had got to him and killed contentment.

Inside the prospects of the parapatterner, the old beggarly man lay, resting his shaggy head on a blue stone. Argustal was too low in spirit to chase him away.

"As your frame of stones will frame words, the words will come forth stones," cried the creature.

"I'll break your bones, old crow!" growled Argustal, but inwardly he wondered at this vile crow's saying and at what he had said the previous day about Argustal's talking to nowhere, for Argustal had discussed the purpose of his structure with nobody, not even Pamitar. Indeed, he had not recognized the purpose of the structure himself until two journeys back – or had it been three or four? The pattern had started simply as a pattern (hadn't it?) and only much later had the obsession become a purpose.

To place the new stones correctly took time. Wherever Argustal walked in his great framework, the old crow followed, sometimes on two legs, sometimes on four. Other personages from the town collected to stare, but none dared step inside the perimeter of the structure, so that they remained far off, like little stalks growing on the margins of Argustal's mind.

Some stones had to touch, others had to be just apart. He walked and stooped and walked, responding to the great pattern that he now knew contained a universal law. The task wrapped him around in an aesthetic daze similar to the one he had experienced traveling the labyrinthine way down to Or, but with greater intensity.

The spell was broken only when the old crow spoke from a few paces away in a voice level and unlike his usual sing-song. And the old crow said, "I remember you planting the very first of these stones here when you were a child."

Argustal straightened.

Cold took him, though the bilious sun shone bright. He could not find his voice. As he searched for it, his gaze went across to the eyes of the beggar-man, festering in his black forehead.

"You know I was once such a phantom – a child?" he asked.

"We are all phantoms. We were all childs. As there is gravy in our bodies, our hours were once few."

"Old crow . . . you describe a different world – not ours!"

"Very true, very true. Yet that other world once was ours."

"Oh, not! Not!"

"Speak to your machine about it! Its tongue is of rock and cannot lie like mine."

He picked up a stone and flung it. "That will I do! Now get away from me!"

The stone hit the old man in his ribs. He groaned, painfully and danced and backward, tripped, lay full length in the sand, hopeless and shapeless.

Argustal, was upon him at once.

"Old crow, forgive me! It was fear at my thoughts made me attack you – and there is a certain sort of horror in your presence!"

"And in your stone-flinging!" muttered the old man, struggling to rise.

"You know of childs! In all the millions of years that I have worked at my design, you have never spoken of this. Why not?"

"Time for all things . . . and that time now draws to a close, even on Yzazys."

They stared into each other's eyes as the old beggar slowly rose, arms and cloak spread in a way that suggested he would either fling himself on Argustal or turn in flight. Argustal did not move. Crouching with his knuckles in the sand, he said, ". . . even on Yzazys? Why do you say so?"

"You are of Yzazys! We humans are not – if I call myself human. Thousands of thousands of years before you were child, I came from the heart stars with many others. There is no life there now! The rot spreads from the center! The sparks fly from sun to sun! Even to Yzazys, the hour is come. Up the galactic chimneys the footprints drum!" Suddenly he fell to the ground, was up again, and made off in haste, limbs whirling in a way that took from him all resemblance to human kind. He pushed through the line of watchers and was gone.

For a while, Argustal squatted where he was, groping through matters that dissolved as they took shape, only to grow large when he dismissed them. The storm blew through him and distorted him, like the trouble on the face of the sun. When he decided there was nothing for it but to complete the parapatterner, still he trembled with the new knowledge: Without being able to understand why, he knew the new knowledge would destroy the old world.

All now was in position, save for the odd-shaped stone from Or, which he carried firm on one shoulder, tucked between ear and hand. For the first time, he realized what a gigantic structure he had wrought. It was a businesslike stroke of insight, no sentiment involved. Argustal was now no more than a bead rolling through the vast interstices around him.

Each stone held its own temporal record as well as its spatial position; each represented different stresses, different epochs, different temperatures, materials, chemicals, molds, intensities. Every stone together represented an anagram of Yzazys, its whole composition and continuity. The last stone was merely a focal point for the whole dynamic, and as Argustal slowly walked between the vibrant arcades, that dynamic rose to pitch.

He heard it grow. He paused. He shuffled now this way, now that. As he did so, he recognized that there was no one focal position but a myriad, depending on position and direction of the key stone.

Very softly, he said, ". . . that my fears might be verified . . ."

And all about him – but softly – came a voice in stone, stuttering before it grew clearer, as if it had long known of words but never practiced them.

"Thou. . . ." Silence, then a flood of sentence.

"Thou thou art, oh, thou art worm thou art sick, rose invisible rose. In the howling storm thou art in the storm. Worm thou art found out, oh, rose thou art sick and found out flies in the night thy bed thy thy crimson life destroy. Oh – oh, rose, thou art sick! The invisible worm, the invisible worm that flies in the night, in the howling storm, has found out – has found out thy bed of crimson joy . . . and his dark dark secret love, his dark secret love does thy life destroy."

Argustal was already running from that place.

In Pamitar's arms he could find no comfort now. Though he huddled there, up in the encaging branches, the worm that flies worked in him. Finally, he rolled away from her and

said, "Who ever heard so terrible a voice? I cannot speak
again with the universe."

"You do not know it was the universe." She tried to tease
him. "Why should the universe speak to little Tapmar?"

"The old crow said I spoke to nowhere. Nowhere is the
universe – where the sun hides at night – where our
memories hide, where our thoughts evaporate. I cannot talk
with it. I must hunt out the old crow and talk to him."

"Talk no more, ask no more questions! All you discover
brings you misery! Look – you will no longer regard me, your
poor wife! You turn your eyes away!"

"If I stare at nothing for all succeeding eons, yet I must
find out what torments us!"

In the center of Gornilo, where many of the Unclassified
lived, bare wood twisted up from the ground like fossilized
sack, creating caves and shelters and strange limbs on which
and in which old pilgrims, otherwise without a home, might
perch. Here at nightfall Argustal sought out the beggar.

The old fellow was stretched painfully beside a broken
pot, clasping a woven garment across his body. He turned in
his small cell, trying to escape, but Argustal had him by the
throat and held him still.

"I want your knowledge, old crow!"

"Get it from the religious men – they know more than I!"

It made Argustal pause, but he slackened his grip on the
other by only the smallest margin.

"Because I have you, you must speak to me. I know that
knowledge is pain, but so is ignorance once one has sensed its
presence. Tell me more about childs and what they did! Tell
me of what you call the heart stars!"

As if in a fever, the old crow rolled about under Argustal's
grip. He brought himself to say, "What I know is so little, so
little, like a blade of grass in a field. And like blades of grass
are the distant bygone times. Through all those times come
the bundles of bodies now on this Earth. Then as now, no
new bodies. But once . . . even before those bygone times . . .
you cannot understand . . ."

"I understand well enough."

"You are scientist! Before bygone times was another time,
and then . . . then was childs and different things that are not

any longer, many animals and birds and smaller things with
frail wings unable to carry them over long time . . ."

"What happened? Why was there change, old crow?"

"Men . . . scientists . . . make understanding of the gravy
of bodies and turn every person and thing and tree to eternal
life. We now continue from that time, a long long time – so
long we have forgotten what was then done."

The smell of him was like an old pie. Argustal asked him,
"And why now are no childs?"

"Childs are just small adults. We are adults, having
become from child. But in that great former time, before
scientists were on Yzazys, adults produced childs. Animals
and trees likewise. But with eternal life, this cannot be –
those child-making parts of the body have less life than
stone."

"Don't talk of stone! So we live forever . . . you old ragbag,
you remember – ah, you remember me as child?"

But the old ragbag was working himself into a kind of fit,
pummeling the ground, slobbering at the mouth.

"Seven shades of lilac, even worse I remember myself a
child, running like an arrow, air, everywhere fresh rosy air.
So I am mad, for I remember!" He began to scream and cry,
and the outcasts round about took up the wail in chorus.
"We remember, we remember!" – whether they did or not.

Clapping his hand over the beggar's mouth, Argustal
said, "But you were not child on Yzazys – tell me about
that!"

Shaking, the other replied, "Earlier I tell you – all humans
come from heart stars. Yzazys here is perched on universe's
end! Once were as many worlds as days in eternity, now all
burned away as smoke up the chimney. Only this last place
was safe."

"What happened? Why?"

"Nothing happened! Life is life is life – only except that
change crept in."

And what was this but an echo of the words of the Tree-
men of Or who, deep in their sinful glade, had muttered of
some unknown element that forced change? Argustal
crouched with bowed head while the beggarman shuddered
beside him, and outside the holy idiots took up his last words

in a chant: "Change crept in! Change crept in! Daylight smoked and change crept in! Change crept in!"

Their dreadful howling worked like spears in Argustal's flank. He had pictures afterward of his panic run through the town, of wall and trunk and ditch and road, but it was all as insubstantial at the time as the pictures afterward. When he finally fell to the ground panting, he was unaware of where he lay, and everything was nothing to him until the religious howling had died into silence.

Then he saw he lay in the middle of his great structure, his cheek against the Or stone where he had dropped it. And as his attention came to it, the great structure around him answered without his having to speak.

He was at a new focal point. The voice that sounded was new, as cool as the previous one had been choked. It blew over him in a cool wind.

"There is no amaranth on this side of the grave, oh Argustal, no name with whatsoever emphasis of passionate love repeated that is not mute at last. Experiment X gave life for eternity to every living thing in the world, but even eternity is punctuated by release and suffers period. The old life had its childhood and its end, the new had no such logic. It found its own after many millennia, and took its cue from individual minds. What a man was, he became; what a tree, it became."

Argustal lifted his tired head from its pillow of stone. Again the voice changed pitch and trend, as if in response to his minute gesture.

"The present is a note in music. That note can no longer be sustained. You find what questions you have found, oh Argustal, because the chord, in dropping to a lower key, rouses you from the long dream of crimson joy that was immortality. What you are finding, others also find, and you can none of you be any longer insensible to change. Even immortality must have an end. Life has passed like a long fire through the galaxy. Now it fast burns out even here, the last refuge of man!"

He stood up then, and hurled the Or stone. It flew, fell, rolled . . . and before it stopped he had awoken a great chorus of universal voice.

All Yzazys roused and a wind blew from the west. As he started again to move, he saw the religious men of the town were on the march, and the great sun-nesting Forces on their midnight wing, and Hrt the flaming stone wheeling overhead, and every majestic object alert as it had never been.

But Argustal walked slowly on his flat simian feet, plodding back to Pamitar. No longer would he be impatient in her arms. There, time would be all too brief.

He knew now the worm that flew and nestled in her cheek, in his cheek, in all things, even in the Tree-men of Or, even in the great impersonal Forces that despoiled the sun, even in the sacred bowels of the universe to which he had lent a temporary tongue. He knew now that back had come that Majesty that previously gave Life its reason, the Majesty that had been away from the world for so long and yet so brief a respite, the Majesty called Death.

GENE WOLFE
The Fifth Head of Cerberus

By early 1970, I was familiar with the name Gene Wolfe, had read one or two of his stories, such as "The Encounter" in *Orbit 3* and "Paul's Treehouse" in *Orbit 4*, and had even, in my capacity as first reader for Dell's SF line, rejected a novel manuscript – never subsequently published – by him. None of which prepared me for attending the Milford Writers Conference in the spring of that year and reading Wolfe's "The Fifth Head of Cerberus" in manuscript there. I remember sitting in the cavernous, high-ceilinged living room of Damon Knight's huge, rambling old wooden house in Milford, Pennsylvania, the manuscript in my lap, stunned by the brilliance of what I had just read. "The Fifth Head of Cerberus" was work a quantum jump better than anything that Wolfe had done up to that time, work that was clearly establishing a new Cutting Edge for the field, and it was plain to me that a new giant of the form had just loomed above the literary horizon.

It was an insight that would be shared by only a few in subsequent years. Although Wolfe went on to produce much of the really superior short fiction of the '70s – pieces such as "The Hero As Werwolf," "Seven American Nights," "Alien Stones," "The Eyeflash Miracles," and "The Island of Doctor Death and Other Stories," among many others – and one of the decade's best novels (the brilliant 1975 novel *Peace*, which, published almost anonymously as a mainstream hardback in a plain tan dustcover, sank without arousing a single ripple), he remained severely underappreciated throughout most of the decade. Perhaps this was because Wolfe was strongly identified with *Orbit* in the early '70s, and, as *Orbit* was the major American recipient for the spleen of the reactionary backlash that developed early in the decade, his reputation may have suffered from the association, as would the reputations of Joanna Russ, Kate Wilhelm, and several other frequent *Orbit* contributors. Wolfe and Russ would become bugbears to the conservatives in much the same way that Heinlein had become a bugbear to the New Wavers, and Wolfe in particular would be loathed and pointed at as an example of the kind of non-rigorous, scientifically illiterate, custardheaded intellectual that the reactionaries saw hiding under every bed. This was strongly ironic, since, as a professional engineer and the editor for many years of the trade publication *Plant Engineering*, Wolfe was probably more conversant with the hard sciences than many of his detractors, and much of his work shows a fine understanding of technology and a concern for the intricacies of its workings.

Wolfe would finally establish his reputation with his landmark *The Book of the New Sun* novel series at the beginning of a new decade, one of the true masterworks of science fiction, and there are few serious critics today who would deny that Wolfe is one of the best writers working in (or out of) the genre in the '90s.

As for "The Fifth Head of Cerberus" itself – lush and rich and strange, evocative and inventive, full of bizarrely transmuted echoes of Proust and Dickens and Kipling and Chesterton – I always believed that it was the best novella of a decade that bristled with good novellas, and doing the research for this anthology has done nothing to dissuade me from that opinion.

Gene Wolfe was born in New York, and grew up in Houston, Texas. Individual volumes of his monumental *The Book of the New Sun* series have won the Nebula Award, the World Fantasy Award and the John W. Campbell Memorial Award, and he also won a Nebula Award for his story "The Death of Doctor Island." His other books include *Peace, The Fifth Head of Cerberus, The Devil in a Forest, Soldier in the Mist,* and *Free Live Free.* His short fiction has been collected in *The Island of Doctor Death and Other Stories, Gene Wolfe's Book of Days, The Wolfe Archipelago* and the recent World Fantasy Award-winning collection *Stories from the Old Hotel.* His most recent books are *Soldier of Arate, There Are Doors, Castleview,* and *Pandora by Holly Hollander.*

> When the ivy-tod is heavy with snow,
> And the owlet whoops to the wolf below,
> That eats the she-wolf's young.
>
> *Samuel Taylor Coleridge*
> "The Rime of the Ancient Mariner"

When I was a boy my brother David and I had to go to bed early whether we were sleepy or not. In summer particularly, bedtime often came before sunset; and because our dormitory was in the east wing of the house, with a broad window facing the central courtyard and thus looking west, the hard, pinkish light sometimes streamed in for hours while we lay staring out at my father's crippled monkey perched on a flaking parapet, or telling stories, one bed to another, with soundless gestures.

Our dormitory was on the uppermost floor of the house, and our window had a shutter of twisted iron which we were forbidden to open. I suppose the theory was that a burglar might, on some rainy morning (this being the only time he could hope to find the roof, which was fitted out as a sort of pleasure garden, deserted) let down a rope and so enter our room unless the shutter was closed.

The object of this hypothetical and very courageous thief would not, of course, be merely to steal us. Children, whether boys or girls, were extraordinarily cheap in Port-Mimizon; and indeed I was once told that my father who had formerly traded in them no longer did so because of the poor market. Whether or not this was true, everyone – or nearly everyone – knew of some professional who would furnish what was wanted, within reason, at a low price. These men made the children of the poor and the careless their study, and should you want, say, a brown-skinned, red-haired little girl or one who was plump or who lisped, a blond boy like David or a pale, brown-haired, brown-eyed boy such as I, they could provide one in a few hours.

Neither, in all probability, would the imaginary burglar seek to hold us for ransom, though my father was thought in some quarters to be immensely rich. There were several reasons for this. Those few people who knew that my brother and I existed knew also, or at least had been led to believe, that my father cared nothing at all for us. Whether this was true or not, I cannot say; certainly I believed it, and my father never gave me the least reason to doubt it, though at the time the thought of killing him had never occurred to me.

And if these reasons were not sufficiently convincing, anyone with an understanding of the stratum in which he had become perhaps the most permanent feature would realize that for him, who was already forced to give large bribes to the secret police, to once disgorge money in that way would leave him open to a thousand ruinous attacks; and this may have been – this and the fear in which he was held – the real reason we were never stolen.

The iron shutter is (for I am writing now in my old dormitory room) hammered to resemble in a stiff and oversymmetrical way the boughs of a willow. In my boyhood it was overgrown by a silver trumpet vine (since dug up) which had scrambled up the wall from the court below, and I used to wish that it would close the window entirely and thus shut out the sun when we were trying to sleep; but David, whose bed was under the window, was forever reaching up to snap off branches so that he could whistle through the hollow stems, making a sort of panpipe of four or five. The piping, of course, growing louder as David grew bolder, would in time attract the attention of Mr Million, our tutor. Mr Million would enter the room in perfect silence, his wide wheels gliding across the uneven floor while David pretended sleep. The panpipe might by this time be concealed under his pillow, in the sheet, or even under the mattress, but Mr Million would find it.

What he did with those little musical instruments after confiscating them from David I had forgotten until yesterday; although in prison, when we were kept in by storms or heavy snow, I often occupied myself by trying to recall it. To have broken them, or dropped them through the shutter onto the patio below would have been completely unlike him; Mr Million never broke anything intentionally, and never wasted anything. I could visualize perfectly the half-sorrowing expression with which he drew the tiny pipes out (the face which seemed to float behind his screen was much like my father's) and the way in which he turned and glided from the room. But what became of them?

Yesterday, as I said (this is the sort of thing that gives me confidence), I remembered. He had been talking to me here while I worked, and when he left it seemed to me – as my glance idly followed his smooth motion through the doorway – that something, a sort of flourish I recalled from my earliest days, was missing. I closed my eyes and tried to remember what the appearance had been, eliminating any skepticism, any attempt to guess in advance what I "must" have seen; and I found that the missing element was a brief flash, the glint of metal, over Mr Million's head.

Once I had established this, I knew that it must have come from a swift upward motion of his arm, like a salute, as he left our room. For an hour or more I could not guess the reason for that gesture, and could only suppose it, whatever it had been, to have been destroyed by time. I tried to recall if the corridor outside our dormitory, in that really not so distant past, held some object now vanished: a curtain or a windowshade, an appliance to be activated, anything that might account for it. There was nothing.

I went into the corridor and examined the floor minutely for marks indicating furniture. I looked for hooks or nails driven into the walls, pushing aside the coarse old tapestries. Craning my neck, I searched the ceiling. Then, after an hour, I looked at the door itself and saw what I had not seen in the thousands of times I had passed through it: that like all the doors in this house, which is very old, it had a massive frame of wooden slabs, and that one of these, forming the lintel, protruded enough from the wall to make a narrow shelf above the door.

I pushed my chair into the hall and stood on the seat. The shelf was thick with dust in which lay forty-seven of my brother's pipes and a wonderful miscellany of other small objects. Objects many of which I recalled, but some of which still fail to summon any flicker of response from the recesses of my mind. . . .

The small blue egg of a songbird, speckled with brown. I suppose the bird must have nested in the vine outside our window, and that David or I despoiled the nest only to be robbed ourselves by Mr Million. But I do not recall the incident.

And there is a (broken) puzzle made of the bronzed viscera of some small animal, and – wonderfully evocative – one of those large and fancifully decorated keys, sold annually, which during the year of its currency will admit the possessor to certain rooms of the city library after hours. Mr Million, I suppose, must have confiscated it when, after expiration, he found it doing duty as a toy; but what memories!

My father had his own library, now in my possession; but we were forbidden to go there. I have a dim memory of standing – at how early an age I cannot say – before that huge carved door. Of seeing it swing back, and the crippled monkey on my father's shoulder pressing itself against his hawk face, with the black scarf and scarlet dressing gown beneath and the rows and rows of shabby books and notebooks behind them, and the sick-sweet smell of formaldehyde coming from the laboratory beyond the sliding mirror.

I do not remember what he said or whether it had been I or another who had knocked, but I do recall that after the door had closed, a woman in pink whom I thought very pretty stooped to bring her face to the level of my own and assured me that my father had written all the books I had just seen, and that I doubted it not at all.

My brother and I, as I have said, were forbidden this room; but when we were a little older Mr Million used to take us, about twice a week, on expeditions to the city library. These were very nearly the only times we were allowed to leave the house, and since our tutor disliked curling the jointed length of his metal modules into a hire cart, and no sedan chair would have withstood his weight or contained his bulk, these forays were made on foot.

For a long time this route to the library was the only part of the city I knew. Three blocks down Saltimbanque Street where our house stood, right at the Rue d'Asticot to the slave market and a block beyond that to the library. A child, not knowing what is extraordinary and what commonplace, usually lights midway between the two, finds interest in incidents adults consider beneath notice and calmly accepts the most improbable occurrences. My brother and I were fascinated by the spurious antiques and bad bargains of the Rue d'Asticot, but often bored when Mr Million insisted on stopping for an hour at the slave market.

It was not a large one, Port-Mimizon not being a center of the trade, and the auctioneers and their merchandise were frequently on a most friendly basis – having met several times previously as a succession of owners discovered the same fault. Mr Million never bid, but watched the bidding, motionless, while we kicked our heels and munched the fried bread he had bought at a stall for us. There were sedan chairmen, their legs knotted with muscle, and simpering bath attendants; fighting slaves in chains, with eyes dulled by drugs or blazing with imbecile ferocity; cooks, house servants, a hundred others – yet David and I used to beg to be allowed to proceed alone to the library.

This library was a wastefully large building which had held government offices in the old French-speaking days. The park in which it had once stood had died of petty corruption, and the library now rose from a clutter of shops and tenements. A narrow thoroughfare led to the main doors, and once we were inside, the squalor of the neighborhood vanished, replaced by a kind of peeling grandeur. The main desk was directly beneath the dome, and this dome, drawing up with it a spiraling walkway lined with the library's main collection, floated five hundred feet in the air: a stony sky whose least chip falling might kill one of the librarians on the spot.

While Mr Million browsed his way majestically up the helix, David and I raced ahead until we were several full turns in advance and could do what we liked. When I was still quite young it would often occur to me that, since my father had written (on the testimony of the lady in pink) a roomful of books, some of them should be here; and I would climb resolutely until I had almost reached the dome, and there rummage. Because the librarians were very lax about reshelving, there seemed always a possibility of finding what I had failed to find before. The shelves towered far above my head, and when I felt myself unobserved I climbed them like ladders, stepping on books when there was no room on the shelves themselves for the square toes of my small brown shoes, and occasionally kicking books to the floor where they remained until our next visit and beyond, evidence of the staff's reluctance to climb that long, coiled slope.

The upper shelves were, if anything, in worse disorder than those more conveniently located, and one glorious day when I attained the highest of all I found occupying that lofty, dusty position (besides a misplaced astronautics text,

The Mile-Long Spaceship, by some German) only a lorn copy of
Monday or Tuesday leaning against a book about the assas-
sination of Trotsky, and a crumbling volume of Vernor
Vinge's short stories that owed its presence there, or so I
suspect, to some long-dead librarian's mistaking the faded *V.
Vinge* on the spine for "Winge."

I never found any books of my father's, but I did not regret
the long climbs to the top of the dome. If David had come
with me, we raced up together, up and down the sloping floor
– or peered over the rail at Mr Million's slow progress while
we debated the feasibility of putting an end to him with one
cast of some ponderous work. If David preferred to pursue
interests of his own farther down I ascended to the very top
where the cap of the dome curved right over my head; and
there, from a rusted iron catwalk not much wider than one of
the shelves I had been climbing (and I suspect not nearly so
strong), opened in turn each of a circle of tiny piercings –
piercings in a wall of iron, but so shallow a wall that when I
had slid the corroded cover plates out of the way I could
thrust my head through and feel myself truly outside, with
the wind and the circling birds and the lime-spotted expanse
of the dome curving away beneath me.

To the west, since it was taller than the surrounding
houses and marked by the orange trees on the roof, I could
make out our house. To the south, the masts of the ships in
the harbor, and in clear weather – if it was the right time of
day – the whitecaps of the tidal race Sainte Anne drew
between the peninsulas called First Finger and Thumb.
(And once, as I very well recall, while looking south I saw the
great geyser of sunlit water when a starcrosser splashed
down.) To east and north spread the city proper, the citadel
and the grand market and the forests and mountains
beyond.

But sooner or later, whether David had accompanied me
or gone off on his own, Mr Million summoned us. Then we
were forced to go with him to one of the wings to visit this or
that science collection. This meant books for lessons. My
father insisted that we learn biology, anatomy, and
chemistry thoroughly, and under Mr Million's tutelage,
learn them we did – he never considering a subject mastered

until we could discuss every topic mentioned in every book catalogued under the heading. The life sciences were my own favorites, but David preferred languages, literature, and law; for we got a smattering of these as well as anthropology, cybernetics, and psychology.

When he had selected the books that would form our study for the next few days and urged us to choose more for ourselves, Mr Million would retire with us to some quiet corner of one of the science reading rooms, where there were chairs and a table and room sufficient for him to curl the jointed length of his body or align it against a wall or bookcase in a way that left the aisles clear. To designate the formal beginning of our class he used to begin by calling roll, my own name always coming first.

I would say, "Here," to show that he had my attention.

"And David."

"Here." (David has an illustrated *Tales from the Odyssey* open on his lap where Mr Million cannot see it, but he looks at Mr Million with bright, feigned interest. Sunshine slants down to the table from a high window, and shows the air as warm with dust.)

"I wonder if either of you noticed the stone implements in the room through which we passed a few moments ago?"

We nod, each hoping the other will speak.

"Were they made on Earth, or here on our own planet?"

This is a trick question, but an easy one. David says, "Neither one. They're plastic." And we giggle.

Mr Million says patiently, "Yes, they're plastic reproductions, but from where did the originals come?" His face, so similar to my father's, but which I thought of at this time as belonging only to him, so that it seemed a frightening reversal of nature to see it on a living man instead of his screen, was neither interested, nor angry, nor bored; but coolly remote.

David answers, "From Sainte Anne." Sainte Anne is the sister planet to our own, revolving with us about a common center as we swing around the sun. "The sign said so, and the aborigines made them – there weren't any abos here."

Mr Million nods, and turns his impalpable face toward me. "Do you feel these stone implements occupied a central place in the lives of their makers? Say no."

"No."

"Why not?"

I think frantically, not helped by David, who is kicking my shins under the table. A glimmering comes.

"Talk. Answer at once."

"It's obvious, isn't it?" (Always a good thing to say when you're not even sure "it" is even possible.) "In the first place, they can't have been very good tools, so why would the abos have relied on them? You might say they needed those obsidian arrowheads and bone fishhooks for getting food, but that's not true. They could poison the water with the juices of certain plants, and for primitive people the most effective way to fish is probably with weirs, or with nets of rawhide or vegetable fiber. Just the same way, trapping or driving animals with fire would be more effective than hunting; and anyway stone tools wouldn't be needed at all for gathering berries and the shoots of edible plants and things like that, which were probably their most important foods – those stone things got in the glass case here because the snares and nets rotted away and they're all that's left, so the people that make their living that way pretend they were important."

"Good. David? Be original, please. Don't repeat what you've just heard."

David looks up from his book, his blue eyes scornful of both of us. "If you could have asked them, they would have told you that their magic and their religion, the songs they sang and the traditions of their people were what were important. They killed their sacrificial animals with flails of seashells that cut like razors, and they didn't let their men father children until they had stood enough fire to cripple them for life. They mated with trees and drowned the children to honor their rivers. That was what was important."

With no neck, Mr Million's face nodded. "Now we will debate the humanity of those aborigines. David negative and first."

(I kick him, but he has pulled his hard, freckled legs up beneath him, or hidden them behind the legs of his chair, which is cheating.) "Humanity," he says in his most objectionable voice, "in the history of human thought implies descent from what we may conveniently call *Adam*; that is, the original Terrestrial stock, and if the two of you don't see that, you're idiots."

I wait for him to continue, but he is finished. To give myself time to think, I say, "Mr Million, it's not fair to let him call me names in a debate. Tell him that's not debating, it's *fighting*, isn't it?"

Mr Million says, "No personalities, David." (David is already peeking at Polyphemus the Cyclops and Odysseus, hoping I'll go on for a long time. I feel challenged and decide to do so.)

I begin, "The argument which holds descent from Terrestrial stock pivotal is neither valid nor conclusive. Not conclusive because it is distinctly possible that the aborigines of Sainte Anne were descendants of some earlier wave of human expansion – one, perhaps, even predating *the Homeric Greeks*."

Mr Million says mildly, "I would confine myself to arguments of higher probability if I were you."

I nevertheless gloss upon the Etruscans, Atlantis, and the tenacity and expansionist tendencies of a hypothetical technological culture occupying Gondwanaland. When I have finished Mr Million says, "Now reverse. David, affirmative without repeating."

My brother, of course, has been looking at his book instead of listening, and I kick him with enthusiasm, expecting him to be stuck; but he says, "The abos are human because they're all dead."

"Explain."

"If they were alive it would be dangerous to let them be human because they'd ask for things, but with them dead it makes it more interesting if they were, and the settlers killed them all."

And so it goes. The spot of sunlight travels across the black-streaked red of the tabletop – traveled across it a hundred times. We would leave through one of the side doors and walk through a neglected areaway between two wings. There would be empty bottles there and wind-scattered papers of all kinds, and once a dead man in bright rags over whose legs we boys skipped while Mr Million rolled silently around him. As we left the areaway for a narrow street, the bugles of the garrison at the citadel (sounding so far away) would call the troopers to their evening mess. In the Rue d'Asticot the lamplighter would be at work, and the shops shut behind their iron grilles. The sidewalks magically clear of old furniture would seem broad and bare.

Our own Saltimbanque Street would be very different, with the first revelers arriving. White-haired, hearty men guiding very young men and boys, men and boys handsome and muscular but a shade overfed; young men who made diffident jokes and smiled with excellent teeth at them. These were always the early ones, and when I was a little older I sometimes wondered if they were early only because the white-haired men wished to have their pleasure and yet a good night's sleep as well, or if it were because they knew the young men they were introducing to my father's establishment would be drowsy and irritable after midnight, like children who have been kept up too late.

Because Mr Million did not want us to use the alleys after dark we came in the front entrance with the white-haired men and their nephews and sons. There was a garden there, not much bigger than a small room and recessed into the windowless front of the house. In it were beds of ferns the size of graves; a little fountain whose water fell upon rods of glass to make a continual tinkling, and which had to be protected from the street boys; and, with his feet firmly planted, indeed almost buried in moss, an iron statue of a dog with three heads.

It was this statue, I suppose, that gave our house its popular name of Maison du Chien, though there may have been a reference to our surname as well. The three heads were sleekly powerful with pointed muzzles and ears. One was snarling and one, the center head, regarded the world of garden and street with a look of tolerant interest. The third, the one nearest the brick path that led to our door, was – there is no other term for it – frankly grinning; and it was the custom for my father's patrons to pat this head between the ears as they came up the path. Their fingers had polished the spot to the consistency of black glass.

*

This, then, was my world at seven of our world's long years, and perhaps for half a year beyond. Most of my days were spent in the little classroom over which Mr Million presided, and my evenings in the dormitory where David and I played and fought in total silence. They were varied by the trips to the library I have described or, very rarely, elsewhere, I pushed aside the leaves of the silver trumpet vine occasionally to watch the girls and their benefactors in the court below, or heard their talk drifting down from the roof garden, but the things they did and talked of were of no great interest to me. I knew that the tall, hatchet-faced man who ruled our house and was called "Maitre" by the girls and servants was my father. I had known for as long as I could remember that there was somewhere a fearsome woman – the servants were in terror of her – called "Madame," but that she was neither my mother nor David's, nor my father's wife.

That life and my childhood, or at least my infancy, ended one evening after David and I, worn out with wrestlings and silent arguments, had gone to sleep. Someone shook me by the shoulder and called me, and it was not Mr Million but one of the servants, a hunched little man in a shabby red jacket. "He wants you," this summoner informed me. "Get up."

I did, and he saw that I was wearing nightclothes. This I think had not been covered in his instructions, and for a moment during which I stood and yawned, he debated with himself. "Get dressed," he said at last. "Comb your hair."

I obeyed, putting on the black velvet trousers I had worn the day before, but (guided by some instinct) a new clean shirt. The room to which he then conducted me (through tortuous corridors now emptied of the last patrons; and others, musty, filthy with the excrement of rats, to which patrons were never admitted) was my father's library – the room with the great carved door before which I had received the whispered confidences of the woman in pink. I had never been inside it, but when my guide rapped discreetly on the door it swung back, and I found myself within, almost before I realized what had happened.

My father, who had opened the door, closed it behind me; and leaving me standing where I was, walked to the most distant end of that long room and threw himself down in a huge chair. He was wearing the red dressing gown and black scarf in which I had most often seen him, and his long, sparse hair was brushed straight back. He stared at me, and I remember that my lip trembled as I tried to keep from breaking into sobs.

"Well," he said, after we had looked at one another for a long time, "and there you are. What am I going to call you?"

I told him my name, but he shook his head. "Not that. You must have another name for me – a private name. You may choose it yourself if you like."

I said nothing. It seemed to me quite impossible that I should have any name other than the two words which were, in some mystic sense I only respected without understanding, *my name*.

"I'll choose for you then," my father said. "You are Number Five. Come here, Number Five."

I came, and when I was standing in front of him, he told me, "Now we are going to play a game. I am going to show you some pictures, do you understand? And all the time you are watching them, you must talk. Talk about the pictures. If you talk you win, but if you stop, even for just a second, I do. Understand?"

I said I did.

"Good. I know you're a bright boy. As a matter of fact, Mr Million has sent me all the examinations he has given you and the tapes he makes when he talks with you. Did you know that? Did you ever wonder what he did with them?"

I said, "I thought he threw them away," and my father, I noticed, leaned forward as I spoke, a circumstance I found flattering at the time.

"No, I have them here." He pressed a switch. "Now remember, you must not stop talking."

But for the first few moments I was much too interested to talk.

There had appeared in the room, as though by magic, a boy considerably younger than I, and a painted wooden soldier almost as large as I was myself, which when I reached out to touch them proved as insubstantial as air. "Say something," my father said. "What are you thinking about, Number Five?"

I was thinking about the soldier, of course, and so was the younger boy, who appeared to be about three. He toddled through my arm like mist and attempted to knock it over.

They were holographs – three-dimensional images formed by the interference of two wave fronts of light – things which had seemed very dull when I had seen them illustrated by flat pictures of chessmen with the phantoms who walked in my father's library at night. All this time my father was saying, "Talk! Say something! What do you think the little boy is feeling?"

"Well, the little boy likes the big soldier, but he wants to knock him down if he can, because the soldier's only a toy, really, but it's bigger than he is. . . ." And so I talked, and for a long time, hours I suppose, continued. The scene changed and changed again. The giant soldier was replaced by a pony, a rabbit, a meal of soup and crackers. But the three-year-old boy remained the central figure. When the hunched man in the shabby coat came again, yawning, to take me back to my bed, my voice had worn to a husky whisper and my throat ached. In my dreams that night I saw the little boy scampering from one activity to another, his personality in some way confused with my own and my father's so that I was at once observer, observed, and a third presence observing both.

The next night I fell asleep almost at the moment Mr Million sent us up to bed, retaining consciousness only long enough to congratulate myself on doing so. I woke when the hunched man entered the room, but it was not me whom he roused from the sheets but David. Quietly, pretending I still slept (for it had occurred to me, and seemed quite reasonable at the time, that if he were to see I was awake he might take both of us), I watched as my brother dressed and struggled to impart some sort of order to his tangle of fair hair. When he returned I was sound asleep, and had no opportunity to question him until Mr Million left us alone, as he sometimes did, to eat our breakfast. I had told him my own experiences as a matter of course, and what he had to tell me was simply that he had had an evening very similar to mine. He had seen holographic pictures, and apparently the same pictures: the wooden soldier, the pony. He had been forced to talk constantly, as Mr Million had so often made us do in debates and verbal examinations. The only way in which his interview with our father had differed from mine, as nearly as I could determine, appeared when I asked him by what name he had been called.

He looked at me blankly, a piece of toast half-raised to his mouth.

I asked again, "What name did he call you by when he talked to you?"

"He called me David. What did you think?"

With the beginning of these interviews the pattern of my life changed, the adjustments I assumed to be temporary becoming imperceptibly permanent, settling into a new shape of which neither David nor I were consciously aware. Our games and stories after bedtime stopped, and David less and less often made his panpipes of the silver trumpet vine. Mr Million allowed us to sleep later and we were in some subtle way acknowledged to be more adult. At about this time too, he began to take us to a park where there was an archery range and provision for various games. This little park, which was not far from our house, was bordered on one side by a canal. And there, while David shot arrows at a goose stuffed with straw or played tennis, I often sat staring at the quiet, only slightly dirty water; or waiting for one of the white ships – great ships with bows as sharp as the scalpel-bills of kingfishers and four, five, or even seven masts – which were, infrequently, towed up from the harbor by ten or twelve spans of oxen.

In the summer of my eleventh or twelfth year – I think the twelfth – we were permitted for the first time to stay after sundown in the park, sitting on the grassy, sloped margin of the canal to watch a fireworks display. The first preliminary flight of rockets had no sooner exhausted itself half a mile above the city than David became ill. He rushed to the water and vomited, plunging his hands half up to the elbows in muck while the red and white stars burned in glory above him. Mr Million took him up in his arms, and when poor David had emptied himself we hurried home.

His disease proved not much more lasting than the tainted sandwich that had occasioned it, but while our tutor was putting him to bed I decided not to be cheated of the remainder of the display, parts of which I had glimpsed between the intervening houses as we made our way home; I was forbidden the roof after dark, but I knew very well where the nearest stair was. The thrill I felt in penetrating that prohibited world of leaf and shadow while fireflowers of purple and gold and blazing scarlet overtopped it affected me like the aftermath of a fever, leaving me short of breath, shaking, and cold in the midst of summer.

There were a great many more people on the roof than I had anticipated, the men without cloaks, hats or sticks (all of which they had left in my father's checkrooms), and the girls, my father's employees, in costumes that displayed their rouged breasts in enclosures of twisted wire like birdcages or gave them the appearance of great height (dissolved only when someone stood very close to them), or gowns whose skirts reflected their wearers' faces and busts as still water does the trees standing near it, so that they appeared, in the intermittent colored flashes, like the queens of strange suits in a tarot deck.

I was seen, of course, since I was much too excited to conceal myself effectively; but no one ordered me back, and I suppose they assumed I had been permitted to come up to see the fireworks.

These continued for a long time. I remember one patron, a heavy, square-faced, stupid-looking man who seemed to be someone of importance, who was so eager to enjoy the company of his protégée – who did not want to go inside until the display was over – that, since he insisted on privacy, twenty or thirty bushes and small trees had to be rearranged on the parterre to make a little grove around them. I helped the waiters carry some of the smaller tubs and pots, and managed to duck into the structure as it was completed. Here I could still watch the exploding rockets and "aerial bombs" through the branches, and at the same time the patron and his *nymphe du bois*, who was watching them a good deal more intently than I.

My motive, as well as I can remember, was not prurience but simple curiosity. I was at that age when we are passionately interested, but the passion is one of science. Mine was nearly satisfied when I was grasped by the shirt by someone behind me and drawn out of the shrubbery.

When I was clear of the leaves I was released, and I turned expecting to see Mr Million, but it was not he. My captor was a little gray-haired woman in a black dress whose skirt, as I noticed even at the time, fell straight from her waist to the ground. I suppose I bowed to her, since she was clearly no servant, but she returned no salutation at all, staring intently into my face in a way that made me think she could see as well in the intervals between the bursting glories as by their light. At last, in what must have been the finale of the display, a great rocket rose screaming on a river of flame, and for an instant she consented to look up. Then, when it had exploded in a mauve orchid of unbelievable size and brilliance, this formidable little woman grabbed me again and led me firmly toward the stairs.

While we were on the level stone pavement of the roof garden she did not, as nearly as I could see, walk at all, but rather seemed to glide across the surface like an onyx chessman on a polished board; and that, in spite of all that has happened since, is the way I still remember her: as the Black Queen, a chess queen neither sinister nor beneficent, and Black only as distinguished from some White Queen I was never fated to encounter.

When we reached the stairs, however, this smooth gliding became a fluid bobbing that brought two inches or more of the hem of her black skirt into contact with each step, as if her torso were descending each as a small boat might a rapids – now rushing, now pausing, now almost backing in the crosscurrents.

She steadied herself on these steps by holding on to me and grasping the arm of a maid who had been waiting for us at the stairhead and assisted her from the other side. I had supposed, while we were crossing the roof garden, that her gliding motion had been the result, merely, of a marvelously controlled walk and good posture, but I now understood her to be in some way handicapped; and I had the impression that without the help the maid and I gave her she might have fallen headfirst.

Once we had reached the bottom of the steps her smooth progress was resumed. She dismissed the maid with a nod and led me down the corridor in the direction opposite to that in which our dormitory and classroom lay until we reached a stairwell far toward the back of the house, a corkscrew, seldom-used flight, very steep, with only a low iron banister between the steps and a six-story drop into the cellars. Here she released me and told me crisply to go down. I went down several steps, then turned to see if she was having any difficulty.

She was not, but neither was she using the stairs. With her long skirt hanging as straight as a curtain she was floating suspended, watching me, in the center of the stairwell. I was so startled I stopped, which made her jerk her head angrily, then began to run. As I fled around and around the spiral she revolved with me, turning toward me always a face extraordinarily like my father's, one hand always on the railing. When we had descended to the second floor she swooped down and caught me as easily as a cat takes charge of an errant kitten, and led me through rooms and passages where I had never been permitted to go until I was as confused as I might have been in a strange building. At last we stopped before a door in no way different from any other. She opened it with an old-fashioned brass key with an edge like a saw and motioned for me to go in.

The room was brightly lit, and I was able to see clearly what I had only sensed on the roof and in the corridors: that the hem of her skirt hung two inches above the floor no matter how she moved, and that there was nothing between the hem and the floor at all. She waved me to a little footstool covered with needlepoint and said, "Sit down," and when I had done so, glided across to a wing-backed rocker and sat facing me. After a moment she asked, "What's your name?" and when I told her she cocked an eyebrow at me and started the chair in motion by pushing gently with her fingers at a floor lamp that stood beside it. After a long time she said, "And what does he call you?"

"He?" I was stupid, I suppose, with lack of sleep.

She pursed her lips. "My brother."

I relaxed a little. "Oh," I said, "you're my aunt then. I thought you looked like my father. He calls me Number Five."

For a moment she continued to stare, the corners of her mouth drawing down as my father's often did. Then she said, "That number's either far too low or too high. Living, there are he and I, and I suppose he's counting the simulator. Have you a sister, Number Five?"

Mr Million had been having us read *David Copperfield*, and when she said this she reminded me so strikingly and unexpectedly of Aunt Betsey Trotwood that I shouted with laughter.

"There's nothing absurd about it. Your father had a sister – why shouldn't you? You have none?"

"No ma'am, but I have a brother. His name is David."

"Call me Aunt Jeannine. Does David look like you, Number Five?"

I shook my head. "His hair is curly and blond instead of like mine. Maybe he looks a little like me, but not a lot."

"I suppose," my aunt said under her breath, "he used one of my girls."

"Ma'am?"

"Do you know who David's mother was, Number Five?"

"We're brothers, so I guess she would be the same as mine, but Mr Million says she went away a long time ago."

"Not the same as yours," my aunt said. "No. I could show you a picture of your own. Would you like to see it?" She rang a bell, and a maid came curtsying from some room beyond the one in which we sat; my aunt whispered to her and she went out again. When my aunt turned back to me she asked, "And what do you do all day, Number Five, besides run up to the roof when you shouldn't? Are you taught?"

I told her about my experiments (I was stimulating unfertilized frogs' eggs to asexual development and then doubling the chromosomes by a chemical treatment so that a futher asexual generation could be produced) and the dissections Mr Million was by then encouraging me to do, and while I talked, happened to drop some remark about how interesting it would be to perform a biopsy on one of the aborigines of Sainte Anne if any were still in existence, since the first explorers' descriptions differed so widely and some pioneers there had claimed the abos could change their shapes.

"Ah," my aunt said, "you know about them. Let me test you, Number Five. What is Veil's Hypothesis?"

We had learned that several years before, so I said, "Veil's Hypothesis supposes the abos to have possessed the ability to mimic mankind perfectly. Veil thought that when the ships came from Earth the abos killed everyone and took their places and the ships, so they're not dead at all, we are."

"You mean the Earth people are," my aunt said. "The human beings."

"Ma'am?"

"If Veil was correct, then you and I are abos from Sainte Anne, at least in origin; which I suppose is what you meant. Do you think he was right?"

"I don't think it makes any difference. He said the imitation would have to be perfect, and if it is, they're the same as we were anyway." I thought I was being clever, but my aunt smiled, rocking more vigorously. It was very warm in the close, bright little room.

"Number Five, you're too young for semantics, and I'm afraid you've been led astray by that word *perfectly*. Dr Veil, I'm certain, meant to use it loosely rather than as precisely as you seem to think. The imitation could hardly have been exact, since human beings don't possess that talent and to imitate them *perfectly* the abos would have to lose it."

"Couldn't they?"

"My dear child, abilities of every sort must evolve. And when they do they must be utilized or they atrophy. If the abos had been able to mimic so well as to lose the power to do so, that would have been the end of them, and no doubt it would have come long before the first ships reached them. Of course there's not the slightest evidence they could do anything of the sort. They simply died off before they could be thoroughly studied, and Veil, who wants a dramatic explanation of the cruelty and irrationality he sees around him, has hung fifty pounds of theory on nothing."

This last remark, especially as my aunt seemed so

friendly, appeared to me to offer an ideal opportunity for a question about her remarkable means of locomotion, but as I was about to frame it we were interrupted, almost simultaneously, from two directions. The maid returned carrying a large book bound in tooled leather, and she had no sooner handed it to my aunt than there was a tap at the door. My aunt said absently, "Get that," and since the remark might as easily have been addressed to me as to the maid I satisfied my curiosity in another form by racing her to answer the knock.

Two of my father's demimondaines were waiting in the hall, costumed and painted until they seemed more alien than any abos, stately as Lombardy poplars and inhuman as specters, with green and yellow eyes made to look the size of eggs and inflated breasts pushed almost shoulder high; and though they maintained an inculcated composure I was pleasantly aware that they were startled to find me in the doorway. I bowed them in, but as the maid closed the door behind them my aunt said absently, "In a moment, girls. I want to show the boy here something, then he's going to leave."

The "something" was a photograph utilizing, as I supposed, some novelty technique which washed away all color save a light brown. It was small, and from its general appearance and crumbling edges very old. It showed a girl of twenty-five or so, thin and as nearly as I could judge rather tall, standing beside a stocky young man on a paved walkway and holding a baby. The walkway ran along the front of a remarkable house, a very long wooden house only a story in height, with a porch or veranda that changed its architectural style every twenty or thirty feet so as to give almost the impression of a number of exceedingly narrow houses constructed with their side walls in contact. I mention this detail, which I hardly noticed at the time, because I have so often since my release from prison tried to find some trace of this house. When I was first shown the picture I was much more interested in the girl's face, and the baby's. The latter was in fact scarcely visible, he being nearly smothered in white wool blankets. The girl had large features and a brilliant smile which held a suggestion of that rarely seen charm which is at once careless, poetic, and sly. Gypsy, was my first thought, but her complexion was surely too fair for that. Since on this world we are all descended from a relatively small group of colonists, we are rather a uniform population, but my studies had given me some familiarity with the original Terrestrial races, and my second guess, almost a certainty, was Celtic. "Wales," I said aloud. "Or Scotland. Or Ireland."

"What?" my aunt said. One of the girls giggled; they were seated on the divan now, their long, gleaming legs crossed before them like the varnished staffs of flags.

"It doesn't matter."

My aunt looked at me acutely and said, "You're right. I'll send for you and we'll talk about this when we've both more leisure. For the present my maid will take you to your room."

I remember nothing of the long walk the maid and I must have had back to the dormitory, or what excuses I gave Mr Million for my unauthorized absence. Whatever they were I suppose he penetrated them, or discovered the truth by questioning the servants, because no summons to return to my aunt's apartment came, although I expected it daily for weeks afterward.

That night – I am reasonably sure it was the same night – I dreamed of the abos of Sainte Anne, abos dancing with plumes of fresh grass on their heads and arms and ankles, abos shaking their shields of woven rushes and their nephrite-tipped spears until the motion affected my bed and became, in shabby red cloth, the arms of my father's valet come to summon me, as he did almost every night, to his library.

That night, and this time I am quite certain it was the same night, that is, the night I first dreamed of the abos, the pattern of my hours with him, which had come over the four or five years past to have a predictable sequence of conversation, holographs, free association, and dismissal – a sequence I had come to think inalterable – changed. Following the preliminary talk designed, I feel sure, to put me at ease (at which it failed, as it always did), I was told to roll up a sleeve and lie down upon an old examining table in a corner of the room. My father then made me look at the wall, which meant at the shelves heaped with ragged notebooks. I felt a needle being thrust into the inner part of my arm, but my head was held down and my face turned away, so that I could neither sit up nor look at what he was doing. Then the needle was withdrawn and I was told to lie quietly.

After what seemed a very long time, during which my father occasionally spread my eyelids to look at my eyes or took my pulse, someone in a distant part of the room began to tell a very long and confusingly involved story. My father made notes of what was said, and occasionally stopped to ask questions I found it unnecessary to answer, since the storyteller did it for me.

The drug he had given me did not, as I had imagined it would, lessen its hold on me as the hours passed. Instead it seemed to carry me progressively further from reality and the mode of consciousness best suited to preserving the individuality of thought. The peeling leather of the examination table vanished under me, and was now the deck of a ship, now the wing of a dove beating far above the world; and whether the voice I heard reciting was my own or my father's I no longer cared. It was pitched sometimes higher, sometimes lower, but then I felt myself at times to be speaking from the depths of a chest larger than my own, and his voice, identified as such by the soft rustling of the pages of his notebook, might seem the high, treble cries of the racing children in the streets as I heard them in summer when I thrust my head through the windows at the base of the library dome.

With that night my life changed again. The drugs – for there seemed to be several, and although the effect I have described was the usual one there were also times when I found it impossible to lie still, but ran up and down for hours as I talked, or sank into blissful or indescribably frightening dreams – affected my health. I often wakened in the morning with a headache that kept me in agony all day, and I became subject to periods of extreme nervousness and apprehensiveness. Most frightening of all, whole sections of days sometimes disappeared, so that I found myself awake and dressed, reading, walking, and even talking, with no memory at all of anything that had happened since I had lain muttering to the ceiling in my father's library the night before.

The lessons I had had with David did not cease, but in some sense Mr Million's role and mine were now reversed. It was I, now, who insisted on holding our classes when they were held at all; and it was I who chose the subject matter and, in most cases, questioned David and Mr Million about it. But often when they were at the library or the park I remained in bed reading, and I believe there were many times when I read and studied from the time I found myself conscious in my bed until my father's valet came for me again.

David's interviews with our father, I should note here, suffered the same changes as my own and at the same time; but since they were less frequent – and they became less and less frequent as the hundred days of summer wore away to autumn and at last to the long winter – and he seemed on the whole to have less adverse reactions to the drugs, the effect on him was not nearly as great.

If at any single time, it was during this winter that I came to the end of childhood. My new ill health forced me away from childish activities, and encouraged the experiments I was carrying out on small animals, and my dissections of the bodies Mr Million supplied in an unending stream of open mouths and staring eyes. Too, I studied or read, as I have said, for hours on end; or simply lay with my hands behind my head while I struggled to recall, perhaps for whole days together, the narratives I had heard myself give my father. Neither David nor I could ever remember enough even to build a coherent theory of the nature of the questions asked us, but I have still certain scenes fixed in my memory which I am sure I have never beheld in fact, and I believe these are my visualizations of suggestions whispered while I bobbed and dove through those altered states of consciousness.

My aunt, who had previously been so remote, now spoke to me in the corridors and even visited our room. I learned that she controlled the interior arrangements of our house, and through her I was able to have a small laboratory of my own set up in the same wing. But I spent the winter, as I have described, mostly at my enamel dissecting table or in bed. The white snow drifted half up the glass of the window, clinging to the bare stems of the silver trumpet vine. My father's patrons, on the rare occasions I saw them, came in with wet boots, the snow on their shoulders and their hats, puffing and red-faced as they beat their coats in the foyer. The orange trees were gone, the roof garden no longer used, and the courtyard under our window only late at night when half a dozen patrons and their protégées, whooping with hilarity and wine, fought with snowballs – an activity invariably concluded by stripping the girls and tumbling them naked in the snow.

Spring surprised me, as she always does those of us who remain most of our lives indoors. One day, while I still thought, if I thought about the weather at all, in terms of winter, David threw open the window and insisted that I go with him into the park – and it was April. Mr Million went with us, and I remember that as we stepped out the front door into the little garden that opened into the street, a garden I had last seen banked with the snow shoveled from the path, but which was now bright with early bulbs and the chiming of the fountain, David tapped the iron dog on its grinning muzzle and recited: " 'And thence the dog/With fourfold head brought to these realms of light.' "

I made some trivial remark about his having miscounted.

"Oh, no. Old Cerberus has four heads, don't you know that? The fourth's her maidenhead, and she's such a bitch no dog can take it from her." Even Mr Million chuckled, but I thought afterward, looking at David's ruddy good health and the foreshadowing of manhood already apparent in the set of his shoulders, that if, as I had always thought of them, the three heads represented Maitre, Madame and Mr Million, that is, my father, my aunt (David's *maidenhead*, I suppose) and my tutor, then indeed a fourth would have to be welded in place soon for David himself.

The park must have been a paradise for him, but in my poor health I found it bleak enough and spent most of the morning huddled on a bench, watching David play squash.

Toward noon I was joined, not on my own bench, but on another close enough for there to be a feeling of proximity, by a dark-haired girl with one ankle in a cast. She was brought there, on crutches, by a sort of nurse or governess who seated herself, I felt sure, deliberately between the girl and me. This unpleasant woman was, however, too straight-backed for her chaperonage to succeed completely. She sat on the edge of the bench, while the girl, with her injured leg thrust out before her, slumped back and thus gave me a good view of her profile, which was beautiful; and occasionally, when she turned to make some remark to the creature with her, I could study her full face – carmine lips and violet eyes, a round rather than an oval face, with a broad point of black hair dividing the forehead; archly delicate black eyebrows and long, curling lashes. When a vendor, an old woman, came selling Cantonese egg rolls (longer than your hand, and still so hot from the boiling fat that they needed to be eaten with great caution as though they were in some way alive), I made her my messenger and, as well as buying one for myself, sent her with two scalding delicacies to the girl and her attendant monster.

The monster, of course, refused; the girl, I was charmed to see, pleaded; her huge eyes and bright cheeks eloquently proclaiming arguments I was unfortunately just too far away to hear but could follow in pantomime: it would be a gratuitous insult to a blameless stranger to refuse; she was hungry and had intended to buy an egg roll in any event – how thriftless to object when what she had wished for was tendered free! The vending woman, who clearly delighted in her role as go-between, announced herself on the point of weeping at the thought of being forced to refund my gold (actually a bill of small denomination nearly as greasy as the paper in which her wares were wrapped, and considerably dirtier), and eventually their voices grew loud enough for me to hear the girl's, which was a clear and very pleasing contralto. In the end, of course, they accepted; the monster conceded me a frigid nod, and the girl winked at me behind her back.

Half an hour later when David and Mr Million, who had been watching him from the edge of the court, asked if I wanted lunch, I told them I did, thinking that when we returned I could take a seat closer to the girl without being brazen about it. We ate, I (at least so I fear) very impatiently, in a clean little café close to the flower market; but when we came back to the park the girl and her governess were gone.

We returned to the house, and about an hour afterward my father sent for me. I went with some trepidation, since it was much earlier than was customary for our interview – before the first patrons had arrived, in fact, while I usually saw him only after the last had gone. I need not have feared. He began by asking about my health, and when I said it seemed better than it had been during most of the winter he began, in a self-conscious and even pompous way, as different from his usual fatigued incisiveness as could be imagined, to talk about his business and the need a young man had to prepare himself to earn a living. He said, "You are a scientific scholar, I believe."

I said I hoped I was in a small way, and braced myself for the usual attack upon the uselessness of studying chemistry or biophysics on a world like ours where the industrial base was so small, of no help at the civil service examinations, does not even prepare one for trade, and so on. He said instead, "I'm glad to hear it. To be frank, I asked Mr Million to encourage you in that as much as he could. He would have done it anyway I'm sure; he did with me. These studies will not only be of great satisfaction to you, but will" – he paused, cleared his throat, and massaged his face and scalp with his hands – "be valuable in all sorts of ways. And they are, as you might say, a family tradition."

I said, and indeed felt, that I was very happy to hear that.

"Have you seen my lab? Behind the big mirror there?"

I hadn't, though I had known that such a suite of rooms existed beyond the sliding mirror in the library, and the servants occasionally spoke of his "dispensary" where he compounded doses for them, examined monthly the girls we employed, and occasionally prescribed treatment for "friends" of patrons, men recklessly imprudent who had failed (as the wise patrons had not) to confine their custom to our establishment exclusively. I told him I should very much like to see it.

He smiled. "But we are wandering from our topic. Science is of great value; but you will find, as I have, that it consumes more money than it produces. You will want apparatus and books and many other things, as well as a livelihood for yourself. We have a not unprofitable business here, and though I hope to live a long time – thanks in part to science – you are the heir, and it will be yours in the end . . .

(So I was older than David!)

". . . every phase of what we do. None of them, believe me, are unimportant."

I had been so surprised, and in fact elated, by my discovery that I had missed a part of what he said. I nodded, which seemed safe.

"Good. I want you to begin by answering the front door. One of the maids has been doing it, and for the first month or so she'll stay with you, since there's more to be learned there than you think. I'll tell Mr Million, and he can make the arrangements."

I thanked him, and he indicated that the interview was over by opening the door of the library. I could hardly believe, as I went out, that he was the same man who devoured my life in the early hours of almost every morning.

I did not connect this sudden elevation in status with the events in the park. I now realize that Mr Million, who has, quite literally, eyes in the back of his head must have reported to my father that I had reached the age at which desires in childhood subliminally fastened to parental figures begin, half consciously, to grope beyond the family.

In any event that same evening I took up my new duties and became what Mr Million called the "greeter" and David (explaining that the original sense of the word was related to *portal*) the "porter," of our house – thus assuming in a practical way the functions symbolically executed by the iron dog in our front garden. The maid who had previously carried them out, a girl named Nerissa who had been selected because she was not only one of the prettiest but one of the tallest and strongest of the maids as well, a large-boned, long-faced, smiling girl with shoulders broader than most men's, remained, as my father had promised, to help.

Our duties were not onerous, since my father's patrons were all men of some position and wealth, not given to brawling or loud arguments except under unusual circumstances of intoxication; and for the most part they had visited our house already dozens, and in a few cases even hundreds of times. We called them by nicknames that were used only here (of which Nerissa informed me *sotto voce* as they came up the walk), hung up their coats, and directed them – or if necessary conducted them – to the various parts of the establishment. Nerissa flounced (a formidable sight, as I observed, to all but the most heroically proportioned patrons), allowed herself to be pinched, took tips, and talked to me afterward, during slack periods, of the times she had been "called upstairs" at the request of some connoisseur of scale, and the money she had made that night. I laughed at jokes and refused tips in such a way as to make the patrons aware that I was a part of the management. Most patrons did not need the reminder, and I was often told that I strikingly resembled my father.

When I had been serving as a receptionist in this way for only a short time, I think on only the third or fourth night, we had an unusual visitor. He came early one evening, but it was the evening of so dark a day, one of the last really wintry days, that the garden lamps had been lit for an hour or more and the occasional carriages that passed on the street beyond, though they could be heard, could not be seen. I answered the door when he knocked, and as we always did with strangers, asked him politely what he wished.

He said, "I should like to speak to Dr Aubrey Veil."

I am afraid I looked blank.

"This is 666 Saltimbanque?"

It was of course; and the name of Dr Veil, though I could not place it, touched a chime of memory. I supposed that one of our patrons had used my father's house as an *adresse d'accommodation*, and since this visitor was clearly legitimate, and it was not desirable to keep anyone arguing in the doorway despite the partial shelter afforded by the garden, I asked him in; then I sent Nerissa to bring us coffee so that we might have a few moments of private talk in the dark little receiving room that opened off the foyer. It was a room very seldom used, and the maids had been remiss in dusting it, as I saw as soon as I opened the door. I made a mental note to speak to my aunt about it, and as I did I recalled where it was that I had heard Dr Veil mentioned. My aunt, on the first occasion I had ever spoken to her, had referred to his theory that we might in fact be the natives of Sainte Anne, having murdered the original Terrestrial colonists and displaced them so thoroughly as to forget our own past.

The stranger had seated himself in one of the musty, gilded armchairs. He wore a beard, very black and more full than the current style, was young, I thought, though of course considerably older than I, and would have been handsome if the skin of his face – what could be seen of it – had not been of so colorless a white as almost to constitute a disfigurement. His dark clothing seemed abnormally heavy, like felt, and I recalled having heard from some patron that a starcrosser from Sainte Anne had splashed down in the bay yesterday, and asked if he had perhaps been on board it. He looked startled for a moment, then laughed. "You're a wit, I see. And living with Dr Veil you'd be familiar with his theory. No, I'm from Earth. My name is Marsch." He gave me his card, and I read it twice before the meaning of the delicately embossed abbreviations registered on my mind. My visitor was a scientist, a doctor of philosophy in anthropology, from Earth.

I said: "I wasn't trying to be witty. I thought you might really have come from Sainte Anne. Here, most of us have a kind of planetary face, except for the gypsies and the criminal tribes, and you don't seem to fit the pattern."

He said, "I've noticed what you mean; you seem to have it yourself."

"I'm supposed to look a great deal like my father."

"Ah," he said. He stared at me. Then, "Are you cloned?"

"Cloned?" I had read the term, but only in conjunction with botany, and as has happened to me often when I have especially wanted to impress someone with my intelligence, nothing came. I felt like a stupid child.

"Parthenogenetically reproduced, so that the new individual – or individuals, you can have a thousand if you want – will have a genetic structure identical to the parent.

It's antievolutionary, so it's illegal on Earth, but I don't suppose things are as closely watched out here."

"You're talking about human beings?"

He nodded.

"I've never heard of it. Really I doubt if you'd find the necessary technology here; we're quite backward compared to Earth. Of course, my father might be able to arrange something for you."

"I don't want to have it done."

Nerissa came in with the coffee then, effectively cutting off anything further Dr Marsch might have said. Actually, I had added the suggestion about my father more from force of habit than anything else, and thought it very unlikely that he could pull off any such biochemical tour de force, but there was always the possibility, particularly if a large sum were offered. As it was, we fell silent while Nerissa arranged the cups and poured, and when she had gone Marsch said appreciatively, "Quite an unusual girl." His eyes, I noticed, were a bright green, without the brown tones most green eyes have.

I was wild to ask him about Earth and the new developments there, and it had already occurred to me that the girls might be an effective way of keeping him here, or at least of bringing him back. I said: "You should see some of them. My father has wonderful taste."

"I'd rather see Dr Veil. Or is Dr Veil your father?"

"Oh, no."

"This is his address, or at least the address I was given. Number 666 Saltimbanque Street, Port-Mimizon, Département de la Main, Sainte Croix."

He appeared quite serious, and it seemed possible that if I told him flatly that he was mistaken he would leave. I said: "I learned about Veil's Hypothesis from my aunt; she seemed quite conversant with it. Perhaps later this evening you'd like to talk to her about it."

"Couldn't I see her now?"

"My aunt sees very few visitors. To be frank, I'm told she quarreled with my father before I was born, and she seldom leaves her own apartments. The housekeepers report to her there and she manages what I suppose I must call our domestic economy, but it's very rare to see Madame outside her rooms, or for any stranger to be let in."

"And why are you telling me this?"

"So that you'll understand that with the best will in the world it may not be possible for me to arrange an interview for you. At least, not this evening."

"You could simply ask her if she knows Dr Veil's present address, and if so what it is."

"I'm trying to help you, Dr Marsch. Really I am."

"But you don't think that's the best way to go about it?"

"No."

"In other words if your aunt were simply asked, without being given a chance to form her own judgment of me, she wouldn't give me information even if she had it?"

"It would help if we were to talk a bit first. There are a great many things I'd like to learn about Earth."

For an instant I thought I saw a sour smile under the black beard. He said, "Suppose I ask you first —"

He was interrupted — again — by Nerissa, I suppose because she wanted to see if we required anything further from the kitchen. I could have strangled her when Dr Marsch halted in midsentence and said instead, "Couldn't this girl ask your aunt if she would see me?"

I had to think quickly. I had been planning to go myself and, after a suitable wait, return and say that my aunt would receive Dr Marsch later, which would have given me an additional opportunity to question him while he waited. But there was at least a possibility (no doubt magnified in my eyes by my eagerness to hear of new discoveries from Earth) that he would not wait — or that, when and if he did eventually see my aunt, he might mention the incident. If I sent Nerissa I would at least have him to myself while she ran her errand, and there was an excellent chance — or at least so I imagined — that my aunt would in fact have some business which she would want to conclude before seeing a stranger. I told Nerissa to go, and Dr Marsch gave her one of his cards after writing a few words on the back.

"Now," I said, "what was it you were about to ask me?"

"Why this house, on a planet that has been inhabited less than two hundred years, seems so absurdly old."

"It was built a hundred and forty years ago, but you must have many on Earth that are far older."

"I suppose so. Hundreds. But for every one of them there are ten thousand that have been up less than a year. Here, almost every building I see seems nearly as old as this one."

"We've never been crowded here, and we haven't had to tear down; that's what Mr Million says. And there are fewer people here now than there were fifty years ago."

"Mr Million?"

I told him about Mr Million, and when I finished he said, "It sounds as if you've got a ten nine unbound simulator here, which should be interesting. Only a few have ever been made."

"A ten nine simulator?"

"A billion, ten to the ninth power. The human brain has several billion synapses, of course; but it's been found that you can simulate its action pretty well –"

It seemed to me that no time at all had passed since Nerissa had left, but she was back. She curtsied to Dr Marsch and said, "Madame will see you."

I blurted, "Now?"

"Yes," Nerissa said artlessly, "Madame said right now."

"I'll take him then. You mind the door."

I escorted Dr Marsch down the dark corridors, taking a long route to have more time, but he seemed to be arranging in his mind the questions he wished to ask my aunt, as we walked past the spotted mirrors and warped little walnut tables, and he answered me in monosyllables when I tried to question him about Earth.

At my aunt's door I rapped for him. She opened it herself, the hem of her black skirt hanging emptily over the untrodden carpet, but I do not think he noticed that. He said, "I'm really very sorry to bother you, Madame, and I only do so because your nephew thought you might be able to help me locate the author of Veil's Hypothesis."

My aunt said, "I am Dr Veil, please come in," and shut the door behind him, leaving me standing open-mouthed in the corridor.

I mentioned the incident to Phaedria the next time we met,

but she was more interested in learning about my father's house. Phaedria, if I have not used her name before now, was the girl who had sat near me while I watched David play squash. She had been introduced to me on my next visit to the park by no one less than the monster herself, who had helped her to a seat beside me and, miracle of miracles, promptly retreated to a point which, though not out of sight, was at least beyond earshot. Phaedria had thrust her broken ankle in front of her, halfway across the graveled path, and smiled a most charming smile. "You don't object to my sitting here?" She had perfect teeth.

"I'm delighted."

"You're surprised too. Your eyes get big when you're surprised, did you know that?"

"I am surprised. I've come here looking for you several times, but you haven't been here."

"We've come looking for you, and you haven't been here either, but I suppose one can't really spend a great deal of time in a park."

"I would have," I said, "if I'd known you were looking for me. I went here as much as I could anyway. I was afraid that she" – I jerked my head at the monster – "wouldn't let you come back. How did you persuade her?"

"I didn't," Phaedria said. "Can't you guess? Don't you know anything?"

I confessed that I did not. I felt stupid, and I was stupid, at least in the things I said, because so much of my mind was caught up not in formulating answers to her remarks but in committing to memory the lilt of her voice, the purple of her eyes, even the faint perfume of her skin and the soft, warm touch of her breath on my cool cheek.

"So you see," Phaedria was saying, "that's how it is with me. When Aunt Uranie – she's only a poor cousin of mother's, really – got home and told him about you he found out who you are, and here I am."

"Yes," I said, and she laughed.

Phaedria was one of those girls raised between the hope of marriage and the thought of sale. Her father's affairs, as she herself said, were "unsettled." He speculated in ship cargoes, mostly from the south – textiles and drugs. He owed, most of the time, large sums which the lenders could not hope to collect unless they were willing to allow him more to recoup. He might die a pauper, but in the meanwhile he had raised his daughter with every detail of education and plastic surgery attended to. If when she reached marriage-able age he could afford a good dowry, she would link him with some wealthy family. If he were pressed for money instead, a girl so reared would bring fifty times the price of a common street child. Our family, of course, would be ideal for either purpose.

"Tell me about your house," she said. "Do you know what the kids call it? 'The Cave Canem,' or sometimes just 'The Cave.' The boys all think it's a big thing to have been there and they lie about it. Most of them haven't."

But I wanted to talk about Dr Marsch and the sciences of Earth, and I was nearly as anxious to find out about her own world, "the kids" she mentioned so casually, her school and family, as she was to learn about us. Also, although I was willing to detail the services my father's girls rendered their benefactors, there were some things, such as my aunt's floating down the stairwell, that I was adverse to discussing. But we bought egg rolls from the same old woman to eat in the chill sunlight and exchanged confidences and somehow parted not only lovers but friends, promising to meet again the next day.

At some time during the night, I believe at almost the same time that I returned – or to speak more accurately *was returned* since I could scarcely walk – to my bed after a session of hours with my father, the weather changed. The musked exhalation of late spring or early summer crept through the shutters, and the fire in our little grate seemed to extinguish itself for shame almost at once. My father's valet opened the window for me and there poured into the room that fragrance that tells of the melting of the last snows beneath the deepest and darkest evergreens on the north sides of mountains. I had arranged with Phaedria to meet at ten, and before going to my father's library I had posted a note on the escritoire beside my bed, asking that I be awakened an hour earlier; and that night I slept with the fragrance in my nostrils and the thought – half-plan, half-dream – in my mind that by some means Phaedria and I would elude her aunt entirely and find a deserted lawn where blue and yellow flowers dotted the short grass.

When I woke, it was an hour past noon, and rain drove in sheets past the window. Mr Million, who was reading a book on the far side of the room, told me that it had been raining like that since six, and for that reason he had not troubled to wake me. I had a splitting headache, as I often did after a long session with my father, and took one of the powders he had prescribed to relieve it. They were gray, and smelled of anise.

"You look unwell," Mr Million said.

"I was hoping to go to the park."

"I know." He rolled across the room toward me, and I recalled that Dr Marsch had called him an "unbound" simulator. For the first time since I had satisfied myself about them when I was quite small, I bent over (at some cost to my head) and read the almost obliterated stampings on his main cabinet. There was only the name of a cybernetics company on Earth and, in French as I had always supposed, his name: M. Million – "Monsieur" or "Mr" Million. Then, as startling as a blow from behind to a man musing in a comfortable chair, I remembered that a dot was employed in some algebras for multiplication. He saw my change of expression at once. "A thousand million word core capacity," he said. "An English billion or a French milliard, the M being the Roman numeral for one thousand, of course. I thought you understood that some time ago."

"You are an unbound simulator. What is a bound simulator, and whom are you simulating – my father?"

"No." The face in the screen, Mr Million's face as I had always thought of it, shook its head. "Call me, call the person simulated, at least, your great-grandfather. He – I – am dead. In order to achieve simulation, it is necessary to examine the cells of the brain, layer by layer, with a beam of accelerated particles so that the neural patterns can be reproduced, we say 'core imaged,' in the computer. The process is fatal."

I asked after a moment, "And a bound simulator?"

"If the simulation is to have a body that looks human the

mechanical body must be linked – 'bound' – to a remote core, since the smallest billion word core cannot be made even approximately as small as a human brain." He paused again, and for an instant his face dissolved into myriad sparkling dots, swirling like dust motes in a sunbeam. "I am sorry. For once you wish to listen but I do not wish to lecture. I was told, a very long time ago, just before the operation, that my simulation – this – would be capable of emotion in certain circumstances. Until today I had always thought they lied." I would have stopped him if I could, but he rolled out of the room before I could recover from my surprise.

For a long time, I suppose an hour or more, I sat listening to the drumming of the rain and thinking about Phaedria and about what Mr Million had said, all of it confused with my father's questions of the night before, questions which had seemed to steal their answers from me so that I was empty, and dreams had come to flicker in the emptiness, dreams of fences and walls and the concealing ditches called ha-has, that contain a barrier you do not see until you are about to tumble on it. Once I had dreamed of standing in a paved court fenced with Corinthian pillars so close set that I could not force my body between them, although in the dream I was only a child of three or four. After trying various places for a long time, I had noticed that each column was carved with a word – the only one that I could remember was *carapace* – and that the paving stones of the courtyard were mortuary tablets like those set into the floors in some of the old French churches, with my own name and a different date on each.

This dream pursued me even when I tried to think of Phaedria, and when a maid brought me hot water – for I now shaved twice a week – I found that I was already holding my razor in my hand, and had in fact cut myself with it so that the blood had streaked my nightclothes and run down onto the sheets.

The next time I saw Phaedria, which was four or five days afterward, she was engrossed by a new project in which she enlisted both David and me. This was nothing less than a theatrical company, composed mostly of girls her own age, which was to present plays during the summer in a natural amphitheater in the park. Since the company, as I have said, consisted principally of girls, male actors were at a premium, and David and I soon found ourselves deeply embroiled. The play had been written by a committee of the cast, and – inevitably – revolved about the loss of political power by the original French-speaking colonists. Phaedria, whose ankle would not be mended in time for our performance, would play the crippled daughter of the French governor; David, her lover (a dashing captain of chasseurs); and I, the governor himself – a part I accepted readily because it was a much better one that David's, and offered scope for a great deal of fatherly affection toward Phaedria.

The night of our performance, which was early in June, I recall vividly for two reasons. My aunt, whom I had not seen since she had closed the door behind Dr Marsch, notified me at the last moment that she wished to attend and that I was to escort her. And we players had grown so afraid of having an empty house that I had asked my father if it would be possible for him to send some of his girls – who would thus lose only the earliest part of the evening, when there was seldom much business in any event. To my great surprise (I suppose because he felt it would be good advertising) he consented, stipulating only that they should return at the end of the third act if he sent a messenger saying they were needed.

Because I would have to arrive at least an hour early to make up, it was no more than late afternoon when I called for my aunt. She showed me in herself, and immediately asked my help for her maid, who was trying to wrestle some heavy object from the upper shelf of a closet. It proved to be a folding wheelchair, and under my aunt's direction we set it up. When we had finished she said abruptly, "Give me a hand in, you two," and taking our arms lowered herself into the seat. Her black skirt, lying emptily against the boards of the chair like a collapsed tent, showed legs no thicker than my wrists; but also an odd thickening, almost like a saddle, below her hips. Seeing me staring she snapped, "Won't be needing that until I come back, I suppose. Lift me up a little. Stand in back and get me under the arms."

I did so, and her maid reached unceremoniously under my

aunt's skirt and drew out a little leather padded device on which she had been resting. "Shall we go?" my aunt sniffed. "You'll be late."

I wheeled her into the corridor, her maid holding the door for us. Somehow, learning that my aunt's ability to hang in the air like smoke was physically, indeed mechanically, derived, made it more disturbing than ever. When she asked why I was so quiet, I told her and added that I had been under the impression that no one had yet succeeded in producing working antigravity.

"And you think I have? Then why wouldn't I use it to get to your play?"

"I suppose because you don't want it to be seen."

"Nonsense. It's a regular prosthetic device. You buy them at the surgical stores." She twisted around in her seat until she could look up at me, her face so like my father's, and her lifeless legs like the sticks David and I used as little boys when, doing parlor magic, we wished Mr Million to believe us lying prone when we were in fact crouched beneath our own supposed figures. "Puts out a superconducting field, then induces eddy currents in the reinforcing rods in the floors. The flux of the induced currents oppose the machine's own flux and I float, more or less. Lean forward to go forward, straighten up to stop. You look relieved."

"I am. I suppose antigravity frightened me."

"I used the iron banister when I went down the stairs with you once; it has a very convenient coil shape."

Our play went smoothly enough, with predictable cheers from members of the audience who were, or at least wished to be thought, descended from the old French aristocracy. The audience, in fact, was better than we had dared hope, five hundred or so besides the inevitable sprinkling of pickpockets, police, and streetwalkers. The incident I most vividly recall came toward the latter half of the first act, when for ten minutes or so I sat with few lines at a desk, listening to my fellow actors. Our stage faced the west, and the setting sun had left the sky a welter of lurid color; purple-reds striped gold and flame and black. Against this violent ground, which might have been the massed banners of Hell, there began to appear, in ones and twos, like the elongate shadows of fantastic grenadiers crenelated and plumed, the heads, the slender necks, the narrow shoulders, of a platoon of my father's demimondaines; arriving late, they were taking the last seats at the upper rim of our theater, encirling it like the soldiery of some ancient, bizarre government surrounding a treasonous mob.

They sat at last, my cue came, and I forgot them; and that is all I can now remember of our first performance, except that at one point some motion of mine suggested to the audience a mannerism of my father's, and there was a shout of misplaced laughter – and that at the beginning of the second act, Sainte Anne rose with its sluggish rivers and great grassy meadow-meres clearly visible, flooding the audience with green light; and at the close of the third I saw my father's crooked little valet bustling among the upper rows, and the girls, green-edged black shadows, filing out.

We produced three more plays that summer, all with some success, and David and Phaedria and I became an accepted partnership, with Phaedria dividing herself more or less equally between us – whether by her own inclination or her parents' orders I could never be quite sure. When her ankle knit she was a companion fit for David in athletics, a better player of all the ball and racket games than any of the other girls who came to the park; but she would as often drop everything and come to sit with me, where she sympathized with (though she did not actually share) my interest in botany and biology, and gossiped, and delighted in showing me off to her friends since my reading had given me a sort of talent for puns and repartee.

It was Phaedria who suggested, when it became apparent that the ticket money from our first play would be insufficient for the costumes and scenery we coveted for our second, that at the close of future performances the cast circulate among the audience to take up a collection; and this, of course, in the press and bustle easily lent itself to the accomplishment of petty thefts for our cause. Most people, however, had too much sense to bring to our theater, in the evening, in the gloomy park, more money than was required to buy tickets and perhaps an ice or a glass of wine during intermission; so no matter how dishonest we were the profit remained small, and we, and especially Phaedria and David, were soon talking of going forward to more dangerous and lucrative adventures.

At about this time, I suppose as a result of my father's continued and intensified probing of my subconscious, a violent and almost nightly examination whose purpose was still unclear to me and which, since I had been accustomed to it for so long, I scarcely questioned, I became more and more subject to frightening lapses of conscious control. I would, so David and Mr Million told me, seem quite myself though perhaps rather more quiet than usual, answering questions intelligently if absently, and then, suddenly, come to myself, start, and stare at the familiar rooms, the familiar faces, among which I now found myself, perhaps after the midafternoon, without the slightest memory of having awakened, dressed, shaved, eaten, gone for a walk.

Although I loved Mr Million as much as I had when I was a boy, I was never able, after that conversation in which I learned the meaning of the familiar lettering on his side, quite to re-establish the old relationship. I was always conscious, as I am conscious now, that the personality I loved had perished years before I was born; and that I addressed an imitation of it, fundamentally mathematical in nature, responding as that personality might to the stimuli of human speech and action. I could never determine whether Mr Million is really aware in that sense which would give him the right to say, as he always has, "I think," and "I feel." When I asked him about it he could only explain that he did not know the answer himself, that having no standard of comparison he could not be positive whether his own mental processes represented true consciousness or not; and I, of course, could not know whether this answer represented the deepest meditation of a soul somehow alive in the dancing abstractions of the simulation, or whether it was merely triggered, a phonographic response, by my question.

Our theater, as I have said, continued through the summer and gave its last performance with the falling leaves drifting, like obscure, perfumed old letters from some discarded trunk, upon our stage. When the curtain calls were over we who had written and acted the plays of our season were too disheartened to do more than remove our costumes and cosmetics, and drift ourselves, with the last of our departing audience, down the whippoorwill-haunted paths to the city streets and home. I was prepared, as I remember, to take up my duties at my father's door, but that night he had stationed his valet in the foyer to wait for me, and I was ushered directly into the library, where he explained brusquely that he would have to devote the latter part of the evening to business and for that reason would speak to me (as he put it) early. He looked tired and ill, and it occurred to me, I think for the first time, that he would one day die – and that I would, on that day, become at once both rich and free.

What I said under the drugs that evening I do not, of course, recall, but I remember as vividly as I might if I had only this morning awakened from it, the dream that followed. I was on a ship, a white ship like one of those the oxen pull, so slowly the sharp prows make no wake at all, through the green water of the canal beside the park. I was the only crewman, and indeed the only living man aboard. At the stern, grasping the huge wheel in such a flaccid way that it seemed to support and guide and steady *him* rather than he it, stood the corpse of a tall, thin man whose face, when the rolling of his head presented it to me, was the face that floated in Mr Million's screen. This face, as I have said, was very like my father's but I knew the dead man at the wheel was not he.

I was aboard the ship a long time. We seemed to be running free, with the wind a few points to port and strong. When I went aloft at night, masts and spars and rigging quivered and sang in the wind, and sail upon sail towered above me, and sail upon white sail spread below me, and more masts clothed in sails stood before me and behind me. When I worked on deck by day, spray wet my shirt and left tear-shaped spots on the planks which dried quickly in the bright sunlight.

I cannot remember ever having really been on such a ship, but perhaps, as a very small child, I was, for the sounds of it, the creaking of the masts in their sockets, the whistling of the wind in the thousand ropes, the crashing of the waves against the wooden hull were all as distinct, and as real, as much *themselves*, as the sounds of laughter and breaking glass overhead had been when, as a child, I had tried to sleep; or the bugles from the citadel which sometimes, then, woke me in the morning.

I was about some work. I do not know just what, aboard this ship. I carried buckets of water with which I dashed clotted blood from the decks, and I pulled at ropes which seemed attached to nothing – or rather, firmly tied to immovable objects still higher in the rigging. I watched the surface of the sea from bow and rail, from the mastheads, and from atop a large cabin amidships, but when a starcrosser, its entry shields blinding-bright with heat, plunged hissing into the sea far off I reported it to no one.

And all this time the dead man at the wheel was talking to me. His head hung limply, as though his neck were broken, and the jerkings of the wheel he held, as big waves struck the rudder, sent it from one shoulder to the other, or back to stare at the sky, or down. But he continued to speak, and the few words I caught suggested that he was lecturing upon an ethical theory whose postulates seemed even to him doubtful. I felt a dread of hearing this talk and tried to keep myself as much as possible toward the bow, but the wind at times carried the words to me with great clarity, and whenever I looked up from my work I found myself much nearer the stern, sometimes in fact almost touching the dead steersman, than I had supposed.

After I had been on this ship a long while, so that I was very tired and very lonely, one of the doors of the cabin opened and my aunt came out, floating quite upright about two feet above the tilted deck. Her skirt did not hang vertically as I had always seen it, but whipped in the wind like a streamer, so that she seemed on the point of blowing away. For some reason I said, "Don't get close to that man at the wheel, Aunt. He might hurt you."

She answered, as naturally as if we had met in the corridor outside my bedroom, "Nonsense. He's far past doing anyone any good, Number Five, or any harm either. It's my brother we have to worry about."

"Where is he?"

"Down there." She pointed at the deck as if to indicate that he was in the hold. "He's trying to find out why the ship doesn't move."

I ran to the side and looked over, and what I saw was not water but the night sky. Stars – innumerable stars were spread at an infinite distance below me, and as I looked at them I realized that the ship, as my aunt had said, did not make headway or even roll, but remained heeled over, motionless. I looked back at her and she told me, "It doesn't move because he has fastened it in place until he finds out why it doesn't move," and at this point I found myself sliding down a rope into what I supposed was the hold of the ship. It smelled of animals. I had awakened, though at first I did not know it.

My feet touched the floor, and I saw that David and Phaedria were beside me. We were in a huge, loftlike room, and as I looked at Phaedria, who was very pretty but tense and biting her lips, a cock crowed.

David said, "Where do you think the money is?" He was carrying a tool kit.

And Phaedria, who I suppose had expected him to say something else, or in answer to her own thoughts, said, "We'll have lots of time; Marydol is watching." Marydol was one of the girls who appeared in our plays.

"If she doesn't run away. Where do you think the money is?"

"Not up here. Downstairs behind the office." She had been crouching, but she rose now and began to creep forward. She was all in black, from her ballet slippers to a black ribbon binding her black hair, with her white face and arms in striking contrast, and her carmine lips an error, a bit of color left by mistake. David and I followed her.

Crates were scatterd, widely separated, on the floor; and as we passed them I saw that they held poultry, a single bird in each. It was not until we were nearly to the ladder which plunged down a hatch in the floor at the opposite corner of the room that I realized that these birds were gamecocks. Then a shaft of sun from one of the skylights struck a crate and the cock rose and stretched himself, showing fierce red eyes and plumage as gaudy as a macaw's. "Come on,"

Phaedria said, "the dogs are next," and we followed her down the ladder. Pandemonium broke out on the floor below.

The dogs were chained in stalls, with dividers too high for them to see the dogs on either side of them and wide aisles between the rows of stalls. They were all fighting dogs, but of every size from ten-pound terriers to mastiffs larger than small horses, brutes with heads as misshapen as the growths that appear on old trees and jaws that could sever both a man's legs at a mouthful. The din of the barking was incredible, a solid substance that shook us as we descended the ladder, and at the bottom I took Phaedria's arm and tried to indicate by signs – since I was certain that we were wherever we were without permission – that we should leave at once. She shook her head and then, when I was unable to understand what she said even when she exaggerated the movements of her lips, wrote on a dusty wall with her moistened forefinger: "They do this all the time – a noise in the street – anything."

Access to the floor below was by stairs, reached through a heavy but unbolted door which I think had been installed largely to exclude the din. I felt better when we had closed it behind us even though the noise was still very loud. I had fully come to myself by this time, and I should have explained to David and Phaedria that I did not know where I was or what we were doing there, but shame held me back. And in any event I could guess easily enough what our purpose was. David had asked about the location of money, and we had often talked – talk I had considered at the time to be more than half empty boasting – about a single robbery that would free us from the necessity of further petty crime.

Where we were I discovered later when we left; and how we had come to be there I pieced together from casual conversations. The building had been originally designed as a warehouse, and stood on the Rue des Egouts close to the bay. Its owner supplied those enthusiasts who stage combats of all kinds for sport, and was credited with maintaining the largest assemblage of these creatures in the Department. Phaedria's father had happened to hear that this man had recently put some of his most valuable stock on ship, had taken Phaedria when he called on him, and, since the place was known not to open its doors until after the last Angelus, we had come the next day a little after the second and entered through one of the skylights.

I find it difficult to describe what we saw when we descended from the floor of the dogs to the next, which was the second floor of the building. I had seen fighting slaves many times before when Mr Million, David, and I had traversed the slave market to reach the library; but never more than one or two together, heavily manacled. Here they lay, sat, and lounged everywhere, and for a moment I wondered why they did not tear one another to pieces, and the three of us as well. Then I saw that each was held by a short chain stapled to the floor, and it was not difficult to tell from the scraped and splintered circles in the boards just how far the slave in the center could reach. Such furniture as they had, straw pallets and a few chairs and benches, was either too light to do harm if thrown or very stoutly made and spiked down. I had expected them to shout and threaten us as I had heard they threatened each other in the pits before closing, but they seemed to understand that as long as they were chained, they could do nothing. Every head turned toward us as we came down the steps, but we had no food for them, and after that first examination they were far less interested in us than the dogs had been.

"They aren't people, are they?" Phaedria said. She was walking erectly as a soldier on parade now, and looking at the slaves with interest; studying her, it occurred to me that she was taller and less plump than the "Phaedria" I pictured to myself when I thought of her. She was not just a pretty, but a beautiful girl. "They're a kind of animal, really," she said.

From my studies I was better informed, and I told her that they had been human as infants – in some cases even as children or older – and that they differed from normal people only as a result of surgery (some of it on their brains) and chemically induced alterations in their endocrine systems. And of course in appearance because of their scars.

"Your father does that sort of thing to little girls, doesn't he? For your house?"

David said, "Only once in a while. It takes a lot of time,

and most people prefer normals, even when they prefer pretty odd normals."

"I'd like to see some of them. I mean the ones he's worked on."

I was still thinking of the fighting slaves around us and said, "Don't you know about these things? I thought you'd been here before. You knew about the dogs."

"Oh, I've seen them before, and the man told me about them. I suppose I was just thinking out loud. It would be awful if they were still people."

Their eyes followed us, and I wondered if they could understand her.

The ground floor was very different from the ones above. The walls were paneled, there were framed pictures of dogs and cocks and of the slaves and curious animals. The windows, opening toward Egouts Street and the bay, were high and narrow and admitted only slender beams of the bright sunlight to pick out of the gloom the arm alone of a rich red-leather chair, a square of maroon carpet no bigger than a book, a half-full decanter. I took three steps into this room and knew that we had been discovered. Striding toward us was a tall, high-shouldered young man – who halted, with a startled look, just when I did. He was my own reflection in a gilt-framed pier glass, and I felt the momentary dislocation that comes when a stranger, an unrecognized shape, turns or moves his head and is some familiar friend glimpsed, perhaps for the first time, from outside. The sharp-chinned, grim-looking boy I had seen when I did not know him to be myself had been myself as Phaedria and David, Mr Million and my aunt, saw me.

"This is where he talks to customers," Phaedria said. "If he's trying to sell something he has his people bring them down one at a time so you don't see the others but you can hear the dogs bark even from way down here, and he took Papa and me upstairs and showed us everything."

David asked, "Did he show you where he keeps the money?"

"In back. See that tapestry? It's really a curtain, because while Papa was talking to him, a man came who owed him for something and paid, and he went through there with it."

The door behind the tapestry opened on a small office, with still another door in the wall opposite. There was no sign of a safe or strongbox. David broke the lock on the desk with a pry bar from his tool kit, but there was only the usual clutter of papers, and I was about to open the second door when I heard a sound, a scraping or shuffling, from the room beyond.

For a minute or more none of us moved. I stood with my hand on the latch. Phaedria, behind me and to my left, had been looking under the carpet for a cache in the floor – she remained crouched, her skirt a black pool at her feet. From somewhere near the broken desk I could hear David's breathing. The shuffling came again, and a board creaked. David said very softly, "It's an animal."

I drew my fingers away from the latch and looked at him. He was still gripping the pry bar and his face was pale, but he smiled. "An animal tethered in there, shifting its feet. That's all."

I said, "How do you know?"

"Anybody in there would have heard us, especially when I cracked the desk. If it were a person he would have come out, or if he were afraid he'd hide and be quiet."

Phaedria said, "I think he's right. Open the door."

"Before I do, if it isn't an animal?"

David said, "It is."

"But if it isn't?"

I saw the answer on their faces; David gripped his pry bar, and I opened the door.

The room beyond was larger than I had expected, but bare and dirty. The only light came from a single window high in the farther wall. In the middle of the floor stood a big chest, of dark wood bound with iron, and before it lay what appeared to be a bundle of rags. As I stepped from the carpeted office the rags moved and a face, a face triangular as a mantis', turned toward me. Its chin was hardly more than an inch from the floor, but under deep brows the eyes were tiny scarlet fires.

"That must be it," Phaedria said. She was looking not at the face but at the iron-banded chest. "David, can you break into that?"

"I think so," David said, but he, like me, was watching the ragged thing's eyes. "What about that?" he said after a moment, and gestured toward it. Before Phaedria or I could answer, its mouth opened showing long, narrow teeth, gray-yellow. "Sick," it said.

None of us, I think, had thought it could speak. It was as though a mummy had spoken. Outside, a carriage went past, its iron wheels rattling on the cobbles.

"Let's go," David said. "Let's get out."

Phaedria said, "It's sick. Don't you see, the owner's brought it down here where he can look in on it and take care of it. It's sick."

"And he chained his sick slave to the cashbox?" David cocked an eyebrow at her.

"Don't you see? It's the only heavy thing in the room. All you have to do is go over there and knock the poor creature in the head. If you're afraid, give me the bar and I'll do it myself."

"I'll do it."

I followed him to within a few feet of the chest. He gestured at the slave imperiously with the steel pry bar. "You! Move away from there."

The slave made a gurgling sound and crawled to one side, dragging his chain. He was wrapped in a filthy, tattered blanket and seemed hardly larger than a child, though I noticed that his hands were immense.

I turned and took a step toward Phaedria, intending to urge that we leave if David were unable to open the chest in a few minutes. I remember that before I heard or felt anything I saw her eyes open wide, and I was still wondering why when David's kit of tools clattered on the floor and David himself fell with a thud and a little gasp. Phaedria screamed, and all the dogs on the third floor began to bark.

All this, of course, took less than a second. I turned to look almost as David fell. The slave had darted out an arm and caught my brother by the ankle, and then in an instant had thrown off his blanket and bounded – that is the only way to describe it – on top of him.

I caught him by the neck and jerked him backward, thinking that he would cling to David and that it would be necessary to tear him away, but the instant he felt my hands he flung David aside and writhed like a spider in my grip. *He had four arms.*

I saw them flailing as he tried to reach me, and I let go of him and jerked back, as if a rat had been thrust in my face. That instinctive repulsion saved me; he drove his feet backward in a kick which, if I had still been holding him tightly enough to give him a fulcrum, would have surely ruptured my liver or spleen and killed me.

Instead it shot him forward and me, gasping for breath, back. I fell and rolled, and was outside the circle permitted him by his chain; David had already scrambled away, and Phaedria was well out of his reach.

For a moment, while I shuddered and tried to sit up, the three of us simply stared at him. Then David quoted wryly:

Arms and the man I sing, who forc'd by fate,
And haughty Juno's unrelenting hate,
Expell'd and exil'd, left the Trojan shore.

Neither Phaedria nor I laughed, but Phaedria let out her breath in a long sigh and asked me, "How did they do that? Get him like that?"

I told her I supposed they had transplanted the extra pair after suppressing his body's natural resistance to the implanted foreign tissue, and that the operation had probably replaced some of his ribs with the donor's shoulder structure. "I've been teaching myself to do the same sort of thing with mice – on a much less ambitious scale, of course – and the striking thing to me is that he seems to have full use of the grafted pair. Unless you've got identical twins to work with, the nerve endings almost never join properly, and whoever did this probably had a hundred failures before he got what he wanted. That slave must be worth a fortune."

David said, "I thought you threw your mice out. Aren't you working with monkeys now?"

I wasn't, although I hoped to; but whether I was or not, it seemed clear that talking about it wasn't going to accomplish anything. I told David that.

"I thought you were hot to leave."

I had been, but now I wanted something else much more.

I wanted to perform an exploratory operation on that creature much more than David or Phaedria had ever wanted money. David liked to think that he was bolder than I, and I knew when I said, "You may want to get away, but don't use me as an excuse, brother," that that would settle it.

"All right, how are we going to kill him?" He gave me an angry look.

Phaedria said: "It can't reach us. We could throw things at it."

"And he could throw the ones that missed back."

While we talked, the thing, the four-armed slave, was grinning at us. I was fairly sure it could understand at least a part of what we were saying, and I motioned to David and Phaedria to indicate that we should go back into the room where the desk was. When we were there I closed the door. "I didn't want him to hear us. If we had weapons on poles, spears of some kind, we might be able to kill him without getting too close. What could we use for the sticks? Any ideas?"

David shook his head, but Phaedria said, "Wait a minute, I remember something." We both looked at her and she knitted her brows, pretending to search her memory and enjoying the attention.

"Well?" David asked.

She snapped her fingers. "Window poles. You know, long things with a little hook on the end. Remember the windows out there where he talks to customers? They're high up in the wall, and while he and Papa were talking one of the men who works for him brought one and opened a window. They ought to be around somewhere."

We found two after a five-minute search. They looked satisfactory: about six feet long and an inch and a quarter in diameter, of hard wood. David flourished his and pretended to thrust at Phaedria, then asked me, "Now what do we use for points?"

The scalpel I always carried was in its case in my breast pocket, and I fastened it to the rod with electrical tape from a roll David had fortunately carried on his belt instead of in the tool kit, but we could find nothing to make a second spearhead for him until he himself suggested broken glass.

"You can't break a window," Phaedria said, "they'd hear you outside. Besides, won't it just snap off when you try to get him with it?"

"Not if it's thick glass. Look here, you two."

I did, and saw – again – my own face. He was pointing toward the large mirror that had surprised me when I came down the steps. While I looked his shoe struck it, and it shattered with a crash that set the dogs barking again. He selected a long, almost straight triangular piece and held it up to the light, where it flashed like a gem. "That's about as good as they used to make them from agate and jasper on Sainte Anne, isn't it?"

By prior agreement we approached from opposite sides. The slave leaped to the top of the chest, and from there, watched us quite calmly, his deep-set eyes turning from David to me until at last when we were both quite close, David rushed him.

He spun around as the glass point grazed his ribs and caught David's spear by the shaft and jerked him forward. I thrust at him but missed, and before I could recover he had dived from the chest and was grappling with David on the far side. I bent over it and jabbed down at him, and it was not until David screamed that I realized I had driven my scalpel into his thigh. I saw the blood, bright arterial blood, spurt up and drench the shaft, and let it go and threw myself over the chest on top of them.

He was ready for me, on his back and grinning, with his legs and all four arms raised like a dead spider's. I am certain he would have strangled me in the next few seconds if it had not been that David, how consciously I do not know, threw one arm across the creature's eyes so that he missed his grip and I fell between those outstretched hands.

There is not a great deal more to tell. He jerked free of David, and pulling me to him, tried to bite my throat; but I hooked a thumb in one of his eye sockets and held him off. Phaedria, with more courage than I would have credited her with, put David's glass-tipped spear into my free hand and I stabbed him in the neck – I believe I severed both jugulars and the trachea before he died. We put a tourniquet on David's leg and left without either the money or the knowledge of technique I had hoped to get from the body of the slave. Marydol helped us get David home, and we told Mr Million he had fallen while we were exploring an empty building – though I doubt that he believed us.

There is one other thing to tell about that incident – I mean the killing of the slave – although I am tempted to go on and describe instead a discovery I made immediately afterward that had, at the time, a much greater influence on me. It is only an impression, and one that I have, I am sure, distorted and magnified in recollection. While I was stabbing the slave, my face was very near his and I saw (I suppose because of the light from the high windows behind us) my own face reflected and doubled in the corneas of his eyes, and it seemed to me that it was a face very like his. I have been unable to forget, since then, what Dr Marsch told me about the production of any number of identical individuals by cloning, and that my father had, when I was younger, a reputation as a child broker. I have tried since my release to find some trace of my mother, the woman in the photograph shown me by my aunt; but that picture was surely taken long before I was born – perhaps even on Earth.

The discovery I spoke of I made almost as soon as we left the building where I killed the slave, and it was simply this: that it was no longer autumn, but high summer. Because all four of us – Marydol had joined us by that time – were so concerned about David and busy concocting a story to explain his injury, the shock was somewhat blunted, but there could be no doubt of it. The weather was warm with that torpid, damp heat peculiar to summer. The trees I remembered nearly bare were in full leaf and filled with orioles. The fountain in our garden no longer played, as it always did after the danger of frost and burst pipes had come, with warmed water: I dabbed my hand in the basin as we helped David up the path, and it was as cool as dew.

My periods of unconscious action then, my sleepwalking, had increased to devour an entire winter and the spring, and I felt that I had lost myself.

When we entered the house, an ape which I thought at

first was my father's sprang to my shoulder. Later Mr
Million told me that it was my own, one of my laboratory
animals I had made a pet. I did not know the little beast, but
scars under his fur and the twist of his limbs showed he knew
me.

(I have kept Popo ever since, and Mr Million took care of
him for me while I was imprisoned. He climbs still in fine
weather on the gray and crumbling walls of this house; and
as he runs along the parapets and I see his hunched form
against the sky, I think, for a moment, that my father is still
alive and that I may be summoned again for the long hours
in his library – but I forgive my pet that.)

My father did not call a physician for David, but treated him
himself; and if he was curious about the manner in which he
had received his injury he did not show it. My own guess –
for whatever it may be worth, this late – is that he believed I
had stabbed him in some quarrel. I say this because he
seemed, after this, apprehensive whenever I was alone with
him. He was not a fearful man, and he had been accustomed
for years to deal occasionally with the worst sort of criminals;
but he was no longer at ease with me – he guarded himself. It
may have been, of course, merely the result of something I
had said or done during the forgotten winter.

Both Marydol and Phaedria, as well as my aunt and Mr
Million, came frequently to visit David, so that his sickroom
became a sort of meeting place for us all, only disturbed by
my father's occasional visits. Marydol was a slight, fair-
haired, kindhearted girl, and I became very fond of her.
Often when she was ready to go home I escorted her, and on
the way back stopped at the slave market, as Mr Million and
David and I had once done so often, to buy fried bread and
the sweet black coffee and to watch the bidding. The faces of
slaves are the dullest in the world; but I would find myself
staring into them, and it was a long time, a month at least,
before I understood – quite suddenly, when I found what I
had been looking for – why I did. A young male, a sweeper,
was brought to the block. His face as well as his back had
been scarred by the whip, and his teeth were broken; but I
recognized him: the scarred face was my own or my father's.

I spoke to him and would have bought and freed him, but he answered me in the servile way of slaves and I turned away in disgust and went home.

That night when my father had me brought to the library – as he had not for several nights – I watched our reflections in the mirror that concealed the entrance to his laboratories. He looked younger than he was; I older. We might almost have been the same man, and when he faced me and I, staring over his shoulder, saw no image of my own body, but only his arms and mine, we might have been the fighting slave.

I cannot say who first suggested we kill him. I only remember that one evening, as I prepared for bed after taking Marydol and Phaedria to their homes, I realized that earlier when the three of us, with Mr Million and my aunt, had sat around David's bed, we had been talking of that.

Not openly, of course. Perhaps we had not admitted even to ourselves what it was we were thinking. My aunt had mentioned the money he was supposed to have hidden; and Phaedria, then, a yacht luxurious as a palace; David talked about hunting in the grand style, and the political power money could buy.

And I, saying nothing, had thought of the hours and weeks, and the months he had taken from me; of the destruction of my *self*, which he had gnawed at night after night. I thought of how I might enter the library that night and find myself when next I woke an old man and perhaps a beggar.

Then I knew that I must kill him, since if I told him those thoughts while I lay drugged on the peeling leather of the old table he would kill *me* without a qualm.

While I waited for his valet to come I made my plan. There would be no investigation, no death certificate for my father. I would replace him. To our patrons it would appear that nothing had changed. Phaedria's friends would be told that I had quarreled with him and left home. I would allow no one to see me for a time, and then, in makeup, in a dim room, speak occasionally to some favored caller. It was an impossible plan, but at the time I believed it possible and even easy. My scalpel was in my pocket and ready. The body could be destroyed in his own laboratory.

He read it in my face. He spoke to me as he always had, but I think he knew. There were flowers in the room, something that had never been before, and I wondered if he had not known even earlier and had them brought in, as for a special event. Instead of telling me to lie on the leather-covered table, he gestured toward a chair and seated himself at his writing desk. "We will have company today," he said.

I looked at him.

"You're angry with me. I've seen it growing in you. Don't you know who –"

He was about to say something further when there was a tap at the door, and when he called, "Come in!" it was opened by Nerissa, who ushered in a demimondaine and Dr Marsch. I was surprised to see him; and still more surprised to see one of the girls in my father's library. She seated herself beside Marsch in a way that showed he was her benefactor for the night.

"Good evening, doctor," my father said. "Have you been enjoying yourself?"

Marsch smiled, showing large, square teeth. He wore clothing of the most fashionable cut now, but the contrast between his beard and the colorless skin of his cheeks was as remarkable as ever. "Both sensually and intellectually," he said. "I've seen a naked girl, a giantess twice the height of a man, walk through a wall."

I said, "That's done with holographs."

He smiled again. "I know. And I have seen a great many other things as well. I was going to recite them all, but perhaps I would only bore my audience; I will content myself with saying that you have a remarkable establishment – but you know that."

My father said, "It is always flattering to hear it again."

"And now are we going to have the discussion we spoke of earlier?"

My father looked at the demimondaine; she rose, kissed Dr Marsch, and left the room. The heavy library door swung shut behind her with a soft click.

Like the sound of a switch, or old glass breaking.

I have thought since, many times, of that girl as I saw her leaving: the high-heeled platform shoes and grotesquely long legs, the backless dress dipping an inch below the coccyx. The bare nape of her neck; her hair piled and teased and threaded with ribbons and tiny lights. As she closed the door she was ending, though she could not have known it, the world she and I had known.

"She'll be waiting when you come out," my father said to Marsch.

"And if she's not, I'm sure you can supply others." The anthropologist's green eyes seemed to glow in the lamplight. "But now, how can I help you?"

"You study race. Could you call a group of similar men thinking similar thoughts a race?"

"And women," Marsch said, smiling.

"And here," my father continued, "here on Sainte Croix, you are gathering material to take back with you to Earth?"

"I am gathering material, certainly. Whether or not I shall return to the mother planet is problematical."

I must have looked at him sharply; he turned his smile toward me, and it became, if possible, even more patronizing than before. "You're surprised?"

"I've always considered Earth the center of scientific thought," I said. "I can easily imagine a scientist leaving it to do field work, but –"

"But it is inconceivable that one might want to stay in the field?

"Consider my position. You are not alone – happily for me – in respecting the mother world's gray hairs and wisdom. As an Earth-trained man I've been offered a department in your university at almost any salary I care to name, with a sabbatical every second year. And the trip from here to Earth requires twenty years of Newtonian time; only six months subjectively for me, of course, but when I return, if I do, my education will be forty years out of date. No, I'm afraid your planet may have acquired an intellectual luminary."

My father said, "We're straying from the subject, I think."

Marsch nodded, then added, "But I was about to say that

an anthropologist is peculiarly equipped to make himself at home in any culture – even in so strange a one as this family has constructed about itself. I think I may call it a family, since there are two members resident besides yourself. You don't object to my addressing the pair of you in the singular?"

He looked at me as if expecting a protest, then when I said nothing: "I mean your son David – that, and not brother is his real relationship to your continuing personality – and the woman you call your aunt. She is in reality daughter to an earlier – shall we say 'version'? – of yourself."

"You're trying to tell me I'm a cloned duplicate of my father, and I see both of you expect me to be shocked. I'm not. I've suspected it for some time."

My father said: "I'm glad to hear that. Frankly, when I was your age the discovery disturbed me a great deal; I came into my father's library – this room – to confront him, and I intended to kill him."

Dr. Marsch asked, "And did you?"

"I don't think it matters – the point is that it was my intention. I hope that having you here will make things easier for Number Five."

"Is that what you call him?"

"It's more convenient since his name is the same as my own."

"He is your fifth clone-produced child?"

"My fifth experiment? No." My father's hunched, high shoulders wrapped in the dingy scarlet of his old dressing gown made him look like some savage bird; and I remembered having read in a book of natural history of one called the red-shouldered hawk. His pet monkey, grizzled now with age, had climbed onto the desk. "No, more like my fiftieth, if you must know. I used to do them for drill. You people who have never tried it think the technique is simple because you've heard it can be done, but you don't know how difficult it is to prevent spontaneous differences. Every gene dominant in myself had to remain dominant, and people are not garden peas – few things are governed by simple Mendelian pairs."

Marsch asked, "You destroyed your failures?"

I said: "He sold them. When I was a child I used to wonder why Mr Million stopped to look at the slaves in the market. Since then I've found out." My scalpel was still in its case in my pocket; I could feel it.

"Mr Million," my father said, "is perhaps a bit more sentimental than I – besides, I don't like to go out. You see, doctor, your supposition that we are all truly the same individual will have to be modified. We have our little variations."

Dr Marsch was about to reply, but I interrupted him. "Why?" I said. "Why David and me? Why Aunt Jeannine a long time ago? Why go on with it?"

"Yes," my father said, "why? We ask the question to ask the question."

"I don't understand you."

"I seek self-knowledge. If you want to put it this way, *we* seek self-knowledge. You are here because I did and do, and I am here because the individual behind me did – who was himself originated by the one whose mind is simulated in Mr Million. And one of the questions whose answer we seek is why we seek. But there is more than that." He leaned forward, and the little ape lifted its white muzzle and bright, bewildered eyes to stare into his face. "We wish to discover why we fail, why others rise and change and we remain here."

I thought of the yacht I had talked about with Phaedria and said, "I won't stay here." Dr Marsch smiled.

My father said, "I don't think you understand me. I don't necessarily mean here physically, but *here*, socially and intellectually. I have traveled, and you may, but –"

"But you end here," Dr Marsch said.

"We end at this level!" It was the only time, I think, that I ever saw my father excited. He was almost speechless as he waved at the notebooks and tapes that thronged the walls. "After how many generations? We do not achieve fame or the rule of even this miserable little colony planet. Something must be changed, but what?" He glared at Dr Marsch.

"You are not unique," Dr Marsch said, then smiled. "That sounds like a truism, doesn't it? But I wasn't referring to your duplicating yourself. I meant that since it became possible, back on Earth during the last quarter of the twentieth century, it has been done in such chains a number of times. We have borrowed a term from engineering to describe it, and call it the process of relaxation – a bad nomenclature, but the best we have. Do you know what relaxation in the engineeering sense is?"

"No."

"There are problems which are not directly soluble, but which can be solved by a succession of approximations. In heat transfer, for example, it may not be possible to calculate initially the temperature at every point on the surface of an unusually shaped body. But the engineer, or his computer, can assume reasonable temperatures, see how nearly stable the assumed values would be, then make new assumptions based on the result. As the levels of approximation progress, the successive sets become more and more similar until there is essentially no change. That is why I said the two of you are essentially one individual."

"What I want you to do," my father said impatiently, "is to make Number Five understand that the experiments I have performed on him, particularly the narcotherapeutic examinations he resents so much, are necessary. That if we are to become more than we have been we must find out – " He had been almost shouting, and he stopped abruptly to bring his voice under control. "That is the reason he was produced, the reason for David too – I hoped to learn something from an outcrossing."

"Which was the rationale, no doubt," Dr Marsch said, "for the existence of Dr Veil as well, in an earlier generation. But as far as your examinations of your younger self are concerned, it would be just as useful for him to examine you."

"Wait a moment," I said. "You keep saying that he and I are identical. That's incorrect. I can see that we're similar in some respects, but I'm not really like my father."

"There are no differences that cannot be accounted for by age. You are what? Eighteen? And you," he looked toward my father, "I should say are nearly fifty. There are only two forces, you see, which act to differentiate between human beings: they are heredity and environment, nature and nurture. And since the personality is largely formed during the first three years of life, it is the environment provided by the home which is decisive. Now every person is born into *some* home environment, though it may be such a harsh one that he dies of it; and no person, except in this situation we call anthropological relaxation, provides that environment himself – it is furnished for him by the preceding generation."

"Just because both of us grew up in this house –"

"Which you built and furnished and filled with the people you chose. But wait a moment. Let's talk about a man neither of you have ever seen, a man born in a place provided by parents quite different from himself: I mean the first of you . . ."

I was no longer listening. I had come to kill my father, and it was necessary that Dr Marsch leave. I watched him as he leaned forward in his chair, his long, white hands making incisive little gestures, his cruel lips moving in a frame of black hair; I watched him and I heard nothing. It was as though I had gone deaf or as if he could communicate only by his thoughts, and I, knowing the thoughts were silly lies had shut them out. I said, "You are from Sainte Anne."

He looked at me in surprise, halting in the midst of a senseless sentence. "I have been there, yes. I spent several years on Sainte Anne before coming here."

"You were born there. You studied your anthropology there from books written on Earth twenty years ago. You are an abo, or at least half-abo; but we are men."

Marsch glanced at my father, then said: "The abos are gone. Scientific opinion on Sainte Anne holds that they have been extinct for almost a century."

"You didn't believe that when you came to see my aunt."

"I've never accepted Veil's Hypothesis. I called on everyone here who had published anything in my field. Really, I don't have time to listen to this."

"You are an abo and not from Earth."

And in a short time my father and I were alone.

Most of my sentence I served in a labor camp in the Tattered Mountains. It was a small camp, housing usually only a hundred and fifty prisoners – sometimes less than eighty when the winter deaths had been bad. We cut wood and burned charcoal and made skis when we found good birch. Above the timberline we gathered a saline moss supposed to be medicinal and knotted long plans for rock slides that would crush the stalking machines that were our guards – though somehow the moment never came, the stones never slid. The work was hard, and these guards administered exactly the mixture of severity and fairness some prison board had decided upon when they were programed and the problem of brutality and favoritism by hirelings was settled forever, so that only well-dressed men at meetings could be cruel or kind.

Or so they thought. I sometimes talked to my guards for hours about Mr Million, and once I found a piece of meat, and once a cake of hard sugar, brown and gritty as sand, hidden in the corner where I slept.

A criminal may not profit by his crime, but the court – so I was told much later – could find no proof that David was indeed my father's son, and made my aunt his heir.

She died, and a letter from an attorney informed me that by her favor I had inherited "a large house in the city of Port-Mimizon, together with the furniture and chattels appertaining thereto." And that this house, "located at 666 Saltimbanque, is presently under the care of a robot servitor." Since the robot servitors under whose direction I found myself did not allow me writing materials, I could not reply.

Time passed on the wings of birds. I found dead larks at the feet of north-facing cliffs in autumn, at the feet of south-facing cliffs in spring.

I received a letter from Mr Million. Most of my father's girls had left during the investigation of his death; the remainder he had been obliged to send away when my aunt died, finding that as a machine he could not enforce the necessary obedience. David had gone to the capital. Phaedria had married well. Marydol had been sold by her parents. The date on his letter was three years later than the date of my trial, but how long the letter had been in reaching me I could not tell. The envelope had been opened and resealed many times and was soiled and torn.

A seabird, I believe a gannet, came fluttering down into our camp after a storm, too exhausted to fly. We killed and ate it.

One of our guards went berserk, burned fifteen prisoners to death, and fought the other guards all night with swords of white and blue fire. He was not replaced.

I was transferred with some others to a camp farther north where I looked down chasms of red stone so deep that if I kicked a pebble in, I could hear the rattle of its descent grow to a roar of slipping rock – and hear that, in half a minute, fade with distance to silence, yet never strike the bottom lost somewhere in darkness.

I pretended the people I had known were with me. When I sat shielding my basin of soup from the wind, Phaedria sat upon a bench nearby and smiled and talked about her friends. David played squash for hours on the dusty ground of our compound, slept against the wall near my own corner. Marydol put her hand in mine while I carried my saw into the mountains.

In time they all grew dim, but even in the last year I never slept without telling myself, just before sleep, that Mr Million would take us to the city library in the morning; never woke without fearing that my father's valet had come for me.

Then I was told that I was to go, with three others, to another camp. We carried our food, and nearly died of hunger and exposure on the way. From there we were marched to a third camp where we were questioned by men who were not prisoners like ourselves but free men in uniforms who made notes of our answers and at last ordered that we bathe, and burned our old clothing, and gave us a thick stew of meat and barley.

I remember very well that it was then that I allowed myself to realize, at last, what these things meant. I dipped my bread into my bowl and pulled it out soaked with the fragrant stock, with bits of meat and grains of barley clinging to it; and I thought then of the fried bread and coffee at the slave market not as something of the past but as something in the future, and my hands shook until I could no longer hold my bowl and I wanted to rush shouting at the fences.

In two more days we, six of us now, were put into a mule cart that drove on winding roads always downhill until the winter that had been dying behind us was gone, and the birches and firs were gone, and the tall chestnuts and oaks beside the road had spring flowers under their branches.

The streets of Port-Mimizon swarmed with people. I would have been lost in a moment if Mr Million had not hired a chair for me, but I made the bearers stop, and bought (with money he gave me) a newspaper from a vendor so that I could know the date with certainty at last.

My sentence had been the usual one of two to fifty years, and though I had known the month and year of the beginning of my imprisonment, it had been impossible to know, in the camps, the number of the current year which everyone counted and no one knew. A man took fever and in ten days, when he was well enough again to work, said that two years had passed or had never been. Then you yourself took fever. I do not recall any headline, any article from the paper I bought. I read only the date at the top, all the way home.

It had been nine years.

I had been eighteen when I had killed my father. I was now twenty-seven. I had thought I might be forty.

The flaking gray walls of our house were the same. The iron dog with his three wolf-heads still stood in the front garden, but the fountain was silent, and the beds of fern and moss were full of weeds. Mr Million paid my chairmen and unlocked with a key the door that was always guard-chained but unbolted in my father's day – but as he did so, an immensely tall and lanky woman who had been hawking pralines in the street came running toward us. It was Nerissa, and I now had a servant and might have had a bedfellow if I wished, though I could pay her nothing.

And now I must, I suppose, explain why I have been writing this account, which has already been the labor of days; and I must even explain why I explain. Very well then. I have written to disclose myself to myself, and I am writing now because I will, I know, sometime read what I am now writing and wonder.

Perhaps by the time I do, I will have solved the mystery of myself; or perhaps I will no longer care to know the solution.

It has been three years since my release. This house, when Nerissa and I re-entered it, was in a very confused state, my aunt having spent her last days, so Mr Million told me, in a search for my father's supposed hoard. She did not find it, and I do not think it is to be found; knowing his character better than she, I believe he spent most of what his girls brought him on his experiments and apparatus. I needed money badly myself at first, but the reputation of the house brought women seeking buyers and men seeking to buy. It is hardly necessary, as I told myself when we began, to do more than introduce them, and I have a good staff now. Phaedria lives with us and works too; the brilliant marriage was a failure after all. Last night while I was working in my surgery I heard her at the library door. I opened it and she had the child with her. Someday they'll want us.

JOANNA RUSS
Nobody's Home

Like Kate Wilhelm and R. A. Lafferty, Joanna Russ would begin selling in the late '50s, but would not become widely known until the late '60s. Even Russ's early work would display the same kind of wit, sophistication, and elegance of style that would characterize her later work, and the best of it – stories like "My Dear Emily," "There Is Another Shore, You Know, Upon the Other Side," and "The New Men" – holds up well even today. Almost all of Russ's early work is fantasy, much of it about vampires – 1962's "My Dear Emily" remains one of the most stylish and fascinating vampire stories of modern times – and she might have established her reputation years earlier than she did if she had continued to steadily produce work like this, but her output was sparse throughout the first half of the decade, and mostly overlooked. (Even at her peak of production, Russ would never be a prolific writer, even when compared to most careful craftsmen, let alone to the high-production sausage factories that have always been common in the genre.)

By 1967, Russ would be attracting attention with her "Alyx" stories, which at first seemed to be merely better-than-usually written sword and sorcery stories, featuring a tough-minded and wily female cutpurse rather than the usual male hero, sort of the Gray Mouser in drag. This may seem an obvious enough reversal now, when the fantasy genre is flooded with sword-swinging Amazons and swashbuckling women adventurers, but it was radical stuff at the time – with even Damon Knight saying that, before Russ, he would have thought that "nobody could get away with a series of heroic fantasies of prehistory in which the central character, the barbarian adventurer, is a woman." The Alyx stories would veer suddenly into science fiction with "The Barbarian" in *Orbit 3*, in which Alyx outwits a degenerate time-traveller, and then Alyx herself would be snatched out of the past and thrown into a decadent and fascinating future for Russ's first novel, 1968's *Picnic on Paradise*, the work with which she would make her first significant impact on the field, and a work which even now strikes me as one of the best novels of the late '60s. (It was one of two books, both Ace Specials – the other was Lafferty's *Past Master*; the impact of Terry Carr's Ace Specials line on the SF world of the late '60s can hardly be overestimated – that I read for the first time during a long and grueling Trans-Atlantic flight, miles above the roof of the world with sunlight gleaming on the clouds far below. I remember thinking how appropriate both books were to the setting in which I was reading them, for both were unlike anything I'd read before; I still maintain a special fondness for both novels.)

By the early '70s, Russ would have published her complex second novel, *And Chaos Died*, by turns brilliantly effective and opaque almost to the point of deliberate obscurity; won a Nebula Award for her controversial feminist story "When It Changed"; and be producing work like the story that follows, "Nobody's Home" – a sleek, sly, and blackly witty story that was years ahead of its time, especially in its brilliant depiction of what the society of the future was going to be like. . . and, more importantly, what the people who *lived* in it were going to be like. The rest of the genre wouldn't catch up to the kind of thing Russ was doing here, with unruffled ease and elegance, until the late '80s.

By the early '70s, Russ was also, in some circles at least, one of the most hated writers in the business. I'm not quite sure why, since there were other writers around who were producing work that ostensibly seemed much further from the aesthetic center of the field. Perhaps it was her large body of critical work – she was the regular reviewer for *F&SF* at one point – in which she would express a lot of unpopular opinions, although her often incisive criticism can be shown to have had a demonstrable effect on other writers such as Le Guin. Maybe it was just that she was an uppity woman who wouldn't stay in her place. Even before "When It Changed," though, her first overtly feminist story, I can remember being on a panel at a science fiction convention in 1970 or 1971, and mentioning that I liked Russ's work, and having the audience actually *boo* me, loudly, with two or three people rising to their feet and shaking their fists. (At another convention, after I'd mentioned the work of Gene Wolfe, another fan, his face contorted with hate, told me that they were going to drive "people like you" out of the field – how quaint all these passions seem now, at this remove, as if we were quarreling about which end of the egg to break!)

Later, when she published her fierce and passionate feminist novel *The Female Man* in 1975, she became a *bête noire* of unparalleled blackness, practically the Antichrist. Perhaps all this furor, added to the general malaise of the late '70s, contributed to her slow drift out of the field. She published two more books in the next three years – including her weakest novel, 1977's *We Who Are About To* – and then fell silent for several years.

She returned to SF in 1982 with her Hugo Award–winning novella "Souls," and with the other stories that would go into making up *Extra(ordinary) People*, and *this* time, ironically, instead of the conservative wing, it was the young, leftist, radical new writers who fiercely attacked her, one of them sneeringly referring to "Souls" as the "Abbess-phone-home" story. Almost nothing has been heard of from Russ in SF since then, perhaps not surprisingly, but I personally miss her work, and hope that she will decide to take another tour of duty on the barricades sometime in the '90s. At her best, she was one of the best writers ever to work in the field, and one of those who helped to shape it the most profoundly.

Russ's other books include the novel *The Two of Them*, the collections *The Zanzibar Cat*, *Extra(ordinary) People*, *The Adventures of Alyx* and *The Hidden Side of the Moon*, and the critical works *Magic Mommas, Trembling Sisters, Puritans, and Perverts*, and *How to Suppress Women's Writing*.

After she had finished her work at the North Pole, Jannina came down to the Red Sea refineries, where she had family business, jumped to New Delhi for dinner, took a nap in a public bed in Queensland, walked from the hotel to the station, bypassed the Leeward Islands (where she thought she might go, but all the stations were busy), and met Charley to watch the dawn over the Carolinas.

"Where've you been, dear C?"

"Tanzonia. And you're married."

"No."

"I heard you were married," he said. "The Lees told the Smiths who told the Kerguelens who told the Utsumbés and we get around, we Utsumbés. A new wife, they said. I didn't know you were especially fond of women."

"I'm not. She's my husbands' wife. And we're not married yet, Charley. She's had hard luck: a first family started in '35, two husbands burned out by an overload while arranging transportation for a concert – of all things, pushing papers, you know! – and the second divorced her, I think, and she drifted away from the third (a big one), and there was some awful quarrel with the fourth, people chasing people around tables, I don't know."

"Poor woman."

In the manner of people joking and talking lightly they had drawn together, back to back, sitting on the ground and rubbing together their shoulders and the backs of their heads. Jannina said sorrowfully, "What lovely hair you have, Charley Utsumbé, like metal mesh."

"All we Utsumbés are exceedingly handsome." They linked arms. The sun, which anyone could chase around the world now, see it rise or set twenty times a day, fifty times a day – if you wanted to spend your life like that – rose dripping out of the cypress swamp. There was nobody around for miles. Mist drifted up from the pools and low places.

"My God," he said, "it's summer! I have to be at Tanga now."

"What?" said Jannina.

"One loses track," he said apologetically. "I'm sorry, love, but I have unavoidable business at home. Tax labor."

"But why summer, why did its being summer –"

"Train of thought! Too complicated" (and already they were out of key, already the mild affair was over, there having come between them the one obligation that can't be put off to the time you like, or the place you like; off he'd go to plug himself into a road-mender or a doctor, though it's of some advantage to mend all the roads of a continent at one time).

She sat cross-legged on the station platform, watching him enter the booth and set the dial. He stuck his head out the glass door.

"Come with me to Africa, lovely lady!"

She thumbed her nose at him. "You're only a passing fancy, Charley U!" He blew a kiss, enclosed himself in the booth, and disappeared. (The transmatter field is larger than the booth, for obvious reasons; the booth flicks on and off several million times a second and so does not get transported itself, but it protects the machinery from the weather and it keeps people from losing elbows or knees or slicing the ends off a package or a child. The booths at the cryogenics center at the North Pole have exchanged air so often with those of warmer regions that each has its own micro-climate; leaves and seeds, plants and earth, are piled about them. *Don't Step on the Grass!* – say the notes pinned to the door, *Wish to Trade Pawlownia Sapling for Sub-arctic Canadian Moss*; *Watch Your Goddamn Bare Six-Toed Feet!*; *Wish Amateur Cellist for Quartet, Six Months' Rehearsal Late Uhl with Reciter*; *I Lost a Squirrel Here Yesterday, Can You Find It Before It Dies? Eight Children Will Be Heartbroken* – Cecilia Ching, Buenos Aires.)

Jannina sighed and slipped on her glass woolly; nasty to get back into clothes, but home was cold. You never knew where you might go, so you carried them. Years ago (she thought) I came here with someone in the dead of winter, either an unmatched man or someone's starting spouse – only two of us, at any rate – and we waded through the freezing water and danced as hard as we could and then proved we could sing and drink beer in a swamp at the same time, good Lord! And then went to the public resort on the Ile de la Cité to watch professional plays, opera, games – you have to be good to get in there – and got into some clothes because it was chilly after sundown in September – no, wait, it was Venezuela – and watched the lights come out and smoked like mad at a café table and tickled the robot waiter and pretended we were old, really old, perhaps a hundred and fifty. . . . Years ago!

But *was* it the same place? she thought, and dismissing the incident forever, she stepped into the booth, shut the door, and dialed home: the Himalayas. The trunk line was clear. The branch stop was clear. The family's transceiver (located in the anteroom behind two doors, to keep the task of heating the house within reasonable limits) had damn well better be clear, or somebody would be blown right into the vestibule. Momentum- and heat-compensators kept Jannina from arriving home at seventy degrees Fahrenheit internal temperature (seven degrees lost for every mile you teleport upward) or too many feet above herself (rise to the east, drop going west, to the north or south you are apt to be thrown right through the wall of the booth). Someday, thought Jannina, everybody will decide to let everybody live in decent climates. But not yet. Not this everybody.

She arrived home singing, "The World's My Back Yard, Yes, The World Is My Oyster," a song that had been popular in her first youth, some seventy years before.

The Komarovs' house was hardened foam with an automatic inside line to the school near Naples. It was good to be brought up on your own feet. Jannina passed through; the seven-year-olds lay with their heads together and their bodies radiating in a six-personed asterisk. In this position (which was supposed to promote mystical thought) they played Barufaldi, guessing the identity of famous dead personages through anagrammatic sentences, the first letters of the words of which (unscrambled into aphorisms or proverbs) simultaneously spelled out a moral and a series of Goedel numbers (in a previously agreed-upon code) which –

"Oh, my darling, how felicitous is the advent of your appearance!" cried a boy (hard to take, the polysyllabic stage). "Embrace me, dearest maternal parent! Unite your valuable upper limbs about my eager person!"

"Vulgar!" said Jannina, laughing.

"*Non sum filius tuus*?" said the child.

"No, you're not my body-child; you're my godchild. Your mother bequeathed me to you when she died. What are you learning?"

"The eternal parental question," he said, frowning. "How to run a helicopter. How to prepare food from its actual, revolting, raw constituents. Can I go now?"

"*Can* you?" she said. "Nasty imp!"

"Good," he said, "I've made you feel guilty. Don't *do* that," and as she tried to embrace him, he ticklishly slid away. "The robin walks quietly up the branch of the tree," he said breathlessly, flopping back on the floor.

"That's not an aphorism." (Another Barufaldi player.)

"It is."
"It isn't."
"It is."
"It isn't."
"It is."
"It –"

The school vanished; the antechamber appeared. In the kitchen Chi Komarov was rubbing the naked back of his sixteen-year-old son. Parents always kissed each other; children always kissed each other. She touched foreheads with the two men and hung her woolly on the hook by the ham radio rig. Someone was always around. Jannina flipped the cover off her wrist chronometer: standard regional time, date, latitude-longitude, family computer hookup clear. "At my age I ought to remember these things," she said. She pressed the computer hookup: Ann at tax labor in the schools, bit-a-month plan, regular Ann; Lee with three months to go, five years off, heroic Lee; Phuong in Paris, still rehearsing; C.E. gone, won't say where, spontaneous C.E.; Ilse making some repairs in the basement, not a true basement, really, but the room farthest down the hillside. Jannina went up the stairs and then came down and put her head round at the living-and-swimming room. Through the glass wall one could see the mountains. Old Al, who had joined them late in life, did a bit of gardening in the brief summers, and generally stuck around the place. Jannina beamed. "Hullo, Old Al!" Big and shaggy, a rare delight, his white body hair. She sat on his lap. "Has she come?"

"The new one? No," he said.

"Shall we go swimming?"

He made an expressive face. "No, dear," he said. "I'd rather go to Naples and watch the children fly helicopters. I'd rather go to Nevada and fly them myself. I've been in the water all day, watching a very dull person restructure coral reefs and experiment with polyploid polyps."

"You mean *you* were doing it."

"One gets into the habit of working."

"But you didn't have to!"

"It was a private project. Most interesting things are."

She whispered in his ear.

With happily flushed faces, they went into Old Al's inner garden and locked the door.

Jannina, temporary family representative, threw the computer helmet over her head and, thus plugged in, she cleaned house, checked food supplies, did a little of the legal business entailed by a family of eighteen adults (two triplet marriages, a quad, and a group of eight). She felt very smug. She put herself through by radio to Himalayan HQ (above two thousand meters) and hooking computer to computer – a very odd feeling, like an urge to sneeze that never comes off – extended a formal invitation to one Leslie Smith ("Come stay, why don't you?"), notifying every free Komarov to hop it back and fast. Six hikers might come for the night – back-packers. More food. First thunderstorm of the year in Albany, New York (North America). Need an extra two rooms by Thursday. Hear the Palnatoki are moving. Can't use a room. Can't use a kitten. Need the geraniums back, Mrs Adam, Chile. The best maker of hand-blown glass in the world has killed in a duel the second-best maker of hand-blown glass for joining the movement toward ceramics. A bitter struggle is foreseen in the global economy. Need a lighting designer. Need fifteen singers and electric pansensicon. Standby tax labor xxxxxpj through xxxyq to Cambaluc, great tectogenic –

With the guilty feeling that one always gets gossiping with a computer, for it's really not reciprocal, Jannina flipped off the helmet. She went to get Ilse. Climbing back through the white foam room, the purple foam room, the green foam room, everything littered with plots and projects of the clever Komarovs or the even cleverer Komarov children, stopping at the baby room for Ilse to nurse her baby. Jannina danced staidly around studious Ilse. They turned on the nursery robot and the television screen. Ilse drank beer in the swimming room, for her milk. She worried her way through the day's record of events – faults in the foundation, some people who came from Chichester and couldn't find C.E. so one of them burst into tears, a new experiment in genetics coming round the gossip circuit, an execrable set of equations from some imposter in Bucharest.

"A duel!" said Jannina.

They both agreed it was shocking. And what fun. A new fashion. You had to be a little mad to do it. Awful.

The light went on over the door to the tunnel that linked the house to the antechamber, and very quickly, one after another, as if the branch line had just come free, eight Komarovs came into the room. The light flashed again; one could see three people debouch one after the other, persons in boots, with coats, packs, and face masks over their woollies. They were covered with snow, either from the mountain terraces above the house or from some other place, Jannina didn't know. They stamped the snow off in the antechamber and hung their clothes outside; "Good heavens, you're not circumcised!" cried someone. There was as much handshaking and embracing all around as at a wedding party. Velet Komarov (the short, dark one) recognized Fung Pao-yu and swung her off her feet. People began to joke, tentatively striking one another's arms. "Did you have a good hike? Are you a good hiker, Pao-yu?" said Velet. The light over the antichamber went on again, though nobody could see a thing since the glass was steamed over from the collision of hot with cold air. Old Al stopped, halfway into the kitchen. The baggage receipt chimed, recognized only by family ears – upstairs a bundle of somebody's things, ornaments, probably, for the missing Komarovs were still young and the young are interested in clothing, were appearing in the baggage receptacle. "Ann or Phuong?" said Jannina; "five to three, anybody? Match me!" but someone strange opened the door of the booth and peered out. Oh, a dizzying sensation. She was painted in a few places, which was awfully odd because really it was old-fashioned; and why do it for a family evening? It was a stocky young woman. It was an awful mistake, thought Jannina. Then the visitor made her second mistake. She said:

"I'm Leslie Smith." But it was more through clumsiness than being rude. Chi Komarov (the tall, blond one) saw this instantly, and snatching off his old-fashioned spectacles, he ran to her side and patted her, saying teasingly:

"Now, haven't we met? Now, aren't you married to someone I know?"

"No, no," said Leslie Smith, flushing with pleasure.

He touched her neck. "Ah, you're a tightrope dancer!"

"Oh, no!" exclaimed Leslie Smith.

"*I'm* a tightrope dancer," said Chi. "Would you believe it?"

"But you're too – too *spiritual*," said Leslie Smith hesitantly.

"Spiritual, how do you like that, family, spiritual?" he cried, delighted (a little more delighted, thought Jannina, than the situation really called for) and he began to stroke her neck.

"What a lovely neck you have," he said.

This steadied Leslie Smith. She said, "I like tall men," and allowed herself to look at the rest of the family. "Who are these people?" she said, though one was afraid she might really mean it.

Fung Pao-yu to the rescue: "Who are these people? Who are they, indeed! I doubt if they are anybody. One might say, 'I have met these people,' but has one? What existential meaning would such a statement convey? I myself, now, I have met them. I have been introduced to them. But they are like the Sahara; it is all wrapped in mystery; I doubt if they even have names," etc. etc. Then lanky Chi Komarov disputed possession of Leslie Smith with Fung Pao-yu, and Fung Pao-yu grabbed one arm and Chi the other; and she jumped up and down fiercely; so that by the time the lights dimmed and the food came, people were feeling better – or so Jannina judged. So embarrassing and delightful to be eating fifteen to a room! "We Komarovs are famous for eating whatever we can get whenever we can get it," said Velet proudly. Various Komarovs in various places, with the three hikers on cushions and Ilse at full length on the rug. Jannina pushed a button with her toe and the fairy lights came on all over the ceiling. "The children did that," said Old Al. He had somehow settled at Leslie Smith's side and was feeding her so-chi from his own bowl. She smiled up at him. "We once," said a hiking companion of Fung Pao-yu's, "arranged a dinner in an amphitheater where half of us played servants to the other half, with forfeits for those who didn't show. It was the result of a bet. Like the bad old days. Did you know there were once *five billion people* in this world?"

"The gulls," said Ilse, "are mating on the Isle of Skye." There were murmurs of appreciative interest. Chi began to develop an erection and everyone laughed. Old Al wanted music and Velet didn't; what might have been a quarrel was ended by Ilse's furiously boxing their ears. She stalked off to the nursery.

"Leslie Smith and I are both old-fashioned," said Old Al, "because neither of us believes in gabbing. Chi – your theater?"

"We're turning people away." He leaned forward, earnestly, tapping his fingers on his crossed knees. "I swear, some of them are threatening to commit suicide."

"It's a choice," said Velet reasonably.

Leslie Smith had dropped her bowl. They retrieved it for her.

"Aiy, I remember – " said Pao-yu. "What I remember! We've been eating dried mush for three days, tax-issue. Did you know one of my dads killed himself?"

"No!" said Velet, surprised.

"Years ago," said Pao-yu. "He said he refused to live to see the time when chairs were reintroduced. He also wanted further genetic engineering, I believe, for even more intelligence. He did it out of spite, I'm sure. I think he wrestled a shark. Jannina, is this tax-issue food? Is it this year's style tax-issue sauce?"

"No, next year's," said Jannina snappishly. Really, some people! She slipped into Finnish, to show up Pao-yu's pronunciation. "Isn't that so?" she asked Leslie Smith.

Leslie Smith stared at her.

More charitably Jannina informed them all, in Finnish, that the Komarovs had withdrawn their membership in a food group, except for Ann, who had taken out an individual, because what the dickens, who had the time? And tax-issue won't kill you. As they finished, they dropped their dishes into the garbage field and Velet stripped a layer off the rug. In that went, too. Indulgently Old Al began a round:

"Red."

"Sun," said Pao-yu.

"The Red Sun Is," said one of the triplet Komarovs.

"The Red Sun Is – High," said Chi.

"The Red Sun Is High, The," Velet said.

"The Red Sun Is High, The Blue —" Jannina finished. They had come to Leslie Smith, who could either complete it or keep it going. She chose to declare for complete, not shyly (as before) but simply by pointing to Old Al.

"The Red Sun Is High, The Blue," he said. "Subtle! Another: Ching."

"*Nü.*"

"*Ching nü ch'i.*"

"*Chin nü ch'i ch'u.*"

"*Ssu.*"

"*Wo.*"

"*Ssu wo yü.*" It had got back to Leslie Smith again. She said, "I can't do that." Jannina got up and began to dance — I'm nice in my nasty way, she thought. The others wandered toward the pool and Ilse reappeared on the nursery monitor screen, saying, "I'm coming down." Somebody said, "What time is it in the Argentine?"

"Five a.m."

"I think I want to go."

"Go then."

"I go."

"Go well."

The red light over the antechamber door flashed and went out.

"Say, why'd you leave your other family?" said Ilse, settling near Old Al where the wall curved out. Ann, for whom it was evening, would be home soon; Chi, who had just got up a few hours back in western America, would stay somewhat longer; nobody ever knew Old Al's schedule and Jannina herself had lost track of the time. She would stay up until she felt sleepy. She followed a rough twenty-eight-hour day, Phuong (what a nuisance that must be at rehearsals!) a twenty-two-hour one, Ilse six hours up, six hours dozing. Jannina nodded, heard the question, and shook herself awake.

"I didn't leave them. They left me."

There was a murmur of sympathy around the pool.

"They left me because I was stupid," said Leslie Smith. Her hands were clasped passively in her lap. She looked very genteel in her blue body paint, a stocky young woman with small breasts. One of the triplet Komarovs, flirting in the pool with the other two, choked. The non-aquatic members of the family crowded around Leslie Smith, touching her with little, soft touches; they kissed her and exposed to her all their unguarded surfaces, their bellies, their soft skins. Old Al kissed her hands. She sat there, oddly unmoved. "But I *am* stupid," she said. "You'll find out." Jannina put her hands over her ears: "A masochist!" Leslie Smith looked at Jannina with a curious, stolid look. Then she looked down and absently began to rub one blue-painted knee. "Luggage!" shouted Chi, clapping his hands together, and the triplets dashed for the stairs. "No, I'm going to bed," said Leslie Smith; "I'm tired," and quite simply, she got up and let Old Al lead her through the pink room, the blue room, the turtle-and-pet room (temporarily empty), the trash room, and all the other rooms, to the guest room with the view that looked out over the cold hillside to the terraced plantings below.

"The best maker of hand-blown glass in the world," said Chi, "has killed in a duel the second-best maker of hand-blown glass in the world."

"For joining the movement to ceramics," said Ilse, awed. Jannina felt a thrill: this was the bitter stuff under the surface of life, the fury that boiled up. A bitter struggle is foreseen in the global economy. Good old tax-issue stuff goes toddling along, year after year. She was, thought Jannina, extra-ordinarily grateful to be living now, to be in such an extraordinary world, to have so long to go before her death. So much to do!

Old Al came back into the living room. "She's in bed."

"Well, which of us. . . ?" said the triplet-who-had-choked, looking mischievously round from one to the other. Chi was about to volunteer, out of his usual conscientiousness, thought Jannina, but then she found herself suddenly standing up, and then just as suddenly sitting down again. "I just don't have the nerve," she said. Velet Komarov walked on his hands toward the stairs, then somersaulted, and vanished, climbing. Ol Al got off the hand-carved chest he had been sitting on and fetched a can of ale from it. He levered off the top and drank. Then he said, "She really is stupid, you know." Jannina's skin crawled.

"Oooh," said Pao-yu. Chi betook himself to the kitchen and returned with a paper folder. It was coated with frost. He shook it, then impatiently dropped it in the pool. The redheaded triplet swam over and took it. "Smith, Leslie," he said. "Adam Two, Leslie. Yee, Leslie. Schwarzen, Leslie."

"What on earth does the woman *do* with herself besides get married?" exclaimed Pao-yu.

"She drove a hovercraft," said Chi, "in some out-of-the-way places around the Pacific until the last underground stations were completed. Says when she was a child she wanted to drive a truck."

"Well, you can," said the redheaded triplet, "can't you? Go to Arizona or the Rockies and drive on the roads. The sixty-mile-an-hour road. The thirty-mile-an-hour road. Great artistic recreation."

"That's not work," said Old Al.

"Couldn't she take care of children?" said the redheaded triplet. Ilse sniffed.

"Stupidity's not much of a recommendation for that," Chi said. "Let's see – no children. No, of course not. Overfulfilled her tax work on quite a few routine matters here. Kim, Leslie. Went to Moscow and contracted a double with some fellow, didn't last. Registered as a singleton, but that didn't last, either. She said she was lonely and they were exploiting her."

Old Al nodded.

"Came back and lived informally with a theater group. Left them. Went into psychotherapy. Volunteered for several experimental, intelligence-enhancing programs, was turned down – hm! -- sixty-five come the winter solstice, muscular coordination average, muscular development above average, no overt mental pathology, empathy, average, prognosis: poor. No, wait a minute, it says, 'More of the same.' Well, that's the same thing."

"What I want to know," added Chi, raising his head, "is who met Miss Smith and decided we needed the lady in this Ice Palace of ours?"

Nobody answered. Jannina was about to say, "Ann,

perhaps?" but as she felt the urge to do so – surely it wasn't right to turn somebody off like that, *just* for that! – Chi (who had been flipping through the dossier) came to the last page, with the tax-issue stamp absolutely unmistakable, woven right into the paper.

"The computer did," said Pao-yu and she giggled idiotically.

"Well," said Jannina, jumping to her feet, "tear it up, my dear, or give it to me and I'll tear it up for you. I think Miss Leslie Smith deserves from us the same as we'd give to anybody else, and I – for one – intend to go *right up there –*"

"After Velet," said Old Al dryly.

"*With* Velet, if I must," said Jannina, raising her eyebrows, "and if you don't know what's due a guest, Old Daddy, I do, and I intend to provide it. Lucky I'm keeping house this month, or you'd probably feed the poor woman nothing but seaweed."

"You won't like her, Jannina," said Old Al.

"I'll find that out for myself," said Jannina with some asperity, "and I'd advise you to do the same. Let her garden with you, Daddy. Let her squirt the foam for the new rooms. And now" – she glared round at them – "I'm going to clean *this* room, so you'd better hop it, the lot of you," and dashing into the kitchen, she had the computer helmet on her head and the hoses going before they had even quite cleared the area of the pool. Then she took the helmet off and hung it on the wall. She flipped the cover off her wrist chronometer and satisfied herself as to the date. By the time she got back to the living room there was nobody there, only Leslie Smith's dossier lying on the carved chest. There was Leslie Smith; there was all of Leslie Smith. Jannina knocked on the wall cupboard and it revolved, presenting its openable side; she took out chewing gum. She started chewing and read about Leslie Smith.

> Q: What have you seen in the last twenty years that you particularly liked?
> A: I don't . . . the museum, I guess. At Oslo. I mean the . . . the mermaid and the children's museum, I don't care if it's a children's museum.
> Q: Do you like children?

A: Oh no.

(No disgrace in *that*, certainly, thought Jannina.)

Q: But you liked the children's museum.

A: Yes, sir. . . . Yes. . . . I liked those little animals, the fake ones, in the – the –

Q: The crèche?

A: Yes. And I liked the old things from the past, the murals with the flowers on them, they looked so real.

(Dear God!)

Q: You said you were associated with a theater group in Tokyo. Did you like it?

A: No . . . yes. I don't know.

Q: Were they nice people?

A: Oh yes. They were awfully nice. But they got mad at me, I suppose. . . . You see . . . well, I don't seem to get things quite right, I suppose. It's not so much the work, because I do that all right, but the other . . . the little things. It's always like that.

Q: What do you think is the matter?

A: You . . . I think you know.

Jannina flipped through the rest of it: normal, normal, normal. Miss Smith was as normal as could be. Miss Smith was stupid. Not even very stupid. It was too damned bad. They'd probably have enough of Leslie Smith in a week, the Komarovs; yes, we'll have enough of her, Jannina thought, never able to catch a joke or a tone of voice, always clumsy, however willing, but never happy, never at ease. You can get a job for her, but what else can you get for her? Jannina glanced down at the dossier, already bored.

Q: You say you would have liked to live in the old days. Why is that? Do you think it would have been more adventurous or would you like to have had lots of children?

A: I . . . you have no right. . . . You're condescending.

Q: I'm sorry. I suppose you mean to say that then you would have been of above-average intelligence. You would, you know.

A: I know. I looked it up. Don't condescend to me.

Well, it *was* too damned bad! Jannina felt tears rise in her eyes. What had the poor woman done? It was just an accident, that was the horror of it, not even a tragedy, as if everyone's forehead had been stamped with the word "Choose" except for Leslie Smith's. She needs money, thought Jannina, thinking of the bad old days when people did things for money. Nobody could take to Leslie Smith. She wasn't insane enough to stand for being hurt or exploited. She certainly wasn't feeble-minded; they couldn't very well put her into a hospital for the feeble-minded or the brain-injured; in fact (Jannina was looking at the dossier again) they had tried to get her to work there and she had taken a good, fast swing at the supervisor. She had said the people there were "hideous" and "revolting." She had no particular mechanical aptitudes. She had no particular interests. There was not even anything for her to read or watch; how could there be? She seemed (back at the dossier) to spend most of her time either working or going on public tours of exotic places, coral reefs and places like that. She enjoyed aqualung diving, but didn't do it often because that got boring. And that was that. There was, all in all, very little one could do for Leslie Smith. You might even say that in her own person she represented all the defects of the bad old days. Just imagine a world made up of such creatures! Jannina yawned. She slung the folder away and padded into the kitchen. Pity Miss Smith wasn't good-looking, also a pity that she was too well balanced (the folder said) to think that cosmetic surgery would make that much difference. Good for you, Leslie, you've got some sense, anyhow. Jannina, half asleep, met Ann in the kitchen, beautiful, slender Ann reclining on a cushion with her so-chi and melon. Dear old Ann. Jannina nuzzled her brown shoulder. Ann poked her.

"Look," said Ann, and she pulled from the purse she wore at her waist a tiny fragment of cloth, stained rusty brown.

"What's that?"

"The second-best maker of hand-blown glass – oh, you know about it – well, this is his blood. When the best maker of hand-blown glass in the world had stabbed to the heart the second-best maker of hand-blown glass in the world, and cut his throat, too, some small children steeped handkerchiefs in his blood and they're sending pieces all over the world."

"Good God!" cried Jannina.

"Don't worry, my dear," said lovely Ann; "it happens every decade or so. The children say they want to bring back cruelty, dirt, disease, glory, and hell. Then they forget about it. Every teacher knows that." She sounded amused. "I'm afraid I lost my temper today, though, and walloped your godchild. It's in the family, after all."

Jannina remembered when she herself had been much younger and Annie, barely a girl, had come to live with them. Ann had played at being a child and had put her head on Jannina's shoulder, saying, "Jannie, tell me a story." So Jannina now laid her head on Ann's breast and said, "Annie, tell me a story."

Ann said: "I told my children a story today, a creation myth. Every creation myth has to explain how death and suffering came into the world, so that's what this one is about. In the beginning, the first man and the first woman lived very contentedly on an island until one day they began to feel hungry. So they called to the turtle who holds up the world to send them something to eat. The turtle sent them a mango and they ate it and were satisfied, but the next day they were hungry again.

"'Turtle,' they said, 'send us something to eat.' So the turtle sent them a coffee berry. They thought it was pretty small, but they ate it anyway and were satisfied. The third day they called on the turtle again and this time the turtle sent them two things: a banana and a stone. The man and woman did not know which to choose, so they asked the turtle which thing it was they should eat. 'Choose,' said the turtle. So they chose the banana and ate that, but they used the stone for a game of catch. Then the turtle said, 'You should have chosen the stone. If you had chosen the stone, you would have lived forever, but now that you have chosen the banana, Death and Pain have entered the world, and it is not I who can stop them.'"

Jannina was crying. Lying in the arms of her old friend, she wept bitterly, with a burning sensation in her chest and the taste of death and ashes in her mouth. It was awful. It was horrible. She remembered the embryo shark she had seen when she was three, in the Auckland Cetacean Research Center, and how she had cried then. She didn't know what she was crying about. "Don't, don't!" she sobbed.

"Don't what?" said Ann affectionately. "Silly Jannina!"

"Don't, don't," cried Jannina, "don't, it's true, it's true!" and she went on in this way for several more minutes. Death had entered the world. Nobody could stop it. It was ghastly. She did not mind for herself but for others, for her godchild, for instance. He was going to die. He was going to suffer. Nothing could help him. Duel, suicide or old age, it was all the same. "This life!" gasped Jannina. "This awful life!" The thought of death became entwined somehow with Leslie Smith, in bed upstairs, and Jannine began to cry afresh, but eventually the thought of Leslie Smith calmed her. It brought her back to herself. She wiped her eyes with her hand. She sat up. "Do you want a smoke?" said beautiful Ann, but Jannina shook her head. She began to laugh. Really, the whole thing was quite ridiculous.

"There's this Leslie Smith," she said, dry-eyed. "We'll have to find a tactful way to get rid of her. It's idiotic, in this day and age."

And she told lovely Annie all about it.

JAMES TIPTREE, Jr
Her Smoke Rose Up Forever

As most of you probably know by now, multiple Hugo- and Nebula-winning author James Tiptree, Jr – at one time a figure reclusive and mysterious enough to be regarded as the B. Traven of science fiction – was actually the pseudonym of the late Dr Alice Sheldon, a semi-retired experimental psychologist who also wrote occasionally under the name of Raccoona Sheldon. Dr Sheldon's tragic death in 1987 put an end to "both" authors' careers, but, before that, she had won two Nebula and two Hugo Awards as Tiptree, won another Nebula Award as Raccoona Sheldon, and established herself, under whatever name, as one of the best writers in SF.

In fact, with her desire for a high bit-rate, her concern for societal goals, her passion for the novel and the unexpected, her taste for extrapolation, her experimenter's interest in the reactions of people to supernormal stimuli and bizarre situations, her fondness for the apocalyptic, her love of color and sweep and dramatic action, and her preoccupation with the mutability of time and the vastness of space, Alice Sheldon was a natural SF writer. I doubt that she would have been able to realize her particular talents as fully in any other genre, and she didn't even seem particularly interested in trying. At a time when many other SF writers would be just as happy – or happier – writing "mainstream" fiction, and chaff at the artistic and financial restrictions of the genre, what *she* wanted to be was a *science-fiction writer*; that was *her* dream, and her passion.

Although "Tiptree" published two reasonably well-received novels – *Up the Walls of the World* and *Brightness Falls From the Air* – she was, like Knight and Sturgeon (two writers she aesthetically resembled), more comfortable with the short story, and more effective with it. She wrote some of the very best short stories of the '70s: "The Screwfly Solution," "The Girl Who Was Plugged In," "The Women Men Don't See," "Beam Us Home," "And I Awoke and Found Me Here on the Cold Hill's

Side," "I'm Too Big But I Love to Play," "The Man Who Walked Home," "Slow Music." Already it's clear that these are stories that will last. They – and a dozen others almost as good –show that Alice Sheldon was simply one of the best short-story writers of our day.

It has become accepted critical dogma recently that her later stories, written after the mystery of her identity had been penetrated, are not worth reading, but, like most things that Everyone Knows, this turns out to be not quite true. The best of the stories she wrote in the years before her death – "Yaqui Doodle," "Beyond the Dead Reef," "Lirios," "The Earth Doth Like a Snake Renew" – are inferior only to Tiptree at the top of her prior form; compared to almost anybody *else*, they look pretty damn good. Even at her worst, she was never less than entertaining, and there was almost always something quirky and interesting to be found in even the most minor of her stories. I once said that much of the future of SF would belong to Tiptree, and indeed she has already had an enormous impact on upcoming generations of SF writers. Her footprints are all over cyberpunk, for instance, and stories like "The Girl Who Was Plugged In" and "Mother in the Sky with Diamonds" can be seen as directly ancestral to that form.

Hope and despair battled continually in Alice Sheldon's work, as in her life. "Her Smoke Rose Up Forever" is Alice at her blackest, and, in fact, may be one of the bleakest science-fiction stories ever written . . . but its power is undeniable. Once you read it, you may never be able to forget it.

As James Tiptree, Jr, Alice Sheldon also published nine short-story collections: *Ten Thousand Light Years From Home*, *Warm Worlds and Otherwise*, *Starsongs of an old Primate*, *Out of the Everywhere*, *Tales of the Quintana Roo*, *Byte Beautiful*, *The Starry Rift*, the posthumously published *Crown of Stars*, and the recent retrospective collection *Her Smoke Rose Up Forever*.

Deliverance quickens, catapults him into his boots on mountain gravel, his mittened hand on the rusty 1935 International truck. Cold rushes into his young lungs, his eyelashes are knots of ice as he peers down at the lake below the pass. He is in a bare bleak bowl of mountains just showing rusty in the dawn; not one scrap of cover anywhere, not a tree, not a rock.

The lake below shines emptily, its wide rim of ice silvered

by the setting moon. It looks small, everything looks small from up here. Is that scar on the edge his boat? Yes – it's there, it's all okay! The black path snaking out from the boat to the patch of tulegrass is the waterway he broke last night. Joy rises in him, hammers his heart. This is it. This – is – *it*.

He squints his lashes, can just make out the black threads of the tules. Black knots among them – sleeping ducks. Just you wait! His grin crackles the ice in his nose. The tules will be his cover – that perfect patch out there. About eighty yards, too far to hit from shore. That's where he'll be when the dawn flight comes over. Old Tom said he was loco. Loco Petey. Just you wait. Loco Tom.

The pickup's motor clanks, cooling, in the huge silence. No echo here, too dry. No wind. Petey listens intently: a thin wailing in the peaks overhead, a tiny croak from the lake below. Waking up. He scrapes back his frozen canvas cuff over the birthday watch, is oddly, fleetingly puzzled by his own knobby fourteen-year-old wrist. Twenty-five – no, twenty-four minutes to the duck season. Opening day! Excitement ripples down his stomach, jumps his dick against his scratchy longjohns. Gentlemen don't beat the gun. He reaches into the pickup, reverently lifts out the brand-new Fox CE double-barrel twelve-gauge.

The barrels strike cold right through his mitts. He'll have to take one off to shoot, too: It'll be fierce. Petey wipes his nose with his cuff, pokes three fingers through his cut mitten and breaks the gun. Ice in the sight. He checks his impulse to blow it out, dabs clumsily. Shouldn't have taken it in his sleeping bag. He fumbles two heavy sixes from his shell pocket, loads the sweet blue bores, is hardly able to breathe for joy. He is holding a zillion dumb bags of the *Albuquerque Herald*, a whole summer of laying adobe for Mr Noff – all transmuted into this: his perfect, agonizingly chosen *own gun*. No more borrowing old Tom's stinky over-and-under with the busted sight. His own gun with his *initials* on the silver stock-plate.

Exaltation floods him, rises perilously. Holding his gun Petey takes one more look around at the enormous barren slopes. Empty, only himself and his boat and the ducks. The sky has gone cold gas-pink. He is standing on a cusp of the

Great Divide at ten thousand feet, the main pass of the western flyway. At dawn on opening day. . . . What if Apaches came around now? Mescalero Apaches own these mountains but he's never seen one out here. His father says they all have TB or something. In the old days, did they come here on horses? They'd look tiny; the other side is ten miles at least.

Petey squints at a fuzzy place on the far shore, decides it's only sagebrush, but gets the keys and the ax out of the pickup just in case. Holding the ax away from his gun he starts down to the lake. His chest is banging, his knees wobble, he can barely feel his feet skidding down the rocks. The whole world seems to be brimming up with tension.

He tells himself to calm down, blinking to get rid of a funny blackness behind his eyes. He stumbles, catches himself, has to stop to rub at his eyes. As he does so everything flashes black-white – the moon jumps out of a black sky like a locomotive headlight, he is sliding on darkness with a weird humming all around. Oh, Jeeze – mustn't get in altitude blackout, not now! And he makes himself breathe deeply, goes on down with his boots crunching hard like rhythmic ski turns, the heavy shell pockets banging his legs, down, going quicker now, down to the waiting boat.

As he gets closer he sees the open water-path has iced over a little during the night. Good job he has the ax. Some ducks are swimming slow circles right by the ice. One of them rears up and quack-flaps, showing the big raked head: canvasback!

"Ah, you beauty," Petey says aloud, starting to run now, skidding, his heart pumping love, on fire for that first boom and rush. "I wouldn't shoot a sitting duck." His nose-drip has frozen, he is seeing himself hidden in those tules when the flights come over the pass, thinking of old Tom squatting in the rocks back by camp. Knocking back his brandy with his old gums slobbering, dreaming of dawns on World War I airdromes, dreaming of shooting a goose, dying of TB. Crazy old fool. Just you wait. Petey sees his plywood boat heaped with the great pearly breasts and red-black Roman noses of the canvasbacks bloodied and stiff, the virgin twelve-gauge lying across them, fulfilled.

And suddenly he's beside the boat, still blinking away a curious unreal feeling. Mysterious to see his own footprints here. The midget boat and the four frosted decoys are okay, but there's ice in the waterway, all right. He lays the gun and ax inside and pushes the boat out from the shore. It sticks, bangs, rides up over the new ice.

Jeeze, it's really thick! Last night he'd kicked through it easily and poled free by gouging in the paddle. Now he stamps out a couple of yards, pulling the boat. The ice doesn't give. Darn! He takes a few more cautious steps – and suddenly hears the *whew-whew, whew-whew* of ducks coming in. Coming in – and he's out here in the open! He drops beside the boat, peers into the bright white sky over the pass.

Oh *Jeeze* – there they are! Ninety miles an hour, coming downwind, a big flight! And he hugs his gun to hide the glitter, seeing the hurtling birds set their wings, become bloodcurdling black crescent-shapes, webs dangling, dropping like dive-bombers – but they've seen him, they veer in a great circle out beyond the tules, all quacking now, away and down. He hears the far rip of water and stands up aching toward them. You wait. Just wait till I get this dumb boat out there!

He starts yanking the boat out over the creaking ice in the brightening light, cold biting at his face and neck. The ice snaps, shivers, is still hard. Better push the boat around ahead of him so he can fall in it when it goes. He does so, makes another two yards, three – and then the whole sheet tilts and slides under with him floundering, and grounds on gravel. Water slops over his boot tops, burns inside his three pairs of socks.

But it's shallow. He stamps forward, bashing ice, slipping and staggering. A yard, a yard, a yard more – he can't feel his feet, he can't get purchase. Crap darn, this is too slow! He grabs the boat, squats, throws himself in and ahead with all his might. The boat rams forward like an ice-breaker. Again! He'll be out of the ice soon now. Another lunge! And again!

But this time the boat recoils, doesn't ram. Darn *shit*, the crappy ice is so thick! How could it get this thick when it was open water last night?

'Cause the wind stopped, that's why, and it's ten above

zero. Old Tom knew, darn him to hell. But there's only about thirty yards left to go to open water, only a few yards between him and the promised land. Get there. Get over it or under it or through it, go!

He grabs the ax, wades out ahead of the boat, and starts hitting ice, trying to make cracks. A piece breaks, he hits harder. But it doesn't want to crack, the ax-head keeps going in, *thunk*. He has to work it out of the black holes. And it's getting deep, he's way over his boots now. So what? *Thunk!* Work it loose. *Thunk!*

But some remaining sanity reminds him he really will freeze out here if he gets his clothes soaked. Shee-it! He stops, stands panting, staring at the ducks, which are now tipping up, feeding peacefully well out of range, chuckling *paducah, paducah* at him and his rage.

Twenty more yards, shit darn, *God*-darn. He utters a caw of fury and hunger and at that moment hears a tiny distant crack. Old Tom, firing. Crack!

Petey jumps into the boat, jerking off his canvas coat, peeling off the two sweaters, pants, the grey longjohns. His fingers can barely open the icy knots of his bootlaces but his body is radiant with heat, it sizzles the air, only his balls are trying to climb back inside as he stands up naked. Twenty yards!

He yanks the sodden boots back on and crashes out into the ice, whacking with the ax-handle, butting whole sheets aside. He's making it! Ten more feet, twenty! He rams with the boat, bangs it up and down like a sledge-hammer. Another yard! Another! His teeth are clattering, his shins are bleeding, and it's cutting his thighs now, but he feels nothing, only joy, joy! – until suddenly he is slewing full-length under water with the incredible cold going up his ass and into his armpits like skewers and ice cutting his nose.

His hands find the edge and he hauls himself up on the side of the boat. The bottom has gone completely. His ax – his ax is gone.

The ice is still there.

A black hand grabs him inside, he can't breathe. He kicks and flails, dragging himself up into the boat to kneel bleeding, trying to make his ribs work and his jaws stop banging. The first sunray slicks him with ice and incredible goosebumps; he gets a breath and can see ahead, see the gleaming ducks. So close!

The paddle. He seizes it and stabs at the ice in front of the boat. It clatters, rebounds, the boat goes backward. With all his force he flails the ice, but it's too thick, the paddle stem is cracking. No bottom to brace on. *Crack!* And the paddle blade skitters away across the ice. He has nothing left.

He can't make it.

Rage, helpless rage vomits through him, his eyes are crying hot ice down his face. So close! *So close!* And sick with fury he sees them come – *whew-whew! whew-whew-whew-whew!* – a torrent of whistling wings in the bright air, the ducks are pouring over the pass. Ten thousand noble canvasbacks hurtling down the sky at him silver and black, the sky is wings beating above him, but too high, too high – they know the range, oh yes!

He has never seen so many, he will never see it again – and he is standing up in the boat now, a naked bleeding loco ice-boy, raging, sweeping the virgin twelve-gauge, firing – *bam-bam!* both barrels at nothing, at the ice, at the sky, spilling out the shells, ramming them in with tearing frozen hands. A drake bullets toward him, nearer – it *has* to be near enough! *Bam! Bam!*

But it isn't, it isn't, and the air-riders, the magic bodies of his love beat over him yelling – canvasback, teal, widgeon, pintails, redheads, every duck in the world rising now, he is in a ten-mile swirl of birds, firing, firing, a weeping maniac under the flashing wings, white-black, black-white. And among the flashing he sees not only ducks but geese, cranes, every great bird that ever rode this wind: hawks, eagles, condors, pterodactyls – *bam-bam! Bam-bam!!* in the crazy air, in the gale of rage, and tears exploding in great black pulses – *black! light! black!* – whirling unbearably, rushing him up . . .

. . . And he surfaces suddenly into total calm and dimness, another self with all fury shrunk to a tiny knot below his mind and his eyes feasting in the open throat of a girl's white shirt. He is in a room, a cool cave humming with secret promise. Behind the girl the windows are curtained with sheer white stuff against the glare outside.

"Your mother said you went to Santa Fe." He hears his throat threaten soprano and digs his fists into the pockets of his Levis.

The girl Pilar – Pee-lar, crazy-name-Pilar – bends to pick at her tanned ankle, feathery brown bob swinging across her cheek and throat.

"Um-m." She is totally absorbed in a thin gold chain around her ankle, crouching on a big red leather thing her parents got in where, Morocco – Pilar of the urgently slender waist curving into her white Levis, the shirt so softly holding swelling softness; everything so white against her golden tan, smelling of soap and flowers and girl. So *clean*. She has to be a virgin, his heart knows it; a marvelous slow-motion happiness is brimming up in the room. She likes me. She's so shy, even if she's a year older, nearly seventeen, she's like a baby. The pathos of her vulnerable body swells in him, he balls his fists to hide the bulge by his fly. Oh Jeeze, I mean Jesus, let her not look, Pilar. But she does look up then, brushing her misty hair back, smiling dreamily up at him.

"I was at the La Fonda, I had a dinner date with René."

"Who's René?"

"I told you, Pe-ter." Not looking at him, she uncurls from the hassock, drifts like a child to the window, one hand rubbing her arm. "He's my cousin. He's old, he's twenty-five or thirty. He's a lieute*nant* now."

"Oh."

"An *older man*." She makes a face, grins secretly, peeking out through the white curtains.

His heart fizzes with relief, with the exultance rising in the room. She's a virgin, all right. From the bright hot world outside comes the sound of a car starting. A horse whickers faintly down at the club stables, answered by the double wheeze of a donkey. They both giggle. Peter flexes his shoulder, opens and grips his hand around an imaginary mallet.

"Does your father know you were out with him?"

"Oh yes." She's cuddling her cheek against her shoulder, pushing the immaculate collar, letting him see the creamy mounds. She wants me, Peter thinks. His guts jump. *She's going to let me do it to her.* And all at once he is calm, richly calm like that first morning at the corral, watching his mare come to him; knowing.

"Pa-*pa* doesn't care, it's nineteen forty-four. René is my cousin."

Her parents are so terribly sophisticated; he knows her father is some kind of secret war scientist: they are all here because of the war, something over at Los Alamos. And her mother talking French, talking about weird places like Dee-jon and Tan-jay. His own mother doesn't know French, his father teaches high school, he never would be going around with these sophisticated strangers except they need him for their sandlot polo. And he can play rings around them all, too, Peter thinks, grinning, all those smooth sweating old young men – even with his one mare for four chukkers and her tendons like big hot balloons, even with his spliced mallet he can cut it over their heads! If he could only get an official rating. Three goals, sure. Maybe four, he muses, seeing himself riding through that twerp Drexel with his four remounts, seeing Pilar smile, not looking at him. She's shy. That time he let her ride the mare she was really frightened, incredibly awkward; he could feel her thighs tremble when he boosted her up.

His own thighs tremble, remembering the weak tenderness of her in his hands. *Always before your voice my soul is as some smooth and awkward foal* – it doesn't sound so wet now, his mother's nutty line. His foal, his velvety vulnerable baby mare. Compared to her he's a gorilla, even if he's technically a virgin too, men are different. And he understands suddenly that weird Havelock Ellis book in her father's den. Gentle. He must be gentle. Not like – a what? – a baboon playing a violin.

"You shouldn't fool around with older men," he says, and is gratified by the gruffness. "You don't know."

She's watching him now under the fall of her hair, coming close, still hugging herself with her hand going slowly up and down her arm, caressing it. A warm soap smell fills his nose, a sharp muskiness under it. She doesn't know what's she's doing, he thinks choking, she doesn't know about men. And he grunts something like "Don't," or "Can it," trying to hold down the leaping heat between them, but is confused by her voice whispering.

"It *hurts*, Pe-ter."

"What, your arm?"

"Here, do-pee," and his hand is suddenly taken hold of by cool small fingers pulling it not to her arm but in wonder to her side, pressed in the rustling shirt under which he feels at first nothing and then shockingly too far in not his own wide ribs but the warm stem of her, and as his paralyzed hand fumbles, clasps, she half turns around so that his ignited hand rides onto a searing soft unnatural swelling – her *breast* – and the room blanks out, whirls up on a brimming, drumming tide as if all the dead buffalo were pounding back. And the window blinks once with lemon light shooting around their two bodies where her hip is butting into his thigh making it wholly impossible to continue standing there with his hands gentle on her tits.

"You don't know what you're doing, Pilar. Don't be a dope, your mother –"

"She's a-way now." And there is a confused interval of mouths and hands trying to be gentle, trying to hold her away from his fly, trying to stuff her into himself in total joy, if he had six hands he couldn't cope with electric all of her – until suddenly she pulls back, is asking inanely, "Pe-ter, don't you have a friend?"

The subtle difference in her voice makes him blink, answering stupidly, "Sure, Tom Ring," while her small nose wrinkles.

"Dopee Pe-ter, I mean a boy friend. Somebody smooth."

He stands trying to pant dignifiedly, thinking Jeeze, I mean Christ, she knows I don't have any smooth friends; if it's for a picnic maybe Diego Martine? But before he can suggest this she has leaned into the window bay, cuddling the silky curtain around her, peeking at him so that his hands go pawing in the cloth.

"René has a friend."

"Uh."

"He's older too, he's twen-tee," she breathes teasingly. "Lieute*nant* Shar-lo. That's Charles to you, see?" And she turns around full into his arms curtain and all and from the press of silk and giggles comes a small voice saying forever, "And Re-*né* and Shar-*lo* and Pee-*lar* all went to bed together and they played with me, Oh, for hours and hours, Pe-ter, it was too marvellous. I will ne-ver do it with just one boy again."

Everything drops then except her face before him horribly heavy and exalted and alien, and just as his heart knows it's dead and an evil so generalized he can hardly recognize it as fury starts tearing emptily at him inside, her hand comes up over her mouth and she is running doubled over past him.

"I'm going to be sick, Peter help me!"

And he stumbles after down the dim cool hall to find her crumpled down, her brown hair flowing into the toilet as she retches, retches, whimpering, convulses unbearably. The white shirt has ridden up to expose her pathetically narrow back, soft knobs of her spine curving down into her pants, her tender buttocks bumping his knees as he stands help-lessly strangling a sopping towel instead of her neck, trying to swab at her hidden forehead. His own gullet is retching too, his face feels doughy, and water is running down into his open mouth while one of her hands grips his, shaking him with her spasms there in the dim hospital-like bathroom. The world is groaning, he is seeing not her father's bay rum bottle but the big tiled La Fonda bedroom, the three bodies writhing on the bed, performing unknown horrors. *Playing with her* . . .

His stomach heaves, only what it is, he is coming in his Levis in a dreadful slow unrelieving ooze like a red-hot wire dragging through his crotch, while he stands by her uselessly as he will stand helplessly by in some near future he can't imagine or remember – and the tension keeps building, pounding, the light flickers – a storm is coming or maybe his eyes are going bad, but he can see below him her pure profile resting spent on the edge of the toilet, oblivious to his furious towel; in the flashing dimness sees the incomprehensible letters *S-E-P-T-I-C A-B-O-R-T-I-O-N* snaking shadowy down the spine of his virgin love, while the universe beats black – Flash! Black! Drumming with hooves harsher than any storm – hurling him through lightning-claps of blinding darkness to a thrumming stasis in which what exists of him senses – something – but is instantly shot away on unimaginable energies –

– And achieves condensement, blooms into the green and open sunlight of another world, into a mellow springtime self – in which a quite different girl is jostling his hip.

"Molly," he hears his older voice say vaguely, seeing with joy how the willow fronds trail in the friendly, dirty Potomac. The bars and caduceus on his collar are pricking his neck.

"Yes sir, doctor sir." She spins around, kneels down in the scruffy grass to open Howard Johnson boxes. "Oh God, the coffee." Handing him up a hot dog, swinging back her fair hair. Her arm is so female with its tender pale armpit, her whole body is edible, even her dress is like lemonade so fresh and clean – no, radiant, he corrects himself. That's the word, radiant. His radiant woman. He shrugs away a tiny darkness, thinking of her hair sliding on his body in the Roger Smith hotel bedroom.

"C'mon sit, Pete. It's only a little dirty."

"Nothing's dirty any more." He flops down beside her, one arm finding its natural way around the opulence of her buttocks on the grass. She chuckles down at him, shaking her head.

"You're a hard case, Pete." She takes a big bite of hot dog with such lips that he considers flinging himself upon her then and there, barely remembers the cars tearing by above them. "I swear," she says, chewing, "I don't think you ever screwed anybody you were friends with before."

"Something like that." He puts his hot dog down to loosen his GI tie.

"Thirty days to civvies, you'll be in Baltimore." She licks her fingers happily. "Oh wow, Pete, I'm so glad you got your fellowship. Try the cole slaw, it's all right. Will you remember us poor slaves when you're a big old pathologist?"

"I'll remember." To distract himself he pokes in the boxes, spills cole slaw on the book. "What you reading?"

"Oh, Whately Carington."

"Whatly what?"

"No, *Whate*-ly. Carington. A Limey. Psychical research man, they do that veddy seddiously, the Limies."

"Uh?" He beams at the river, blinks to get rid of a flicker back of his eyes. Amphetamine withdrawal, after six months?

"He has this theory, about K-objects. Whatever thing you feel most intense about, part of you lives on – Pete, what's wrong?"

"Nothing."

But the flicker won't quit, it is suddenly worse; through it he can just make out her face turned nurse-wary, coming close, and he tries to hang on through a world flashing black – green – BLACK! – is trapped for unbreathing timelessness in dark nowhere, a phantom landscape of grey tumbled ash under a hard black sky, seeing without eyes a distant tangle of wreckage on the plain so menacing that his unbodied voice screams at the shadow of a metal scrap beside him in the ashes, 2004 the ghostly unmeaning numbers – *stop it!* – And he is back by the river under Molly's springtime eyes, his hands gripping into the bones of her body.

"Hey-y-y, honey, the war's over." Sweet sensual pixie-smile now watchful, her nurse's hand inside his shirt. "Korea's ten thousand miles away, you're in good old DC, doctor."

"I know. I saw a license plate." He laughs unconvincingly, makes his hands relax. Will the ghosts of Seoul never let him go? And his body guiltily intact, no piece of him in the stained waste cans into which he has – Stop it! Think of Molly. I like Ike. Johns Hopkins research fellowship. Some men simply aren't cut out for surgical practice.

"I'm a gutless wonder, Molly. Research."

"Oh for Christ's sake, Pete," she says with total warmth, nurse-hand satisfied, changing to lover's on his chest. "We've been *over* all that."

And of course they have, he knows it and only mutters, "My dad wanted me to be an Indian doctor," which they have been over too; and the brimming gladness is back now, buoyantly he seizes the cole slaw, demands entertainment, demonstrating reality-grasp.

"So what about Whately?"

"It's serious-s-s," she protests, snickering, and is mercurially almost serious too. "I mean, I'm an atheist,

Pete, I don't believe there's anything afterwards, but this theory. . . ." And she rattles on about K-objects and the pool of time, intense energic structures of the mind undying – sweet beddable girl in the springtime who has taught him unclaiming love. His friend. Liberated him.

He stretches luxuriously, relishes a cole slaw belch. Free male beside a willing woman. No problems. "What is it men in women do require? The lineaments of gratified desire." The radiance of her. He has gratified her. Will gratify her again . . .

"It's kind of spooky, though." She flings the box at the river with tremendous effort, it flies twenty feet. "Damn! But think of parts of yourself whirling around forever sticking to whatever you loved!" She settles against the willow, watching the box float away. "I wonder if part of me is going to spend eternity hanging around a dumb cat. I loved that old cat. Henry. He died, though."

The ghost of a twelve-gauge fires soundlessly across his mind, a mare whickers. He sneezes and rolls over onto her lap with his nose in her warm scented thighs. She peers dreamily down at him over her breasts, is almost beautiful.

"Whatever you love, forever. Be careful what you love." She squints wickedly. "Only with you I think it'd be whatever you were maddest at – no, that's a horrible thought. Love *has* to be the most intense."

He doubts it but is willing to be convinced, rooting in her lap while she pretends to pound on him and then squirms, stretching up her arms, giving herself to the air, to him, to life.

"I want to spend eternity whirling around you." He heaves up to capture her, no longer giving a damn about the cars, and as the sweet familiar body comes pliantly under him he realizes it's true, he's known it for some time. Not friendship at all, or rather, the best of friendships. The real one. "I love you, Molly. We love."

"Ooh, Pete."

"You're coming to Baltimore with me. We'll get married," he tells her warm neck, feeling the flesh under her skirt heavy in his hand, feeling also an odd stillness that makes him draw to where he can see her face, see her lips whispering.

"I was afraid of that."

"Afraid?" His heart jumps with relief, jumps so hard that the flicker comes back in the air, through which he sees her lying too composed under his urgency. "Don't be afraid, Molly. I *love* you."

But she is saying softly, "Oh, damn, damn, Pete, I'm so sorry, it's a lousy thing women do. I was just so happy, because. . . ." She swallows, goes on in an absurd voice. "Because someone very dear to me is coming home. He called me this morning from Honolulu."

This he cannot, will not understand among the flashing pulses, but repeats patiently, "You love me, Molly. I love you. We'll get married in Baltimore," while she fights gently away from him saying, "Oh I do, Pete, I *do*, but it's not the same."

"You'll be happy with me. You love me."

They are both up crouching now in the blinking, pounding sunlight.

"No, Pete, I never *said*. I didn't – " Her hands are out seeking him like knives.

"I *can't* marry you, honey. I'm going to marry a man called Charlie McMahon."

McMahon – Maaa – honn – aa – on-n-n the idiot sound flaps through the universe, his carotids are hammering, the air is drumming with his hurt and rage as he stands foolishly wounded, unable to believe the treachery of everything – which is now strobing in great blows of blackness as his voice shouts "Whore!" shouts "Bitch-bitch-bitch . . ." into a dwindling, flashing chaos –

– And explodes silently into a non-being which is almost familiar, is happening this time more slowly as if huge energy is tiding to its crest so slowly that some structure of himself endures to form in what is no longer a brain the fear that he is indeed dead and damned to live forever in furious fragments. And against this horror his essence strains to protest *But I did love!* at a horizon of desolation – a plain of endless, lifeless rubble under a cold black sky, in which he or some pattern of energies senses once more that distant presence: wreckage, machines, huge structures incomprehensibly operative, radiating dark force in the nightmare world, the force which now surges –

*

– To incorporate him anew within familiar walls, with the words "But I did love" meaninglessly on his lips. He leans back in his familiarly unoiled swivel chair, savoring content. Somewhere within him weak darkness stirs, has power only to send his gaze to the three-di portraits behind the pile of print-outs on his desk.

Molly smiles back at him over the computer sheets, her arm around their eldest daughter. For the first time in years the thought of poor Charlie McMahon crosses his mind, triggers the automatic incantation: Molly-never-would-have-been-happy-with-him. They had a bad time around there, but it worked out. Funny how vividly he recalls that day by the river, in spite of all the good years since. *But I did love*, his mind murmurs uneasily, as his eyes go lovingly to the computer print-outs.

The lovely, elegant results. All confirmed eight ways now, the variance all pinned down. Even better than he'd hoped. The journal paper can go in the mail tomorrow. Of course the pub-lag is nearly three years now; never mind: the AAAS panel comes next week. That's the important thing. Lucky timing, couldn't be neater. The press is bound to play it up. . . . Going to be hard not to watch Gilliam's face, Peter muses, his own face ten years younger, sparkling, all lines upturned.

I do love it, that's what counts, he thinks, a jumble of the years of off-hours drudgery in his mind. . . . Coffee-ringed clipboards, the new centrifuge, the animal mess, a girl's open lab coat, arguments with Ferris in Analysis, arguments about space, about equipment, about costs – and arching over it like a laser-grid the luminous order of his hypothesis. His proven – no, mustn't say it – his meticulously *tested* hypothesis. The lucky lifetime break. The beauty one. Never do it again, he hasn't another one like this left in him; no matter! This is it, the peak. Just in time. Don't think of what Nathan said, don't think the word. (Nobel) – That's stupid. (Nobel) – Think of the work itself, the explanatory power, the clarity.

His hand has been wandering toward the in-basket under the print-outs where his mail has been growing moss (he'll get a secretary out of this, that's for sure!) but the idea of light turns him to the window. The room feels tense, brimming with a tide of energy. Too much coffee, he thinks, too much joy. I'm not used to it. Too much of a loner. From here in I share. Spread it around, encourage younger men. Herds of assistants now . . .

Across his view of tired Bethesda suburbs around the NIH Annex floats the train of multiple-author papers, his name as senior, a genial myth; sponsoring everybody's maiden publication. A fixture in the mainstream. . . . Kids playing down there, he sees, shooting baskets by a garage, will some of them live to have a myeloma cured by the implications of his grubby years up here? If the crystallization can be made easier. Bound to come. But not by me, he thinks, trying to focus on the running figures through a faint stroboscopic blink which seems to arise from the streets below although he knows it must be in his retinae.

Really too much caffeine, he warns himself. Let's not have a hypertensive episode, not *now* for God's sake. Exultation is almost tangible in the room, it's not distracting but integrative; as if he were achieving some higher level of vitality, a norepinephrine-like effect. Maybe I really will live on a higher level, he muses, rubbing the bridge of his nose between two fingers to get rid of a black after-image which seems almost like an Apollo moonscape behind his eyes, a trifle unpleasant.

Too much doom, he tells himself, vigorously polishing his glasses, too much bomb-scare, ecology-scare, fascism-scare, race-war-scare, death-of-everything scare. He jerks his jaw to stop the tinnitis thrumming in his inner ear, glancing at the big 1984 desk calendar with its scrawled joke: *If everything's okay why are we whispering?* Right. Let's get at it and get home. To Molly and Sue and little Pete, their late-born.

He grins, thinking of the kid running to him, and thrusts his hand under the print-outs to his packet of stale mail – and as his hand touches it an icicle rams into his heart.

For an instant he thinks he really is having a coronary, but it isn't his heart, it's a horrible cold current of knowledge striking from his fingers to his soul, from that hideous sleazy tan-covered foreign journal which he now pulls slowly out to see the penciled note clipped to the cover, the personally delivered damned journal which has been lying under there like a time-bomb for how long? Weeks?

Pete, you better look at this. Sorry as hell.

But he doesn't need to look, riffling through the wretchedly printed pages with fingers grown big and cold as clubs; he already knows what he'll find inside there published so neatly, so sweetly, and completely, with the confirmation even stronger and more elegant, the implication he hadn't thought of – and all so modest and terse. So young. Despair takes him as the page opens. *Djakarta University* for Jesus Christ's sake. And some Hindu's bloody paradigm . . .

Sick fury fulminates, bile and ashes rain through his soul as his hands fumble the pages, the gray unreal unreadable pages which are now strobing – Flash! Black! Flash! Black! –swallowing the world, roaring him in or up or out on a phantom whirlwind. . . .

. . . till unsensation crescendos past all limit, bursts finally into the silence of pure energy, where he – or what is left of him, or momentarily reconstituted of him – integrates to terrified insight, achieves actual deathly awareness of its extinct self immaterially spinning in the dust of an aeons-gone NIH Annex on a destroyed planet. And comprehends with agonized lucidity the real death of everything that lived – excepting only that in himself which he would most desperately wish to be dead.

What happened? He does not know, can never know which of the dooms or some other had finally overtaken them, nor when; only that he is registering eternity, not time, that all that lived here has been gone so long that even time is still. Gone, all gone; centuries or millennia gone, all gone to ashes under pulseless stars in the icy dark, gone forever. Saving him alone and his trivial pain.

He alone. . . . But as the mercilessly reifying force floods higher there wakes in him a dim uncomforting sense of presence; a bodiless disquiet in the dust tells him he is companioned, is but a node in a ghostly film of dead life shrouding the cold rock-ball. Unreachable, isolate – he strains for contact and is incorporeally stricken by new dread. *Are they too in pain?* Was pain indeed the fiercest fire in our nerves, alone able to sustain its flame through death? What of love, of joy? . . . There are none here.

He wails voicelessly as conviction invades him, he who had believed in nothing before. All the agonies of earth, uncanceled? Are broken ghosts limping forever from Stalingrad and Salamis, from Gettysburg and Thebes and Dunkirk and Khartoum? Do the butchers' blows still fall at Ravensbruck and Wounded Knee? Are the dead of Carthage and Hiroshima and Cuzco burning yet? Have ghostly women waked again only to resuffer violation, only to watch again their babies slain? Is every nameless slave still feeling the iron bite, is every bomb, every bullet and arrow and stone that ever flew still finding its screaming mark – atrocity without end or comfort, forever?

Molly. The name forms in his canceled heart. She who was love. He tries to know that she or some fragment of her is warm among her children, but can summon only the image of her crawling forever through wreckage to Charlie McMahon's bloody head.

Let it not be! He would shriek defiance at the wastes, finding himself more real as the strange energy densens; he struggles bodilessly, flails perished non-limbs to conjure love out of extinction to shield him against hell, calling with all his obliterated soul on the ultimate talisman: the sound of his little son's laugh, the child running to him, clasping his leg in welcome home.

For an instant he thinks he has it – he can see the small face turn up, the mouth open – but as he tries to grasp, the ghost-child fades, frays out, leaving in his destroyed heart only another echo of hurt – *I want Mommy, Mommy, my mommy.* And he perceives that what he had taken for its head are forms. Presences intrusive, alien as the smooth, bleak regard of sharks met under water.

They move, precess obscurely – they *exist* here on this time-lost plain! And he understands with loathing that it is from *them* or *those* – machines or beings, he cannot tell – that the sustaining energy flows. It is *their* dark potency which has raised him from the patterns of the dust.

Hating them he hungers, would sway after them to suck

his death-life, as a billion other remnants are yearning, dead sunflowers thirsting toward their black sun – but finds he cannot, can only crave helplessly as they recede.

They move, he perceives, toward those black distant cenotaphs, skeletal and alien, which alone break the dead horizon. What these can be, engines or edifices, is beyond his knowing. He strains sightlessly, sensing now a convergence, an inflowing as of departure like ants into no earthly nest. And at this he understands that the energy upbuoying him is sinking, is starting to ebb. The alien radiance that raised him is going and he is guttering out. *Do you know?* he voicelessly cries after them, *Do you know? Do you move oblivious among our agonies?*

But he receives no answer, will never receive one; and as his tenuous structure fails he has consciousness only to wonder briefly what unimaginable errand brought such beings here to his dead cinder. Emissaries, he wonders, dwindling; explorers, engineers? Or is it possible that they are only sightseers? Idling among our ruins, perhaps even cognizant of the ghosts they raise to wail – turning us on, recreating our dead-show for their entertainment?

Shriveling, he watches them go in, taking with them his lacerating life, returning him to the void. Will they return? Or – his waning self forms one last desolation – have they returned already on their millennial tours? Has this recurred, to recur and recur again? Must he and all dead life be borne back each time helplessly to suffer, to jerk anew on the same knives and die again until another energy exhumes him for the next performance?

Let us die! But his decaying identity can no longer sustain protest, knows only that it is true, is unbearably all true, has all been done to him before and is all to do again and again and again without mercy forever.

And as he sinks back through the collapsing levels he can keep hold only of despair, touching again the deadly limp brown journal – *Djakarta University?* Flash – and he no longer knows the cause of the terror in his soul as he crumbles through lost springtime – *I don't love you that way, Pete* – and is betrayed to aching joy as his hand closes over the young breast within her white shirt – *Pe-ter, don't you have a friend?* –

while his being shreds out, disperses among a myriad draining ghosts of anguish as the alien life deserts them, strands them lower and lower toward the final dark – until with uncomprehending grief he finds himself, or a configuration that was himself, for a last instant real – his boots on gravel in the dawn, his hand on a rusty pickup truck.

A joy he cannot bear rises in his fourteen-year-old heart as he peers down at the magic ducks, sees his boat safe by the path he's cut; not understanding why the wind shrieks pain through the peaks above as he starts leaping down the rocks holding his ax and his first own gun, down to the dark lake under the cold stars, forever.

URSULA K. LE GUIN
The Barrow

Like Zelazny, Ursula K. Le Guin started publishing in 1962 in the pages of Cele Goldsmith's *Amazing*, but her career would rise in a less meteoric way, even if, in the end, its arc would take her as high or higher. Her first novel, *Rocannon's World*, published in 1966, was another one of those garishly covered Ace Doubles, and was resolutely ignored. Her next few novels, the excellent and still-underrated *Planet of Exile*, and the complex (perhaps too complex) and Van Vogtian *City of Illusions*, were also mostly overlooked, and would only be discovered retrospectively by most readers (in the same fashion as was Delany's early work) after her plunge into wide public notice was accomplished by the publication of *The Left Hand of Darkness* in 1969 as part of Terry Carr's new Ace Specials line.

Rarely has a novel had as sharp and sudden an impact, or been accepted as widely as a modern masterpiece. *The Left Hand of Darkness* won both the Hugo Award and Nebula Award that year, and it deserved them. A starkly poetic, emotionally charged, and deeply moving exploration into the nature of humanness and the question of sexual identity, it would be the most influential novel of the new decade, and shows every sign of becoming one of the enduring classics of the genre – even ignoring the rest of Le Guin's work, the impact of this one novel on future SF and future SF writers would be incalculably strong. (Her 1968 fantasy novel, *A Wizard of Earthsea*, would be almost as influential on future generations of High Fantasy writers.)

By the middle of the decade, Le Guin was possibly the most talked-about SF writer of the '70s, rivaled for that position only by Robert Silverberg, James Tiptree, Jr, and Philip K. Dick. By the end of the decade, she had won Hugo and Nebula Awards, for her monumental Utopian novel *The Dispossessed*, two other Hugo Awards and a Nebula Award for her short fiction, and the National Book Award for Children's Literature for her novel

The Farthest Shore, and was probably one of the best-known and most universally respected SF writers in the world. She won another Hugo in 1988 for her story "Buffalo Gals, Won't You Come Out Tonight?"

"The Barrow" is an almost unknown Le Guin story, but it is a stunning evocation of period and place, and it packs a powerful impact into a very short package. Like all Le Guin stories, it is about responsibility and consequences – and the making of hard choices.

Le Guin's other novels include *The Lathe of Heaven, The Beginning Place, The Tombs of Atuan. The World for World Is Forest, The Eye of the Heron,* and the controversial multi-media novel (it sold with a tape cassette of music, and included drawings and recipes) *Always Coming Home,* which critics seem either to love or loathe. There are four collections of her short work: *The Wind's Twelve Quarters, Orsinian Tales, The Compass Rose,* and, most recently, *Buffalo Gals and Other Animal Presences.* Her most recent novel is *Tehanu,* a continuation of her Earthsea trilogy.

Night came down along the snowy road from the mountains. Darkness ate the village, the stone tower of Vermare Keep, the barrow by the road. Darkness stood in the corners of the rooms of the Keep, sat under the great table and on every rafter, waited behind the shoulders of each man at the hearth.

The guest sat in the best place, a corner seat projecting from one side of the twelve-foot fireplace. The host, Freyga, Lord of the Keep, Count of the Montayna, sat with everybody else on the hearth-stones, though nearer the fire than some. Cross-legged, his big hands on his knees, he watched the fire steadily. He was thinking of the worst hour he had known in his twenty-three years, a hunting trip, three autumns ago, to the mountain lake Malafrena. He thought of how the thin barbarian arrow had stuck up straight from his father's throat; he remembered how the cold mud had oozed against his knees as he knelt by his father's body in the reeds, in the circle of the dark mountains. His father's hair had stirred a little in the lake-water. And there had been a strange taste in his own mouth, the taste of death, like licking bronze. He tasted bronze now. He listened for the women's voices in the room overhead.

The guest, a traveling priest, was talking about his travels. He came from Solariy, down in the southern plains. Even merchants had stone houses there, he said. Barons had palaces, and silver platters, and ate roast beef. Count Freyga's liege men and servants listened open-mouthed. Freyga, listening to make the minutes pass, scowled. The guest had already complained of the stables, of the cold, of mutton for breakfast dinner and supper, of the dilapidated condition of Vermare Chapel and the way Mass was said there – "Arianism!" he had muttered, sucking in his breath and crossing himself. He told old Father Egius that every soul in Vermare was damned: they had received heretical baptism. "Arianism, Arianism!" he shouted. Father Egius, cowering, thought Arianism was a devil and tried to explain that no one in his parish had ever been possessed, except one of the count's rams, who had one yellow eye and one blue one and had butted a pregnant girl so that she miscarried her child, but they had sprinkled holy water on the ram and it made no more trouble, indeed was a fine breeder, and the girl, who had been pregnant out of wedlock, had married a good peasant from Bara and borne him five little Christians, one a year. "Heresy, adultery, ignorance!" the foreign priest had railed. Now he prayed for twenty minutes before he ate his mutton, slaughtered, cooked, and served by the hands of heretics. What did he want? thought Freyga. Did he expect comfort, in winter? Did he think they were heathens, with his "Arianism"? No doubt he had never seen a heathen, the little, dark, terrible people of Malafrena and the farther hills. No doubt he had never had a pagan arrow shot at him. That would teach him the difference between heathens and Christian men, thought Freyga.

When the guest seemed to have finished boasting for the time being, Freyga spoke to a boy who lay beside him chin in hand: "Give us a song, Gilbert." The boy smiled and sat up, and began at once in a high, sweet voice:

King Alexander forth he came,
Armored in gold was Alexander,
Golden his greaves and great helmet,
His hauberk all of hammered gold.

Clad in gold came the king,
Christ he called on, crossing himself,
　In the hills at evening,
Forward the army of King Alexander
Rode on their horses, a great host,
Down to the plains of Persia
To kill and conquer, they followed the King,
　In the hills at evening.

The long chant droned on; Gilbert had begun in the middle and stopped in the middle, long before the death of Alexander "in the hills at evening." It did not matter; they all knew it from beginning to end.

"Why do you have the boy sing of pagan kings?" said the guest.

Freyga raised his head. "Alexander was a great king of Christendom."

"He was a Greek, a heathen idolator."

"No doubt you know the song differently than we do," Freyga said politely. "As we sing it, it says, 'Christ he called on, crossing himself.'"

Some of his men grinned.

"Maybe your servant would sing us a better song," Freyga added, for his politeness was genuine. And the priest's servant, without much urging, began to sing in a nasal voice a canticle about a saint who lived for twenty years in his father's house, unrecognized, fed on scraps. Freyga and his household listened in fascination. New songs rarely came their way. But the singer stopped short, interrupted by a strange, shrieking howl from somewhere outside the room. Freyga leapt to his feet, staring into the darkness of the hall. Then he saw that his men had not moved, that they sat silently looking up at him. Again the faint howl came from the room overhead. The young count sat down. "Finish your song," he said. The priest's servant gabbled out the rest of the song. Silence closed down upon its ending.

"Wind's coming up," a man said softly.

"An evil winter it's been."

"Snow to your thighs, coming through the pass from Malafrena yesterday."

"It's their doing."

"Who? The mountain folk?"

"Remember the gutted sheep we found last autumn? Kass said then it was an evil sign. They'd been killing to Odne, he meant."

"What else would it mean?"

"What are you talking about?" the foreign priest demanded.

"The mountain folk, Sir Priest. The heathen."

"What is Odne?"

A pause.

"What do you mean, killing to Odne?"

"Well, sir, maybe it's better not to talk about it."

"Why?"

"Well, sir, as you said of the singing, holy things are better, tonight." Kass the blacksmith spoke with dignity, only glancing up to indicate the room overhead; but another man, a young fellow with sores around his eyes, murmured, "The Barrow has ears, the Barrow hears . . ."

"Barrow? That hillock by the road, you mean?"

Silence.

Freyga turned to face the priest. "They kill to Odne," he said in his soft voice, "on stones beside the barrows in the mountains. What's inside the barrows, no man knows."

"Poor heathen men, unholy men," old Father Egius murmured sorrowfully.

"The altarstone of our chapel came from the Barrow," said the boy Gilbert.

"What?"

"Shut your mouth," the blacksmith said. "He means, sir, that we took the top stone from the stones beside the Barrow, a big marble stone, Father Egius blessed it and there's no harm in it."

"A fine altarstone," Father Egius agreed, nodding and smiling, but on the end of his words another howl rang out from overhead. He bent his head and muttered prayers.

"You pray too," said Freyga, looking at the stranger. He ducked his head and began to mumble, glancing at Freyga now and then from the corner of his eye.

There was little warmth in the Keep except at the hearth,

and dawn found most of them still there: Father Egius curled up like an aged dormouse in the rushes, the stranger slumped in his chimney corner, hands clasped across his belly, Freyga sprawled out on his back like a man cut down in battle. His men snored around him, started in their sleep, made unfinished gestures. Freyga woke first. He stepped over the sleeping bodies and climbed the stone stairs to the floor above. Ranni the midwife met him in the ante-room, where several girls and dogs were sleeping in a heap on a pile of sheepskins. "Not yet, count."

"But it's been two nights now –"

"Ah, she's hardly begun," the midwife said with contempt. "Has to rest, hasn't she?"

Freyga turned and went heavily down the twisted stairs. The woman's contempt weighed upon him. All the women, all yesterday; their faces were stern, preoccupied; they paid no attention to him. He was outside, out in the cold, insignificant. He could not do anything. He sat down at the oaken table and put his head in his hands, trying to think of Galla, his wife. She was seventeen; they had been married ten months. He thought of her round white belly. He tried to think of her face but there was nothing but the taste of bronze on his tongue. "Get me something to eat!" he shouted, bringing his fist down on the board, and the Tower Keep of Vermare woke with a jump from the grey paralysis of dawn. Boys ran about, dogs yelped, bellows roared in the kitchen, men stretched and spat by the fire. Freyga sat with his head buried in his hands.

The women came down, one or two at a time, to rest by the great hearth and have a bite of food. Their faces were stern. They spoke to each other, not to the men.

The snow had ceased and a wind blew from the mountains, piling snowdrifts against the walls and byres, a wind so cold it cut off breath in the throat like a knife.

"Why has God's word not been brought to these mountain folk of yours, these sacrificers of sheep?" That was the potbellied priest, speaking to Father Egius and the man with sores around his eyes, Stefan.

They hesitated, not sure what "sacrificers" meant.

"It's not just sheep they kill," said Father Egius, tentatively.

Stefan smiled. "No, no, no," he said, shaking his head.

"What do you mean?" The stranger's voice was sharp; and Father Egius, cowering slightly, said, "They – they kill goats, too."

"Sheep or goats, what's that to me? Where do they come from, these pagans? Why are they permitted to live in a Christian land?"

"They've always lived here," the old priest said, puzzled.

"And you've never tried to bring the Holy Church among them?"

"Me?"

It was a good joke, the idea of the little old priest going up into the mountains; there was a good deal of laughter for quite a while. Father Egius, though without vanity, was perhaps a little hurt, for he finally said in a rather stiff tone, "They have their gods, sir."

"Their idols, their devils, their what do you call it – Odne!"

"Be quiet, priest," Freyga said suddenly. "Must you say that name? Do you know no prayers?"

After that the stranger was less haughty. Since the count had spoken harshly to him the charm of hospitality was broken, the faces that looked at him were hard. That night he was again given the corner seat by the fire, but he sat huddled up there, not spreading his knees to the warmth.

There was no singing at the hearth that night. The men talked low, silenced by Freyga's silence. The darkness waited at their shoulders. There was no sound but the howling of the wind outside the walls and the howling of the woman upstairs. She had been still all day, but now the hoarse, dull yell came again and again. It seemed impossible to Freyga that she could still cry out. She was thin and small, a girl, she could not carry so much pain in her. "What good are they, up there!" he broke out. His men looked at him, saying nothing. "Father Egius! There is some evil in this house."

"I can only pray, my son," the old man said, frightened.

"Then pray! At the altar!" He hurried Father Egius before him out into the black cold, across the courtyard where dry snow whirled invisible on the wind, to the chapel. After some while he returned alone. The old priest had promised to spend the night on his knees by the fire in his little cell behind the chapel. At the great hearth only the foreign priest was still awake. Freyga sat down on the hearthstone and for a long time said nothing.

The stranger looked up and winced, seeing the count's blue eyes staring straight at him.

"Why don't you sleep?"

"I'm not sleepy, count."

"It would be better if you slept."

The stranger blinked nervously, then closed his eyes and tried to look asleep. He peered now and then under half-closed lids at Freyga and tried to repeat, without moving his lips, a prayer to his patron saint.

To Freyga he looked like a fat black spider. Rays of darkness spread out from his body, enwebbing the room.

The wind was sinking, leaving silence, in which Freyga heard his wife moaning, a dry, weak sound.

The fire died down. Ropes and webs of darkness tangled thicker and thicker around the man-spider in the corner of the hearth. A tiny glitter showed under his brows. The lower part of his face moved a little. He was casting his spells deeper, deeper. The wind had fallen. There was no sound at all.

Freyga stood up. The priest looked up at the broad golden figure looming against darkness, and when Freyga said, "Come with me," he was too frightened to move. Freyga took his arm and pulled him up. "Count, count, what do you want?" he whispered, trying to free himself.

"Come with me," Freyga said, and led him over the stone floor, through darkness, to the door.

Freyga wore a sheepskin tunic; the priest only a woollen gown. "Count," he gasped, trotting beside Freyga across the court, "it's cold, a man could freeze to death, there might be wolves —"

Freyga shot the arm-thick bolts of the outer gates of the Keep and swung one portal open. "Go on," he said, gesturing with his sheathed sword.

The priest stopped short. "No," he said.

Freyga unsheathed his sword, a short, thick blade.

Jabbing its point at the rump beneath the woolen gown, he drove the priest before him out the gate, down the village street, out onto the rising road that led to the mountains. They went slowly, for the snow was deep and their feet broke through its crust at each step. The air was perfectly still now, as if frozen. Freyga looked up at the sky. Overhead between high faint clouds stood the star-shape with a swordbelt of three bright stars. Some called the figure the Warrior, others called it the Silent One, Odne the Silent.

The priest muttered one prayer after another, a steady pattering mumble, drawing breath with a whistling sound. Once he stumbled and fell face down in the snow. Freyga pulled him to his feet. He looked up at the young man's face in the starlight, but said nothing. He shambled on, praying softly and steadily.

The tower and village of Vermare were dark behind them; around them were empty hills and plains of snow, pale in the starlight. Beside the road was a hillock, less than a man's height, grave-shaped. Beside it, bared of snow by the wind, stood a short thick pillar or altar built of uncut stones. Freyga took the priest's shoulder, forcing him off the road and to the altar beside the Barrow. "Count, count –" the priest gasped when Freyga seized his head and forced it back. His eyes looked white in the starlight, his mouth was open to scream, but the scream was only a bubbling wheeze as Freyga slit his throat.

Freyga forced the corpse to bend over the altar, and cut and tore the thick gown away till he could slash the belly open. Blood and entrails gushed out over the dry stones of the altar and smoked on the dry snow. The gutted corpse fell forward over the stones like an empty coat, the arms dangling.

The living man sank down on the thin, wind-scoured snow beside the Barrow, sword still in hand. The earth rocked and heaved, and voices went crying past him in the darkness.

When he lifted his head and looked about him everything had changed. The sky, starless, rose in a high pale vault. Hills and far mountains stood distinct, unshadowed. The shapeless corpse slumped over the altar was black, the snow at the foot of the Barrow was black, Freyga's hands and sword-blade were black. He tried to wash his hands with snow, and the sting of it woke him. He got up, his head swimming, and stumbled back to Vermare on numb legs. As he went he felt the west wind, soft and damp, rising with the day around him, bringing the thaw.

Ranni was standing by the great hearth while the boy Gilbert built up the fire. Her face was puffy and grey. She spoke to Freyga with a sneer: "Well, count, high time you're back!"

He stood breathing heavily, slack-faced, and did not speak.

"Come along, then," said the midwife. He followed her up the twisting stairs. The straw that had covered the floor was swept aside into the fireplace. Galla lay again in the wide box-like bed, the marriage bed. Her closed eyes were deep-sunken. She was snoring faintly. "Shh!" the midwife said, as he started to her. "Be quiet! Look here."

She was holding up a tightly wrapped bundle.

After some while, as he still said nothing, she whispered sharply, "A boy. Fine, big."

Freyga put out one hand towards the bundle. His fingernails were caked and checked with brown.

The midwife drew the bundle closer to herself. "You're cold," she said in the sharp, contemptuous whisper. "Here." She drew back a fold to show for a moment a very tiny, purplish human face in the bundle, then rewrapped it.

Freyga went to the foot of the bed and knelt on the floor there, bending till his head was on the stones of the floor. He murmured, "Lord Christ, be praised, be thanked . . ."

The Bishop of Solariy never found out what had become of his envoy to the northwest. Probably, being a zealous man, he had ventured too far into the mountains where heathen folk still lived, and had suffered martyrdom.

Count Freyga's name lived long in the history of his province. During his lifetime the Benedictine monastery on the mountain above Lake Malafrena was established. Count Freyga's flocks and Count Freyga's sword fed and defended the monks in their first hard winters there. In the bad Latin of their chronicles, in black ink on the lasting vellum, he and his son after him are named with gratitude, staunch defenders of the Church of God.

EDWARD BRYANT
Particle Theory

Edward Bryant became a full-time writer in 1969, at the tag-end of the New Wave days, and over the last twenty years has established himself as one of the most respected writers of his generation . . . something not easy to do without publishing novels, for Bryant is a consummate short-story writer, and has devoted himself almost entirely to that form, rarely writing anything even at novella length. A number of writers in the field are far better known for their short fiction than for their novels –Tiptree, Knight, Bradbury, and so on – but Bryant is almost unique in having written *no* real solo novels at all . . . in this, he resembles his mentor, Harlan Ellison (who wrote some early mainstream novels, but has so far produced no SF novels). It says something for Bryant's mastery of the form that he has managed to secure a solid reputation *anyway*, without novels (also like Ellison). You'll see something of that mastery in the story that follows, Bryant's best, in my opinion, and perhaps one of the best stories written by anyone in the '70s, a dazzling exploration of the interface between the vast, inimical cosmos and one man's private reality.

Bryant has won two Nebula Awards for his short fiction, which has appeared in almost all of the well-known magazines and anthologies, as well as in markets outside the genre such as *Penthouse* and *National Lampoon*. Bryant is also well-known as a critic, his reviews appearing regularly in such places as *Mile-High Futures* and *Locus*. His books include the acclaimed short-story collections *Particle Theory*, *Cinnabar*, *Among the Dead*, and *Wyoming Sun*, a novelization of a television script by Harlan Ellison, *Phoenix Without Ashes*, and, as editor, the anthology *2076: The American Tricentennial*. Bryant lives in Denver, Colorado.

I see my shadow flung like black iron against the wall. My sundeck blazes with untimely summer. Eliot was wrong: Frost, right.

Nanoseconds . . .

Death is as relativistic as any other apparent constant. I wonder: *Am I dying?*

I thought it was a cliché with no underlying truth.

"Lives *do* flash in a compressed instant before dying eyes," said Amanda. She poured me another glass of Burgundy the color of her hair. The fire highlighted both. "A psychologist named Noyes –" She broke off and smiled at me. "You really want to hear this?"

"Sure." The fireplace light softened the taut planes of her face. I saw a flicker of the gentler beauty she had possessed thirty years before.

"Noyes catalogued testimonial evidence for death's-door phenomena in the early seventies. He termed it 'life review,' the second of three clearly definable steps in the process of dying; like a movie, and not necessarily linear."

I drink, I have a low threshold of intoxication, I ramble. "Why does it happen? How?" I didn't like the desperation in my voice. We were suddenly much farther apart than the geography of the table separating us; I looked in Amanda's eyes for some memory of Lisa. "Life goes shooting off – or we recede from it – like Earth and an inter-stellar probe irrevocably severed. Mutual recession at light-speed, and the dark fills in the gap." I held my glass by the stem, rotated it, peered through the distorting bowl.

Pine logs crackled. Amanda turned her head and her eyes' image shattered in the flames.

The glare, the glare –

When I was thirty I made aggrieved noises because I'd screwed around for the past ten years and not accomplished nearly as much as I should. Lisa only laughed, which sent me into a transient rage and a longer-lasting sulk before I realized hers was the only appropriate response.

"Silly, silly," she said. "A watered-down Byronic character, full of self-pity and sloppy self-adulation." She blocked my exit from the kitchen and said, millimeters from my face,

"It's not as though you're waking up at thirty to discover that only fifty-six people have heard of you."

I stuttered over a weak retort.

"Fifty-seven?" She laughed; I laughed.

Then I was forty and went through the same pseudo-menopausal trauma. Admittedly, I hadn't done any work at all for nearly a year, and any *good* work for two. Lisa didn't laugh this time; she did what she could, which was mainly to stay out of my way while I alternately moped and raged around the coast house southwest of Portland. Royalties from the book I'd done on the fusion break-through kept us in groceries and mortgage payments.

"Listen, maybe if I'd go away for a while –" she said. "Maybe it would help for you to be alone." Temporary separations weren't alien to our marriage: we'd once figured that our relationship got measurably rockier if we spent more than about sixty percent of our time together. It had been a long winter and we were overdue; but then Lisa looked intently at my face and decided not to leave. Two months later I worked through the problems in my skull, and asked her for solitude. She knew me well – well enough to laugh again because she knew I was waking out of another mental hibernation.

She got onto a jetliner on a gray winter day and headed east for my parents' old place in southern Colorado. The jetway for the flight was out of commission that afternoon, so the airline people had to roll out one of the old wheeled stairways. Just before she stepped into the cabin, Lisa paused and waved back from the head of the stairs; her dark hair curled about her face in the wind.

Two months later I'd roughed out most of the first draft for my initial book about the reproduction revolution. At least once a week I would call Lisa and she'd tell me about the photos she was taking river-running on an icy Colorado or Platte. Then I'd use her as a sounding board for speculations about ectogenesis heterogynes, or the imminent emergence of an exploited human host-mother class.

"So what'll we do when you finish the first draft, Nick?"

"Maybe we'll take a leisurely month on the Trans-Canadian Railroad."

"Spring in the provinces . . ."

Then the initial draft was completed and so was Lisa's Colorado adventure. "Do you know how badly I want to see you?" she said.

"Almost as badly as I want to see you."

"Oh, no," she said. "Let me tell you –"

What she told me no doubt violated state and federal laws and probably telephone-company tariffs as well. The frustration of only hearing her voice through the wire made me twine my legs like a contortionist.

"Nick, I'll book a flight out of Denver. I'll let you know."

I think she wanted to surprise me. Lisa didn't tell me when she booked the flight. The airline let me know.

And now I'm fifty-one. The pendulum has swung and I again bitterly resent not having achieved more. There is so much work left undone; should I live for centuries, I still could not complete it all. That, however, will not be a problem.

I am told that the goddamned level of acid phosphatase in my goddamned blood is elevated. How banal that single fact sounds, how sterile; and how self-pitying the phraseology. Can't I afford a luxurious tear, Lisa?

Lisa?

Death: I wish to determine my own time.

"Charming," I had said. "End of the world."

My friend Denton, the young radio astronomer, said, "Christ almighty! Your damned jokes. How can you make a pun about this?"

"It keeps me from crying," I said quietly. "Wailing and breast-beating won't make a difference."

"Calm, so calm." She looked at me peculiarly.

"I've seen the enemy," I said. "I've had time to consider it."

Her face was thoughtful, eyes focused somewhere beyond this cluttered office. "*If* you're right," she said, "it could be the most fantastic event a scientist could observe and record." Her eyes refocused and met mine. "Or it might be the most frightening; a final horror."

"Choose one," I said.

"If I believed you at all."

"I'm dealing in speculations."

"Fantasies," she said.

"However you want to term it." I got up and moved to the door. "I don't think there's much time. You've never seen where I live. Come" – I hesitated – "visit me if you care to. I'd like that – to have you there."

"Maybe," she said.

I should not have left the situation ambiguous.

I didn't know that in another hour, after I had left her office, pulled my car out of the Gamow Peak parking lot, and driven down to the valley, Denton would settle herself behind the wheel of her sports car and gun it onto the Peak road. Tourists saw her go off the switchback. A Highway Department crew pried her loose from the embrace of Lotus and lodgepole.

When I got the news I grieved for her, wondering if this were the price of belief. I drove to the hospital and, because no next of kin had been found and Amanda intervened, the doctors let me stand beside the bed.

I had never seen such still features, never such stasis short of actual death. I waited an hour, seconds sweeping silently from the wall clock, until the urge to return home was overpowering.

I could wait no longer because daylight was coming and I would tell no one.

Toward the beginning:

I've tolerated doctors as individuals; as a class they terrify me. It's a dread like that of shark attacks or dying by fire. But eventually I made the appointment for an examination, drove to the sparkling white clinic on the appointed day, and spent a surly half hour reading a year-old issue of *Popular Science* in the waiting room.

"Mr Richmond?" the smiling nurse finally said. I followed her back to the examination room. "Doctor will be here in just a minute." She left, I sat apprehensively on the edge of the examination table. After two minutes I heard the rustling of my file being removed from the outside rack. Then the door opened.

"How's it going?" said my doctor. "I haven't seen you in a while."

"Can't complain," I said, reverting to accustomed medical ritual. "No flu so far this winter. The shot must have been soon enough."

Amanda watched me patiently. "You're not a hypo-chondriac. You don't need continual reassurance – or sleeping pills, anymore. You're not a medical groupie, God knows. So what is it?"

"Uh," I said. I spread my hands helplessly.

"Nicholas." Get-on-with-it-I'm-busy-today sharpness edged her voice.

"Don't imitate my maiden aunt."

"All right. *Nick*," she said. "What's wrong?"

"I'm having trouble urinating."

She jotted something down. Without looking up: "What kind of trouble?"

"Straining."

"For how long?"

"Six, maybe seven months. It's been a gradual thing."

"Anything else you've noticed?"

"Increased frequency."

"That's all?"

"Well," I said, "afterwards, I, uh, dribble."

She listed, as though by rote: "Pain, burning, urgency, hesitancy, change in stream of urine? Incontinence, change of size of stream, change in appearance of urine?"

"What?"

"Darker, lighter, cloudy, blood discharge from penis, VD exposure, fever, night sweats?"

I answered with a variety of nods and monosyllables.

"Mmh." She continued to write on the pad, then snapped it shut. "Okay, Nick, would you get your clothes off?" And when I had stripped: "Please lie on the table. On your stomach."

"The greased finger?" I said. "Oh, shit."

Amanda tore a disposable glove off the roll. It crackled as she put it on. "You think I get a thrill out of this?" She's been my GP for a long time.

When it was over and I sat gingerly and uncomfortably on the edge of the examining table, I said, "Well?"

Amanda again scribbled on a sheet. "I'm sending you to a urologist. He's just a couple of blocks away. I'll phone over. Try to get an appointment in – oh, inside of a week."

"Give me something better," I said, "or I'll go to the library and check out a handbook of symptoms."

She met my eyes with a candid blue gaze. "I want a specialist to check out the obstruction."

"You found something when you stuck your finger in?"

"Crude, Nicholas." She half-smiled. "Your prostate is hard – stony. There could be a number of reasons."

"What John Wayne used to call the Big C?"

"Prostatic cancer," she said, "is relatively infrequent in a man of your age." She glanced down at my records. "Fifty."

"Fifty-one," I said, wanting to shift the tone, trying, failing. "You didn't send me a card on my birthday."

"But it's not impossible," Amanda said. She stood. "Come on up to the front desk. I want an appointment with you after the urology results come back." As always, she patted me on the shoulder as she followed me out of the examination room. But this time there was slightly too much tension in her fingers.

I was seeing grassy hummocks and marble slabs in my mind and didn't pay attention to my surroundings as I exited the waiting room.

"Nick?" A soft Oklahoma accent.

I turned back from the outer door, looked down, saw tousled hair. Jackie Denton, one of the bright young minds out at the Gamow Peak Observatory, held the well-thumbed copy of *Popular Science* loosely in her lap. She honked and snuffled into a deteriorating Kleenex. "Don't get too close. Probably doesn't matter at this point. Flu. You?" Her green irises were red-rimmed.

I fluttered my hands vaguely. "I had my shots."

"Yeah." She snuffled again. "I was going to call you later on from work. See the show last night?"

I must have looked blank.

"Some science writer," she said. "Rigel went supernova."

"Supernova," I repeated stupidly.

"Blam, you know? *Blooie*." She illustrated with her hands

and the magazine flipped onto the carpet. "Not that you missed anything. It'll be around for a few weeks – biggest show in the skies."

A sudden ugly image of red and white aircraft warning lights merging in an actinic flare sprayed my retinas. I shook my head. After a moment I said, "First one in our galaxy in – how long? Three hundred and fifty years? I wish you'd called me."

"A little longer. Kepler's star was in 1604. Sorry about not calling – we were all a little busy, you know?"

"I can imagine. When did it happen?"

She bent to retrieve the magazine. "Just about midnight. Spooky. I was just coming off shift." She smiled. "Nothing like a little cosmic cataclysm to take my mind off jammed sinuses. Just as well; no sick leave tonight. That's why I'm here at the clinic. Kris says no excuses."

Krishnamurthi was the Gamow director. "You'll be going back up to the peak soon?" She nodded. "Tell Kris I'll be in to visit. I want to pick up a lot of material."

"For sure."

The nurse walked up to us. "Ms Denton?"

"Mmph." She nodded and wiped her nose a final time. Struggling up from the soft chair, she said, "How come you didn't read about Rigel in the papers? It made every morning edition."

"I let my subscriptions lapse."

"But the TV news? The radio?"

"I didn't watch, and I don't have a radio in the car."

Before disappearing into the corridor to the examination rooms, she said, "That country house of yours must really be isolated."

The ice drips from the eaves as I drive up and park beside the garage. Unless the sky deceives me there is no new weather front moving in yet; no need to protect the car from another ten centimeters of fresh snow.

Sunset comes sooner at my house among the mountains; shadows stalk across the barren yard and suck heat from my skin. The peaks are, of course, deliberate barriers blocking off light and warmth from the coastal cities. Once I personified them as friendly giants, amiable *lummoxen* guarding us. No more. Now they are only mountains again, the Cascade Range.

For an instant I think I see a light flash on, but it is just a quick sunset reflection on a window. The house remains dark and silent. The poet from Seattle's been gone for three months. My coldness – her heat. I thought that transference would warm me. Instead she chilled. The note she left me in the vacant house was a sonnet about psychic frostbite.

My last eleven years have not been celibate, but sometimes they feel like it. Entropy ultimately overcomes all kinetic force.

Then I looked toward the twilight east and saw Rigel rising. Luna wouldn't be visible for a while, so the brightest object in the sky was the exploded star. It fixed me to this spot by my car with the intensity of an aircraft landing light. The white light that shone down on me had left the supernova five hundred years before (a detail to include in the inevitable article – a graphic illustration of interstellar distances never fails to awe readers).

Tonight, watching the hundred-billion-degree baleful eye that was Rigel convulsed, I know *I* was awed. The cataclysm glared, brighter than any planet. I wondered whether Rigel – unlikely, I knew – had had a planetary system; whether guttering mountain ranges and boiling seas had preceded worlds frying. I wondered whether, five centuries before, intelligent beings had watched stunned as the stellar fire engulfed their skies. Had they had time to rail at the injustice? There are one hundred billion stars in our galaxy; only an estimated three stars go supernova per thousand years. Good odds: Rigel lost.

Almost hypnotized, I watched until I was abruptly rocked by the wind rising in the darkness. My fingers were stiff with cold. But as I started to enter the house I looked at the sky a final time. Terrifying Rigel, yes – but my eyes were captured by another phenomenon in the north. A spark of light burned brighter than the surrounding stars. At first I thought it was a passing aircraft, but its position remained stationary. Gradually, knowing the odds and unwilling to believe, I recognized the new supernova for what it was.

In five decades I've seen many things. Yet watching the sky I felt as if I were a primitive, shivering in uncured furs. My teeth chattered from more than the cold. I wanted to hide from the universe. The door to my house was unlocked, which was lucky – I couldn't have fitted a key into the latch. Finally I stepped over the threshold. I turned on all the lights, denying the two stellar pyres burning in the sky.

My urologist turned out to be a dour black man named Sharpe who treated me, I suspected, like any of the other specimens that turned up in his laboratory. In his early thirties, he'd read several of my books. I appreciated his having absolutely no respect for his elders or for celebrities.

"You'll give me straight answers?" I said.

"Count on it."

He also gave me another of those damned urological fingers. When I was finally in a position to look back at him questioningly, he nodded slowly and said, "There's a nodule."

Then I got a series of blood tests for an enzyme called acid phosphatase. "Elevated," Sharpe said.

Finally, at the lab, I was to get the cystoscope, a shiny metal tube which would be run up my urethra. The biopsy forceps would be inserted through it. "Jesus, you're kidding." Sharpe shook his head. I said, "If the biopsy shows a malignancy . . ."

"I can't answer a silence."

"Come on," I said. "You've been straight until now. What are the chances of curing a malignancy?"

Sharpe had looked unhappy ever since I'd walked into his office. Now he looked unhappier. "Ain't my department," he said. "Depends on many factors."

"Just give me a simple figure."

"Maybe thirty percent. All bets are off if there's a metastasis." He met my eyes while he said that, then busied himself with the cystoscope. Local anesthetic or not, my penis burned like hell.

I had finally gotten through to Jackie Denton on a private line the night of the second supernova. "I thought last night was a madhouse?" she said. "You should see us now. I've only got a minute."

"I just wanted to confirm what I was looking at," I said. "I saw the damn thing actually blow."

"You're ahead of everybody at Gamow. We were busily focusing on Rigel –" Electronic *wheeps* garbled the connection. "Nick, are you still there?"

"I think somebody wants the line. Just tell me a final thing: Is it a full-fledged supernova?"

"Absolutely. As far as we can determine now, it's a genuine Type II."

"Sorry it couldn't be the biggest and best of all."

"Big enough," she said. "It's good enough. This time it's only about nine light-years away. Sirius A."

"Eight-point-seven light-years," I said automatically. "What's that going to mean?"

"Direct effects? Don't know. We're thinking about it." It sounded as if her hand cupped the mouthpiece; then she came back on the line. "Listen, I've got to go. Kris is screaming for my head. Talk to you later."

"All right," I said. The connection broke. On the dead line I thought I heard the twenty-one-centimeter basic hydrogen hiss of the universe. Then the dial tone cut in and I hung up the receiver.

Amanda did not look at all happy. She riffled twice through what I guessed were my laboratory test results. "All right," I said from the patient's side of the wide walnut desk. "Tell me."

"Mr Richmond? Nicholas Richmond?"

"Speaking."

"This is Mrs Kurnick, with Trans-West Airways. I'm calling from Denver."

"Yes?"

"We obtained this number from a charge slip. A ticket was issued to Lisa Richmond –"

"My wife. I've been expecting her sometime this weekend. Did she ask you to phone ahead?"

"Mr Richmond, that's not it. Our manifest shows your wife boarded our Flight 903, Denver to Portland, tonight."

"So? What's wrong? Is she sick?"

"I'm afraid there's been an accident."

Silence choked me. "How bad?" The freezing began.

"Our craft went down about ten miles northwest of Glenwood Springs, Colorado. The ground parties at the site say there are no survivors. I'm sorry, Mr Richmond."

"No one?" I said. "I mean –"

"I'm truly sorry," said Mrs Kurnick. "If there's any change in the situation, we will be in touch immediately."

Automatically I said, "Thank you."

I had the impression that Mrs Kurnick wanted to say something else; but after a pause, she only said, "Good night."

On a snowy Colorado mountainside I died.

"The biopsy was malignant," Amanda said.

"Well," I said. "That's pretty bad." She nodded. "Tell me about my alternatives." *Ragged bits of metal slammed into the mountainside like teeth.*

My case was unusual only in a relative sense. Amanda told me that prostatic cancer is the penalty men pay for otherwise good health. If they avoid every other health hazard, twentieth-century men eventually get zapped by their prostates. In my case, the problem was about twenty years early; my bad luck. *Cooling metal snapped and sizzled in the snow, was silent.*

Assuming that the cancer hadn't already metastasized, there were several possibilities; but Amanda had, at this stage, little hope for either radiology or chemotherapy. She suggested a radical prostatectomy.

"I wouldn't suggest it if you didn't have a hell of a lot of valuable years left," she said. "It's not usually advised for older patients. But you're in generally good condition; you could handle it."

Nothing moved on the mountainside. "What all would come out?" I said.

"You already know the ramifications of 'radical.'"

I didn't mind so much the ligation of the spermatic tubes – I should have done that a long time before. At fifty-one I could handle sterilization with equanimity, but –

"Sexually dysfunctional?" I said. "Oh, my God." I was aware of my voice starting to tighten. "I can't do that."

"You sure as hell can," said Amanda firmly. "How long have I known you?" She answered her own question. "A long time. I know you well enough to know that what counts isn't all tied up in your penis."

I shook my head silently.

"Listen, damn it, cancer death is worse."

"No," I said stubbornly. "Maybe. Is that the whole bill?"

It wasn't. Amanda reached my bladder's entry on the list. It would be excised as well.

"Tubes protruding from me?" I said. "*If* I live, I'll have to spend the rest of my life toting a plastic bag as a drain for my urine?"

Quietly she said, "You're making it too melodramatic."

"But am I right?"

After a pause, "Essentially, yes."

And all that was the essence of it; the *good* news, all assuming that the carcinoma cells wouldn't jar loose during surgery and migrate off to other organs. "No," I said. The goddamned lousy, loathsome unfairness of it all slammed home. "Goddamn it, no. It's my choice; I won't live that way. If I just die, I'll be done with it."

"Nicholas! Cut the self-pity."

"Don't you think I'm entitled to some?"

"Be reasonable."

"You're supposed to comfort me," I said. "Not argue. You've taken all those death-and-dying courses. *You* be reasonable."

The muscles tightened around her mouth. "I'm giving you suggestions," said Amanda. "You can do with them as you damned well please." It had been years since I'd seen her angry.

We glared at each other for close to a minute. "Okay," I said. "I'm sorry."

She was not mollified. "Stay upset, even if it's whining. Get angry, be furious. I've watched you in a deep-freeze for a decade."

I recoiled internally. "I've survived. That's enough."

"No way. You've been sitting around for eleven years in suspended animation, waiting for someone to chip you free of the glacier. You've let people carom past, occasionally bouncing off you with no effect. Well, now it's not some*one* that's shoving you to the wall – it's some*thing*. Are you going to lie down for it? Lisa wouldn't have wanted that."

"Leave her out," I said.

"I can't. You're even more important to me because of her. She was my closest friend, remember?"

"Pay attention to her," Lisa had once said. "She's more sensible than either of us." Lisa had known about the affair; after all, Amanda had introduced us.

"I know." I felt disoriented; denial, resentment, numbness – the roller coaster clattered toward a final plunge.

"Nick, you've got a possibility for a healthy chunk of life left. I want you to have it, and if it takes using Lisa as a wedge, I will."

"I don't want to survive if it means crawling around as a piss-dripping cyborg eunuch." The roller coaster teetered on the brink.

Amanda regarded me for a long moment, then said earnestly, "There's an outside chance, a long shot. I heard from a friend there that the New Mexico Meson Physics Facility is scouting for a subject."

I scoured my memory. "Particle-beam therapy?"

"Pions."

"It's chancy," I said.

"Are you arguing?" She smiled.

I smiled too. "No."

"Want to give it a try?"

My smile died. "I don't know. I'll think about it."

"That's encouragement enough," said Amanda. "I'll make some calls and see if the facility's as interested in you as I expect you'll be in them. Stick around home? I'll let you know."

"I haven't said yes. We'll let each other know." I didn't tell Amanda, but I left her office thinking only of death.

Melodramatic as it may sound, I went downtown to visit the hardware stores and look at their displays of pistols. After two hours, I tired of handling weapons. The steel seemed uniformly cold and distant.

When I returned home late that afternoon, there was a single message on my phone-answering machine:

"Nick, this is Jackie Denton. Sorry I haven't called for a while, but you know how it's been. I thought you'd like to know that Kris is going to have a press conference early in the week – probably Monday afternoon. I think he's worried because he hasn't come up with a good theory to cover the three Type II supernovas and the half dozen standard novas that have occurred in the last few weeks. But then nobody I know has. We're all spending so much time awake nights, we're turning into vampires. I'll get back to you when I know the exact time of the conference. I think it must be about thirty seconds now, so I –" The tape ended.

I mused with winter bonfires in my mind as the machine rewound and reset. Three Type II supernovas? One is merely nature, I paraphrased. Two mean only coincidence. Three make a conspiracy.

Impulsively I dialed Denton's home number; there was no answer. Then the lines to Gamow Peak were all busy. It seemed logical to me that I needed Jackie Denton for more than being my sounding board, or for merely news about the press conference. I needed an extension of her friendship. I thought I'd like to borrow the magnum pistol I knew she kept in a locked desk drawer at her observatory office. I knew I could ask her a favor. She ordinarily used the pistol to blast targets on the peak's rocky flanks after work.

The irritating regularity of the busy signal brought me back to sanity. Just a second, I told myself. Richmond, what the hell are you proposing?

Nothing, was the answer. Not yet. Not . . . quite.

Later in the night, I opened the sliding glass door and disturbed the skiff of snow on the second-story deck. I shamelessly allowed myself the luxury of leaving the door partially open so that warm air would spill out around me while I watched the sky. The stars were intermittently visible between the towering banks of stratocumulus scudding over the Cascades. Even so, the three supernovas dominated the night. I drew imaginary lines with my eyes;

connect the dots and solve the puzzle. How many enigmas can you find in this picture?

I reluctantly took my eyes away from the headline phenomena and searched for old standbys. I picked out the red dot of Mars.

Several years ago I'd had a cockamamie scheme that sent me to a Mesmerist – that's how she'd billed herself – down in Eugene. I'd been driving up the coast after covering an aerospace medical conference in Oakland. Somewhere around Crescent City, I capped a sea-bass dinner by getting blasted on prescribed pills and proscribed Scotch. Sometime during the evening, I remembered the computer-enhancement process JPL had used to sharpen the clarity of telemetered photos from such projects as the Mariner flybys and the Viking Mars lander. It seemed logical to me at the time that memories from the human computer could somehow be enhanced, brought into clarity through hypnosis. Truly stoned fantasies. But they somehow sufficed as rationale and incentive to wind up at Madame Guzmann's "Advice/Mesmerism/Health" establishment across the border in Oregon. Madame Guzmann had skin the color of her stained hardwood door; she made a point of looking and dressing the part of a stereotype we *gajos* would think of as Gypsy. The scarf and crystal ball strained the image. I think she was Vietnamese. At any rate she convinced me she could hypnotize, and then she nudged me back through time.

Just before she ducked into the cabin, Lisa paused and waved back from the head of the stairs; her dark hair curled about her face in the wind.

I should have taken to heart the lesson of stasis; entropy is not so easily overcome.

What Madam Guzmann achieved was to freeze-frame that last image of Lisa. Then she zoomed me in so close it was like standing beside Lisa. I sometimes still see it in my nightmares: Her eyes focus distantly. Her skin has the graininess of a newspaper photo. I look but cannot touch. I can speak but she will not answer. I shiver with cold –

– and slid the glass door farther open.

There! An eye opened in space. A glare burned as cold as a

refrigerator light in a night kitchen. Mars seemed to disappear, swallowed in the glow from the nova distantly behind it. Another one, I thought. The new eye held me fascinated, pinned as securely as a child might fasten a new moth in the collection.

Nick?

Who is it?

Nick . . .

You're an auditory hallucination.

There on the deck the sound of laughter spiraled around me. I thought it would shake loose the snow from the trees. The mountain stillness vibrated.

The secret, Nick.

What secret?

You're old enough at fifty-one to decipher it.

Don't play with me.

Who's playing? Whatever time is left –

Yes?

You've spent eleven years now dreaming, drifting, letting others act on you.

I know.

Do you? Then act on that. Choose your actions. No lover can tell you more. Whatever time is left –

Shivering uncontrollably, I gripped the rail of the deck. A fleeting pointillist portrait in black and white dissolved into the trees. From branch to branch, top bough to bottom, crusted snow broke and fell, gathering momentum. The trees shed their mantle. Powder swirled up to the deck and touched my face with stinging diamonds.

Eleven years was more than half what Rip Van Winkle slept. "Damn it," I said. "Damn you." We prize our sleep. The grave rested peacefully among the trees. "Damn you," I said again, looking up at the sky.

On a snowy Oregon mountainside I was no longer dead.

And yes, Amanda. Yes.

After changing planes at Albuquerque, we flew into Los Alamos on a small feeder line called Ross Airlines. I'd never flown before on so ancient a DeHavilland Twin Otter, and I hoped never to again; I'd take a Greyhound out of Los

Alamos first. The flight attendant and half the other sixteen passengers were throwing up in the turbulence as we approached the mountains. I hadn't expcted the mountains. I'd assumed Los Alamos would lie in the same sort of southwestern scrub desert surrounding Albuquerque. Instead I found a small city nestled a couple of kilometers up a wooded mountainside.

The pilot's unruffled voice came on the cabin intercom to announce our imminent landing, the airport temperature, and the fact that Los Alamos has more Ph.Ds per capita than any other American city. "Second only to Akademgorodok," I said, turning away from the window toward Amanda. The skin wrinkled around her closed eyes. She hadn't had to use her airsick bag. I had a feeling that despite old friendships, a colleague and husband who was willing to oversee the clinic, the urgency of helping a patient, and the desire to observe an exotic experiment, Amanda might be regretting accompanying me to what she'd termed "the meson factory."

The Twin Otter made a landing approach like a strafing run and then we were down. As we taxied across the apron I had a sudden sensation of déjà vu: the time a year ago when a friend had flown me north in a Cessna. The airport in Los Alamos looked much like the civil air terminal at Sea-Tac where I'd met the Seattle poet. It happened that we were both in line at the snack counter. I'd commented on her elaborate Haida-styled medallion. We took the same table and talked; it turned out she'd heard of me.

"I really admire your stuff," she said.

So much for my ideal poet using only precise images. Wry thought. She was – is – a first-rate poet. I rarely think of her as anything but "the poet from Seattle." Is that kind of depersonalization a symptom?

Amanda opened her eyes, smiled wanly, said, "I could use a doctor." The flight attendant cracked the door and thin New Mexican mountain air revived us both.

Most of the New Mexico Meson Physics Facility was buried beneath a mountain ridge. Being guest journalist as well as experimental subject, I think we were given a more exhaustive tour than would be offered most patients and their doctors. Everything I saw made me think of expensive sets for vintage science-fiction movies: the interior of the main accelerator ring, glowing eggshell white and curving away like the space-station corridors in *2001*; the linac and booster areas; the straightaway tunnel to the meson medical channel; the five-meter bubble chamber looking like some sort of time machine.

I'd visited both FermiLab in Illinois and CERN in Geneva, so I had a general idea of what the facilities were all about. Still I had a difficult time trying to explain to Amanda the *Alice in Wonderland* mazes that constituted high energy physics. But then so did Delaney, the young woman who was the liaison biophysicist for my treatment. It became difficult sorting out the mesons, pions, hadrons, leptons, baryons, J's, fermions and quarks, and such quantum qualities as strangeness, color, baryonness and charm. Especially charm, that ephemeral quality accounting for why certain types of radioactive decay should happen, but don't. I finally bogged down in the midst of quarks, antiquarks, charmed quarks, neoquarks, and quarklets.

Some wag had set a sign on the visitors' reception desk in the administration center reading: Charmed to meet you. "It's a joke, right?" said Amanda tentatively.

"It probably won't get any funnier," I said.

Delaney, who seemed to load every word with deadly earnestness, didn't laugh at all. "Some of the technicians think it's funny. I don't."

We rehashed the coming treatment endlessly. Optimistically I took notes for the book: *The primary problem with a radiological approach to the treatment of cancer is that hard radiation not only kills the cancerous cells, it also irradiates the surrounding healthy tissue. But in the mid-nineteen-seventies, cancer researchers found a more promising tool: shaped beams of subatomic particles which can be selectively focused on the tissue of tumors.*

Delaney had perhaps two decades on Amanda; being younger seemed to give her a perverse satisfaction in playing the pedagogue. "Split atomic nuclei on a small scale –"

"Small?" said Amanda innocently.

"– smaller than a fission bomb. Much of the binding force of the nucleus is miraculously transmuted to matter."

"Miraculously?" said Amanda. I looked up at her from the easy cushion shot I was trying to line up on the green velvet. The three of us were playing rotation in the billiards annex of the NMMPF recreation lounge.

"Uh," said Delaney, the rhythm of her lecture broken. "Physics shorthand."

"Reality shorthand," I said, not looking up from the cue now. "Miracles are as exact a quality as charm."

Amanda chuckled. "That's all I wanted to know."

The miracle pertinent to my case was atomic glue, mesons, one of the fission-formed particles. More specifically, my miracle was the negatively charged pion, a subclass of meson. Electromagnetic fields could focus pions into a controllable beam and fire it into a particular target – me.

"There are no miracles in physics," said Delaney seriously. "I used the wrong term."

I missed my shot. A gentle stroke, and gently the cue ball rolled into the corner pocket, missing the eleven. I'd set things up nicely, if accidentally, for Amanda.

She assayed the table and smiled. "Don't come unglued."

"That's very good," I said. Atomic glue does become unstuck, thanks to pions' unique quality. When they collide and are captured by the nucleus of another atom, they reconvert to pure energy; a tiny nuclear explosion.

Amanda missed her shot too. The corners of Delaney's mouth curled in a small gesture of satisfaction. She leaned across the table, hands utterly steady. "Multiply pions, multiply target nuclei, and you have a controlled aggregate explosion releasing considerably more energy than the entering pion beam. *Hah!*"

She sank the eleven and twelve; then ran the table. Amanda and I exchanged glances. "Rack 'em up," said Delaney.

"Your turn," Amanda said to me.

In my case the NMMPF medical channel would fire a directed pion beam into my recalcitrant prostate. If all went as planned, the pions intercepting the atomic nuclei of my cancer cells would convert back into energy in a series of atomic flares. The cancer cells being more sensitive, tissue damage should be restricted, localized in my cancerous nodule.

Thinking of myself as a nuclear battlefield in miniature was wondrous. Thinking of myself as a new Stagg Field or an Oak Ridge was ridiculous.

Delaney turned out to be a pool shark *par excellence*. Winning was all-important and she won every time. I decided to interpret that as a positive omen.

"It's time," Amanda said.

"You needn't sound as though you're leading a condemned man to the electric chair." I tied the white medical smock securely about me, pulled on the slippers.

"I'm sorry. Are you worried?"

"Not so long as Delaney counts me as part of the effort toward a Nobel Prize."

"She's good." Her voice rang too hollow in the sterile tiled room. We walked together into the corridor.

"Me, I'm bucking for a Kalinga Prize," I said.

Amanda shook her head. Cloudy hair played about her face. "I'll just settle for a positive prognosis for my patient." Beyond the door, Delaney and two technicians with a gurney waited for me.

There is a state beyond indignity that defines being draped naked on my belly over a bench arrangement, with my rear spread and facing the medical channel. Rigidly clamped, a ceramic target tube opened a separate channel through my anus to the prostate. Monitoring equipment and shielding shut me in. I felt hot and vastly uncomfortable. Amanda had shot me full of chemicals, not all of whose names I'd recognized. Now dazed, I couldn't decide which of many discomforts was the most irritating.

"Good luck," Amanda had said. "It'll be over before you know it." I'd felt a gentle pat on my flank.

I thought I heard the phasing-up whine of electrical equipment. I could tell my mind was closing down for the duration; I couldn't even remember how many billion electron volts were about to route a pion beam up my backside. I heard sounds I couldn't identify; perhaps an enormous metal door grinding shut.

My brain swam free in a chemical river; I waited for something to happen.

I thought I heard machined ball bearings rattling down a chute; no, particles screaming past the giant bending magnets into the medical channel at three hundred thousand kilometers per second; flashing toward me through the series of adjustable filters; slowing, slowing, losing energy as they approach; then through the final tube and into my body.

Inside . . .

The pion sails the inner atomic seas for a relativistically finite time. Then the perspective inhabited by one is inhabited by two. The pion drives toward the target nucleus. At a certain point the pion is no longer a pion; what was temporarily matter transmutes back to energy. The energy flares, expands, expends, and fades. Other explosions detonate in the spaces within the patterns underlying larger patterns.

Darkness and light interchange.

The light coalesces into a ball; massive, hot, burning against the darkness. Pierced, somehow stricken, the ball begins to collapse in upon itself. Its internal temperature climbs to a critical level. At six hundred million degrees, carbon nuclei fuse. Heavier elements form. When the fuel is exhausted, the ball collapses further; again the temperature is driven upward; again heavier elements form and are in turn consumed. The cycle repeats until the nuclear furnace manufactures iron. No further nuclear reaction can be triggered; the heart's fire is extinguished. Without the outward balance of fusion reaction, the ball initiates the ultimate collapse. Heat reaches one hundred billion degrees. Every conceivable nuclear reaction is consummated.

The ball explodes in a final convulsive cataclysm. Its energy flares, fades, is eaten by entropy. The time it took is no more than the time it takes Sol-light to reach and illuminate the Earth.

"How do you feel?" Amanda leaned into my field of vision, eclipsing the fluorescent rings overhead.

"Feel?" I seemed to be talking through a mouthful of cotton candy.

"Feel."

"Compared to what?" I said.

She smiled. "You're doing fine."

"I had one foot on the accelerator," I said.

She looked puzzled, then started to laugh. "It'll wear off

soon." She completed her transit and the lights shone back in my face.

"No hand on the brake," I mumbled. I began to giggle. Something pricked my arm.

I think Delaney wanted to keep me under observation in New Mexico until the anticipated ceremonies in Stockholm; I didn't have time for that. I suspected none of us did. Amanda began to worry about my moody silences; she ascribed them at first to my medication and then to the two weeks' tests Delaney and her colleagues were inflicting on me.

"To hell with this," I said. "We've got to get out of here." Amanda and I were alone in my room.

"What?"

"Give me a prognosis."

She smiled. "I think you may as well shoot for the Kalinga."

"Maybe." I quickly added, "I'm not a patient anymore; I'm an experimental subject."

"So what do we do about it?"

We exited NMMPF under cover of darkness and struggled a half-kilometer through brush to the highway. There we hitched a ride into town.

"This is crazy," said Amanda, picking thistle out of her sweater.

"It avoids a strong argument," I said as we neared the lights of Los Alamos.

The last bus of the day had left. I wanted to wait until morning. Over my protests, we flew out on Ross Airlines. "Doctor's orders," said Amanda, teeth tightly together, as the Twin Otter bumped onto the runway.

I dream of pions. I dream of colored balloons filled with hydrogen, igniting and flaming up in the night. I dream of Lisa's newsprint face. Her smile is both proud and sorrowful.

Amanda had her backlog of patients and enough to worry about, so I took my nightmares to Jackie Denton at the observatory. I told her of my hallucinations in the accelerator chamber. We stared at each other across the small office.

"I'm glad you're better, Nick, but –"

"That's not it," I said. "Remember how you hated my article about poetry glorifying the new technology? Too fanciful?" I launched into speculation, mixing with abandon pion beams, doctors, supernovas, irrational statistics, cancerous nodes, fire balloons and gods.

"Gods?" she said. "*Gods?* Are you going to put that in your next column?"

I nodded.

She looked as though she were inspecting a newly found-out psychopath. "No one needs that in the press now, Nick. The whole planet's upset already. The possibility of nova radiation damaging the ozone layer, the potential for genetic damage, all that's got people spooked."

"It's only speculation."

She said, "You don't yell 'Fire!' in a crowded theater."

"Or in a crowded world?"

Her voice was unamused. "Not now."

"And if I'm right?" I felt weary. "What about it?"

"A supernova? No way. Sol simply doesn't have the mass."

"But a nova?" I said.

"Possibly," she said tightly. "But it shouldn't happen for a few billion years. Stellar evolution –"

"– is theory," I said. "*Shouldn't* isn't *won't*. Tonight look again at that awesome sky."

Denton said nothing.

"Could you accept a solar flare? A big one?"

I read the revulsion in her face and knew I should stop talking; but I didn't. "Do you believe in God? Any god?" She shook her head. I had to get it all out. "How about concentric universes, one within the next like Chinese carved ivory spheres?" Her face went white. "Pick a card," I said, "any card. A wild card."

"God damn you, shut up." On the edge of her desk, her knuckles were as white as her lips.

"Charming," I said, ignoring the incantatory power of

words, forgetting what belief could cost. I do not think she deliberately drove her Lotus off the Peak road. I don't want to believe that. Surely she was coming to join me.

Maybe, she'd said.

Nightmares should be kept home. So here I stand on my sundeck at high noon for the Earth. No need to worry about destruction of the ozone layer and the consequent skin cancer. There will be no problem with mutational effects and genetic damage. I need not worry about deadlines or contractual commitments. I regret that no one will ever read my book about pion therapy.

All that – maybe.

The sun shines bright – The tune plays dirgelike in my head.

Perhaps I am wrong. The flare may subside. Maybe I am not dying. No matter.

I wish Amanda were with me now, or that I were at Jackie Denton's bedside, or even that I had time to walk to Lisa's grave among the pines. Now there is no time.

At least I've lived as long as I have now by choice.

That's the secret, Nick . . .

The glare illuminates the universe.

HOWARD WALDROP
The Ugly Chickens

Howard Waldrop has been called "the resident Weird Mind of his generation," and he has one of the most individual and quirky voices (and visions) in letters today. Nobody but Howard could possibly have written one of Howard's stories; in most cases, nobody but Howard could possibly have even *thought* of them. Nor is any one Waldrop story ever much like any previous Waldrop story, and in that respect (as well as in the *panache* and pungency of the writing, the sweep of imagination, and the depth of offbeat erudition), he resembles those other two great uniques, R. A. Lafferty and Avram Davidson. And, like them, in a climate where the familiar is desirable and originality is viewed with suspicion, if not with outright fear, he remains seriously underappreciated, while writers inferior in mind and skill and heart march on to garner the big bucks, and the audiences of millions.

Waldrop's first story was sold to John W. Campbell in 1970, and appeared in *Analog* in 1972, but, like Kate Wilhelm before him, Waldrop made an unlikely *Analog* writer, and soon was seen no more in its pages. He began cropping up here and there instead, *Universe, Galaxy*, during the first few years of the '70s, and even published a novel (*The Texas-Israeli War*, co-authored with Jake Saunders – interesting, but uneven), but to no great effect. His remained one of those names that were vaguely in the air during the early part of the decade, new writers whom you would hear of now and then, but who had yet to really make a mark. That would change in 1976, the year when the first of the really good Waldrop stories started coming out, "Mary Margaret Road-Grader" and (in collaboration with Steven Utley) "Custer's Last Jump," work a quantum jump better than anything that he'd done before. From then on, he'd produce some of the best short work of the '70s and '80s, stories like "God's Hooks," "Flying Saucer Rock & Roll," "Ike at the Mike," "Save a Place in the Lifeboat for Me," "Man Mountain

Gentian," "Fair Game," "The Lions Are Asleep This Night," "Heirs of the Perisphere," "He-We-Await," "Do Ya, Do Ya Wanna Dance?," "Night of the Cooters."

And the story that follows, "The Ugly Chickens," one of only two SF stories about dodos that I can call to mind (I leave the identity of the other story as an exercise for the reader), and perhaps one of the single best stories of the '80s.

"The Ugly Chickens" won both the Nebula Award and the World Fantasy Award in 1981. Waldrop's short work has been gathered in two collections: *Howard Who?* and *All About Strange Monsters of the Recent Past: Neat Stories by Howard Waldrop* (published in Britain in a combined edition as *Strange Things in Close Up: The Nearly Complete Howard Waldrop*), and another collection, *Night of the Cooters*, is coming up. Although Waldrop has had more effect with his short fiction than at novel length, he published a well-received solo novel, *Them Bones*, in 1984, as part of the resurrected Ace Specials line, and is reported to be at work on another solo novel, tentatively entitled *I, John Mandeville*. He lives in Austin, Texas.

My car was broken, and I had a class to teach at eleven. So I took the city bus, something I rarely do.

I spent last summer crawling through the Big Thicket with cameras and tape recorder, photographing and taping two of the last ivory-billed woodpeckers on the earth. You can see the films at your local Audubon Society showroom.

This year I wanted something just as flashy but a little less taxing. Perhaps a population study on the Bermuda cahow, or the New Zealand *takahe*. A month or so in the warm (not hot) sun would do me a world of good. To say nothing of the advance of science.

I was idly leafing through Greenway's *Extinct and Vanishing Birds of the World*. The city bus was winding its way through the ritzy neighborhoods of Austin, stopping to let off the chicanas, black women and Vietnamese who tended the kitchens and gardens of the rich.

"I haven't seen any of those ugly chickens in a long time," said a voice close by.

A gray-haired lady was leaning across the aisle toward me.

I looked at her, then around. Maybe she was a shopping-bag lady. Maybe she was just talking. I looked straight at her. No doubt about it, she was talking to me. She was waiting for an answer.

"I used to live near some folks who raised them when I was a girl," she said. She pointed.

I looked down at the page my book was open to.

What I should have said was: "That is quite impossible, madam. This is a drawing of an extinct bird of the island of Mauritius. It is perhaps the most famous dead bird in the world. Maybe you are mistaking this drawing for that of some rare Asiatic turkey, peafowl or pheasant. I am sorry, but you *are* mistaken."

I should have said all that.

What she said was, "Oops, this is my stop," and got up to go.

My name is Paul Lindberl. I am twenty-six years old, a graduate student in ornithology at the University of Texas, a teaching assistant. My name is not unknown in the field. I have several vices and follies, but I don't think foolishness is one of them.

The stupid thing for me to do would have been to follow her.

She stepped off the bus.

I followed her.

I came into the departmental office, trailing scattered papers in the whirlwind behind me. "Martha! Martha!" I yelled.

She was doing something in the supply cabinet.

"Jesus, Paul! What do you want?"

"Where's Courtney?"

"At the conference in Houston. You know that. You missed your class. What's the matter?"

"Petty cash. Let me at it!"

"Payday was only a week ago. If you can't . . . ."

"It's business! It's fame and adventure and the chance of a lifetime! It's a long sea voyage that leaves . . . a plane ticket. To either Jackson, Mississippi or Memphis. Make it Jackson, it's closer. I'll get receipts! I'll be famous. Courtney will be famous. *You'll* even be famous! This university will make even *more* money! I'll pay you back. Give me some paper. I gotta write Courtney a note. When's the next plane out? Could you get Marie and Chuck to take over my classes Tuesday and Wednesday? I'll try to be back Thursday unless something happens. Courtney'll be back tomorrow, right? I'll call him from, well, wherever. Do you have some coffee? . . ."

And so on and so forth. Martha looked at me like I was crazy. But she filled out the requisition anyway.

"What do I tell Kemejian when I ask him to sign these?"

"Martha, babe, sweetheart. Tell him I'll get his picture in *Scientific American*."

"He doesn't read it."

"*Nature*, then!"

"I'll see what I can do," she said.

The lady I had followed off the bus was named Jolyn (Smith) Jimson. The story she told me was so weird that it had to be true. She knew things only an expert, or someone with firsthand experience, could know. I got names from her, and addresses, and directions, and tidbits of information. Plus a year: 1927.

And a place. Northern Mississippi.

I gave her my copy of the Greenway book. I told her I'd call her as soon as I got back into town. I left her standing on the corner near the house of the lady she cleaned up for twice a week. Jolyn Jimson was in her sixties.

Think of the dodo as a baby harp seal with feathers. I know that's not even close, but it saves time.

In 1507, the Portuguese, on their way to India, found the (then un-named) Mascarene Islands in the Indian Ocean – three of them a few hundred miles apart, all east and north of Madagascar.

It wasn't until 1598, when that old Dutch sea captain Cornelius van Neck bumped into them, that the islands received their names – names which changed several times through the centuries as the Dutch, French and English changed them every war or so. They are now known as Rodriguez, Réunion and Mauritius.

The major feature of these islands were large flightless, stupid, ugly, bad-tasting birds. Van Neck and his men named them *dod-aarsen*, stupid ass, or dodars, silly birds, or solitaires.

There were three species – the dodo of Mauritius, the real gray-brown, hooked-beak clumsy thing that weighed twenty kilos or more; the white, somewhat slimmer, dodo of Réunion; and the solitaires of Rodriguez and Réunion, which looked like very fat, very dumb light-colored geese.

The dodos all had thick legs, big squat bodies twice as large as a turkey's, naked faces, and big long downcurved beaks ending in a hook like a hollow linoleum knife. They were flightless. Long ago they had lost the ability to fly, and their wings had degenerated to flaps the size of a human hand with only three or four feathers in them. Their tails were curly and fluffy, like a child's afterthought at decoration. They had absolutely no natural enemies. They nested on the open ground. They probably hatched their eggs wherever they happened to lay them.

No natural enemies until van Neck and his kind showed up. The Dutch, French and Portuguese sailors who stopped at the Mascarenes to replenish stores found that besides looking stupid, dodos *were* stupid. They walked right up to them and hit them on the head with clubs. Better yet, dodos could be herded around like sheep. Ship's logs are full of things like: "Party of ten men ashore. Drove half-a-hundred of the big turkey-like birds into the boat. Brought to ship where they are given the run of the decks. Three will feed a crew of one hundred and fifty."

Even so, most of the dodo, except for the breast, tasted bad. One of the Dutch words for them was *walghvogel*, disgusting bird. But on a ship three months out on a return from Goa to Lisbon, well, food was where you found it. It was said, even so, that prolonged boiling did not improve the flavor.

Even so, the dodos might have lasted, except that the Dutch, and later the French, colonized the Mascarenes. The islands became plantations and dumping-places for religious refugees. Sugar cane and other exotic crops were raised there.

With the colonists came cats, dogs, hogs and the cunning *Rattus norwegicus* and the Rhesus monkey from Ceylon. What dodos the hungry sailors left were chased down (they were dumb and stupid, but they could run when they felt like it) by dogs in the open. They were killed by cats as they sat on their nests. Their eggs were stolen and eaten by monkeys, rats and hogs. And they competed with the pigs for all the low-growing goodies of the islands.

The last Mauritius dodo was seen in 1681, less than a hundred years after man first saw them. The last white dodo walked off the history books around 1720. The solitaires of Rodriguez and Réunion, last of the genus as well as the species, may have lasted until 1790. Nobody knows.

Scientists suddenly looked around and found no more of the Didine birds alive, anywhere.

This part of the country was degenerate before the first Snopes ever saw it. This road hadn't been paved until the late fifties, and it was a main road between two county seats. That didn't mean it went through civilized country. I'd traveled for miles and seen nothing but dirt banks red as Billy Carter's neck and an occasional church. I expected to see Burma Shave signs, but realized this road had probably never had them.

I almost missed the turn-off onto the dirt and gravel road the man back at the service station had marked. It led onto the highway from nowhere, a lane out of a field. I turned down it and a rock the size of a golf ball flew up over the hood and put a crack ten centimeters long in the windshield of the rent-a-car I'd gotten in Grenada.

It was a hot muggy day for this early. The view was obscured in a cloud of dust every time the gravel thinned. About a mile down the road, the gravel gave out completely. The roadway turned into a rutted dirt pathway, just wider than the car, hemmed in on both sides by a sagging three-strand barbed wire fence.

In some places the fenceposts were missing for a few meters. The wire lay on the ground and in some places disappeared under it for long stretches.

The only life I saw was a mockingbird raising hell with

something under a thorn bush the barbed wire had been nailed to in place of a post. To one side now was a grassy field which had gone wild, the way everywhere will look after we blow ourselves off the face of the planet. The other was fast becoming woods – pine, oak, some black gum and wild plum, fruit not out this time of the year.

I began to ask myself what I was doing here. What if Ms Jimson were some imaginative old crank who – but no. Wrong, maybe, but even the wrong was worth checking. But I knew she hadn't lied to me. She had seemed incapable of lies – a good ol' girl, backbone of the South, of the earth. Not a mendacious gland in her being.

I couldn't doubt her, or my judgement, either. Here I was, creeping and bouncing down a dirt path in Mississippi, after no sleep for a day, out on the thin ragged edge of a dream. I *had* to take it on faith.

The back of the car sometimes slid where the dirt had loosened and gave way to sand. The back tire stuck once, but I rocked out of it. Getting back out again would be another matter. Didn't anyone ever use this road?

The woods closed in on both sides like the forest primaeval, and the fence had long since disappeared. My odometer said ten kilometers and it had been twenty minutes since I'd turned off the highway. In the rearview mirror, I saw beads of sweat and dirt in the wrinkles of my neck. A fine patina of dust covered everything inside the car. Clots of it came through the windows.

The woods reached out and swallowed the road. Branches scraped against the windows and the top. It was like falling down a long dark leafy tunnel. It was dark and green in there. I fought back an atavistic urge to turn on the headlights. The roadbed must be made of a few centuries of leaf mulch. I kept constant pressure on the accelerator and bulled my way through.

Half a log caught and banged and clanged against the car bottom. I saw light ahead. Fearing for the oil pan, I punched the pedal and sped out.

I almost ran through a house.

It was maybe ten meters from the trees. The road ended

under one of the windows. I saw somebody waving from the corner of my eye.

I slammed on the brakes.

A whole family was on the porch, looking like a Walker Evan Depression photograph, or a fever dream from the mind of a "Hee Haw" producer. The house was old. Strips of peeling paint a meter long tapped against the eaves.

"Damned good thing you stopped," said a voice. I looked up. The biggest man I had ever seen in my life leaned down into the driver-side window.

"If we'd have heard you sooner, I'd've sent one of the kids down to the end of the driveway to warn you," he said.

Driveway?

His mouth was stained brown at the corners. I figured he chewed tobacco until I saw the sweet-gum snuff brush sticking from the pencil pocket in the bib of his overalls. His hands were the size of catcher's mitts. They looked like they'd never held anything smaller than an axe handle.

"How y'all?" he said, by way of introduction.

"Just fine," I said. I got out of the car.

"My name's Lindberl," I said, extending my hand. He took it. For an instant, I thought of bear traps, shark's mouths, closing elevator doors. The thought went back to wherever it is they stay.

"This the Gudger place?" I asked.

He looked at me blankly with his grey eyes. He wore a diesel truck cap, and had on a checked lumberjack shirt beneath the coveralls. His rubber boots were the size of the ones Karloff wore in *Frankenstein*.

"Naw. I'm Jim Bob Krait. That's my wife Jenny, and there's Luke and Skeeno and Shirl." He pointed to the porch.

The people on the porch nodded.

"Lessee? Gudger? No Gudgers round here I know of. I'm sorta new here." I took that to mean he hadn't lived here for more than twenty years or so.

"Jennifer!' he yelled. "You know of anybody named Gudger?" To me he said, "My wife's lived around here all her life."

His wife came down onto the second step of the porch

landing. "I think they used to be the ones what lived on the Spradlin place before the Spradlins. But the Spradlins left around the Korean War. I didn't know any of the Gudgers myself. That's while we was living over to Water Valley."

"You an insurance man?" asked Mr Krait.

"Uh . . . no," I said. I imagined the people on the porch leaning toward me, all ears. "I'm a . . . I teach college."

"Oxford?" asked Krait.

"Uh, no. University of Texas."

"Well, that's a damn long way off. You say you're looking for the Gudgers?"

"Just their house. The area. As your wife said, I understand they left. During the Depression, I believe."

"Well, they musta had money," said the gigantic Mr Krait. "Nobody around here was rich enough to *leave* during the Depression.

"Luke!" he yelled. The oldest boy on the porch sauntered down. He looked anemic and wore a shirt in vogue with the Twist. He stood with his hands in his pockets.

"Luke, show Mr Lindbergh –"

"Lindberl."

"Mr Lindberl here the way up to the old Spradlin place. Take him as far as the old log bridge, he might get lost before then."

"Log bridge broke down, Daddy."

"When?"

"October, Daddy."

"Well, hell, somethin' else to fix! Anyway, to the creek."

He turned to me. "You want him to go along on up there, see you don't get snakebit?"

"No, I'm sure I'll be fine."

"Mind if I ask what you're going up there for?" he asked. He was looking away from me. I could see having to come right out and ask was bothering him. Such things usually came up in the course of conversation.

"I'm a – uh, bird scientist. I study birds. We had a sighting – someone told us the old Gudger place – the area around here – I'm looking for a rare bird. It's hard to explain."

I noticed I was sweating. It was hot.

"You mean like a goodgod? I saw a goodgod about twenty-five years ago, over next to Bruce," he said.

"Well, no." (A goodgod was one of the names for an ivory-billed woodpecker, one of the rarest in the world. Any other time I would have dropped my jaw. Because they were thought to have died out in Mississippi by the teens, and by the fact that Krait knew they *were* rare.)

I went to lock my car up, then thought of the protocol of the situation. "My car be in your way?" I asked.

"Naw. It'll be just fine," said Jim Bob Krait. "We'll look for you back by sundown, that be all right?"

For a minute, I didn't know whether that was a command or an expression of concern.

"Just in case I get snakebit," I said. "I'll try to be careful up there."

"Good luck on findin' them rare birds," he said. He walked up to the porch with his family.

"Les go," said Luke.

Behind the Krait house was a henhouse and pigsty where hogs lay after their morning slop like islands in a muddy bay, or some Zen pork sculpture. Next we passed broken farm machinery gone to rust, though there was nothing but uncultivated land as far as the eye could see. How the family made a living I don't know. I'm told you can find places just like this throughout the South.

We walked through woods and across fields, following a sort of path. I tried to memorize the turns I would have to take on my way back. Luke didn't say a word the whole twenty minutes he accompanied me, except to curse once when he stepped into a bull nettle with his tennis shoes.

We came to a creek which skirted the edge of a woodsy hill. There was a rotted log forming a small dam. Above it the water was nearly a meter deep, below it, half that much.

"See that path?" he asked.

"Yes."

"Follow it up around the hill, then across the next field. Then you cross the creek again on the rocks, and over the hill. Take the left-hand path. What's left of the house is about three quarters the way up the next hill. If you come to a big bare rock cliff, you've gone too far. You got that?"

I nodded.

He turned and left.

The house had once been a dog-run cabin, like Ms Jimson had said. Now it was fallen in on one side, what they call sigoglin (or was it antisigoglin?). I once heard a hymn on the radio called "The Land Where No Cabins Fall." This was the country songs like that were written in.

Weeds grew everywhere. There were signs of fences, a flattened pile of wood that had once been a barn. Further behind the house were the outhouse remains. Half a rusted pump stood in the backyard. A flatter spot showed where the vegetable garden had been; in it a single wild tomato, pecked by birds, lay rotting. I passed it. There was lumber from three outbuildings, mostly rotten and green with algae and moss. One had been a smokehouse and woodshed combination. Two had been chicken roosts. One was larger than the other. It was there I started to poke around and dig.

Where? Where? I wish I'd been on more archaeological digs, knew the places to look. Refuse piles, midden heaps, kitchen scrap piles, compost boxes. Why hadn't I been born on a farm so I'd know instinctively where to search.

I prodded around the grounds. I moved back and forth like a setter casting for the scent of quail. I wanted more, more. I still wasn't satisfied.

Dusk. Dark, in fact. I trudged into the Kraits' front yard. The toe sack I carried was full to bulging. I was hot, tired, streaked with fifty years of chicken shit. The Kraits were on their porch. Jim Bob lumbered down like a friendly mountain.

I asked him a few questions, gave them a Xerox of one of the dodo pictures, left them addresses and phone numbers where they could reach me.

Then into the rent-a-car. Off to Water Valley, acting on information Jennifer Krait gave me. I went to the postmaster's house at Water Valley. She was getting ready for bed. I asked questions. She got on the phone. I bothered people until one in the morning. Then back into the trusty rent-a-car.

On to Memphis as the moon came up on my right. Interstate 55 was a glass ribbon before me. WLS from Chicago was on the radio.

I hummed along with it, I sang at the top of my voice.

The sack full of dodo bones, beaks, feet and eggshell fragments kept me company on the front seat.

Did you know a museum once traded an entire blue whale skeleton for one of a dodo?

Driving, driving.

the dance of the dodos

I used to have a vision sometimes – I had it long before this madness came up. I can close my eyes and see it by thinking hard. But it comes to me most often, most vividly when I am reading and listening to classical music, especially Pachelbel's "Canon in D."

It is near dusk in The Hague, and the light is that of Frans Hals, of Rembrandt. The Dutch royal family and their guests eat and talk quietly in the great dining hall. Guards with halberds and pikes stand in the corners of the room. The family is arranged around the table; the King, Queen, some princesses, a prince, a couple of their children, an invited noble or two. Servants come out with plates and cups but they do not intrude.

On a raised platform at one end of the room an orchestra plays dinner music – a harpsichordist, viola, cello, three violins and woodwinds. One of the royal dwarfs sits on the edge of the platform, his foot slowly rubbing the back of one of the dogs sleeping near him.

As the music of Pachelbel's "Canon in D" swells and rolls through the hall, one of the dodos walks in clumsily, stops, tilts its head, its eyes bright as a pool of tar. It sways a little, lifts its foot tentatively, one then another, rocks back and forth in time to the cello.

The violins swirl. The dodo begins to dance, its great ungainly body now graceful. It is joined by the other two dodos who come into the hall, all three turning in sort of a circle.

The harpsichord begins its counterpoint. The fourth dodo, the white one from Réunion, comes from its place under the table and joins the circle with the others.

It is most graceful of all, making complete turns where the others only sway and dip on the edge of the circle they have formed.

The music rises in volume; the first violinist sees the dodos and nods to the King. But he and the others at the table have already seen. They are silent, transfixed – even the servants stand still, bowls, pots and kettles in their hands forgotten.

Around the dodos dance with bobs and weaves of their ugly heads. The white dodo dips, takes a half step, pirouettes on one foot, circles again.

Without a word the King of Holland takes the hand of the Queen, and they come around the table, children before the spectacle. They join in the dance, waltzing (anachronism) among the dodos while the family, the guests, the soldiers watch and nod in time with the music.

Then the vision fades, and the afterimage of a flickering fireplace and a dodo remains.

The dodo and its kindred came by ships to the ports of civilized men. The first we have record of is that of Captain van Neck who brought back two in 1599 – one for the King of Holland, and one which found its way through Cologne to the menagerie of Emperor Rudolf II.

This royal aviary was at Schloss Neugebau, near Vienna. It was here the first paintings of the dumb old birds were done by Georg and his son Jacob Hoefnagel, between 1602 and 1610. They painted it among more than ninety species of birds which kept the Emperor amused.

Another Dutch artist named Roelandt Savery, as someone said, "made a career out of the dodo." He drew and painted them many times, and was no doubt personally fascinated by them. Obsessed, even. Early on, the paintings are consistent; the later ones have inaccuracies. This implies he worked from life first, then from memory as his model went to that place soon to be reserved for all its species. One of his drawings has two of the Raphidae scrambling for some goodie on the ground. His works are not without charm.

Another Dutch artist (they seemed to sprout up like mushrooms after a spring rain) named Peter Withoos also stuck dodos in his paintings, sometimes in odd and exciting places – wandering around during their owner's music lessons, or stuck with Adam and Eve in some Edenic idyll.

The most accurate representation, we are assured, comes from half a world away from the religious and political turmoil of the seafaring Europeans. There is an Indian miniature painting of the dodo which now rests in a museum in Russia. The dodo could have been brought by the Dutch or Portuguese in their travels to Goa and the coasts of the Indian subcontinent. Or they could have been brought centuries before by the Arabs who plied the Indian Ocean in their triangular-sailed craft, and who may have discovered the Mascarenes before the Europeans cranked themselves up for the First Crusade.

At one time early in my bird-fascination days (after I stopped killing them with BB guns but before I began to work for a scholarship), I once sat down and figured out where all the dodos had been.

Two with van Neck in 1599, one to Holland, one to Austria. Another was in Count Solms's park in 1600. An account speaks of "one in Italy, one in Germany, several to England, eight or nine to Holland." William Boentekoe van Hoorn knew of "one shipped to Europe in 1640, another in 1685" which he said was "also painted by Dutch artists." Two were mentioned as "being kept in Surrat House in India as pets," perhaps one of which is the one in the painting. Being charitable, and considering "several" to mean at least three, that means twenty dodos in all.

There had to be more, when boatloads had been gathered at the time.

What do we know of the Didine birds? A few ships' logs, some accounts left by travellers and colonists. The English were fascinated by them. Sir Hamon L'Estrange, a contemporary of Pepys, saw exhibited "a Dodar from the Island of Mauritius . . . it is not able to flie, being so bigge." One was stuffed when it died, and was put in the Museum Tradescantum in South Lambeth. It eventually found its way into the Ashmolean Museum. It grew ratty and was burned, all but a leg and the head, in 1750. By then there were no more dodos, but nobody had realized that yet.

Francis Willughby got to describe it before its incineration. Earlier, old Carolus Clusius in Holland studied the one in Count Solms's park. He collected everything known about the Raphidae, describing a dodo leg Pieter Pauw kept in his natural history cabinet, in *Exoticarium libri decem* in 1605, eight years after their discovery.

François Leguat, a Huguenot who lived on Réunion for some years, published an account of his travels in which he mentioned the dodos. It was published in 1690 (after the Mauritius dodo was extinct) and included the information that "some of the males weigh forty-five pound. One egg, much bigger than that of a goos is laid by the female, and takes seven weeks hatching time."

The Abbé Pingre visited the Mascarenes in 1761. He saw the last of the Rodriguez solitaires, and collected what information he could about the dead Mauritius and Réunion members of the genus.

After that, only memories of the colonists, and some scientific debate as to *where* the Raphidae belonged in the great taxonomic scheme of things – some said pigeons, some said rails – were left. Even this nitpicking ended. The dodo was forgotten.

When Lewis Carroll wrote *Alice in Wonderland* in 1865, most people thought he invented the dodo.

The service station I called from in Memphis was busier than a one-legged man in an ass-kicking contest. Between bings and dings of the bell, I finally realized the call had gone through.

The guy who answered was named Selvedge. I got nowhere with him. He mistook me for a real estate agent, then a lawyer. Now he was beginning to think I was some sort of a con man. I wasn't doing too well, either. I hadn't slept in two days. I must have sounded like a speed freak. My only progress was that I found that Ms Annie Mae Gudger (childhood play-mate of Jolyn Jimson) was now, and had been, the respected Ms Annie Mae Radwin. This guy Selvedge must have been a secretary or toady or something.

We were having a conversation comparable to that between a shrieking macaw and a pile of mammoth bones. Then there was another click on the line.

"Young man?" said the other voice, an old woman's voice, Southern, very refined but with a hint of the hills in it.

"Yes? Hello! Hello!"

"Young man, you say you talked to a Jolyn somebody? Do you mean Jolyn Smith?"

"Hello! Yes! Ms Radwin, Ms Annie Mae Radwin who used to be Gudger? She lives in Austin now. Texas. She used to live near Water Valley, Mississippi. Austin's where I'm from. I —"

"Young man," asked the voice again, "are you sure you haven't been put up to this by my hateful sister Alma?"

"Who? No, ma'am. I met a woman named Jolyn —"

"I'd like to talk to you, young man," said the voice. Then offhandedly, "Give him directions to get here, Selvedge."

Click.

I cleaned out my mouth as best I could in the service station restroom, tried to shave with an old clogged Gillette disposable in my knapsack and succeeded in gapping up my jawline. I changed into a clean pair of jeans, the only other shirt I had with me and combed my hair. I stood in front of the mirror.

I still looked like the dog's lunch.

The house reminded me of Presley's mansion, which was somewhere in the neighborhood. From a shack on the side of a Mississippi hill to this, in forty years. There are all sorts of ways of making it. I wondered what Anne Mae Gudger's had been. Luck? Predation? Divine intervention? Hard work? Trover and replevin?

Selvedge led me toward the sun room. I felt like Philip Marlowe going to meet a rich client. The house was filled with that furniture built sometime between the turn of the century and the 1950s – the ageless kind. It never looks great, it never looks ratty, and every chair is comfortable.

I think I was expecting some formidable woman with sleeve blotters and a green eyeshade hunched over a roll-top desk with piles of paper whose acceptance or rejection meant life or death for thousands.

Who I met was a charming lady in a green pantsuit. She was in her sixties, her hair still a straw wheat color. It didn't look dyed. Her eyes were blue as my first-grade teacher's had been. She was wiry and looked as if the word fat was not in her vocabulary.

"Good morning, Mr Lindberl." She shook my hand. "Would you like some coffee? You look as if you could use it."

"Yes, thank you."

"Please sit down." She indicated a white wicker chair at a glass table. A serving tray with coffeepot, cups, tea bags, croissants, napkins and plates lay on the tabletop.

After I swallowed half a cup of coffee at a gulp, she said, "What you wanted to see me about must be important?"

"Sorry about my manners," I said. "I know I don't look it, but I'm a biology assistant at the University of Texas. An ornithologist. Working on my master's. I met Ms Jolyn Jimson two days ago –"

"How is Jolyn? I haven't seen her in, oh, Lord, it must be on to fifty years. The time gets away."

"She seemed to be fine. I only talked to her half an hour or so. That was –"

"And you've come to see me about. . . ?"

"Uh. The . . . about some of the poultry your family used to raise, when they lived near Water Valley."

She looked at me a moment. Then she began to smile.

"Oh, you mean the ugly chickens?" she said.

I smiled. I almost laughed. I knew what Oedipus must have gone through.

It is now four-thirty in the afternoon. I am sitting at the downtown Motel 6 in Memphis. I have to make a phone call and get some sleep and catch a plane.

Annie Mae Gudger Radwin talked for four hours, answering my questions, setting me straight on family history, having Selvedge hold all her calls.

The main problem was that Annie Mae ran off in 1928, the year *before* her father got his big break. She went to Yazoo

City, and by degrees and stages worked her way northward to Memphis and her destiny as the widow of a rich mercantile broker.

But I get ahead of myself.

Grandfather Gudger used to be the overseer for Colonel Crisby on the main plantation near McComb, Mississippi. There was a long story behind that. Bear with me.

Colonel Crisby himself was the scion of a seafaring family with interests in both the cedars of Lebanon (almost all cut down for masts for His Majesty's and others' navies) and Egyptian cotton. Also teas, spices and any other saleable commodity which came their way.

When Colonel Crisby's grandfather reached his majority in 1802, he waved good-bye to the Atlantic Ocean at Charleston, SC and stepped westward into the forest. When he stopped, he was in the middle of the Chickasaw Nation, where he opened a trading post and introduced slaves to the Indians.

And he prospered, and begat Colonel Crisby's father, who sent back to South Carolina for everything his father owned. Everything – slaves, wagons, horses, cattle, guinea fowl, peacocks, and dodos, which everybody thought of as atrociously ugly poultry of some kind, one of the seafaring uncles having bought them off a French merchant in 1721. (I surmised these were white dodos from Réunion, unless they had been from even earlier stock. The dodo of Mauritius was already extinct by then.)

All this stuff was herded out west to the trading post in the midst of the Chickasaw Nation. (The tribes around there were of the confederation of the Dancing Rabbits.)

And Colonel Crisby's father prospered, and so did the guinea fowl and the dodos. Then Andrew Jackson came along and marched the Dancing Rabbits off up the Trail of Tears to the heaven of Oklahoma. And Colonel Crisby's father begat Colonel Crisby, and put the trading post in the hands of others, and moved his plantation westward still to McComb.

Everything prospered but Colonel Crisby's father, who died. And the dodos, with occasional losses to the avengin' weasel and the egg-sucking dog, reproduced themselves also.

Then along came Granddaddy Gudger, a Simon Legree role model, who took care of the plantation while Colonel Crisby raised ten companies of men and marched off to fight the War of the Southern Independence.

Colonel Crisby came back to the McComb plantation earlier than most, he having stopped much of the same volley of Minié balls that caught his commander, General Beauregard Hanlon, on a promontory bluff during the Siege of Vicksburg.

He wasn't dead, but death hung round the place like a gentlemanly bill collector for a month. The colonel languished, went slap-dab crazy and freed all his slaves the week before he died (the war lasted another two years after that). Not having any slaves, he didn't need an overseer.

Then comes the Faulkner part of the tale, straight out of *As I Lay Dying*, with the Gudger family returning to the area of Water Valley (before there was a Water Valley), moving through the demoralized and tattered displaced persons of the South, driving their dodos before them. For Colonel Crisby had given them to his former overseer for his faithful service. Also followed the story of the bloody murder of Granddaddy Gudger at the hands of the Freedman's militia during the rising of the first Klan, and of the trials and tribulations of Daddy Gudger in the years between 1880 and 1910, when he was between the ages of four and thirty-four.

Alma and Annie Mae were the second and fifth of Daddy Gudger's brood, born three years apart. They seemed to have hated each other from the very first time Alma looked into little Annie Mae's crib. They were kids by Daddy Gudger's second wife (his desperation had killed the first) and their father was already on his sixth career. He had been a lumber-man, a stump preacher, a plowman-for-hire (until his mules broke out in farcy buds and died of the glanders), a freight hauler (until his horses died of overwork and the hardware store repossessed the wagon), a politician's roadie (until the politician lost the election). When Alma and Annie Mae were born, he was failing as a sharecropper. Somehow Gudger had made it through the Depression of 1898 as a boy, and was too poor after that to notice more about economics than the price of Beech-Nut tobacco at the store.

Alma and Annie Mae fought, and it helped none at all that Alma, being the oldest daughter, was both her mother and father's darling. Annie Mae's life was the usual unwanted poor-white-trash-child's hell. She vowed early to run away, and recognized her ambition at thirteen.

All this I learned this morning. Jolyn (Smith) Jimson was Annie Mae's only friend in those days – from a family even poorer than the Gudgers. But somehow there was food, and an occasional odd job. And the dodos.

"My father hated those old birds," said the cultured Annie Mae Radwin, nee Gudger, in the solarium. "He always swore he was going to get rid of them someday, but just never seemed to get around to it. I think there was more to it than that. But they were so much *trouble*. We always had to keep them penned up at night, and go check for their eggs. They wandered off to lay them, and forgot where they were. Sometimes no new ones were born at all in a year.

"And they got so *ugly*. Once a year. I mean, terrible-looking, like they were going to die. All their feathers fell off, and they looked like they had mange or something. Then the whole front of their beaks fell off, or worse, hung halfway on for a week or two. They looked like big old naked pigeons. After that they'd lose weight, down to twenty or thirty pounds, before their new feathers grew back.

"We were always having to kill foxes that got after them in the turkey house. That's what we called their roost, the turkey house. And we found their eggs all sucked out by cats and dogs. They were so stupid we had to drive them into their roost at night. I don't think they could have found it standing ten feet from it."

She looked at me.

"I think much as my father hated them, they meant something to him. As long as he hung on to them, he knew he was as good as Granddaddy Gudger. You may not know it, but there was a certain amount of family pride about Granddaddy Gudger. At least in my father's eyes. His rapid fall in the world had a sort of grandeur to it. He'd gone from a relatively high position in the old order, and maintained some grace and stature after the Emancipation. And though he lost everything, he managed to keep those ugly old chickens the colonel had given him as sort of a symbol.

"And as long as he had them, too, my daddy thought himself as good as his father. He kept his dignity, even when he didn't have anything else."

I asked what happened to them. She didn't know, but told me who did and where I could find her.

That's why I'm going to make a phone call.

"Hello. Dr Courtney. Dr Courtney? This is Paul. Memphis. Tennessee. It's too long to go into. No, of course not, not yet. But I've got evidence. What? Okay, how do trochanters, coracoids, tarsometatarsi and beak sheaths sound? From their henhouse, where else? Where would you keep *your* dodos, then?

"Sorry. I haven't slept in a couple of days. I need some help. Yes, yes. Money. Lots of money.

"Cash. Three hundred dollars, maybe. Western Union, Memphis, Tennessee. Whichever one's closest to the airport. Airport. I need the department to set up reservations to Mauritius for me . . .

"No. No. Not wild goose chase, wild *dodo* chase. Tame dodo chase. I *know* there aren't any dodos on Mauritius! I know that. I could explain. I know it'll mean a couple of grand . . . if . . . but . . .

"Look, Dr Courtney. Do you want *your* picture in *Scientific American*, or don't you?"

I am sitting in the airport café in Port Louis, Mauritius. It is now three days later, five days since that fateful morning my car wouldn't start. God bless the Sears Diehard people. I have slept sitting up in a plane seat, on and off, different planes, different seats, for twenty-four hours, Kennedy to Paris, Paris to Cairo, Cairo to Madagascar. I felt like a brand-new man when I got here.

Now I feel like an infinitely sadder and wiser brand-new man. I have just returned from the hateful sister Alma's house in the exclusive section of Port Louis, where all the French and British officials used to live.

Courtney will get his picture in *Scientific American*, me too, all right. There'll be newspaper stories and talk shows for a few weeks for me, and I'm sure Annie Mae Gudger Radwin on one side of the world and Alma Chandler Gudger Moliere on the other will come in for their share of glory.

I am putting away cup after cup of coffee. The plane back to Tananarive leaves in an hour. I plan to sleep all the way back to Cairo, to Paris, to New York, pick up my bag of bones, sleep back to Austin.

Before me on the table is a packet of documents, clippings and photographs. I have come half the world for this. I gaze from the package, out the window across Port Louis to the bulk of Mt Pieter Boothe, which overshadows the city and its famous racecourse.

Perhaps I should do something symbolic. Cancel my flight. Climb the mountain and look down on man and all his handiworks. Take a pitcher of martinis with me. Sit in the bright semitropical sunlight (it's early dry winter here). Drink the martinis slowly, toasting Snuffo, God of Extinction. Here's one for the Great Auk. This is for the Carolina Parakeet. Mud in your eye, Passenger Pigeon. This one's for the Heath Hen. Most importantly, here's one each for the Mauritius dodo, the white dodo of Réunion, the Réunion solitaire, the Rodriguez solitaire. Here's to the Raphidae, great Didine birds that you were.

Maybe I'll do something just as productive, like climbing Mt Pieter Boothe and pissing into the wind.

How symbolic. The story of the dodo ends where it began, on this very island. Life imitates cheap art. Like the Xerox of the Xerox of a bad novel. I never expected to find dodos still alive here (this is the one place they would have been noticed). I still can't believe Alma Chandler Gudger Moliere could have lived here twenty-five years and not *know* about the dodo, never set foot inside the Port Louis Museum, where they have skeletons, and a stuffed replica the size of your little brother.

After Annie Mae ran off, the Gudger family found itself prospering in a time the rest of the country was going to hell. It was 1929. Gudger delved into politics again, and backed a man who knew a man who worked for Theodore "Sure

Two-Handed Sword of God" Bilbo, who had connections everywhere. Who introduced him to Huey "Kingfish" Long just after that gentleman lost the Louisiana governor's election one of the times. Gudger stumped around Mississippi, getting up steam for Long's Share the Wealth plan, even before it had a name.

The upshot was that the Long machine in Louisiana knew a rabble-rouser when it saw one, and invited Gudger to move to the Sportsman's Paradise, with his family, all expenses paid, and start working for the Kingfish at the unbelievable salary of sixty-two dollars fifty a week. Which prospect was like turning a hog loose under a persimmon tree, and before you could say Backwoods Messiah, the Gudger clan was on its way to the land of pelicans, graft and Mardi Gras.

Almost. But I'll get to that.

Daddy Gudger prospered all out of proportion with his abilities, but many men did that during the Depression. First a little, thence to more, he rose in bureaucratic (and political) circles of the state, dying rich and well-hated with his fingers in *all* the pies.

Alma Chandler Gudger became a debutante (she says Robert Penn Warren put her in his book) and met and married Jean Carl Moliere, only heir to rice, indigo and sugar cane growers. They had a happy wedded life, moving first to the West Indies, later to Mauritius, where the family sugar cane holdings were one of the largest on the island. Jean Carl died in 1959. Alma was his only survivor.

So local family makes good. Poor sharecropping Mississippi people turn out to have a father dying with a smile on his face, and two daughters who between them own a large portion of the planet.

I open the envelope before me. Ms Alma Moliere had listened politely to my story (the university had called ahead and arranged an introduction through the director of the Port Louis Museum, who knew Ms Moliere socially) and told me what she could remember. Then she sent a servant out to one of the storehouses (large as a duplex) and he and two others came back with boxes of clippings, scrapbooks and family photos.

"I haven't looked at any of this since we left St Thomas," she said. "Let's go through it together."

Most of it was about the rise of Citizen Gudger.

"There's not many pictures of us before we came to Louisiana. We were so frightfully poor then, hardly anyone we knew had a camera. Oh, look. Here's one of Annie Mae. I thought I threw all those out after Mamma died."

This is the photograph. It must have been taken about 1927. Annie Mae is wearing some unrecognizable piece of clothing that approximates a dress. She leans on a hoe, smiling a snaggle-toothed smile. She looks to be ten or eleven. Her eyes are half hidden by the shadow of the brim of a gapped straw hat she wears. The earth she is standing in barefoot has been newly turned. Behind her is one corner of the house, and the barn beyond has its upper hay-windows open. Out-of-focus people are at work there.

A few feet behind her, a huge male dodo is pecking at something on the ground. The front two thirds of it shows, back to the stupid wings and the edge of the upcurved tail feathers. One foot is in the photo, having just scratched at something, possibly an earthworm, in the new-plowed clods. Judging by its darkness, it is the gray, or Mauritius, dodo.

The photograph is not very good, one of those three-and-a-half by five jobs box cameras used to take. Already I can see this one, and the blowup of the dodo, taking up a double-page spread in *SA*. Alma told me around then they were down to six or seven of the ugly chickens, two whites, the rest gray-brown.

Besides this photo, two clippings are in the package, one from the Bruce *Banner-Times*, the other from the Oxford newspaper; both are columns by the same woman dealing with "Doings in Water Valley." Both mention the Gudger family moving from the area to seek its fortune in the swampy state to the west, and telling how they will be missed. Then there's a yellowed clipping from the front page of the Oxford paper with a small story about the Gudger Farewell Party in Water Valley the Sunday before (dated October 19, 1929).

There's a handbill in the package, advertising the Gudger Family Farewell Party, Sunday Oct. 15, 1929 Come One

Come All. (The people in Louisiana who sent expense money to move Daddy Gudger must have overestimated the costs by an exponential factor. I said as much.)

"No," Alma Moliere said. "There was a lot, but it wouldn't have made any difference. Daddy Gudger was like Thomas Wolfe and knew a shining golden opportunity when he saw one. Win, lose or draw, he was never coming back *there* again. He would have thrown some kind of soiree whether there had been money for it or not. Besides, people were much more sociable then, you mustn't forget."

I asked her how many people came.

"Four or five hundred," she said. "There's some pictures here somewhere." We searched awhile, then we found them.

Another thirty minutes to my flight. I'm not worried sitting here. I'm the only passenger, and the pilot is sitting at the table next to mine talking to an RAF man. Life is much slower and nicer on these colonial islands. You mustn't forget.

I look at the other two photos in the package. One is of some men playing horseshoes and washer-toss, while kids, dogs and women look on. It was evidently taken from the east end of the house looking west. Everyone must have had to walk the last mile to the old Gudger place. Other groups of people stand talking. Some men, in shirtsleeves and suspenders, stand with their heads thrown back, a snappy story, no doubt, just told. One girl looks directly at the camera from close up, shyly, her finger in her mouth. She's about five. It looks like any snapshot of a family reunion which could have been taken anywhere, anytime. Only the clothing marks it as backwoods 1920s.

Courtney will get his money's worth. I'll write the article, make phone calls, plan the talk show tour to coincide with publication. Then I'll get some rest. I'll be a normal person again; get a degree, spend my time wading through jungles after animals which will all be dead in another twenty years, anyway.

Who cares? The whole thing will be just another media

event, just this year's Big Deal. It'll be nice getting normal again. I can read books, see movies, wash my clothes at the laundromat, listen to Jonathan Richman on the stereo. I can study and become an authority on some minor matter or other.

I can go to museums and see all the wonderful dead things there.

"That's the memory picture," said Alma. "They always took them at big things like this, back in those days. Everybody who was there would line up and pose for the camera. Only we couldn't fit everybody in. So we had two made. This is the one with us in it."

The house is dwarfed by people. All sizes, shapes, dress and age. Kids and dogs in front, women next, then men at the back. The only exceptions are the bearded patriarchs seated towards the front with the children – men whose eyes face the camera but whose heads are still ringing with something Nathan Bedford Forrest said to them one time on a smoke-filled field. This photograph is from another age. You can recognize Daddy and Mrs Gudger if you've seen their photographs before. Alma pointed herself out to me.

But the reason I took the photograph is in the foreground. Tables have been built out of sawhorses, with doors and boards nailed across them. They extend the entire width of the photograph. They are covered with food, more food than you can imagine.

"We started cooking three days before. So did the neighbors. Everybody brought something," said Alma.

It's like an entire Safeway had been cooked and set out to cool. Hams, quarters of beef, chickens by the tubful, quail in mounds, rabbit, butterbeans by the bushel, yams, Irish potatoes, an acre of corn, eggplant, peas, turnip greens, butter in five-pound molds, cornbread and biscuits, gallon cans of molasses, redeye gravy by the pot.

And five huge birds – twice as big as turkeys, legs capped like for Thanksgiving, drumsticks the size of Schwarzenegger's biceps, whole-roasted, lying on their backs on platters large as cocktail tables.

The people in the crowd sure look hungry.

"We ate for days," said Alma.

I already have the title for the *Scientific American* article. It's going to be called "The Dodo Is *Still* Dead."

JACK DANN
Going Under

As a writer, Jack Dann has always been ahead of his time, a quality that has garnered him wildly enthusiastic fan letters from people like Philip K. Dick, and has earned him the respect of his peers, by whom he is considered to be a writer's writer, but which has perhaps kept him underappreciated by the public at large. By the time they catch up to where he *was*, some years before, he is already gone, off ahead somewhere, breaking new ground. In this, as in the complex weight of ideas he piles one atop the other, and the elegance and intensity of his prose, he reminds me of Charles Harness, who had the uncomfortable honor of writing stories like "The New Reality" in the '50s that ninety percent of his potential audience would not be aesthetically equipped to appreciate until the late '80s. This is not the surest formula for a comfortable career.

Dann began writing in 1970, and first attracted wide notice with the critically acclaimed novella "Junction," which was a Nebula finalist in 1973; he has been a Nebula finalist nine more times since then, and twice a finalist for the World Fantasy Award. Later in that decade, he expanded the already strange "Junction" into the even *stranger* novel *Junction*, one of the truly weird books of the '70s, and later followed it up with *Starhiker*, which has to be a prime candidate for the most bizarre book ever published ostensibly as a Young Adult novel. Both of these novels bristle with enough new ideas, strange bits of business and offbeat conceptualization to keep less original writers going through two or three four hundred-page trilogies, although the bit-rate in them is so high that they are both actually rather slender books. Throughout the last years of the '70s, he contributed memorable stories like the searing "Camps," "A Quiet Revolution for Death," "I'm Waiting for You in Rockland," and "The Dybbuk Dolls" to various magazines and anthologies. And then, at the beginning of the '80s, he began to publish the stories that would later be melded

into his brilliant novel, *The Man Who Melted*, in my opinion one
of the best novels of the decade.

This was work a quantum jump better even than Dann's own
previous high standard, and the best of the lot was the story that
follows, "Going Under," one of the most memorable stories of
the '80s, and one with a vision of the future as strange,
sophisticated, and elegantly kinky as any I've ever seen.

Dann's other books include *Counting Coup*, a powerful – and,
inexplicably, as yet unsold – mainstream novel, and *Timetipping*,
a collection of his short fiction. He edited one of the best-known
anthologies of the '70s, *Wandering Stars*, a collection of fantasy
and SF on Jewish themes; his other anthologies include *More
Wandering Stars*, *Immortal*, *Faster Than Light* (co-edited with
George Zebrowski), and several anthologies co-edited with
Gardner Dozois. His most recent books are an acclaimed
anthology of Vietnam stories, edited in collaboration with
Jeanne Van Buren Dann, called *In the Field of Fire*, and a
collection of his collaborative short work, *Slow Dancing Through
Time*. Upcoming is a major new novel called *The Path of
Remembrance*. Dann lives with his family in Binghamton, New
York.

She was beautiful, huge, as graceful as a racing liner. She
was a floating Crystal Palace, as magnificent as anything
J. P. Morgan could conceive. Designed by Alexander
Carlisle and built by Harland and Wolff, she wore the golden
band of the company along all nine hundred feet of her. She
rose one hundred and seventy-five feet like the side of a cliff,
with nine steel decks, four sixty-two-foot funnels, over two
thousand windows and sidelights to illuminate the luxurious
cabins and suites and public rooms. She weighed forty-six
thousand tons, and her reciprocating engines and Parsons-
type turbines could generate over fifty-thousand horsepower
and speed the ship over twenty knots. She had a gymnasium,
a Turkish bath, squash and racket courts, a swimming pool,
libraries and lounges and sitting rooms. There were rooms
and suites to accommodate seven hundred and thirty-five
first-class passengers, six hundred and seventy-four in
second class, and over a thousand in steerage.

She was the RMS *Titanic*, and Stephen met Esme on her
Promenade Deck as she pulled out of her Southampton dock,
bound for New York on her maiden voyage.

Esme stood beside him, resting what appeared to be a cedar box on the rail, and gazed out over the cheering crowds on the docks below. She was plain-featured and quite young. She had a high forehead, a small, straight nose, wet brown eyes which peeked out from under plucked, arched eyebrows, and a mouth that was a little too full. Her blonde hair, although clean, was carelessly brushed and tangled in the back.

To Stephen she seemed beautiful.

"Hello," he said. Coloured ribbons and confetti snakes were coiling through the air, and anything seemed possible.

Esme glanced at him. "Hello you," she said.

"Pardon?"

"I said 'hello, you.' That's an expression that was in vogue when this boat first sailed, if you'd care to know. It means, 'Hello, I think you're interesting and would consider sleeping with you if I were so inclined.'"

"You must call it a ship," Stephen said.

She laughed and for an instant looked at him intently, as if in that second she could see everything about him – that he was taking this voyage because he was bored with his life, that nothing had ever *really* happened to him. He felt his face become hot. "Okay, 'ship,' does that make you feel better?" she asked. "Anyway, I *want* to pretend that I'm living in the past. I don't ever want to return to the present. I suppose you do, want to return, that is."

"What makes you think that?"

"Look how you're dressed. You shouldn't be wearing modern clothes on this ship. You'll have to change later, you know." She was perfectly dressed in a powder-blue walking suit with matching jacket, a pleated, velvet-trimmed front blouse, and an ostrich-feather hat. She looked as if she had stepped out of another century.

"What's your name?" Stephen asked.

"Esme." She turned the box that she was resting on the rail and opened the side facing the deck. "You see," she said to the box, "we really *are* here."

"What did you say?" Stephen asked.

"I was just talking to Poppa," she said, closing and latching the box.

"Who?"

"I'll show you later if you like." Bells began to ring and the ship's whistles cut the air. There was a cheer from the dock and on board, and the ship moved slowly out to sea. To Stephen it seemed that the land, not the ship, was moving. The whole of England floated peacefully away while the string band on the ship's bridge played Oskar Straus.

They watched until the land had dwindled to a thin line on the horizon, then Esme reached for Stephen's hand, squeezed it for a moment and hurried away.

Stephen found her again in the Café Parisien, sitting in a large wicker chair beside an ornately trellised wall.

"Well, hello you," Esme said, smiling. She was the model of a smart, stylish young lady.

"Does that mean you're still interested?" Stephen asked, standing before her. Her smile was infectious, and Stephen felt himself losing his poise, as he couldn't stop grinning.

"But *mais oui*," she said. "That's French, which no one uses anymore, but it was *the* language of the world when this ship first sailed." She relaxed suddenly in her chair, slumped down as if she could revert instantly to being a child, and looked around the room as though Stephen had suddenly disappeared.

"I believe it was English," he said.

"Well," she said, looking up at him, "whatever, it means that I might be interested *if* you'd kindly sit down instead of looking at me from the heights." Stephen sat beside her. "It took you long enough to find me," Esme said.

"Well, I had to dress. Remember? You didn't find my previous attire –"

"I agree and I apologize," she said quickly, as if suddenly afraid of hurting his feelings. She folded her hands behind the box that she had centered perfectly on the damask-covered table. Her leg brushed his; indeed, he did look fine dressed in gray-striped trousers, spats, black morning coat, blue vest, and a silk cravat tied under a butterfly collar. "Now don't you feel better?"

Stephen was taken with her; this had never happened to him before. A tall waiter disturbed him by asking if he wished to order cocktails, but Esme asked for a Narcodrine instead.

"I'm sorry, madam, but Narcodrines or inhalers are not publicly sold on the ship."

"Well, that's what I *want*."

"One would have to ask the steward for more modern refreshments."

"You did say you wanted to live in the past," Stephen said. He ordered a Campari for her and a Drambuie for himself.

"Right now I would prefer a robot to take my order," Esme said.

"I'm sorry, but we have no robots on this ship either," the waiter said before turning away.

"Are you going to show me what's inside the box?" Stephen asked.

"It might cause a stir if I opened it here."

"I would think you'd like that," Stephen said.

"You see, you know me intimately already." Esme smiled and winked at someone four tables away. "Isn't he cute?"

"Who?"

"The little boy with the black hair parted in the middle." She waved at him, but the boy ignored her and made an obscene gesture at a woman who looked to be his nanny. Then Esme opened the box, which drew the little boy's attention. She pulled out a full-sized head of a man and placed it gently beside the box.

"Jesus," Stephen said.

"Stephen, I'd like you to meet Poppa. Poppa, this is Stephen."

"Who is Stephen?" Poppa said. "Where am I? Why is this going on? I'm frightened."

Esme leaned toward the head and whispered into its ear. "He sometimes gets disoriented on awakening," she said to Stephen confidentially. "He still isn't used to it yet. But he'll be all right in a moment."

"I'm scared," Poppa said in a fuller voice. "I'm alone in the dark."

"Not anymore," Esme said positively. "Poppa, this is my friend, Stephen."

"Hello, Poppa," Stephen said awkwardly.

"Hello, Stephen," the head said. Its voice was powerful now, commanding. "I'm pleased to meet you." It rolled its eyes and then said to Esme, "Turn me a bit now so I can see your friend without eyestrain." The head had white hair, which was a bit yellowed on the ends. It was neatly trimmed at the sides and combed into a rather seedy pompadour in the front. The face was strong, although dissipated. It was the face of a man in his late sixties, lined and tanned.

"My given name is Elliot," the head said. "Call me that, please."

"Hello, Elliot," Stephen said. He had heard of such things, but had never seen one before.

"These are going to be all the rage in the next few months," Esme said. "They aren't on the mass market yet, but you can imagine their potential for both adults and children. They can be programmed to talk and react very realistically."

"So I see," Stephen said.

The head smiled, accepting the compliment.

"He also learns and thinks quite well," Esme continued.

"I should hope so," said the head.

"Is your father alive?" Stephen asked.

"I *am* her father," the head said, its face betraying impatience. "At least give me *some* respect."

"Be civil, Poppa, or I'll close you up," Esme said, piqued. She looked at Stephen. "Yes, he died recently. That's the reason I'm taking this trip and that's the reason –" She nodded at the head. "He's marvelous, though. He *is* my father in every way." Mischievously she added, "Well, I *did* make a few changes. Poppa was very demanding."

"You're ungrateful –"

"Shut up, Poppa."

Poppa shut his eyes.

"That's all I have to say," Esme said, "and he turns himself off."

The little boy who had been staring unabashedly came over to the table just as Esme was putting Poppa back in the box. "Why'd you put him away?" he asked. "I want to talk to him. Take him out."

"No," Esme said firmly, "he's sleeping now. And what's your name?"

"Michael, and can I please see the head, just for a minute?"

"If you like, Michael, you can have a private audience with Poppa tomorrow," Esme said. "How's that?"

"I want to talk to him now."

"Shouldn't you be getting back to your nanny?" Stephen asked, standing and indicating that Esme do the same. They would have no privacy here.

"Stuff it," Michael said. "She's not my nanny, she's my sister." Then he pulled a face at Stephen; he was able to contort his lips, drawing the right side toward the left and left toward the right as if they were made of rubber. Stephen and Esme walked out of the café and up the staircase to the Boat Deck, and Michael followed them.

The Boat Deck was not too crowded at least; it was brisk out and the breeze had a chill to it. Looking forward, Stephen and Esme could see the ship's four huge smokestacks to their left and a cluster of four lifeboats to their right. The ocean was a smooth, deep green expanse turning to blue toward the horizon. The sky was empty, except for a huge, nuclear-powered airship that floated high over the *Titanic* . . . this was the dirigible *California*, a French luxury liner capable of carrying two thousand passengers.

"Are you two married?" Michael asked.

"No we are not," Esme said impatiently. "Not yet, at least," and Stephen felt exhilarated at the thought of her really wanting him. Actually, it made no sense for he could have any young woman he wanted. Why Esme? Simply because just now she was perfect.

"You're quite pretty," Michael said to Esme.

"Well, thank you," Esme replied, warming to him. "I like you, too."

"Are you going to stay on the ship and die when it sinks?"

"No!" Esme said, as if taken aback.

"What about your friend?"

"You mean Poppa?"

Vexed, the boy said, "No, *him*," giving Stephen a nasty look.

"Well, I don't know," Esme said. Her face was flushed. "Have you opted for a lifeboat, Stephen?"

"Yes, of course I have."

"Well, *we're* going to die on the ship."

"Don't be silly," Esme said.

"Well, we are."

"Who's we?" Stephen asked.

"My sister and I. We've made a pact to go down with the ship."

"I don't believe it," Esme said. She stopped beside one of the lifeboats, rested the box containing Poppa on the rail, and gazed downwards at the ocean spume curling away from the side of the ship.

"He's just baiting us," Stephen said. "Anyway, he's too young to make such a decision, and his sister, if she is his sister, couldn't decide such a thing for him, even if she were his guardian. It would be illegal."

"We're at sea," Michael said in the nagging tone children use. "I'll discuss the ramifications of my demise with Poppa tomorrow. I'm sure *he's* more conversant with these things than you."

"Shouldn't you be getting back to your sister now?" Stephen asked.

Michael made the rubber-lips face at him and then walked away, tugging at the back of his shorts as if his undergarments had bunched up beneath. He only turned around to wave goodbye to Esme, who blew him a kiss.

"Intelligent little brat," Stephen said to be ingratiating.

But Esme looked as if she had just now forgotten all about Stephen and the little boy. She stared at the box as tears rolled from her eyes.

"Esme?"

"I love him and now he's dead," she said. She seemed to brighten then. She took Stephen's hand and they went inside, down the stairs, through several noisy corridors – stateroom parties were in full swing – to her suite. Stephen was a bit nervous, but all things considered, everything was progressing at a proper pace.

Esme's suite had a parlor and a private promenade deck with Elizabethan half-timbered walls. She led him directly into the plush-carpeted, velour-papered bedroom, which contained a huge four-poster bed, an antique night table, and a desk and stuffed chair beside the door. The ornate, harp-sculpture desk lamp was on, as was the lamp just inside the bedcurtains. A porthole gave a view of sea and sky, but to Stephen it seemed that the bed overpowered the room.

Esme pushed the desk lamp aside, and then took Poppa out of the box and placed him carefully in the center of the desk. "There," she said. At rest the head seemed even more handsome and quite peaceful although now and then an eyelid twitched. Then she undressed quickly, looking shyly away from Stephen who was taking his time. She slipped between the parted curtains of the bed and complained that she could hear the damn engines thrumming right through these itchy pillows – she didn't like silk. After a moment, she sat up in bed and asked him if he intended to get undressed or just stand there.

"I'm sorry," Stephen said, "but it's just –" He nodded toward the head.

"Poppa *is* turned off you know," Esme said.

The head's left eyelid fluttered.

Michael knocked on Esme's door at seven-thirty the next morning.

"Good morning," Michael said, looking Esme up and down. She had not bothered to put anything on before answering the door. "I came to see Poppa. I won't disturb you."

"Jesus, Michael, it's too early –"

"Early bird gets the worm."

"Oh," Esme said, "and what the hell does that mean?"

"I calculated that my best chance of talking with Poppa was if I woke you up. You'll go back to bed and I can talk with him in peace. My chances would be greatly diminished if –"

"Come in."

"The steward in the hall just saw you naked."

"Big deal. Look, why don't you come back later, I'm not ready for this, and I don't know why I let you in the room."

"You see, it worked." Michael looked around. "He's in the bedroom, right?"

Esme nodded and followed him in. Michael was wearing the same wrinkled shirt and shorts that he had worn yesterday; his hair was not combed, just tousled.

"Is *he* with you, too?" Michael asked.

"If you mean Stephen, yes."

"I thought so," said Michael. Then he sat down at the desk. "Hello Poppa," he said.

"I'm frightened," the head said. "It's so dark; I'm scared."

Michael gave Esme a look.

"He's always like that when he's been shut off for a while," Esme said. "Talk to him a bit more."

"It's Michael," the boy said. "I came in here to talk to you. We're on the *Titanic*."

"Oh Michael," the head said, more confidently. "I think I remember you. Why are you on the *Titanic?*"

"Because it's going to sink."

"That's a silly reason," the head said confidently. "There must be others."

"There are lots of others."

"Can't we have *any* privacy?" Stephen said, sitting up in the bed. Esme sat beside him, shrugged, and took a pull at her inhaler. Drugged, she looked even softer, more vulnerable. "I thought you told me that Poppa was turned off all night," he continued angrily.

"I'll tell you all about the *Titanic*," Michael said confidentially to the head. He leaned close to it and whispered intensely.

"He *was* turned off," Esme said. "I just now turned him back on for Michael." She cuddled up to Stephen, as intimately as if they had been in love for days. That seemed to mollify him.

"Do you have a spare Narcodrine in there?" Michael shouted.

Stephen looked at Esme, who laughed. "No," Esme said, "you're too young for such things." She pulled the curtain so that the bed was now shut off from Michael and the head. "Let him talk to Poppa," she said. "He'll be dead soon, anyway."

"You mean you believe him?" Stephen said. "I'm going to talk to his sister or whoever she is about this."

Michael peered through the curtain. "I heard what you said. I have very good hearing, I heard everything. Go ahead and talk to her, talk to the captain if you like. It won't do you any good. I'm an international hero if you'd like to know. That girl who wears the camera in her hair already did an interview for me for the poll." He closed the curtain.

"What does he mean?" Esme asked.

"The woman reporter from *Interfax*," Stephen said.

Michael opened the curtains again. "Her job is to guess which passengers will opt to die and why. She interviews the most interesting passengers, then gives her predictions to her viewers, and she has a lot of them. They respond immediately to a poll taken several times every day. Keeps us in their minds, and everybody loves the smell of death." The curtain closed.

"Well, she hasn't tried to interview *me*," Esme said, pouting.

"Do you really want her to?"

"And why not? I'm for conspicuous consumption, and I want so much for this experience to be a success. Goodness, let the whole world watch us sink if they want. They might just as well take bets." Then, in a conspiratorial whisper, she said, "None of us knows who's really opted to die. *That's* part of the excitement."

"I suppose," Stephen said.

"Oh you're such a prig," Esme said. "One would think you're a doer."

"A what?"

"A doer. All of us are either doers or voyeurs, isn't that right? But the doers mean business," and to illustrate she cocked her head, stuck out her tongue, and made gurgling noises as if she were drowning. "The voyeurs, however, are just along for the ride. Are you *sure* you're not a doer?"

Michael, who had been eavesdropping again, said referring to Stephen, "He's not a doer, you can bet on that! He's a voyeur of the worst sort. He takes it all seriously."

"Now that's enough disrespect from both of you," Poppa said richly. "Michael, stop goading Stephen. Esme says she loves him. Esme, be nice to Michael. He just made my day. And you don't have to threaten to turn me off. I'm turning myself off. I've got some thinking to do." Poppa closed his eyes.

"*Well*," Esme said to Michael who was now standing before the bed and trying to place his feet as wide apart as possible, "he's never done that before. He's usually so afraid of being afraid when he wakes up. What did you say to him?"

"Nothing much."

"Come on, Michael, *I* let you into the room, remember?"

"I remember. Can I come into bed with you?"

"Hell, no," Stephen said.

"He's only a child," Esme said as she moved over to make room for Michael, who climbed in between her and Stephen. "Be a sport. *You're* the man I love."

Stephen moved closer to Esme so that Michael could come into the bed. They discussed the transmigration of souls. Michael was sure of it, but Esme thought it all too confusing. Stephen had no real opinion.

They finally managed to lose Michael by lunchtime. Esme seemed happy enough to be rid of the boy, and they spent the rest of the day discovering the ship. They tried a quick dip in the pool, but the water was too cold and it was chilly outside. If the dirigible was floating above, they did not see it because the sky was covered with heavy, gray clouds. They changed clothes, strolled along the glass-enclosed lower Promenade Deck, looked for the occasional flying fish, and spent an interesting half hour being interviewed by the woman from *Interfax*. Then they took a snack in the opulent first-class smoking room. Esme loved the mirrors and stained-glass windows. After they explored cabin and tourist class, Esme talked Stephen into a quick game of squash, which he played rather well. By dinnertime they found their way into the garish, blue-tiled Turkish bath. It was empty and hot, and they made gentle but exhausting love on one of the Caesar couches. Then they changed clothes again, danced in the lounge, and took a late supper in the café.

He spent the night with Esme in her suite. It was about four in the morning when he was awakened by a hushed conversation. Rather than make himself known, Stephen feigned sleep and listened.

"I can't make a decision," Esme said as she carefully paced back and forth beside the desk upon which Poppa rested.

"I'm still scared," Poppa said in a weak voice. "Just give me a minute, this was so *sudden*. Where did you say I am?"

"The *Titanic*," Esme said angrily, "and I have to make a decision. Come to your senses."

"You've told me over and over what you know you must do, haven't you?" Poppa said. His voice sounded better; the disorientation was leaving him. "Now you change your mind?"

"I think things have changed."

"And how is that?"

"Stephen. He –"

"Ah," Poppa said, "so now *love* is the escape. But do you know how long that will last?"

"I didn't expect to meet him, to feel better about everything."

"It will pass."

"But right now I don't want to die."

"You've spent a fortune on this trip, and on me. And now you want to throw it away. Look, the way you feel about Stephen is all for the better, don't you understand? It will make your passing away all the sweeter because you're happy, in love, whatever you want to claim for it. But now you want to throw everything away that we've planned and take your life some other time, probably when you're desperate and unhappy and don't have me around to help you. You wish to die as mindlessly as you were born."

"That's not so, Poppa. But it's up to *me* to choose."

"You've made your choice, now stick to it or you'll drop dead like I did."

"Esme, what the hell are you talking about?" Stephen said.

Esme looked startled in the dim light and then said to Poppa, "You were purposely talking loudly to wake him up, weren't you?"

"*You* had me programmed to help you. I love you and I care about you. You can't undo that!"

"I can do whatever I wish," Esme said petulantly.

"Then let me help you, as I always have. If I were alive and had my body I would tell you exactly what I'm telling you now."

"What *is* going on?" Stephen asked.

"She's fooling you," Poppa said gently to Stephen. "She's using you because she's frightened. She's grasping at anyone she can find."

"What the hell is he telling you?" Stephen asked.

"The truth," Poppa said. "I know all about fear, don't you know that?"

Esme sat beside Stephen on the bed and began to cry, then, as if sliding easily into a new role, she looked at him and said, "I did program Poppa to help me die. Poppa and I talked everything over very carefully, we even discussed what to do if something like this came about."

"You mean if you fell in love and wanted to live."

"And she decided that under no circumstances would she undo what she had done," Poppa said. "She has planned the best possible death for herself, a death to be experienced and savored. She's given everything up and spent all her money to do it. She's broke. She can't go back now, isn't that right, Esme?"

Esme folded her hands, swallowed, and looked at Stephen. "Yes," she said.

"But you're not sure," Stephen said. "I can see that."

"I will help her as I always have," Poppa said.

"Jesus, shut that thing up," Stephen shouted.

"He's not a— "

"Please," Stephen said, "at least give us a chance. You're the first authentic experience I've ever had, I love you, I don't want it to end . . ."

Poppa pleaded his own case eloquently until Esme told him to shut up.

The great ship hit an iceberg on the fourth night of her voyage, exactly one day earlier than scheduled. Stephen and Esme were standing by the rail of the Promenade Deck. Both were dressed in the early twentieth-century accouterments provided by the ship – he in woolen trousers, jacket, motoring cap, and caped overcoat with a long scarf; she in a fur coat, a stylish "Merry Widow" hat, high button shoes and a black-velvet, two-piece suit edged with white silk. She looked ravishing and very young, despite the clothes.

"Throw it away," Stephen said authoritatively. "Now."

Esme brought the cedar box containing Poppa to her chest, as if she were about to throw it forward, then slowly placed it atop the rail again. "I *can't.*"

"Do you want me to do it?"

"I don't see why I must throw him away."

"Because we're starting a new life together."

At that moment someone shouted, and as if in the distance, a bell rang three times.

"Could there be another ship nearby?" Esme asked.

"Esme, throw the box away!" Stephen snapped; and then he saw it. He pulled Esme backward, away from the rail. An iceberg as high as the forecastle deck scraped against the side of the ship; it almost seemed that the bluish, glistening mountain of ice was another ship passing, that the ice rather than the ship was moving. Pieces of ice rained upon the deck, slid across the varnished wood, and then the iceberg was lost in the darkness astern. It must have been at least one hundred feet high.

"Oh my God!" Esme screamed, rushing to the rail.

"What is it?"

"Poppa! I dropped him when you pulled me away from the iceberg."

"It's too late for that– "

Esme disappeared into the crowd, crying for Poppa.

It was bitter cold and the Boat Deck was filled with people, all rushing about, shouting, scrambling for the lifeboats, and, inevitably, those who had changed their minds at the last moment about going down with the ship were shouting the loudest, trying to be permitted into the boats, not one of which had been lowered yet. There were sixteen wooden lifeboats and four canvas Engelhardts, the collapsibles. But they could not be lowered away until the davits were cleared of the two forward boats. "We'll let you know when it's time to board," shouted an officer to the families crowding around him.

The floor was listing. Esme was late, and Stephen wasn't going to wait. At this rate, the ship would be bow down in the water in no time.

She must be with Michael, he thought. The little bastard has talked her into dying.

Michael had a stateroom on C-Deck. Stephen knocked, called to Michael and Esme, tried to open the door, and finally kicked the lock free.

Michael was sitting on the bed, which was a Pullman berth. His sister lay beside him, dead.

"Where's Esme?" Stephen said, repelled by the sight of Michael sitting so calmly beside his dead sister.

"Not here. Obviously." Michael smiled and made the rubber-lips face.

"Jesus," Stephen said. "Put your coat on, you're coming with me."

Michael laughed and patted down his hair. "I'm already dead, just like my sister, almost. I took a pill too, see?" He held up a small brown bottle. "Anyway, they wouldn't let me on a lifeboat. I didn't sign up for one, remember?"

"You're a baby– "

"I thought Poppa explained all that to you." Michael lay down beside his sister and watched Stephen like a puppy with its head cocked at an odd angle.

"You do know where Esme is, now tell me."

"You never understood her. She came here to die."

An instant later, Michael stopped breathing.

Stephen searched the ship, level by level, broke in on the parties where those who had opted for death were having a last fling, looking into the lounges where many old couples sat, waiting for the end. He made his way down to F-Deck, where he had made love to Esme in the Turkish bath. The water was up to his knees; it was green and soapy. He was afraid, for the list was becoming worse minute by minute. The water rose even as he walked.

He had to get to the stairs, had to get up and out, onto a lifeboat, away from the ship, but on he walked, looking for Esme, unable to stop. He had to find her. She might even be on the Boat Deck right now, he thought, wading through a corridor. But he had to satisfy himself that she wasn't down here.

The Turkish bath was filling with water, and the lights were still on, giving the room a ghostly illumination. Oddments floated in the room: blue slippers, a comb, scraps of paper, cigarettes, and several seamless, plastic packages.

On the farthest couch, Esme sat meditating, her eyes closed and hands folded on her lap. She wore a simple white dress. Overjoyed, he shouted to her. She jerked awake, looking disoriented, and without a word waded toward the other exit, dipping her hands into the water as if to speed her on her way.

"Esme, where are you going?" Stephen called, following. "Don't run from *me*."

An explosion pitched them both into the water and a wall gave way. A solid sheet of water seemed to be crashing into the room, smashing Stephen, pulling him under and sweeping him away. He fought to reach the surface and tried to swim back, to find Esme. A lamp broke away from the ceiling, just missing him. "Esme," he shouted, but he couldn't see her, and then he found himself choking, swimming, as the water carried him through a corridor and away from her.

Finally, Stephen was able to grab the iron curl of a railing and pull himself onto a dry step. There was another explosion, the floor pitched. He looked down at the water, which filled the corridor, the Turkish bath, the entire deck, and he screamed for Esme.

The ship shuddered, then everything was quiet. In the great rooms, chandeliers hung at angles; tables and chairs had skidded across the floors and seemed to squat against the walls like wooden beasts. Still the lights burned, as if all was quite correct, except gravity, which was misbehaving. Stephen walked and climbed, followed by the sea, as if in a dream.

Numbed, he found himself back on the Boat Deck. Part of the deck was already submerged. Almost everyone had moved aft, climbing uphill as the bow dipped farther into the water.

The lifeboats were gone, as were the crew. There were a few men and women atop of the officers' quarters. They were working hard, trying to launch Collapsibles C and D, their only chance of getting safely away from the ship.

"Hey," Stephen called to them, just now coming to his senses. "Do you need any help up there?"

He was ignored by those who were pushing one of the freed collapsibles off the port side of the roof. Someone shouted, "Damn!" The boat had landed upside down in the water.

"It's better than nothing," a woman shouted, and she and her friends jumped after the boat.

Stephen shivered; he was not yet ready to leap into the twenty-eight-degree water, although he knew there wasn't much time left, and he had to get away from the ship before it went down. Everyone on or close to the ship would be sucked under. He crossed to the starboard side, where some other men were trying to push the boat to the edge of the deck. The great ship was listing heavily to port.

This time Stephen just joined the work. No one complained. They were trying to slide the boat over the edge on planks. All these people looked to be in top physical shape – Stephen noticed that about half of them were women wearing the same warm coats as the men. This was a game to all of them, he suspected, and they were enjoying it. Each one was going to beat the odds, one way or another; the very thrill was to outwit fate, opt to die and yet survive.

But then the bridge was under water.

There was a terrible crashing and Stephen slid along the floor as everything tilted. Everyone was shouting. "She's going down!" someone screamed. Indeed, the stern of the ship was swinging upward. The lights flickered. there was a roar as the entrails of the ship broke loose: anchor chains, the huge engines and boilers. One of the huge, black funnels fell, smashing into the water amid sparks. But still the ship was brilliantly lit, every porthole afire. The crow's nest before him was almost submerged, but Stephen swam for it nevertheless. Then he caught himself and tried to swim away from the ship, but it was too late. He felt himself being sucked back, pulled under. He was being sucked into the ventilator, which was in front of the forward funnel; he gasped, swallowed water, and felt the wire mesh, the air-shaft grating that prevented him from being sucked under. He held his breath desperately.

Water was surging all around him, and then there was another explosion. Stephen felt warmth on his back, as a blast of hot air pushed him upward. Then he broke out into the freezing air. He swam for his life, away from the ship, away from the crashing and thudding of glass and wood, away from the debris of deck chairs, planking, and ropes, and especially away from the other people who were moaning, screaming at him, and trying to grab him as a buoy, trying to pull him down as the great ship sank.

Swimming, he heard voices nearby and saw a dark shape. For a moment it didn't register, then he realized that he was near an overturned lifeboat, the collapsible he had seen pushed into the water. There were almost thirty men and women standing on it. Stephen tried to climb aboard and someone shouted, "You'll sink us, we've too many already." A woman tried to hit Stephen with an oar, just missing his head. Stephen swam around to the other side of the boat. He grabbed hold again, found someone's foot, and was kicked back into the water.

"Come on," a man said, "take my arm and I'll pull you up."

'There's no *room!*" someone else said.

"There's enough room for one more."

"No there's not."

The boat began to rock.

"We'll all be in the water if we don't stop this," shouted the man who was holding Stephen afloat. Then he pulled Stephen aboard. He stood with the others; truly there was barely enough room. Everyone had formed a double line now, facing the bow, and leaned in the direction opposite the swells. Slowly the boat inched away from the site where the ship had gone down, away from the people in the water, all begging for life, for one last chance. As he looked back to where the ship had once been, Stephen thought of Esme. He couldn't bear to think of her as dead, floating through the corridors of the ship.

Those in the water could be easily heard; in fact the calls seemed magnified, as if meant to be heard clearly by everyone who was safe as a punishment for past sins.

"We're all deaders," said a woman standing beside Stephen. "I'm sure no one's coming to get us before dawn, when they have to pick up survivors."

"We'll be the last pickup, that's if they intend to pick us up at all."

"Those in the water have to get their money's worth. And since we opted for death– "

"I didn't," Stephen said, almost to himself.

"Well, you've got it anyway."

Stephen was numb but no longer cold. As if from far away, he heard the splash of someone falling from the boat, which was very slowly sinking as air was lost from under the hull. At times the water was up to Stephen's knees, yet he wasn't even shivering. Time distended or contracted. He measured it by the splashing of his companions as they fell overboard. He heard himself calling Esme, as if to say goodbye, or perhaps to greet her.

By dawn, Stephen was so muddled by the cold that he thought he was on land, for the sea was full of debris . . . cork, steamer chairs, boxes, pilasters, rugs, carved wood, clothes, and of course the bodies of those unfortunates who could not or would not survive – and the great icebergs and the smaller ones called growlers looked like cliffs and mountainsides. The icebergs were sparkling and many-hued, all brilliant in the light, as if painted by some cheerless Gauguin of the north.

"There," someone said, a woman's hoarse voice. "It's coming down, it's coming down!" The dirigible, looking like a huge white whale, seemed to be descending through its more natural element, water, rather than the thin, cold air. Its electric engines could not be heard.

In the distance, Stephen could see the other lifeboats. Soon the airship would begin to rescue those in the boats, which were now tied together in a cluster. As Stephen's thoughts wandered and his eyes watered from the reflected morning sunlight, he saw a piece of carved oak bobbing up and down near the boat, and noticed a familiar face in the debris that seemed to surround the lifeboat. There, just below the surface in his box, the lid open, eyes closed, floated Poppa. Poppa opened his eyes and looked at Stephen. Stephen screamed, lost his balance on the hull, and plunged like a knife into the cold black water.

The Laurel Lounge of the dirigible *California* was dark and filled with survivors. Some sat in the flowered, stuffed chairs; others just milled about. But they were all watching the lifelike, holographic tapes of the sinking of the *Titanic*. The images filled the large room.

Stephen stood in the back, away from the others who cheered each time there was a close-up of someone jumping overboard or slipping under the water. He pulled the scratchy woolen blanket around him and shivered. He had been on the dirigible for over twenty-four hours, and he was still chilled. A crewman had told him it was because of the injections he had received when he boarded the airship.

There was another cheer and, horrified, he saw that they were cheering for *him*. He watched himself being sucked into the ventilator and then blown upward to the surface. His body ached from the battering. But he had saved himself. He had survived and that had been an actual experience. It was worth it for that, but poor Esme . . .

"You had one of the *most* exciting experiences," a woman said to him as she touched his hand. He recoiled and she shrugged, then moved on.

"I wish to register a complaint," said a stocky man dressed in period clothing to one of the *Titanic* officers, who was standing beside Stephen and sipping a cocktail.

"Yes?"

"I was saved against my wishes. I specifically took this voyage that I might pit myself against the elements."

"Did you sign one of our protection waivers?"

"I was not aware that we were required to sign any such thing."

"All such information was provided," the officer said, looking disinterested. "Those passengers who are truly committed to taking their chances sign, and we leave them to their own devices. Otherwise, we are responsible for every passenger's life."

"I might just as well have jumped into the ocean at the beginning and gotten pulled out," the passenger said bitterly.

The officer smiled. "Most want to test themselves as long as they can. Of course, if you want to register a formal complaint . . ."

The passenger stomped away.

"The man's trying to save face," the officer said to Stephen. "We see quite a bit of that. But *you* seemed to have an interesting ride. You gave us quite a start; we thought you were going to take a lifeboat with the others, but you disappeared below deck. It was a bit more difficult to monitor you, but we managed – that's the fun for *us*. You were never in any danger, of course. Well, maybe a little."

Stephen was shaken. He had felt that his experiences had been authentic, that he had really saved himself. But none of that had been *real*. Only Esme . . .

And then he saw her step into the room.

"Esme?" He couldn't believe it. "Esme!"

She walked over to him and smiled as she had the first time they'd met. She was holding a water-damaged, cedar box. "Hello, Stephen. Wasn't it exciting?"

Stephen threw his arms around her, but she didn't respond. She waited a proper time, then disengaged herself.

"And look," she said, "they've even found Poppa." She opened the box and held it up to him.

Poppa's eyes fluttered open. For a moment his eyes were vague and unfocused, then they fastened on Esme and sharpened. "Esme . . ." Poppa said, uncertainly, and then he smiled. "Esme, I've had the strangest dream." He laughed. "I dreamed I was a head in a box . . ."

Esme snapped the box closed. "Isn't he marvelous?" she said. She patted the box and smiled. "He almost had me talked into going through with it this time."

LUCIUS SHEPARD
Salvador

Lucius Shepard was perhaps the most popular and influential new writer of the '80s, rivaled for that title only by William Gibson, Connie Willis, and Kim Stanley Robinson . . . and, as he is far more prolific than any of them, especially at shorter lengths, his impact on the short-fiction market of the decade was perhaps even more profound. In fact, pound for pound, Shepard may have produced the most vital and consistently excellent body of short work of the '80s, and may come to be seen as one of the best short-fiction writers ever to enter the field.

Shepard made his first sale to Terry Carr's *Universe* in 1983. That particular story attracted little notice at the time, but the floodgates were about to open, and the next seven years would see a steady stream of bizarre and powerfully compelling stories, such as the landmark novella "R&R," "The Jaguar Hunter," "Black Coral," "A Spanish Lesson," "The Man Who Painted the Dragon Griaule," "Shades," "Aymara," "A Traveler's Tale," "How the Wind Spoke at Madaket," "On the Border," "Fire Zone Emerald," and "The Scalehunter's Beautiful Daughter," among literally dozens of others . . . for even Shepard's second-rate tales are strong enough to serve as first-rate stuff for many another writer. The field had not seen such a concentrated outpouring of outstanding work from a single writer since Robert Silverberg's most prolific days in the early '70s.

Shepard's work is both nightmarish and hallucinatorily beautiful, a strange and contradictory mixture of wild romance, vivid eroticism, brutal violence, intricate metaphysical structures, radical politics, and intensely concentrated Lovecraftian horror – all peopled by low-life bums and winos and junkies who also turn out to be psychologically complex and broodingly introverted characters, and who often find themselves enmeshed in a desperate quest for personal transcendence. All this is frequently set in authentically described Third World milieus, often structured by an almost Victorian concern with personal ethics and moral responsibility, and expressed in a mannered, cadenced, complexly structured, formal prose that would probably be considered old-fashioned and fustian if it wasn't at the same time so vivid and supple.

The cyberpunks were so impressed with Shepard's dark power and political passion that they tried to co-opt him for the Movement for a while, in spite of the fact that he almost never writes about technology in any kind of really convincing way, and spends very little time speculating on the future effect of scientific principles or hardware on our lives. His *sociological* speculations, on the other hand, have often been brilliant, as witness the powerful little story that follows, one that shows us that we *do* learn something from the experience of war – the only question is, learn *what*?

Since Shepard began writing in 1983, no year since has gone by without him adorning the final ballot for one major award or another, and often for several. He won the John W. Campbell Award in 1985 as the year's Best New Writer. In 1987, he won the Nebula Award for his powerful novella "R & R," and in 1988 he picked up a World Fantasy Award for his monumental short-story collection *The Jaguar Hunter*, one of the most memorable collections of the '80s. He has had less impact at novel length, although his novels have been generally well-received. His first novel was *Green-Eyes*, published as part of the revived Ace Specials series; his second was the bestselling *Life During Wartime*, which was printed as non-SF, in spite of one of its sections having won a Nebula Award . . . which may be an indication of which way his novelistic career will go in the future. He is at work on several new novels. Born in Lynchburg, Virginia, he now lives somewhere in the wilds of Nantucket, Massachusetts.

Three weeks before they wasted Tecolutla, Dantzler had his baptism of fire. The platoon was crossing a meadow at the foot of an emerald-green volcano, and being a dreamy sort, he was idling along, swatting tall grasses with his rifle barrel and thinking how it might have been a first-grader with crayons who had devised this elementary landscape of a perfect cone rising into a cloudless sky, when cap-pistol noises sounded on the slope. Someone screamed for the medic, and Dantzler dove into the grass, fumbling for his ampules. He slipped one from the dispenser and popped it under his nose, inhaling frantically; then, to be on the safe side, he popped another – "A double helpin' of martial arts," as DT would say – and lay with his head down until the drugs had worked their magic. There was dirt in his mouth, and he was very afraid.

Gradually his arms and legs lost their heaviness, and his heart rate slowed. His vision sharpened to the point that he could see not only the pinpricks of fire blooming on the slope, but also the figures behind them, half-obscured by brush. A bubble of grim anger welled up in his brain, hardened to a fierce resolve, and he started moving towards the volcano. By the time he reached the base of the cone, he was all rage and reflexes. He spent the next forty minutes spinning acrobatically through the thickets, spraying shadows with bursts of his M-18; yet part of his mind remained distant from the action, marveling at his efficiency, at the comic-strip enthusiasm he felt for the task of killing. He shouted at the men he shot, and he shot them many more times than was necessary, like a child playing soldier.

"Playin' my ass!" DT would say. "You just actin' natural."

DT was a firm believer in the ampules; though the official line was that they contained tailored RNA compounds and pseudoendorphins modified to an inhalant form, he held the opinion that they opened a man up to his inner nature. He was big, black, with heavily muscled arms and crudely stamped features, and he had come to the Special Forces direct from prison, where he had done a stretch for attempted murder; the palms of his hands were covered by jail tattoos – a pentagram and a horned monster. The words DIE HIGH were painted on his helmet. This was his second tour in Salvador, and Moody – who was Dantzler's buddy – said the drugs had addled DT's brains, that he was crazy and gone to hell.

"He collects trophies," Moody had said. "And not just ears like they done in 'Nam."

When Dantzler had finally gotten a glimpse of the trophies, he had been appalled. They were kept in a tin box in DT's pack and were nearly unrecognizable; they looked like withered brown orchids. But despite his revulsion, despite the fact that he was afraid of DT, he admired the man's capacity for survival and had taken to heart his advice to rely on the drugs.

On the way back down the slope they discovered a live casualty, an Indian kid about Dantzler's age, nineteen or twenty. Black hair, adobe skin, and heavy-lidded brown eyes. Dantzler, whose father was an anthropologist and had done fieldwork in Salvador, figured him for a Santa Ana tribesman; before leaving the States, Dantzler had pored over his father's notes, hoping this would give him an edge, and had learned to identify the various regional types. The kid had a minor leg wound and was wearing fatigue pants and a faded COKE ADDS LIFE T-shirt. This T-shirt irritated DT no end.

"What the hell you know 'bout Coke?" he asked the kid as they headed for the chopper that was to carry them deeper into Morazán Province. "You think it's funny or somethin'?" He whacked the kid in the back with his rifle butt, and when they reached the chopper, he slung him inside and had him sit by the door. He sat beside him, tapped out a joint from a pack of Kools, and asked, "Where's Infante?"

"Dead," said the medic.

"Shit!" DT licked the joint so it would burn evenly. "Goddamn beaner ain't no use 'cept somebody else know Spanish."

"I know a little," Dantzler volunteered.

Staring at Dantzler, DT's eyes went empty and unfocused. "Naw," he said. "You don't know no Spanish."

Dantzler ducked his head to avoid DT's stare and said nothing; he thought he understood what DT meant, but he ducked away from the understanding as well. The chopper bore them aloft, and DT lit the joint. He let the smoke out his nostrils and passed the joint to the kid, who accepted gratefully.

"*Qué sabor!*" he said, exhaling a billow; he smiled and nodded, wanting to be friends.

Dantzler turned his gaze to the open door. They were flying low between the hills, and looking at the deep bays of shadow in their folds acted to drain away the residue of the drugs, leaving him weary and frazzled. Sunlight poured in, dazzling the oil-smeared floor.

"Hey, Dantzler!" DT had to shout over the noise of the rotors. "Ask him whass his name!"

The kid's eyelids were drooping from the joint, but on hearing Spanish he perked up; he shook his head, though, refusing to answer. Dantzler smiled and told him not to be afraid.

"Ricardo Quu," said the kid.

"Kool!" said DT with false heartiness. "Thass my brand!" He offered his pack to the kid.

"*Gracias*, no." The kid waved the joint and grinned.

"Dude's named for a goddamn cigarette," said DT disparagingly, as if this were the height of insanity.

Dantzler asked the kid if there were more soldiers nearby, and once again received no reply; but, apparently sensing in Dantzler a kindred soul, the kid leaned forward and spoke rapidly, saying that his village was Santander Jiménez, that his father was – he hesitated – a man of power. He asked where they were taking him. Dantzler returned a stony glare. He found it easy to reject the kid, and he realized later this was because he had already given up on him.

Latching his hands behind his head, DT began to sing – a wordless melody. His voice was discordant, barely audible above the rotors; but the tune had a familiar ring and Dantzler soon placed it. The theme from "Star Trek." It brought back memories of watching TV with his sister, laughing at the low-budget aliens and Scotty's Actors' Equity accent. He gazed out the door again. The sun was behind the hills, and the hillsides were unfeatured blurs of dark green smoke. Oh, God, he wanted to be home, to be anywhere but Salvador! A couple of the guys joined in the singing at DT's urging, and as the volume swelled, Dantzler's emotion peaked. He was on the verge of tears, remembering tastes and sights, the way his girl Jeanine had smelled, so clean and fresh, not reeking of sweat and perfume like the whores around Ilopango – finding all this substance in the banal touchstone of his culture and the illusions of the hillsides rushing past. Then Moody tensed beside him, and he glanced up to learn the reason why.

In the gloom of the chopper's belly, DT was as unfeatured as the hills – a black presence ruling them, more the leader of a coven than a platoon. The other two guys were singing their lungs out, and even the kid was getting into the spirit of things. "*Música!*" he said at one point, smiling at everybody, trying to fan the flame of good feeling. He swayed to the rhythm and essayed a "la-la" now and again. But no one else was responding.

The singing stopped, and Dantzler saw that the whole platoon was staring at the kid, their expressions slack and dispirited.

"Space!" shouted DT, giving the kid a little shove. "The final frontier!"

The smile had not yet left the kid's face when he toppled out the door. DT peered after him; a few seconds later he smacked his hand against the floor and sat back, grinning. Dantzler felt like screaming, the stupid horror of the joke was so at odds with the languor of his homesickness. He looked to the others for reaction. They were sitting with their heads down, fiddling with trigger guards and pack straps, studying their bootlaces, and seeing this, he quickly imitated them.

Morazán Province was spook country. Santa Ana spooks. Flights of birds had been reported to attack patrols; animals appeared at the perimeters of campsites and vanished when you shot at them; dreams afflicted everyone who ventured there. Dantzler could not testify to the birds and animals, but he did have a recurring dream. In it the kid DT had killed was pinwheeling down through a golden fog, his T-shirt visible against the roiling back-drop, and sometimes a voice would boom out of the fog, saying, "You are killing my son." No, no, Dantzler would reply, it wasn't me, and besides, he's already dead. Then he would wake covered with sweat, groping for his rifle, his heart racing.

But the dream was not an important terror, and he assigned it no significance. The land was far more terrifying. Pine-forested ridges that stood out against the sky like fringes of electrified hair; little trails winding off into thickets and petering out, as if what they led to had been magicked away; gray rock faces along which they were forced to walk, hopelessly exposed to ambush. There were innumerable booby traps set by the guerrillas, and they lost several men to rockfalls. It was the emptiest place of Dantzler's experience. No people, no animals, just a few hawks circling the solitudes between the ridges. Once in a while they found tunnels, and these they blew with the new gas grenades; the gas ignited the rich concentrations of hydrocarbons and sent flame sweeping through the entire system. DT would praise whoever had discovered the tunnel and would estimate in a loud voice how many beaners they had "refried." But Dantzler knew they were traversing pure emptiness and burning empty holes. Days, under debilitating heat, they humped the mountains, traveling seven, eight, even ten klicks up trails so steep that frequently the feet of the guy ahead of you would be on a level with your face; nights, it was cold, the darkness absolute, the silence so profound that Dantzler imagined he could hear the great humming vibration of the earth. They might have been anywhere or nowhere. Their fear was nourished by the isolation, and the only remedy was "martial arts."

Dantzler took to popping the pills without the excuse of combat. Moody cautioned him against abusing the drugs, citing rumors of bad side effects and DT's madness; but even he was using them more and more often. During basic training, Dantzler's DI had told the boots that the drugs were available only to the Special Forces, that their use was optional; but there had been too many instances of lackluster battlefield performance in the last war, and this was to prevent a reoccurrence.

"The chickenshit infantry take 'em," the DI had said. "You bastards are brave already. You're born killers, right?"

"Right, sir!" they had shouted.

"What are you?"

"Born killers, sir!"

But Dantzler was not a born killer; he was not even clear as to how he had been drafted, less clear as to how he had been manipulated into the Special Forces, and he had learned that nothing was optional in Salvador, with the possible exception of life itself.

The platoon's mission was reconnaissance and mop-up. Along with other Special Forces platoons, they were to secure Morazán prior to the invasion of Nicaragua; specifically, they were to proceed to the village of Tecolutla, where a Sandinista patrol had recently been spotted, and following that they were to join up with the First Infantry and take part in the offensive against León, a provincial capital just across the Nicaraguan border. As Dantzler and Moody walked together, they frequently talked about the offensive, how it would be good to get down into flat country; occasionally they talked about the possibility of reporting DT, and once, after he had led them on a forced night march, they toyed with the idea of killing him. But most often they discussed the ways of the Indians and the land, since this was what had caused them to become buddies.

Moody was slightly built, freckled, and red-haired; his eyes had the "thousand-yard stare" that came from too much war. Dantzler had seen winos with such vacant, lusterless stares. Moody's father had been in 'Nam, and Moody said it had been worse than Salvador because there had been no real commitment to win; but he thought Nicaragua and Guatemala might be the worst of all, especially if the Cubans sent in troops as they had threatened. He was adept at locating tunnels and detecting booby traps, and it was for this reason Dantzler had cultivated his friendship. Essentially a loner, Moody had resisted all advances until learning of Dantzler's father; thereafter he had buddied up, eager to hear about the field notes, believing they might give him an edge.

"They think the land has animal traits," said Dantzler one day as they climbed along a ridgetop. "Just like some kinds of fish look like plants or sea bottom, parts of the land look like plain ground, jungle . . . whatever. But when you enter them, you find you've entered the spirit world, the world of *Sukias*."

"What's *Sukias?*" asked Moody.

"Magicians." A twig snapped behind Dantzler, and he spun around, twitching off the safety of his rifle. It was only Hodge – a lanky kid with the beginnings of a beer gut. He stared hollow-eyed at Dantzler and popped an ampule.

Moody made a noise of disbelief. "If they got magicians, why ain't they winnin'? Why ain't they zappin' us off the cliffs?"

"It's not their business," said Dantzler. "They don't believe in messing with worldly affairs unless it concerns them directly. Anyway, these places – the ones that look like normal land but aren't – they're called. . . ." He drew a blank on the name. "*Aya*-something. I can't remember. But they have different laws. They're where your spirit goes to die after your body dies."

"Don't they got no Heaven?"

"Nope. It just takes longer for your spirit to die, and so it goes to one of these places that's between everything and nothing."

"Nothin'," said Moody disconsolately, as if all his hopes for an afterlife had been dashed. "Don't make no sense to have spirits and not have no Heaven."

"Hey," said Dantzler, tensing as wind rustled the pine boughs. "They're just a bunch of damn primitives. You know what their sacred drink is? Hot chocolate! My old man was a guest at one of their funerals, and he said they carried cups of hot chocolate balanced on these little red towers and acted like drinking it was going to wake them to the secrets of the universe." He laughed, and the laughter sounded tinny and psychotic to his own ears. "So you're going to worry about fools who think hot chocolate's holy water?"

"Maybe they just like it," said Moody. "Maybe somebody dyin' just give 'em an excuse to drink it."

But Dantzler was no longer listening. A moment before, as they emerged from pine cover onto the highest point of the ridge, a stony scarp open to the winds and providing a view of rumpled mountains and valleys extending to the horizon, he had popped an ampule. He felt so strong, so full of righteous purpose and controlled fury, it seemed only the sky was around him, that he was still ascending, preparing to do battle with the gods themselves.

Tecolutla was a village of whitewashed stone tucked into a notch between two hills. From above, the houses – with their shadow-blackened windows and doorways – looked like an

unlucky throw of dice. The streets ran uphill and down,
diverging around boulders. Bougainvilleas and hibiscuses
speckled the hillsides, and there were tilled fields on the
gentler slopes. It was a sweet, peaceful place when they
arrived, and after they had gone it was once again peaceful;
but its sweetness had been permanently banished. The
reports of Sandinistas had proved accurate, and though they
were casualties left behind to recuperate, DT had decided
their presence called for extreme measures. Fu gas, frag
grenades, and such. He had fired an M-60 until the barrel
melted down, and then had manned the flamethrower.
Afterward, as they rested atop the next ridge, exhausted and
begrimed, having radioed in a chopper for resupply, he
could not get over how one of the houses he had torched had
come to resemble a toasted marshmallow.

"Ain't that how it was, man?" he asked, striding up and
down the line. He did not care if they agreed about the house;
it was a deeper question he was asking, one concerning the
ethics of their actions.

"Yeah," said Dantzler, forcing a smile. "Sure did."

DT grunted with laughter. "You *know* I'm right, don'tcha
man?"

The sun hung directly behind his head, a golden corona
rimming a black oval, and Dantzler could not turn his eyes
away. He felt weak and weakening, as if threads of himself
were being spun loose and sucked into the blackness. He had
popped three ampules prior to the firefight, and his experience of Tecolutla had been a kind of mad whirling dance
through the streets, spraying erratic bursts that appeared to
be writing weird names on the walls. The leader of the
Sandinistas had worn a mask – a gray face with a surprised
hole of a mouth and pink circles around the eyes. A ghost
face. Dantzler had been afraid of the mask and had poured
round after round into it. Then, leaving the village, he had
seen a small girl standing beside the shell of the last house,
watching them, her colorless rag of a dress tattering in the
breeze. She had been a victim of that malnutrition disease,
the one that paled your skin and whitened your hair and left
you retarded. He could not recall the name of the disease –
things like names were slipping away from him – nor could

he believe anyone had survived, and for a moment he had thought the spirit of the village had come out to mark their trail.

That was all he could remember of Tecolutla, all he wanted to remember. But he knew he had been brave.

Four days later, they headed up into a cloud forest. It was the dry season, but dry season or not, blackish gray clouds always shrouded these peaks. They were shot through by ugly glimmers of lightning, making it seem that malfunctioning neon signs were hidden beneath them, advertisements for evil. Everyone was jittery, and Jerry LeDoux – a slim dark-haired Cajun kid – flat-out refused to go.

"It ain't reasonable," he said. "Be easier to go through the passes."

"We're on recon, man! You think the beaners be waitin' in the passes, wavin' their white flags?" DT whipped his rifle into firing position and pointed it at LeDoux. "C'mon, Louisiana man. Pop a few, and you feel different."

As LeDoux popped the ampules, DT talked to him.

"Look at it this way, man. This is your big adventure. Up there it be like all them animal shows on the tube. The savage kingdom, the unknown. Could be like Mars or somethin'. Monsters and shit, with big red eyes and tentacles. You wanna miss that, man? You wanna miss bein' the first grunt on Mars?"

Soon LeDoux was raring to go, giggling at DT's rap.

Moody kept his mouth shut, but he fingered the safety of his rifle and glared at DT's back. When DT turned to him, however, he relaxed. Since Tecolutla he had grown taciturn, and there seemed to be a shifting of lights and darks in his eyes, as if something were scurrying back and forth behind them. He had taken to wearing banana leaves on his head, arranging them under his helmet so the frayed ends stuck out the side like strange green hair. He said this was camouflage, but Dantzler was certain it bespoke some secretive irrational purpose. Of course DT had noticed Moody's spiritual erosion, and as they prepared to move out, he called Dantzler aside.

"He done found someplace inside his head that feel good

to him," said DT. "He's tryin' to curl up into it, and once he do that he ain't gon' be responsible. Keep an eye on him."

Dantzler mumbled his assent, but was not enthused.

"I know he your fren', man, but that don't mean shit. Not the way things are. Now me, I don't give a damn 'bout you personally. But I'm your brother-in-arms, and thass somethin' you can count on . . . y'understand."

To Dantzler's shame, he did understand.

They had planned on negotiating the cloud forest by nightfall, but they had underestimated the difficulty. The vegetation beneath the clouds was lush – thick, juicy leaves that mashed underfoot, tangles of vines, trees with slick, pale bark and waxy leaves – and the visibility was only about fifteen feet. They were gray wraiths passing through grayness. The vague shapes of the foliage reminded Dantzler of fancifully engraved letters, and for a while he entertained himself with the notion that they were walking among the half-formed phrases of a constitution not yet manifest in the land. They barged off the trail, losing it completely, becoming veiled in spiderwebs and drenched by spills of water; their voices were oddly muffled, the tag ends of words swallowed up. After seven hours of this, DT reluctantly gave the order to pitch camp. They set electric lamps around the perimeter so they could see to string the jungle hammocks; the beam of light illuminated the moisture in the air, piercing the murk with jeweled blades. They talked in hushed tones, alarmed by the eerie atmosphere. When they had done with the hammocks, DT posted four sentries – Moody, LeDoux, Dantzler, and himself. Then they switched off the lamps.

It grew pitch-dark, and the darkness was picked out by plips and plops, the entire spectrum of dripping sounds. To Dantzler's ears they blended into a gabbling speech. He imagined tiny Santa Ana demons talking about him, and to stave off paranoia he popped two ampules. He continued to pop them, trying to limit himself to one every half hour; but he was uneasy, unsure where to train his rifle in the dark, and he exceeded his limit. Soon it began to grow light again, and he assumed that more time had passed than he had thought. That often happened with the ampules – it was easy to lose yourself in being alert, in the wealth of perceptual detail available to your sharpened senses. Yet on checking his watch, he saw it was only a few minutes after two o'clock. His system was too inundated with the drugs to allow panic, but he twitched his head from side to side in tight little arcs to determine the source of the brightness. There did not appear to be a single source; it was simply that filaments of the cloud were gleaming, casting a diffuse golden glow, as if they were elements of a nervous system coming to life. He started to call out, then held back. The others must have seen the light, and they had given no cry; they probably had a good reason for their silence. He scrunched down flat, pointing his rifle out from the campsite.

Bathed in the golden mist, the forest had acquired an alchemic beauty. Beads of water glittered with gemmy brilliance; the leaves and vines and bark were gilded. Every surface shimmered with light . . . everything except a fleck of blackness hovering between two of the trunks, its size gradually increasing. As it swelled in his vision, he saw it had the shape of a bird, its wings beating, flying toward him from an inconceivable distance – inconceivable, because the dense vegetation did not permit you to see very far in a straight line, and yet the bird was growing larger with such slowness that it must have been coming from a long way off. It was not really flying, he realized; rather, it was as if the forest were painted on a piece of paper, as if someone were holding a lit match behind it and burning a hole, a hole that maintained the shape of a bird as it spread. He was transfixed, unable to react. Even when it had blotted out half the light, when he lay before it no bigger than a mote in relation to its huge span, he could not move or squeeze the trigger. And then the blackness swept over him. He had the sensation of being borne along at incredible speed, and he could no longer hear the dripping of the forest.

"Moody!" he shouted. "DT!"

But the voice that answered belonged to neither of them. It was hoarse, issuing from every part of the surrounding blackness, and he recognized it as the voice of his recurring dream.

"You are killing my son," it said. "I have led you here, to this *ayahuamaco*, so he may judge you."

Dantzler knew to his bones the voice was that of the Sukia of the village of Santander Jiménez. He wanted to offer a denial, to explain his innocence, but all he could manage was, "No." He said it tearfully, hopelessly, his forehead resting on his rifle barrel. Then his mind gave a savage twist, and his soldiery self regained control. He ejected an ampule from his dispenser and popped it.

The voice laughed – malefic, damning laughter whose vibrations shuddered Dantzler. He opened up with the rifle, spraying fire in all directions. Filigrees of golden holes appeared in the blackness, tendrils of mist coiled through them. He kept on firing until the blackness shattered and fell in jagged sections toward him. Slowly. Like shards of black glass dropping through water. He emptied the rifle and flung himself flat, shielding his head with his arms, expecting to be sliced into bits; but nothing touched him. At last he peeked between his arms; then – amazed, because the forest was now a uniform lustrous yellow – he rose to his knees. He scraped his hands on one of the crushed leaves beneath him, and blood welled from the cut. The broken fibers of the leaf were as stiff as wires. He stood, a giddy trickle of hysteria leaking up from the bottom of his soul. It was no forest, but a building of solid gold worked to resemble a forest – the sort of conceit that might have been fabricated for the child of an emperor. Canopied by golden leaves, columned by slender golden trunks, carpeted by golden grasses. The water beads were diamonds. All the gleam and glitter soothed his apprehension; here was something out of a myth, a habitat for princesses and wizards and dragons. Almost gleeful, he turned to the campsite to see how the others were reacting.

Once, when he was nine years old, he had sneaked into the attic to rummage through the boxes and trunks, and he had run across an old morocco-bound copy of *Gulliver's Travels*. He had been taught to treasure old books, and so he had opened it eagerly to look at the illustrations, only to find that the centers of the pages had been eaten away, and there, right in the heart of the fiction, was a nest of larvae. Pulpy, horrid things. It had been an awful sight, but one unique in his experience, and he might have studied those crawling scraps of life for a very long time if his father had not interrupted. Such a sight was now before him, and he was numb with it.

They were all dead. He should have guessed they would be; he had given no thought to them while firing his rifle. They had been struggling out of their hammocks when the bullets hit, and as a result they were hanging half-in, half-out, their limbs dangling, blood pooled beneath them. The veils of golden mist made them look dark and mysterious and malformed, like monsters killed as they emerged from their cocoons. Dantzler could not stop staring, but he was shrinking inside himself. It was not his fault. That thought kept swooping in and out of a flock of less acceptable thoughts; he wanted it to stay put, to be true, to alleviate the sick horror he was beginning to feel.

"What's your name?" asked a girl's voice behind him.

She was sitting on a stone about twenty feet away. Her hair was a tawny shade of gold, her skin a half-tone lighter, and her dress was cunningly formed out of the mist. Only her eyes were real. Brown heavy-lidded eyes – they were at variance with the rest of her face, which had the fresh, unaffected beauty of an American teenager.

"Don't be afraid," she said, and patted the ground, inviting him to sit beside her.

He recognized the eyes, but it was no matter. He badly needed the consolation she could offer; he walked over and sat down. She let him lean his head against her thigh.

"What's your name?" she repeated.

"Dantzler," he said. "John Dantzler." And then he added, "I'm from Boston. My father's . . ." It would be too difficult to explain about anthropology. "He's a teacher."

"Are there many soldiers in Boston?" She stroked his cheek with a golden finger.

The caress made Dantzler happy. "Oh, no," he said. "They hardly know there's a war going on."

"This is true?" she said, incredulous.

"Well, they *do* know about it, but it's just news on the TV to them. They've got more pressing problems. Their jobs, families."

"Will you let them know about the war when you return home?" she asked. "Will you do that for me?"

Dantzler had given up hope of returning home, of surviving, and her assumption that he would do both acted to awaken his gratitude. "Yes," he said fervently. "I will."

"You must hurry," she said. "If you stay in the *ayahuamaco* too long, you will never leave. You must find the way out. It is a way not of directions or trails, but of events."

"Where is this place?" he asked, suddenly aware of how much he had taken it for granted.

She shifted her leg away, and if he had not caught himself on the stone, he would have fallen. When he looked up, she had vanished. He was surprised that her disappearance did not alarm him; in reflex he slipped out a couple of ampules, but after a moment's reflection he decided not to use them. It was impossible to slip them back into the dispenser, so he tucked them into the interior webbing of his helmet for later. He doubted he would need them, though. He felt strong, competent and unafraid.

Dantzler stepped carefully between the hammocks; not wanting to brush against them; it might have been his imagination, but they seemed to be bulged down lower than before, as if death had weighed out heavier than life. That heaviness was in the air, pressuring him. Mist rose like golden steam from the corpses, but the sight no longer affected him – perhaps because the mist gave the illusion of being their souls. He picked up a rifle with a full magazine and headed off into the forest.

The tips of the golden leaves were sharp, and he had to ease past them to avoid being cut; but he was at the top of his form, moving gracefully, and the obstacles barely slowed his pace. He was not even anxious about the girl's warning to hurry; he was certain the way out would soon present itself. After a minute or so he heard voices, and after another few seconds he came to a clearing divided by a stream, one so perfectly reflecting that its banks appeared to enclose a wedge of golden mist. Moody was squatting to the left of the stream, staring at the blade of his survival knife and singing under his breath – a wordless melody that had the erratic rhythm of a trapped fly. Beside him lay Jerry LeDoux, his throat slashed from ear to ear. DT was sitting on the other side of the stream; he had been shot just above the knee, and though he had ripped up his shirt for bandages and tied off the leg with a tourniquet, he was not in good shape. He was sweating, and a gray chalky pallor infused his skin. The entire scene had the weird vitality of something that had materialized in a magic mirror, a bubble of reality enclosed within a gilt frame.

DT heard Dantzler's footfalls and glanced up. "Waste him!" he shouted, pointing to Moody.

Moody did not turn from contemplation of the knife. "No," he said, as if speaking to someone whose image was held in the blade.

"Waste him, man!" screamed DT. "He killed LeDoux!"

"Please," said Moody to the knife. "I don't want to."

There was blood clotted on his face, more blood on the banana leaves sticking out of his helmet.

"Did you kill Jerry?" asked Dantzler; while he addressed the question to Moody, he did not relate to him as an individual, only as part of a design whose message he had to unravel.

"Jesus Christ! Waste him!" DT smashed his fist against the ground in frustration.

"Okay," said Moody. With an apologetic look, he sprang to his feet and charged Dantzler, swinging the knife.

Emotionless, Dantzler stitched a line of fire across Moody's chest; he went sideways into the bushes and down.

"What the hell was you waitin' for!" DT tried to rise, but winced and fell back. "Damn! Don't know if I can walk."

"Pop a few," Dantzler suggested mildly.

"Yeah. Good thinkin', man." DT fumbled for his dispenser.

Dantzler peered into the bushes to see where Moody had fallen. He felt nothing, and this pleased him. He was weary of feeling.

DT popped an ampule with a flourish, as if making a toast, and inhaled. "Ain't you gon' to do some, man?"

"I don't need them," said Dantzler. "I'm fine."

The stream interested him; it did not reflect the mist, as he had supposed, but was itself a seam of the mist.

"How many you think they was?" asked DT.

"How many what?"

"Beaners, man! I wasted three or four after they hit us, but I couldn't tell how many they was."

Dantzler considered this in light of his own interpretation of events and Moody's conversation with the knife. It made sense. A Santa Ana kind of sense.

"Beats me," he said. "But I guess there's less than there used to be."

DT snorted. "You got *that* right!" He heaved to his feet and limped to the edge of the stream. "Gimme a hand across."

Dantzler reached out to him, but instead of taking his hand, he grabbed his wrist and pulled him off-balance. DT teetered on his good leg, then toppled and vanished beneath the mist. Dantzler had expected him to fall, but he surfaced instantly, mist clinging to his skin. Of course, thought Dantzler; his body would have to die before his spirit would fall.

"What you doin', man?" DT was more disbelieving than enraged.

Dantzler planted a foot in the middle of his back and pushed him down until his head was submerged. DT bucked and clawed at the foot and managed to come to his hands and knees. Mist slithered from his eyes, his nose, and he choked out the words ". . . kill you. . . ." Dantzler pushed him down again; he got into pushing him down and letting him up, over and over. Not so as to torture him. Not really. It was because he had suddenly understood the nature of the *ayahuamaco's* laws, that they were approximations of normal laws, and he further understood that his actions had to approximate those of someone jiggling a key in a lock. DT was the key to the way out, and Dantzler was jiggling him, making sure all the tumblers were engaged.

Some of the vessels in DT's eyes had burst, and the whites were occluded by films of blood. When he tried to speak, mist curled from his mouth. Gradually his struggles subsided; he clawed runnels in the gleaming yellow dirt of the bank and shuddered. His shoulders were knobs of black land foundering in a mystic sea.

For a long time after DT sank from view, Dantzler stood

beside the stream, uncertain of what was left to do and unable to remember a lesson he had been taught. Finally he shouldered his rifle and walked away from the clearing. Morning had broken, the mist had thinned, and the forest had regained its usual coloration. But he scarcely noticed these changes, still troubled by his faulty memory. Eventually, he let it slide – it would all come clear sooner or later. He was just happy to be alive. After a while he began to kick the stones as he went, and to swing his rifle in a carefree fashion against the weeds.

When the First Infantry poured across the Nicaraguan border and wasted León, Dantzler was having a quiet time at the VA hospital in Ann Arbor, Michigan; and at the precise moment the bulletin was flashed nationwide, he was sitting in the lounge, watching the American League playoffs between Detroit and Texas. Some of the patients ranted at the interruption, while others shouted them down, wanting to hear the details. Dantzler expressed no reaction whatsoever. He was solely concerned with being a model patient; however, noticing that one of the staff was giving him a clinical stare, he added his weight on the side of the baseball fans. He did not want to appear too controlled. The doctors were as suspicious of that sort of behavior as they were of its contrary. But the funny thing was – at least it was funny to Dantzler – that his feigned annoyance at the bulletin was an exemplary proof of his control, his expertise at moving through life the way he had moved through the golden leaves of the cloud forest. Cautiously, gracefully, efficiently. Touching nothing, and being touched by nothing. That was the lesson he had learned – to be as perfect a counterfeit of a man as the *ayahuamaco* had been of the land; to adopt the various stances of a man, and yet, by virtue of his distance from things human, to be all the more prepared for the onset of crisis or a call to action. He saw nothing aberrant in this; even the doctors would admit that men were little more than organized pretense. If he was different from other men, it was only that he had a deeper awareness of the principles on which his personality was founded.

When the battle of Managua was joined, Dantzler was

living at home. His parents had urged him to go easy in readjusting to civilian life, but he had immediately gotten a job as a management trainee in a bank. Each morning he would drive to work and spend a controlled, quiet eight hours; each night he would watch TV with his mother, and before going to bed, he would climb to the attic and inspect the trunk containing his souvenirs of war – helmet, fatigues, knife, boots. The doctors had insisted he face his experiences, and this ritual was his way of following their instructions. All in all, he was quite pleased with his progress, but he still had problems. He had not been able to force himself to venture out at night, remembering too well the darkness in the cloud forest, and he had rejected his friends, refusing to see them or answer their calls – he was not secure with the idea of friendship. Further, despite his methodical approach to life, he was prone to a nagging restlessness, the feeling of a chore left undone.

One night his mother came into his room and told him that an old friend, Phil Curry, was on the phone. "Please talk to him, Johnny," she said. "He's been drafted, and I think he's a little scared."

The word *drafted* struck a responsive chord in Dantzler's soul, and after brief deliberation he went downstairs and picked up the receiver.

"Hey," said Phil. "What's the story, man? Three months, and you don't even give me a call."

"I'm sorry," said Dantzler. "I haven't been feeling so hot."

"Yeah, I understand." Phil was silent a moment. "Listen, man. I'm leavin', y'know, and we're havin' a big send-off at Sparky's. It's goin' on right now. Why don't you come down?"

"I don't know."

"Jeanine's here, man. Y'know, she's still crazy 'bout you, talks 'bout you alla time. She don't go out with nobody."

Dantzler was unable to think of anything to say.

"Look," said Phil, "I'm pretty weirded out by this soldier shit. I hear it's pretty bad down there. If you got anything you can tell me 'bout what it's like, man, I'd 'preciate it."

Dantzler could relate to Phil's concern, his desire for an

edge, and besides, it felt right to go. Very right. He would take some precautions against the darkness.

"I'll be there," he said.

It was a foul night, spitting snow, but Sparky's parking lot was jammed. Dantzler's mind was flurried like the snow, crowded like the lot – thoughts whirling in, jockeying for position, melting away. He hoped his mother would not wait up, he wondered if Jeanine still wore her hair long, he was worried because the palms of his hands were unnaturally warm. Even with the car windows rolled up, he could hear loud music coming from inside the club. Above the door the words SPARKY'S ROCK CITY were being spelled out a letter at a time in red neon, and when the spelling was complete, the letters flashed off and on and a golden neon explosion bloomed around them. After the explosion, the entire sign went dark for a split second, and the big ramshackle building seemed to grow large and merge with the black sky. He had an idea it was watching him, and he shuddered – one of those sudden lurches downward of the kind that take you just before you fall asleep. He knew the people inside did not intend him any harm, but he also knew that places have a way of changing people's intent, and he did not want to be caught off-guard. Sparky's might be such a place, might be a huge black presence camouflaged by neon, its true substance one with the abyss of the sky, the phosphorescent snow-flakes, jittering in his headlights, the wind keening through the side vent. He would have liked very much to drive home and forget about his promise to Phil; however, he felt a responsibility to explain about the war. More than a responsibility, an evangelistic urge. He would tell them about the kid falling out of the chopper, the white-haired girl in Tecolutla, the emptiness. God, yes! How you went down chock-full of ordinary American thoughts and dreams, memories of smoking weed and chasing tail and hanging out and freeway flying with a case of something cold, and how you smuggled back a human-shaped container of pure Salvadorian emptiness. Primo grade. Smuggled it back to the land of silk and money, of mindfuck video games and topless tennis matches and fast-food solutions to the nutritional problem. Just a taste of Salvador would banish all those trivial obsessions. Just a taste. It would be easy to explain.

Of course, some things beggared explanation.

He bent down and adjusted the survival knife in his boot so the hilt would not rub against his calf. From the coat pocket he withdrew the two ampules he had secreted in his helmet that long-ago night in the cloud forest. As the neon explosion flashed once more, glimmers of gold coursed along their shiny surfaces. He did not think he would need them; his hand was steady, and his purpose was clear. But to be on the safe side, he popped them both.

PAT CADIGAN

Pretty Boy Crossover

One of the most brilliant and versatile of all the decade's new writers, Pat Cadigan remains underappreciated to date, in spite of the fact that she is responsible for some of the best short work done by anybody in the '80s.

Cadigan first came to the attention of the SF world as co-editor, along with husband Arnie Fenner, of the long-running semiprozine *Shayol*, perhaps the best of the semiprozines of the late '70s and early '80s; it was honored with a World Fantasy Award in the "Special Achievement, Non-Professional" category in 1981. She made her first professional sale in 1980 to *New Dimensions*, and soon her jazzy, elegant, and incisive stories were turning up with some frequency in magazines like *Omni*, *The Magazine of Fantasy and Science Fiction*, and *Isaac Asimov's Science Fiction Magazine*, as well as in horror markets like *Shadows*, *Fears*, *The Twilight Zone Magazine*, *Ripper!* and *Tropical Chills*.

This wideness of range, in fact, may go a long way toward explaining why she is underappreciated. If you look only at her body of supernatural horror tales, stuff like "The Boys in the Rain," "Two," "The Pond," "The Edge," "My Brother's Keeper," "The Power and the Passion," and "It Was the Heat," you could make a pretty good argument that she was one of the rising young stars of the horror genre. But then, you look at all the pure-quill *science fiction* she's written, much of it hard science fiction, at that . . . and *then* someone points out all the stuff by her that's hard to categorize at all, stories like "Second Comings – Reasonable Rates," "The Coming of the Doll," "Another One Hits the Road," "The Day the Martels Got the Cable." Fantasy? Surrealism? Magic Realism? No, it's been my experience that the harder a writer is to critically pigeonhole, the easier that writer is to ignore; this is a problem Cadigan shares with a number of other writers who refuse to stick within strict genre boundaries, or, worse, write unclassifiable stuff that blurs the distinctions between several genres – Cadigan does both.

Within the SF field itself, Cadigan was best known in the mid-'80s for her sequence of hard-edged and elegant stories about "Deadpan Allie," a sort of high-tech psychoanalyst of the future who can hook directly into another person's mind to seek out the root causes of their psychological troubles; these stories were melded into her well-received first novel, *Mindplayers*. Toward the end of the '80s, however, she began to produce work a quantum jump better than even her previous high standard, one of them the amazing story that follows, "Pretty Boy Crossover," to my mind one of the very best stories of the decade.

Besides being stylish, intelligent, and vivid, and accomplishing the difficult feat of being simultaneously compassionate *and* hard-edged, the best of Cadigan's short works are marvels of compression and economy, with hardly a wasted word or an ounce of fat. At a time when the bookstore shelves are groaning with bloated and hugely padded four hundred-page novels that would have worked better as novelettes instead, Cadigan – in stories like "Pretty Boy Crossover," "Rock On," and "Angel" – is creating new and unique future societies, jam-packed with enough new ideas and background concepts and colorful bits of business for a four-hundred-page novel, and doing it all within the confines of four-thousand-word short stories. I suspect that Tiptree, who always admired elegance combined with a high-bit rate, and who had an absolute horror of padding, would have approved . . . and, in fact, much of Cadigan's work reminds me strongly of Tiptree.

(Speaking of Tiptree, it annoys me that several critics have ignored Cadigan in discussing – at great length – cyberpunk, and that least one critic has summarily read her out of the movement altogether, in spite of the fact that much of her work is aesthetically more central to that canon than the work of a couple of the core writers who are inevitably invoked in the usual cyberpunk litany. I suspect that some of these critics are made very uncomfortable by the idea that a girl should be allowed to play in the boys' exclusive clubhouse – and I suspect that they would have been just as uncomfortable with Tiptree as well, in spite of her being an undoubted cyberpunk ancestor, if she had showed up wearing her Alice Sheldon suit.)

Most of Cadigan's best short fiction to date has been collected in *Patterns*, one of the two collections released in 1989 (the other is Bruce Sterling's *Crystal Express*) that are vital if you want an idea of where the SF short story is going to be going in the '90s.

She has a new novel out, *Synners*, and she is working on another. She was born in Schenectady, New York, and now lives with her family in Overland Park, Kansas.

First you see video. Then you wear video. Then you eat video. Then you *be* video.

The Gospel According to Visual Mark

Watch or Be watched.

Pretty Boy Credo

"Who made you?"

"You mean recently?"

Mohawk on the door smiles and takes his picture. "You in. But only you, okay? Don't try to get no friends in, hear that?"

"I hear. And I ain't no fool, fool. I got no friends."

Mohawk leers, leaning forward. "Pretty Boy like you, no friends?"

"Not in this world." He pushes past the Mohawk, ignoring the kissy-kissy sounds. He would like to crack the bridge of the Mohawk's nose and shove bone splinters into his brain but he is lately making more effort to control his temper and besides, he's not sure if any of that bone splinters in the brain stuff is really true. He's a Pretty Boy, all of sixteen years old, and tonight could be his last chance.

The club is Noise. Can't sneak into the bathroom for quiet, the Noise is piped in there, too. Want to get away from Noise? Why? No reason. But this Pretty Boy has learned to think between the beats. Like walking between the raindrops to stay dry, but he can do it. This Pretty Boy thinks things all the time – *all* the time. Subversive (and, he thinks so much that he knows that word *subversive*, sixteen, Pretty, or not). He thinks things like *how many Einsteins have died of hunger and thirst under a hot African sun* and *why can't you remember being born* and *why is music common to every culture* and especially *how much was there going on that he didn't know about and how could he find out about it.*

And this is all the time, one thing after another running in his head, you can see by his eyes. It's for def not much like a

Pretty Boy but it's one reason why they want him. That he *is* a Pretty Boy is another and one reason why they're halfway home getting him.

He knows all about them. Everybody knows about them and everybody wants them to pause, look twice, and cough up a card that says, Yes, we see possibilities, please come to the following address during regular business hours on the next regular business day for regular further review. Everyone wants it but this Pretty Boy, who once got five cards in a night and tore them all up. But here he is, still a Pretty Boy. He thinks enough to know this is a failing in himself, that he likes being Pretty and chased and that is how they could end up getting him after all and that's b-b-b-bad. When he thinks about it, he thinks it with the stutter. B-b-b-bad. B-b-b-bad for him because he doesn't God help him want it, no, no n-n-n-no. Which may make him the strangest Pretty Boy still live tonight and every night.

Still live and standing in the Club where only the Prettiest Pretty Boys can get in any more. Pretty Girls are too easy, they've got to be better than Pretty and besides, Pretty Boys like to be Pretty all alone, no help thank you so much. This Pretty Boy doesn't mind Pretty Girls or any other kind of girls. Lately, though he has begun to wonder how much longer it will be for him. Two years? Possibly a little longer? By three it will be for def over and Mohawk on the door will as soon spit on his face as leer in it.

If they don't get to him.

And if they *do* get to him, then it's never over and he can be wherever he chooses to be and wherever that is will be the center of the universe. They promise it, unlimited access in your free hours and endless hot season, endless youth. Pretty Boy Heaven, and to get there, they say, you don't even really have to die.

He looks up to the dj's roost, far above the bobbing, boogieing crowd on the dance floor. They still call them djs even though they aren't discs any more, they're chips and there's more than just sound on a lot of them. The great hyper-program, he's been told, the ultimate of ultimates, a short walk from there to the fourth dimension. He suspects this stuff comes from low-steppers shilling for them, hoping they'll get auditioned if they do a good enough shuck job. Nobody knows what it's really like except the ones who are there and you can't trust them, he figures. Because maybe they *aren't*, any more. Not really.

The dj sees his Pretty upturned face, recognizes him even though it's been awhile since he's come back here. Part of it was wanting to stay away from them and part of it was that the thug on the door might not let him in. And then, of course, he *had* to come, to see if he could get in, to see if anyone still wanted him. What was the point of Pretty if there was nobody to care and watch and pursue? Even now, he is almost sure he can feel the room rearranging itself around his presence in it and the dj confirms this is true by holding up a chip and pointing it to the left.

They are squatting on the make-believe stairs by the screen, reminding him of pigeons plotting to take over the world. He doesn't look too long, doesn't want to give them the idea he'd like to talk. But as he turns away, one, the younger man, starts to get up. The older man and the woman pull him back.

He pretends a big interest in the figures lining the nearest wall. Some are Pretty, some are female, some are undecided, some are very bizarre, or wealthy, or just charity cases. They all notice him and adjust themselves for his perusal.

Then one end of the room lights up with the color and new noise. Bodies dance and stumble back from the screen where images are forming to rough music.

It's Bobby, he realizes.

A moment later, there's Bobby's face on the screen, sixteen feet high, even Prettier than he'd been when he was loose among the mortals. The sight of Bobby's Pretty-Pretty face fills him with anger and dismay and a feeling of loss so great he would strike anyone who spoke Bobby's name without his permission.

Bobby's lovely slate-gray eyes scan the room. They've told him senses are heightened after you make the change and go over but he's not so sure how that's supposed to work. Bobby looks kind of blind up there on the screen. A few people wave at Bobby – the dorks they let in so the rest can have someone to be hip in front of – but Bobby's eyes move slowly back and forth, back and forth, and then stop, looking right at him.

"Ah . . ." Bobby whispers it, long and drawn out. "Aaaaaahhhh."

He lifts his chin belligerently and stares back at Bobby.

"You don't have to die any more," Bobby says silkily. Music bounces under his words. "It's beautiful in here. The dreams can be as real as you want them to be. And if you want to be, you can be with me."

He knows the commercial is not aimed only at him but it doesn't matter. This is *Bobby*. Bobby's voice seems to be pouring over him, caressing him, and it feels too much like a taunt. The night before Bobby went over, he tried to talk him out of it, knowing it wouldn't work. If they'd actually refused him, Bobby would have killed himself, like Franco had.

But now Bobby would live forever and ever, if you believed what they said. The music comes up louder but Bobby's eyes are still on him. He sees Bobby mouth his name.

"Can you really see me, Bobby?" he says. His voice doesn't make it over the music but if Bobby's senses are so heightened, maybe he hears it anyway. If he does, he doesn't choose to answer. The music is a bumped-up remix of a song Bobby used to party-till-he-puked to. The giant Bobby-face fades away to be replaced with a whole Bobby, somewhat larger than life, dancing better than the old Bobby ever could, whirling along changing scenes of streets, rooftops and beaches. The locales are nothing special but Bobby never did have all that much imagination, never wanted to go to Mars or even to the South Pole, always just to the hottest club. Always he liked being the exotic in plain surroundings and he still likes it. He always loved to get the looks. To be watched, worshiped, pursued. Yeah. He can see this is Bobby-heaven. The whole world will be giving him the looks now.

The background on the screen goes from street to the inside of a club; *this* club, only larger, better, with an even hipper crowd, and Bobby shaking it with them. Half the real crowd is forgetting to dance now because they're watching Bobby, hoping he's put some of them into his video. Yeah, that's the dream, get yourself remixed in the extended dance version.

His own attention drifts to the fake stairs that don't lead anywhere. They're still perched on them, the only people who are watching *him* instead of Bobby. The woman, looking overaged in a purple plastic sac-suit, is fingering a card.

He looks up at Bobby again. Bobby is dancing in place and looking back at him, or so it seems. Bobby's lips move soundlessly but so precisely he can read the words: *This can be you. Never get old, never get tired, it's never last call, nothing happens unless you want it to and it could be you. You. You.* Bobby's hands point to him on the beat. *You. You. You.*

Bobby. Can you really see me?

Bobby suddenly breaks into laughter and turns away, shaking it some more.

He sees the Mohawk from the door pushing his way through the crowd, the real crowd, and he gets anxious. The Mohawk goes straight for the stairs, where they make room for him, rubbing the bristly red strip of hair running down the center of his head as though they were greeting a favored pet. The Mohawk looks as satisfied as a professional glutton after a foodrace victory. He wonders what they promised the Mohawk for letting him in. Maybe some kind of limited contract. Maybe even a try-out.

Now they are all watching him together. Defiantly, he touches a tall girl dancing nearby and joins her rhythm. She smiles down at him, moving between him and them purely by chance but it endears her to him anyway. She is wearing a flap of translucent rag over secondskins, like an old-time showgirl. Over six feet tall, not beautiful with that nose, not even pretty, but they let her in so she could be tall. She probably doesn't know that; she probably doesn't know anything that goes on and never really will. For that reason, he can forgive her the hard-tech orange hair.

A Rude Boy brushes against him in the course of a dervish turn, asking acknowledgement by ignoring him. Rude Boys haven't changed in more decades than anyone's kept track of, as though it were the same little group of leathered and chained troopers buggering their way down the years. The

Rude Boy isn't dancing with anyone. Rude Boys never do. But this one could be handy, in case of an emergency.

The girl is dancing hard, smiling at him. He smiles back, moving slightly to her right, watching Bobby possibly watching him. He still can't tell if Bobby really sees anything. The scene behind Bobby is still a double of the club, getting hipper and hipper if that's possible. The music keeps snapping back to its first peak passage. Then Bobby gestures like God and he sees *himself*. He is dancing next to Bobby, Prettier than he ever could be, just the way they promise. Bobby doesn't look at the phantom but at him where he really is, lips moving again. *If you want to be, you can be with me. And so can she.*

His tall partner appears next to the phantom himself. She is also much improved, though still not Pretty, or even pretty. The real girl turns and sees herself and there's no mistaking the delight in her face. Queen of the Hop for a minute or two. Then Bobby sends her image away so that it's just the two of them, two Pretty Boys dancing the night away, private party, stranger go find your own time. How it used to be sometimes in real life, between just the two of them. He remembers hard.

"B-b-b-bobby!" he yells, the old stutter reappearing. Bobby's image seems to give a jump, as though he finally heard. He forgets everything, the girl, the Rude Boy, the Mohawk, them on the stairs, and plunges through the crowd toward the screen. People fall away from him as though they were re-enacting the Red Sea. He dives for the screen, for Bobby, not caring how it must look to anyone. What would they know about it, any of them. He can't remember in his whole sixteen years ever hearing one person say, *I love my friend*. Not Bobby, not even himself.

He fetches up against the screen like a slap and hangs there, face pressed to the glass. He can't see it now but on the screen Bobby would seem to be looking down at him. Bobby never stops dancing.

The Mohawk comes and peels him off. The others swarm up and take him away. The tall girl watches all this with the expression of a woman who lives upstairs from Cinderella and wears the same shoe size. She stares longingly at the screen. Bobby waves bye-bye and turns away.

"Of course, the process isn't reversible," says the older man. The steely hair has a careful blue tint; he had sense enough to stay out of hip clothes.

They have laid him out on a lounger with a tray of refreshments right by him. Probably slap his hand if he reaches for any, he thinks.

"Once you've distilled something to pure information, it just can't be reconstituted in a less efficient form," the woman explains, smiling. There's no warmth to her. A *less efficient form*. If that's what she really thinks, he knows he should be plenty scared of these people. Did she say things like that to Bobby? And did it make him even *more* eager?

"There may be no more exalted a form of existence than to live as sentient information," she goes on. "Though a lot more research must be done before we can offer conversation on a larger scale."

"Yeah?" he says. "Do they know that, Bobby and the rest?"

"Oh, there's nothing to worry about," says the younger man. He looks as though he's still getting over the pain of having outgrown his boogie shoes. "The system's quite perfected. What Grethe means is we want to research more applications for this new form of existence."

"Why not go over yourselves and do that, if it's so *exalted*."

"There are certain things that need to be done on this side," the woman says bitchily. "Just because – "

"Grethe." The older man shakes his head. She pats her slicked-back hair as though to soothe herself and moves away.

"We have other plans for Bobby when he gets tired of being featured in clubs," the older man says. "Even now, we're educating him, adding more data to his basic information configuration – "

"That would mean he ain't really *Bobby* any more, then, huh?"

The man laughs. "Of course he's Bobby. Do you change into someone else every time you learn something new?"

"Can you prove I *don't?*"

The man eyes him warily. "Look. You *saw* him. Was that Bobby?"

"I saw a video of Bobby dancing on a giant screen."

"That *is* Bobby and it will remain Bobby no matter what, whether he's poured into a video screen in a dot pattern or transmitted the length of the universe."

"That what you got in mind for him? Send a message to nowhere and the message is him?"

"We could. But we're not going to. We're introducing him to the concept of higher dimensions. The way he is now, he could possibly break out of the three-dimensional level of existence, pioneer a whole new plane of reality."

"Yeah? And how do you think you're gonna get Bobby to do *that?*"

"We convince him it's entertaining."

He laughs. "That's a good one. Yeah. Entertainment. You get to a high level of existence and you'll open a club there that only the hippest can get into. It figures."

The older man's face gets hard. "That's what all you Pretty Boys are crazy for, isn't it? Entertainment?"

He looks around. The room must have been a dressing room or something back in the days when bands had been live. Somewhere overhead he can hear the faint noise of the club but he can't tell if Bobby's still on. "You call this entertainment?"

"I'm tired of this little prick," the woman chimes in. "He's thrown away opportunities other people would kill for – "

He makes a rude noise. "Yeah, we'd all kill to be someone's data chip. You think I really believe Bobby's real just because I can see him on a *screen?*"

The older man turns to the younger one. "Phone up and have them pipe Bobby down here." Then he swings the lounger around so it faces a nice modern screen implanted in a shored-up cement-block wall.

"Bobby will join us shortly. Then he can tell you whether he's real or not himself. How will that be for you?"

He stares hard at the screen, ignoring the man, waiting for Bobby's image to appear. As though they really bothered to communicate regularly with Bobby this way. Feed in that kind of data and memory and Bobby'll believe it. He shifts uncomfortably, suddenly wondering how far he could get if he moved fast enough.

"My *boy*," says Bobby's sweet voice from the speaker on either side of the screen and he forces himself to keep looking as Bobby fades in, presenting himself on the same kind of lounger and looking mildly exerted, as though he's just come off the dance floor for real. "Saw you shakin' it upstairs awhile ago. You haven't been here for such a long time. What's the story?"

He opens his mouth but there's no sound. Bobby looks at him with boundless patience and indulgence. So Pretty, hair the perfect shade now and not a bit dry from the dyes and lighteners, skin flawless and shining like a healthy angel. Overnight angel, just like the old song.

"My *boy*," says Bobby. "Are you struck, like, shy or *dead?*"

He closes his mouth, takes one breath. "I don't like it, Bobby. I don't like it this way."

"Of course not, lover. You're the Watcher, not the Watchee, that's why. Get yourself picked up for a reason or two and your disposition will *change*."

"You really like it, Bobby, being a blip on a chip?"

"Blip on a chip, your ass. I'm a universe now. I'm, like, *everything*. And, hey, dig – I'm on every channel." Bobby laughed. "I'm happy I'm sad!"

"S-A-D," comes in the older man. "Self-Aware Data."

"Ooo-eee," he says. "Too clever for me. Can I get out of here now?"

"What's your hurry?" Bobby pouts. "Just because I went over you don't love me any more?"

"You always were screwed up about that, Bobby. Do you know the difference between being loved and being watched?"

"Sophisticated boy," Bobby says. "So wise, so learned. So fully packed. On this side, there *is* no difference. Maybe there never was. If you love me, you watch me. If you don't look, you don't care and if you don't care I don't matter. If I don't matter, I don't exist. Right?"

He shakes his head.

"No, my boy, I *am* right." Bobby laughs. "You believe I'm

right, because if you *didn't*, you wouldn't come shaking your
Pretty Boy ass in a place like *this*, now, would you? You *like* to
be watched, get seen. You see me, I see you. Life goes on."

He looks up at the older man, needing relief from Bobby's
pure Prettiness. "How does he see me?"

"Sensors in the equipment. Technical stuff, nothing you
care about."

He sighs. He should be upstairs or across town, shaking it
with everyone else, living Pretty for as long as he could.
Maybe in another few months, this way would begin to look
good to him. By then they might be off Pretty Boys and
looking for some other type and there he'd be, out in the
cold-cold, sliding down the other side of his peak and no one
would *want* him. Shut out of something going on that he
might want to know about after all. Can he face it? He
glances at the younger man. All grown up and no place to
glow. Yeah, but can *he* face it?

He doesn't know. Used to be there wasn't much of a choice
and now that there is, it only seems to make it worse. Bobby's
image looks like it's studying him for some kind of sign,
Pretty eyes bright, hopeful.

The older man leans down and speaks low into his ear.
"We need to get you before you're twenty-five, before the
brain stops growing. A mind taken from a still-growing
brain will blossom and adapt. Some of Bobby's predecessors
have made marvellous adaptation to their new medium.
Pure video: there's a staff that does nothing all day but watch
and interpret their symbols for breakthroughs in thought.
And we'll be taking Pretty Boys for as long as they're
publicly sought-after. It's the most efficient way to find the
best performers, go for the ones everyone wants to see or be.
The top of the trend is closest to heaven. And even if you
never make a breakthrough, you'll still be entertainment.
Not such a bad way to live for a Pretty Boy. Never have to
age, to be sick, to lose touch. You spent most of your life
young, why learn how to be old? Why learn how to live
without all the things you have now – "

He puts his hands over his ears. The older man is still
talking and Bobby is saying something and the younger man
and the woman come over to try to do something about him.

Refreshments are falling off the tray. He struggles out of the lounger and makes for the door.

"Hey, my *boy*," Bobby calls after him. "Gimme a minute here, gimme what the problem is."

He doesn't answer. What can you tell someone made of pure information anyway?

There's a new guy on the front door, bigger and meaner than His Mohawkness but he's only there to keep people out, not to keep anyone *in*. You want to jump ship, go to, you poor un-hip asshole. Even if you are a Pretty Boy. He reads it in the guy's face as he passes from noise into the 3 a.m. quiet of the street.

They let him go. He doesn't fool himself about that part. They *let* him out of the room because they know all about him. They know he lives like Bobby lived, they know he loves what Bobby loved – the clubs, the admiration, the lust of strangers for his personal magic. He can't say he doesn't love that, because he *does*. He isn't even sure if he loves it more than he ever loved Bobby, or if he loves it more than being alive. Than being live.

And here it is 3 a.m., clubbing prime time, and he is moving toward home. Maybe he *is* a poor up-hip asshole after all, no matter what he loves. Too stupid even to stay in the club, let alone grab a ride to heaven. Still he keeps moving, unbothered by the chill but feeling it. Bobby doesn't have to go home in the cold any more, he thinks. Bobby doesn't even have to get through the hours between the club-times if he doesn't want to. All times are now prime time for Bobby. Even if he gets unplugged, he'll never know the difference. Poof, it's a day later, poof, it's a year later, poof, you're out for good. Painlessly.

Maybe Bobby has the right idea, he thinks, moving along the empty sidewalk. If he goes over tomorrow, who will notice? Like when he left the dance floor – people will come and fill up the space. Ultimately, it wouldn't make any difference to anyone.

He smiles suddenly. Except *them*. As long as they don't have him, he makes a difference. As long as he has flesh to shake and flaunt and feel with, he makes a pretty goddamn big difference to *them*. Even after they don't want him any more, he will still be the one they didn't get. He rubs his hands together against the chill, feeling the skin rubbing skin, really *feeling* it for the first time in a long time, and he thinks about sixteen million things all at once, maybe one thing for every brain cell he's using, or maybe one thing for every brain cell yet to come.

He keeps moving, holding to the big thought, making a difference, and all the little things they won't be making a program out of. He's lightheaded with joy – he doesn't know what's going to happen.

Neither do they.

JOHN KESSEL
The Pure Product

Born in Buffalo, New York, John Kessel now lives in Raleigh, North Carolina, where he is a professor of American literature and creative writing at North Carolina State University. Kessel made his first sale in 1975, and has since become a frequent contributor to *The Magazine of Fantasy and Science Fiction* and *Isaac Asimov's Science Fiction Magazine*, as well as to many other magazines and anthologies.

Kessel's novel *Good News from Outer Space* was released in 1989 to wide critical acclaim, but before that he had made his mark on the genre primarily as a writer of highly imaginative, finely crafted short stories . . . the best of which, to date, is the taut, hard-edged, casually and cold-bloodedly horrifying story that follows, one of the most adroit and chilling examinations of its theme ever to appear anywhere.

Kessel won a Nebula Award in 1983 for his superlative novella "Another Orphan," which was also a Hugo finalist that year, and has just been released as a Tor Double. His other books include the novel *Freedom Beach*, written in collaboration with James Patrick Kelly, and, coming up, a collection of his short fiction, from Arkham House.

I arrived in Kansas City at one o'clock on the afternoon of the thirteenth of August. A Tuesday. I was driving the beige 1983 Chevrolet Citation that I had stolen two days earlier in Pocatello, Idaho. The Kansas plates on the car I'd taken from a different car in a parking lot in Salt Lake City. Salt Lake City was founded by the Mormons, whose God tells them that in the future Jesus Christ will come again.

I drove through Kansas City with the windows open and the sun beating down through the windshield. The car had no air-conditioning and my shirt was stuck to my back from seven hours behind the wheel. Finally I found a hardware store, "Hector's" on Wornall. I pulled into the lot. The Citation's engine dieseled after I turned off the ignition; I pumped the accelerator once and it coughed and died. The heat was like syrup. The sun drove shadows deep into corners, left them flattened at the feet of the people on the sidewalk. It made the plate glass of the store window into a dark negative of the positive print that was Wornall Avenue. August.

The man behind the counter in the hardware store I took to be Hector himself. He looked like Hector, slain in vengeance beneath the walls of paintbrushes – the kind of semi-friendly, publicly optimistic man who would tell you about his good wife and his ten-penny nails. I bought a gallon of kerosene and a plastic paint funnel, put them into the trunk of the Citation, then walked down the block to the Mark Twain Bank. Mark Twain died at the age of seventy-five with a heart full of bitter accusations against the Calvinist God and no hope for the future of humanity. Inside the bank I went to one of the desks, at which sat a Nice Young Lady. I asked about starting a business checking account. She gave me a form to fill out, then sent me to the office of Mr Graves.

Mr Graves wielded a formidable handshake. "What can I do for you, Mr. . . ?"

"Tillotsen. Gerald Tillotsen," I said. Gerald Tillotsen, of Tacoma, Washington, died of diphtheria at the age of four weeks – on September 24, 1938. I have a copy of his birth certificate.

"I'm new to Kansas City. I'd like to open a business account here, and perhaps take out a loan. I trust this is a reputable bank? What's your exposure in Brazil?" I looked around the office as if Graves were hiding a woman behind the hatstand, then flashed him my most ingratiating smile.

Mr Graves did his best. He tried smiling back, then looked as if he had decided to ignore my little joke. "We're very sound, Mr Tillotsen."

I continued smiling.

"What kind of business do you own?"

"I'm in insurance. Mutual Assurance of Hartford. Our regional office is in Oklahoma City, and I'm setting up an agency here, at 103rd and State Line." Just off the interstate.

He examined the form I had given him. His absorption was too tempting.

"Maybe I can fix you up with a life policy? You look like dead meat."

Graves' head snapped up, his mouth half open. He closed it and watched me guardedly. The dullness of it all! How I tire. He was like some cow, like most of the rest of you in this silly age, unwilling to break the rules in order to take offense. Did he really say that? he was thinking. If he did say that, was that his idea of a joke? What is he after? He looks normal enough. I did look normal, exactly like an insurance agent. I was the right kind of person, and I could do anything. If at times I grate, if at times I fall a little short of or go a little beyond convention, there is not one of you who can call me to account.

Mr Graves was coming around. All business.

"Ah – yes, Mr Tillotsen. If you'll wait a moment, I'm sure we can take care of this checking account. As for the loan . . ."

"Forget it."

That should have stopped him. He should have asked after my credentials, he should have done a dozen things. He looked at me, and I stared calmly back at him. And I knew that, looking into my honest blue eyes, he could not think of a thing.

"I'll just start the checking account now with this money order," I said, reaching into my pocket. "That will be acceptable, won't it?"

"It will be fine," he said. He took the completed form and the order over to one of the secretaries while I sat at the desk. I lit a cigar and blew some smoke rings. The money order had been purchased the day before in a post office in Denver. It was for thirty dollars. I didn't intend to use the account very long. Graves returned with my sample checks, shook hands earnestly, and wished me a good day. Have a *good* day, he said. I *will*, I said.

Outside, the heat was still stifling. I took off my sportcoat. I was sweating so much I had to check my hair in the sideview mirror of my car. I walked down the street to a liquor store and bought a bottle of chardonnay and a bottle of Chivas Regal. I got some paper cups from a nearby grocery. One final errand, then I could relax for a few hours.

In the shopping center I had told Graves would be the location for my non-existent insurance office, there was a sporting goods store. It was about three o'clock when I parked in the lot and ambled into the shop. I looked at various golf clubs: irons, woods, even one set with fiberglass shafts. Finally I selected a set of eight Spaulding irons with matching woods, a large bag, and several boxes of Topflites. The salesman, who had been occupied with another customer at the rear of the store, hustled up his eyes full of commission money. I gave him little time to think. The total cost was six hundred and twelve dollars and thirty-two cents. I paid with a check drawn on my new account, cordially thanked the man, and had him carry all the equipment out to the trunk of the car.

I drove to a park near the bank; Loose Park, they called it. I felt loose. Cut loose, drifting free, like one of the kites people were flying in the park that had broken its string and was ascending into the sun. Beneath the trees it was still hot, though the sunlight was reduced to a shuffling of light and shadow on the brown grass. Kids ran, jumped, swung on playground equipment. I uncorked my bottle of wine, filled one of the paper cups, and lay down beneath a tree, enjoying the children, watching young men and women walking along the paths of the park.

A girl approached along the path. She did not look any older than seventeen. She was short and slender, with clean blonde hair cut to her shoulders. Her shorts were very tight. I watched her unabashedly; she saw me watching her and left the path to come over to me. She stopped a few feet away, her hands on her hips. "What are you looking at?" she asked.

"Your legs," I said. "Would you like some wine?"

"No thanks. My mother told me never to accept wine from strangers." She looked right through me.

"I take whatever I can get from strangers," I said. "Because I'm a stranger, too."

I guess she liked that. She was different. She sat down and we chatted for a while. There was something wrong about her imitation of a seventeen-year-old; I began to wonder whether hookers worked the park. She crossed her legs and her shorts got tighter. "Where are you from?" she asked.

"San Francisco. But I've just moved here to stay. I have a part interest in the sporting goods store at the Eastridge Plaza."

"You live near here?"

"On West 89th." I had driven down 89th on my way to the bank.

"I live on 89th! We're neighbors."

An edge of fear sliced through me. A slip? It was exactly what one of my own might have said to test me. I took a drink of wine and changed the subject. "Would you like to visit San Francisco some day?"

She brushed her hair back behind one ear. She pursed her lips, showing off her fine cheekbones. "Have you got something going?" she asked, in queerly accented English.

"Excuse me?"

"I said, have you got something going," she repeated, still with the accent – the accent of my own time.

I took another sip. "A bottle of wine," I replied in good Midwestern 1980s.

She wasn't having any of it. "No artwork, please. I don't like artwork."

I had to laugh: my life was devoted to artwork. I had not met anyone real in a long time. At the beginning I hadn't wanted to and in the ensuing years I had given up expecting it. If there's anything more boring than you people it's us people. But that was an old attitude. When she came to me in KC I was lonely and she was something new.

"Okay," I said. "It's not much, but you can come for the ride. Do you want to?"

She smiled and said yes.

As we walked to my car, she brushed her hip against my leg. I switched the bottle to my left hand and put my arm around her shoulders in a fatherly way. We got into the front seat, beneath the trees on a street at the edge of the park. It was quiet. I reached over, grabbed her hair at the nape of her neck and jerked her face toward me, covering her little mouth with mine. Surprise: she threw her arms round my neck, sliding across the seat and awkwardly onto my lap. We did not talk. I yanked at the shorts; she thrust her hand into my pants. Saint Augustine asked the Lord for chastity, but not right away.

At the end she slipped off me, calmly buttoned her blouse, brushed her hair back from her forehead. "How about a push?" she asked. She had a nailfile out and was filing her index fingernail to a point.

I shook my head, and looked at her. She resembled my grandmother. I had never run into my grandmother but she had a hellish reputation. "No thanks. What's your name?"

"Call me Ruth." She scratched the inside of her left elbow with her nail. She leaned back in her seat, sighed deeply. Her eyes became a very bright, very hard blue.

While she was aloft I got out, opened the trunk, emptied the rest of the chardonnay into the gutter and used the funnel to fill the bottle with kerosene. I plugged it with part of the cork and a kerosene-soaked rag. Afternoon was sliding into evening as I started the car and cruised down one of the residential streets. The houses were like those of any city or town of that era of the midwest USA: white frame, forty or fifty years old, with large porches and small front yards. Dying elm trees hung over the street. Shadows stretched across the sidewalks. Ruth's nose wrinkled; she turned her face lazily toward me, saw the kerosene bottle, and smiled.

Ahead on the left-hand sidewalk I saw a man walking leisurely. He was an average sort of man, middle-aged, probably just returning from work, enjoying the quiet pause dusk was bringing to the hot day. It might have been Hector; it might have been Graves. It might have been any one of you. I punched the cigarette lighter, readied the bottle in my right hand, steering with my leg as the car moved slowly forward. "Let me help," Ruth said. She reached out and steadied the wheel with her slender fingertips. The lighter popped out. I touched it to the rag; it smouldered and caught. Greasy smoke stung my eyes. By now the man had noticed us. I hung my arm, holding the bottle, out the window. As we passed him, I tossed the bottle at the sidewalk like a newsboy tossing a rolled-up newspaper. The rag flamed brighter as it whipped through the air; the bottle landed at his feet and exploded, dousing him with burning kerosene. I floored the accelerator; the motor coughed, then roared, the tires and Ruth both squealing in delight. I could see the flaming man in the rear-view mirror as we sped away.

On the Great American Plains, the summer nights, are not silent. The fields sing the summer songs of insects – not individual sounds, but a high-pitched drone of locusts, cicadas, small chirping things for which I have no names. You drive along the superhighway and that sound blends with the sound of wind rushing through your opened windows, hiding the thrum of the automobile, conveying the impression of incredible velocity. Wheels vibrate, tires beat against the pavement, the steering wheel shudders, alive in your hands, droning insects alive in your cars. Reflecting posts at the roadside leap from the darkness with metronomic regularity, glowing amber in the headlights, only to vanish abruptly into the ready night when you pass. You lose track of time, how long you have been on the road, where you are going. The fields scream in your ears like a thousand lost, mechanical souls, and you press your foot to the accelerator, hurrying away.

When we left Kansas City that evening we were indeed hurrying. Our direction was in one sense precise: Interstate 70, more or less due east, through Missouri in a dream. They might remember me in Kansas City, at the same time wondering who and why. Mr Graves checks the morning paper over his grapefruit: "Man Burned by Gasoline Bomb." The clerk wonders why he ever accepted an unverified check, a check without even a name or address printed on it, for six-hundred dollars. The check bounces. They discover it was a bottle of chardonnay. The story is pieced together. They would eventually figure out how – I wouldn't lie to myself about that – I never lie to myself – but the why would always escape them. Organized crime, they would say. A plot that misfired.

Of course, they still might have caught me. The car became more of a liability the longer I held onto it. But Ruth, humming to herself, did not seem to care, and neither did I. You have to improvise those things; that's what gives them whatever interest they have.

Just shy of Columbia, Missouri, Ruth stopped humming and asked me, "Do you know why Helen Keller can't have any children?"

"No."

"Because she's dead."

I rolled up the window so I could hear her better. "That's pretty funny," I said.

"Yes. I overheard it in a restaurant." After a minute she asked, "Who's Helen Keller?"

"A dead woman." An insect splattered itself against the windshield. The lights of the oncoming cars glinted against the smear it left.

"She must be famous," said Ruth. "I like famous people. Have you met any? Was that man you burned famous?"

"Probably not. I don't care about famous people anymore." The last time I had anything to do, even peripherally, with anyone famous was when I changed the direction of the tape over the lock in the Watergate so Frank Wills would see it. Ruth did not look like the kind who would know about that. "I was there for the Kennedy assassination," I said, "but I had nothing to do with it."

"Who was Kennedy?"

That made me smile. "How long have you been here?" I pointed at her tiny purse. "That's all you've got with you?"

She slid across the seat and leaned her head against my shoulder. "I don't need anything else."

"No clothes?"

"I left them in Kansas City. We can get more."

"Sure," I said.

She opened the purse and took out a plastic Bayer aspirin case. From it she selected two blue-and-yellow caps. She shoved her sweaty palm up under my nose. "Serometh?"

"No thanks."

She put one of the caps back into the box and popped the other under her nose. She sighed and snuggled tighter against me. We had reached Columbia and I was hungry. When I pulled in at a McDonald's she ran across the lot into the shopping mall before I could stop her. I was a little nervous about the car and sat watching it as I ate (Big Mac, small Dr Pepper). She did not come back. I crossed the lot to the mall, found a drugstore and bought some cigars. When I strolled back to the car she was waiting for me, hopping from one foot to another and tugging at the door handle. Serometh makes you impatient. She was wearing a pair of shiny black pants, pink and white checked sneakers and a hot pink blouse. " 's go!" she hissed at me.

I moved even slower. She looked like she was about to wet herself, biting her soft lower lip with a line of perfect white teeth. I dawdled over my keys. A security guard and a young man in a shirt and tie hurried out of the small entrance and scanned the lot. "Nice outfit," I said. "Must have cost you something."

She looked over her shoulder, saw the security guard, who saw her. "Hey!" he called, running toward us. I slid into the car, opened the passenger door. Ruth had snapped open her purse and pulled out a small gun. I grabbed her arm and yanked her into the car; she squawked and her shot went wide. The guard fell down anyway, scared shitless. For the second time that day I tested the Citation's acceleration; Ruth's door slammed shut and we were gone.

"You scut," she said as we hit the entrance ramp of the interstate. "You're a scut-pumping Conservative. You made me miss." But she was smiling, running her hand up the inside of my thigh. I could tell she hadn't ever had so much fun in the twentieth century.

For some reason I was shaking. "Give me one of those seromeths," I said.

Around midnight we stopped in St Louis at a Holiday Inn. We registered as Mr and Mrs Gerald Bruno (an old acquaintance) and paid in advance. No one remarked on the apparent difference in our ages. So discreet. I bought a copy of the *Post-Dispatch* and we went to the room. Ruth flopped down on the bed, looking bored, but thanks to her gunplay I had a few more things to take care of. I poured myself a glass of Chivas, went into the bathroom, removed the toupee and flushed it down the toilet, showered, put a new blade in my old razor and shaved the rest of the hair from my head. The Lex Luthor look. I cut my scalp. That got me laughing, and I could not stop. Ruth peeked through the doorway to find me dabbing the crown of my head with a bloody Kleenex.

"You're a wreck," she said.

I almost fell off the toilet laughing. She was absolutely right. Between giggles I managed to say, "You must not stay anywhere too long, if you're as careless as you were tonight."

She shrugged. "I bet I've been at it longer than you." She stripped and got into the shower. I got into bed.

The room enfolded me in its gold-carpet, green-bedspread mediocrity. Sometimes it's hard to remember that things were ever different. In 1596 I rode to court with Essex; I slept in a chamber of supreme garishness (gilt escutcheons in the corners of the ceiling, pink cupids romping on the walls), in a bed warmed by any of the trollops of the city I might want. And there in the Holiday Inn I sat with my drink, in my pastel blue pajama bottoms, reading a late-twentieth-century newspaper, smoking a cigar. An earthquake in Peru estimated to have killed eight thousand in Lima alone. Nope. A steelworker in Gary, Indiana, discovered to be the murderer of six pre-pubescent children, bodies found buried in his basement. Perhaps. The President refuses to enforce the ruling of his Supreme Court because it "subverts the will of the American people." Probably not.

We are everywhere. But not everywhere.

Ruth came out of the bathroom, saw me, did a double take. "You look – perfect!" she said. She slid in the bed beside me, naked, and sniffed at my glass of Chivas. Her lip curled. She looked over my shoulder at the paper. "You can understand that stuff?"

"Don't kid me. Reading is a survival skill. You couldn't last here without it."

"Wrong."

I drained the scotch. Took a puff of the cigar. Dropped the paper to the floor beside the bed. I looked her over. Even relaxed, the muscles in her thighs were well-defined.

"You even smell like one of them," she said.

"How did you get the clothes past their store security? They have those beeper tags clipped to them."

"Easy. I tried on the shoes and walked out when they weren't looking. In the second store I took the pants into a dressing room, cut off the bottoms, along with the alarm tag, and put them on. I held the alarm tag that was clipped to the blouse in my armpit and walked out of that store, too. I put the blouse on in the mall women's room."

"If you can't read, how did you know which was the women's room?"

"There's a picture on the door."

I felt very tired and very old. Ruth moved close. She rubbed her foot up my leg, drawing the pajama leg up with it. Her thigh slid across my groin. I started to get hard. "Cut it out," I said. She licked my nipple.

I could not stand it. I got off the bed. "I don't like you."

She looked at me with true innocence. "I don't like you either."

Although he was repulsed by the human body, Jonathan Swift was passionately in love with a woman named Esther Johnson. "What you did at the mall was stupid," I said. "You would have killed that guard."

"Which would have made us even for the day."

"Kansas City was different."

"We should ask the cops there what they think."

"You don't understand. That had some grace to it. But what you did was inelegant. Worst of all it was not gratuitous. You stole those clothes for yourself, and I hate that." I was shaking.

"Who made all these laws?"

"I did."

She looked at me with amazement. "You're not just a Conservative. You've gone native!"

I wanted her so much I ached. "No I haven't," I said, but even to me, my voice sounded frightened.

Ruth got out of the bed. She glided over, reached one hand around to the small of my back, pulled herself close. She looked up at me with a face that held nothing but avidity. "You can do whatever you want," she whispered. With a feeling that I was losing everything, I kissed her. You don't need to know what happened then.

I woke when she displaced herself: there was a sound like the sweep of an arm across fabric, a stirring of air to fill the place where she had been. I looked around the still brightly lit room. It was not yet morning. The chain was across the door; her clothes lay on the dresser. She had left the aspirin box beside my bottle of scotch.

She was gone. Good, I thought, now I can go on. But I found I could not sleep, could not keep from thinking. Ruth must be very good at that, or perhaps her thought is a different kind of thought from mine. I got out of the bed, resolved to try again but still fearing the inevitable. I filled the tub with hot water. I got in, breathing heavily. I took the blade from my razor. Holding my arm just beneath the surface of the water, hesitating only a moment, I cut deeply one, two, three times along the veins in my left wrist. The shock was still there, as great as ever. With blood streaming from me I cut the right wrist. Quickly, smoothly. My heart beat fast and light, the blood flowed frighteningly; already the water was stained. I felt faint – yes – it was going to work this time, yes. My vision began to fade – but in the last moments before consciousness fell away I saw, with sick despair, the futile wounds closing themselves once again, as they had so many time before. For in the future the practice of medicine may progress to the point where men need have no fear of death.

The dawn's rosy fingers found me still unconscious. I came to myself about eleven, my head throbbing, so weak I could hardly rise from the cold, bloody water. There were no scars. I stumbled into the other room and washed down one of Ruth's megamphetamines with two fingers of scotch. I felt better immediately. It's funny how that works sometimes, isn't it? The maid knocked as I was cleaning the bathroom. I shouted for her to come back later, finished as quickly as possible and left the motel immediately. I ate shredded wheat with milk and strawberries for breakfast. I was full of ideas. A phone book gave me the location of a likely country club.

The Oak Hill Country Club of Florisant, Missouri, is not a spectacularly wealthy institution, or at least it does not give that impression. I'll bet you that the membership is not as purely white as the stucco clubhouse. That was all right with me. I parked the Citation in the mostly empty parking lot, hauled my new equipment from the trunk, and set off for the locker room, trying hard to look like a dentist. I successfully ran the gauntlet of the pro shop, where the proprietor was busy telling a bored caddy why the Cardinals would fade in the stretch. I could hear running water from the shower as I shuffled into the locker room and slung the bag into a corner. Someone was singing the "Ode to Joy," abominably.

I began to rifle through the lockers, hoping to find an open one with someone's clothes in it. I would take the keys from my benefactor's pocket and proceed along my merry way. Ruth would have accused me of self-interest; there was a moment in which I accused myself. Such hesitation is the seed of failure: as I paused before a locker containing a likely set of clothes, another golfer entered the room along with the locker room attendant. I immediately began undressing, lowering my head so that the locker door would obscure my face. The golfer was soon gone, but the attendant sat down and began to leaf through a worn copy of *Penthouse*. I could come up with no better plan than to strip and enter the showers. Amphetamine daze. Perhaps the kid would develop a hard-on and go to the john to take care of it.

There was only one other man in the shower, the operatic soloist, a somewhat portly gentleman who mercifully shut up as soon as I entered. He worked hard at ignoring me. I ignored him in return: neither of us was much to look at. I waited a long five minutes after he left; two more men came into the showers and I walked out with what composure I could muster. The locker room boy was stacking towels on the table. I fished a five from my jacket in the locker and walked up behind him. Casually I took a towel.

"Son, get me a pack of Marlboros, will you?"

He took the money and left.

In the second locker I found a pair of pants that contained the keys to some sort of Audi. I was not choosy. Dressed in record time, I left the new clubs beside the rifled locker. My note read: *The pure products of America go crazy.* There were three eligible cars in the lot, two 4000s and a Fox. The key would not open the door of the Fox. I was jumpy, but almost home free, coming around the front of a big Chrysler . . .

"Hey!"

My knee gave way and I ran into the fender of the car. The keys slipped out of my hand and skittered across the hood to the ground, jingling. Grimacing, I hopped toward them, plucked them up, glancing over my shoulder at my pursuer as I stopped. It was the locker room attendant.

"Your cigarettes." He was looking at me the way a sixteen-year-old looks at his father, that is, with bored skepticism. All our gods in the end become pitiful. It was time for me to be abruptly friendly. As it was he would remember me too well.

"Thanks," I said. I limped over, put the pack into my shirt pocket. He started to go, but I couldn't help myself. "What about my change?"

Oh, such an insolent silence! I wonder what you told them when they asked you about me, boy. He handed over the money. I tipped him a quarter, gave him a piece of Mr Graves' professional smile. He studied me. I turned and inserted the key into the lock of the Audi. A fifty percent chance. Had I been the praying kind I might have prayed to one of those pitiful gods. The key turned without resistance; the door opened. The kid slouched back toward the clubhouse, pissed at me and his lackey's job. Or perhaps he found it in his heart to smile. Laughter – the Best Medicine.

A bit of a racing shift, then back to Interstate 70. My hip twinged all the way across Illinois.

I had originally intended to work my way east to Buffalo, New York, but after the Oak Hill business I wanted to cut it short. If I stayed on the interstate I was sure to get caught; I had been lucky to get as far as I had. Just outside of Indianapolis I turned onto Route 37 north to Ft Wayne and Detroit.

I was not, however, entirely cowed. Twenty-five years in one time had given me the right instincts, and with the coming of evening and the friendly insects to sing me along, the boredom of the road became a new recklessness. Hadn't I already been seen by too many people in those twenty-five years? Thousands had looked into my honest face – and where were they? Ruth had reminded me that I was not stuck here. I would soon make an end to this latest adventure one way or another, and once I had done so, there would be no reason in god's green world to suspect me.

And so: north of Ft Wayne, on Highway 6 east, a deserted country road (what was he doing there?), I pulled over to pick up a young hitchhiker. He wore a battered black leather jacket. His hair was short on the sides, stuck up in spikes on top, hung over his collar in back; one side was carrot-orange, the other brown with a white streak. His sign, pinned to a knapsack, said "?" He threw the pack into the back seat and climbed into the front.

"Thanks for picking me up." He did not sound like he meant it. "Where you going?"

"Flint. How about you?"

"Flint's as good as anywhere."

"Suit yourself." We got up to speed. I was completely calm. "You should fasten your seat belt," I said.

"Why?"

The surly type. "It's not just a good idea. It's the Law."

"How about turning on the light." He pulled a crossword puzzle book and a pencil from his jacket pocket. I flicked on the domelight for him.

"I like to see a young man improve himself," I said.

His look was an almost audible sigh. "What's a five-letter word for 'the lowest point?' "

"Nadir," I replied.

"That's right. How about 'widespread'; four letters."

"Rife."

"You're pretty good." He stared at the crossword for a minute, then suddenly rolled down his window and threw the book, and the pencil, out of the car. He rolled up the window and stared at his reflection in it, his back to me. I couldn't let him get off that easily. I turned off the interior light and the darkness leapt inside.

"What's your name, son? What are you so mad about?"

"Milo. Look, are you queer? If you are, it doesn't matter to me but it will cost you . . . if you want to do anything about it."

I smiled and adjusted the rear-view mirror so I could watch him – and he could watch me. "No, I'm not queer.

The name's Loki." I extended my right hand, keeping my eyes on the road.

He looked at the hand. "Loki?"

As good a name as any. "Yes. Same as the Norse god."

He laughed. "Sure, Loki. Anything you like. Fuck you."

Such a musical voice. "Now there you go. Seems to me, Milo – if you don't mind me giving you my unsolicited opinion – that you have something of an attitude problem." I punched the cigarette lighter, reached back and pulled a cigar from my jacket on the back seat, in the process weaving the car all over Highway 6. I bit the end off the cigar and spat it out the window, stoked it up. My insects wailed. I cannot explain to you how good I felt.

"Take for instance this crossword puzzle book. Why did you throw it out the window?"

I could see Milo watching me in the mirror, wondering whether he should take me seriously. The headlights fanned out ahead of us, the white lines at the center of the road pulsing by like a rapid heartbeat. Take a chance, Milo. What have you got to lose?

"I was pissed," he said. "It's a waste of time. I don't care about stupid games."

"Exactly. It's just a game, a way to pass the time. Nobody ever really learns anything from a crossword puzzle. Corporation lawyers don't get their Porsches by building their word power with crosswords, right?"

"I don't care about Porsches."

"Neither do I, Milo. I drive an Audi."

Milo sighed.

"I know, Milo. That's not the point. The point is that it's all a game, crosswords or corporate law. Some people devote their lives to Jesus; some devote their lives to artwork. It all comes to pretty much the same thing. You get old. You die."

"Tell me something I don't already know."

"Why do you think I picked you up, Milo? I saw your question mark and it spoke to me. You probably think I'm some pervert out to take advantage of you. I have a funny name. I don't talk like your average middle-aged business-man. Forget about that." The old excitement was upon me; I was talking louder, leaning on the accelerator. The car sped along. "I think you're as troubled by the materialism and cant of life in America as I am. Young people like you, with orange hair, are trying to find some values in a world that offers them nothing but crap for ideas. But too many of you are turning to extremes in response. Drugs, violence, religious fanaticism, hedonism. Some, like you I suspect, to suicide. Don't do it, Milo. Your life is too valuable." The speedometer touched eighty, eighty-five. Milo fumbled for his seatbelt but couldn't find it.

I waved my hand, holding the cigar, at him. "What's the matter, Milo? Can't find the belt?" Ninety now. A pickup went by us going the other way, the wind of its passing beating at my head and shoulder. Ninety-five.

"Think, Milo! If you're upset with the present, with your parents and the schools, think about the future. What will the future be like if this trend toward valuelessness continues in the next hundred years? Think of the impact of new technologies! Gene splicing, gerontological research, artificial intelligence, space exploration, biological weapons, nuclear proliferation! All accelerating this process! Think of the violent reactionary movements that could arise – are arising already, Milo, as we speak – from people's efforts to find something to hold onto. Paint yourself a picture, *Milo*, of the kind of man or woman another hundred years of this process might produce!"

"What are you talking about?" He was terrified.

"I'm talking about the survival of values in America! Simply that." Cigar smoke swirled in front of the dashboard lights, and my voice had reached a shout. Milo was gripping the sides of his seat. The speedometer read 105. "And you, *Milo*, are at the heart of this process! If people continue to think the way they do, *Milo*, throwing their crossword puzzle books out the windows of their Audis across America, *the future will be full of absolutely valueless people!* Right, MILO?" I leaned over, taking my eyes off the road, and blew smoke into his face, screaming, "ARE YOU LISTENING, MILO? MARK MY WORDS!"

"Y – yes."

"GOO, GOO, GA-GA-GAA!"

I put my foot all the way to the floor. The wind howled through the window; the gray highway flew beneath us.

"Mark my words, Milo," I whispered. He never heard me. "Twenty-five across. Eight letters. N-i-h-i-l – "

My pulse roared in my ears, there joining the drowned choir of the fields and the roar of the engine. My body was slimy with sweat, my fingers clenched through the cigar, fists clamped on the wheel, smoke stinging my eyes. I slammed on the brakes, downshifting immediately, sending the transmission into a painful whine as the car slewed and skidded off the pavement, clipping a reflecting marker and throwing Milo against the windshield. The car stopped with a jerk in the gravel at the side of the road, just shy of a sign announcing *Welcome to Ohio*.

There were no other lights on the road; I shut off my own and sat behind the wheel, trembling, the night air cool on my skin. The insects wailed. The boy was slumped against the dashboard. There was a star fracture in the glass above his head, and warm blood came away on my fingers when I touched his hair. I got out of the car, circled around to the passenger's side, and dragged him from the seat into a field adjoining the road. He was surprisingly light. I left him there, in a field of Ohio soybeans on the evening of a summer's day.

The city of Detroit was founded by the French adventurer Antoine de la Mothe Cadillac, a supporter of Comte de Pontchartrain, minister of state to the Sun King, Louis XIV. All of these men worshipped the Roman Catholic God, protected their political positions, and let the future go hang. Cadillac, after whom an American automobile was named, was seeking a favorable location to advance his own economic interests. He came ashore on July 24, 1701 with fifty soldiers, an equal number of settlers, and about one hundred friendly Indians near the present site of the Veterans Memorial Building, within easy walking distance of the Greyhound Bus Terminal.

The car had not run well after the accident, developing a reluctance to go into fourth, but I did not care. The encounter with Milo had gone exactly as such things should go, and was especially pleasing because it had been totally unplanned. An accident – no order, one would guess – but exactly as if I had laid it all out beforehand. I came into Detroit late at night via Route 12, which eventually turned into Michigan Avenue. The air was hot and sticky. I remember driving past the Cadillac Plant; multitudes of red, yellow and green lights glinting off dull masonry and the smell of auto exhaust along the city streets. The sort of neighborhood I wanted was not far from Tiger Stadium: pawnshops, an all-night deli, laundromats, dimly lit bars with red Stroh's signs in the windows. Men on streetcorners walked casually from noplace to noplace.

I parked on a side street just around the corner from a Seven-Eleven. I left the motor running. In the store I dawdled over a magazine rack until at last I heard the racing of an engine and saw the Audi flash by the window. I bought a copy of *Time* and caught a downtown bus at the corner. At the Greyhound station I purchased a ticket for the next bus to Toronto and sat reading my magazine until departure time.

We got onto the bus. Across the river we stopped at customs and got off again. "Name?" they asked me.

"Gerald Spotsworth."

"Place of birth?"

"Calgary." I gave them my credentials. The passport photo showed me with hair. They looked me over. They let me go.

I work in the library of the University of Toronto. I am well-read, a student of history, a solid Canadian citizen. There I lead a sedentary life. The subways are clean, the people are friendly, the restaurants are excellent. The sky is blue. The cat is on the mat.

We got back on the bus. There were few other passengers, and most of them were soon asleep; the only light in the darkened interior was that which shone above my head. I was very tired, but I did not want to sleep. Then I remembered that I had Ruth's pills in my jacket pocket. I smiled, thinking of the customs people. All that was left in the box were a couple of tiny pink tabs. I did not know what they were, but I broke one down the middle with my fingernail and took it anyway. It perked me up immediately. Everything I could see seemed sharply defined. The dark green plastic of the seats. The rubber mat in the aisle. My fingernails. All details were separate and distinct, all interdependent. I must have been focused on the threads in the weave of my pants leg for ten minutes when I was surprised by someone sitting down next to me. It was Ruth. "You're back!" I exclaimed.

"We're all back," she said. I looked around and it was true: on the opposite side of the aisle, two seats ahead, Milo sat watching me over his shoulder, a trickle of blood running down his forehead. One corner of his mouth pulled tighter in a rueful smile. Mr Graves came back from the front seat and shook my hand. I saw the fat singer from the country club, still naked. The locker room boy. A flickering light from the back of the bus: when I turned around there stood the burning man, his eye sockets two dark hollows behind the wavering flames. The shopping mall guard. Hector from the hardware store. They all looked at me.

"What are you doing here?" I asked Ruth.

"We couldn't let you go on thinking like you do. You act like I'm some monster. I'm just a person."

"A rather nice-looking young lady," Graves added.

"People are monsters," I said.

"Like you, huh?" Ruth said. "But they can be saints, too."

That made me laugh. "Don't feed me platitudes. You can't even read."

"You make such a big deal out of reading. Yeah, well, times change. I get along fine, don't I?"

The mall guard broke in. "Actually, miss, the reason we caught on to you is that someone saw you go into the men's room." He looked embarrassed.

"But you didn't catch me, did you?" Ruth snapped back. She turned to me. "You're afraid of change. No wonder you live back here."

"This is all in my imagination," I said. "It's because of your drugs."

"It is all in your imagination," the burning man repeated. His voice was a whisper. "What you see in the future is what you are able to see. You have no faith in God or your fellow man."

"He's right," said Ruth.

"Bull. Psychobabble."

"Speaking of babble," Milo said, "I figured out where you got that goo-goo-goo stuff. Talk – "

"Never mind that," Ruth broke in. "Here's the truth. The future is just a place. The people there are just people. They live differently. So what. People make what they want of the world. You can't escape human failings by running into the past." She rested her hand on my leg. "I'll tell you what you'll find when you get to Toronto," she said. "Another city full of human beings."

This was crazy. I knew it was crazy. I knew it was all unreal, but somehow I was getting more and more afraid. "So the future is just the present writ large," I said bitterly. "More bull."

"You tell her, pal," the locker room boy said.

Hector, who had been listening quietly, broke in, "For a man from the future, you talk a lot like a native."

"You're the king of bullshit, man," Milo said. " 'Some people devote themselves to artwork!' Jesus!"

I felt dizzy. "Scut down, Milo. That means 'Fuck you too.' " I shook my head to try to make them go away. That was a mistake: the bus began to pitch like a sailboat. I grabbed for Ruth's arm but missed. "Who's driving this thing?" I asked, trying to get out of the seat.

"Don't worry," said Graves. "He knows what he's doing."

"He's brain-dead," Milo said.

"You couldn't do any better," said Ruth, pulling back down.

"No one is driving," said the burning man.

"We'll crash!" I was so dizzy now that I could hardly keep from vomiting. I closed my eyes and swallowed. That seemed to help. A long time passed; eventually I must have fallen asleep.

When I woke it was late morning and we were entering the city, cruising down Eglinton Avenue. The bus has a driver after all – a slender black man with neatly trimmed sideburns who wore his uniform hat at a rakish angle. A sign above the windshield said *Your driver – safe, courteous*, and below that, on the slide-in name plate, *Wilbert Caul*. I felt like

I was coming out of a nightmare. I felt happy. I stretched some of the knots out of my back. A young soldier seated across the aisle from me looked my way; I smiled, and he returned it briefly.

"You were mumbling to yourself in your sleep last night," he said.

"Sorry. Sometimes I have bad dreams."

"It's okay. I do too, sometimes." He had a round, open face, an apologetic grin. He was twenty, maybe. Who knew where his dreams came from? We chatted until the bus reached the station; he shook my hand and said he was pleased to meet me. He called me "sir."

I was not due back at the library until Monday, so I walked over to Yonge Street. The stores were busy, the tourists were out in droves, the adult theaters were doing a brisk business. Policemen in sharply creased trousers, white gloves, sauntered along among the pedestrians. It was a bright, cloudless day, but the breeze coming up the street from the lake was cool. I stood on the sidewalk outside one of the strip joints and watched the videotaped come-on over the closed circuit. The Princess Laya. Sondra Nieve, the Human Operator. Technology replaces the traditional barker, but the bodies are more or less the same. The persistence of your faith in sex and machines is evidence of your capacity to hope.

Francis Bacon, in his masterwork *The New Atlantis*, foresaw the utopian world that would arise through the application of experimental science to social problems. Bacon, however, could not solve the problems of his own time and was eventually accused of accepting bribes, fined forty thousand pounds, and imprisoned in the Tower of London. He made no appeal to God, but instead applied himself to the development of the virtues of patience and acceptance. Eventually he was freed. Soon after, on a freezing day in late March, we were driving near Highgate when I suggested to him that cold might delay the process of decay. He was excited by the idea. On impulse he stopped the carriage, purchased a hen, wrung its neck and stuffed it with snow. He eagerly looked forward to the results of his experiment. Unfortunately, in haggling with the street vendor he had exposed himself thoroughly to the cold and was seized with a chill which rapidly led to pneumonia, of which he died on April 9, 1626.

There's no way to predict these things.

When the videotape started repeating itself I got bored, crossed the street, and lost myself in the crowd.

WILLIAM GIBSON
The Winter Market

Almost unknown only a few years ago, William Gibson won the Nebula Award, the Hugo Award, and the Philip K. Dick Award in 1985 for his remarkable first novel *Neuromancer* – a rise to prominence as fiery and meteoric as any in SF history. Gibson sold his first story in 1977 to the now-defunct semiprozine *Unearth*, but it was seen by practically no one, and Gibson's name remained generally unknown until 1981, when he sold to *Omni* a taut and vivid story called "Johnny Mnemonic," a Nebula finalist that year. He followed it up in 1982 with another and even more compelling *Omni* story called "Burning Chrome," which was also a Nebula finalist . . . and all at once Gibson was very much A Writer To Watch.

Those watching him did not have long to wait. The appearance of *Neuromancer* and its sequels, *Count Zero*, and *Mona Lisa Overdrive*, made him the most talked-about and contro- versial new SF writer of the decade – one might almost say "writer," leaving out the "SF" part, for Gibson's reputation spread far outside the usual boundaries of the genre. Wildly enthusiastic notices about him and interviews with him appeared in places like *Rolling Stone*, *Spin* and *The Village Voice*, and pop-culture figures like Timothy Leary (not someone ordinarily much given to close observation of the SF world) embraced him with open arms. Gibson was also at the heart of the acrimonious Cyberpunk Wars of the mid-'80s (although more as a somewhat aloof figurehead than as one of the sweaty strugglers up on the barricades), with most critics acclaiming him as the foremost cyberpunk, and some even saying that he was the *only* true cyberpunk. By the beginning of the '90s, he was a bestseller in Britain, and was practically worshipped as a god in SF circles in Japan. Gibson stood aside from all this foofrah, smiling politely, and by the time the dust had settled, even most of his harshest critics had been forced to admit – sometimes grudgingly – that a major new talent had entered the field, the kind of major talent that comes along maybe once or twice in a literary generation.

You'll see why in the vivid, brilliant story that follows, a story in which he suggests that people who know *exactly* what they want can be a little frightening – particularly if they need *you* to get it for them . . .

Gibson's short fiction has been collected in *Burning Chrome*. His most recent book is a novel written in collaboration with Bruce Sterling, *The Difference Engine*, and he also has a new solo novel coming up. Born in South Carolina, he now lives in Vancouver, Canada, with his wife and family.

It rains a lot, up here; there are winter days when it doesn't really get light at all, only a bright, indeterminate gray. But then there are days when it's like they whip aside a curtain to flash you three minutes of sunlit, suspended mountain, the trademark at the start of God's own movie. It was like that the day her agents phoned, from deep in the heart of their mirrored pyramid on Beverly Boulevard, to tell me she'd merged with the net, crossed over for good, that *Kings of Sleep* was going triple-platinum. I'd edited most of *Kings*, done the brain-map work and gone over it all with the fast-wipe module, so I was in line for a share of royalties.

No, I said, no. Then yes, yes, and hung up on them. Got my jacket and took the stairs three at a time, straight out to the nearest bar and an eight-hour blackout that ended on a concrete ledge two meters above midnight. False Creek water. City lights, that same gray bowl of sky smaller now, illuminated by neon and mercury-vapor arcs. And it was snowing, big flakes but not many, and when they touched black water, they were gone, no trace at all. I looked down at my feet and saw my toes clear of the edge of concrete, the water between them. I was wearing Japanese shoes, new and expensive, glove-leather Ginza monkey boots with rubber-capped toes. I stood there for a long time before I took that first step back.

Because she was dead, and I'd let her go. Because, now, she was immortal, and I'd helped her get that way. And because I knew she'd phone me, in the morning.

My father was an audio engineer, a mastering engineer. He

went way back, in the business, even before digital. The processes he was concerned with were partly mechanical, with that clunky quasi-Victorian quality you see in twentieth-century technology. He was a lathe operator, basically. People brought him audio recordings and he burned their sounds into grooves on a disk of lacquer. Then the disk was electroplated and used in the construction of a press that would stamp out records, the black things you see in antique stores. And I remember him telling me, once, a few months before he died, that certain frequencies – transients, I think he called them – could easily burn out the head, the cutting head, on a master lathe. These heads were incredibly expensive, so you prevented burnouts with something called an accelerometer. And that was what I was thinking of, as I stood there, my toes out over the water: that head, burning out.

Because that was what they did to her.

And that was what she wanted.

No accelerometer for Lise.

I disconnected my phone on my way to bed. I did it with the business end of a West German studio tripod that was going to cost a week's wages to repair.

Woke some strange time later and took a cab back to Granville Island and Rubin's place.

Rubin, in some way that no one quite understands, is a master, a teacher, what the Japanese call a *sensei*. What he's the master of, really, is garbage, kipple, refuse, the sea of cast-off goods our century floats on. *Gomi no sensei*. Master of junk.

I found him, this time, squatting between two vicious-looking drum machines I hadn't seen before, rusty spider arms folded at the hearts of dented constellations of steel cans fished out of Richmond dumpsters. He never calls the place a studio, never refers to himself as an artist. "Messing around," he calls what he does there, and seems to view it as some extension of boyhood's perfectly bored backyard afternoons. He wanders through his jammed, littered space, a kind of minihangar cobbled to the water side of the Market, followed by the smarter and more agile of his creations, like some vaguely benign Satan bent on the elaboration of still stranger processes in his ongoing Inferno of *gomi*. I've seen Rubin program his constructions to identify and verbally abuse pedestrians wearing garments by a given season's hot designer; others attend to more obscure missions, and a few seem constructed solely to deconstruct themselves with as much attendant noise as possible. He's like a child, Rubin; he's also worth a lot of money in galleries in Tokyo and Paris.

So I told him about Lise. He let me do it, get it out, then nodded. "I know," he said. "Some CBC creep phoned eight times." He sipped something out of a dented cup. "You wanna Wild Turkey sour?"

"Why'd they call you?"

"Cause my name's on the back of *Kings of Sleep*. Dedication."

"I didn't see it yet."

"She try to call you yet?"

"No."

"She will."

"Rubin, she's dead. They cremated her already."

"I know," he said. "And she's going to call you."

Gomi.

Where does the *gomi* stop and the world begin? The Japanese, a century ago, had already run out of *gomi* space around Tokyo, so they came up with a plan for creating space out of *gomi*. By the year 1969 they had built themselves a little island in Tokyo Bay, out of *gomi*, and christened it Dream Island. But the city was still pouring out its nine thousand tons per day, so they went on to build New Dream Island, and today they coordinate the whole process, and new Nippons rise out of the Pacific. Rubin watches this on the news and says nothing at all.

He has nothing to say about *gomi*. It's his medium, the air he breathes, something he's swum in all his life. He cruises Greater Van in a spavined truck-thing chopped down from an ancient Mercedes airporter, its roof lost under a wallowing rubber bag half-filled with natural gas. He looks for things that fit some strange design scrawled on the inside of his forehead by whatever serves him as Muse. He brings home more *gomi*. Some of it still operative. Some of it, like Lise, human.

I met Lise at one of Rubin's parties. Rubin had a lot of parties. He never seemed particularly to enjoy them, himself, but they were excellent parties. I lost track, that fall, of the number of times I woke on a slab of foam to the roar of Rubin's antique espresso machine, a tarnished behemoth topped with a big chrome eagle, the sound outrageous off the corrugated steel walls of the place, but massively comforting, too: There was coffee. Life would go on.

First time I saw her: in the Kitchen Zone. You wouldn't call it a kitchen, exactly, just three fridges and a hot plate and a broken convection oven that had come in with the *gomi*. First time I saw her: She had the all-beer fridge open, light spilling out, and I caught the cheekbones and the determined set of that mouth, but I also caught the black glint of polycarbon at her wrist, and the bright slick sore the exoskeleton had rubbed there. Too drunk to process, to know what it was, but I did know it wasn't party time. So I did what people usually did, to Lise, and clicked myself into a different movie. Went for the wine instead, on the counter beside the convection oven. Never looked back.

But she found me again. Came after me two hours later, weaving through the bodies and junk with that terrible grace programmed into the exoskeleton. I knew what it was, then, as I watched her homing in, too embarrassed now to duck it, to run, to mumble some excuse and get out. Pinned there, my arm around the waist of a girl I didn't know, while Lise advanced – *was advanced*, with that mocking grace – straight at me now, her eyes burning with wizz, and the girl had wriggled out and away in a quiet social panic, was gone, and Lise stood there in front of me, propped up in her pencil-thin polycarbon prosthetic. Looked into those eyes and it was like you could hear her synapses whining, some impossibly high-pitched scream as the wizz opened every circuit in her brain.

"Take me home," she said, and the words hit me like a whip. I think I shook my head. "Take me home." There were levels of pain there, and subtlety, and an amazing cruelty. And I knew then that I'd never been hated, ever, as deeply or thoroughly as this wasted little girl hated me now, hated me for the way I'd looked, then looked away, beside Rubin's all-beer refrigerator.

So – if that's the word – I did one of those things you do and never find out why, even though something in you knows you could never have done anything else.

I took her home.

I have two rooms in an old condo rack at the corner of Fourth and MacDonald, tenth floor. The elevators usually work, and if you sit on the balcony railing and lean out backward, holding on to the corner of the building next door, you can see a little upright slit of sea and mountain.

She hadn't said a word, all the way back from Rubin's, and I was getting sober enough to feel very uneasy as I unlocked the door and let her in.

The first thing she saw was the portable fast-wipe I'd brought home from the Pilot the night before. The exoskeleton carried her across the dusty broadloom with that same walk, like a model down a runway. Away from the crash of the party, I could hear it click softly as it moved her. She stood there, looking down at the fast-wipe. I could see the thing's ribs when she stood like that, make them out across her back through the scuffed black leather of her jacket. One of those diseases. Either one of the old ones they've never quite figured out or one of the new ones – the all too obviously environmental kind – that they've barely even named yet. She couldn't move, not without that extra skeleton, and it was jacked straight into her brain, myoelectric interface. The fragile-looking polycarbon braces moved her arms and legs, but a more subtle system handled her thin hands, galvanic inlays. I thought of frog legs twitching in a high-school lab tape, then hated myself for it.

"This is a fast-wipe module," she said, in a voice I hadn't heard before, distant, and I thought then that the wizz might be wearing off. "What's it doing here?"

"I edit," I said, closing the door behind me.

"Well, now," and she laughed. "You do. Where?"

"On the Island. Place called the Autonomic Pilot."

She turned; then, hand on thrust hip, she swung – it swung her – and the wizz and the hate and some terrible parody of lust stabbed out at me from those washed-out gray eyes. "You wanna make it, editor?"

And I felt the whip come down again, but I wasn't going to take it, not again. So I cold-eyed her from somewhere down in the beer-numb core of my walking, talking, live-limbed, and entirely ordinary body and the words came out of me like spit: "Could you feel it, if I did?"

Beat. Maybe she blinked, but her face never registered. "No," she said, "but sometimes I like to watch."

Rubin stands at the window, two days after her death in Los Angeles, watching snow fall into False Creek. "So you never went to bed with her?"

One of his push-me-pull-yous, little roller-bearing Escher lizards, scoots across the table in front of me, in curl-up mode.

"No," I say, and it's true. Then I laugh. "But we jacked straight across. That first night."

"You were crazy," he says, a certain approval in his voice. "It might have killed you. Your heart might have stopped, you might have stopped breathing. . . ." He turns back to the window. "Has she called you yet?"

We jacked, straight across.

I'd never done it before. If you'd asked me why, I would have told you that I was an editor and that it wasn't professional.

The truth would be something more like this.

In the trade, the legitimate trade – I've never done porno – we call the raw product dry dreams. Dry dreams are neural output from levels of consciousness that most people can only access in sleep. But artists, the kind I work with at the Autonomic Pilot, are able to break the surface tension, dive down deep, down and out, out into Jung's sea, and bring back – well, dreams. Keep it simple. I guess some artists have always done that, in whatever medium, but neuro-electronics lets us access the experience, and the net gets it all out on the wire, so we can package it, sell it, watch how it moves in the market. Well, the more things change. . . . That's something my father liked to say.

Ordinarily I get the raw material in a studio situation, filtered through several million dollars' worth of baffles, and I don't even have to see the artist. The stuff we get out to the consumer, you see, has been structured, balanced, turned into art. There are still people naive enough to assume that they'll actually enjoy jacking straight across with someone they love. I think most teenagers try it, once. Certainly it's easy enough to do; Radio Shack will sell you the box and the trodes and the cables. But me, I'd never done it. And now that I think about it, I'm not so sure I can explain why. Or that I even want to try.

I do know why I did it with Lise, sat down beside her on my Mexican futon and snapped the optic lead into the socket on the spine, the smooth dorsal ridge, of the exoskeleton. It was high up, at the base of her neck, hidden by her dark hair.

Because she claimed she was an artist, and because I knew that we were engaged, somehow in total combat, and I was *not* going to lose. That may not make sense to you, but then you never knew her, or know her through *Kings of Sleep*, which isn't the same at all. You never felt that hunger she had, which was pared down to a dry need, hideous in its singleness of purpose. People who know *exactly* what they want have always frightened me, and Lise had known what she wanted for a long time, and wanted nothing else at all. And I was scared, then, of admitting to myself that I was scared, and I'd seen enough strangers' dreams, in the mixing room at the Autonomic Pilot, to know that most people's inner monsters are foolish things, ludicrous in the calm light of one's own consciousness. And I was still drunk.

I put the trodes on and reached for the stud on the fast-wipe. I'd shut down its studio functions, temporarily converting eighty thousand dollars' worth of Japanese electronics to the equivalent of one of those little Radio Shack boxes. "Hit it," I said, and touched the switch.

Words. Words cannot. Or, maybe, just barely, if I even knew how to begin to describe it, what came up out of her, what she did . . .

There's a segment on *Kings of Sleep*; it's like you're on a motorcycle at midnight, no lights but somehow you don't need them, blasting out along a cliff-high stretch of coast highway, so fast that you hang there in a cone of silence, the bike's thunder lost behind you. Everything, lost behind you. . . . It's just a blink, on *Kings*, but it's one of the thousand things you remember, go back to, incorporate into your own vocabulary of feelings. Amazing. Freedom and death, right there, right there, razor's edge, forever.

What I got was the big-daddy version of that, raw rush, the king hell killer uncut real thing, exploding eight ways from Sunday into a void that stank of poverty and loveless-ness and obscurity.

And that was Lise's ambition, that rush, *seen from the inside*.

It probably took all of four seconds.

And, course, she'd won.

I took the trodes off and stared at the wall, eyes wet, the framed posters swimming.

I couldn't look at her. I heard her disconnect the optic lead. I heard the exoskeleton creak as it hoisted her up from the futon. Heard it tick demurely as it hauled her into the kitchen for a glass of water.

Then I started to cry.

Rubin inserts a skinny probe in the roller-bearing belly of a sluggish push-me-pull-you and peers at the circuitry through magnifying glasses with miniature headlights mounted at the temples.

"So? You got hooked." He shrugs, looks up. It's dark now and the twin tensor beams stab at my face, chill damp in his steel barn and the lonesome hoot of a foghorn from somewhere across the water. "So?"

My turn to shrug. "I just did. . . . There didn't seem to be anything else to do."

The beams duck back to the silicon heart of his defective toy. "Then you're okay. It was a true choice. What I mean is, she was set to be what she is. You had about as much to do with where she's at today as that fast-wipe module did. She'd have found somebody else if she hadn't found you . . ."

I made a deal with Barry, the senior editor, got twenty

minutes at five on a cold September morning. Lise came in and hit me with that same shot, but this time I was ready, with my baffles and brain maps, and I didn't have to feel it. It took me two weeks, piecing out the minutes in the editing room, to cut what she'd done down into something I could play for Max Bell, who owns the Pilot.

Bell hadn't been happy, not happy at all, as I explained what I'd done. Maverick editors can be a problem, and eventually most editors decide that they've found someone who'll be it, the next monster, and then they start wasting time and money. He'd nodded when I'd finished my pitch, then scratched his nose with the cap of his red feltpen. "Uh-huh. Got it. Hottest thing since fish grew legs, right?"

But he'd jacked it, the demo soft I'd put together, and when it clicked out of its slot in his Braun desk unit, he was staring at the wall, his face blank.

"Max?"

"Huh?"

"What do you think?"

"Think? I. . . . What did you say her name was?" He blinked. "Lisa? Who you say she's signed with?"

"Lise. Nobody, Max. She hasn't signed with anybody yet."

"Jesus Christ." He still looked blank.

"You know how I found her?" Rubin asks, wading through ragged cardboard boxes to find the light switch. The boxes are filled with carefully sorted *gomi*: lithium batteries, tantalum capacitors, RF connectors, breadboards, barrier strips, ferroresonant transformers, spools of bus bar wire. . . . One box is filled with the severed heads of hundreds of Barbie dolls, another with armored industrial safety gauntlets that look like space-suit gloves. Light floods the room and a sort of Kandinski mantis in snipped and painted tin swings its golfball-size head toward the bright bulb. "I was down Granville on a *gomi* run, back in an alley, and I found her just sitting there. Caught the skeleton and she didn't look so good, so I asked her if she was okay. Nothin'. Just closed her eyes. Not my lookout, I think. But I happen back by there about four hours later and she hasn't moved. 'Look, honey,' I tell her, 'maybe your hardware's buggered up. I can help you, okay?' Nothin'. 'How long you been back here?' Nothin'. So I take off." He crosses to his workbench and strokes the thin metal limbs of the mantis thing with a pale forefinger. Behind the bench, hung on damp-swollen sheets of ancient pegboard, are pliers, screw-drivers, tie-wrap guns, a rusted Daisy BB rifle, coax strippers, crimpers, logic probes, heat guns, a pocket oscilloscope, seemingly every tool in human history, with no attempt ever made to order them at all, though I've yet to see Rubin's hand hesitate.

"So I went back," he says. "Gave it an hour. She was out by then, unconscious, so I brought her back here and ran a check on the exoskeleton. Batteries were dead. She'd crawled back there when the juice ran out and settled down to starve to death, I guess."

"When was that?"

"About a week before you took her home."

"But what if she'd died? If you hadn't found her?"

"Somebody was going to find her. She couldn't *ask* for anything, you know? Just *take*. Couldn't stand a favor."

Max found the agents for her, and a trio of awesomely slick junior partners Leared into YVR a day later. Lise wouldn't come down to the Pilot to meet them, insisted we bring them up to Rubin's, where she still slept.

"Welcome to Couverville," Rubin said as they edged in the door. His long face was smeared with grease, the fly of his ragged fatigue pants held more or less shut with a twisted paper clip. The boys grinned automatically, but there was something marginally more authentic about the girl's smile. "Mr Stark," she said, "I was in London last week. I saw your installation at the Tate."

"*Marcello's Battery Factory*," Rubin said. "They say it's scatological, the Brits. . . ." He shrugged. "Brits. I mean, who knows?"

"They're right. It's also very funny."

The boys were beaming like tabled-tanned lighthouses, standing there in their suits. The demo had reached Los Angeles. They knew.

"And you're Lise," she said, negotiating the path between Rubin's heaped *gomi*. "You're going to be a very famous person soon, Lise. We have a lot to discuss . . ."

And Lise just stood there, propped in polycarbon, and the look on her face was the one I'd seen that first night, in my condo, when she'd asked me if I wanted to go to bed. But if the junior agent lady saw it, she didn't show it. She was a pro.

I told myself that I was a pro, too.

I told myself to relax.

Trash fires gutter in steel canisters around the Market. The snow still falls and kids huddle over the flames like arthritic crows, hopping from foot to foot, wind whipping their dark coats. Up in Fairview's arty slum-tumble, someone's laundry had frozen solid on the line, pink squares of bedsheet standing out against the background dinge and the confusion of satellite dishes and solar panels. Some ecologist's eggbeater windmill goes round and round, round and round, giving a whirling finger to the Hydro rates.

Rubin clumps along in paint-spattered L.L. Bean gumshoes, his big head pulled down into an oversize fatigue jacket. Sometimes one of the hunched teens will point him out as we pass, the guy who builds all the crazy stuff, the robots and shit.

"You know what your trouble is?" he says when we're under the bridge, headed up to Fourth. "You're the kind who *always reads the handbook*. Anything people build, any kind of technology, it's going to have some specific purpose. It's for doing something that somebody already understands. But if it's new technology, it'll open areas nobody's ever thought of before. You read the manual, man, and you won't play around with it, not the same way. And yet get all funny when somebody else uses it to do something you never thought of. Like Lise."

"She wasn't the first." Traffic drums past overhead.

"No, but she's sure as hell the first person *you* ever met who went and translated themselves into a hardwired program. You lose any sleep when whatsisname did it, three-four years ago, the French kid, the writer?"

"I didn't really think about it, much. A gimmick. PR . . ."

"He's still writing. The weird thing is, he's going to *be* writing, unless somebody blows up his mainframe . . ."

I wince, shake my head. "But it's not *him*, is it? It's just a program."

"Interesting point. Hard to say. With Lise, though, we find out. She's not a writer."

She had it all in there, *Kings*, locked up in her head the way her body was locked in that exoskeleton.

The agents signed her with a label and brought in a production team from Tokyo. She told them she wanted me to edit. I said no; Max dragged me into his office and threatened to fire me on the spot. If I wasn't involved, there was no reason to do the studio work at the Pilot. Vancouver was hardly the center of the world, and the agents wanted her in Los Angeles. It meant a lot of money to him, and it might put the Autonomic Pilot on the map. I couldn't explain to him why I'd refused. It was too crazy, too personal; she was getting a final dig in. Or that's what I thought then. But Max was serious. He really didn't give me any choice. We both knew another job wasn't going to crawl into my hand. I went back out with him and we told the agents that we'd worked it out: I was on.

The agents showed us lots of teeth.

Lise pulled out an inhaler full of wizz and took a huge hit. I thought I saw the agent lady raise one perfect eyebrow, but that was the extent of censure. After the papers were signed, Lise more or less did what she wanted.

And Lise always knew what she wanted.

We did *Kings* in three weeks, the basic recording. I found any number of reasons to avoid Rubin's place, even believed some of them myself. She was still staying there, although the agents weren't too happy with what they saw as a total lack of security. Rubin told me later that he'd had to have *his* agent call them up and raise hell, but after that they seemed to quit worrying. I hadn't known that Rubin had an agent. It was always easy to forget that Rubin Stark was more famous, then, than anyone else I knew, certainly more famous than I thought Lise was ever likely to become. I knew we were working on something strong, but you never know how big anything's liable to be.

But the time I spent in the Pilot, I was *on*. Lise was amazing.

It was like she was born to the form, even though the technology that made that form possible hadn't even existed when she was born. You see something like that and you wonder how many thousands, maybe millions, of phenomenal artists have died mute, down the centuries, people who could never have been poets or painters or saxophone players, but who had this stuff inside, these psychic waveforms waiting for the circuitry required to tap in . . .

I learned a few things about her, incidentals, from our time in the studio. That she was born in Windsor. That her father was American and served in Peru and came home crazy and half-blind. That whatever was wrong with her body was congenital. That she had those sores because she refused to remove the exoskeleton, ever, because she'd start to choke and die at the thought of that utter helplessness. That she was addicted to wizz and doing enough of it daily to wire a football team.

Her agents brought in medics, who padded the polycarbon with foam and sealed the sores over with micropore dressings. They pumped her up with vitamins and tried to work on her diet, but nobody ever tried to take that inhaler away.

They brought in hairdressers and makeup artists, too, and wardrobe people and image builders and articulate little PR hamsters, and she endured it with something that might almost have been a smile.

And, right through those three weeks, we didn't talk. Just studio talk, artist-editor stuff. Very much a restricted code. Her imagery was so strong, so extreme, that she never really needed to explain a given effect to me. I took what she put out and worked with it, and jacked it back to her. She'd either say yes or no, and usually it was yes. The agents noted this and approved, and clapped Max Bell on the back and took him out to dinner, and my salary went up.

And I was pro, all the way. Helpful and thorough and polite. I was determined not to crack again, and never thought about the night I cried, and was also doing the best work I'd ever done, and knew it, and that's a high in itself.

And then, one morning, about six, after a long, long session – when she'd first gotten that eerie cotillion sequence out, the one the kids call the Ghost Dance – she spoke to me. One of the two agent boys had been there, showing teeth, but he was gone now and the Pilot was dead quiet, just the hum of a blower somewhere down by Max's office.

"Casey," she said, her voice hoarse with the wizz, "sorry I hit on you so hard."

I thought for a minute she was telling me something about the recording we'd just made. I looked up and saw her there, and it struck me that we were alone, and hadn't been alone since we'd made the demo.

I had no idea at all what to say. Didn't even know what I felt.

Propped up in the exoskeleton, she was looking worse than she had that first night, at Rubin's. The wizz was eating her, under the stuff the makeup team kept smoothing on, and sometimes it was like seeing a death's-head surface beneath the face of a not very handsome teenager. I had no idea of her real age. Not old, not young.

"The ramp effect," I said, coiling a length of cable.

"What's that?"

"Nature's way of telling you to clean up your act. Sort of mathematical law, says you can only get off real good on a stimulant x number of times, even if you increase the doses. But you can't *ever* get off as nice as you did the first few times. Or you shouldn't be able to, anyway. That's the trouble with designer drugs; they're too clever. That stuff you're doing has some tricky tail on one of its molecules, keeps you from turning the decomposed adrenaline into adrenochrome. If it didn't, you'd be schizophrenic by now. You got any little problems, Lise? Like apneia? Sometimes maybe you stop breathing if you go to sleep?"

But I wasn't even sure I felt the anger that I heard in my own voice.

She stared at me with those pale gray eyes. The wardrobe people had replaced her thrift-shop jacket with a butter-tanned matte black blouson that did a better job of hiding the polycarbon ribs. She kept it zipped to the neck, always, even though it was too warm in the studio. The hairdressers had tried something new the day before, and it hadn't worked out, her rough dark hair a lopsided explosion above the drawn, triangular face. She stared at me and I felt it again, her singleness of purpose.

"I don't sleep, Casey."

It wasn't until later, much later, that I remembered she'd told me she was sorry. She never did again, and it was the only time I ever heard her say anything that seemed to be out of character.

Rubin's diet consists of vending-machine sandwiches, Pakistani takeout food, and espresso. I've never seen him eat anything else. We eat samosas in a narrow shop on Fourth that has a single plastic table wedged between the counter and the door to the can. Rubin eats his dozen samosas, six meat and six veggie, with total concentration, one after another, and doesn't bother to wipe his chin. He's devoted to the place. He loathes the Greek counterman; it's mutual, a real relationship. If the counterman left, Rubin might not come back. The Greek glares at the crumbs on Rubin's chin and jacket. Between samosas, he shoots daggers right back, his eyes narrowed behind the smudged lenses of his steel-rimmed glasses.

The samosas are dinner. Breakfast will be egg salad on dead white bread, packed in one of those triangles of milky plastic, on top of six little cups of poisonously strong espresso.

"You didn't see it coming, Casey." He peers at me out of the thumbprinted depths of his glasses. " 'Cause you're no good at lateral thinking. You read the handbook. What else did you think she was after? Sex? More wizz? A world tour? She was past all that. That's what made her so strong. She was past it. That's why *Kings of Sleep*'s as big as it is, and why the kids buy it, why they *believe* it. They know. Those kids back down the Market, warming their butts around the fires and wondering if they'll find someplace to sleep tonight, they believe it. It's the hottest soft in eight years. Guy at a shop on Granville told me he gets more of the damned things lifted than he sells of anything else. Says it's a hassle to even stock it. . . . She's big because she was what they are, only more so. She knew, man. No dreams, no hope. You can't see the cages on those kids, Casey, but more and more they're twigging to it, that they aren't going *anywhere*." He brushes a greasy crumb of meat from his chin, missing three more. "So she sang it for them, said it the way they can't, painted them a picture. And she used the money to buy herself a way out, that's all."

I watch the steam bead and roll down the window in big drops, streaks in the condensation. Beyond the window I can make out a partially stripped Lada, wheels scavenged, axles down on the pavement.

"How many people have done it, Rubin? Have any idea?"

"Not too many. Hard to say, anyway, because a lot of them are probably politicians we think of as being comfortably and reliably dead." He gives me a funny look. "Not a nice thought. Anyway, they had first shot at the technology. It still costs too much for any ordinary dozen millionaires, but I've heard of at least seven. They say Mitsubishi did it to Weinberg before his immune system finally went tits up. He was head of their hybridoma lab in Okayama. Well, their stock's still pretty high, in monoclonals, so maybe it's true. And Langlais, the French kid, the novelist . . ." He shrugs. "Lise didn't have the money for it. Wouldn't now, even. But she put herself in the right place at the right time. She was about to croak, she was in Hollywood, and they could already see what *Kings* was going to do."

The day we finished up, the band stepped off a JAL shuttle out of London, four skinny kids who operated like a well-oiled machine and displayed a hypertrophied fashion sense and a total lack of affect. I set them up in a row at the Pilot, in identical white Ikea office chairs, smeared saline paste on their temples, taped the trodes on, and ran the rough version of what was going to become *Kings of Sleep*. When they came out of it, they all started talking at once, ignoring me totally, in the British version of that secret language all studio musicians speak, four sets of pale hands zooming and chopping the air.

I could catch enough of it to decide that they were excited. That they thought it was good. So I got my jacket and left. They could wipe their own saline paste off, thanks.

And that night I saw Lise for the last time, though I didn't plan to.

Walking back down to the Market, Rubin noisily digesting his meal, red taillights reflected on wet cobbles, the city beyond the Market a clean sculpture of light, a lie, where the broken and the lost burrow into the *gomi* that grows like humus at the bases of the towers of glass . . .

"I gotta go to Frankfurt tomorrow, do an installation. You wanna come? I could write you off as a technician." He shrugs his way deeper into the fatigue jacket. "Can't pay you, but you can have airfare, you want . . ."

Funny offer, from Rubin, and I know it's because he's worried about me, thinks I'm too strange about Lise, and it's the only thing he can think of, getting me out of town.

"It's colder in Frankfurt now than it is here."

"You maybe need a change, Casey. I dunno . . ."

"Thanks, but Max has a lot of work lined up. Pilot's a big deal now, people flying in from all over . . ."

"Sure."

When I left the band at the Pilot, I went home. Walked up to Fourth and took the trolley home, past the windows of the shops I see every day, each one lit up jazzy and slick, clothes and shoes and software, Japanese motorcycles crouched like clean enamel scorpions, Italian furniture. The windows change with the seasons, the shops come and go. We were into the preholiday mode now, and there were more people on the street, a lot of couples, walking quickly and purposefully past the bright windows, on their way to score that perfect little whatever for whomever, half the girls in those padded thigh-high nylon boot things that came out of New York the winter before, the ones that Rubin said made them look like they had elephantiasis. I grinned, thinking about that, and suddenly it hit me that it really was over, that I was done with Lise, and that now she'd be sucked off to Hollywood as inexorably as if she'd poked her toe into a black hole, drawn down by the unthinkable gravitic tug of Big Money. Believing that, that she was gone – probably was gone, by then – I let down some kind of guard in myself and felt the edges of my pity. But just the edges, because I didn't want my evening screwed up by anything. I wanted partytime. It had been a while.

Got off at my corner and the elevator worked on the first try. Good sign, I told myself. Upstairs, I undressed and showered, found a clean shirt, microwaved burritos. Feel normal, I advised my reflection while I shaved. You have been working too hard. Your credit cards have gotten fat. Time to remedy that.

The burritos tasted like cardboard, but I decided I liked them because they were so aggressively normal. My car was in Burnaby, having its leaky hydrogen cell repacked, so I wasn't going to have to worry about driving. I could go out, find partytime, and phone in sick in the morning. Max wasn't going to kick; I was his star boy. He owed me.

You owe me, Max, I said to the subzero bottle of Moskovskaya I fished out of the freezer. Do you ever owe me. I have just spent three weeks editing the dreams and nightmares of one very screwed up person, Max. On your behalf. So that you can grow and prosper, Max. I poured three fingers of vodka into a plastic glass left over from the party I'd thrown the year before and went back into the living room.

Sometimes it looks to me like nobody in particular lives there. No that it's that messy; I'm a good if somewhat robotic housekeeper, and even remember to dust the tops of framed posters and things, but I have these times when the place abruptly gives me a kind of low-grade chill, with its basic accumulation of basic consumer goods. I mean, it's not like I want to fill it up with cats or houseplants or anything, but there are moments when I see that anyone could be living there, could own those things, and it all seems sort of interchangeable, my life and yours, my life and any-body's. . .

I think Rubin sees things that way, too, all the time, but for him it's a source of strength. He lives in other people's garbage, and everything he drags home must have been new and shiny once, must have meant something, however briefly, to someone. So he sweeps it all up into his crazy-looking truck and hauls it back to his place and lets it compost there until he thinks of something new to do with it. Once he was showing me a book of twentieth-century art he liked, and there was a picture of an automated sculpture called "Dead Birds Fly Again," a thing that whirled real dead birds around and around on a string, and he smiled and nodded, and I could see he felt the artist was a spiritual ancestor of some kind. But what could Rubin do with my framed posters and my Mexican futon from the Bay and my temperfoam bed from Ikea? Well, I thought, taking a first chilly sip, he'd be able to think of something, which was why he was a famous artist and I wasn't.

I went and pressed my forehead against the plate-glass window, as cold as the glass in my hand. Time to go, I said to myself. You are exhibiting symptoms of urban singles angst. There are cures for this. Drink up. Go.

I didn't attain a state of partytime that night. Neither did I exhibit adult common sense and give up, go home, watch some ancient movie, and fall asleep on my futon. The tension those three weeks had built up in me drove me like the mainspring of a mechanical watch, and I went ticking off through nighttown, lubricating my more or less random progress with more drinks. It was one of those nights, I quickly decided, when you slip into an alternate continuum, a city that looks exactly like the one where you live except for the peculiar difference that it contains not one person you love or know or have even spoken to before. Nights like that, you can go into a familiar bar and find that the staff has just been replaced; then you understand that your real motive in going there was simply to see a familiar face, on a waitress or a bartender, whoever. . . . This sort of thing has been known to mediate against partytime.

I kept it rolling, though, through six or eight places, and eventually it rolled me into a West End club that looked as if it hadn't been redecorated since the nineties. A lot of peeling chrome over plastic, blurry holograms that gave you a headache if you tried to make them out. I think Barry had told me about the place, but I can't imagine why. I looked around and grinned. If I was looking to be depressed, I'd come to the right place. Yes, I told myself as I took a corner stool at the bar, this was genuinely sad, really the pits. Dreadful enough to halt the momentum of my shitty evening, which was undoubtedly a good thing. I'd have one more for the road, admire the grot, and then cab it on home.

And then I saw Lise.

She hadn't seen me, not yet, and I still had my coat on, tweed collar up against the weather. She was down the bar and around the corner with a couple of empty drinks in front of her, big ones, the kind that come with little Hong Kong parasols of plastic mermaids in them, and as she looked up at the boy beside her, I saw the wizz flash in her eyes and knew that those drinks had never contained alcohol, because the levels of drug she was running couldn't tolerate the mix. The kid, though, was gone, numb grinning drunk and about ready to slide off his stool, and running on about something as he made repeated attempts to focus his eyes and get a better look at Lise, who sat there with her wardrobe team's black leather blouson zipped to her chin and her skull about to burn through her white face like a thousand-watt bulb. And seeing that, seeing her there, I knew a whole lot of things at once.

That she really was dying, either from the wizz or her disease or the combination of the two. That she damned well knew it. That the boy beside her was too drunk to have picked up on the exoskeleton, but not too drunk to register the expensive jacket and the money she had for drinks. And that what I was seeing was exactly what it looked like.

But I couldn't add it up, right away, couldn't compute. Something in me cringed.

And she was smiling, or anyway doing a thing she must have thought was like a smile, the expression she knew was appropriate to the situation, and nodding in time to the kid's slurred inanities, and that awful line of hers came back to me, the one about liking to watch.

And I know something now. I know that if I hadn't happened in there, hadn't seen them, I'd have been able to accept all that came later. Might even have found a way to rejoice on her behalf, or found a way to trust in whatever it is that she's since become, or had built in her image, a program that pretends to be Lise to the extent that it believes it's her. I could have believed what Rubin believes, that she was so truly past it, our hi-tech Saint Joan burning for union with that hardwired godhead in Hollywood, that nothing mattered to her except the hour of her departure. That she threw away that poor sad body with a cry of release, free of the bonds of polycarbon and hated flesh. Well, maybe, after all, she did. Maybe it was that way. I'm sure that's the way she expected it to be.

But seeing her there, that drunken kid's hand in hers, that hand she couldn't even feel, I knew, once and for all, that no human motive is ever entirely pure. Even Lise, with that corrosive, crazy drive to stardom and cybernetic immortality, had weaknesses. Was human in a way I hated myself for admitting.

She'd gone out that night, I knew, to kiss herself goodbye. To find someone drunk enough to do it for her. Because, I knew then, it was true: She did like to watch.

I think she saw me, as I left. I was practically running. If she did, I suppose she hated me worse than ever, for the horror and the pity in my face.

I never saw her again.

Someday I'll ask Rubin why Wild Turkey sours are the only drink he knows how to make. Industrial-strength, Rubin's sours. He passes me the dented aluminum cup, while his place ticks and stirs around us with the furtive activity of his smaller creations.

"You ought to come to Frankfurt," he says again.

"Why, Rubin?"

"Because pretty soon she's going to call you up. And I think maybe you aren't ready for it. You're still screwed up about this, and it'll sound like her and think like her, and you'll get too weird behind it. Come over to Frankfurt with me and you can get a little breathing space. She won't know you're there . . ."

"I told you," I say, remembering her at the bar in that club, "lots of work. Max – "

"Stuff Max. Max you just made rich. Max can sit on his

hands. You're rich yourself, from your royalty cut on *Kings*, if you weren't too stubborn to dial up your bank account. You can afford a vacation."

I look at him and wonder when I'll tell him the story of that final glimpse. "Rubin, I appreciate it, man, but I just . . ."

He sighs, drinks. "But what?"

"Rubin, if she calls me, is it *her?*"

He looks at me a long time. "God only knows." His cup clicks on the table. "I mean, Casey, the technology is there, so who, man, really who, is to say?"

"And you think I should come with you to Frankfurt?"

He takes off his steel-rimmed glasses and polishes them inefficiently on the front of his plaid flannel shirt. "Yeah, I do. You need the rest. Maybe you don't need it now, but you're going to, later."

"How's that?"

"When you have to edit her next release. Which will almost certainly be soon, because she needs money bad. She's taking up a lot of ROM on some corporate mainframe, and her share of *Kings* won't come close to paying for what they had to do to put her there. And you're her editor, Casey. I mean, who else?"

And I just stare at him as he puts the glasses back on, like I can't move at all.

"Who else, man?"

And one of his constructs clicks right then, just a clear and tiny sound, and it comes to me, he's right.

CONNIE WILLIS

Chance

Connie Willis lives in Greeley, Colorado, with her family. She first attracted attention as a writer in the late '70s with a number of outstanding stories for the now defunct magazine *Galileo*, and in the subsequent few years has made a large name for herself very fast indeed. In 1982, she won two Nebula Awards, one for her superb novelette "Fire Watch," and one for her poignant short story "A Letter from the Clearys;" a few months later, "Fire Watch" went on to win her a Hugo Award as well. In 1989, her powerful novella "The Last of the Winnebagoes" won both the Nebula and the Hugo, and she won another Nebula last year for her novelette "At the Rialto." Her books include the novel *Water Witch*, written in collaboration with Cynthia Felice, and *Fire Watch*, a collection of her short fiction. Her most recent book was the outstanding *Lincoln's Dreams*, her first solo novel. Upcoming is another novel in collaboration with Cynthia Felice, and a new solo novel.

Willis's is a unique and powerful voice, comfortable with either comedy or tragedy – she may well come to be seen as one of the greatest talents ever to enter the field. "Chance" may be one of the best stories of the last decade, in or out of the genre; by rights, it should have been published in *Esquire* or *Harper's*, and be being reprinted in Martha Foley's *Best American Short Stories* . . . but, things being as they are, it will have to settle instead for having appeared in *Isaac Asimov's Science Fiction Magazine*, and for being reprinted in this anthology.

On Wednesday Elizabeth's next-door neighbor came over. It was raining hard, but she had run across the yard without a raincoat or an umbrella, her hands jammed in her cardigan sweater pockets.

"Hi," she said breathlessly. "I live next door to you, and I just thought I'd pop in and say hi and see if you were getting settled in." She reached in one of the sweater pockets and pulled out a folded piece of paper. "I wrote down the name of our trash pickup. Your husband asked about it the other day."

She handed it to her. "Thank you," Elizabeth said. The young woman reminded her of Tib. Her hair was short and blonde and brushed back in wings. Tib had worn hers like that when they were freshmen.

"Isn't this weather awful?" the young woman said. "It usually doesn't rain like this in the fall."

It had rained all fall when Elizabeth was a freshman. "Where's your raincoat?" Tib had asked her when she unpacked her clothes and hung them up in the dorm room.

Tib was little and pretty, the kind of girl who probably had dozens of dates, the kind of girl who brought all the right clothes to college. Elizabeth hadn't known what kind of clothes to bring. The brochure the college had sent the freshmen had said to bring sweaters and skirts for class, a suit for rush, a formal. It hadn't said anything about a raincoat.

"Do I need one?" Elizabeth had said.

"Well, it's raining right now if that's any indication," Tib had said.

"I thought it was starting to let up," the neighbor said, "but it's not. And it's so cold."

She shivered. Elizabeth saw that her cardigan was damp.

"I can turn the heat up," Elizabeth said.

"No, I can't stay. I know you're trying to get unpacked. I'm sorry you had to move in all this rain. We usually have beautiful weather here in the fall." She smiled at Elizabeth. "Why am I telling you that? Your husband told me you went to school here. At the university."

"It wasn't university back then. It was a state college."

"Oh, right. Has the campus changed a lot?"

Elizabeth went over and looked at the thermostat. It showed the temperature as sixty-eight, but it felt colder. She turned it up to seventy-five. "No," she said. "It's just the same."

"Listen, I can't stay," the young woman said. "And you've probably got a million things to do. I just came over to say hello and see if you'd like to come over tonight. I'm having a Tupperware party."

A Tupperware party, Elizabeth thought sadly. No wonder she reminds me of Tib.

"You don't have to come. And if you come you don't have to buy anything. It's not going to be a big party. Just a few friends of mine. I thought it would be a good way for you to meet some of the neighbors. I'm really only having the party because I have this friend who's trying to get started selling Tupperware and . . ." She stopped and looked anxiously at Elizabeth, holding her arms against her chest for warmth.

"I used to have a friend who sold Tupperware," Elizabeth said.

"Oh, then you probably have tons of it."

The furnace came on with a deafening blow. "No," Elizabeth said. "I don't have any."

"Please come," the young woman had continued to say even on the front porch. "Not to buy anything. Just to meet everybody."

The rain was coming down hard again. She ran back across the lawn to her house, her arms wrapped tightly around her and her head down.

Elizabeth went back in the house and called Paul at his office.

"Is this really important, Elizabeth?" he said. "I'm supposed to meet with Dr Brubaker in Admissions for lunch at noon, and I have a ton of paperwork."

"The girl next door invited me to a Tupperware party," Elizabeth said. "I didn't want to say yes if you had anything planned for tonight."

"A Tupperware party?!" he said. "I can't believe you called me about something like that. You know how busy I am. Did you put your application in at Carter?"

"I'm going over there right now," she said. "I was going to go this morning, but the – "

"Dr Brubaker's here," he said, and hung up the phone.

Elizabeth stood by the phone a minute, thinking about Tib, and then put on her raincoat and walked over to the old campus.

"It's exactly the same as it was when we were freshmen," Tib had said when Elizabeth told her about Paul's new job. "I was up there last summer to get some transcripts, and I couldn't believe it. It was raining, and I swear the sidewalks were covered with exactly the same worms as they always were. Do you remember that yellow slicker you bought when you were a freshman?"

Tib had called Elizabeth from Denver when they came out to look for a house. "I read in the alumni news that Paul was the new assistant dean," she had said as if nothing had ever happened. "The article didn't say anything about you, but I thought I'd call on the off-chance that you were still married. I'm not." Tib had insisted on taking her to lunch in Larimer Square. She had let her hair grow out, and she was too thin. She ordered a peach daiquiri and told Elizabeth all about her divorce. "I found out Jim was screwing some little slut at the office," she had said, twirling the sprig of mint that had come with her drink, "and I couldn't take it. He couldn't see what I was upset about. 'So I fooled around, so what?' he told me. 'Everybody does it. When are you going to grow up?' I never should have married the creep, but you don't know you're ruining your life when you do it, do you?"

"No," Elizabeth said.

"I mean, look at you and Paul," she said. She talked faster than Elizabeth remembered, and when she called the waiter over to order another daiquiri, her voice shook a little. "Now that's a marriage I wouldn't have taken bets on, and you've been married, what? Fifteen years?"

"Seventeen," Elizabeth said.

"You know, I always thought you'd patch things up with Tupper," she said. "I wonder whatever became of him." The waiter brought the daiquiri and took the empty one away. She took the mint sprig out and laid it carefully on the tablecloth.

"Whatever became of Elizabeth and Tib, for that matter," she said.

The campus wasn't really just the same. They had added a wing onto Frasier and cut down most of the elms. It wasn't even really the campus anymore. The real campus was west and north of here, where there had been room for the new concrete classroom buildings and high-rise dorms. The music department was still in Frasier, and the PE department used the old gym in Gunter for women's sports, but most of the old classroom buildings and the small dorms at the south end of the campus were offices now. The library was now the administration building and Kepner belonged to the campus housing authority, but in the rain the campus looked the same.

The leaves were starting to fall, and the main walk was wet and covered with worms. Elizabeth picked her way among them, watching her feet and trying not to step on them. When she was a freshman she had refused to walk on the sidewalks at all. She had ruined two pairs of flats that fall by cutting through the grass to get to her classes.

"You're a nut, you know that?" Tib had shouted, sprinting to catch up to her. "There are worms in the grass, too."

"I know, but I can't see them."

When there was no grass, she had insisted on walking in the middle of the street. That was how they had met Tupper. He almost ran them down with his bike.

It had been a Friday night. Elizabeth remembered that because Tib was in her ROTC Angel Flight uniform and after Tupper had swerved wildly to miss them, sending up great sprays of water and knocking his bike over, the first thing he said was, "Cripes! She's a cop!"

They had helped him pick up the plastic bags strewn all over the street. "What are these?" Tib had said, stooping because she couldn't bend over in her straight blue skirt and high heels.

"Tupperware," he had said. "The latest thing. You girls wouldn't need a lettuce crisper, would you? They're great for keeping worms in."

Carter Hall looked just the same from the outside, ugly beige stone and glass brick. It had been the student union, but now it housed Financial Aid and Personnel. Inside it had been completely remodeled. Elizabeth couldn't even tell where the cafeteria had been.

"You can fill it out here if you want," the girl who gave her the application said, and gave her a pen. Elizabeth hung her coat over the back of a chair and sat down at a desk by a window. It felt chilly, though the window was steamy.

They had all gone to the student union for pizza. Elizabeth

had hung her yellow slicker over the back of the booth. Tupper had pretended to wring out his jean jacket and draped it over the radiator. The window by the booth was so steamed up they couldn't see out. Tib had written "I hate rain" on the window with her finger, and Tupper had told them how he was putting himself through college selling Tupperware.

"They're great for keeping cookies in," he said, hauling up a big pink box he called a cereal keeper. He put a piece of pizza inside and showed them how to put the lid on and burp it. "There. It'll keep for weeks. Years. Come on. You need one. I'll bet your mothers send you cookies all the time."

He was a junior. He was tall and skinny and when he put his damp jean jacket back on the sleeves were too short, and his wrists stuck out. He had sat next to Tib on one side of the booth and Elizabeth had sat on the other. He had talked to Tib most of the evening, and when he was paying the check he had bent toward Tib and whispered something to her. Elizabeth was sure he was asking her out on a date, but on the way home, Tib had said, "You know what he wanted, don't you? Your telephone number."

Elizabeth stood up and put her coat back on. She gave the girl in the sweater and skirt back her pen. "I think I'll fill this out at home and bring it back."

"Sure," the girl said.

When Elizabeth went back outside, the rain had stopped. The trees were still dripping, big drops that splattered onto the wet walk. She walked up the wide center walk toward her old dorm, looking at her feet so she wouldn't step on any worms. The dorm had been converted into the university's infirmary. She stopped and stood a minute under the center window, looking up at the room that had been hers and Tib's.

Tupper had stood under the window and thrown pebbles at it. Tib had opened the window and yelled, "You'd better stop throwing rocks, you. . . ." Something hit her in the chest. "Oh, hi, Tupper," she said, and picked it up off the floor and handed it to Elizabeth. "It's for you," she said. It wasn't a pebble. It was a pink plastic gadget, one of the favors he passed out at his Tupperware parties.

"What's this supposed to be?" Elizabeth had said, leaning out of the window and waving it at him. It was raining. Tupper had the collar of his jean jacket turned up, and he looked cold. The sidewalk around him was covered with pink plastic favours.

"A present," he said. "It's an egg separator."

"I don't have any eggs."

"Wear it around your neck then. We'll be officially scrambled."

"Or separated."

He grabbed at his chest with his free hand. "Never!" he said. "Want to come out in the worms with me? I've got some deliveries to make." He held up a clutch of plastic bags full of bowls and cereal keepers.

"I'll be right down," she had said, but she had stopped and found a ribbon to string the egg separator on before she went downstairs.

Elizabeth looked down at the sidewalk, but there were no plastic favors on the wet cement. There was a big puddle out by the curb, and a worm lay at the edge of it. It moved a little as she watched, in that horrid boneless way that she had always hated, and then lay still.

A girl brushed past her, walking fast. She stepped in the puddle, and Elizabeth took a half-step back to avoid being splashed. The water in the puddle rippled and moved out in a wave. The worm went over the edge of the sidewalk and into the gutter.

Elizabeth looked up. The girl was already halfway down the center walk, late for class or angry or both. She was wearing an Angel Flight uniform and high heels, and her short blonde hair was brushed back in wings along the side of her garrison cap.

Elizabeth stepped off the curb into the street. The gutter was clogged with dead leaves and full of water. The worm lay at the bottom. She sat down on her heels, holding the application form in her right hand. The worm would drown, wouldn't it? That was what Tupper had told her. The reason they came out on the sidewalks when it rained was that their tunnels filled up with water, and they would drown if they didn't.

She stood up and looked down the central walk again, but the girl was gone, and there was nobody else on the campus. She stooped again and transferred the application to her other hand, and then reached in the icy water, and scooped up the worm in her cupped hand, thinking that as long as it didn't move she would be able to stand it, but as soon as her fingers touched the soft pink flesh, she dropped it and clenched her fist.

"I can't," Elizabeth said, rubbing her wet hand along the side of her raincoat, as if she could wipe off the memory of the worm's touch.

She took the application in both hands and dipped it into the water like a scoop. The paper went a little limp in the water, but she pushed it into the dirty, wet leaves and scooped the worm up and put it back on the sidewalk. It didn't move.

"And thank God they do come out on the sidewalks!" Tupper had said, walking her home in the middle of the street from his Tupperware deliveries. "You think they're disgusting lying there! What if they didn't come out on the sidewalks? What if they all stayed in their holes and drowned? Have you ever had to do mouth-to-mouth resuscitation on a worm?"

Elizabeth straightened up. The job application was wet and dirty. There was a brown smear where the worm had lain, and a dirty line across the top. She should throw it away and go back to Carter to get another one. She unfolded it and carefully separated the wet pages so they wouldn't stick together as they dried.

"I had first aid last semester, and we had to do mouth-to-mouth resuscitation in there," Tupper had said, standing in the middle of the street in front of her dorm. "What a great class! I sold twenty-two square rounds for snake bite kits. Do you know how to do mouth-to-mouth resuscitation?"

"No."

"It's easy," Tupper had said, and put his hand on the back of her neck under her hair and kissed her, in the middle of the street in the rain.

The worm still hadn't moved. Elizabeth stood and

watched it a little longer, feeling cold, and then went out in the middle of the street and walked home.

Paul didn't come home till after seven. Elizabeth had kept a casserole warm in the oven.

"I ate," he said. "I thought you'd be at your Tupperware party."

"I don't want to go," she said, reaching into the hot oven to get the casserole out. It was the first time she had felt warm all day.

"Brubaker's wife is going. I told him you'd be there, too. I want you to get to know her. Brubaker's got a lot of influence around here about who gets tenure."

She put the casserole on top of the stove and then stood there with the oven door half open. "I went over to apply for a job today," she said, "and I saw this worm. It had fallen in the gutter and it was drowning and I picked it up and put it back on the sidewalk."

"And did you apply for the job or do you think you can make any money picking up worms?"

She had turned up the furnace when she got home and put the application on the vent, but it had wrinkled as it dried, and there was a big smear down the middle where the worm had lain. "No," she said, "I was going to, but when I was over on the campus, there was this worm lying on the sidewalk. A girl walked by and stepped in a puddle, and that was all it took. The worm was right on the edge, and when she stepped in the puddle, it made a kind of wave that pushed it over the edge. She didn't even know she'd done it."

"Is there a point to this story, or have you decided to stand here and talk until you've completely ruined my chance at tenure?" He shut off the oven and went into the living room. She followed him.

"All it took was somebody walking past and stepping in a puddle, and the worm's whole life was changed. Do you think things happen like that? That one little action can change your whole life forever?"

"What I think," he said, "is that you didn't want to move here in the first place, and so you are determined to sabotage my chances. You know what this move is costing us, but you won't go apply for a job. You know how important my getting tenure is, but you won't do anything to help. You won't even go to a goddamn Tupperware party!" He turned the thermostat down. "It's like an oven in here. You've got the heat turned up to seventy-five. What's the matter with you?"

"I was cold," Elizabeth said.

She was late to the Tupperware party. They were in the middle of a game where they told their name and something they liked that began with the same letter.

"My name's Sandy," an overweight woman in brown polyester pants and a rust print blouse was saying, "and I like sundaes." She pointed at Elizabeth's neighbor. "And you're Meg, and you like marshmallows, and you're Janice," she said, glaring at a woman in a pink suit with her hair teased and sprayed the way girls had worn it when Elizabeth was in college. "You're Janice and you like Jesus," she said, and moved rapidly on to the next person. "And you're Barbara and you like bananas."

She went all the way around the circle until she came to Elizabeth. She looked puzzled for a moment, and then said, "And you're Elizabeth, and you went to college here, didn't you?"

"Yes," she said.

"That doesn't begin with an E," the woman in the center said. Everyone laughed. "I'm Terry, and I like Tupperware," she said, and there was more laughter. "You got here late. Stand up and tell us your name and something you like."

"I'm Elizabeth," she said, still trying to place the woman in the brown slacks. Sandy. "And I like. . . ." She couldn't think of anything that began with an E.

"Eggs," Sandy whispered loudly.

"And I like eggs," Elizabeth said, and sat back down.

"Great," Terry said. "Everybody else got a favor, so you get one, too." She handed Elizabeth a pink plastic egg separator.

"Somebody gave me one of those," she said.

"No problem," Terry said. She held out a shallow plastic

box full of plastic toothbrush holders and grapefruit slicers. "You can put it back and take something else if you've already got one."

"No. I'll keep this." She knew she should say something good-natured and funny, in the spirit of things, but all she could think of was what she had said to Tupper when he gave it to her. "I'll treasure this always," she had told him. A month later she had thrown it away.

"I'll treasure it always," Elizabeth said, and everyone laughed.

They played another game, unscrambling words like "autumn" and "schooldays" and "leaf," and then Terry passed out order forms and pencils and showed them the Tupperware.

It was cold in the house, even though Elizabeth's neighbor had a fire going in the fireplace, and after she had filled out her order form, Elizabeth went over and sat in front of the fire, looking at the plastic egg separator.

The woman in the brown pants came over, holding a coffee cup and a brownie on a napkin. "Hi, I'm Sandy Konkel. You don't remember me, do you?" she said. "I was an Alpha Phi. I pledged the year after you did."

Elizabeth looked earnestly at her, trying to remember her. She did not look like she had ever been an Alpha Phi. Her mustard-colored hair looked as if she had cut it herself. "I'm sorry, I . . ." Elizabeth said.

"That's okay," Sandy said. She sat down next to her. "I've changed a lot. I used to be skinny before I went to all these Tupperware parties and ate brownies. And I used to be a lot blonder. Well, actually, I never was any blonder, but I looked blonder, if you know what I mean. You look just the same. You were Elizabeth Wilson, right?"

Elizabeth nodded.

"I'm not really a whiz at remembering names," she said cheerfully, "but they stuck me with being alum rep this year. Could I come over tomorrow and get some info from you on what you're doing, who you're married to. Is your husband an alum, too?"

"No," Elizabeth said. She stretched her hands out over

the fire, trying to warm them. "Do they still have Angel Flight at the college?"

"At the university, you mean," Sandy said, grinning. "It used to be a college. Gee, I don't know. They dropped the whole ROTC thing back in sixty-eight. I don't think they ever reinstated it. I can find out. Were you in Angel Flight?"

"No," Elizabeth said.

"You know, now that I think about it, I don't think they did. They always had that big fall dance, and I don't remember them having it since . . . what was it called, the Autumn Something?"

"The Harvest Ball," Elizabeth said.

Thursday morning Elizabeth walked back over to the campus to get another job application. Paul had been late going to work. "Did you talk to Brubaker's wife?" he had said on his way out the door. Elizabeth had forgotten all about Mrs Brubaker. She wondered which one she had been, Barbara who liked bananas or Meg who liked marshmallows.

"Yes," she said. "I told her how much you liked the university."

"Good. There's a faculty concert tomorrow night. Brubaker asked if we were going. I invited them over for coffee afterwards. Did you turn the heat up again?" he said. He looked at the thermostat and turned it down to sixty. "You had it turned up to eighty. I can hardly wait to see what our first gas bill is. The last thing I need is a two-hundred-dollar gas bill, Elizabeth. Do you realize what this move is costing us?"

"Yes," Elizabeth said. "I do."

She had turned the thermostat back up as soon as he left, but it didn't seem to do any good. She put on a sweater and her raincoat and walked over to the campus.

The rain had stopped sometime during the night, but the central walk was still wet. At the far end, a girl in a yellow slicker stepped up on the curb. She took a few steps on the sidewalk, her head bent, as if she were looking at something on the ground, and then cut across the wet grass toward Gunter.

*

Elizabeth went into Carter Hall. The girl who had helped her the day before was leaning over the counter, taking notes from a textbook. She was wearing a pleated skirt and sweater like Elizabeth had worn in college.

"The styles we wore have all come back," Tib had said when they had lunch together. "Those matching sweater and skirt sets and those horrible flats that we never could keep on our feet. And penny loafers." She was on her third peach daiquiri and her voice had gotten calmer with each one, so that she almost sounded like her old self. "And cocktail dresses! Do you remember that rust formal you had, with the scoop neck and the long skirt with the raised design? I always loved that dress. Do you remember that time you loaned it to me for the Angel Flight dance?"

"Yes," Elizabeth said, and picked up the bill.

Tib tried to stir her peach daiquiri with its mint sprig, but it slipped out of her fingers and sank to the bottom of the glass. "He really only took me to be nice."

"I know," Elizabeth had said. "Now how much do I owe? Six-fifty for the crepes and two for the wine cooler. Do they add on the tip here?"

"I need another job application," Elizabeth said to the girl.

"Sure thing." When the girl walked over to the files to get it, Elizabeth could see that she was wearing flat-heeled shoes like she had worn in college. Elizabeth thanked her and put the application in her purse.

She walked up past her dorm. The worm was still lying there. The sidewalk around it was almost dry, and the worm was a darker red than it had been. "I should have put it in the grass," she said out loud. She knew it was dead, but she picked it up and put it in the grass anyway, so no one would step on it. It was cold to the touch.

Sandy Konkel came over in the afternoon wearing a gray polyester pantsuit. She had a wet high school letter jacket over her head. "John loaned me his jacket," she said. "I wasn't going to wear a coat this morning, but John told me I was going to get drenched. Which I was."

"You might want to put it on," Elizabeth said. "I'm sorry it's so cold in here. I think there's something wrong with the furnace."

"I'm fine," Sandy said. "You know, I wrote that article on your husband being the new assistant dean, and I asked him about you, but he didn't say anything about your having gone to college here."

She had a thick notebook with her. She opened it at tabbed sections. "We might as well get this alum stuff out of the way first, and then we can talk. This alum rep job is a real pain, but I must admit I get kind of a kick out of finding out what happened to everybody. Let's see," she said, thumbing through the sections. "Found, lost, hopelessly lost, deceased. I think you're one of the hopelessly lost. Right? Okay." She dug a pencil out of her purse. "You were Elizabeth Wilson."

"Yes," Elizabeth said. "I was." She had taken off her light sweater and put on a heavy wool one when she got home, but was still cold. She rubbed her hands along her upper arms. "Would you like some coffee?"

"Sure," she said. She followed Elizabeth to the kitchen and asked her questions about Paul and his job and whether they had any children while Elizabeth made coffee and put out the cream and sugar and a plate of the cookies she had baked for after the concert.

"I'll read you some names off the hopelessly lost list, and if you know what happened to them, just stop me. Carolyn Waugh, Pam Callison, Linda Bohlender." She was several names past Cheryl Tibner before Elizabeth realized that was Tib.

"I saw Tib in Denver this summer," she said. "Her married name's Scates, but she's getting a divorce, and I don't know if she's going to go back to her maiden name or not."

"What's she doing?" Sandy said.

She's drinking too much, Elizabeth thought, and she let her hair grow out, and she's too thin. "She's working for a stockbroker," she said and went to get the address Tib had given her. Sandy wrote it down, and then flipped to the tabbed section marked *Found* and entered the name and address again.

"Would you like some more coffee, Mrs Konkel?" Elizabeth said.

"You still don't remember me, do you?" Sandy said. She stood up and took off her jacket. She was wearing a short-sleeved gray knit shell underneath it. "I was Karen Zamora's roommate. Sondra Dickeson?"

Sondra Dickeson. She had pale blonde hair that she wore in a pageboy, and a winter white cashmere sweater and a matching white skirt with a kick pleat. She had worn it with black heels and a string of real pearls.

Sandy laughed. "You should see the expression on your face. You remember me now, don't you?"

"I'm sorry. I just didn't . . . I should have . . ."

"Listen, it's okay," she said. She took a sip of coffee. "At least you didn't say, 'How could you let yourself go like that?' like Janice Brubaker did." She bit into a cookie. "Well, aren't you going to ask me whatever became of Sondra Dickeson? It's a great story."

"What happened to her?" Elizabeth said. She felt suddenly colder. She poured herself another cup of coffee and sat back down, wrapping her hands around the cup for warmth.

Sandy finished the cookie and took another one. "Well, if you remember, I was kind of a snot in those days. I was going to this Sigma Chi dinner dance with Chuck Pagano. Do you remember him? Well, anyway, we were going to this dance clear out in the country somewhere and he stopped the car and got all clutchy grabby and I got mad because he was messing up my hair and my makeup so I got out of the car. And he drove off. So there I was, standing out in the middle of nowhere in a formal and high heels. I hadn't even grabbed my purse or anything, and it's getting dark, and Sondra Dickeson is such a snot that it never even occurs to her to walk back to town or try to find a phone or something. No, she just stands there like an idiot in her brocade formal and her orchid corsage and her dyed satin pumps and thinks, He can't do this to me. Who does he think he is?"

She was talking about herself as if she had been another person, which Elizabeth supposed she had been, an ice-blonde with a pageboy and a formal like the one Elizabeth had loaned Tib for the Harvest Ball, a rust satin bodice and a bell skirt out of sculptured rust brocade. After the dance Elizabeth had given it to the Salvation Army.

"Did Chuck come back?" she said.

"Yes," Sandy said, frowning, and then grinned. "But not soon enough. Anyway, it's almost dark and along comes this truck with no lights on, and this guy leans out and says, 'Hiya, gorgeous. Wanta ride?' " She smiled at her coffee cup as if she could still hear him saying it. "He was awful. His hair was down to his ears and his fingernails were black. He wiped his hand on his shirt and helped me into the truck. He practically pulled my arm out of its socket, and then he said, 'I thought there for a minute I was going to have to go around behind and shove. You know, you're lucky I came along. I'm not usually out after dark on account of my lights being out, but I had a flat tire.' "

She's happy, Elizabeth thought, putting her hand over the top of her cup to try to warm herself with the steam.

"And he took me home and I thanked him and the next week he showed up at the Phi house and asked me out for a date, and I was so surprised that I went, and I married him, and we have four kids."

The furnace kicked on, and Elizabeth could feel the air coming out of the vent under the table, but it felt cold. "You went out with him?" she said.

"Hard to believe, isn't it? I mean, at that age all you can think about is your precious self. You're so worried about getting laughed at or getting hurt, you can't even see anybody else. When my sorority sister told me he was downstairs, all I could think of was how he must look, his hair all slicked back with water and cleaning those black fingernails with a penknife, and what everybody would say. I almost told her to tell him I wasn't there."

"What if you had done that?"

"I guess I'd still be Sondra Dickeson, the snot, a fate worse than death."

"A fate worse than death," Elizabeth said, almost to herself, but Sandy didn't hear her. She was plunging along, telling the story that she got to tell everytime somebody new moved to town, and no wonder she liked being alum rep.

"My sorority sister said, 'He's really got intestinal

fortitude coming here like this, thinking you'd go out with him,' and I thought about him, sitting down there being laughed at, being hurt, and I told my roommate to go to hell and went downstairs and that was that." She looked at the kitchen clock. "Good lord, is it that late? I'm going to have to pick up the kids pretty soon." She ran her finger down the hopelessly lost list. "How about Dallas Tindall, May Matsumoto, Ralph DeArvill?"

"No," Elizabeth said. "Is Tupper Hofwalt on that list?"

"Hofwalt." She flipped several pages over. "Was Tupper his real name?"

"No. Phillip. But everybody called him Tupper because he sold Tupperware."

She looked up. "I remember him. He had a Tupperware party in our dorm when I was a freshman." She flipped back to the Found section and started paging through it.

He had talked Elizabeth and Tib into having a Tupperware party in the dorm. "As co-hostess you'll be eligible to earn points toward a popcorn popper," he had said. "You don't have to do anything except come up with some refreshments, and your mothers are always sending you cookies, right? And I'll owe you guys a favor."

They had had the party in the dorm lounge. Tupper pinned the names of famous people on their backs and they had to figure out who they were by asking questions about themselves.

Elizabeth was Twiggy. "Am I a girl?" she had asked Tib. "Yes."

"Am I pretty?"

"Yes," Tupper had said before Tib could answer.

After she guessed it she went over and stooped down next to the coffee table where Tupper was setting up his display of plastic bowls. "Do you really think Twiggy's pretty?" she asked.

"Who said anything about Twiggy?" he said. "Listen, I wanted to tell you . . ."

"Am I alive?" Sharon Oberhausen demanded.

"I don't know," Elizabeth said. "Turn around so I can see who you are."

The sign on her back said Mick Jagger.

"It's hard to tell," Tupper said.

Tib was King Kong. It had taken her forever to figure it out. "Am I tall?" she asked.

"Compared to what?" Elizabeth said.

She stuck her hands on her hips. "I don't know. The Empire State Building."

"Yes," Tupper said.

He had had a hard time getting them to stop talking so he could show them his butter keeper and cake taker and popsicle makers. While they were filling out their order forms, Sharon Oberhausen said to Tib, "Do you have a date yet for the Harvest Ball?"

"Yes," Tib said.

"I wish I did," Sharon said. She leaned across Tib. "Elizabeth, do you realize everybody in ROTC has to have a date or they put you on weekend duty? Who are you going with, Tib?"

"Listen, you guys," Tib said, "the more you buy, the better our chances at that popcorn popper, which we are willing to share."

They had bought a cake and chocolate chip ice cream. Elizabeth cut the cake in the dorm's tiny kitchen while Tib dished it up.

"You didn't tell me you had a date to the Harvest Ball," Elizabeth said. "Who is it? That guy in your Ed Psych class?"

"No." She dug into the ice cream with a plastic spoon.

"Who?"

Tupper came into the kitchen with a catalog. "You're only twenty points away from a popcorn popper," he said. "You know what you girls need?" He folded back a page and pointed to a white plastic box. "An ice-cream keeper. Holds a half-gallon of ice cream, and when you want some, all you do is slide this tab out," he pointed to a flat rectangle of plastic, "and cut off a slice. No more digging around in it and getting your hands all messy."

Tib licked ice cream off her knuckles. "That's the best part."

"Get out of here, Tupper," Elizabeth said. "Tib's trying to tell me who's taking her to the Harvest Ball."

Tupper closed the catalog. "I am."

"Oh," Elizabeth said.

Sharon stuck her head around the corner. "Tupper, when do we have to pay for this stuff?" she said. "And when do we get something to eat?"

Tupper said, "You pay before you eat," and went back out to the lounge.

Elizabeth drew the plastic knife across the top of the cake, making perfectly straight lines in the frosting. When she had the cake divided into squares, she cut the corner piece and put it on the paper plate next to the melting ice cream. "Do you have anything to wear?" she said. "You can borrow my rust formal."

Sandy was looking at her, the thick notebook opened almost to the last page. "How well did you know Tupper?" she said.

Elizabeth's coffee was ice cold, but she put her hand over it, as if to try to catch the steam. "Not very well. He used to date Tib."

"He's on my deceased list, Elizabeth. He killed himself five years ago."

Paul didn't get home till after ten. Elizabeth was sitting on the couch wrapped in a blanket.

He went straight to the thermostat and turned it down. "How high do you have this thing turned up?" He squinted at it. "Eighty-five. Well, at least I don't have to worry about you freezing to death. Have you been sitting there like that all day?"

"The worm died," she said. "I didn't save it after all. I should have put it over on the grass."

"Ron Brubaker says there's an opening for a secretary in the dean's office. I told him you'd put in an application. You have, haven't you?"

"Yes," Elizabeth said. After Sandy left, she had taken the application out of her purse and sat down at the kitchen table to fill it out. She had had it nearly all filled out before she realized it was a retirement fund withholding form.

"Sandy Konkel was here today," she said. "She met her husband on a dirt road. They were both there by chance. By chance. It wasn't even his route. Like the worm. Tib just walked by, she didn't even know she did it, but the worm was too near the edge, and it went over into the water and it drowned." She started to cry. The tears felt cold running down her cheeks. "It drowned."

"What did you and Sandy Konkel do? Get out the cooking sherry and reminisce about old times?"

"Yes," she said. "Old times."

In the morning Elizabeth took back the retirement fund withholding form. It had rained off and on all night, and it had turned colder. There were patches of ice on the central walk.

"I had it almost all filled out before I realized what it was," she told the girl. A boy in a button-down shirt and khaki pants had been leaning on the counter when Elizabeth came in. The girl was turned away from the counter, filing papers.

"I don't know what you're so mad about," the boy had said and then stopped and looked at Elizabeth. "You've got a customer," he said, and stepped away from the counter.

"All these dumb forms look alike," the girl said, handing the application to Elizabeth. She picked up a stack of books. "I've got a class. Did you need anything else?"

Elizabeth shook her head and stepped back so the boy could finish talking to her, but the girl didn't even look at him. She shoved the books into a backpack, slung it over her shoulder, and went out the door.

"Hey, wait a minute," the boy said, and started after her. By the time Elizabeth got outside, they were halfway up the walk. Elizabeth heard the boy say, "So I took her out once or twice. Is that a crime?"

The girl jerked the backpack out of his grip and started off down the walk toward Elizabeth's old dorm. In front of the dorm a girl in a yellow slicker was talking to another girl with short upswept blonde hair. The girl in the slicker turned suddenly and started down the walk.

A boy went past Elizabeth on a bike, hitting her elbow and knocking the application out of her hand. She grabbed for it and got it before it landed on the walk.

"Sorry," he said without glancing back. He was wearing a jean jacket. Its sleeves were too short, and his bony wrists stuck out. He was steering the bike with one hand and holding a big plastic sack full of pink and green bowls in the other. That was what he had hit her with.

"Tupper," she said, and started to run after him.

She was down on the ice before she even knew she was going to fall, her hands splayed out against the sidewalk and one foot twisted under her. "Are you all right, ma'am?" the boy in the button-down shirt said. He knelt down in front of her so she couldn't see up the walk.

Tupper would call me "ma'am," too, she thought. He wouldn't even recognize me.

"You shouldn't try to run on this sidewalk. It's slicker than shit."

"I thought I saw somebody I knew."

He turned, balancing himself on the flat of one hand, and looked down the long walk. There was nobody there now. "What did they look like? Maybe I can still catch them."

"No," Elizabeth said. "He's long gone."

The girl came over. "Should I go call 911 or something?" she said.

"I don't know," he said to her, and then turned back to Elizabeth. "Can you stand up?" he said, and put his hand under her arm to help her. She tried to bring her foot out from its twisted position, but it wouldn't come. He tried again, from behind, both hands under her arms and hoisting her up, then holding her there by brute force till he could come around to her bad side. She leaned shamelessly against him, shivering.

"If you can get my books and this lady's purse, I think I can get her up to the infirmary," he said. "Do you think you can walk that far?"

"Yes," Elizabeth said, and put her arm around his neck. The girl picked up Elizabeth's purse and her retirement fund application.

"I used to go to school here. The central walk was heated back then." She couldn't put any weight on her foot at all. "Everything looks the same. Even the college kids. The girls wear skirts and sweaters just like we wore and those little flat shoes that never will stay on your feet, and the boys wear button-down shirts and jean jackets and they look just like the boys I knew when I went here to school, and it isn't fair. I keep thinking I see people I used to know."

"I'll bet," the boy said politely. He shifted his weight, hefting her up so her arm was more firmly on his shoulder.

"I could maybe go get a wheelchair. I bet they'd loan me one," the girl said, sounding concerned.

"You know it can't be them, but it looks just like them, only you'll never see them again, never. You'll never even know what happened to them." She had thought she was getting hysterical, but instead her voice was getting softer and softer until her words seemed to fade away to nothing. She wondered if she had even said them aloud.

The boy got her up the stairs and into the infirmary.

"You shouldn't let them get away," she said.

"No," the boy said, and eased her onto the couch. "I guess you shouldn't."

"She slipped on the ice on the central walk," the girl told the receptionist. "I think maybe her ankle's broken. She's in a lot of pain." She came over to Elizabeth.

"I can stay with her," the boy said. "I know you've got a class."

She looked at her watch. "Yeah, Ed psych. Are you sure you'll be all right?" she said to Elizabeth.

"I'm fine. Thank you for all your help, both of you."

"Do you have a way to get home?" the boy said.

"I'll call my husband to come and get me. There's really no reason for either of you to stay. I'm fine. Really."

"Okay," the boy said. He stood up. "Come on," he said to the girl. "I'll walk you to class and explain to old Harrigan that you were being an angel of mercy." He took the girl's arm, and she smiled up at him.

They left, and the receptionist brought Elizabeth a clipboard with some forms on it. "They were having a fight," Elizabeth said.

"Well, I'd say whatever it was about, it's over now."

"Yes," Elizabeth said. Because of me. Because I fell down on the ice.

"I used to live in this dorm," Elizabeth said. "This was the lounge."

"Oh," the receptionist said. "I bet it's changed a lot since then."

"No," Elizabeth said. "It's just the same."

Where the reception desk was there had been a table with a phone on it where they had checked in and out of the dorm, and along the far wall the couch that she and Tib had sat on at the Tupperware party. Tupper had been sitting on it in his tuxedo when she came down to go to the library.

The receptionist was looking at her. "I bet it hurts," she said.

"Yes," Elizabeth said.

She had planned to be at the library when Tupper came, but he was half an hour early. He stood up when he saw her on the stairs and said, "I tried to call you this afternoon. I wondered if you wanted to go study at the library tomorrow." He had brought Tib a corsage in a white box. He came over and stood at the foot of the stairs, holding the box in both hands.

"I'm studying at the library tonight," Elizabeth said, and walked down the stairs past him, afraid he would put his hand out to stop her, but they were full of the corsage box. "I don't think Tib's ready yet."

"I know. I came early because I wanted to talk to you."

"You'd better call her so she'll know you're here," she said, and walked out the door. She hadn't even checked out, which could have gotten her in trouble with the dorm mother. She found out later that Tib had done it for her.

The receptionist stood up. "I'm going to see if Dr Larenson can't see you right now," she said. "You are obviously in a lot of pain."

Her ankle was sprained. The doctor wrapped it in an Ace bandage. Halfway through, the phone rang, and he left her sitting on the examining table with her foot propped up while he took the call.

The day after the dance Tupper had called her. "Tell him I'm not here," Elizabeth had told Tib.

"You tell him," Tib had said, and stuck the phone at her, and she had taken the receiver and said, "I don't want to talk to you, but Tib's here. I'm sure she does," and handed the phone back to Tib and walked out of the room. She was halfway across the campus before Tib caught up with her.

It had turned colder in the night, and there was a sharp wind that blew the dead leaves across the grass. Tib had brought Elizabeth her coat.

"Thank you," Elizabeth said, and put it on.

"At least you're not totally stupid," Tib said. "Almost, though."

Elizabeth jammed her hands deep in the pockets. "What did Tupper have to say? Did he ask you out again? To one of his Tupperware parties?"

"He didn't ask me out. I asked him to the Harvest Ball because I needed a date. They put you on weekend duty if you didn't have a date, so I asked him. And then after I did it, I was afraid you wouldn't understand."

"Understand what?" Elizabeth said. "You can date whoever you want."

"I don't want to date Tupper, and you know it. If you don't stop acting this way, I'm going to get another roommate."

And she had said, without any idea how important little things like that could be, how hanging up a phone or having a flat tire or saying something could splash out in all directions and sweep you over the edge, she had said, "Maybe you'd better do just that."

They had lived in silence for two weeks. Sharon Oberhausen's roommate didn't come back after Thanksgiving, and Tib moved in with her until the end of the quarter. Then Elizabeth pledged Alpha Phi and moved into the sorority house.

The doctor came back and finished wrapping her ankle. "Do you have a ride home? I'm going to give you a pair of crutches. I don't want you walking on this any more than absolutely necessary."

"No, I'll call my husband." The doctor helped her off the table and onto the crutches. He walked her back out to the waiting room and punched buttons on the phone so she could make an outside call.

She dialed her own number and told the ringing to come

pick her up. "He'll be over in a minute," she told the receptionist. "I'll wait outside for him."

The receptionist helped her through the door and down the steps. She went back inside, and Elizabeth went out and stood on the curb, looking up at the middle window.

After Tupper took Tib to the Angel Flight dance, he had come and thrown things at her window. She would see them in the mornings when she went to class, plastic jar openers and grapefruit slicers and kitchen scrubber holders, scattered on the lawn and the sidewalk. She had never opened the window, and after a while he had stopped coming.

Elizabeth looked down at the grass. At first she couldn't find the worm. She parted the grass with the tip of her crutch, standing on her good foot. It was there, where she had put it, shrivelled now and darker red, almost black. It was covered with ice crystals.

Elizabeth looked in the front window at the receptionist. When she got up to go file Elizabeth's chart, Elizabeth crossed the street and walked home.

The walk home had made Elizabeth's ankle swell so badly she could hardly move by the time Paul came home.

"What's the matter with you?" he said angrily. "Why didn't you call me?" He looked at his watch. "Now it's too late to call Brubaker. He and his wife were going out to dinner. I suppose you don't feel like going to the concert."

"No," Elizabeth said. "I'll go."

He turned down the thermostat without looking at it. "What in the hell were you doing anyway?"

"I thought I saw a boy I used to know. I was trying to catch up to him."

"A boy you used to know?" Paul said disbelievingly. "In college? What's he doing here? Still waiting to graduate?"

"I don't know," Elizabeth said. She wondered if Sandy ever saw herself on the campus, dressed in the winter white sweater and pearls, standing in front of her sorority house talking to Chuck Pagano. She's not there, Elizabeth thought. Sandy had not said, "Tell him I'm not here." She had not said, "Maybe you'd better just do that," and because of that and a flat tire, Sondra Dickeson isn't trapped on the campus, waiting to be rescued. Like they are.

"You don't even realize what this little move of yours has cost, do you?" Paul said. "Brubaker told me this afternoon he'd gotten you the job in the dean's office."

He took off the Ace bandage and looked at her ankle. She had gotten the bandage wet walking home. He went to look for another one. He came back carrying the wrinkled job application. "I found this in the bureau drawer. You told me you turned your application in."

"It fell in the gutter," she said.

"Why didn't you throw it away?"

"I thought it might be important," she said, and hobbled over on her crutches and took it away from him.

They were late to the concert because of her ankle, so they didn't get to sit with the Brubakers, but afterward they came over. Dr Brubaker introduced his wife.

"I'm so sorry about this," Janice Brubaker said. "Ron's been telling them for years they should get that central walk fixed. It used to be heated." She was the woman Sandy had pointed at at the Tupperware party and said was Janice who loved Jesus. She was wearing a dark red suit and had her hair teased into a bouffant, the way girls had worn their hair when Elizabeth was in college. "It was so nice of you to ask us over, but of course now with your ankle we understand."

"No," Elizabeth said. "We want you to come. I'm doing great, really. It's just a little sprain."

The Brubakers had to go talk to someone backstage. Paul told the Brubakers how to get to their house and took Elizabeth outside. Because they were late there hadn't been anyplace to park. Paul had had to park up by the infirmary. Elizabeth said she thought she could walk as far as the car, but it took them fifteen minutes to make it three-fourths of the way up the walk.

"This is ridiculous," Paul said angrily, and strode off the walk to get the car.

She hobbled slowly on up to the end of the walk and sat down on one of the cement benches that had been vents for the heating system. Elizabeth had worn a wool dress and her warmest coat, but she was still cold. She laid her crutches against the bench and looked across at her old dorm.

Someone was standing in front of the dorm, looking up at the middle window. He looked cold. He had his hands jammed in his jean jacket pockets, and after a few minutes he pulled something out of one of the pockets and threw it at the window.

It's no good, Elizabeth thought, she won't come.

He had made one last attempt to talk to her. It was spring quarter. It had been raining again. The walk was covered with worms. Tib was wearing her Angel Flight uniform, and she looked cold.

Tib had stopped Elizabeth after she came out of the dorm and said, "I saw Tupper the other day. He asked about you, and I told him you were living in the Alpha Phi house."

"Oh," Elizabeth had said, and tried to walk past her, but Tib had kept her there, talking as if nothing had happened, as if they were still roommates. "I'm dating this guy in ROTC. Jim Scates. He's gorgeous!" she had said, as if they were still roommates.

"I'm going to be late for class," she said. Tib glanced nervously down the walk, and Elizabeth looked, too, and saw Tupper bearing down on them on his bike. "Thanks a lot," she said angrily.

"He just wants to talk to you."

"About what? How he's taking you to the Alpha Sig dinner dance?" she had said, and turned and walked back into the dorm before he could catch up to her. He had called her on the dorm phone for nearly half an hour, but she hadn't answered, and after awhile he had given up.

But he hadn't given up. He was still there, under her windows, throwing grapefruit slicers and egg separators at her, and she still, after all these years, wouldn't come to the window. He would stand there forever, and she would never, never come.

She stood up. The rubber tip of one of her crutches skidded on the ice under the bench, and she almost fell. She steadied herself against the hard cement bench.

Paul honked and pulled over beside the curb, his turn-lights flashing. He got out of the car. "The Brubakers are already going to be there, for God's sake," he said. He took the crutches away from her and hurried her to the car, his hand jammed under her armpit. When they pulled away, the boy was still there, looking up at the window, waiting.

The Brubakers were there, waiting in the driveway. Paul left her in the car while he unlocked the door. Dr Brubaker opened the car door for her and tried to help her with her crutches. Janice kept saying, "Oh, really, we would have understood." They both stood back, looking helpless, while Elizabeth hobbled into the house.

Janice offered to make the coffee, and Elizabeth let her, sitting at the kitchen table, her coat still on. Paul had set out the cups and saucers and the plate of cookies before they left.

"You were at the Tupperware party, weren't you?" Janice said, opening the cupboards to look for the coffee filters. "I never really got a chance to meet you. I saw Sandy Konkel had her hooks in you."

"At the party you said you liked Jesus," Elizabeth said. "Are you a Christian?"

Janice had been peeling off a paper filter. She stopped and looked hard at Elizabeth. "Yes," she said. "I am. You know, Sandy Konkel told me a Tupperware party was no place for religion, and I told her that any place was the place for a Christian witness. And I was right, because that witness spoke to you, didn't it, Elizabeth?"

"What if you did something, a long time ago, and you found out it had ruined everything?"

" 'For behold your sin will find you out,' " Janice said, holding the coffee pot under the faucet.

"I'm not talking about sin," Elizabeth said. "I'm talking about little things that you wouldn't think would matter so much, like stepping in a puddle or having a fight with somebody. What if you drove off and left somebody standing in the road because you were mad, and it changed their whole life, it made them into a different person? Or what if you turned and walked away from somebody because your feelings were hurt or you wouldn't open your window, and because of that one little thing their whole lives were changed and now she's getting a divorce and she drinks too much, and he killed himself! He killed himself, and you didn't even know you did it."

Janice had opened her purse and started to get out a Bible. She stopped with the Bible only half out of the purse and stared at Elizabeth. "You made somebody kill himself?"

"No," Elizabeth said. "I didn't make him kill himself and I didn't make her get a divorce, but if I hadn't turned and walked away from them that day, everything would have been different."

"Divorce?" Janice said.

"Sandy was right. When you're young all you think about is yourself. All I could think about was how much prettier she was and how she was the kind of girl who had dozens of dates, and when he asked her out, I thought that he'd liked her all along, and I was so hurt. I threw away the egg separator, I was so hurt, and that's why I wouldn't talk to him that day, but I didn't know it was so important! I didn't know there was a puddle there and it was going to sweep me over into the gutter."

Janice laid the Bible on the table. "I don't know what you've done, Elizabeth, but whatever it is, Our Lord can forgive you. I want to read you something." She opened the Bible at a cross-shaped bookmark. " 'For God so loved the world that He gave his only begotten Son that whosoever believeth in Him should not perish, but have everlasting life.' Jesus, God's own son, died on a cross and rose again so we could be forgiven for our sins."

"What if he didn't?" Elizabeth said impatiently. "What if he just lay there in the tomb getting colder and colder, until ice crystals formed on him and he never knew if he'd saved them or not?"

"Is the coffee ready yet?" Paul said, coming into the kitchen with Dr Brubaker. "Or did you womenfolk get to talking and forget all about it?"

"What if they were waiting there for him to save them, they'd been waiting for him all those years and he didn't know it? He'd have to try to save them, wouldn't he? He couldn't just leave them there, standing in the cold looking up at her window? And maybe he couldn't. Maybe they'd get a divorce or kill themselves anyway." Her teeth had started to chatter. "Even if he did save them, he wouldn't be able to save himself. Because it was too late. He was already dead."

Paul moved around the table to her. Janice was paging through the Bible, looking frantically for the right scripture. Paul took hold of Elizabeth's arm, but she shook it off impatiently. "In Matthew we see that he was raised from the dead and is alive today. Right now," Janice said, sounding frightened. "And no matter what sin you have in your heart he will forgive you if you accept him as your personal Savior."

Elizabeth brought her fist down hard on the table so that the plate of cookies shook. "I'm not talking about sin. I'm talking about opening a window. She stepped in the puddle and the worm went over the edge and drowned. I shouldn't have left it on the sidewalk." She hit the table with her fist again. Dr Brubaker picked up the stack of coffee cups and put them on the counter, as if he were afraid she might start throwing them at the wall. "I should have put it in the grass."

Paul left for work without even having breakfast. Elizabeth's ankle had swollen up so badly she could hardly get her slippers on, but she got up and made the coffee. The filters were still lying on the counter where Janice Brubaker had left them.

"Weren't you satisfied that you'd ruined your chances for a job, you had to ruin mine, too?"

"I'm sorry about last night," she said. "I'm going to fill out my job application today and take it over to the campus. When my ankle heals . . ."

"It's supposed to warm up today," Paul said. "I turned the furnace off."

After he was gone, she filled out the application. She tried to erase the dark smear that the worm had left, but it wouldn't come out, and there was one question that she couldn't read. Her fingers were stiff with cold, and she had to stop and blow on them several times, but she filled in as many questions as she could, and folded it up and took it over to the campus.

The girl in the yellow slicker was standing at the end of the walk, talking to a girl in an Angel Flight uniform. She hobbled toward them with her head down, trying to hurry, listening for the sound of Tupper's bike.

"He asked about you," Tib said, and Elizabeth looked up.

She didn't look at all the way Elizabeth remembered her. She was a little overweight and not very pretty, the kind of girl who wouldn't have been able to get a date for the dance. Her short hair made her round face look even plumper. She looked hopeful and a little worried.

Don't worry, Elizabeth thought. I'm here. She didn't look at herself. She concentrated on getting up even with them at the right time.

"I told him you were living in the Alpha Phi house," Tib said.

"Oh," she heard her own voice, and under it the hum of a bicycle.

"I'm dating this guy in ROTC. He's absolutely gorgeous!"

There was a pause, and then Elizabeth's voice said, "Thanks a lot," and Elizabeth pushed the rubber end of her crutch against a patch of ice and went down.

For a minute she couldn't see anything for the pain. "I've broken it," she thought, and clenched her fists to keep from screaming.

"Are you all right?" Tib said, kneeling in front of her so she couldn't see anything. No, not you! Not you! For a minute she was afraid that it hadn't worked, that the girl had turned and walked away. But after all this was not a stranger but only herself, who was too kind to let a worm drown. She had only gone around to Elizabeth's other side, where she couldn't see her. "Did she break it?" she said. "Should I go call an ambulance or something?"

No. "No," Elizabeth said. "I'm fine. If you could just help me up."

The girl who had been Elizabeth Wilson put her books down on the cement bench and came and knelt down by Elizabeth. "I hope we don't collapse in a heap," she said, and smiled at Elizabeth. She was a pretty girl. I didn't know that either, Elizabeth thought, even when Tupper told me.

She took hold of Elizabeth's arm and Tib took hold of the other.

"Tripping innocent passersby again, I see. How many times have I told you not to do that?" And here, finally, was Tupper. He laid his bike flat in the grass and put his bag of Tupperware beside it.

Tib and the girl that had been herself let go and stepped back, and he knelt beside her. "They're not bad girls, really. They just like to play practical jokes. But banana peels is going too far, girls," he said, so close she could feel his warm breath on her cheek. She turned to look at him, suddenly afraid that he would be different, too, but it was only Tupper, who she had loved all these years. He put his arm around her. "Now just put your arm around my neck, sweetheart. That's right. Elizabeth, come over here and atone for your sins by helping this pretty lady up."

She had already picked her boots up and was holding them against her chest, looking angry and eager to get away. She looked at Tib, but Tib was picking up the crutches, stooping down in her high heels because she couldn't bend over in her Angel Flight skirt.

She put her books down again and came around to Elizabeth's other side to take hold of her arm, and Elizabeth grabbed for her hand instead and held it tightly so she couldn't get away. "I took her to the dance because she helped with the Tupperware party. I told her I owed her a favor," he said, and Elizabeth turned and looked at him.

He was not looking at her really. He was looking past her at that other Elizabeth, who would not answer the phone, who would not come to the window, but he seemed to be looking at her, and on his young remembered face there was a look of such naked, vulnerable love that it was like a blow.

"I told you so," Tib said. She laid the crutches against the bench.

"I'm sure this lady doesn't want to hear this," Elizabeth said.

"I was going to tell you at the party, but that idiot Sharon Oberhausen . . ."

Tib brought over the crutches. "After I asked him, I thought, 'What if she thinks I'm trying to steal her boyfriend?' and I got so worried I was afraid to tell you. I really only asked him to get out of weekend duty. I mean, I don't like him or anything."

Tupper grinned at Elizabeth. "I try to pay my debts, and this is the thanks I get. You wouldn't get mad at me if I took your roommate to a dance, would you?"

"I might," Elizabeth said. It was cold sitting on the cement. She was starting to shiver. "But I'd forgive you."

"You see that?" he said.

"I see," Elizabeth said disgustedly, but she was smiling at him now. "Don't you think we'd better get this innocent passerby up off the sidewalk before she freezes to death?"

"Upsy-daisy, sweetheart," Tupper said, and in one easy motion she was up sitting on the stone bench.

"Thank you," she said. Her teeth were chattering with the cold.

Tupper knelt in front of her and examined her ankle. "It looks pretty swollen," he said. "Do you want us to call somebody?"

"No, my husband will be along any minute. I'll just sit here till he comes."

Tib fished Elizabeth's application out of the puddle. "I'm afraid it's ruined," she said.

"It doesn't matter."

Tupper picked up his bag of bowls. "Say," he said, "you wouldn't be interested in having a Tupperware party? As hostess, you could earn valuable points toward . . ."

"Tupper!" Tib said.

"Will you leave this poor lady alone?" Elizabeth said.

He held up the sack. "Only if you'll go with me to deliver my lettuce crispers to the Sigma Chi house."

"I'll go," Tib said. "There's this darling Sigma Chi I've been wanting to meet."

"And I'll go," Elizabeth said, putting her arm around Tib. "I don't trust the kind of boyfriend you find on your own. Jim Scates is a real creep. Didn't Sharon tell you what he did to Marilyn Reed?"

Tupper handed Elizabeth the sack of bowls while he stood his bike up. Elizabeth handed them to Tib.

"Are you sure you're all right?" Tupper said. "It's cold out here. You could wait for your husband in the student union."

She wished she could put her hand on his cheek just once. "I'll be fine," she said.

The three of them went down the walk toward Frasier, Tupper pushing the bike. When they got even with Carter Hall, they cut across the grass toward Frasier. She watched them until she couldn't see them anymore, and then sat there awhile longer on the cold bench. She had hoped that something might happen, some sign that she had rescued them, but nothing happened. Her ankle didn't hurt anymore. It had stopped the minute Tupper touched it.

She continued to sit there. It seemed to her to be getting colder, though she had stopped shivering, and after awhile she got up and walked home, leaving the crutches where they were.

It was cold in the house. Elizabeth turned the thermostat up and sat down at the kitchen table, still in her coat, waiting for the heat to come on. When it didn't, she remembered that Paul had turned the furnace off, and she went and got a blanket and wrapped up in it on the couch. Her ankle did not hurt at all, though it felt cold. When the phone rang, she could hardly move it. It took her several rings to make it to the phone.

"I thought you weren't going to answer," Paul said. "I made an appointment with Dr Jamieson for you for this afternoon at three. He's a psychiatrist."

"Paul," she said. She was so cold it was hard to talk. "I'm sorry."

"It's a little too late for that, isn't it?" he said. "I told Dr Brubaker you were on muscle relaxants for your ankle. I don't know whether he bought it or not." He hung up.

"Too late," Elizabeth said. She hung up the phone. The back of her hand was covered with ice crystals. "Paul," she tried to say, but her lips were stiff with cold, and no sound came out.

MICHAEL SWANWICK
The Edge of the World

One of the most popular and respected of all the decade's new
writers, Michael Swanwick made his debut in 1980 with two
strong and compelling stories, "The Feast of St. Janis" and
"Ginungagap," both of which were Nebula Award finalists that
year. Since then, he has gone on to become a finalist for the
Hugo Award, the World Fantasy Award, and the John W.
Campbell Award as well, and to win the Theodore Sturgeon
Award and the *IAsfm* Reader's Award, with intense and
powerful stories such as "Mummer Kiss," "The Man Who Met
Picasso," "Trojan Horse," "Dogfight" (written with William
Gibson), "Covenant of Souls," "The Dragon Line," "Snow
Angles," "A Midwinter's Tale," and many others – all of which
have earned him a reputation as one of the most powerful and
consistently inventive short-story writers of his generation.

Swanwick's reputation as a novelist has been growing as well.
His evocative first novel, *In the Drift*, was published in 1985 as
part of the resurrected Ace Specials line. His second novel was
the critically acclaimed *Vacuum Flowers*, and he has just
published a third novel, *Stations of the Tide*, that may well
establish him among the vanguard of the hot new novelists of
the '90s. His most recent book is *Griffin's Egg*. Upcoming is a
collection of his short fiction, titled *Gravity's Angels*, and a
collection of his collaborative work, *Slow Dancing Through Time*.
Swanwick lives in Philadelphia, Pennsylvania, with his wife
Marianne Porter and their young son Sean.

In the intense, scary, evocative and mystiçal story that
follows, he takes us to the Edge of the World – and beyond.

The day that Donna and Piggy and Russ went to see the
Edge of the World was a hot one. They were sitting on the
curb by the gas station that noontime, sharing a Coke and
watching the big Starlifters lumber up into the air, one by
one, out of Toldenarba AFB. The sky rumbled with their

passing. There'd been an accident in the Persian Gulf, and half the American forces in the Twilight Emirates were on alert.

"My old man says when the Big One goes up, the base will be the first to go," Piggy said speculatively. "Treaties won't allow us to defend it. One bomber comes in high and *whaboom*" – he made soft nuclear explosion noises – "it's all gone." He was wearing camouflage pants and a khaki T-shirt with an iron-on reading: KILL 'EM ALL AND LET GOD SORT 'EM OUT. Donna watched as he took off his glasses to polish them on his shirt. His face went slack and vacant, then livened as he put them back on again, as if he were playing with a mask.

"You should be so lucky," Donna said. "Mrs Khashoggi is still going to want that paper done on Monday morning, Armageddon or not."

"Yeah, can you believe her?" Piggy said. "That weird accent! And all that memorization! Cut me some slack. I mean, who cares whether Ackronnion was part of the Mezentian Dynasty?"

"You ought to care, dipshit," Russ said. "Local History's the only decent class the school's got." Russ was the smartest boy Donna had ever met, never mind the fact that he was flunking out. He had soulful eyes and a radical haircut, short on the sides with a dyed-blond punklock down the back of his neck. "Man, I opened the *Excerpts from Epics* text that first night, thinking it was going to be the same old bullshit, and I stayed up 'til dawn. Got to school without a wink of sleep. But I'd managed to read every last word. This is one weird part of the world; its history is full of dragons and magic and all kinds of weird monsters. Do you realize that in the eighteenth century three members of the British legation were eaten by demons? That's in the historical record!"

Russ was an enigma to Donna. The first time they'd met, hanging with the misfits at an American School dance, he'd tried to put a hand down her pants, and she'd slugged him good, almost breaking his nose. She could still hear his surprised laughter as blood ran down his chin. They'd been friends ever since. Only there were limits to friendship, and now she was waiting for him to make his move and hoping he'd get down to it before her father was rotated out.

In Japan she'd known a girl who had taken a razor blade and carved her boyfriend's name in the palm of her hand. How could she do that, Donna had wanted to know? Her friend had shrugged, said, "As long as it gets me noticed." It wasn't until Russ that Donna understood.

"Strange country," Russ said dreamily. "The sky beyond the Edge is supposed to be full of demons and serpents and shit. They say that if you stare into it long enough, you'll go mad."

They all three looked at one another.

"Well, hell," Piggy said. "What are we waiting for?"

The Edge of the World lay beyond the railroad tracks. They bicycled through the American enclave into the old native quarter. The streets were narrow here, the sideyards crammed with broken trucks, rusted-out buses, even yachts up in cradles with staved-in sides. Garage doors were black mouths hissing and spitting welding sparks, throbbing to the hammered sound of worked metal. They hid their bikes in a patch of scrub apricot trees where the railroad crossed the industrial canal and hiked across.

Time had altered the character of the city where it bordered the Edge. Gone were the archers in their towers, vigilant against a threat that never came. Gone were the rose quartz palaces with their thousand windows, not a one of which overlooked the Edge. The battlements where blind musicians once piped up the dawn now survived only in Mrs Khashoggi's texts. Where they had been was now a drear line of weary factory buildings, their lower windows cinderblocked or bricked up and those beyond reach of vandals' stones painted over in patchwork squares of gray and faded blue.

A steam whistle sounded and lines of factory workers shambled back inside, brown men in chinos and white shirts, Syrian and Lebanese laborers imported to do work no native Toldenarban would touch. A shredded net waved forlornly from a basketball hoop set up by the loading dock.

There was a section of hurricane fence down. They scrambled through.

As they cut across the grounds, a loud whine arose from

within the factory building. Down the way another plant lifted its voice in a solid wham-wham-wham as rhythmic and unrelenting as a headache. One by one the factories shook themselves from their midday drowse and went back to work. "Why do they locate these things along the Edge?" Donna asked.

"It's so they can dump their chemical waste over the Edge," Russ explained. "These were all erected before the Emir nationalized the culverts that the Russian Protectorate built."

Behind the factory was a chest-high concrete wall, rough-edged and pebbly with the slow erosion of cement. Weeds grew in clumps at its foot. Beyond was nothing but sky.

Piggy ran ahead and spat over the Edge. "Hey, remember what Nixon said when he came here? *It is indeed a long way down.* What a guy!"

Donna leaned against the wall. A film of haze tinted the sky gray, intensifying at the focal point to dirty brown, as if a dead spot were burned into the center of her vision. When she looked down, her eyes kept grabbing for ground and finding more sky. There were a few wispy clouds in the distance and nothing more. No serpents coiled in the air. She should have felt disappointed but, really, she hadn't expected better. This was of a piece with all the natural wonders she had ever seen, the waterfalls, geysers and scenic vistas that inevitably included power lines, railings and parking lots absent from the postcards. Russ was staring intently ahead, hawklike, frowning. His jaw worked slightly, and she wondered what he saw.

"Hey, look what I found!" Piggy whooped. "It's a stairway!"

They joined him at the top of an institutional-looking concrete and iron stairway. It zigzagged down the cliff toward an infinitely distant and non-existent Below, dwindling into hazy blue. Quietly, as if he'd impressed himself, Piggy said, "What do you suppose is down there?"

"Only one way to find out, isn't there?" Russ said.

Russ went first, then Piggy, then Donna, the steps ringing dully under their feet. Graffiti covered the rocks, worn spraypaint letters in yellow and black and red scrawled one over the other and faded by time and weather into mutual unreadability, and on the iron railings, words and arrows and triangles had been markered onto or dug into the paint with knife or nail: JURGEN BIN SCHEISSKOPF. MOTLEY CRUE. DEATH TO SATAN AMERICA IMPERIALIST. Seventeen steps down, the first landing was filthy with broken brown glass, bits of crumbled concrete, cigarette butts, soggy, half-melted cardboard. The stairway folded back on itself and they followed it down.

"You ever had *fugu?*" Piggy asked. Without waiting for an answer, he said, "It's Japanese poisonous blowfish. It has to be prepared very carefully – they license the chefs – and even so, several people die every year. It's considered a great delicacy."

"Nothing tastes that good," Russ said.

"It's not the flavor," Piggy said enthusiastically. "It's the poison. Properly prepared, see, there's a very small amount left in the sashimi and you get a threshold dose. Your lips and the tips of your fingers turn cold. Numb. That's how you know you're having the real thing. That's how you know you're living right on the edge."

"I'm already living on the edge," Russ said. He looked startled when Piggy laughed.

A fat moon floated in the sky, pale as a disk of ice melting in blue water. It bounced after them as they descended, kicking aside loose soda bottles in styrofoam sleeves, crushed Marlboro boxes, a scattering of carbonized spark plugs. On one landing they found a crumpled shopping cart, and Piggy had to muscle it over the railing and watch it fall. "Sure is a lot of crap here," he observed. The landing smelled faintly of urine.

"It'll get better farther down," Russ said. "We're still near the top, where people can come to get drunk after work." He pushed on down. Far to one side they could see the brown flow from the industrial canal where it spilled into space, widening and then slowly dispersing into rainbowed mist, distance glamoring it beauty.

"How far are we planning to go?" Donna asked apprehensively.

"Don't be a weak sister," Piggy sneered. Russ said nothing.

The deeper they went, the shabbier the stairway grew, and the spottier its maintenance. Pipes were missing from the railing. Where patches of paint had fallen away the bolts anchoring the stair to the rock were walnut-sized lumps of rust.

Needle-clawed marsupials chittered warningly from niches in the rock as they passed. Tufts of grass and moth-white gentians grew in the loess-filled cracks.

Hours passed. Donna's feet and calves and the small of her back grew increasingly sore, but she refused to be the one to complain. By degrees she stopped looking over the side and out into the sky, and stared instead at her feet flashing in and out of sight while one hand went slap-grab-tug on the rail. She felt sweaty and miserable.

Back home she had a half-finished paper on the Three Days Incident of March, 1810, when the French Occupation, by order of Napoleon himself had fired cannonade after cannonade over the Edge into nothingness. They had hoped to make rainstorms of devastating force that would lash and destroy their enemies, and created instead only a gunpowder haze, history's first great failure in weather control. This descent was equally futile, Donna thought, an endless and wearying exercise in nothing. Just the same as the rest of her life. Every time her father was reposted, she had resolved to change, to be somebody different this time around, whatever the price, even if – no, especially if – it meant playacting something she was not. Last year in Germany when she'd gone out with that local boy with the Alfa Romeo and instead of jerking him off had used her mouth, she had thought: Everything's going to be different now. But no.

Nothing ever changed.

"Heads up!" Russ said. "There's some steps missing here!" He leaped and the landing gonged hollowly under his sneakers. Then again as Piggy jumped after.

Donna hesitated. There were five steps gone and a drop of twenty feet before the stairway cut back beneath itself. The cliff bulged outward here, and if she slipped she'd probably miss the stairs altogether.

She felt the rock draw away from her to either side, and was suddenly aware that she was connected to the world by the merest speck of matter, barely enough to anchor her feet. The sky wrapped itself about her, extending in infinity, depthless and absolute. She could extend her arms and fall into it forever. What would happen to her then, she wondered. Would she die of thirst and starvation, or would the speed of her fall grow so great that the oxygen would be sucked from her lungs, leaving her to strangle in a sea of air? "Come on Donna!" Piggy shouted up at her. "Don't be a pussy!"

"Russ – " she said quaveringly.

But Russ wasn't looking her way. He was frowning downward, anxious to be going. "Don't push the lady," he said. "We can go on by ourselves."

Donna choked with anger and hurt and desperation all at once. She took a deep breath and, heart scudding, leaped. Sky and rock wheeled over her head. For an instant she was floating, falling, totally lost and filled with a panicky awareness that she was about to die. Then she crashed onto the landing. It hurt like hell, and at first she feared she'd pulled an ankle. Piggy grabbed her shoulders and rubbed the side of her head with his knuckles. "I knew you could do it, you wimp."

Donna knocked away his arm. "Okay, wise-ass. How are you expecting to get us back up?"

The smile disappeared from Piggy's face. His mouth opened, closed. His head jerked fearfully upward. An acrobat could leap across, grab the step and flip up without any trouble at all. "I – I mean, I – "

"Don't worry about it," Russ said impatiently. "We'll think of something." He started down again.

It wasn't natural, Donna realized, his attitude. There was something obsessive about his desire to descend the stairway. It was like the time he'd brought his father's revolver to school along with a story about playing Russian roulette that morning before breakfast. "Three times!" he'd said proudly.

He'd had that same crazy look on him, and she hadn't the slightest notion then or now how she could help him.

*

Russ walked like an automaton, wordlessly, tirelessly, never hurrying up or slowing down. Donna followed in concerned silence, while Piggy scurried between them, chattering like somebody's pet Pekingese. This struck Donna as so apt as to be almost allegorical: the two of them together yet alone, the distance between filled with noise. She thought of this distance, this silence, as the sun passed behind the cliff and the afternoon heat lost its edge.

The stairs changed to cement-jacketed brick with small buttresses cut into the rock. There was a pile of stems and cherry pits on one landing, and the railing above them was white with bird droppings. Piggy leaned over the rail and said, "Hey, I can see seagulls down there. Flying around."

"Where?" Russ leaned over the railing, then said scornfully, "Those are pigeons. The Ghazoddis used to release them for rifle practice."

As Piggy turned to follow Russ down again, Donna caught a glimpse into his eyes, liquid and trembling with helplessness and despair. She'd seen that fear in him only once before, months ago, when she'd stopped by his house on the way to school, just after the Emir's assassination.

The living-room windows were draped and the room seemed unnaturally gloomy after being out in the morning sun. Blue television light flickered over shelves of shadowy ceramic figurines: Dresden milkmaids, Chantilly Chinamen, Meissen pug-dogs connected by a gold chain held in their champed jaws, naked Delft nymphs dancing.

Piggy's mother sat in a limp dressing gown, hair unbrushed, watching the funeral. She held a cup of oily-looking coffee in one hand. Donna was surprised to see her up so early. Everyone said that she had a bad problem with alcohol, that even by service-wife standards she was out of control.

"Look at them," Piggy's mother said. On the screen were solemn processions of camels and Cadillacs, sheikhs in jellaba, keffiyeh and mirrorshades, European dignitaries with wives in tasteful gray Parisian fashions. "They've got their nerve."

"Where did you put my lunch?" Piggy said loudly from the kitchen.

"Making fun of the Kennedys like that!" The Emir's youngest son, no more than four years old, salaamed his father's casket as it passed before him. "That kid's bad enough, but you should see the mother, crying as if her heart were broken. It's enough to turn your stomach. If I were Jackie, I'd – "

Donna and Piggy and Russ had gone bowling the night the Emir was shot. This was out in the ruck of cheap joints that surrounded the base, catering almost exclusively to service-men. When the Muzak piped through overhead speakers was interrupted for the news bulletin, everyone had stood up and cheered. *Up we go*, someone had begun singing, and the rest had joined in, *into the wild blue yonder*. . . . Donna had felt so sick with fear and disgust she had thrown up in the parking lot. "I don't think they're making fun of anyone," Donna said. "They're just – "

"Don't talk to her!" The refrigerator door slammed shut. A cupboard door slammed open.

Piggy's mother smiled bitterly. "This is exactly what you'd expect from these ragheads. Pretending they're white people, deliberately mocking their betters. Filthy brown animals."

"*Mother!* Where is my fucking lunch?"

She looked at him then, jaw tightening. "Don't you use that kind of language on me, young man."

"All right!" Piggy shouted. "All right, I'm going to school without lunch! Shows how much you care!"

He turned to Donna and in the instant before he grabbed her wrist and dragged her out of the house, Donna could no longer hear the words, could only see that universe of baffled futility haunting Piggy's eyes. That same look she glimpsed today.

The railings were wooden now, half the posts rotting at their bases, with an occasional plank missing, wrenched off and thrown over the side by previous visitors. Donna's knees buckled and she stumbled, almost lurching into the rock. "I have to stop," she said, hating herself for it. "I cannot go one more step."

Piggy immediately collapsed on the landing. Russ

hesitated, then climbed up to join them. They three sat staring out into nothing, legs over the Edge, arms clutching the rail.

Piggy found a Pepsi can, logo in flowing Arabic, among the rubble. He held it in his left hand and began sticking holes in it with his butterfly knife, again and again, cackling like a demented sex criminal. "Exterminate the brutes!" he said happily. Then, with absolutely no transition he asked, "How are we ever going to get back up?" so dolorously Donna had to bite back her laughter.

"Look, I just want to go on down a little bit more," Russ said.

"Why?" Piggy sounded petulant.

"So I can get down enough to get away from this garbage." He gestured at the cigarette butts, the broken brown glass, sparser than above but still there. "Just a little further, okay guys?" There was an edge to his voice, and under that the faintest hint of a plea. Donna felt helpless before those eyes. She wished they were alone, so she could ask him what was wrong.

Donna doubted that Russ himself knew what he expected to find down below. Did he think that if he went down far enough, he'd never have to climb back? She remembered the time in Mr Herriman's algebra class when a sudden tension in the air had made her glance across the room at Russ, and he was, with great concentration, tearing the pages out of his math text and dropping them one by one on the floor. He'd taken a five-day suspension for that, and Donna had never found out what it was all about. But there was a kind of glorious arrogance to the act; Russ had been born out of time. He really should have been a medieval prince, a Medici or one of the Sabakan pretenders.

"Okay," Donna said, and Piggy of course had to go along.

Seven flights farther down the modern stairs came to an end. The wooden railing of the last short, septambic flight had been torn off entire, and laid across the steps. They had to step carefully between the uprights and the rails. But when they stood at the absolute bottom, they saw that there were stairs beyond the final landing, steps that had been cut into the stone itself. They were curving swaybacked things that millennia of rain and foot traffic had worn so uneven they were almost unpassable.

Piggy groaned. "Man, you *can't* expect us to go down that thing."

"Nobody's asking you," Russ said.

They descended the old stairway backwards and on all fours. The wind breezed up, hitting them with the force of an expected shove first to one side and then the other. There were times when Donna was so frightened she thought she was going to freeze up and never move again. But at last the stone broadened and became a wide, even ledge, with caves leading back into the rock.

The cliff face here was green-white with lichen, and had in ancient times been laboriously smoothed and carved. Between each cave (their mouths alone left in a natural state, unaltered) were heavy-thighed women – goddesses, perhaps, or demons or sacred dancers – their breasts and faces chipped away by the image-hating followers of the Prophet at a time when Mohammed yet lived. Their hands held loops of vines in which were entangled moons, cycling from new through waxing quarter and gibbous to full and then back through gibbous and waning quarter to dark. Piggy was gasping, his face bright with sweat, but he kept up his blustery front. "What the fuck is all this shit, man?"

"It was a monastery," Russ said. He walked along the ledge dazedly, a wondering half smile on his lips. "I read about this." He stopped at a turquoise automobile door someone had flung over the Edge to be caught and tossed by fluke winds, the only piece of trash that had made it down this far. "Give me a hand."

He and Piggy lifted the door, swung it back and forth three times to build up momentum, then lofted it over the lip of the rock. They all three lay down on their stomachs to watch it fall away, turning end over end and seeming finally to flicker as it dwindled smaller and smaller, still falling. At last it shrank below the threshold of visibility and became one of a number of shifting motes in the downbelow, part of the slow, mazy movement of dead blood cells in the eyes' vitreous humors. Donna turned over on her back, drew her head back from the rim, stared upward. The cliff seemed to be slowly tumbling forward, all the world inexorably, dizzyingly leaning down to crush her.

"Let's go explore the caves," Piggy suggested.

They were empty. The interiors of the caves extended no more than thirty feet into the rock, but they had all been elaborately worked, arched ceilings carved with thousands of *faux tesserae*, walls adorned with bas-relief pillars. Between the pillars the walls were taken up with long shelves carved into the stone. No artifacts remained, not so much as a potsherd or a splinter of bone. Piggy shone his pocket flash into every shadowy niche. "Somebody's been here before us and taken everything," he said.

"The Historic Registry people, probably." Russ ran a hand over one shelf. It was the perfect depth and height for a line of three-pound coffee cans. "This is where they stowed the skulls. When a monk grew so spiritually developed he no longer needed the crutch of physical existence, his fellows would render the flesh from his bones and enshrine his skull. They poured wax in the sockets, then pushed in opals while it was still warm. They slept beneath the faintly gleaming eyes of their superiors."

When they emerged it was twilight, the first stars appearing from behind a sky fading from blue to purple. Donna looked down on the moon. It was as big as a plate, full and bright. The rilles, dry seas and mountain chains wre preternaturally distinct. Somewhere in the middle was Tranquility Base, where Neil Armstrong had planted the American flag.

"Jeez, it's late," Donna said. "If we don't start home soon, my mom is going to have a cow."

"We still haven't figured a way to get back up," Piggy reminded her. Then, "We'll probably have to stay here. Learn to eat owls and grow crops sideways on the cliff face. Start our own civilization. Our only serious problem is the imbalance of sexes, but even that's not insurmountable." He put an arm around Donna's shoulders, grabbed at her breast. "You'd pull the train for us, wouldn't you, Donna?"

Angrily she pushed him away and said, "You keep a clean mouth! I'm so tired of your juvenile talk and behavior."

"Hey, calm down, it's cool." That panicky look was back in his eyes, the forced knowledge that he was not in control, could never be in control, that there was no such thing as control. He smiled weakly, placatingly.

"No, it is not. It is most emphatically not 'cool.'" Suddenly she was white and shaking with fury. Piggy was a spoiler. His simple presence ruined any chance she might have had to talk with Russ, find out just what was bugging him, get him to finally, really notice her. "I am sick of having to deal with your immaturity, your filthy language and your crude behavior."

Piggy turned pink and began stuttering.

Russ reached a hand into his pocket, pulled out a chunk of foil-wrapped hash, and a native tin pipe with a carved coral bowl. The kind of thing the local beggar kids sold for twenty-nine cents. "Anybody want to get stoned?" he asked suavely.

"You bastard!" Piggy laughed. "You told me you were out!"

Russ shrugged. "I lied." He lit the pipe carefully, drew in, passed it to Donna. She took it from his fingers, felt how cold they were to her touch, looked up over the pipe and saw his face, thin and ascetic, eyelids closed, pale and Christlike through the blue smoke. She loved him intensely in that instant and wished she could sacrifice herself for his happiness. The pipe's stem was overwarm, almost hot, between her lips. She drew in deep.

The smoke was raspy in her throat, then tight and swirling in her lungs. It shot up into her head, filled it with buzzing harmonics: the air, the sky, the rock behind her back all buzzing, ballooning her skull outward in a visionary rush that forced wide-open first her eyes and then her mouth. She choked and spasmodically coughed. More smoke than she could imagine possibly holding in her lungs gushed out into the universe.

"Hey, watch that pipe!" Piggy snatched it from her distant fingers. They tingled with pinpricks of pain like tiny stars in the darkness of her flesh. "You were spilling the hash!" The evening light was abuzz with energy, the sky swarming up into her eyes. Staring out into the darkening air, the moon rising below her and the stars as close and friendly as those in a children's book illustration, she felt at peace, detached from worldly cares. "Tell us about the monastery, Russ," she said, in the same voice she might have used a decade before to ask her father for a story.

"Yeah, tell us about the monastery, Unca Russ," Piggy said, but with jeering undertones. Piggy was always sucking up to Russ, but there was tension there too, and his sarcastic little challenges were far from rare. It was classic beta male jealousy, straight out of Primate Psychology 101.

"It's very old," Russ said. "Before the Sufis, before Mohammed, even before the Zoroastrians crossed the gulf, the native mystics would renounce the world and go to live in cliffs on the Edge of the World. They cut the steps down, and once down, they never went back up again."

"How did they eat then?" Piggy asked skeptically.

"They wished their food into existence. No, really! It was all in their creation myth: In the beginning all was Chaos and Desire. The world was brought out of Chaos – by which they meant unformed matter – by Desire, or Will. It gets a little inconsistent after that, because it wasn't really a religion, but more like a system of magic. They believed that the world wasn't complete yet, that for some complicated reason it could never be complete. So there's still traces of the old Chaos lingering just beyond the Edge, and it can be tapped by those who desire it strongly enough, if they have distanced themselves from the things of the world. These mystics used to come down here to meditate against the moon and work miracles.

"This wasn't sophisticated stuff like the Tantric monks in Tibet or anything, remember. It was like a primitive form of animism, a way to force the universe to give you what you wanted. So the holy men would come down here and they'd wish for . . . like riches, you know? Filigreed silver goblets with rubies, mounds of moonstones, elfinbone daggers sharper than Damascene steel. Only once they got them they weren't supposed to want them. They'd just throw them over the Edge. There were these monasteries all along the cliffs. The farther from the world they were, the more spiritually advanced."

"So what happened to the monks?"

"There was a king – Althazar? I forget his name. He was this real greed-head, started sending his tax collectors down to gather up everything the monks brought into existence. Must've figured, hey, the monks weren't using them. Which as it turned out was like a real major blasphemy, and the monks got pissed. The boss mystics, all the real spiritual heavies, got together for this big confab. Nobody knows how. There's one of the classics claims they could run sideways on the cliff just like it was the ground, but I don't know. Doesn't matter. So one night they all of them, every monk in the world, meditated at the same time. They chanted together, saying, 'It is not enough that Althazar should die, for he has blasphemed. He must suffer a doom such as has been visited on no man before. He must be unmade, uncreated, reduced to less than has ever been.' And they prayed that there be no such king as Althazar, that his life and history be unmade, so that there never had been such king as Althazar.

"And he was no more.

"But so great was their yearning for oblivion that when Althazar ceased to be, his history and family as well, they were left feeling embittered and did not know why. And not knowing why, their hatred turned upon themselves, and their wish for destruction, and they too all of a single night, ceased to be." He fell silent.

At last Piggy said, "You believe that crap?" Then, when there was no answer, "It's none of it true, man! Got that? There's no magic, and there never was." Donna could see that he was really angry, threatened on some primal level by the possibility that someone he respected could even begin to believe in magic. His face got pink, the way it always did when he lost control.

"No, it's all bullshit," Russ said bitterly. "Like everything else."

They passed the pipe around again. Then Donna leaned back, stared straight out, and said, "If I could wish for anything, you know what I'd wish for?"

"Bigger tits?"

She was so weary now, so pleasantly washed out, that it was easy to ignore Piggy. "I'd wish I knew what the situation was."

"What situation?" Piggy asked. Donna was feeling langorous, not at all eager to explain herself, and she waved away the question. But he persisted. "What situation?"

"Any situation. I mean, all the time, I find myself talking with people and I don't know what's really going on. What games they're playing. Why they're acting the way they are. I wish I knew what the situation was."

The moon floated before her, big and fat and round as a griffin's egg, shining with power. She could feel that power washing through her, the background radiation of decayed chaos spread across the sky at a uniform three degrees Kelvin. Even now, spent and respent, a coin fingered and thinned to the worn edge of non-existence, there was power out there, enough to flatten planets.

Staring out at that great fat boojum snark of a moon, she felt the flow of potential worlds, and within the cold silver disk of that jester's skull, rank with magic, sensed the invisible presence of Russ's primitive monks, men whose minds were nowhere near comprehensible to her, yet vibrated with power, existing as matrices of patterned stress, no more actual than Donald Duck, but no less powerful either. She was caught in a waking fantasy, in which the sky was full of power and all of it accessible to her. Monks sat empty-handed over their wishing bowls, separated from her by the least fictions of time and reality. For an eternal instant all possibilities fanned out to either side, equally valid, no one more real than any other. Then the world turned under her, and her brain shifted back to realtime.

"Me," Piggy said, "I just wish I knew how to get back up the stairs."

They were silent for a moment. Then it occurred to Donna that here was the perfect opportunity to find out what was bugging Russ. If she asked cautiously enough, if the question hit him just right, if she were just plain lucky, he might tell her everything. She cleared her throat. "Russ? What do you wish?"

In the bleakest voice imaginable, Russ said, "I wish I'd never been born."

She turned to ask him why, and he wasn't there.

"Hey," Donna said. "Where'd Russ go?"

Piggy looked at her oddly. "Who's Russ?"

It was a long trip back up. They carried the length of wooden railing between them, and every now and then Piggy said, "Hey, wasn't this a great idea of mine? This'll make a swell ladder."

"Yeah, great," Donna would say, because he got mad when she didn't respond. He got mad, too, whenever she started to cry, but there wasn't anything she could do about that. She couldn't even explain why she was crying, because in all the world – of all his friends, acquaintances, teachers, even his parents – she was the only one who remembered that Russ had ever existed.

The horrible thing was that she had no specific memories of him, only a vague feeling of what his presence had been like, and a lingering sense of longing and frustration.

She no longer even remembered his face.

"Do you want to go first or last?" Piggy had asked her.

When she'd replied, "Last. If I go first, you'll stare at my ass all the way up," he'd actually blushed. Without Russ to show off in front of, Piggy was a completely different person, quiet and not at all abusive. He even kept his language clean. But that didn't help, for just being in his presence was enough to force understanding on her: that his bravado was fueled by his insecurities and aspirations, that he masturbated nightly and with self-loathing, that he despised his parents and longed in vain for the least sign of love from them. That the way he treated her was the sum and total of all of this and more.

She knew exactly what the situation was.

Dear God, she prayed, let it be that I won't have this kind of understanding when I reach the top. Or else make it so that situations won't be so painful up there, that knowledge won't hurt like this, that horrible secrets won't lie under the most innocent word.

They carried their wooden burden upward, back toward the world.

BRUCE STERLING
Dori Bangs

One of the most powerful and innovative new talents to enter SF in recent years, a man with a rigorously worked-out and aesthetically convincing vision of what the future may have in store for humanity, Bruce Sterling is as yet better known to the *cognoscenti* than to the population at large. If you look behind the scenes, though, you will find him everywhere, and he has had almost as much to do, as writer, critic, propagandist, aesthetic theorist, and tireless polemicist, with the shaping and evolution of SF in the '80s as Michael Moorcook did with the shaping of SF in the '60s; it is not for nothing that many of the other new writers of the decade refer to him, half-ruefully, half-admiringly, as "Chairman Bruce." And if I had to limit myself to guessing which single author in this book will have the most to do with shaping the SF of the '90s (and it would be a damn tough call), I'd probably in the end have to place my money on Sterling.

Sterling published his first story in 1976, in an obscure anthology of stories by Texas writers called *Lone Star Universe*, and followed it up in 1977 with his first novel, *Involution Ocean*. Neither story or novel attracted much attention, nor would his second novel, *The Artificial Kid*, in 1980 – indeed, both novels remain fundamentally unread even today, although, in retrospect, *The Artificial Kid* is interesting because it is clearly an early cyberpunk work; at the time, the few critics who mentioned it seemed to be puzzled by it, and dismissed it as a grotesque curiosity.

Like many another new writer of the day, Sterling would have to wait for "steam-engine time," for the revolutionary surge of new creative energy that would sweep into the field around 1982, before his work was suddenly accessible to, and ready to be appreciated by, the SF readership. And like many another new writer, he first caught on with his short fiction, attracting interest and acclaim with a series of stories he published in the middle '80s in places like *The Magazine of Fantasy and Science Fiction*, *Omni*, and *Universe*. Stories such as "Swarm," "Cicada Queen," "Spider Rose," and "Sunken Gardens" were among the strongest work of the decade, all set against the backdrop of his exotic Shaper/Mechanist future, a complex and disturbing future where warring political factions struggle to control the shape of human destiny, and the nature of humanity itself. This vision of the future would reach its purest expression in his landmark 1985 novel *Schismatrix*, a vivid, complex, Stapel-donian meditation on cultural evolution, rivaled only by Gibson's somewhat more accessible *Neuromancer* as the prime cyberpunk work. (Sterling's hard-science stuff has a ferociously high bit-rate, more densely packed new ideas per page than anything seen in the field since Van Vogt or Harness, which prompted Brian Aldiss to remark that Sterling's work had gone beyond Future Shock to "Future Blitzkrieg.")

At the same time, Sterling would be up to his hips in blood as one of the chief antagonists in the newly launched Cyberpunk War in SF, relentlessly hyping cyperpunk in his agitprop organ, *Cheap Truth*, almost certainly the most influential, admired, and loathed critical magazine of the '80s, even though it was only a shoddy-looking mimeographed fanzine sent out to a reader list – selected personally by Sterling – of only a few hundred people. What would be obscured by all the fierce polemics and bitter infighting was the fact that Sterling was undoubtedly the best new hard-science writer of the decade, rivaled for the title only by Greg Bear. Ironically, the traditional hard-science audience, centered now around *Analog* and Jim Baen's *Far Frontiers*, would be put off by Sterling's political stance and by the punk flavor of his work, and would have nothing to do with him, while he would receive most of his support outside of his own core clique from the leftist literary intellectuals like John Kessel that *Cheap Truth* would devote a good deal of its energy to attacking.

With the partial exception of his Shaper/Mechanist stories, no two stories by Sterling are ever much alike in tone or setting or style . . . so much so that I was seriously tempted to use *two* stories by Sterling in this book, just because there is so much difference between the Sterling of "Dinner in Audoghast" and the Sterling of "The Beautiful and the Sublime" and the Sterling of "Green Days in Brunei" and the Sterling of "Flowers of Edo," that they might as well all be different individual writers. The Sterling I finally settled on, the Sterling of "Dori Bangs," is not much like *any* of them . . . but he wrote a story that could not be ignored, quite probably the single best story of 1989, an odd kind of alternate worlds story, unlike any you've ever seen anywhere else.

Sterling's other books include the critically acclaimed novel *Islands in the Net* and, as editor, *Mirrorshades: the Cyberpunk Anthology*. His most recent books are the landmark collection *Crystal Express*, and a new novel, *The Difference Engine*, in collaboration with William Gibson. He lives with his family in Austin, Texas.

True facts, mostly: Lester Bangs was born in California in 1948. He published his first article in 1969. It came in over the transom at *Rolling Stone*. It was a frenzied review of the MC5's "Kick Out the Jams."

Without much meaning to, Lester Bangs slowly changed from a Romilar-guzzling college kid into a "professional rock critic." There wasn't much precedent for this job in 1969, so Lester kinda had to make it up as he went along. Kind of *smell* his way into the role, as it were. But Lester had a fine set of cultural antennae. For instance, Lester invented the tag "punk rock." This is posterity's primary debt to the Bangs oeuvre.

Lester's not as famous now as he used to be, because he's been dead for some time, but in the '70s Lester wrote a million record reviews, for *Creem* and the *Village Voice* and *NME* and *Who Put the Bomp*. He liked to crouch over his old manual typewriter, and slam out wild Beat-influenced copy, while the Velvet Underground or Stooges were on the box. This made life a hideous trial for the neighborhood, but in Lester's opinion the neighborhood pretty much had it coming. *Épater les bourgeois*, man!

Lester was a party animal. It was a professional obligation, actually. Lester was great fun to hang with, because he usually had a jagged speed-edge, which made him smart and bold and rude and crazy. Lester was a one-man band, until he got drunk. Nutmeg, Romilar, belladonna, crank, those substances Lester could handle. But booze seemed to crack him open, and an unexpected black dreck of rage and pain would come dripping out, like oil from a broken crankcase.

Toward the end – but Lester had no notion that the end was nigh. He'd given up the booze, more or less. Even a single beer often triggered frenzies of self-contempt. Lester was thirty-three, and sick of being groovy; he was restless, and the stuff he'd been writing lately no longer meshed with the surroundings that had made him what he was. Lester told his friends that he was gonna leave New York and go to Mexico and work on a deep, serious novel, about deep serious issues, man. The real thing, this time. He was really gonna pin it down, get into the guts of Western Culture, what it really was, how it really felt.

But then, in April '82, Lester happened to catch the flu. Lester was living alone at the time, his mom, the Jehovah's Witness, having died recently. He had no one to make him chicken soup, and the flu really took him down. Tricky stuff, flu; it has a way of getting on top of you.

Lester ate some Darvon, but instead of giving him that buzzed-out float it usually did, the pills made him feel foggy and dull and desperate. He was too sick to leave his room, or hassle with doctors or ambulances, so instead he just did more Darvon. And his heart stopped.

There was nobody there to do anything about it, so he lay there for a couple of days, until a friend showed up and found him.

More true fax, pretty much: Dori Seda was born in 1951. She was a cartoonist, of the "underground" variety. Dori wasn't ever famous, certainly not in Lester's league, but then she didn't beat her chest and bend every ear in the effort to make herself a Living Legend, either. She had a lot of friends in San Francisco, anyway.

Dori did a "comic book" once, called *Lonely Nights*. An unusual "comic book" for those who haven't followed the "funnies" trade lately, as *Lonely Nights* was not particularly "funny," unless you really get a hoot from deeply revealing tales of frustrated personal relationships. Dori also did a lot of work for *WEIRDO* magazine, which emanated from the artistic circles of R. Crumb, he of "Keep On Truckin' " and "Fritz the Cat" fame.

R. Crumb once said: "Comics are words and pictures. You can do anything with words and pictures!" As a manifesto, it was a typically American declaration, and it was a truth that Dori held to be self-evident.

Dori wanted to be a True Artist in her own real-gone little '80s-esque medium. Comix, or "graphic narrative" if you want a snazzier cognomen for it, was a breaking thing, and she had to feel her way into it. You can see the struggle in her "comics" – always relentlessly autobiographical – Dori hanging around in the Café La Boheme trying to trade food stamps for cigs; Dori living in drafty warehouses in the Shabby Hippie Section of San Francisco, sketching under the skylight and squabbling with her roommate's boyfriend; Dori trying to scrape up money to have her dog treated for mange.

Dori's comics are littered with dead cig-butts and toppled wine-bottles. She was, in a classic nutshell, Wild, Zany, and Self-Destructive. In 1988 Dori was in a car-wreck which cracked her pelvis and collarbone. She was laid up, bored and in pain. To kill time, she drank and smoked and took painkillers.

She caught the flu. She had friends who loved her, but nobody realized how badly off she was; probably she didn't know it herself. She just went down hard, and couldn't get up alone. On February 26 her heart stopped. She was thirty-six.

So enough "true facts." Now for some comforting lies.

As it happens, even while a malignant cloud of flu virus was lying in wait for the warm hospitable lungs of Lester Bangs, the Fate, Atropos, she who weaves the things that are to be, accidentally dropped a stitch. Knit one? Purl two? What the hell does it matter, anyway? It's just human lives, right?

So Lester, instead of inhaling a cloud of invisible contagion from the exhalations of a passing junkie, is almost hit by a Yellow Cab. This mishap on his way back from the deli shocks Lester out of his dogmatic slumbers. High time, Lester concludes, to get out of this burg and down to sunny old Mexico. He's gonna tackle his great American novel: *All My Friends are Hermits*.

So true. None of Lester's groovy friends go out much any more. Always ahead of their time, Lester's Bohemian cadre are no longer rock-and-roll animals. They still wear black leather jackets, they still stay up all night, they still hate Ronald Reagan with fantastic virulence; but they never leave home. They pursue an unnamed lifestyle that sociologist Faith Popcorn – (and how can you doubt anyone with a name like *Faith Popcorn*) – will describe years later as "cocooning."

Lester has eight zillion rock, blues, and jazz albums, crammed into his grubby NYC apartment. Books are piled feet deep on every available surface: Wm. Burroughs, Hunter Thompson, Celine, Kerouac, Huysmans, Foucault, and dozens of unsold copies of *Blondie*, Lester's book-length band-bio.

More albums and singles come in the mail every day. People used to send Lester records in the forlorn hope he would review them. But now it's simply a tradition. Lester has transformed himself into a counter-cultural info-sump. People send him vinyl just because he's *Lester Bangs*, man!

Still jittery from his thrilling brush with death, Lester looks over this lifetime of loot with a surge of Sartrean nausea. He resists the urge to raid the fridge for his last desperate can of Blatz Beer. Instead, Lester snorts some speed, and calls an airline to plan his Mexican wanderjahr. After screaming in confusion at the hopeless stupid bitch of a receptionist, he gets a ticket to San Francisco, best he can do on short notice. He packs in a frenzy and splits.

Next morning finds Lester exhausted and wired and on the wrong side of the continent. He's brought nothing with him but an Army duffel-bag with his Olympia portable, some typing paper, shirts, assorted vials of dope, and a paperback copy of *Moby Dick*, which he's always meant to get around to rereading.

Lester takes a cab out of the airport. He tells the cabbie to drive nowhere, feeling a vague compulsive urge to soak up the local vibe. San Francisco reminds him of his *Rolling Stone* days, back before Wenner fired him for being nasty to rock-stars. Fuck Wenner, he thinks. Fuck this city that was almost Avalon for a few months in '67 and has been on greased skids to Hell ever since.

The hilly half-familiar streets creep and wriggle with memories, avatars, talismans. Decadence, man, a no-kidding *death of affect*. It all ties in for Lester, in a bilious mental stew: snuff movies, discos, the cold-blooded whine of synthesizers, Pet Rocks, S&M, mindfuck self-improvement cults, Winning Through Intimidation, every aspect of the invisible war slowly eating the soul of the world.

After an hour or so he stops the cab at random. He needs coffee, white sugar, human beings, maybe a cheese Danish. Lester glimpses himself in the cab's window as he turns to pay: a chunky jobless thirty-three-year-old in a biker jacket, speed-pale dissipated New York face, Fu Manchu mustache looking pasted on. Running to fat, running for shelter . . . no excuses, Bangs! Lester hands the driver a big tip. Chew on that, pal – you just drove the next Oswald Spengler.

Lester staggers into the café. It's crowded and stinks of patchouli and clove. He sees two chainsmoking punkettes hanging out at a formica table. CBGB's types, but with California suntans. The kind of women, Lester thinks, who sit crosslegged on the floor and won't fuck you but are perfectly willing to describe in detail their highly complex postexistential *weltanschauung*. Tall and skinny and crazy-looking and bad news. Exactly his type, really. Lester sits down at their table and gives them his big rubber grin.

"Been having fun?" Lester says.

They look at him like he's crazy, which he is, but he wangles their names out: "Dori" and "Krystine." Dori's wearing fishnet stockings, cowboy boots, a strapless second-hand bodice-hugger covered with peeling pink feathers. Her long brown hair's streaked blonde. Krystine's got a black knit tank top and a leather skirt and a skull-tattoo on her stomach.

Dori and Krystine have never heard of "Lester Bangs." They don't read much. They're *artists*. They do cartoons. Underground comix. Lester's mildly interested. Manifestations of the trash aesthetic always strongly appeal to him. It seems so American, the *good* America that is: the righteous wild America of rootless European refuse picking up discarded pop-junk and making it shine like the Koh-i-noor. To make "comic books" into *Art* – what a hopeless fucking effort, worse than rock and roll and you don't even get heavy bread for it. Lester says as much, to see what they'll do.

Krystine wanders off for a refill. Dori, who is mildly weirded-out by this tubby red-eyed stranger with his loud come-on, gives Lester her double-barreled brush-off. Which consists of opening up this Windex-clear vision into the Vent of Hell that is her daily life. Dori lights another Camel from the butt of the last, smiles at Lester with her big gappy front teeth and says brightly:

"You like *dogs*, Lester? I have this dog, and he has eczema and disgusting open sores all over his body, and he smells *really* bad . . . I can't get friends to come over becuse he likes to shove his nose right into their, you know, *crotch* . . . and go *Snort! Snort!*"

" 'I want to scream with wild dog joy in the smoking pit of a charnel house,' " Lester says.

Dori stares at him. "Did you make that up?"

"Yeah," Lester says. "Where were you when Elvis died?"

"You taking a survey on it?" Dori says.

"No, I just wondered," Lester says. "There was talk of having Elvis's corpse dug up, and the stomach analyzed. For dope, y'know. Can you *imagine* that? I mean, the *thrill* of sticking your hand and forearm into Elvis's rotted guts and slopping around in the stomach lining and liver and kidneys and coming up out of dead Elvis's innards triumphantly clenching some crumbs off a few Percodans and Desoxyns and 'ludes . . . and then this is the *real* kick, Dori: you pop these crumbled-up bits of pills in your *own mouth* and bolt 'em down and get high on drugs that not only has Elvis Presley, the *King*, gotten high on, not the same brand mind you but the same *pills*, all slimy with little bits of his innards, so you've actually gotten to *eat* the King of Rock and Roll!"

"*Who* did you say you were?" Dori says. "A rock journalist? I thought you were putting me on. 'Lester Bangs,' that's a fucking weird name!"

Dori and Krystine have been up all night, dancing to the heroin head banger vibes of Darby Crash and the Germs. Lester watches through hooded eyes: this Dori is a woman over thirty, but she's got this wacky airhead routine down smooth, the Big Shiny Fun of the American Pop Bohemia. "Fuck you for believing I'm this shallow." Beneath the skin of her Attitude he can sense a bracing skeleton of pure desperation. There is hollow fear and sadness in the marrow of her bones. He's been writing about a topic just like this lately.

They talk a while, about the city mostly, about their variant scenes. Sparring, but he's interested. Dori yawns with pretended disinterest and gets up to leave. Lester notes that Dori is taller than he is. It doesn't bother him. He gets her phone number.

Lester crashes in a Holiday Inn. Next day he leaves town. He spends a week in a flophouse in Tijuana with his Great American Novel, which sucks. Despondent and terrified he writes himself little cheering notes: "*Burroughs was almost fifty when he wrote* Nova Express! *Hey boy, you only thirty-three! Burnt-out! Washed up! Finished! A bit of flotsam! And in that flotsam your salvation! In that one grain of wood. In that one bit of that irrelevance. If you can bring yourself to describe it . . .*"

It's no good. He's fucked. He knows he is, too, he's been reading over his scrapboks lately, those clippings of yellowing newsprint, thinking: it was all a box, man! *El Cajon!* You'd think: wow, a groovy youth-rebel Rock Writer, he can talk about *anything*, can't he? Sex, dope, violence, Mazola parties with teenage Indonesian groupies, Nancy Reagan publicly fucked by a herd of clapped-out bull walruses . . . but when you actually *read* a bunch of Lester Bangs Rock Reviews in a row, the whole shebang has a delicate hermetic whiff, like so many eighteenth-century sonnets. It is to dance in chains; it is to see the whole world through a little chromed window of Silva-Thin 'shades. . . .

Lester Bangs is nothing if not a consummate romantic. He is, after all, a man who *really no kidding believes* that Rock and Roll Could Change the World, and when he writes something which isn't an impromptu free lesson on what's wrong with Western Culture and how it can't survive without grabbing itself by the backbrain and turning itself inside-out, he feels like he's wasted a day. Now Lester, fretfully abandoning his typewriter to stalk and kill flophouse roaches, comes to realize that *he* will have to turn himself inside out. Grow, or die. Grow into something but he has no idea what. He feels beaten.

So Lester gets drunk. Starts with Tecate, works his way up

to tequila. He wakes up with a savage hangover. Life seems hideous and utterly meaningless. He abandons himself to senseless impulse. Or, in alternate terms, Lester allows himself to follow the numinous artistic promptings of his holy intuition. He returns to San Francisco and calls Dori Seda.

Dori, in the meantime, has learned from friends that there is indeed a rock journalist named "Lester Bangs" who's actually kind of *famous*. He once appeared on stage with the J. Geils Band "playing" his typewriter. He's kind of a big deal, which probably accounts for his being kind of an asshole. On a dare, Dori calls Lester Bangs in New York, gets his answering machine, and recognizes the voice. It was him, all right. Through some cosmic freak, she met Lester Bangs and he tried to pick her up! No dice, though. More Lonely Nights, Dori!

Then Lester calls. He's back in town again. Dori's so flustered she ends up being nicer to him on the phone than she means to be.

She goes out with him. To rock clubs. Lester never has to pay; he just mutters at people, and they let him in and find him a table. Strangers rush up to gladhand Lester and jostle round the table and pay court. Lester finds the music mostly boring, and it's no pretense; he actually *is* bored, he's heard it all. He sits there sipping club sodas and handing out these little chips of witty guru insight to these sleaze-ass Hollywood guys and bighaired coke-whores in black Spandex. Like it was his *job*.

Dori can't believe he's going to all this trouble just to jump her bones. It's not like he can't get women, or like their own relationship is all that tremendously scintillating. Lester's whole set-up is alien. But it *is* kind of interesting, and doesn't demand much. All Dori has to do is dress in her sluttiest Goodwill get-up, and be This Chick With Lester. Dori likes being invisible, and watching people when they don't know she's looking. She can see in their eyes that Lester's people wonder Who The Hell Is She? Dori finds this really funny, and makes sketches of his creepiest acquaintances on cocktail napkins. At night she puts them in her sketch books and writes dialogue balloons. It's all really good material.

Lester's also very funny, in a way. He's smart, not just hustler-clever but scary-crazy smart, like he's sometimes profound without knowing it or even *wanting* it. But when he thinks he's being most amusing, is when he's actually the most depressing. It bothers her that he doesn't drink around her; it's a bad sign. He knows almost nothing about art or drawing, he dresses like a jerk, he dances like a trained bear. And she's fallen in love with him and she knows he's going to break her goddamn heart.

Lester has put his novel aside for the moment. Nothing new there; he's been working on it, in hopeless spasms, for ten years. But now juggling this affair takes all he's got.

Lester is terrified that this amazing woman is going to go to pieces on him. He's seen enough of her work now to recognize that she's possessed of some kind of genuine demented genius. He can smell it; the vibe pours off her like Everglades swamp-reek. Even in her frowsy houserobe and bunny slippers, hair a mess, no makeup, half-asleep, he can see something there like Dresden china, something fragile and precious. And the world seems like a maelstrom of jungle hate, sinking into entropy or gearing up for Armageddon, and what the hell can anybody do? How can he be happy with her and not be punished for it? How long can they break the rules before the Nova Police show?

But nothing horrible happens to them. They just go on living.

Then Lester blunders into a virulent cloud of Hollywood money. He's written a stupid and utterly commercial screenplay about the laff-a-minute fictional antics of a heavy-metal band, and without warning he gets eighty thousand dollars for it.

He's never had so much money in one piece before. He has, he realizes with dawning horror, sold out.

To mark the occasion Lester buys some freebase, six grams of crystal meth, and rents a big white Cadillac. He fast-talks Dori into joining him for a supernaturally cool Kerouac adventure into the Savage Heart of America, and they get in the car laughing like hyenas and take off for parts unknown.

Four days later they're in Kansas City. Lester's lying in

the back seat in a jittery Hank Williams half-doze and Dori is driving. They have nothing left to say, as they've been arguing viciously ever since Albuquerque.

Dori, white-knuckled, sinuses scorched with crack, loses it behind the wheel. Lester's slammed from the back seat and wakes up to find Dori knocked out and drizzling blood from a scalp wound. The Caddy's wrapped messily in the buckled ruins of a sidewalk mailbox.

Lester holds the resultant nightmare together for about two hours, which is long enough to flag down help and get Dori into a Kansas City trauma room.

He sits there, watching over her, convinced he's lost it, blown it; it's over, she'll hate him forever now. My God, she could have died! As soon as she comes to, he'll have to face her. The thought of this makes something buckle inside him. He flees the hospital in headlong panic.

He ends up in a sleazy little rock dive downtown where he jumps onto a table and picks a fight with the bouncer. After he's knocked down for the third time, he gets up screaming for the manager, how he's going to *ruin that motherfucker!* and the club's owner shows up, tired and red-faced and sweating. The owner, whose own tragedy must go mostly unexpressed here, is a fat white-haired cigar-chewing third-rater who attempted, and failed, to model his life on Elvis's Colonel Parker. He hates kids, he hates rock and roll, he hates the aggravation of smart-ass doped-up hippies screaming threats and pimping off the hard work of businessmen just trying to make a living.

He has Lester hauled to his office backstage and tells him all this. Toward the end, the owner's confused, almost plaintive, because he's never seen anyone as utterly, obviously, and desperately fucked-up as Lester Bangs, but who can still be coherent about it and use phrases like "rendered to the factor of machinehood" while mopping blood from his punched nose.

And Lester, trembling and red-eyed, tells him: fuck you Jack, I could run this jerkoff place, I could do everything you do blind drunk, and make this place a fucking *legend in American culture*, you booshwah sonofabitch.

Yeah punk if you had the money, the owner says.

I've *got* the money! Let's see your papers, you evil cracker bastard! In a few minutes Lester is the owner-to-be on a handshake and an earnestcheck.

Next day he brings Dori roses from the hospital shop downstairs. He sits next to the bed; they compare bruises, and Lester explains to her that he has just blown his fortune. They are now tied down and beaten in the corn-shucking heart of America. There is only one possible action left to complete this situation.

Three days later they are married in Kansas City by a justice of the peace.

Needless to say marriage does not solve any of their problems. It's a minor big deal for a while, gets mentioned in rock-mag gossip columns; they get some telegrams from friends, and Dori's mom seems pretty glad about it. They even get a nice note from Julie Burchill, the Marxist Amazon from *New Musical Express* who has quit the game to write for fashion mags, and her husband Tony Parsons the proverbial "hip young gunslinger" who now writes weird potboiler novels about racetrack gangsters. Tony & Julie seem to be making some kind of a go of it. Kinda inspirational.

For a while Dori calls herself Dori Seda-Bangs, like her good friend Aline Kominsky-Crumb, but after a while she figures what's the use? and just calls herself Dori Bangs which sounds plenty weird enough on its own.

Lester can't say he's really *happy* or anything, but he's sure *busy*. He renames the club "Waxy's Travel Lounge," for some reason known only to himself. The club loses money quickly and consistently. After the first month Lester stops playing Lou Reed's *Metal Machine Music* before sets, and that helps attendance some, but Waxy's is still a club which books a lot of tiny weird college-circuit acts that Albert Average just doesn't get yet. Pretty soon they're broke again and living on Lester's reviews.

They'd be even worse off, except Dori does a series of promo posters for Waxy's that are so amazing that they draw people in, even after they've been burned again and again on weird-ass bands only Lester can listen to.

After a couple of years they're still together, only they have shrieking crockery-throwing fights and once, when he's been drinking, Lester wrenches her arm so badly Dori's truly afraid it's broken. It isn't, luckily, but it's sure no great kick being Mrs Lester Bangs. Dori was always afraid of this: that what he does is *work* and what she does is *cute*. How many Great Women Artists are there anyway, and what happened to 'em? They went into patching the wounded ego and picking up the dropped socks of Mr Wonderful, that's what. No big mystery about it.

And besides, she's thirty-six and still barely scraping a living. She pedals her beat-up bike through the awful Kansas weather and sees these yuppies cruise by with these smarmy grins: hey we don't *have* to invent our lives, our lives are *invented for us* and boy does that ever save a lot of soul-searching.

But still somehow they blunder along; they have the occasional good break. Like when Lester turns over the club on Wednesdays to some black kids for (eeeh!) "disco nite" and it turns out to be the beginning of a little Kansas City rap-scratch scene, which actually makes the club some money. And Polyrock, a band Lester hates at first but later champions to global megastardom, cuts a live album in Waxy's.

And Dori gets a contract to do one of those twenty-second animated logos for MTV, and really gets into it. It's fun, so she starts doing video animation work for (fairly) big bucks and even gets a Macintosh II from a video-hack admirer in Silicon Valley. Dori had always loathed feared and despised *computers* but this thing is *different*. This is a kind of art that *nobody's ever done before* and has to be invented from leftovers, sweat and thin air! It's wide open and way rad!

Lester's novel doesn't get anywhere, but he does write a book called *A Reasonable Guide to Horrible Noise* which becomes a hip coffeetable cult item with an admiring introduction by a trendy French semiotician. Among other things, this book introduces the term "chipster" which describes a kind of person who, well, didn't really *exist* before Lester described them but once he'd pointed 'em out it was *obvious to everybody*.

But they're still not *happy*. They both have a hard time taking the "marital fidelity" notion with anything like seriousness. They have a vicious fight once, over who gave who herpes, and Dori splits for six months and goes back to California. Where she looks up her old girlfriends and finds the survivors married with kids, and her old boyfriends are even seedier and more pathetic than Lester. What the hell, it's not happiness but it's something. She goes back to Lester. He's gratifyingly humble and appreciative for almost six weeks.

Waxy's does in fact become a cultural legend of sorts, but they don't pay you for that; and anyway it's hell to own a bar while attending sessions of Alcoholics Anonymous. So Lester gives in, and sells the club. He and Dori buy a house, which turns out to be far more hassle than it's worth, and then they go to Paris for a while, where they argue bitterly and squander all their remaining money.

When they come back Lester gets, of all the awful things, an academic gig. For a Kansas state college. Lester teaches Rock and Popular Culture. In the '70s there'd have been no room for such a hopeless skidrow weirdo in a, like, Serious Academic Environment, but it's the late '90s by now, and Lester has outlived the era of outlawhood. Because who are we kidding? Rock and Roll is a satellite-driven worldwide information industry which is worth billions and *billions*, and if they don't study *major industries* then what the hell are the taxpayers funding colleges for?

Self-destruction is awfully tiring. After a while, they just give it up. They've lost the energy to flame-out, and it hurts too much; besides it's less trouble just to live. They eat balanced meals, go to bed early, and attend faculty parties where Lester argues violently about the parking privileges.

Just after the turn of the century, Lester finally gets his novel published, but it seems quaint and dated now, and gets panned and quickly remaindered. It would be nice to say that Lester's book was rediscovered years later as a Klassic of Litratchur but the truth is that Lester's no novelist; what he is, is a cultural mutant, and what he has in the way of insight and energy has been eaten up. Subsumed by the Beast, man. What he thought and said made some kind of difference, but nowhere near as big a difference as he'd dreamed.

In the year 2015, Lester dies of a heart attack while shoveling snow off his lawn. Dori has him cremated, in one of those plasma flash-cremators that are all the mode in the twenty-first-century undertaking business. There's a nice respectful retrospective on Lester in the *New York Times Review of Books* but the truth is Lester's pretty much a forgotten man; a colorful footnote for cultural historians who can see the twentieth century with the unflattering advantage of hindsight.

A year after Lester's death they demolish the remnants of Waxy's Travel Lounge to make room for a giant high-rise. Dori goes out to see the ruins. As she wanders among the shockingly staid and unromantic rubble, there's another of those slips in the fabric of Fate, and Dori is approached by a Vision.

Thomas Hardy used to call it the Immanent Will and in China it might have been the Tao, but we late twentieth-century postmoderns would probably call it something soothingly pseudoscientific like the "genetic imperative." Dori, being Dori, recognizes this glowing androgynous figure as The Child They Never Had.

"Don't worry, Mrs Bangs," the Child tells her, "I might have died young of some ghastly disease, or grown up to shoot the President and break your heart, and anyhow you two woulda been no prize as parents." Dori can see herself and Lester in this Child, there's a definite nacreous gleam in its right eye that's Lester's, and the sharp quiet left eye is hers; but behind the eyes where there should be a living breathing human being there's *nothing*, just kind of chill galactic twinkling.

"And don't feel guilty for outliving him either," the Child tells her, "because you're going to have what we laughingly call a natural death, which means you're going to die in the company of strangers hooked up to tubes when you're old and helpless."

"But did it *mean* anything?" Dori says.

"If you mean were you Immortal Artists leaving indelible graffiti in the concrete sidewalk of Time, no. You've never walked the earth as gods, you were just people. But it's better to have a real life than no life." The Child shrugs. "You weren't all that happy together, but you *did* suit each other, and if you'd both married other people instead, there would have been *four* people unhappy. So here's your consolation: you helped each other."

"So?" Dori says.

"So that's enough. Just to shelter each other, and help each other up. Everything else is gravy. Someday, no matter what, you go down forever. Art can't make you immortal. Art can't Change the World. Art can't even heal your soul. All it can do is maybe ease the pain a bit or make you feel more awake. And that's enough. It only matters as much as it matters, which is zilch to an ice-cold interstellar Cosmic Principle like yours truly. But if you try to live by my standards it will only kill you faster. By your own standards, you did pretty good, really."

"Well okay then," Dori says.

After this purportedly earth-shattering mystical encounter, her life simply went right on, day following day, just like always. Dori gave up computer-art; it was too hairy trying to keep up with the hotshot high-tech cutting edge, and kind of undignified, when you came right down to it. Better to leave that to hungry kids. She was idle for a while, feeling quiet inside, but finally she took up watercolors. For a while Dori played the Crazy Old Lady Artist and was kind of a mainstay of the Kansas regionalist art scene. Granted, Dori was no Georgia O'Keeffe, but she was working, and living, and she touched a few people's lives.

Or, at least, Dori surely would have touched those people, if she'd been there to do it. But of course she wasn't, and didn't. Dori Seda never met Lester Bangs. Two simple real-life acts of human caring, at the proper moment, might have saved them both; but when those moments came, they had no one, not even each other. And so they went down into darkness, like skaters, breaking through the hard bright shiny surface of our true-facts world.

Today I made this white paper dream to cover the holes they left.

Afterword

You have to be a little crazy to try to do good work in science fiction, a field where indifferent, run-of-the-mill, lowest-common-denominator work is often not only tolerated but actively rewarded, and where good work is often not only ignored, but, in many cases, greeted with outright hostility. About the only thing that has saved SF, kept it evolving, is the constant influx of new writers, writers young and enthusiastic enough to actually work *harder* than they need to for the same kind of money they'd have gotten for producing a formula space opera or a sharecropper book. Eventually, many of them burn out, wear themselves smooth, get tired and cynical, and either fall silent or opt for the easier way. But SF has so far been lucky in always having a new generation of writers waiting to snatch up the torch (with naive enthusiasm, of course) as the previous generation lets it slip from numbed hands.

And those new generations are still marching in, right on schedule, here at the beginning of the '90s.

In Britain, new writers ("new," of course, being a relative term, hard to define objectively) who have been attracting attention for the last few years include Geoff Ryman, Ian MacDonald, Paul J. McAuley, Ian R. MacLeod, Iain Banks, Richard Calder, Greg Egan (actually an Australian), Gwyneth Jones, Jamil Nasir, Ian Lee, William King and Kim Newman, among many others.

In the United States, strong work has been being done by new (or "new") writers such as Judith Moffett, Alexander Jablokov, Kathe Koja, John Barnes, Allen Steele, Eileen Gunn, Steven Popkes, D. Alexander Smith, R. V. Branham, Lisa Mason, Maureen McHugh, Janet Kagan, Kristine Kathryn Rusch, Susan Casper, R. Garcia y Robertson,

Megan Lindholm, Don Webb, Robert Frazier, Richard Paul Russo, Philip C. Jennings, and Dean Whitlock, among many others.

And right behind *them* are marching still "newer" generations of writers, some of whom have not even yet had their first professional sales hit print as I write this (I'm in a better position to know this about the American scene than I am about the British, which is why there are no British writers on the following list; I'm positive that they are marching along there too, though): Mary Rosenblum, Tony Daniel, Deborah Wessell, Jonathan Lethem, Sage Walker, Peni Griffin, Lawrence Person, Kathleen Ann Goonan, Mark Tiedemann, Patricia Anthony, Diane Mapes, Charles Oberndorf, and *many* others.

Some of the above writers will falter and fall by the wayside, some will turn out to be minor writers or occasional writers (not necessarily the same thing), but some of them will be among the Big Names of 2001.

And as long as good new writers like them – and the as yet faceless ranks behind even the newest of *them* – keep coming along, science fiction will survive, and even prosper.